ESCAPE

Also by Robert K. Tanenbaum

Fiction

Malice

Counterplay

Fury

Hoax

Resolved

Absolute Rage

Enemy Within

True Justice

Act of Revenge

Reckless Endangerment

Irresistible Impulse

Falsely Accused

Corruption of Blood

Justice Denied

Material Witness

Reversible Error

Immoral Certainty

Depraved Indifference

No Lesser Plea

Nonfiction

The Piano Teacher: The True Story of a Psychotic Killer

Badge of the Assassin

ESCAPE

ROBERT K. TANENBAUM

Vanguard Press
A Member of the Perseus Books Group

Designed by Trish Wilkinson
Set in Goudy

ISBN-13: 978-1-59315-474-5

To those blessings in my life:
Patti, Rachael, Roger and Billy

ACKNOWLEDGMENTS

To my legendary mentors, District Attorney Frank S. Hogan and Henry Robbins, both of whom were larger in life than in legend, everlasting gratitude and respect; to my special friends and brilliant tutors at the Manhattan DAO, Bob Lehner, Mel Glass, and John Keenan, three of the best who ever served and whose passion for justice was unequaled and uncompromising, my heartfelt appreciation, respect, and gratitude; to Steve Jackson, an extraordinarily talented and gifted scrivener whose genius flows throughout the manuscript and whose contribution to it cannot be overstated, a dear friend for whom I have the the utmost respect; to Roger Cooper and Georgina Levitt, many thanks for your enthusiasm and support; and to my agents, Mike Hamilburg and Bob DiForio who in exemplary fashion have always represented my best interests.

PROLOGUE

Roger "Butch" Karp sat on the desk, which protested briefly before accepting its burden, and looked out at his audience. He was a big man—big enough to have played pro basketball, if a knee injury in college hadn't derailed that dream. Instead, he'd pursued a different course and worked for the New York District Attorney's Office most of his life.

Now, thirty-plus years after law school, he was the elected DA of New York County, essentially the island of Manhattan. And he was sitting on a desk at the front of a classroom in a synagogue, getting ready to speak to bar mitzvah and bat mitzvah candidates as a "role model" from the Jewish community.

He marveled at the resilience of youth. Considering what had happened at the synagogue just a month and a half earlier, it was amazing that these kids were smiling, flirting, and laughing, seemingly undaunted by a sometimes-insane world that paralyzed many adults with fear. Yes, they had been afraid. No, they had not been defeated.

Two of the students were Karp's twin sons, Isaac and Giancarlo, and it was because of them that he had agreed to teach the class. That his children were interested in religion at all was something of a surprise. The twins, as well as their older sister, Lucy, had been exposed to a smattering of their mother's Roman Catholic upbringing—Marlene Ciampi had been raised in an Italian American

1

family in Queens, and it was this heritage, more than any devotion on her part, that had predestined the children to learn the tenets of the faith.

Of the three, Lucy had been the most spiritual, having shown an inclination toward Catholic mysticism that included "visitations" from—or hallucinations of— the fifteenth-century saint Teresa of Avila during times of stress and danger. Of late her spirituality had been undergoing a transformation due to her acquaintance with John Jojola, the police chief of the Taos Indian Pueblo in New Mexico, who had become something of a Native American spiritual guide for both Lucy and Marlene. But none of the kids had ever shown much interest in the spiritual side of Judaism.

In fact, the twins' previous religiosity had centered on holiday avarice. Giancarlo, the youngest by several minutes and the more artistically inclined, especially as a musician, had demonstrated an appreciation for the art, music, and historical significance of his parents' heritage. However, they both were more interested in the present count at Christmas, with a little Chanukah thrown in for the food and family togetherness, than in the stories or scriptures behind the celebrations.

Then, nearly two years ago, they had suddenly announced that they wanted to go through the bar mitzvah ceremony that celebrated a Jewish boy's passage into manhood. As that meant studying Hebrew, as well as the Torah, Karp suspected that they'd heard about the monetary gains common to bar mitzvah graduates. When he'd leveled that charge, they'd howled their protests and sulked in aggrieved innocence.

When they'd actually signed up for classes, he'd had to admit that maybe they were serious. Marlene had suggested that Lucy's continuing quest for spiritual growth and the twins' new interest could be a reaction to having been individually, and as a family, subjected to a host of violent attacks—bombings, kidnappings, shootings, stabbings, and run-ins with a variety of sociopaths and terrorists—some attributable to their father's employment as the chief law-enforcement official in Manhattan. The family seemed to attract trouble like bread crumbs attract ants, with a regularity that made Karp's head hurt when he considered the implausibilities.

When the rabbi responsible for teenage education had asked Karp if he'd take part in the "role model" classes that were part of the bar mitzvah instruction, Karp had protested that his own bar mitzvah was only a hazy memory, and his knowledge of Hebrew abysmal. But Rabbi Greg Romberg had laughed and said, "Leave the Hebrew and Torah to me. The purpose of these classes is to talk to *them about what it means to be productive, responsible, and thinking members of the community."*

Karp had felt his involvement would give him more time with the boys in a setting where they could discuss moral choices without the discomfort typical of arranged father-son talks. However, he had found that he enjoyed teaching the classes and the challenge of coming up with lessons that would make the boys in the class—as well as the girls who were studying for their bat mitzvah—think in terms of how decisions made by the individual affect society.

It was a good thing he enjoyed it, because the twins' bar mitzvah preparation was taking longer than anticipated. The boys had started behind their classmates, most of whom came from more traditional Jewish families and therefore had at least some background. And then there had been the interruptions in life's usual pattern that were par for the course with the Karp-Ciampi clan. If they weren't being shot at by murderous hillbillies—in fact, Giancarlo had only recently recovered from surgery to restore his eyesight after being struck by a shotgun pellet—then it was nearly being incinerated along with the rest of the New Year's Eve crowd at Times Square, or being targeted for execution by the sociopath Andrew Kane. So Isaac, better known as Zak, and Giancarlo were now repeating the classes with a new group, most of them a year younger, and the boys and girls they'd started with were now officially Jewish men and women. It was Karp's second time through as a teacher as well.

"It feels like we're dummies who got held back in school," Zak had complained. Larger, stronger, plenty smart, and streetwise, he'd been the bigger surprise when the boys announced that they wanted to take the classes in the first place. Even now, in with the "little kids," he stayed with it.

Allowed free rein by Rabbi Romberg, Karp had led the class through a wide range of discussions, including the historical implications of Jesus as a rabbi and whether Jews at the time had conspired to murder him. Such topics had shocked the more orthodox children and engendered a few alarmed telephone calls from their parents to the rabbi, though to Romberg's credit he'd insisted that exposing the kids to different viewpoints on controversial subjects was important to their growth.

Karp often drew his lessons from modern ethical and legal dilemmas he saw in his role as the district attorney. Such as this evening's topic, which stemmed from a recent murder trial he'd prosecuted, as well as a terrorist attack months earlier on that very synagogue.

When he had their attention, Karp took a moment to look over the faces of these sons and daughters of some of New York City's most influential Jewish families. He wondered how this generation would meet the challenges of the future. "I'm sure we all know the story about God commanding Abraham to sacrifice his son, Isaac," he began.

"I do. I do. I was named after the dude," shouted Zak, who had a tendency to get loud when excited.

"Actually, you were named after a relative who was named after a relative who was named after a few hundred generations of relatives who were named after this particular Isaac."

"Same difference," Zak shrugged.

"Mr. Karp! Mr. Karp!" the equally excited and loud voice of Elisa Robyn interjected. "Wasn't it the 'Angel of the Lord' who told Abraham that God wanted him to sacrifice Isaac?"

Zak crossed his eyes. Elisa sat directly behind him and, as he said after nearly every class, she drove him crazy. "She's such a know-it-all, a female Giancarlo," he once said. He swore he hated her and wished she'd leave for someplace far away . . . "like California, where they like know-it-alls." However, Karp suspected that some of Zak's disdain was due to the fact that Elisa, with her budding figure, wild mane of curly dark hair, and flashing brown eyes, seemed to prefer his brother.

"According to some accounts," Karp agreed. "However, I believe that it's generally accepted that 'Angel of the Lord' and God are one and the same."

"Maybe angels are an extension of God," Giancarlo volunteered.

"Perhaps," Karp conceded. "But for the purposes of this story, I guess we could agree that if the 'Angel of the Lord' was not God personified, then the Angel was acting on behalf of God. A co-conspirator, you might say."

The last comment brought wary looks to the faces of the more conservative students. He could see it in their eyes.

"An accessory anyway," young Miss Robyn agreed. She was not one of the conservatives and easily mixed the secular with the divine. More than once, he'd told himself to keep an eye on her; in ten years or so—if he was still in office—she'd make a hell of a good assistant district attorney for the New York DAO.

"If the evidence supports the charge," Karp responded with a nod that he noticed bothered Zak. "Anyway, the premise of the story is that Abraham believed *that God had instructed him to sacrifice his only son, Isaac. So first Abraham planned how to do it. Then he procured a sharp knife and some rope to bind his son. He led Isaac out into the desert, away from prying eyes, where he'd prepared an altar ahead of time."*

Karp looked around the room to see if they were paying attention, or if he'd lost them already. He didn't have to worry; he'd had the boys at the mention of a sacrifice involving a knife, and the girls with the idea that a father could kill his son, who, according to every story they'd ever heard, was about their age at the time of this big event, a guy who could carry a pile of firewood up a mountain-side—to them, no doubt, a hottie.

"Abraham tied up his son and placed him on the altar," Karp continued. "He was just about to slit Isaac's throat when suddenly God called his name. 'Abraham!' So Abraham stopped and answered, 'Hineini!'"

"What's that?" someone asked from the back of the classroom.

"It means, 'Here I am!' in Hebrew," Giancarlo answered. "It's how the old prophets and Jewish patriarchs answered whenever God called to them . . . usually for something they'd done wrong, or some tough job He wanted them to do."

Elisa raised her hand. "Sometimes it was God who answered them by saying, 'Hineini,'" she noted. "Like when God appeared to Moses in a burning bush, He spoke Hebrew, 'Hineini!' Here I am." She looked at Giancarlo and sighed. Giancarlo smiled at Elisa, who smiled back. Zak pretended to gag.

Karp was not surprised that Elisa would be attracted to Giancarlo. There was something about the boy, with his porcelain skin, his fine, delicate features, and the dark, gentle curls framing his face, that seemed to draw women of any age, bringing out motherly instincts in the grown-ups and flirtatious behavior in his peers. There was something about him that made him look like one of the angels in a Renaissance painting. It wasn't that he was better looking than the macho, tough-talking Zak. But Zak, with his rugged demeanor, looked more like a soldier than an angel.

Karp thought it was time to move on. "Right on both counts," he said. "'Hineini! Here I am!' Abraham replied. He stopped with the knife poised above Isaac's neck. Good thing, too, as God granted a stay of execution. Instead, he now told Abraham, 'Do not lay your hand on the boy, or do anything to him; for now I know that you fear God, since you have not withheld your son, your only son, from Me.'"

The boys in the class looked somewhat disappointed. They'd all probably heard the story at some point, but there was always the hope for a new, surprise ending . . . something with a twist and preferably violence.

"Now the question I wanted to ask you is," Karp continued, "if you had been the district attorney back then and God had not intervened to save Isaac, would you have charged Abraham with a homicide?"

Karp smiled as a dozen mouths dropped open in astonishment. "Well, no," Zak replied first. "God told him to do it. You have to do what God says!"

"Really?" Karp replied, raising an eyebrow. "Even commit murder?"

1

Six months earlier . . .

Setting aside her copy of the *New York Times*, Jessica Campbell smiled as her husband, Charlie, hurried into the kitchen and over to the espresso maker. He poured himself a double-shot and took a sip before putting the cup down to fumble at his tie.

"Here, let me help with that," Jessica said, standing. "I fixed breakfast—a western omelette, bacon, and an English muffin."

"No time," Charlie replied, turning his face away from her as she stood on her tiptoes to complete a Windsor knot. "I'm expected at campaign headquarters by 8, and I have to stop by and pick up Diane." He stepped back and gave her a funny look. "What's with all the domesticity?"

An angry expression sailed quickly across Jessica's face, but she forced a smile in its wake. *Act normal, no tantrums or crying.* Her laugh was brittle. "Can't a wife cook breakfast for her husband, the future congressman from the 8th Congressional District, without losing her feminist credentials?"

Charlie caught the strain in her voice. "Sure, she can," he said, forcing a smile of his own. "Just checking to see if you're feeling okay."

They both knew that the question was as loaded as a pimp's gun in Spanish Harlem. She wondered for a moment if he was on to her. *Careful, or he'll ruin everything.* "I'm fine, silly," she said. "I just wish I could be more of a help to you with your campaign. It's already March and you've hardly started fund-raising."

Politics was a safe subject, unlike the state of her mental health or their marriage. And despite everything that had happened of late, she had her admirers and friends in the media, and he needed to keep her on his side.

———————

Jessica had been inducted into grassroots liberal politics by her parents, Benjamin and Liza Gupperstein, who liked to boast at cocktail parties that they'd hung out with Bob Dylan and Allen Ginsberg at the Chelsea Hotel. Abbie Hoffman had once crashed on their couch. Their daughter had been born in 1968, just a few weeks after they were arrested in Chicago for protesting at the Democratic National Convention. They'd also marched in Selma, worked for Eugene McCarthy, and burned flags to protest the war in Vietnam. Many years later their stories gave them a sort of rock-star credibility among the wealthy liberal crowd of upper-crust Manhattan. But they hadn't always hobnobbed with the rich.

In fact, Jessica had spent her first decade living with her parents in a tenement building at 120th Street and Fifth Avenue across from Marcus Garvey Park in Harlem. The white, non-practicing Jewish couple had explained to their horrified Modern Orthodox families that the reason they chose to live "among the oppressed" was to "immerse our child in an environment surrounded by the suffering and discrimination faced by blacks so that she will learn to be sympathetic to the plight of those less fortunate."

However, their home had been broken into more often than a methadone clinic; the Guppersteins were robbed and mugged so many times that when Benjamin's parents were killed in a car accident in 1978, he and Liza quickly decided that the lesson had been learned and moved into the now-vacant Gupperstein Sr.'s walk-up in SoHo. It was the first of many steps up the ladder. A few years later, Benjamin's more capitalist-minded brother, Sam, a computer-software savant, talked them into giving him their life savings so that he could buy stock for them in a young company he worked for, a little startup called Microsoft. This was shortly before the company went public. And the rest—you guessed it—was history.

The Guppersteins assuaged the guilt of sudden riches by contributing large checks to the NAACP, the American Civil Liberties Union, and the Anti-Defamation League. Every Christmas Eve, which they referred to as "Winter Solstice," Benjamin, Liza, and Jessica had the chauffeur drive them to a soup kitchen just a few blocks from the old family tenement in Harlem to serve turkey and ladle mashed potatoes and gravy onto the plates of their former neighbors. They then went home where the adults quietly thanked their lucky stars for insider trading and multiple stock splits.

That kind of money bought the Guppersteins seats at every liberal charity and political event in the Five Boroughs, including the cocktail parties, where they trotted out their former radical left-wing bona fides. Unfortunately for family tranquility, however, teen-aged Jessica saw her father—in his designer tie-dyed T-shirts, Birkenstock sandals, and cell phone with its speed-dial set to his stock broker, lawyer, and hair stylist—as a sellout, and she frequently told him so. Even her mother's seat on several boards of nonprofit organizations and charities did little to mollify Jessica's abhorrence of all things smacking of capitalism, though she made no complaint about the money spent on her private schooling and the latest teen fashions. She gladly took her free ride through Vassar College in Poughkeepsie, where she majored in art, and then through graduate school in political science at Columbia. And she also accepted her parents' wedding present of a $2 million brownstone on the Upper West Side when she married Charlie Campbell.

At the time she met Charlie, Jessica had been involved in a lesbian relationship—not because she was particularly attracted to women, but it seemed the right thing for an avowed feminist to at least sample. She and her lover had gone to a coffeehouse one night where Charlie, an aspiring writer, was trying out his poetry on an unsuspecting crowd during Open Mic Night. His poetry was predictably neo-Beat and self-indulgent, but he was so earnest and so obviously interested in Jessica that she'd shown up the next week without her girlfriend and gone home with him to his flat in the East Village. They'd been together ever since.

The son of a third-generation Detroit autoworker, Charlie was tall, slightly overweight, and slope-shouldered but handsome in a cherubic kind of way—pouty lips, round flushed cheeks, and wavy brown hair. She, on the other hand, was short, dishwater blonde, flat-chested, thin-lipped, shaped like Anjou pear, and in need of thick glasses to see much of anything with her watery blue eyes.

Despite their physical disparities, their politics and interest in social issues meshed like peanut butter and jelly or lox and bagels (depending on which side of the family was talking). She admired how he wanted to make the world a better place; he liked the way she admired him, and besides, her family had more money than God.

Only the most cynical of Jessica's friends, such as her former lesbian lover, pointed out that Charlie had proposed marriage the night after he'd met her parents and discovered the extent of their wealth and political connections. The former lover also noted—at the wedding reception—that for an avowed feminist, Jessica had been quick to announce that she was dropping Gupperstein for Campbell as a last name. "Quite the transformation," the woman complained. "Jew dyke to WASP breeder practically overnight."

Such bitter pronouncements and their owners were soon left to the past. The young couple moved into the brownstone at 95th and Columbus where they hosted meet-the-candidate, or avant-garde-artist, or hip-new-musician dinner parties, after which the hosts and guests retired to the living room for heated political and social debates fueled by dense clouds of Lebanese hashish and expensive Spanish wines. Meanwhile, Jessica worked on her Ph.D. in political science—specializing in feminist revisions of history—while Charlie decided with his in-laws' financial blessing to pursue a law degree at Columbia University.

After Jessica received her doctorate, her parents' connections and financial resources landed her a job teaching at New York City University, where she made it a point to introduce herself to her students as a "left-wing femi-socialist." Always good for an anti-government or anti-business quote in the school newspaper, she was soon enjoying her reputation as a campus radical. But it wasn't until November 2001 that she made front-page headlines by chaining herself, along with her three-year-old daughter, Hillary, to the gate of Trinity Church on Broadway, just down the street from the still-smoldering ruins of the World Trade Center.

Running low on post-9/11 stories, the press was happy to give her a soap-box. With her daughter in her arms, she accused the United States of being "the true terrorist nation." The publicity and hate mail that followed had been the highlight of her life to that date. She'd even had the photograph from the *Times* article enlarged and framed to hang in her campus office. It showed her handing off Hillary to Charlie as she was being hauled off to jail.

Another child, Chelsea, was born into the Campbell household just before the beginning of the Iraq War in 2003. Which is when Jessica became Public Enemy Number One on conservative local radio talk shows. Both hosts and callers were angered by her proclamation that Islamic extremists were "at least fighting for Allah, which is a more ethical reason than our troops fighting for Big Oil, the god of the United States."

There just seemed to be something about childbirth that got her radical juices flowing. In late 2005, when she was pregnant with their third child, Benjamin, she wrote an essay entitled "What Goes Around, Comes Around," published in a left-of-center national magazine, which suggested that the people who'd died in the World Trade Center were "casualties of war . . . no different from civilians the U.S. government kills daily in Fallujah." Indeed, she wrote, the WTC dead shouldn't be considered victims, or even "collateral damage," because they were "the economic foot soldiers of the American war machine." "Therefore," she said, "it can be argued that they were legitimate military targets." She also noted that Islamic jihadists believed that they were obeying the will of God when they blew up other people along with themselves. "Thus they consider themselves, with some degree of accuracy . . . at least in an abstract sense, to be operating on a higher moral plane."

Throwing rocket fuel on the fire, she'd concluded that "the Christian Right, who run this country, should be the last to judge someone who believes that they are obeying the will of God."

After the article was published, Jessica eagerly awaited the deluge of hate mail and telephone death-threats she'd receive and pass on to her friends in the media as badges of honor. This time, however, the fallout was more than she'd anticipated. It was one thing to be pilloried by conservative talk-show hosts, but this time, even the *New York Times*, while defending her right to express her opinion, tepidly admonished her for "opening wounds that are still healing."

The public was not so timid. The Families of 9/11 Victims, as well as various conservative groups, organized a protest march on the NYCU campus that turned into a near-riot when anti-war and pro-Jessica supporters showed up. Heated words quickly turned to fisticuffs and an all-out brawl before the police moved in to separate the combatants. After the incident, members of the New York state legislature, including some middle-of-the-road Democrats, threatened to cut funding to the university for what the sponsor of the budget appropriations bill called Campbell's "hate speech."

NYCU's board of regents voted to censure her for "actions detrimental to the reputation of the school" because she'd signed the piece as "by Jessica Campbell, professor of political science at New York City University," without permission from the administration. Jessica threatened to sue on First Amendment grounds, and a settlement was reached. But part of the agreement was that she take an extended maternity leave for the birth of baby Benjamin in January.

The brouhaha might have ended there. However, Ariadne Stupenagel, a reporter for the normally liberal Manhattan weekly the *New York Guardian*, received a tip from an anonymous member of the NYCU faculty that Jessica's work wasn't entirely her own. The reporter began digging and found several instances where Jessica had apparently plagiarized the work of other scholars for a number of her essays, including her Ph.D. treatise, *A Feminist View of the Criminality of White Males in American Politics*. Stupenagel's investigation, published under the headline "What Goes Around, Comes Around for NYCU Prof," uncovered evidence that Campbell regularly made up facts and falsified research to support her writings.

Jessica's lawyer protested to her friends at other media outlets, as well as to the school's Board of Regents at a hastily arranged ethics hearing, that "these small irregularities, if they can even be described as such, were at worst accidental, and the product of carelessness and poor editing, not intentional academic fraud." He then hinted to the press that Stupenagel's story was essentially ghost-written for her by right-wing pundits, noting that the reporter was in an apparently amorous relationship with an aide to the New York district attorney, himself a notorious conservative.

Campbell's lawyer lambasted the university for using "these minor and out-of-context accusations to punish my client, not for alleged academic fraud, but for her essay regarding the people who died in the World Trade

Center." And that, he wagged his finger, "is a reprehensible assault on Jessica Campbell's constitutionally protected free speech." Any effort by the university to punish her, he warned, would have "a chilling effect on academic freedom" and result in a hefty lawsuit against the school.

However, with public sentiment decidedly against Jessica, and even the governor pronouncing that taxpayers should not have to fund "radical demagoguery disguised as free speech," the Board of Regents felt safe to begin an official inquest to determine if the charges of academic fraud and plagiarism warranted dismissal. In the meantime, they told Jessica and her attorney that her maternity leave was now a "sabbatical" until the review was complete.

Jessica wanted to fight. But gazing at an accordion file full of evidence that damned his client, the attorney shook his head. "No. You're going to take a break until this all blows over. Then you're going to throw yourself on your knees in front of the regents and beg to keep your job. *Comprende?*"

Jessica saw the look in his eyes and nodded. As high as she'd been while working on the article and immediately following its publication, her spirits plummeted like Icarus back to Earth.

In the kitchen, Charlie Campbell patted Jessica on the shoulder, the insincerity of which they both noticed but said nothing about. "Maybe when you get . . . better," he said, "you can help with the campaign. But you know what Dr. Winkler said about avoiding stress and getting plenty of rest. Just enjoy this time with the kids. Like Diane said the other day, they grow up fast, and it won't be long before they're out of the house."

Charlie thought he saw a look of irritation on his wife's face. His smile collapsed into a frown. He had watched her increasingly vitriolic mood swings with growing concern for their potential impact on his forthcoming congressional race.

Charlie was a politically ambitious man whose marriage to Jessica had given him the financial and personal wherewithal to pursue his goals. After graduating from Columbia Law School, he'd gone straight into politics, and by age thirty he had become borough president of Manhattan.

When he began wooing the predominantly liberal voters of Manhattan, his wife's outspokenness had been an asset. She'd also been astute with her political advice. He was still thankful that she'd encouraged him to denounce the war in Iraq early on, before he'd done much more than test the waters of a congressional campaign. Now he looked like a prophet, while other politicians were trying to explain why they'd initially approved of the war.

The 8th Congressional District included most of Manhattan's Upper West Side and points south encompassing Chelsea, SoHo, Greenwich Village, TreBeCa, and downtown Manhattan, as well as Sunset Park, Bay Ridge, Bensonhurst, Coney Island, Brighton Beach, and Gravesend in Brooklyn. As such, the district was composed of the most left-leaning voters in the entire state, who were only too willing to believe that a Republican administration had lied to lead Americans into a disastrous war and was possibly even responsible for the destruction of the World Trade Center.

Personally, Charlie had a hard time swallowing the notion that the Bush administration could have carried out what would have been the most complex and well-executed conspiracy and cover-up ever conceived by any government anywhere. *Hell, they can't even keep their sexual peccadilloes off the front pages and newscasts,* he thought, *much less pull off 9/11 and blame it on the fucking camel jockeys.* But publicly, he bent in whatever direction the voters in the district leaned.

Even up to Jessica's declaration that Islamic extremists were fighting for Allah, rather than Big Oil, Charlie had been able—when the press called asking for comment—to shake his head, plaster an affectionate smile on his face, and fall back on his wife's First Amendment rights while pointing out that being married did not mean that they shared all the same views. "At least not necessarily to the same degree of . . . vigor," he'd add, with a "what can you do" chuckle.

Charlie's own idealism had mellowed with age and political realities. As he had pointed out to his wife numerous times when asking for a bit more discretion in her comments, radical leftists rarely had their husbands elected to high office in the United States. The caution usually had the desired effect, because she wanted it as much as he did. She positively dreamed of becoming the darling of the Left within the D.C. beltway and being offered an endowed chair at Georgetown University.

Still, she couldn't seem to shut up for long. Something would set her off, and the next thing he knew, he'd be speed-dialing for the public-relations spin doctors.

At the same time that NYCU was trying to distance itself from his wife's comments, Charlie's political handlers, who privately referred to her as the "C-word," prepared Charlie's responses to the media. To wit, she had been taken out of context, and even at that her comments were "devil's advocate–type provocation intended to make people think about how our actions are perceived in other countries."

"My wife was merely trying to say that if U.S. foreign policy is based on violence, then violence is to be expected in return," he'd explained during an impromptu speech at Columbia University, where he could expect a sympathetic crowd. It was a few days after the birth of Benjamin, and he had said, "My wife and I have a new baby boy . . . yes, thank you for your applause, we like him too . . . and he's why I'm running for Congress. We need more voices for reason and diplomacy, not more dead soldiers or a draft of our sons and even our daughters. Our current adventurism in the Middle East has only created more enemies and a more dangerous world for all of our children."

Charlie and his team thought the speech had gone over well. But when Jessica saw the clip on the evening news, she'd lashed out. "I don't need you interpreting me for the masses," she'd hissed, "or using our son for cheap political theatrics."

"Great, here we go again," he'd snarled back, then ducked when she hurled a crystal ashtray at him. "You're nuts! I can't keep up with your fucking moods." He'd stomped out of the house and didn't return that night.

———

But that's all water under the bridge, Jessica thought, standing in the kitchen. Today, she'd save her children from that evil man.

Charlie finished his espresso and gave her a wink. "Well, got to run," he said. "You sure you're all right?"

Jessica hesitated. A part of her wanted to tell him that no, she wasn't all right—that there was a voice she believed to be the voice of God and it was telling her to do a terrible thing . . . that she needed help and he shouldn't leave. *But that would ruin everything.*

"I'm good," she replied and pecked him on the cheek. "Really, I am. Now get going to your meeting . . . mustn't keep Diane waiting."

Charlie scanned her face for evidence of sarcasm. Diane was usually a sore point in their relationship. *With good reason*, he thought, hoping he could still make it across town to her apartment for a quick romp in bed before heading to the campaign office. But his wife's face was the picture of innocence. He shook his head and headed out the door for the waiting cab.

Jessica walked over to a window facing the street and looked out. It was mid-March, and the leaf buds were opening on the trees in front of the brownstone. Her husband glanced back at the house but didn't see her, then climbed into the cab. She kept her vigil for several more minutes to make sure the taxi and Charlie didn't return.

Then she picked up the telephone and called the nanny. "Hi, Rebecca, I won't be needing you today," she said. "I'm going to take care of the children myself."

"Are you sure, ma'am?" Rebecca replied, the worry in her Jamaican-accented voice unmistakable. "Perhaps, I should come over just to help a little bit, dearie."

"That won't be necessary," Jessica said evenly. "But thank you, Rebecca. In fact, thank you for everything. And goodbye."

Jessica hung up with a sense of relief. With Charlie gone and the nanny accounted for, the steps of her plan were being checked off like a grocery list. She went down to the brownstone's underground garage where she opened up the back of the family Volvo station wagon and pulled a large footlocker from the interior. Charlie rarely, if ever, drove; he always taxied or had a driver, so the car had been a good hiding place.

Bumping the footlocker up the stairs, Jessica lugged it into the hallway outside the main floor bathroom and opened it. Inside were her "supplies"—two new pretty white dresses for the girls and a white gown for Benjamin; a padlock still in its packaging from the hardware store; and a hunting knife purchased at a sporting goods emporium in Newark. She picked the knife up and examined the blade; the weight of the weapon felt empowering in her hand. *Just like the knife Abraham planned to use on his son Isaac*, the voice noted approvingly.

Jessica left the trunk in the hallway and carried the clothing and the knife into the bathroom. The knife she laid on the vanity, and then she hung up the dresses and the gown before turning on the bathwater—testing the water on her wrist to make sure it wasn't too hot. She wanted the children to be clean and freshly scrubbed for their trip.

She heard the voice humming—the sort of sound, she imagined, that the universe makes, or how God communicates without words. She turned off the water, but the humming persisted.

Jessica turned and walked to the nursery and stood next to Benjamin's crib. She looked down at her sleeping child for a moment, then picked him up and held him against her shoulder. He felt warm and trusting nestled against her, making little sounds associated with baby dreams and contentment.

Suddenly she sobbed, overcome by what she knew she had to do. *Murderer!* cried a voice that sounded more like her own.

Don't listen to that, replied the other voice. *Your children's souls are at stake. The sins of their father run in their blood. Send them to me if you want to save them.*

Jessica willed herself to turn to the door of the nursery and begin to walk. Tears clouded her vision. She stumbled to the bathroom, where she sank to her knees next to the tub. Cradling her baby, she looked down into Benjamin's adoring eyes. A tear fell from her cheek onto his forehead, startling him. Lying him on the rug, she unzipped and removed his sleeper, and then his heavy, wet diaper. "God, do I have to do this?" she cried when he was naked.

I command it! The voice was insistent, angry. *Jessica, answer me!*

"*Hineini!*" Jessica shouted her reply. The Hebrew word confused her for a moment; she hadn't heard it since her childhood, when she'd visited her grandparents' home in Mount Vernon and listened to stories from the Torah. But she knew what it meant. "Here I am!" she shouted again.

The ancient word gave her the strength to pick up the child, who gurgled happily and kicked his feet. "Oh such a good baby," she cooed. "Don't worry little lamb, we'll meet again someday."

Jessica hesitated. She feared God, and in the Torah that had been enough to satisfy Him and spare Isaac. But now the voice was silent. "*Hineini,*" she whispered again and plunged her baby beneath the warm, soapy waters of the tub.

2

A young black man paced back and forth on the sidewalk outside of the Third Avenue synagogue on the Upper East Side of Manhattan, his fingers nervously combing through his frizzy beard and scratching at the old pock-marks on his cheeks. Stopping at the bottom of the stairs leading up to the temple, he closed his eyes and allowed the warmth of the sunny July morning to soak into his face.

Ever since his childhood growing up in the tenement apartment at 126th and Madison Avenue in Harlem he shared with his grandparents and younger sister, he'd loved this time of year. On a day like this, the memory of shivering through a long winter in the rat-infested building would be forgotten. On a day like this, the sunlight would last forever and the games of stickball, punchball, and hoops would go on well beyond his normal bedtime.

Back then, his grandmother, a large woman who favored loud floral-print dresses, would be hanging out the window of their apartment, fanning herself and complaining to the neighbor woman in the next window over that the city smelled "like a big ol' garbage truck." But the heat also meant the arrival each evening of heaven on wheels.

It would begin as just a few notes heard in the distance, a sound no boy or girl sweating it out on the baked city streets could resist. Every kid on the block would stop what they were doing and swivel their heads like radar antennae, trying to determine the direction of the music. Then around a corner it would appear, driving slowly, calling out like the Pied Piper of cold sugar treats, the Good Humor Ice Cream truck.

He'd look up at the old woman in the windowsill, the only mom he'd ever really known, and wouldn't have to say a thing. Her eyes might have been going, but her hearing was as good as his and she knew the sound of the ice cream man when she heard it, too. She'd disappear for a moment to fetch her purse and then drop a dollar bill to "buy a little treat" for himself and his sister.

The young man shook his head. All of that had been long ago and they were both dead—one of old age, the other murdered during a drug deal. But today he was ready to join them, ready to place himself in the hands of Allah.

Beneath his calf-length wool coat and the heavy vest he wore, sweat trickled down his chest and back. He wanted to scratch, but he didn't dare. *It's time to do this,* he thought, yet he lingered, soaking in the sounds and smells and sights.

To the east he could see a small section of the Queensboro Bridge and the Memorial Sloan-Kettering Cancer Center where his mother had died, writhing in pain, when he was eight. Death had frightened him then, but not anymore. He welcomed it. *Inshallah, as God wills.*

Sighing, he thought about his young son—Abdullah, only four years old. The boy would be in religious school, the *madrasah,* in his *hifz* introductory course, memorizing the Qur'an. He was also studying Arabic so that some-day he could read the words as they'd been written by the Prophet Muham-mad—*blessings be upon him.* Someday, if it was Allah's plan, his son would also study Qur'anic interpretation, called *tafsir;* Islamic law, or *shar'iah;* and *hadith,* the recorded sayings and deeds of the Prophet.

May Allah grant him peace, the young man recited to himself. He hoped that his son would grow up to be a man of God, perhaps even an imam in the new world—a Muslim world subject to Islamic law. *I'm doing this for him,* he assured himself.

Baptized in the Harlem Baptist Church some twenty-five years earlier as Rondell James, he'd suffered a case of smallpox at the age of ten. It left his complexion scarred and his psyche battered, especially when the other kids nicknamed him "Scratchy."

His grandparents had tried to fill the void left by a father he'd never known and the death of his mother, but he'd misspent a miserable youth running with gangs, dealing crack, drinking malt liquor until he couldn't stand up or shoot straight, fathering illegitimate children, and serving time upstate for armed robbery. His life had no purpose, no meaning. If he had ever dreamed of something better when he was a boy, the notion had been drummed out of him as a teenager by his so-called community leaders and activists who convinced him he was a victim of racism. It wasn't his fault he had nothing. Society owed him but wasn't going to pay up. It was the white man's world, and he was just taking up space in it. A real nobody.

But he wasn't going to be a victim anymore. On September 11, 2001, the martyrs had flown the jetliners into the World Trade Center, and he'd seen the power that a few men of faith could wield if they obeyed the will of Allah. Even as the city mourned, a part of him had thrilled that men with brown faces like him had terrified the world's most powerful nation.

It had also been Allah's will that shortly after the attack, as he happened to be walking down Frederick Douglass Boulevard, he had seen a man standing on a milk crate, preaching to the crowd. Tall and so thin that the skin of his face seemed to have been pulled and stretched over the bones, which made his protruding eyes and thick lips more pronounced, the man drew attention to himself like a red cape attracts a bull. He was dressed all in white, including a small, round white cap on his head. And in his brown hand was a microphone hooked up to a boombox held above the passersby—most of whom tried to ignore him—by another, even larger and much heavier man, also wearing only white.

As he moved closer, Rondell saw that the two were surrounded by yet more black men similarly dressed—tough-looking men in dark glasses, who stood with their arms crossed and their jaws set. Even the local gangbangers and street criminals gave them a wide berth.

"Hear me, my brothers and sisters," the man on the milk crate shouted into the microphone. "Christianity is the white man's religion. He's used it to keep our people in shackles from the days when they were brought here in chains from Africa. There is only one faith for the black man whether he is in Africa or America, the one true faith of Islam."

The man spoke in clipped, three- or four-word bursts, but without pausing in his train of thought. "Only men of the One True Faith would have the courage to strike at the World Trade Center where the white man forged his economic chains every bit as cruel and binding as the iron shackles of slavery. They were men of purpose. Those of you who have been living lives without purpose, find a purpose here with us in serving Allah. Return with us to our mosque and join us in prayers that the Prophet, blessings and peace be upon him, taught us so that we might live as we were intended."

A few hecklers across the street shouted slurs from a safe distance, but Rondell James stood mesmerized. It was as if the man was speaking to him directly. He'd never embraced Christianity like his mother or grandparents; he couldn't identify with a white Jesus hanging on a cross. And, like the man said, he was almost twenty-five years old and still living a life without purpose. Jobless, pointless, he couldn't even make child support payments—not that he'd tried very hard to do so—without resorting to crime.

When the man stepped down, Rondell walked toward him, intending to ask him more about Islam. But when he got to within several feet, one of the big bodyguards put out a hand and stopped him. Embarrassed, he assumed the man thought he wasn't good enough. He was about to turn away when the tall speaker placed his own hand on the bodyguard's arm and lowered it.

"Salaam, Brother Abdul," the man said. "I believe we have a seeker of the One True Faith."

In that moment, Rondell knew he'd found a home. He went back to the Al-Aqsa mosque at 124th and Malcolm X Boulevard with the men in white and several other prospects, including his friend Suleiman Abdalla, who, like him, had a physical deformity, a disease that affected his skin's pigmentation. After a quick introductory course, the young men had found themselves kneeling and rising, kneeling and rising—praying in the direction of Mecca. Afterward, Rondell's knees were sore, but his soul was lifted, and he resolved to change his life.

He'd thrown himself into his new religion with all the zeal of the recent convert. Never much of a reader in school, having dropped out in eighth grade, he took the *hifz* course to memorize the Qur'an, so that he would be known as a *hafiz*, someone who knew the book by heart. He prayed five times a day with such fervor that some of his fellow converts thought he was "putting on a show," and he always listened intently to the exhortations of the tall man in white, Imam Sharif Jabbar.

The imam gave him a new name, Muhammad Jamal Khalifa. "Be proud," Jabbar told him. "It is also the name of one of Sheik Osama bin Laden's brothers-in-law. He has arranged the financing of many spectacular projects on behalf of *jihad*."

The new Khalifa was thrilled to bear the name of one of the great men of Al Qaeda who, as Imam Jabbar lectured, were "fighting the white man and his decadent culture on behalf of people of color, not just Muslims, everywhere." Of course, such virulent speeches were reserved for "special converts" like Khalifa and not heard by the general congregation at the mosque. Most of the members of the congregation, in fact, had no reason to suspect that their imam's politics were any more radical than his soapbox oratory, or that he would ever suggest acting on the ideas he privately espoused.

Soon, Khalifa was one of the men in white standing in a circle around Imam Jabbar as he proselytized on the street corners of Harlem, reaching out to other young black men like himself. The imam was a heroic figure to him, the father he'd never known—a real man who wasn't afraid to speak out on his convictions, and damn the authorities if they didn't like it. He'd even been on *hajj*, the pilgrimage to Mecca that every Muslim was obligated to make during his lifetime, if he could afford to do so.

Khalifa was ready to do whatever the imam asked. He'd even helped beat a man senseless for his sake. The man, claiming to have lost his wife in the 9/11 attack, had tried to push his way through the bodyguards one Sunday afternoon to get at Jabbar. After Khalifa was arrested, he had pleaded to a reduced charge of misdemeanor assault and spent three months in jail, praising Allah that the authorities had not matched his current name to his old felony record.

After such a show of loyalty, he'd moved into the imam's innermost circle of trusted men. Only then was he told the story of how the imam had gone from the hajj to Afghanistan, where he'd spent a month training in an Al Qaeda camp. That's how Khalifa learned that the tens of thousands of dollars the mosque's congregation raised every year for "Muslim charities" actually ended up in the hands of the *mujahideen* for their holy war against the West.

"*Who are they to call us 'terrorists'?*" the imam had railed at one of the secret meetings attended by the bodyguards and a dozen other newer converts like Khalifa and Abdalla. *"The Jews in Israel murder Palestinians all the time, and no one calls them terrorists. White American soldiers drop bombs on innocent people in Afghanistan and Iraq, slaughtering thousands, but no one calls them terrorists. The attack on the World Trade Center was not an act of terrorism, it was a military strike in a war declared by Sheik Osama bin Laden and others five years earlier. It's war if the atrocities are carried out by the West, but it's terrorism if Muslims defend themselves."*

The men at that meeting had been asked to line up so that the imam could speak to each in turn. Then, the imam had placed a hand on each man's shoulder and looked him squarely in the eyes. *"We need our own mujahideen who are not afraid to die for Allah,"* he had said to them. *"Are you such a man?"*

"I am," Khalifa had sworn when it was his turn. *"Tell me how I can serve."*

The imam had smiled. *"Soon, my brother, soon."*

———

That had been two years ago. Now, Khalifa looked up at the simple rectangular, gray granite sides of the synagogue with its modest, unadorned windows and Star of David above the wide doors. *At least the Jews are not idolaters—unlike Christians with their blasphemous paintings of God, the prophets, and their false saints,* he thought and then caught himself before he let any other decent thoughts about Jews slip into his mind.

He was aware that Jews were also "People of the Book," who followed the same general teachings regarding the worship of the God of Ibrahim, the father of Islam, Judaism, and Christianity, though the latter two had bastardized the teachings and strayed from the true path. He also knew that the Qur'an generally preached tolerance of the Jews in Muslim lands. However, as Imam Jabbar had explained, all that had changed when the Zionists stole Palestine from its rightful Muslim owners. The Israelis were the enemy, as were all Jews and the Western governments they controlled, especially the United States.

"Yes, the Prophet Muhammad, peace be upon him, wrote that Jews should be allowed to live in Muslim lands without converting so long as they, in his blessed words, 'pay the tax of acknowledgment of superiority and are in a state of subjection,'" Jabbar had said. *"After all, there must be Jews in Jerusalem at the end of*

the world for the prophecies to be fulfilled. However, the Prophet, blessings upon his name, often made war on Jews if, like today's Zionist murderers, they harmed or insulted Muslims. And has not Sheik Rahman issued fatwas permitting Muslims to kill Jews and Americans? Who are we to argue with such a great man!"

Learned men like the "blind sheik" Omar Abdul Rahman, who had been behind the first attempt to destroy the World Trade Center, bin Laden, and Jabbar impressed Khalifa. He admired how they could find ways to resolve apparent contradictions within the Qur'an through *fatwas,* decrees by Islamic clerics that absolved individual Muslims of actions that would otherwise be considered crimes. The fatwas were a necessary tool of jihad, otherwise suicide bombers and jihadis would have been committing sins. He had studied the writings of Sayyid Qutb, the martyred Egyptian writer of the 1950s and '60s, and one of the founders of the Islamic fundamentalist movement. Qutb had argued that the establishment of Israel, and the West's support of the Zionists, were insufferable humiliations for Muslims that had to be rectified. But Allah had allowed it because Muslims had turned from the righteous path by adopting Western culture, including immodest clothing, ideas about women's rights, and secular democracy. Only by returning to fundamentalist doctrine, establishing nations governed by shar'iah, and waging jihad on those who oppressed them would Muslims regain the blessing of Allah and attain eventual world domination.

The father of the movement from which Al Qaeda and like-minded organizations would spring, Qutb, who'd been hung in Egypt for sedition in 1966, also had a lot to say that spoke directly to young black men living in Harlem. *"The white man in Europe or America is our number-one enemy,"* he'd written. *"The white man crushes us underfoot while we teach our children about his civilization, his universal principles, and noble objectives. . . . Let us plant the seeds of hatred, disgust, and revenge in the souls of these children."* Heeding that advice, Khalifa had enrolled his son, Abdullah, in the madrasah established at the mosque.

Now, as he stood outside the synagogue, Khalifa imagined the seeds being planted in his son's mind. If it was the will of Allah, Abdullah would someday blossom into a American mujahideen like his father.

He wondered what his wife would have to say about that. He'd met Miriam Juma soon after joining the mosque. She and her family were illegal immigrants from Kenya who'd come to the mosque hoping to find work as well as a place to worship. The imam had noted the way that Khalifa looked at the sixteen-year-old, and after several weeks of negotiations with her father—and repeated reminders that such a union would help her immigration status—a marriage between Khalifa and Miriam was arranged.

Miriam was unlike any of the women Khalifa had known in Harlem. As a wife, she knew her place and did not argue or "sass" him; she had his meals ready for him when he returned home from the mosque, where he earned a meager living as a member of the imam's "security team," and quickly bore him a son. She was a model of female Muslim propriety—she wore the *hajib*, a long scarf that covered her hair and shielded her face, as well as loose-fitting gowns that modestly hid the curves of her body when in public.

Miriam had hoped that their son, Abdullah, would go to public school kindergarten when he turned four that previous fall. But she did not fight Khalifa when he insisted that Abdullah be enrolled instead in the madrasah.

Only when he began talking about jihad and fantasizing about going to Afghanistan or Sudan to train with Al Qaeda did she argue with him. Islamic extremists were not true Muslims, she insisted. *"They are apostate, and doomed to hell for killing innocent people . . . especially making war on women and children, which the Qur'an forbids. These fatwas are false absolutions that twist and bend the law for their own ends. Their fatwas have no legitimacy with true Muslims, only the ignorant who cannot read and therefore do not know the Qur'an."*

As she spoke, Khalifa felt doubt, and that made him react angrily; he told her to be quiet. But Miriam was not to be silenced on this matter. *"Islam is a religion of peace and tolerance,"* she insisted. *"We greet each other, and even strangers, with 'salaam,' which means peace. Osama bin Laden, Sheik Rahman, and these others are nothing more than murderers who use the Qur'an for their own political ends."*

Miriam pointed to her own father, Mahmoud Juma, as the sort of Muslim man Khalifa should try to emulate. *"He works hard to support his family,"* she said. *"And worships Allah in his prayers five times a day without strutting around with his chest puffed out saying, 'I am mujahideen and going on jihad' when he has a wife and children who depend on him. He lives his life by the Qur'an. He doesn't need fatwas to absolve him of things that he knows—that every human knows—are sinful. Murdering people in the name of Allah is a sin that will never be forgiven."*

Khalifa stormed out of the apartment and went to the mosque to pray. He had grown to love his wife—he was even surprised at the tenderness he felt toward her—and when he prayed he thanked Allah for her. When he was honest with himself, it was at such times that he saw the true beauty of his faith. He had noted how content his father-in-law was to have the opportunity to make a living, even though he was only a janitor in a building in the Financial District. The former Kenyan fisherman wanted nothing more, it seemed, than better lives for his children, legal resident status (*"and perhaps someday, Allah willing, citizenship"*), and to worship according to his beliefs.

"All these I found in America, not a supposedly Muslim country, where they try to dictate which 'version' of Islam is correct," he'd pointed out one night when Khalifa was railing on about American injustices. But it only made Khalifa angry and confused.

Imam Jabbar must have sensed his follower's discomfiture after one of Khalifa's arguments with his wife that past winter. He'd just ended one of the secret meetings with the inner circle, in which he'd announced that two special visitors involved in a "very special project" would be arriving the next fall. They would all be called upon to make great sacrifices in the cause of Islam. As the others filed out, he'd pulled Khalifa aside.

"So, my brother," he'd begun, placing his hands on Khalifa's shoulders. "You seem troubled. Are you having doubts?"

Khalifa shook his head. For a moment, he thought he'd heard a veiled threat in the other man's tone, but then dismissed it as paranoia. "No, imam," he said. "I am committed to jihad. It's just my wife . . . she . . . well, she . . ."

"Yes, she what?" the imam said sternly. "You haven't told her about our discussions?"

"Oh no, imam."

The imam smiled and changed his tone to that of a father figure counseling a favorite son on "woman troubles." "Good. Then, perhaps, she has been immodest? Has she shamed you?"

Khalifa wished he hadn't brought up the subject of his wife. The things she said were troubling and contradicted what the imam taught; Jabbar might not appreciate her opinion. He might even order him to divorce her. So Khalifa, on the spot, made up a lie. "Well, I have been concerned that she is picking up bad habits from non-believer women. As you know, she works at a grocery store as a clerk, and sometimes she says things that aren't right for a Muslim woman."

The imam relaxed. He'd heard this complaint many times. Among couples who converted to Islam, it was the man who usually stayed with it. Give women raised in Harlem a few months, or even weeks, of kowtowing to her man, and there was a tendency to revolt . . . and if the man wasn't careful, that included a swift kick to his backside. Then the women would be out of the gowns and back into their tight pants and blouses with their breasts bouncing around for all to see, and they often took their men with them.

Miriam was different because she was an immigrant and raised a Muslim. Her father was one of the most respected men in the mosque, even though he did not agree with Jabbar's politics and said so frequently. The daughter was young and couldn't help but be influenced by the overwhelming decadence of American culture. Jabbar didn't want to come down too hard on her, which could cause her to revolt and leave the mosque, taking her husband with her. He'd spent too much time grooming Khalifa to lose him now. So he counseled him to be firm "but understanding of her age" when she seemed to stray from the path.

"Perhaps, you should buy her something—a new scarf or comfortable undergarments to wear in the privacy of your bedroom," Jabbar said with a knowing smile, pulling a roll of cash from his pocket. He peeled off several twenties and handed the money to Khalifa, who protested but then accepted the cash and thanked the imam.

"It is my pleasure, Muhammad Jamal Khalifa," Jabbar said. "You are a good man, and soon, if it is the will of Allah, all of Islam will know your name."

3

Some eighty blocks south of where Khalifa stood, Darla Milquetost leaned back in her chair at the receptionist's desk, trying to decipher the raised voices coming from behind the door leading to the private office of the District Attorney for the County of New York. Then she noticed that the two young assistant district attorneys sitting on the couch in her office, waiting to meet with her boss, were entirely too interested in the argument for her liking.

"Is there something you need?" Milquetost's tone and stare could have chilled the toes off a penguin. It was one thing for her to eavesdrop on the boss; after all, she had his best interests at heart. However, whatever was being said on the other side of the closed doors was certainly none of their business.

Startled, the ADAs found something eminently fascinating about the months-old reading material on the coffee table in front of them. Rookie assistant district attorneys might have slugged their way to the top of their class at Harvard Law, or fought for the prestige of clerking for one of the imperious justices of the U.S. Circuit Court of Appeals, but they all quickly learned that there was one person you didn't mess with on the eighth floor of the Criminal Courts building at 100 Centre Street in downtown Manhattan. That person wasn't so much The Man Himself, District Attorney

Roger "Butch" Karp, though he could be intimidating and demanding; it was the ferocious middle-aged woman who guarded his inner sanctum. Cross Mrs. Milquetost, and requests for audiences with her boss, or recommendations for promotions and plum assignments, had a way of being shuffled to the bottom of a pile of papers. Legend had it that a multiple-offender was now practicing traffic court law on Staten Island.

In particular, woe be it to the newbie who read the nameplate on her desk and pronounced her name "Milk Toast." Frost would form on all glass surfaces as her voice iced over, "It's Mil-kay-tossed . . . that's French in case they didn't teach foreign languages at whatever school you graduated—I assume you graduated—from. Do not forget—Mil . . . kay . . . tossed." Mispronounce it once, and you were on her bad side until a lot of ass-kissing thawed the glacier that surrounded her heart. But do it twice and it was a one-way ticket to the Outer Boroughs.

Satisfied that the ADAs were appropriately occupied with dog-eared copies of *Law Enforcement Magazine*, Mrs. Milquetost inclined her brunette bouffant toward where the voices had grown suddenly quieter. A moment later, she nearly launched to her feet when the door to the office popped open with a bang.

A short, dapper man emerged and fixed her with an angry glare from his intense blue eyes. Normally, the mere presence of assistant district attorney Vinson Talcott "V. T." Newbury would have sent Mrs. Milquetost happily aflutter. He was extraordinarily handsome—even if his sandy blond hair was thinning and the lines in his face deepening—as well as charming and impeccably mannered.

If she hadn't had a nice new boyfriend, Mrs. Milquetost, a widow, would have liked to demonstrate to Newbury that beneath her proper business persona beat the heart of a poetically passionate woman. *Oh who are you kidding, you'd drop Bill like a wormy apple if Mr. Newbury showed the slightest interest, which he hasn't,* Mrs. Milquetost thought gloomily.

V. T., as she'd never had the nerve to call him, was the opposite of "The Beast," otherwise known as assistant district attorney Ray Guma, who in her opinion was a boorish, hairy ape of a man whose only manners were bad ones. Where Mr. Newbury was bluebloodedly well-spoken, Guma grunted with the irritating accent of his native borough, which he laid on especially thick when trying to rile her. He also seemed to take great delight in mispronouncing her name, but there was little she could do about it. The Beast had unfettered access to Mr. Karp and was untouchable.

Both men were longtime friends of her boss, though she didn't understand how two such opposite characters could possibly coexist or why Mr. Karp put up with Guma. She certainly wouldn't have; she read the *New York Post* on the subway every morning on the way to work, hoping to find a story about some terrible accident befalling Ray Guma. Finding nothing could put her in a bad mood for the rest of the day.

Usually the pendulum of her moods swung the other way at the appearance of V. T. Newbury in the office. But he'd stalked in that morning and without so much as an "Is he in?" stormed the inner office, from which the sounds of discord soon emanated. It broke her heart that Newbury and Karp seemed to be at such odds these days, and she continued to hope that they would reconcile. But the shouting matches had been growing more frequent and angry of late. As she had confided to her boyfriend, work at the New York DAO wasn't so pleasant anymore.

———

A deep, irritated voice followed Newbury out of the office. "Damn it, V. T., come back, we can talk this over. You're overreacting."

Newbury whirled and faced the open door. His pale complexion turned bright red. "I think we've said all that needs to be said," he replied. "As for my 'overreactions,' they are none of your business."

Not knowing what else to do, Mrs. Milquetost picked up her telephone and placed a call to the building's janitorial services to complain about "mildew in the air conditioner." She'd actually planned on making the call later, but now seemed a good time with all the tension in the room. She hazarded a glance at the ADAs on the couch, who'd looked up when V. T. stormed out of the inner sanctum but now had their noses buried even further in their reading material. She wished she, too, had a copy of *Law Enforcement Magazine* to hide behind.

V. T. Newbury had only recently returned to the DAO after he'd been badly beaten during a robbery. His assailants had broken his nose and fractured a cheek bone—both requiring the services of plastic surgeons to repair—as well as cracking several ribs and giving him a concussion. But from what she gathered listening in on conversations among those who had known him for many years, the most serious injuries weren't physical.

Despite his refined features and somewhat effete mannerisms, V. T. Newbury was said to be as tough and fearless a prosecutor as anyone in the New York DAO. Specializing in white-collar and organized crimes, he'd taken on the CEOs of Fortune 500 companies and reduced them to common felons doing time, and put away a dozen supposedly "untouchable" mob bosses on racketeering and criminal conspiracy charges. He currently headed up the New York DAO bureau of racketeering and public corruption, which for more than a year had been pursuing recently discovered cases against New York City police officers that had been shoved under the rug. None of them had ever been able to intimidate V. T. Newbury—not billionaires, not gangsters, and not crooked cops.

But not anymore . . . not since the beating that put him in the hospital for two weeks. The old fire and zest for the fight seemed extinguished, as was the sense of humor that, while dry as a Silver Bullet martini, was also as integral to his personality as monogrammed handkerchiefs were to his wardrobe. As he walked through the halls of the Criminal Courts building, he looked like a dog that expected to get beat for some unknown infraction.

The rumor around the office was that he was going to accept an offer from his uncle, Dean Newbury, to join the family's white-shoe law firm in Midtown. He would be taking the place of his father, Vincent Newbury, who'd died suddenly that past fall of a heart attack. Along with a guaranteed, and substantial, rise in income and nicer digs—on the top floor of a Fifth Avenue skyscraper with a view of Central Park, instead of a tiny office in the Criminal Courts building—he'd gain a ticket out of the primordial swamp of prosecuting New York's criminals. Little wonder the office pool was running four to one that he'd be gone within a month. And no one blamed him.

No one except Butch Karp, apparently. A legendarily straight arrow who saw prosecuting criminals on behalf of the citizens of New York City as a calling nearly on par with the priesthood, the district attorney had been overheard discussing V. T.'s possible "defection" in terms that were border-line insulting—and unexpected, given the longtime friendship between the two men.

The friendship was not very apparent now as Newbury stalked over to the door leading out to the hallway. He grabbed the doorknob just as Karp appeared from his office.

"I just want you to reconsider before you do something you'll regret," Karp said to his colleague's back.

Newbury set his jaw and replied, "Shall I announce this at the meeting on Monday, or are you going to save me the trouble?"

Karp shrugged. "Fine. Never thought I'd see the day when you'd let a couple of punks chase you out of this office for a Fifth Avenue day spa, but money talks and bullshit walks I guess. I'll let the others know and save you the . . . embarrassment."

Newbury paused at the insult, then flung open the door. He stomped out, slamming the door behind him so that the glass pane rattled dangerously.

After a long pause, Karp turned toward the ADAs. Reluctantly, like pris-oners ordered to look into the eyes of the firing squad, they raised their heads to meet the infamous Karp glare. It was worse than they'd heard. He was a big man—six-foot-five and 240 pounds—which made the fire in his gold-flecked gray eyes all the more imposing. A sound like steam from a tea kettle escaped his pursed lips.

Gazing down at them, Karp knew that the latest episode of the rift be-tween himself and V. T. would now become the buzz of the office. It was sure to inspire wonder in those who knew how far he and V. T. went back. He would never have believed it himself.

They'd been friends and colleagues for thirty years, ever since they both arrived fresh out of law school to work at the New York DAO when the of-fice was run by the legendary, seemingly immortal Francis Garrahy. V. T. came from a family of wealth and social prominence. His mother traced her ancestry back to the Pilgrims of Plymouth Colony, while his father's side had been knocking around since the Revolutionary War. From the moment he'd graduated from Harvard Law, V. T. had seemed destined to eventually take over his paternal family's two-hundred-year-old law firm, but to every-one's surprise and consternation, he'd joined the DAO instead. Ever since, his family had waited for him to "get it out of his system," but except for a brief stint with the U.S. Attorney General's Office, he'd remained at 100 Centre Street.

Karp, on the other hand, was a Brooklyn Jew whose predecessors had emigrated from Poland fleeing Cossacks and pogroms. His mother had been an elementary school teacher, and while his father, Julius, had graduated from law school, he'd made his living as a businessman manufacturing and selling women's hair products. Their son, "Butch," had attended the University of California–Berkeley on a basketball scholarship until a knee injury ended the possibility of an athletic career and put him on the path to law school. After graduating, he'd applied to one place and one place only, the New York District Attorney's Office, with the aim of making it to the homicide bureau.

In between then and now, Karp had dabbled in private practice, but he'd hated it and returned to the DAO. He still took on the occasional off-the-clock case to help a friend—in one recent trial, he'd helped a coach in Idaho, the brother of an old basketball friend, defend himself against charges trumped up to get him fired. But he was where he wanted to be, though it was still hard to imagine that he was now the duly elected district attorney, the heir to Garrahy's legacy.

Their family backgrounds were not the only differences between Karp and Newbury. In a court of law, V. T. was the meticulous, low-key technician who prosecuted cases like an engineer building a bridge. The more complex the crime, the more he enjoyed the challenge of piecing it together so quietly and efficiently that defendants hardly knew that he'd made a case against them until the jury returned with a guilty verdict.

Karp, however, was the courtroom brawler. A tactician in the sense of military warfare, he wasted little time cutting to the chase, tearing the heart out of defense strategies while ripping the truth out of hostile witnesses and defendants who dared to lie on the stand. He was a true believer—a champion of the U.S. Constitution, which to him was as sacrosanct as any Torah, Bible, or Qur'an, and a modern, laser-focused, metro-savvy Don Quixote committed to the ultimate victory of right over wrong, good over evil. . . . Which earned him a great deal of teasing from Guma, who occasionally referred to him as Miss Goody Two-Shoes.

Despite their differences, however, Newbury, Guma, and Karp shared a common dedication to the cause of justice. Early on they'd come to respect each other's strengths and joke about their foibles. They always knew where they could find someone to lean on when the frustrations and burden of trying cases in the busiest district attorney's office in the country weighed heavily.

Although he would himself have been a plum recruit for any private law firm in the city, Karp also admired Newbury's dedication to a career of public service when he could have easily given in to his father's yearly invitation to join the family firm. But all of that had changed when Newbury, responding to an anonymous tip regarding the NYPD investigations, went to meet the source only to be accosted by two young black men who'd beat the living hell out of him.

A few days after the assault, Karp had arrived outside his friend's hospital room when he overheard V. T.'s uncle, Dean Newbury, head of the family firm, urging him to give up the DAO for private practice. A subsequent exchange between Karp and the older man had grown heated and then ended when V. T. had sided with his uncle and said that he was thinking about accepting the offer.

Karp had backed off. One of his oldest friends was lying in a hospital bed, and he had a right to consider what was best for him. "What he needs is space," he'd confided to Mrs. Milquetost in a rare moment of openness. "But this is where he belongs, he'll be back."

But when V. T. got out of the hospital and returned to work at the DAO, word soon spread that he was going to quit. Karp even brought it up at one of the Monday morning staff meetings, telling those assembled not to worry about the rumor, because V. T. would never be "happy kissing fat-cat asses and whoring himself to oil companies." He'd meant it as a joke, but Newbury reacted by gathering his papers and walking out without a word, leaving the room filled with an embarrassed silence and averted eyes.

The discord between Karp and Newbury had quickly become common knowledge among the several hundred assistant district attorneys and bureau chiefs, as well as several hundred more support staffers. Even some of the regular street people who hung around the Criminal Courts building knew that closed-door meetings between him and V. T. were growing increasingly rancorous.

And now there was even more fuel for the gossip-mongers, Karp thought as he glanced at his receptionist, who kept looking under the pile of papers on her desk as if whatever it was she was searching for would magically appear where it had not been before.

He was about to invite the wide-eyed ADAs into his office when a large black man burst through the door. Clay Fulton pulled up short when he saw Karp standing a few feet from him. Fulton nodded toward the inner office. "Can I speak to you for a minute?" he asked.

Karp walked back into his office with a knot growing in the pit of his stomach. A former college football player who still looked like he could tote the rock, as well as a New York Police Department detective, Fulton wasn't the sort to make dramatic entrances or mysterious requests for a private audience unless something important was up. He was in charge of the NYPD detectives assigned to investigate cases for the DAO, as well as to provide security for Karp, and he took his job very, very seriously.

Fulton followed Karp into the office and shut the door. His big, broad face was creased into an angry scowl. "Boss, we got a problem," he said. "It finally happened."

4

"*All of Islam will know your name.*" Khalifa could still hear the promise above the honking of the taxis and general roar of traffic on Third Avenue. *I will be somebody. And, with Allah's blessing, they will pay.*

Imam Jabbar had been saying that Khalifa and his other "American mujahideen" would soon be called upon to wage jihad against white America and the Jews. Then in March, the imam had announced that they would begin their training for a "spectacular" task. Soon a man whom he called only "The Sheik," along with one of the foremost mujahideen in the world, known as Tatay, would arrive, and together—with the help of Jabbar's hand-picked jihadis—they would rock the world.

They needed to prepare themselves physically as well as spiritually for the event, which in all likelihood would result in their martyrdom—and, Jabbar noted quickly, their automatic admittance to Paradise. If anyone had reservations about his ability to make the sacrifice, he needed to make it known then and there, the imam warned.

When no one bowed out, Jabbar hugged each man, saying how proud he was to be their imam. It was clear that he had no real idea of what the event would be, but he asked if there were any questions.

A quiet, bookish man named Omar Al-Hassan raised his hand, as Khalifa and the others cast knowing sideways glances at one another. Omar, a native of Pakistan and the only one in the room not raised in Harlem, was a computer genius, and for unexplained reasons, that gave him special status with Jabbar. The imam even seemed to put up with what Khalifa and the others considered a lukewarm commitment to jihad. So it did not surprise them that he asked again to hear how his family would be taken care of *if* they did not return from the mission.

"Your families will receive a generous stipend provided by some of our wealthy benefactors in Saudi Arabia," the imam promised, with a grand flourish of his large, spider-like hands.

"And, as the widows and orphaned children of martyrs, they will have the goodwill of Muslims all over the world and be blessed in the eyes of Allah." The imam fixed the questioner with his protruding eyes the way a large brown lizard sizes up a bug. "However, be forewarned; it is highly unlikely that you will return from this mission. Resign yourself to the will of Allah, or leave now."

Omar averted his eyes. But Khalifa and his friend Abdalla could see his face and later told each other that they thought the man looked troubled. Not the right attitude for a mujahideen.

Abdalla raised his hand next. Most of the others in the room didn't like him because he had a skin disease that was turning him white. Even Khalifa, who was about his only companion, thought he tended to be a bit of an ass-kisser. "I have a question, imam," Abdalla said.

"Yes, Suleiman?"

"Would this sheik be Osama?" he said, turning to inform the others, "Osama is sometimes referred to as a sheik by Al Qaeda."

Jabbar raised an eyebrow. "No, it is not Osama," he said. "He is the new Osama, but more than that I cannot say at this time."

Training was broken into two phases. Phase One, they were told, would be conducted in the administration building on the mosque grounds, late at night after all worshipers and staff had left.

At the first meeting, the mujahideen were introduced to a woman who spoke with what sounded like an Eastern European accent of some sort. She said she would be leading one of two teams on the mission. However, her purpose at this phase was to teach them what they would need to know for Phase Two.

Khalifa was surprised by her presence. For one thing, she was a woman, and Jabbar rarely spoke of women except as property, and for another she was white. In fact, she was a good-looking blonde of about forty years, immodestly dressed in pants and a cotton shirt that accented her breasts. But even Jabbar deferred to her.

"You may call me Ajmaani," she said. "You will do exactly as I say, when I say it."

Despite her gender, no one voiced doubts about her intensity. Someone later said he thought she might be from Chechnya, "one of them little countries over there by Russia where the Muslim brothers are trying to break free. I hear they're vicious motherfucking holy warriors; they cut the throats of any Russian soldiers they catch."

At first, they'd trained like any new military recruits. They learned to address their superiors—Ajmaani and Jabbar—in a respectful manner and do as told without comment or question. They were taught to disassemble, clean, and reassemble a variety of weapons, and they studied tactics for fighting inside a building.

Each man was taught how to create vest bombs for the purpose of killing as many people as possible while seeking martyrdom. ("We do not say 'suicide,'" Jabbar had instructed them. "Suicide is prohibited by the Qur'an. You are seeking martyrdom. These are martyr's vests.") The vests were lined with C-4 plastic explosives and filled with ball-bearings; they were triggered by yanking on a cord attached to a small detonator that would in turn ignite the explosives.

They were instructed to keep the vests handy in their homes in case they were called upon to make an impromptu sacrifice, or if the police showed up. If the latter, they were to strap on the vest before the police could come through the door, and then yank the cord.

As the group trained, they became more and more curious about the mission and this mysterious leader who would be arriving to take command of what was to be a two-pronged attack. Ajmaani wouldn't talk about either mission specifically, but she did reveal a little about The Sheik.

The Sheik was indeed "the successor" to Osama bin Laden, who was a great warrior but whose value to jihad was diminished because he was hiding in the mountains of Pakistan. "He served Allah well and now waits for glorious martyrdom," Ajmaani said as Jabbar stood behind her, nodding sagely.

"But his time has passed. This is a new era that requires constant adjustments to counter the enemy's strategies. It is time to move beyond merely shedding the blood of infidels, though that still is an objective, toward the primary goal of destroying the United States. But such a blow will take more than talk, it will take a man with a greater vision than Osama. The Sheik is such a man."

Jabbar added that The Sheik would lead the Muslim world to the establishment of a single Islamic state that would stretch from Spain to China as it had in the past. "Which will be the next step toward the ultimate victory of Islam over the West."

As he listened, Khalifa day-dreamed of what the event might entail and his role in it. Perhaps he would receive flight training and destroy a building. Or maybe it would be a poison gas attack in the subway system. His name would live forever, his son would be proud of him, and his wife would come to understand that he'd done what needed to be done for the glory and praise of Allah. Someday they would meet again in Paradise, and she would apologize for the bad things she'd said.

———

However, with just two months to go, Allah's plan for Khalifa took an unexpected turn after he got into another fight with Miriam. He'd never told her what he was doing, afraid that she'd try to talk him out of it or report him to the police. Instead, he told her he was taking special classes to become an Islamic scholar, possibly even an imam someday. She'd happily congratulated him. At least imams were paid by the congregation—not much, but it would be more regular, and more honorable, than providing security for Imam Jabbar, whom she did not like.

However, the next time he told her the lie, Miriam started asking why class was being conducted at such a late hour instead of in the evening. He explained that these particular classes were for especially dedicated students; Jabbar did not want to make anyone who had not been selected jealous.

Then she'd apparently started asking around about the late-night classes at the mosque, and she did not like what she learned. In particular, Miriam did not like who his classmates were. "These 'chosen' few are not spiritual men," she said. "They are extremists and sheep; many of them have been gangsters and criminals."

"I was a gangster and a criminal," Khalifa reminded her.

"Yes, my husband," Miriam responded tenderly. "But you've changed. I've seen the peace that worshiping Allah gives you sometimes, and I know that in your heart, you are a good man . . . a good father . . . and a good husband. But sometimes you don't separate reality from the nonsense that Jabbar spouts."

The criticism of Jabbar angered Khalifa, partly because it was probably true, but that didn't alter how he felt about the man. "Yes, I have changed through the grace of Allah," he retorted. "And it was the imam who brought me to the true path. What kind of man would I be if I did not honor that and do as he asks, and what I believe Allah commands me to do?"

"And what is it that Allah commands you to do, Jamal?" her dark eyes sparkled in her pretty round face. "I hope for your eternal soul that you do nothing that brings shame on Islam and do not blame Allah for any sins you commit."

Khalifa had no response to that except to storm out of the apartment and go for a walk. It seemed that two voices argued in his head for his conscience. *"Jabbar saved you from a pointless life, a life as a nobody,"* said one voice. *"Look in your heart, you know Miriam is telling you the truth,"* replied the other, which eventually won the debate. He was about to return to the apartment to apologize when a voice from the past interrupted his thoughts.

"Well, if it ain't our old homeboy, Scratchy!"

Khalifa turned around. Several of his former gang friends approached from behind. The one whose voice he had recognized, a big hulking brute nicknamed Killah with a lazy eye, chortled and said, "Say niggah, where you been?"

"Praying to Allah, brother," Khalifa responded. Saying it, he felt a moral superiority to his old friends, who, by the look of them, were still gangbanging. Every inch of exposed skin on their bodies—hands and arms, necks, chests—was covered with black prison tattoos.

"Oh thass right," Killah snarked. "You a Muslim now."

"Praise Allah for that," he responded. "He saved me from my wicked ways. Ain't you brothers tired of banging? Ain't you getting a little ol' to be committing crimes and chasing loose women? Maybe you should get your black asses over to the mosque."

Killah laughed, "Ain't never too old for easy money and booty," he said. "I like to see my ho's big backdoor before I get busy with her. What them Muslim women hiding 'neath them gowns anyway? Two pussies? Or, maybe just big ol' hairy legs, like a gorilla."

Khalifa thought about Miriam's beautiful figure and thanked Allah that her body was his and his alone to view. Again, the feeling of superiority washed over him, and he accepted the ribbing good-naturedly. He'd grown up on the streets with Killah and the others, and there'd been times when they had been his only family. That was why now, he let them talk him into going with them to another part of the park, where they were meeting up with a couple more of Khalifa's old running mates. They found the others sitting on a picnic table, passing brown bags containing 40-ounce bottles of malt liquor.

In his sinful past, Khalifa had developed quite a taste for malt liquor and the respite it gave him from feeling like a nobody. Alcohol had always been involved when he got into trouble, and he thought he'd now put the desire for it behind him. Ever since converting, he'd done his best to adhere to the teachings of Islam and its principles of self-denial, including staying away from alcohol and his old gang. *Praise Allah.* But the sight of the bags and the smell of the malt liquor on the breath of the others revived old memories, and he watched the others drink while licking his lips.

The first time the bottle came his way, he held up his hand and said his new faith didn't allow it. Then someone offered a joint of marijuana. He suspected that Jabbar would frown on it, too, but he knew that some Muslims in the Middle East smoked hashish, and he didn't see the harm in taking a puff or two. Or three, so that when his friends pressed the bottle of malt liquor on him again, he let himself be talked into taking a sip *"for old times' sake."*

Three hours later, he'd shown up drunk for evening prayers at the mosque. He wouldn't have gone, except that they were supposed to meet afterward to discuss Phase Two of their training.

The imam listened to his slurred excuses and looked into his bloodshot eyes, then declared that he was no longer mujahideen. "You have disgraced yourself, Jamal," he said scornfully. "And this mission is too important to trust to someone who cannot resist the temptation of alcohol. I need men whose minds and souls are clean for the task ahead."

Khalifa begged to be forgiven. "Give me one more chance," he pleaded. "I'm ready to die for Allah!"

"Then rededicate yourself to your prayers and ask that there will be another time," the imam rebuked him. "The Sheik has sent instructions that I am to select only the most trusted men . . . those who can resist all temptation and put away all Earthly vices."

Ashamed and despondent, Khalifa stopped at the liquor store on the way home, where he purchased four more forties. Back at his apartment, he guzzled two of them, and when Miriam complained, he beat her until their son begged him to leave her alone.

The next morning, he woke up with his head pounding from the aftershock of the alcohol. He yelled for his wife, but she didn't answer and wasn't in the apartment. Nor could he find her at the mosque. Finally, he called his father-in-law, who admitted that she was there—with their son—and she would also remain there. "And if you come here," Mr. Juma spat, "I will cut you open and gut you like I used to gut fish. What kind of a man would beat a woman when she was only trying to save you from yourself? You are not Muslim, you are nobody."

The man hung up without waiting for Khalifa's response. The word "nobody" stung and left him speechless. He spent the day sitting in the dark, alternately crying and throwing their few possessions around, until the neighbor below pounded on the ceiling and threatened to call the police. That night he faced east and said his prayers alone, too ashamed to go to the mosque. He would be nothing more than the drunken mujahideen, too drunk to be trusted with an important mission—a laughingstock, a nobody, as his father-in-law had reminded him.

His life had tumbled downhill ever since. He no longer had his job with the imam, and he'd had to sell almost everything he and Miriam had bought together just to pay rent in the crummy little flat he'd moved to. He had a mattress on the floor, a lamp, and a framed photograph of his wife and son. If not for food stamps, he wouldn't have had anything to eat. He kept an old video camera they'd bought to record Abdullah's progress, but that was only so that he could watch the tapes and remember when he had been a father.

He was lying on the floor of his bedroom crying again when he noticed the martyr's vest lying beneath a pile of clothes. *"You will feel no pain,"* Ajmaani had assured them. *"One moment, you are looking into the terrified eyes of your enemies when they realize what is about to happen, and the next moment, you awake in Paradise."*

As he picked up the vest, he heard another voice. Not Ajmaani. Not his own. He didn't know where it came from. But he was sure it was the voice of God, and it was telling him how he would earn his place in Paradise. *"And all of Islam will know your name,"* it said.

As Khalifa stood looking up at the synagogue, a young white couple walked toward him. She was laughing, but when she saw him she stopped and clung more tightly to her boyfriend's arm.

But Khalifa hardly noticed their wary looks, and they gave him a wide berth and passed. He was too busy wishing that he was with his wife and that they were the ones walking down a sidewalk arm in arm. But that could never be.

His hand dipped into the pocket of his coat and felt a piece of paper. He pulled it out—a food-stamp certificate good for twenty dollars. *Might as well give it to someone,* he thought. A young black woman approached, and he held it out. But she shook her head like he was one of the addict-hustlers in Times Square handing out leaflets advertising "Gentlemen's Clubs . . . All Nude Dancers," and hurried past without making eye contact. *Thinks I'm some sort of junkyard dog.* He crumpled up the certificate and tossed it to the ground.

His attention was drawn to an old couple at the bottom of the steps leading up to the synagogue door. They were both short, shorter even than Miriam, who had only come up to his chest. The man had a big nose and ears that jutted from the side of his head like a monkey's; everything about the woman was tiny, as if she'd never quite left childhood, and she wore her short red hair in small ringlets.

The woman kissed her husband on the cheek as he patted her affectionately on her arm. They reminded him of his grandparents, though they looked nothing like them; maybe it was just the way they seemed to belong together.

The woman did not speak but stepped back from her husband and signed something with her hands. The man responded with other signs. *One of them is deaf*, Khalifa thought.

As if she'd heard his mind, the woman glanced down the sidewalk, and her eyes met Khalifa's. She smiled, and unable to resist the simple act of friendliness, he smiled back. Then she turned and walked away, while her husband climbed the steps to the synagogue.

Khalifa hardened his heart. *They're Jews*, he told himself. *Don't be fooled by appearances. They're the enemy.* And he would be the sword of Allah.

He was committed now. He'd even videotaped his last will and testament, explaining the reasons for his actions this day and his last instructions for his son. He'd placed the tape in a large envelope, addressed it to the imam, and then dropped it in a mailbox before catching a taxi to the synagogue. He hoped that the imam would send it to Al Jazeera television and, as the imam had predicted, that he would be a martyr known throughout the Muslim world. The Sheik and Tatay would hear his name and use his death as an inspiration when the others went forward with their missions.

Khalifa strode up the stairs and entered the synagogue. He found himself in a wide, deserted lobby and quickly walked over to a bulletin board where he began reading the postings. Most of the notices on the board were for synagogue services and charitable events. But then his eyes fastened on a request for contributions to fund the purchase of "supplemental supplies for an elite paratrooper unit" in the Israeli army that had been "adopted" by the synagogue. It said that the "brave soldiers are fighting terrorists" and that the congregation was being asked to raise money to purchase "custom-fitted combat vests."

Murderers, Khalifa swore silently. *Jew pigs. Well, I have a combat vest, too!* His mind, which had been clouded by the trickery of the old couple, was as clear and filled with purpose as it had ever been. He walked along the wall, studying a series of photographs depicting Israeli presidents, prime ministers, and generals; chief Jewish rabbis; and Knesset members who had visited the synagogue.

Good, he thought, *they'll hear of this soon in Israel. And all of these impor-*
tant Jews will be able to picture the blood on the walls when they read about what
I have done.

Several old men entered the lobby from the temple, but other than a curious glance or two, they paid no attention to him. *Allah has made me invisi-*
ble so that I can walk into their temple to serve his purpose! he thought. *Truly*
God has spoken to me.

He'd heard stories of similar miracles from visiting "freedom fighters"
who'd come to the mosque from Muslim countries to raise money. They
talked about mujahideen in Afghanistan and Iraq who had walked through
clouds of bullets, or emerged from homes destroyed by cruise missiles, without injury.

"The warrior who has given his life to Allah is invincible," they claimed.
"Only when Allah is ready to reward their faith can they be killed so that
they can enter Paradise."

Their voices and stories filled Khalifa's mind as he found himself standing in front of the door leading into the temple. He had few regrets. He'd
never been to Mecca on the hajj and, in fact, had rarely ever left the
island of Manhattan. His son would not have a father, his young wife
would be a widow. But these were inconsequential in the face of eternity.
He was ready.

Pulling open the door, he stepped inside. It took a moment for his eyes
to adjust to the shadowed interior, but when they did, he saw perhaps as
many as fifty men sitting in the pews. They were facing away from him,
their heads nodding in cadence as they recited their prayers. He was reminded of the faithful praying in the mosque. The thought that the two
scenes were similar was disconcerting.

With sweat now running in rivulets down his body, he forced himself to
dwell on the differences, such as the strange little round caps the Jews wore
and the shawls draped across their shoulders. Some had what appeared to
be small boxes strapped to their foreheads, and others wore girlish curls instead of sideburns.

The temple hummed with their prayers, and he became aware of a presence that could not be seen or understood. His knees nearly buckled. "All
of Islam will know your name," he whispered to give himself strength.

A strange affliction seemed to be taking over his eyes, as if he were look-ing down a glass-walled tunnel. He was aware of images to either side, but all that he could see clearly was what was straight in front of him, and what he saw now was a young man walking toward him. The man wore a beard and was smiling, but there was a wary look in his eyes.

———

When Rabbi Greg Romberg saw the young black man enter the temple, he thought at first that the stranger was one of the city's many homeless. The beard was long and scraggly and the long wool coat too warm for such a hot day. The man looked like he had not slept well in several days and might have been hoping for a pew to curl up on.

Then the thought occurred to him that the stranger might also be a black Jew. A surprisingly large community of them lived in New York, though he'd been largely unaware of them until he was in rabbinical school. The new-comer was not wearing a yarmulke, or *kippah*, on his head, but that didn't necessarily mean he was not a Jew. Though some Jews believed that Talmu-dic law commanded them to cover their heads in the temple, it was actually more of a custom than a religious requirement—a reminder that God was above them. Still, he didn't know if that was also the custom of black Jewish communities.

The synagogue on Third Avenue billed itself as Modern Orthodox, but even within Modern Orthodoxy there was a lot of diversity in personal styles of worship. For instance, some members wore the *phylacteries*, some-times called *tefillin*—small boxes containing portions of the Torah—during *Shacharit*, the morning prayer service. Others thought this was too old-fashioned and didn't bother. However, nearly all wore the *tallit*, the prayer shawl, which was a reminder of the tents the Israelites had lived in when they had wandered in the desert with Moses.

Romberg was a modern rabbi who respected all the different variations of Judaism. He saw them as reminders of all that Jews had been through since the Diaspora. And yet, they remained one people. God's Chosen People.

"*Shalom*," the rabbi greeted the stranger, using the Hebrew word for peace. "May I help you?"

"*Salaam*," the young man replied.

In the moment he heard the Arabic response, Romberg knew what was going to happen. *Such is the darkness of these days,* he thought sadly. *But haven't we been expecting this?* He watched the young man open the long coat to reveal the vest beneath it. He'd never seen one before, but he'd heard a lot about them during a recent trip to Israel—about what they'd done to school buses and crowded discothèques and shopping malls.

There was no time to give a warning that would do any good. Instead, he used the deep, resonant voice he'd worked so hard to train in rabbinical school to shout the *Shema*, the declaration of Jewish faith.

"*Shema Yisrael Adonai Eloheinu Adonai Echad!*" Hear O Israel, the Lord is our God, the Lord is One.

The black man responded in kind as he reached for the cord at his waist. "*Lu Ilaha illal lah! Allah-u-Akbar! Allah-u-Akbar!*" There is no God but God! God is Great! God is Great!

———

Those who lived told the police of the voices shouting in the ancient languages of two closely related peoples.

"Like prophets in the wilderness," said an old man, a baker by trade. He and his wife had seen the man outside the synagogue. "He seemed sad, not dangerous," he said.

The baker had not seen the man enter but had heard the shouts from inside the synagogue just before the explosion. "Then there was a flash and an enormous roar," he recalled, wiping tears from his eyes. "I was struck by a hot wind and flung through the air like a leaf. It is only by God's grace that I survived . . . again."

5

Karp listened with interest and a mouth full of peach pancakes as the old men debated at the table next to him on the sidewalk outside of The Kitchenette, a small café on West Broadway. One of them, a former newspaper editor named Bill Florence, had fished an article out of the day's *Times* about the Islamic Society of America, which had complained about television shows portraying Muslims as "the bad guys."

"I guess I can see how they'd be concerned that sort of stereotyping might lead to antagonism against Muslim Americans," said Murray Epstein, who'd retired as one of the top defense attorneys in Manhattan, though he frequently appeared on CNN when they needed a legal mind with a liberal viewpoint.

"Oh puleeeeze," moaned Dennis Hall, the former U.S. Attorney for the Southern District of New York and Epstein's conservative counterpart on Fox News. "It's not like we're at war with blond Swedish Catholics. I haven't noticed any Episcopalian Icelanders becoming suicide bombers and charging into any synagogues. I guess they're saying that if somebody makes another movie about World War II in the Pacific, they shouldn't use Japanese actors because it might offend someone in Japan."

"But isn't it true that the people attacking us are terrorists who happen to be Muslims?" a handsome man with a short gray crewcut and a priest's collar said.

"Oh come on, Father Jim," Hall argued. "We identify them by how they identify themselves. They claim to be Islamic, to a man, and they are terrorists; therefore, they are Islamic terrorists. Now, if the rest of the Muslim world wants to disown them, or better yet, get involved in stopping them, instead of playing 'see no evil' and couching every denunciation of someone murdering other people in the name of Allah with a denunciation of Israel, then welcome to the circle of humanity."

"Says here that Americans are insensitive to Muslims," said Florence, a short man with thick bushy dark eyebrows who looked a bit like Albert Einstein on a bad hair day.

"Bullshit," exclaimed Saul Silverstein, an ex-Marine who'd survived Iwo Jima and then made a fortune in women's apparel. "Six months after a bunch of terrorists—who claimed to be acting in the name of Islam—murdered a few thousand people in the World Trade Center, Columbia University held a one-day, in-service training session for more than one hundred New York City high school teachers to teach them how to be more sensitive to Muslim students. The whole thing was paid for by the Ford Foundation. It's like we're apologizing because some of their fellow Muslims have declared war on us. It's not as if every Jap in Japan personally attacked Pearl Harbor in 1941 either, but we sure as hell were at war with Japan and the Japanese people for the next four years. They can kiss my hairy Semper Fi ass."

"Well, on that patriotic note, I guess there's nothing further to debate," Epstein said dryly as the others burst out laughing. "Not unless you'd like to comment, Mr. District Attorney sir?"

"Pretty much says it all. I don't think there's anything I could add to the sentiment," Karp responded to more laughter.

"The Sons of Liberty Breakfast Club and Girl-Watching Society" met several times a week at The Kitchenette to haggle over politics, the arts, the law, and foreign affairs. And, of course, girls, particularly those walking by on sunny days. But they were more than—as self-described by their resident artist and poet, Geoffrey Gilbert—"a bunch of dirty old men who like to argue."

Although they were all now retired, they'd all been successful in their careers—Hall and Epstein as attorneys; Gilbert as an artist; Florence as manager of the newsroom at the *New York Post*; Silverstein as a trendsetter in the apparel industry, making pants culturally acceptable attire for women in the 1950s; and Sunderland, a Catholic priest, as a social activist and writer. The only one missing from the group today was Frank Plaut, who, while currently sporting a silver ponytail and Neil Young–style muttonchops, had been a respected federal judge with the 2nd Circuit Court of Appeals and a professor of law at Columbia University.

Karp had been told when he arrived at 7 for breakfast that Plaut was on a "secret mission." He didn't doubt it. The group seemed to have any number of secrets. For instance, Karp had only recently discovered that they'd all known his dad, Julius. The lawyers and the judge had all gone to law school with him, and they'd attended the Saturday evening socials at his house in Brooklyn. There, they had talked law and politics over cigars and glasses of whiskey. Most remembered Karp as a boy, sitting at the foot of his father's easy chair to listen in on the conversations.

He'd been introduced to the group by Sunderland, whom he'd met by accident. Or, rather, by attempted assassination. Nearly a year ago, Karp's political opponent for the district attorney's seat, a former sex crimes bureau chief named Rachel Rachman, had tried to win the election by gunning him down from a moving car. Unfortunately for Rachman, Marlene had been there—armed as usual—to terminate her candidacy. Fortunately for Karp, the priest had been present to help Marlene apply pressure to his wounds.

Karp had almost died, but as he rehabilitated from wounds to his shoulder, chest, and leg, Sunderland had volunteered to be his walking companion. Then one day he'd brought him over to The Kitchenette, where Karp had discovered peach pancakes drowned in strawberry butter—and met The Breakfast Club.

"Anything you can tell us about the bombing at the synagogue?" asked Gilbert, who could be counted on to blurt out whatever was on his mind.

"Terrible business," Sunderland said.

"Yes, it was. But there's not much I can tell you," Karp replied. "It's a federal case, for now anyway. About all I know is what you've read in the newspapers. So far no one has identified the bomber, or claimed responsibility for the attack. It appears that he was acting alone."

"I read that there's a competency hearing for Jessica Campbell tomorrow," Florence said, changing the subject.

"Correct," Karp replied.

"Are you still trying the case?" Epstein asked. "An insanity defense I presume."

"Yes, though my colleague, Kenny Katz, is co-counsel, and he'll be handling the competency hearing." Karp looked at his watch. "Speaking of which, I have a meeting this morning that I need to get to in ten minutes. I'll see you gentlemen the next time my diet prescribes peach pancakes."

———————

Even though it was only 8 A.M. on a Monday, the sidewalk in front of the Criminal Courts building was already swarming when Karp pulled up in a taxi. At that hour, most of the people out and about were men and women in business attire making their way to the government buildings and the Financial District farther to the south. Some were content to fall in and move at the pace of traffic; others dashed in and out of the stream of pedestrians when they saw openings. But they all walked with single-minded purposefulness, like salmon swimming up a river to spawn.

Karp noted dour expressions and vacant looks. Mondays were never the best day for Joe Blow office-worker; however, today their expressions were a bit tighter than usual. People seemed more lost than usual in their own concerns. *They've been struck again in the gut by the madness of terrorism,* Karp thought, grabbing a copy of the *New York Times* from the newsstand in front of the courts building.

At the top in bold, 72-point type, the paper blared: **"WHO WAS HE?"** The subhead complained that the feds were still withholding the identification of the suicide bomber—if they had it—under provisions of the Patriot Act, which these days seemed to override the rights of a free press.

No one knew how long the secret would be kept. Karp had heard over the weekend from Ariadne Stupenagel, the investigative reporter who was shacking up with his aide-de-camp, Gilbert Murrow, that the *Times*, as well as the rest of the media—including the *New York Guardian*, the weekly she was currently working for—intended to go to U.S. District Court to force the government to release the bomber's name, or, if they did not have it, to at least admit that fact. She'd also learned that they would be joined in court by U.S. Senator Tom McCullum, a tough-talking politician from Montana who'd been the chief critic on Capitol Hill of overreaching actions by federal law-enforcement agencies using the Patriot Act as their carte blanche to "spy on U.S. citizens."

Karp noted that the main story wrapped around a sidebar report on eye-witness accounts from the bombing site. Several described the bomber as a black man in his late twenties or early thirties, dressed in a long dark coat.

"I saw the guy outside," Lydia Sheffield, a twenty-two-year-old cosmetology student, was quoted as saying. She had walked past the synagogue with her boyfriend a few minutes before the blast. "He gave me the creeps," she added.

Other accounts described the horror of a man blowing himself up, along with an innocent rabbi, and sending the blast, along with thousands of steel ball bearings, through men who'd gathered peacefully to pray.

———

Over the years, Karp had witnessed the aftereffects of dozens of heinous crimes—the viciousness of sadistic serial killers, the gut-wrenching horror caused by child killers, the senseless deeds of men and women armed with shotguns and knives, and even the gory aftermath of bombings. But he'd been stunned by the carnage at the synagogue that day.

Within minutes of Fulton announcing "it finally happened," the two of them were in the DAO's armored Lincoln with a blue flashing light on top heading north on Third Avenue. By the time they arrived, the block had already been cordoned off by the cops while bomb-sniffing dogs circulated in the gathering crowd as well as inside the police perimeter.

Looking up as he got out of the car, Karp saw police snipers on rooftops scanning the spectators from open windows of nearby buildings. He re-called what a speaker had once told the Five Boroughs Anti-Terrorism Task Force: that unlike lightning, terrorists often struck the same place twice. The purpose of the second attack was to kill those who responded to the first, especially medical and police personnel.

A wadded-up piece of colored paper lay on the ground near his feet. He bent over to pick it up—a $20 food-stamp voucher. *I'll give it to Booger or one of the others,* he thought, and stuffed it into his pocket.

Inside the perimeter, police officers, firefighters, and paramedics rushed about on errands or stood in small clusters with a hand on a comrade's shoulder. An undercurrent of cries and sobs punctuated the space between siren screams. Some of the relatives and friends of the victims had been allowed past the yellow tape to help the wounded as they were loaded onto ambulances, or to identify the dead, who had already been placed in body bags off to the side of the front entrance.

Aside from the activity, the front of the synagogue looked the same as it had when he'd last taught one of the bar mitzvah classes. As Karp climbed the stairs with Fulton at his side, he felt an anger rising in him that was personal, unrelated to the job. The bomber had attacked "his" synagogue. He rarely attended services or other functions, but he'd met many of the parents of his students, and he hoped that they were not among the casualties, though he knew that only transferred the ramifications to someone else. *What if the twins had been here, or any of the other kids?* The thought enraged him as he entered the synagogue.

Inside, Karp and Fulton crossed the lobby to the temple entrance, where they stopped to adjust to what they were seeing. The interior was brightly lit by klieg lights, which lent a harsh texture and stark reality to a sanctuary Karp remembered as softly lit and dedicated to the worship of the divine. The air that had once been filled with the praise of God now carried the acrid smell of an explosion and fire, plus a sweet, metallic scent that always took him a moment to recognize. *Blood.*

A crime-scene technician in a white HAZMAT suit walked up and handed them both respirators. "Please, wear these and stay back, Mr. Karp," the technician said. "There is biological material all over the place that we haven't got to yet."

Other technicians were working throughout the temple, looking like astronauts on the moon. Karp recalled that at the same task force meeting where the speaker had addressed the issue of second attacks, a crime-scene investigator from Israel had spoken about the dangers to first-responders and survivors from exposure to pathogens in blood and body parts following a bombing. The Israeli ended his talk with a slide depicting people fleeing the billowing gray clouds that had chased them down the streets when the WTC's twin towers crumbled. "That's not just crushed concrete and glass," he'd noted. "It's also the pulverized remains of several thousand human beings. Along with all the other crap, breathing that was an extreme biohazard."

Once his mind adjusted to the scene, Karp was able to grasp what had happened. The side of the synagogue closest to where it appeared the bomb detonated looked like the disaster path of a tornado. Pews lay overturned and shattered; splintered pieces of wood and pieces of clothing, including blood-stained prayer shawls, littered the ground. The wall and floor nearest to the blast looked like something the artist Jackson Pollock could have done if he'd been turned loose with cans of red paint.

As Karp watched, a crime-scene technician carefully plucked what appeared to be a human finger from a pile of rubble and bloody rags. He held it up for a moment, then dropped it into an evidence bag. Karp learned later that night, at a briefing of the task force, that the finger belonged to an ex-con named Rondell James. The briefing was led by a spokesman from the Department of Homeland Security, who said they still had no clue why this Rondell James had blown himself up, or whether he was working alone.

Now, standing at the newsstand on Centre Street in front of the court-house, Karp looked up and met the gaze of the little vendor with the pointed, perpetually dripping nose, who peered at him through filthy, half-inch thick glasses that magnified his watery blue eyes to make him look like some cartoon character.

"Hey, fu-fu-fuck ass shit," the newsstand operator said, "you gonna pay for that . . . crap, oohhh boy, oohhh boy . . . paper or what?"

Dirty Warren didn't necessarily mean to curse; he suffered from Tourette's Syndrome—faulty wiring in his brain that caused, along with a variety of involuntary muscle tics and random noises, a compulsion to spew a seemingly endless and colorfully imaginative torrent of profanity. Every once in a while, Karp was pretty sure that Warren threw a few extra expletives in for effect, but he couldn't prove it . . . and besides, he liked the little guy's moxie.

Fishing into his pocket, Karp pulled out two dollars. "Keep the change," he said, slapping the bills on the newsstand counter.

"Gee, thanks . . . lick me asswipe . . . think you can afford it?"

Karp's eyes narrowed. This was one of those times when he was pretty sure the foul language wasn't necessary. But Dirty Warren just smiled innocently as if he'd politely inquired what Karp thought of the Yankees' season so far. "You're welcome," Karp said. "I think."

Dirty Warren's face grew serious. "In the movie *Contact*, the scientist, Dr. David Drumlin, is . . . oohhh boy, you're a whore . . . killed by a religious fanatic trying to prevent him . . . penis vagina ooop ooop . . . from contacting an alien civilization. How does Drumlin die?"

Karp rolled his eyes. They'd been playing the movie trivia game since they first met years ago. He had yet to lose a single round, but today he wasn't in the mood, especially for this particular line of questioning. "Uh, let's see . . . given the present circumstances . . . the assassin wrapped himself in explosives. . . . It was a suicide bombing. . . . Come on, Warren, maybe now's not the time for this."

"Yeah, well . . . fuck you balls and titties . . . humor me," Dirty Warren insisted. "Tom Skerritt played Drumlin, but who played Dr. Eleanor Arroway, the scientist who travels to the star Vega and makes contact with an alien?"

Karp looked at his watch in the universal sign language for he didn't have the time or patience, but answered, "Jodie Foster. Now, Warren, I really need to get going."

"Okay, but what reason did . . . oohhh boy MOTHER FUCKER! . . . the alien give for his civilization to bring Arroway to them . . . no shit bastard?"

The question stumped Karp. "That's not the game, Warren, that's script, not trivia. . . . And I don't like science fiction movies."

Warren waved the protest off. "I know, I . . . piss off . . . know. This doesn't count but I just wanted to . . . ah crap bite me eat my shorts . . . tell you anyway." The man's face screwed up in a knot of concentration as he fought off a wave of tics and grimaces.

"The alien tells her that the human race is an interesting species . . . oohhh BOY. . . ." He waited patiently as the muscles in his face went through a series of spasms before he could continue. "Capable of such extremes of love and hate and it was that . . . God dammit! . . . mix that prompted their curiosity about us. It wasn't a . . . oohhh oohhh . . . trick, or a test, it's just that the im-im-im-immensity of space is lonely, and the only thing that makes it bearable . . . oohhh please oohhh please . . . is each other."

For a moment, Karp thought Dirty Warren might pass out from the strain of trying to hold it together to get his message across. But the little man got it out and stood there panting from the exertion. Only then did

Karp notice the tears in his eyes. *Yeah, we're all a little scared, Warren,* he thought. "I hear you, pal," he said. "'The only thing that makes it bearable is each other.' Thanks, that's a good one to remember on a day like today."

The newspaper vendor wiped at his nose and eyes and held out Karp's dollars. "Paper's on me . . . asswipe," he said, his voice raspy.

Karp started to protest but realized it was a point of pride with the newspaper vendor. He took the bills and put them back in his pocket, then stuck out his hand for Dirty Warren to shake. The little man had looked at the hand for a moment, like he wasn't sure what he was supposed to do, but then accepted the offer and shook hands.

They stood there hand in hand until Dirty Warren shyly let go. Karp tried to recall if he'd ever made the gesture to Dirty Warren before. He couldn't recall a single instance. *That has to change,* he thought.

The newspaper vendor seemed to sense Karp's discomfiture. "Better hur-hur-hurry . . . twat did you say I cunt hear you . . . to your meeting," he sputtered with a grin.

Karp nodded and saluted with his rolled-up newspaper. "Yeah, I better do that. Take care, Warren, and thanks again for the thought."

Turning, Karp straightened his shoulders and looked up at the Criminal Courts building, a massive monument to simple linear architecture on a grand and imposing scale. To some—usually those who had good reason to fear justice—it was a frightening place. But to Karp, it had been home for more than thirty years, a rock-solid anchor in an unstable world.

As he passed the concrete barriers erected around the front of the building post-9/11, he reflected on how long it would be before such barriers would be necessary in front of synagogues, churches, and schools. Would going out to dinner mean passing through metal detectors and allowing bomb dogs to sniff ladies' purses?

The synagogue bombing was more real to him than even the attack on the World Trade Center, where the number of victims had just been so massive, so incomprehensible, that five years later he still had a hard time getting his mind around it. It was easier to visualize a single man blowing himself up and killing six other men, including Rabbi Greg Romberg, as gentle a soul as Karp had ever known. Twenty others had been injured, half of them seriously, by flying ball bearings and bits of wood; only the fact that they'd been seated and partly shielded by the heavy wooden pews saved more.

The twins had been devastated by the news that the friendly rabbi had been murdered. They couldn't comprehend that their friend's death had been caused by a man who in his last moment had claimed to be acting on behalf of God, and they had insisted on joining in a candlelight ceremony in front of the synagogue after sundown on Saturday.

Inside the Criminal Courts building, Karp hurried through the lobby, which, given the hour, was empty of the usual potpourri of jaded lawyers; angry, frightened, or indifferent defendants; confused citizens "just trying to pay a parking ticket and get the hell out of here"; and frustrated fathers reminding weeping mothers, "I told you that damn kid was no good." He rode an elevator to the eighth floor, which housed the administrative offices of the New York District Attorney.

Opening the door leading to the reception area outside his office, he hardly got a foot inside before Mrs. Milquetost handed him his first message. "Mr. Newbury called," she announced. "He said to tell you that his mind is made up and that he intends to let the others know at this morning's meeting."

She was obviously upset by the news and dying to know more, so he thought he'd add to the rumor mill. "What a wonderful beginning and end to the weekend," he growled. "Somebody decides to commit murder by blowing himself up in a synagogue on Friday, and Monday one of my best prosecutors decides to take the money and run. Lovely."

As he turned to go into his office, Mrs. Milquetost wrinkled her nose. "Oh, and Mr. Guma is waiting for you. I tried to get him to wait out here, like everybody else, but he just won't listen." It was obvious from her tone that the receptionist was hoping that he'd promise to give Ray a good talking to, if not order his outright dismissal. "That's okay, Mrs. Milquetost," he said. "He hasn't listened to anybody for years. But he's a damn good prosecutor, and I guess that and longevity have earned him certain forbearance."

Mrs. Milquetost frowned, obviously disappointed. Karp tried to ease the sting. "Look, I know Guma's rough ways can wear on a person," he said, "but honestly, he's a good man at heart. The best way to handle him is to ignore him, and he'll give up and go find someone else to pick on."

The receptionist blushed. "I'll do my best," she sighed.

"I'm sure you will, as you have since the day you started here," Karp replied, pleased to see her smile broaden.

The office had changed little since the days of Francis Garrahy. Karp was usually indifferent to décor, but there was something about the dark wood and the preponderance of leather furniture that made him feel connected to the past. The massive mahogany desk looked like it belonged to another era, as did the stuffed bookshelves that went from floor to ceiling along an entire wall. A large window overlooked Centre Street below. Other than that, the only light source was provided by green-shaded floor and desk lamps; Karp did not like fluorescent lights any more than his mentor had. A visitor with a keen nose may have also noticed the lingering ghosts of old cigar smoke and hard liquor, even though Karp rarely touched either.

Not so with Ray Guma, who lounged in one of the leather chairs facing his desk, chomping on a sausage-sized cigar. Not that Karp, who disliked tobacco smoke, would have let him, but "Goom" wasn't allowed to light the things up anymore. New York law prohibited smoking in public buildings, and his doctors had ordered him not to anyway; cancer had already nearly killed him once, and they warned that it might return to finish the job. The cigar was as much a part of Guma's hand as one of his fingers, however, and even what he referred to as "unwarranted government interference in personal habits" couldn't remove it.

Tough, irreverent, and unself-consciously loud, Ray Guma had grown up in the Bath Beach section of Brooklyn, one of six children of an Italian plumber. Rumor had it that some of his family members and childhood friends were "made men" in the mob; nevertheless, Goom had wanted to work homicide cases for the New York DAO ever since he could remember, and he'd prosecuted Mafioso with the same fervor as he had the unaffiliated criminal element. The rumor mill also said he'd maintained "an understanding" with mobbed-up members of his family and friends. They kept their business out of Manhattan, or risked prosecution, and helped out with certain delicate requests—like supplying information—and he showed up for Sunday spaghetti and meatballs with his cornucopia of cousins. He even occasionally went to the neighborhood bar to shoot the breeze with his old high-school buddies.

ESCAPE 59

As Guma turned to him with his usual sly smile, Karp took a moment to study his friend. Goom always sort of resembled an ape with his large protruding ears, thick Mediterranean features, and permanent five o'clock shadow. Although a former college baseball player, he even carried himself like an ape—bowlegged and swinging his long arms in great arcs when he walked. But he'd changed a lot physically over the past few years.

They were about the same age and had even started working for Garrahy within months of each other. However, Guma now looked like a spent old man with his wizened frame; snow-white hair; sunken, dark eyes; and loose, pale skin—all compliments of the radiation and chemotherapy nightmare he'd lived through to beat colon cancer.

The disease was currently in remission, but Goom didn't have the energy for full-time work anymore. So Karp let him work "cold cases," as well as special assignments, on a part-time basis. Part of that was because, as he'd told Mrs. Milquetost, his colleague was a damned fine prosecutor—one of the best, especially in the knock-down, drag-out brawl types of trials. But Karp also gave him the assignments because he knew Guma needed to work. Assistant District Attorney for the County of New York was who Goom was, and Karp believed that if that had been taken from him, the cancer might have won the fight, or might outlast him in Round Two.

After the suicide bombing at the synagogue, Karp had assigned Guma to head up the case for the DAO, working with the NYPD and the feds, who weren't exactly playing nice. Within an hour of the attack, the U.S. Department of Homeland Security had taken over the investigation. It was definitely a "keep the locals happy" political afterthought when somebody thought to invite Karp to send someone to "act as a liaison," as well as take over the case should they decide to give it back for local prosecution. But the square-jawed types at Homeland Security weren't interested in including New York City law enforcement in the investigation, barely deigning to share some information at carefully controlled "briefings."

Guma knew the score. He'd made a few choice remarks to the feds in Italian, disguising their meaning behind his crocodile smile—not that he cared if they had somebody who could interpret, except that Karp had asked him to play along and get what he could. Then, with his boss's approval, he had shrugged off Homeland Security's "suggestion" that New York City law enforcement "let us handle this" and started his own investigation with the aid of Clay Fulton, who headed the NYPD detectives assigned to the DAO, and his team.

Given Fulton's abilities and Guma's mob connections, Karp was betting on his old friend putting the case together before the feds could. "Morning, Goom. I hear you're still working at getting under Darla Milquetost's skin." He took a seat next to his friend rather than behind his desk.

Guma grinned. "Actually, doesn't require any work," he replied. "I swear I don't know why, but that broad has it in for me."

"Uh, maybe it's because you still think of women as 'broads.'"

"I'd never say that to their faces . . . at least not any more. But she's one of them old-school broads—uptight, overcompensating because she thinks everybody is looking down their noses at her, needs a good banging to get over herself." He studied his cigar as if his comment had constructed a new idea in his head. "In fact, I bet she'd be a real tiger in the sack."

Karp shook his head. "Same old Guma . . . Some things never change. Death, taxes, and the certainty that Ray Guma will remain an unrepentant male chauvinist pig. . . . But Darla Milquetost? Are there any women you don't consider having sex with?"

"Not many—but only out of professional curiosity these days. I'm afraid the glorious era of the Italian Stallion is over; the vast majority of my current fantasies will remain, alas, unfulfilled, because where the mind is willing, the flesh is weak."

"Well, in the interests of inner-office harmony, as well as avoiding sexual harassment complaints, please do remember to control your dirty mind and your cavalier attitude around Mrs. Milquetost."

Guma held up his hands in mock surrender. "Hey, no worries. Actually, I sort of like the old Dragon Lady—and no, not like that. She doesn't take shit from nobody, and I can respect that. So I'll see if I can't make a better impression in the future."

"Thanks, I appreciate it, Ray," Karp nodded. "And thanks for coming in early. I wanted to catch up on the bombing investigation before the bureau chiefs meeting. Some of this is 'need-to-know only' type stuff. We've got a leak in the office; so best to keep this close to the vest for now."

Guma fished a small notebook out of his inner suitcoat pocket and flipped it open. "Well, the feds still aren't saying a lot. As you know from the task force briefing on Saturday night, they've identified the perpetrator as Rondell James, black, age thirty, has a rap sheet going back to Juvenile Hall, spent some time at Attica for armed robbery, but then not much else on him for the past five years. In fact, the feds had nothing more at all after 2001, at least that they're willing to share."

Guma squinted at his notebook. "He caught a cab on 117th Street to the synagogue. Clay Fulton's guys talked to the cabbie before the feds shut him up, so we were able to get a little out of him. The cabbie said he didn't notice anything unusual about his customer, except that he was wearing a long, heavy coat and it was such a warm day."

"I guess now we'll have to start looking twice at anybody in long black coats," Karp muttered.

"Yeah, or maybe just put metal detectors and bomb dogs at the entrance of every public building. Anyway, the cabbie said that the guy was friendly enough when talking about day-to-day things. But when they passed a group of Hasidic Jews standing on a sidewalk, he started in on how Jews were the cause of all the world's problems."

"That's a new one," Karp noted dryly. "So unusual to blame Jews."

Guma smiled at the sarcasm. "Yes, according to James, Jews have taken over Congress and control the U.S. military." He flipped forward a few more pages. "I went and talked to the cabbie, Aman al-Barak, a Muslim immigrant from Yemen. He was a little ticked off that James paid his cab fare in food stamps, but otherwise he considers James to be a 'jihadi martyr.' Interesting because the feds don't have anything linking James to Muslims— at least nothing they're telling me about."

Guma seemed about to say something more but hesitated. Karp, who was used to listening for nuances in the way people said things, especially when answering questions, decided to ask about it. "You keep emphasizing that 'the feds' don't seem to have much, with the implication that perhaps you have more?"

Guma grinned mischievously. "Well, I hope this doesn't get me in trouble," he said. "And I suppose in the spirit of cooperation, I should have passed it on directly to our friends at the Department of Homeland Security, but since they're treating us like second cousins twice removed, I thought maybe I'd share it with you first."

"As I'm your boss, I don't see the problem," Karp said.

"Well, it seemed odd to me that this guy is a career criminal until 9/11 goes down," Guma replied. "Then all of the sudden, nothing . . . until he decides to blow himself up in a synagogue. I start thinking, 'Maybe the feds are looking at the big picture and missed some of the small stuff.' So when everybody was otherwise occupied, I bribed their nebbish fingerprint guy into e-mailing me a copy of the print from the perp's right index finger, which was about all that was left."

"Bribed?" Karp asked, not sure he wanted to know.

"Yeah," Guma replied. "This guy is from Boston—I could tell by that ridiculous accent. So happens that the damn Red Sox are playing at Yankee Stadium next week, and I got tickets. He drove a hard bargain; it was both my tickets or nothing."

"That's rough," Karp said, hiding a smile.

"Yeah, you owe me big," Guma agreed. "And even then he was pretty nervous—said everything was supposed to be on lock down, top secret bull-shit—but I convinced him that it was just for my files, and if I turned up anything I'd report it right away. Which is what I'm doing now . . . only it's to you."

"So noted," Karp said.

"I ran the fed print through the guys at the NYPD lab, and all that stuff from James's pre-2001 life popped up," he said. "But this time, there was something else on the misdemeanors screen from a more recent case; in fact, just a couple of years ago. Even then it was just a name and a case number. So I spent a few hours down here yesterday morning until I found the file. Apparently, James was one of three bodyguards for a Muslim religious leader over in Harlem, and they beat the shit out of a guy who had some beef with their boss. Only James wasn't going by that name; he was calling himself Muhammad Jamal Khalifa."

"Tell me how you're certain it's the same guy?" Karp asked, intrigued. "Fingerprints don't lie, but they have been known to be misplaced, as in misfiled."

"The feds had a mugshot of him from Rikers, and I found the booking photo from the assault case," Guma replied. "It was the same guy—lots of pockmarks—different name. Easy to miss the misdemeanor, and it's apparently not on the national computer. The case file, however, indicated that he and the others were originally charged with felony assault, but we let him plead to a misdemeanor assault. The victim started the physical stuff, and I guess there was a concern that we might not win at trial."

"He do any time?"

Guma referred to his notepad. "Yeah, three months at Rikers and a year's probation. . . . It's hindsight, but I wish we'd stayed on him for the felony and sent him away longer."

Karp caught the edge in his colleague's voice. They both knew that plea deals were a necessary evil for prosecutors. There was no way the DAO had the manpower or the money to go to trial on every case, and sometimes the best they could do was get the guy off the street for a while and hope it would save a few more people from being victimized.

To avoid "turnstile justice," Karp had senior ADAs review the incoming caseload daily to ensure that serious cases were not plea-bargained away. He'd also instituted the "No Lesser Plea" files. While the defendant could plead to the top count of the indictment, no sweetheart agreements on sentencing would apply to those cases marked NLP; on those, the ADAs asked for max time, no bargaining.

But every once in a while, they'd have to plead a case for some bad guy who should have been looking at hard time in Attica—maybe because the case was weak—and they had to settle for probation or time-served. Then the asshole would go out and kill somebody; after which, the press and politicians would be all over the DAO for being "soft on crime" and making too many plea deals. Of course, when it came time to pay for more prisons and more prosecutors, the press and the politicians became fiscal conservatives.

It was a damning conundrum. "There's no crystal ball in this business," Karp said. "No way we could have singled him out from ten thousand other assault cases that year as a potential suicide bomber."

"I know," Guma said. "But when something like this happens, it really hits you and you wonder if we're doing any good. Anyway, he did three months at Rikers for misdemeanor assault, which is maybe why the feds' computer didn't pick it up. Turns out the religious leader runs that mosque in Harlem that gets in the news all the time."

"Imam Sharif Jabbar," Karp said, wrinkling his nose as if a bad odor had entered the room.

Everybody knew the rabble-rousing religious leader of the Al-Aqsa mosque. In September 2001, there'd been a near riot outside the mosque after a local television station had aired aerial footage of men dancing in its courtyard, apparently celebrating the attack on the World Trade Center. An angry crowd had gathered on the sidewalk and shouted epithets, and when shoving matches started between some of the mob and the mosque security people, the police came in to break it up.

At a press conference inside the mosque the next day, Jabbar contended that neither he nor his congregation condoned violence. "But unlike the United States government and Israel, through Allah's blessings and insight, we understand the root causes that drive desperate people to take rash actions." He demanded extra police protection, which the city council— worried about escalating tensions between groups threatening to march on the Harlem mosque and blacks sympathetic to Muslims—granted.

In the years followings the attacks, Jabbar had been a frequent and vehement critic of U.S. foreign policy and the War on Terror. "That's just another way of saying 'War on People of Color,' and 'War on Muslims,'" he'd shouted into a microphone, addressing several thousand protesters at Marcus Garvey Park at the start of the Iraq War. "The U.S. government wants their oil, and the U.S. government wants to humiliate Muslims. The U.S. government forces them to defend themselves in the only way they can against a superior military, and then the U.S. government calls them terrorists so it can justify killing them . . . men, women, AND, may Allah protect them, little children."

When NYCU political science professor Jessica Campbell—then only a campus radical, not an accused mass murderer—published her provocative essay "What Goes Around, Comes Around," Jabbar had happily gone on the *Off the Hook Show with Barry Queen*, a syndicated television program, to defend her. "And I ain't just talking about her right to publish that essay," he'd proclaimed to a national audience. "I'm talking about her just telling the truth. It was a military strike in a declared war . . . and what's more, the U.S. government knew about it, and Allah strike me down if this isn't the truth, let it happen . . . maybe even helped."

The appearance had earned him threats deemed serious enough that the mosque again received extra police protection.

Quite the irony, Karp thought, that Jessica Campbell was charged with mass murder, and her defender, Imam Jabbar, had possibly just been connected by Guma to another mass murderer. *God does work in mysterious ways*, he thought.

"Anything else connecting Khalifa to the mosque?"

"Gee, tough audience," Guma replied. "I thought I'd already thrown a couple of strikes to the plate."

Karp shrugged. "I just didn't want to assume that your arm was tired."

"Well, you got it right, because when Khalifa got popped for the assault, he gave his address as 126th and Madison."

"Jabbar's mosque."

"Yep. And get this, turns out Khalifa had a wife and a four-year-old kid. According to the file, she and her dad, Khalifa's father-in-law, showed up at his sentencing hearing as character witnesses. I did a little checking. Her name is Miriam Juma Khalifa, an immigrant here illegally with her family from Kenya. She applied for permanent resident status as Khalifa's wife, but it hasn't come through."

"Might be a little harder to get now," Karp noted.

"She may not have done anything wrong, except marry a sociopath."

"But maybe she'd know if her husband had any co-conspirators. By the way, where'd you learn about their kid?"

"The Internet. I went online and found the birth records for a male infant born to Jamal and Miriam Khalifa in Harlem Hospital four years ago."

"You can get that off the Internet?" asked Karp, feeling like a dinosaur.

"Easy."

Karp tapped on a yellow legal pad with a no. 2 pencil. "So what's your guess? Was James, aka Khalifa, acting alone? Or is the Al-Aqsa mosque turning out suicide bombers?"

Closing his notebook, Guma looked at him, his bushy white eyebrows knitted into a single line. "Really, at this point, I can't say, and your guess is as good as mine. I think any way you look at it, with the sort of rhetoric coming out of some of these U.S. mosques, including this one, it's only a wonder that someone didn't do this sooner. But does that mean that somebody put Khalifa up to it—at least to where we could prove a conspiracy case? I don't know, these guys like Jabbar are good at walking just this side of criminal intent."

As Guma spoke, Karp jotted down notes on the legal pad, but he was thinking about all the times the two of them and Fulton had talked about when, not if, suicide bombers would start turning the country upside down. Now that it had happened, it was still just as much of a shock.

"Sure as hell would like to know if he had help putting that bomb together," Guma noted.

"Can't you get that off the Internet, too?" Karp asked. "I thought the Internet was omnipotent, as well as omnipresent."

"Pretty much," Guma agreed, oblivious to Karp's snipe at modernity's techno-Frankenstein. "Yes, if you know where to look you can get instructions on how to create anything from a vest bomb to a nuclear weapon. But in either case, there's something you can't get off the Internet—at least not yet—and that's the stuff that goes boom. The feds said he used military-grade plastic explosives, which are particularly difficult to get and can be traced. No word on that yet. But I don't think this guy was the sort to be surfing the Net on his own. Nor do I think he had the financial wherewithal or connections to make a bomb. My opinion is that he had help."

Guma paused. "There is one more thing that I thought was kind of unusual."

"What's that?"

"Well, this guy, Khalifa, was basically indigent, and so were his codefendants. But the day of their arraignment on that assault case, they show up with an attorney from one of the priciest firms in town."

"Maybe the imam collected a little extra from the worshipers that week to help his guys," Karp said. "Or the attorney was doing a little pro bono work."

"You mean 'a lot' extra from the worshipers. This guy charges five hundred bucks an hour; plus he's white, in his late fifties, and according to campaign contribution lists, which are also available on the Internet, a regular contributor to the GOP. I don't think he's the sort to do pro bono work for a bunch of black Muslims. But he shows up in the morning, and an hour later, all three defendants agree to plead to a misdemeanor, three months max on Rikers Island, no state prison time."

"So who was this guy?"

Guma wiggled his bushy eyebrows dramatically. "Actually that's what's more interesting than just the fact that these thugs had an expensive lawyer. His name is William White, and he's a junior partner at the firm of Newbury, Newbury and White."

The Newbury name hung in the air like a bubble. "Interesting," Karp remarked, tapping again on the legal pad.

"I thought you'd think so," Guma said. "So do I tell them?"

"Tell who?"

"The feds . . . about Khalifa."

Karp made a note on the pad. "When's your next meeting with them?"

"They haven't said when they might be so kind as to give me an update."

"Then I don't think there's any reason to bother them at this moment. Apparently, they aren't interested in anything we might have to say anyway."

"Fine with me, but they'll probably find out themselves at some point," Guma noted. "And when they do, and if they figure out we already had it, they might get pissed."

"Let me worry about that," Karp said. "Let's keep this quiet until they do. Something doesn't smell right about this investigation."

"My lips are sealed. Now, shall I send you a bill for those Yankee tickets?"

"Tell Fulton to take it out of his investigations budget."

"You mean his beer slush fund?"

"Whatever works."

Both men stopped laughing at the sound of a knock at the side door leading out of Karp's office. The door led to a private elevator that went to the ground floor and the main entrance to the DAO off the Franklin Street side of the building. The elevator was reserved for judges and the DA, and only someone with a special key could use it.

6

Dr. Louise "Niki" Nickles, a tiny woman with pink, oversized glasses and a page-boy haircut that was much too Clairol blonde and young for her lined, sixty-year-old face, smiled as she pushed a clipboard across the coffee table to Jessica Campbell. "This is . . . um . . . an MDQ, a Mood Disorder Questionnaire, that . . . I, ah, yes . . . would like you to fill out . . . please."

They were sitting in a visiting room in the psychiatric wing of Bellevue Hospital—Nickles in a high-backed chair on one end of a low, glass-topped coffee table, Jessica on a chair meant for a child, while her defense attorney, Linda Lewis, sat between them on a couch.

"What's it for?" Jessica asked. The psychiatrist's voice reminded her of sweet warm milk. But rather than soothing, she found it condescending and difficult to follow—filled with odd pauses and sighs, as if the doctor were suddenly reminded of something she'd forgotten to do.

"Well, it will . . . um, ah . . . help me assess your mental illness for the purposes of your defense at trial," Nickles said pleasantly. She folded her hands in front of her as if to indicate that there'd been enough discussion.

"There's still going to be a trial?" Jessica asked, giving her attorney a worried glance. "I thought we didn't have to . . . that they'd just let me stay in a hospital until I was better."

Lewis reached over and patted her client on the knee. She was a large woman, attractive but diminished by a dour personality. "We've been over this," she said. "Tomorrow there's going to be another competency hearing to determine if you're able to stand trial. The first time, right after your arrest, you were so obviously disturbed that the judge wanted to wait and see how you responded to treatment. But since that time, you have been examined by two doctors here at Bellevue and they've reported that you are presently competent to stand trial. We will, of course, that is to say, Dr. Nickles and I, attempt to prove differently at the hearing. But even if we win tomorrow, it will only delay the trial."

Lewis explained that the psychiatrists at Bellevue were only supposed to determine two very narrow questions: "whether you know and can appreciate—or understand—the nature and possible consequences of the charges against you, and whether you are capable of assisting your lawyer, me, with your defense."

It was an entirely separate issue from an insanity defense, Lewis added, "which is what we will argue at the trial. In that case, the questions become: Did you, at the time of the deaths of your children, understand the nature and consequences of your actions—in other words, did you know what you were doing to your children? And did you know it was wrong?"

Lewis smiled again to reassure Jessica Campbell. *Jesus, how many times have I given that speech over the past ten years,* she wondered. *It never gets old.*

She'd made a legal career out of that one point of law—as well as a lot of money. She'd sold millions of books on the topic, and she'd made a small fortune in speaking fees. She had even been invited to talk on various television and radio shows, such as the *Off the Hook Show with Barry Queen* that she was scheduled to appear on soon to discuss the Campbell case. It was good timing since she'd be able to promote her newest book, *By Any Means Necessary: One Defense Attorney's Manifesto for Winning!*

In the 1980s, she'd been among the first defense attorneys to use the "battered wife syndrome" as a defense in murder cases. She'd won dozens of acquittals for women who'd killed their abusive husbands by claiming they'd killed in self-defense. Sometimes, she figured, it actually was self-defense; other times, it was a nice excuse to get rid of the bum.

These days it was all about postpartum depression for mothers who killed their infants, and/or bipolar mood swings in which the defendant lashed out either during an extremely low point or during a manic stage. *One of these days I'm going to find a great menopause defense case,* she thought with a wry smile. *"Your honor, my client was experiencing a hot flash, and when it was over, her unsympathetic bastard of a husband was lying on the kitchen floor with a steak knife in his heart."*

Of course, Lewis had hoped that the Bellevue psychiatrists would deem Jessica incompetent to stand trial—or, if they wouldn't, bring in Nickles to see if she could persuade the judge. If that happened, Jessica would be sent to a mental institution where she would be examined regularly until judged competent to stand trial; and if Jessica did as she was told, that could take a long time. Lewis's scheme was to delay the criminal trial for as long as possible—buying plenty of time to stack up medical witnesses who were willing to testify about the seriousness of Jessica's mental condition and say what a gentle and caring person Jessica truly was. Also, with enough time, perhaps a more sympathetic DA would be elected, someone who would not want to prosecute a mom who was obviously insane at the time she "innocently" spared her children life's torment.

As a defense attorney, Lewis had helped cold-blooded murderers exchange a few years of acting crazy in a mental hospital—drawing disturbing pictures and acting out—for what would have otherwise been a very long stretch in prison. She had no qualms about teaching them how to play this game; her conscience did not trouble her even when former clients got out and committed other murders. That's how the system was set up, she reasoned, and all she was doing was using it to represent her clients to the best of her ability.

One of her favorite ploys was known in legal circles as the Ganser Syndrome. Essentially, it described the behavior of a defendant who became "psychotic" only when he realized that the evidence against him was so overwhelming that conviction was likely. She once had a client who liked to strangle the prostitutes he pimped but got away with it by perfecting the syndrome. Every time he was judged competent to stand trial, he'd start crowing like a rooster as soon as he entered the courtroom and attempt to

hop up onto the defense table to flap his wings. Then they'd haul him back
to the mental hospital where the process of finding him competent to stand
trial would start all over again. He'd keep it up until the DA would plead his
case down to a mere pittance of the time he deserved—turnstile justice at its
worst. But Lewis had not lost any more sleep over thwarting justice in his
case than she had when she heard that one of his prostitutes had sliced off
his penis with a straight razor. He'd bled to death on the way to the hospital.

Of course, it was quite possible that none of these games were going to
work for Jessica Campbell. She wasn't crafty enough to work the Ganser
Syndrome, the DAO wasn't offering any plea deals, and Butch Karp, a man
she detested, had just won an uncontested election and didn't appear to be
going anywhere for awhile. Of course, Karp had designated Jessica Campbell's case file NI P

There was still hope, and that was where Dr. Nickles came in. She was
not just to assess Jessica's mental state, but to help teach her how to play
the game. Still, it looked like they were going to have to win at trial by
convincing the jury that Jessica Campbell, as a result of mental disease or
defect, did not know or appreciate the nature and consequences of her acts
or understand that they were wrong at the time she murdered her children.

Right now, they weren't going to win at the competency hearing.
Dr. Nickles was going to testify that Jessica wasn't competent, but that was
more to set the grounds for an appeal if she was found guilty at trial. The
doctor was an expensive addition to the defense team, which consisted of
Lewis and her investigators—she preferred to try cases alone—but that was
all right; Jessica's parents were wealthy and had essentially given her carte
blanche. "Whatever it takes to keep our daughter out of prison," Liza Gupperstein had insisted, handing over the first $250,000 retainer check.

"Eventually, we'll have to go to trial," Lewis told Jessica. "So we need to
start preparing now by answering the doctor's questionnaire."

Jessica looked over at Nickles, who took a pen out of her pink briefcase,
clicked it, and handed it to her. "Let's begin. There are . . . um . . . thirteen
questions in the first part, and then a . . . single question in parts two . . .
and um . . . three. Please answer yes . . . or no. For instance, Question One:
Has there ever been a period of time . . . um . . . when you were not your
usual self, while not on drugs or alcohol and . . . ah, yes . . . you were so irri-
table that you shouted at people or started fights or arguments?"

Jessica recognized irony when she heard it. "I'm a political science pro-fessor, of course I shout and argue."

Nickles and Lewis exchanged a meaningful glance; they would have to tone down that assertive personality in the courtroom. "Uh-huh . . . I see . . . so then you would mark . . . 'Yes,'" the psychiatrist said, pointing at the clipboard.

———

Jessica had never wanted children in the first place. Her career came first, and the way she saw it, that would leave little room for anyone but herself and her husband.

But Charlie had decided in 1997 that it would be good for his political ambitions to be perceived as a "family man." He was thinking of the photo ops that playing ball with a son would produce. But to convince Jessica, he'd recast the idea as an opportunity for them to demonstrate to the rest of the world how a modern couple raised a morally conscientious child.

"You could write a book about it," he said. "After all, what kind of a coun-try will this be if the only ones having children are the Christian Right?"

It was the perfect button to push. He saw her shiver as she contemplated the thought of a nation full of little Pat Robertsons and Jerry Falwells.

Having made the decision, she concentrated on getting pregnant. She'd always been "reserved" in her love-making, though she'd kept her ambiva-lence mostly hidden until after they were married. But now she was almost enthusiastic, so long as the deed was done while she was ovulating.

Once the pregnancy was confirmed, she shifted gears. Sex was no longer part of her equation, and she spent her free time reading everything she could find on child-rearing with liberal sensibilities. And she read impor-tant works to the fetus: *The Autobiography of Malcolm X* and Gloria Steinem's *Feminist Family Values*.

Soon, Jessica pictured herself as the perfect modern mother—a career woman who would balance a meaningful life with the needs of a child, at least for the first few weeks or so until an au pair could take over. And as the day approached, she interviewed several dozen nannies before settling on a large black woman from Jamaica named Rebecca. Perfect.

Thus it was an embarrassment when something went haywire with her brain chemistry following the birth of her first daughter in March 1998. Instead of joy and pride, she just felt blue. When the nurse brought the infant in to nurse for the first time, Jessica burst into tears, rolled over onto her stomach, and went to sleep.

After her discharge, she went home determined to do her best to be "Super Mom." But the ups and downs of her moods continued and even grew worse after a few weeks. Euphoric reactions to something like her baby's smile, or a kind word from Charlie, would be followed by thirty-minute crying jags that she alleviated by downing a quart of mint-chocolate-chip ice cream.

As her blues grew bluer, she spent entire days in her "dark place," refusing to attend to her child despite the pleadings of the nanny, indifferent to Charlie's endeavors to settle on a name—he'd eventually chosen Hillary, after the president's wife—and unable to get out of bed any longer than it took her to use the bathroom.

Charlie saw that something needed to be done when he came home on the nanny's day off and found Jessica cutting off her stringy hair "because it's ugly," while Hillary, who had obviously not been changed all day, wailed in her crib. Mindful of keeping "family business" out of the media, he quietly took her to their family physician, who diagnosed Jessica's behavior as postpartum depression. The doctor explained that what she was experiencing was due to a chemical imbalance in Jessica's brain brought on by all the hormonal changes and stresses that came with pregnancy. He prescribed Prozac and assured Charlie that Jessica would soon be back to normal.

The anti-depressant had the desired effect. Jessica came out of her blues and became the devoted mother she'd envisioned. Still, she was glad to get back to the university and resume indoctrinating her students on the evils of old, white males and their negative impact on the United States. It was a good balance. She saw Hillary briefly in the morning before leaving for work, and then again for a couple of hours in the evening before the nanny put the infant to bed. On weekends, she happily pushed the baby carriage to art museums and political rallies as part of Hillary's education.

The September 11, 2001, attack on the World Trade Center, and Jessica's subsequent protest at Trinity Church with Hillary in her arms, gave even more meaning to Jessica's life. At least until Charlie started talking about having another child.

Jessica thought that having one child was more than sufficient—and more socially responsible. But Charlie still wanted a son, which resulted in shouting matches. He called her "frigid" and "self-centered." She sneered at him *"needing an heir with a dick to pass on the family sperm. How typically male."*

However, he eventually wore her down. Before Hillary, she would never have let him get his way. But she was aware that despite his increasing paunch and receding hairline, Charlie was attractive to other women—especially the "whore-bitch" Diane Castrano, who'd started working in his borough president's office in 2001.

Barely out of Brown University, Diane's main attribute—at least from Jessica's viewpoint—was that she had big, creamy white breasts that she flaunted with low-cut blouses. Charlie described her as *"intelligent and invaluable"* and told Jessica to quit being jealous. *"Jesus,"* he'd exclaim, shaking his head as if she were crazy, *"she's just an enthusiastic kid."*

At first Jessica ignored the younger woman's "enthusiastic" fawning over her husband and the exchanging of meaningful glances whenever the two were in the same room. Then, when it was impossible to ignore any longer, she decided that she would be "open-minded" about the relationship. After all, if the President of the United States could accept blowjobs from interns in the Oval Office, who was she to deny Charlie his "fling"? In truth, she found sex to be a messy, unwanted chore. So if Diane could relieve her—pun intended—of that responsibility, then it was okay by her, so long as Charlie came home to roost.

However, after the birth of Hillary, she became increasingly conscious of the fact that she'd never regained her figure, which had been nothing to shout about to begin with. Now, ever since the pregnancy, the Anjou pear had more closely resembled a gourd. But her insecurity went further than the broadening of her ass.

She'd once believed that Charlie would never risk losing her family's money and influence, or risk the damage a messy divorce might do to his political career. But now that he was more established, she began to worry that he might leave her for the younger woman. *Especially if the whore is willing to give him the son he wants,* she'd think to herself as she lay alone in bed at night.

So in the end, Jessica acquiesced to his desire to impregnate her again. She was convinced that with another addition to the family he would be even less likely to abandon her.

When Chelsea was born in the spring of 2003, not only was the disappointment of another daughter written all over Charlie's face, but within a week the postpartum depression returned with a vengeance. Jessica could hardly stand to look at the infant, or Hillary, and she recoiled from any effort her husband made to encourage her toward motherhood as if he were a serpent who'd poisoned her with another child.

———

She began hearing the voice in her head. At first it was no more than a whisper, as though from down a long hallway. But as the days passed, the voice grew stronger, more like someone talking to her through a closed door.

It explained that her aversion to her children was to be expected and was quite normal. After all, they were the product of her fornicating with an evil man. But she dismissed the assertion. She didn't consider her husband "evil"—a lying, sneaking adulterer whose political convictions changed with expediency, yes, but "evil" was an ignorant and inappropriate term tossed about by the Christian Right to vilify anyone who didn't agree with their agenda. Philosophically, she didn't believe in a metaphysical concept of good and evil existing as forces within the universe any more than she believed in the existence of God, Satan, heaven, or hell.

Jessica did not mention the voice to her husband. He'd already warned her not to talk to anyone, especially someone who might leak it to the press, about the fact that she was taking "brain medicine" for depression. He pointed out that revelations about mental illness had ruined the political career of Senator Thomas Eagleton and could well spoil any aspirations she had of being the wife of a congressman in Washington, D.C., or getting a position at Georgetown University. It had to be their secret.

Jessica hated Charlie for making her feel ashamed. She was clinically depressed, which the doctor had explained wasn't her fault. It was like having the flu, or cancer—a person didn't ask for it. Nor could she just "snap out of it." But Charlie didn't buy the "mumbo-jumbo."

Meanwhile, the voice was nothing if not persistent. It was now more like listening to someone in the same room with her, though she could not see him. Eventually, the voice convinced her that evil did exist, and it was personified by her husband, the lying, cheating son of a bitch who was going to hell. Unfortunately, the voice said, that also meant her children were damned, too.

———

Thus, she found herself one night standing in the nursery clutching a pillow as she stared blankly down at sleeping Chelsea. The voice urged her to place the pillow over the child's face and then repeat the effort with Hillary. *Your children's souls are at risk,* said the voice. *They are the spawn of Satan. If you want to save them, send them to God.*

Crying out from the effort, she flung the pillow aside and fled the room. She crawled into bed next to her snoring husband and spent the rest of the night shivering and telling the voice to leave her alone.

Charlie had not wakened to comfort her. Nor did he seem to notice the bags beneath her eyes or the haunted look on her face the next morning. In fact, he hardly acknowledged that she was alive until he received a panicked call from the nanny telling him that his wife had swallowed her entire bottle of Prozac and was being rushed to Mount Sinai Hospital uptown on Fifth Avenue.

At the hospital, Jessica had her stomach pumped full of a charcoal solution to absorb the drug and induce vomiting. However, retching until she thought that her internal organs would fly out of her mouth wasn't the worst part of the experience—the worst part was the angry look on Charlie's face and the icy hardness in his voice after the doctor left the room.

"What the hell are you trying to do, ruin me?" he snarled. "That's all I need for headlines: Candidate's depressed wife tries to kill herself." Even when Jessica started crying he didn't let up. "Diane is doing everything she can to keep this quiet," he warned. "Right now, your name is Betty Jones, and you're here for an appendectomy. If word of this gets out, I'll . . ." He stopped before he said anything else, but she got the idea.

Charlie did keep his promise to take her to a psychiatrist, though this one was in Newark, where Diane thought they would be less likely to be spotted. But he wasn't happy when the psychiatrist, Harry Winkler, asked to speak to Jessica alone first.

"First of all," Winkler said when he was alone with Jessica, "you have nothing to be ashamed of. This is not your fault, no matter what your husband, or any others, may imply."

Winkler's kind and understanding tone gave Jessica hope. She told him everything. Well, almost everything. Tearfully choking over the words, she recalled how she'd stood above her daughter's crib prior to her suicide attempt and contemplated murdering her children. But she didn't tell him about the voice in her head. That was her secret.

The doctor had listened to the entire story as if he were being told about a trip to the zoo—mildly interesting but nothing to write home about. "Chemicals," he said when she finished talking. "It's just chemicals. First adolescence, and then pregnancy and giving birth, simply threw off the chemical balance in your brain." He said he was going to prescribe lithium as a mood stabilizer and to combat the depression.

The psychiatrist had then called Charlie into the office and explained what was going on in his wife's life and why. Then he dropped the bombshell. "It is my professional opinion that it would not be advisable for Jessica to have any more children."

Charlie blinked several times like he'd just been told that he was going to die. "So what are you saying?" he demanded.

"Well, on rare occasions," Winkler pontificated, "postpartum depression can be dangerous, not just to the mother—as you've recently experienced— but also to the children. And I'm afraid, there is some history, an incident during which your wife considered doing harm to your children."

"What!?" Charlie scoffed. "I don't believe it. Jessica let her mood get her down and she acted out . . . what you shrinks call a 'cry for help.' That doesn't mean she would have hurt the kids. That's nuts!" He turned toward Jessica. "This isn't true?"

Jessica nodded but kept her eyes on her hands folded on her lap. As if trying to wake from a dream, he shook his head rapidly and turned back to the doctor, clearly angry. "So again, what are you telling me . . . us?"

"I'm saying that the chemical imbalances brought on by pregnancy and . . . childbirth exacerbate what I'm diagnosing as clinical depression," Winkler said. "And, it could get worse with each childbirth. So as I said, I strongly advise against having any more children, unless you want to adopt."

Charlie took the final warning in silence, and he remained quiet for the remainder of the consultation. However, once back in the car, he let loose. "I think he's full of bullshit. Psychology isn't a real science; it's a bunch of guesswork and theories."

"I don't agree, Charlie," Jessica said evenly. "And besides, we have two beautiful kids. I think that's plenty."

Charlie gave her a dark look but fell back into silent mode for the rest of the ride back to the Upper West Side. He then made an excuse and went out for the evening.

―――――――

The lithium took the edge off Jessica's mood swings, but it also caused her to gain weight. Looking in the mirror one morning several months later, she thought she looked like one of the "Before" photographs from a weight-loss advertisement. She started hearing comments about her "big backdoor" and sniggers from some of the students at NYCU. And Charlie didn't even bother to make his half-hearted attempts at sex with her anymore.

Jessica quit taking the drug. The excess pounds started to come off, though the mood swings returned. But they were mild, and she decided that she could deal with them without pharmaceuticals. In fact, she found once again that she was capable of prodigious amounts of work and creative thinking during the "up" swings. And whenever she was depressed, she found that smoking a little pot and sleeping a lot helped.

It wasn't like Charlie was around much to notice, especially after he announced that he would be running for the 8th Congressional seat in the November 2008 election. He was always off with Diane at some fundraising dinner or "fact-finding" junket.

The surprising thing was that in the middle of all this she'd let Charlie talk her into having a third child. It began when he started talking about trying one more time to have a son to "complete our family," not to mention how good it would look in his campaign literature.

When she pointed out that the psychiatrist said it could be dangerous for her to have any more children, he'd grown angry. "What does that quack know? This is all in your mind."

"Are you blaming me?" Jessica scowled. *"Of course he's blaming you,"* said the voice, which had returned when she stopped taking the lithium. *"That's what evil people do. Blame others to hide from their own sins."*

"I just think that you could handle it if you wanted to," Charlie said, then decided that he'd rather avoid a scene. He tried to soften his approach. "Look, the girl I met, fell in love with, and married was so strong. She wouldn't have let some witch doctor tell her what she could and couldn't do with her own body. Where's my old pro-choice hellraiser?"

"Adulterer," whispered the voice. *"Fornicator."*

"Don't be so fucking condescending," Jessica snapped. "Why do you want to have sex with me? Aren't you getting enough from your whore Diane?"

The understanding look disappeared from Charlie's face and was replaced with a sneer. "At least she's not fucking crazy . . . or a fat cow," he spat. He leaned forward into her face. "If you do this, I'll stay with you. You can be a congressman's wife and attend your stupid little left-wing parties in Washington, D.C.—as long as you don't embarrass me. But I want a son, and if you won't give me one, then Diane will."

Jessica knew that the only reason Charlie was offering to stay married was because he needed her family's money and political connections. Otherwise, he'd probably be willing to take his chances on the fallout of the divorce and the exposure of his affair. So she agreed to have sex with him in order to be impregnated.

It was a clinical, loveless act. She would lay down on the bed at the appointed time, and he would finish as quickly as he could. There was no kissing, no lovemaking. Only procreation at its bleakest.

In January she'd given birth, and to Charlie's delight the infant was a boy. Charlie agreed to name him Benjamin, after her father. Afterward, he'd even treated her a little nicer. If not his lover, she could be the appreciated mother of his children and his political partner. He even started talking about the high-brow functions they would attend in Washington, D.C., after the election and suggesting that she apply to Georgetown if there were any openings in the political science department.

Jessica embraced the idea of being the political wife. She didn't need Charlie as a mate; it was more of a business partnership. The fantasies of life in Washington, D.C., even helped her deal with the familiar depression that returned with Benjamin's birth.

In fact, there were days when she had so much energy, she didn't know how to fill them. She'd written the essay "What Goes Around, Comes Around" by staying up all of one night, feverishly pecking at the keyboard. But it all came crashing down. First, there were the attacks on the article, which she'd expected and relished until the university regents sided with her detractors. And then that bitch reporter Stupenagel started looking into the allegations from jealous colleagues about the efficacy of her work, followed by more accusations of plagiarism and inaccuracies—all of which had some basis in fact; but everyone did it—she was just being attacked because of the essay.

Then came the night when she turned on the news and heard Charlie trying to put his spin on her work. "I don't need you interpreting me for the masses," she'd screamed. "Or using our son for cheap political theatrics!"

"Great, here we go again with one of your fucking mood swings."

She grabbed the crystal ashtray and flung it at him. *"You're evil! Fornicator! Adulterer!"* the voice screamed in her head.

"You're fucking nuts!" he'd shouted and stormed out of the brownstone.

———————

Charlie hadn't come home that night or the next. As she lay in her empty marital bed, Jessica listened to the voice consoling her. Only then did she realize that it was more than just some disembodied figment of her imagination. It was the voice of God.

Still, she recoiled from God's repeated demand that her children needed to be sacrificed to save them from Satan. "Why them?" she complained. "Why not kill Charlie? He's the evil one. He's the lying, cheating son of a bitch."

"His soul is already lost," replied the voice. *"But you can still save the souls of your children."*

"But it's wrong," she cried. "It's murder."

"Is it murder to save souls from eternal damnation?" the voice argued. *"I command it!"*

"But I'll get caught," she whimpered. "They'll send me to prison."

"Oh, but you'll have an excuse," the voice reasoned. *"You heard Charlie. Everybody will think you were crazy. They'll put you in a hospital for a little while and then all will be forgiven. But you have to be careful; if Charlie suspects, he'll have them put you away before you can save your children. They'll put you in that hospital anyway and force you to take the pills that make it hard to hear the voice of the Lord thy God."*

"But I love my children," Jessica cried out in the dark. "I don't want to kill them."

"If you love your children, you'll do as I say," the voice said.

And at last Jessica had agreed.

———

As the day of the sacrifice approached, the voice told her to be more cautious. *"You need to be the perfect wife and mother,"* it said. So outwardly, she accepted Charlie's infidelity and lack of affection. She talked eagerly of returning to her classrooms and didn't complain when he left for overnight trips and took Diane with him. But inwardly, the fire of holy retribution burned brighter and hotter with each day.

Adulterer. Fornicator. Liar.

He would lose his bid to damn her children to hell. Yes, she understood that others would accuse her of murder, but that was because they didn't see that in this case, the ends justified the means. Occasionally she quailed at the thought of what could happen to her—prison, or even the death penalty. *But not if they think you're crazy, and think of what it will do to Charlie's fucking political career.*

The warmer days of March arrived. The time was at hand. She'd taken the family Volvo and gone shopping in Newark to pick up the supplies she needed. She also found a map and planned where she would take the bodies so that no one would ever know what had really happened, and Charlie wouldn't be able to find them.

On the big day, she woke with her spirits soaring. She would do God's work, her children would go to heaven, and someday she would be rewarded by meeting them there. *While Charlie burns in hell!*

Jessica got up and fixed her husband a western omelette, bacon, and an English muffin. When she heard him stirring, she fired up the espresso machine so that the coffee would be good and hot when he came down. She'd finished knotting his tie, resisting the urge to tighten it until the veins in his head burst. Then she'd kissed him goodbye and sent him out the door.

Are you ready? God asked.

Hineini, she replied. Here I am!

In the visiting room at Bellevue, Nickles guided Jessica through the questions. "Has there . . . ever, um, yes . . . been a period of time . . . when you felt . . . much more . . . self-confident than usual?"

Jessica considered the question. It had been a while, but yes, whenever she'd seen her name in the newspaper, fighting for a cause, she'd felt more self-confident then. She shrugged and marked "Yes."

Most of the remaining questions seemed no more penetrating or revealing. Was there ever a time . . .

. . . she got much less sleep than usual and found she didn't really miss it? *Well sure.*

. . . she was much more talkative or spoke faster than usual? *Yes, but didn't everybody?*

. . . that thoughts raced through her head and she couldn't slow her mind down? *Wasn't that just because she was smart?*

. . . she was much more active or did many more things than usual? *Everybody has energy highs and lows.*

She began to wonder if anyone answered no to any of the questions, and if not, what did that mean for the entire population? *That we're all crazy, I guess.*

The only two questions she'd answered no to were about whether there'd ever been a time when she was more interested in sex than usual . . . *no, never* . . . or if there'd been a time when she was much more social or outgoing than usual. "For example, you telephoned . . . um . . . friends in the middle of the . . . night?" Nickles explained.

"I don't really have those sorts of friends," Jessica responded. The thought made her sad.

"Then you would mark 'No' on the MDQ."

When Jessica finished the questionnaire, Nickles studied the results before putting the clipboard back down on the coffee table and peered over the top of her pink glasses. "I believe . . . um, ah, yes . . . that my diagnosis is . . . um hmph . . . that you're bipolar," the psychiatrist said, "or what used to . . . ah, yes . . . to be referred to as 'manic-depressive,' which . . . um . . . is characterized by mood . . . ah . . . swings from abnormally high energy, the 'manic' stage, to debilitating depression, which in extreme . . . ah, yes, um . . . cases can be dangerous to others."

The psychiatrist turned to Lewis. "I will . . . ah . . . of course, write this up officially, but in essence the complete . . . ah, um, yes . . . diagnosis is Bipolar One with psychotic episodes—exacerbated by severe postpartum psychosis—with a . . . ummmm . . . schizophrenic personality disorder."

Nickles removed her glasses and leaned across the table toward Jessica. "Let me ask you something, my dear," she said. "When you were . . . ummm, yes . . . sending your children to God, didn't it feel as if someone else was using your body?"

"Well, yes. It did sort of feel like God was moving me."

Nickles sat back. "There, you see," she said to Lewis, "classic schizophrenia . . . ah, ummm, hmmm. . . . I believe that you have a . . . hmmm . . . insanity defense."

Lewis smiled like she'd just won the lottery. She patted Jessica on the knee again. "Don't worry, honey. When this unpleasantness is over, we'll find you a nice clinic where you can get well."

Nickles nodded. "Yes, there are some very nice institutions in upstate New York, as well as Vermont. Your parents are . . . ummmm, aaaah . . . quite wealthy I hear, and I'm quite certain that I can arrange my . . . hmmmm . . . schedule so that I can work with you on a . . . ah, yes, hmmm . . . consultation basis."

Jessica looked from one smiling woman to the other. She began to hope, but then a voice spoke, only it wasn't God's. *Murderer*, it said. *You killed your three babies and deserve to be punished.* "Maybe I should plead guilty and get this over with," she blurted.

The other women scowled. "I don't want you to say anything like that ever again, especially where anyone else can hear you—not to your family, not to your best friend," Lewis said, her mouth now tight with anger. "It wasn't your fault, Jessica. You are suffering from a mental illness, which is why you said what you said and did what you did. But no more, do you understand me?"

Jessica looked again from lawyer to psychiatrist. She wanted to believe. "Well, God did tell me to do it," she said.

7

At the sound of the second knock, Karp answered, "Yeah, come in." The door opened and a lean-faced man with a pewter-colored crewcut poked his head into the room. "Coast clear?"

"No one here but us chickens. Have a seat, Espey." Karp walked around to his desk chair so that the new arrival could sit next to Guma.

As he had with Guma, Karp studied his friend for a moment. Tall and tan, S. P. "Espey" Jaxon moved with the fluid grace of a bullfighter. Even sitting down in the chair, he seemed poised to move his lean, muscular body in an instant.

Karp had known Jaxon for about as long as he'd known Marlene, V. T., and Guma, which placed the federal agent among his oldest friends. He'd been another of that generation of prosecutors who got started under Garrahy, but he'd grown tired of dealing with criminals by using law books and training in the art of trial practice. He opted for the FBI Academy in Quantico, Virginia. He'd spent a lot of time in various posts, but his latest assignment with the bureau had been post 9/11 as special agent in charge of the New York office, specializing in anti-terrorism intelligence. Then, almost a year ago now, he'd suddenly quit the bureau and opted for a lucrative position with a private firm providing security for VIP clients.

Karp was one of a handful of people who knew that Jaxon's resignation was a ruse to allow him to operate under the radar to ferret out suspected double-agents and provocateurs within federal law-enforcement and intelligence agencies. That past spring, he'd become interested in a shadowy domestic group called the Sons of Man, who were apparently well-insinuated within the country's political, financial, legal, and military systems. How well, no one knew for sure, but apparently they weren't above using Islamic extremists to accomplish their own ends, which weren't completely clear either, except that they involved power and wealth.

There was no hard evidence proving it, but if there'd been any doubt that such a group existed outside of the imaginations of conspiracy buffs, it had disappeared when Jon Ellis, an assistant director of special operations for Homeland Security, was exposed as working for an independent organization bent on bringing the United States, and eventually the world, under a single all-powerful government. Trying to prevent his unmasking, Ellis had tried to kill Karp, but had fallen into a trap instead, and ended up killing himself to protect his secrets.

Jaxon's role in Ellis's capture and demise, as well as the suspected existence of the Sons of Man, had been kept quiet. Still, he was in a dangerous position. Ellis had the resources of his agency, as well as the people he really worked for. It could be assumed that whoever replaced him would also have access to these resources. Meanwhile, Jaxon was operating "unofficially," and if he ran into trouble, he and his team were on their own; he was persona non grata with the other agencies, including his own—a sellout who couldn't be trusted.

Karp was okay with the *Mission: Impossible* stuff as far as his friend was concerned. Jaxon was a big boy and knew what he was doing. What Karp didn't like was that Espey had recruited his own daughter, Lucy, onto his team. A savant with languages, having mastered more than sixty-plus, she was more Madam Librarian than Mata Hari. But following the murder of a friend who'd helped her and Espey uncover the existence, if not the identities, of the Sons of Man, she'd signed on full time. She seemed to have her mother's DNA for wanting vengeance.

When Karp appealed to his friend, as a father might, to dissuade Lucy, Jaxon explained that he needed people he could trust who were "off the grid"—that is, who had no prior history with federal and local law-enforcement agencies. For the same reason, he'd also recruited Lucy's boyfriend, Ned Blanchet, a ranch hand she'd met in New Mexico, as well as John Jojola, the police chief of the Taos Indian Pueblo, which was independent of other agencies, and one of Marlene's longtime associates, a Vietnamese teacher-turned-Viet-Cong-guerrilla-turned-gangster named Tran Vinh Do. Along with a few handpicked FBI agents, these four made up the team Jaxon created to "try to save the world."

Karp tried to reason with his daughter to convince her that she wasn't cut out for espionage. But he'd had no luck there, either; in response, she'd started spouting French philosophers at him.

"*Every man is guilty of all the good he did not do,*'" she'd answered when he asked why she felt that this was her responsibility.

"I appreciate the Voltaire," he said, "*but there's plenty of good you can do without putting your life on the line.*"

"*Sorry, Dad, but I think we can't afford to sit on the sidelines in this one. This is one of those times in history—like stopping the Nazis—when good people need to stand up against evil or it will be too late when the bad guys come for the rest of us. And in some way, these Islamic extremists are maybe more dangerous than the Nazis; they actually believe that God wants them to commit mass murder. And the Sons of Man are worse still because I think they're using these terrorists to put themselves in power.*"

"Or as Voltaire also wrote, 'Anyone who has the power to make you believe absurdities has the power to make you commit injustices. As long as people believe in absurdities they will continue to commit atrocities.' Yes, I know the drill," Karp said. "And I know they have to be stopped, or we're all in trouble. But that doesn't mean I have to like my daughter being on the front lines, especially as you've already experienced more than your fair share of danger."

"*But that's just it,*" Lucy said, stepping forward to give him a hug. "*I've been trying to tell you for years that it's no accident that this family, including but not limited to me, has been in the epicenter of this storm—at least as far as New York City is concerned. I know you aren't into all the mysticism and apocalyptic signs, but I think it's for a reason that is a lot bigger than just our family's attraction to hot water.*"

Lucy had always been headstrong, especially when she believed that she was on the moral high ground. The debate had ended as he'd known in his heart that it would; he had to accept that she was committed.

But so was Muhammad Jamal Khalifa, Karp thought. He filled Jaxon in on what Guma had told him regarding the bombing. "So what do you think?"

No longer officially a federal agent, Jaxon had no direct access to the investigation, nor was he invited to the briefing. There were people on the inside of the investigation who could be trusted, but they reported what they knew to the mysterious entity Jaxon worked for, who in turn passed it on to the agent. It was a cumbersome method and lacked detail.

"What do I think?" Jaxon repeated the question. "Well, I think that was nice work by Mr. Guma and company here. My people didn't have the name change to Jamal Khalifa or his connection to the mosque, either; this misdemeanor assault conviction isn't on the National Crime Computer, although I couldn't tell you why not. Anyway, if this checks out with Jamal Khalifa it presents me with a whole new can of worms."

"What's that?" Guma asked.

"I've got a 'client' coming in from Saudi Arabia," Jaxon explained. "Some playboy prince with more money than the combined Gross National Product of South America. Somebody in the State Department put in a request that I baby-sit this guy, and my 'employer' thought it was a good idea for our own reasons. There's been a lot of Internet chatter about some character known only as 'The Sheik,' and something big going down here in Gotham."

"Where else? Manhattan must look like a bull's-eye from the sky," Karp said dryly, then asked, "So you think the bombing was maybe a trial run, or a threat? These extremists don't like the Saudi royal family, and somebody with that kind of money and connections might make a good target. Maybe The Sheik is going to assassinate your guy."

"We thought of that, but then why tip their hand with this bombing?" Jaxon countered. "Unless, like you say, it was meant as just a threat in order to keep the prince from showing up at all."

"But why?"

"I have a couple of theories. Both are connected to the prince's itinerary. First, the main reason he's coming is that he's the president of one of the world's largest hedge funds—without getting technical, that boils down to being in control of billions of dollars' worth of stock. So he's going to be wined and dined by all the big banks and brokerage houses competing for the right to take care of that money for him when he wants to buy or sell. And a lot of that money belongs to his extended family, along with their wealthiest friends. Maybe, The Sheik and his terrorist pals think that killing this guy and disrupting their business will destabilize the royal family."

"Works for me," Karp noted again, taking up his pad and pencil. "And the second reason for his trip?"

"Well, as you said, the Saudi royals aren't particularly popular with the poor people in their own country, which is why that assassination theory works. So the royals are constantly doing a high-wire act balancing their financial interests with keeping their own version of the Religious Right placated. The Wahabi sect is the most anti-West and anti-American brand of conservative Islam there is, and it's native to Saudi Arabia. In fact, the Saudi government, and their rich friends, support these Wahabi imams and their madrasah religious schools teaching jihad to keep them from inciting the masses, while out of the other corner of their mouths, they're talking about all their efforts in the 'War on Terrorism.' But the Saudi royals are one misstatement from inciting those imams, who could unleash an Islamic revolution on the Arabian Peninsula that will make the 1979 Iranian revolution look tame. The Saudi royals and friends stave it off by paying the imams to keep the Saudi public in check, while these same imams incite terrorism in other countries. Sort of like feeding the man-eating crocodile you keep in your bathtub, knowing some day that you're going to be what's for dinner."

"What's this have to do with the prince?" Guma asked.

"Well, the second publicized reason for his trip is that he plans to present a large check to fund the construction of a new madrasah on the grounds of a certain mosque in Harlem."

Karp leaned back in his chair and whistled. "Let me guess, the lucky mosque sits at 126th and Madison?"

"You got it," the agent nodded. "The Al-Aqsa mosque."

Flipping to a blank sheet on his legal pad, Karp said, "So let's do the math: If Jamal Khalifa is connected to this mosque; and if some person or persons also connected to the mosque want to assassinate this prince; then why does Khalifa blow himself up in a synagogue and bring all this attention to his comrades?"

Jaxon shrugged. "Dissension in the ranks? Some splintering? Maybe it's a warning that if the Saudi royals don't do something, perhaps an agreement with Al Qaeda, then the prince is going to get it here?"

"Or," Guma pointed out, "maybe the locals were making a demonstration of their abilities and commitment to their friends overseas."

The three men were silent for a minute, then Karp tossed his pencil onto the pad. "We're not seeing something here."

"I agree," Jaxon said. "But thanks to Guma, I've got a little bit of a heads-up. I think I'll be paying a visit to the mosque—routine security for the prince's visit. Oh, and I agree that we should keep this to ourselves for now. I'm like you, something doesn't quite smell right with this investigation, or maybe it's just the usual floundering around that troubles me."

"No problem," Karp replied. "I never have liked it when you snotty G-men come to my town and take over my cases."

Jaxon held up his hands. "You don't have to tell this cowboy who the sheriff is around these here parts."

"So is that it for this morning?" Guma asked.

Karp opened the middle drawer of his desk. "Nope. I was going to get to this when Jaxon knocked on the door. It has to do with your sleuthing regarding the cab driver."

"About what?"

"About Khalifa paying with food stamps." Karp tossed the crumpled food-stamp certificate that he'd found on the street outside the police perimeter. "I picked this up off the street outside the synagogue. I didn't give it much thought. I was going to give it to one of the street people, but maybe you guys can use it."

Jaxon picked up the certificate and spread it out. "There are registration numbers on these things," he said. "Maybe they keep track of who they give these to."

———

With their meeting over, the three men shook hands. Jaxon went back out the side door for the private elevator while Karp and Guma walked out into the receptionist area.

"Good morning, Mrs. Milquetost," Guma said pleasantly, pronouncing her name correctly. "Forgive my abruptness this morning. I'm afraid my mind was elsewhere."

Darla Milquetost looked like she might fall off her chair. She gave an appreciative glance toward Karp and sniffed. "That's quite all right, Mr. Guma. I'm just trying to treat everyone equally . . . no special favors."

Guma gave a little bow. "And I would *never* ask for any . . . *special favors* . . . from you, Darla."

A confused look passed over Mrs. Milquetost's face. She'd have to tell her new boyfriend, Bill, about this—he was interested in everything about her job, and so good at counseling her to not let Mr. Ray Guma get to her.

Karp used the moment to hustle Guma out of the office. They walked down the hall to the large staff meeting room where every Monday morning, in the tradition of his mentor Garrahy, Karp met with his bureau chiefs and a select few other assistant district attorneys. It was a chance for up-and-comers among the ADAs to present their cases and have older hands attempt to rip them to shreds to find any hole a defense attorney might exploit and get it plugged before trial. Rigorous preparation was a hallmark of a prosecutor trained by Garrahy—or now by Karp.

When Karp entered, the attorneys quieted; those who were standing quickly found seats. Some of the rookie ADAs hovered over the case files on the table in front of them like college students doing last-minute cramming before a final exam. Careers had been made, and lost, based on how a young prosecutor fared in these staff meetings.

As everybody else found their seats, Karp quickly noted that a lot of eyes were flicking back and forth between him and V. T. Newbury, who sat alone about halfway down the table with no one on either side of him. V. T. twirled a fountain pen—one of his blueblood eccentricities—in his fingers as he stared straight ahead.

Just as cancer seemed to have reduced Ray Guma to a shell, the assault seemed to have affected Newbury's physical presence. He wasn't a big man, but he'd been a rowing champion at Yale, and he'd previously never lacked for self-confidence.

"All right, everybody, let's get this party started," proclaimed a high-pitched male voice to Karp's right. "Take your seats—and that includes you, Guma. . . . Thank you very much for showing me your middle finger, Ray, but I've seen it before."

Gilbert Murrow narrowed his eyes to show the unrepentant Guma that he was serious. He adjusted his round, wire-rimmed glasses on his nose, tugged at the edges of his ubiquitous bow tie, and cleared his throat. He was ready.

Although hired as an assistant district attorney, Murrow had never parked his five-foot-eight-inch, egg-shaped body much in a courtroom. Instead, he was one of those attorneys whose best asset is their ability to run an office full of other attorneys. Some did it for big law firms; Murrow did it for Butch Karp, and he excelled at it. As such, he kept the boss's calendar, intercepted press inquiries, and made sure he was where he was supposed to be when he was supposed to be there. If Mrs. Milquetost was the guardian at the gate, Murrow was the counselor behind the throne. He'd also run Karp's political campaign for the district attorney's seat in the last election, and only recently gotten over the post-campaign blues.

This morning, Murrow's job was to call the meeting to order and then keep it on schedule. "First to bat, ladies and gentlemen," he announced with all the verve of a circus ringmaster, "I give you the young and audacious Mr. Kenny Katz, who as you all know is propping up the boss on the Jessica Campbell case. Kenny, the floor is yours."

There was a smattering of applause, which Kenny acknowledged with a gap-toothed smile below a large nose that appeared to have been broken in several different directions. He was another of the new young hotshot ADAs, a recent appointment to the homicide bureau after working for Narcotics and Vice.

"Can somebody tear this guy a new one for me?" Karp asked.

"Let 'em try, I ain't afraid of none of youse guys," Katz said, laying on his native Queens accent extra thick. When the laughter stopped, he quickly gave a synopsis of the case: Husband leaves for work, defendant waits until he's gone, defendant kills couple's three young children, husband comes home, children are missing, wife tells him that God told her to save their souls by sending them to heaven.

"Jessica Campbell is charged with three counts of murder," Katz concluded. "That's pretty much it in a nutshell."

"Have they found the children yet?" someone asked.

"No, the bodies have not been located. Nor the family station wagon." He gave Karp a meaningful look, then added, "However, my co-counsel has been in contact with a few magicians who have agreed to accomplish what the best detectives in the state have not."

Karp smiled. He understood where Katz's remarks regarding the 221b Baker Street Irregulars came from; he'd had much the same reaction when introduced to the volunteer organization whose members, he thought originally, just wanted to play detective. However, the Baker Street gang specialized in finding the clandestine graves of murder victims through applications of various scientific methods, and now several successful cases later, he was a firm believer in their abilities.

"For those of you, like my young but misinformed co-counsel, who don't know, the 221b Baker Street Irregulars—a name taken from the address of Sherlock Holmes—are scientists, as well as a few folks already involved in law-enforcement specialties," Karp said. "They've provided an excellent service to this and other law-enforcement offices, as well as a case my wife, Marlene, was working on in which they located a car that had been buried in a gravel pit and were able to exhume the body of a murder victim from its interior. All defendants in the case have either pled guilty or are being tried and convicted."

"I stand corrected," Kenny said. "And look forward to whatever assistance the Baker Street Highly Irregulars can give us."

"Sticks and stones, my boy," Karp said.

"So what's next?" asked a voice to Karp's immediate left. Second-in-command at the DAO, Harry "Hotspur" Kipman was the office's appellate bureau chief, and as such he knew more about the minutia of the law than any five men in the room, including Karp. He was the guy, along with his team, who handled any appeals. He tended to pay more attention at these meetings than most; after all, he would have to deal with any fuckups they, or the judge, made at trial. His motto was that an ounce of prevention was worth a case coming back for retrial.

"The competency hearing is on for tomorrow," Katz replied. Normally a quick wit—read smartass—with anyone else, he held Kipman in reverential awe for his knowledge of the law. "We, of course, expect them to argue that she's not competent to stand trial. But the shrinks say she is and so will the judge."

"So we're still going forward with the murder charges?" The voice came from the far end of the table, where Joanie Kern, the newly appointed bureau chief of the sex crimes unit, sat.

"Yes," Katz replied. "But we've decided against seeking the death penalty. . . . Too tough a row to hoe, obviously because of the mitigating circumstances of her mental illness."

"I should say so," the woman answered.

"Is there a reason we shouldn't, Mrs. Kern?" Karp asked.

"You mean other than the fact that she's incompetent to stand trial?"

"I see," Karp replied. "By 'incompetent' do you mean that she's unable to assist her attorney with her defense and doesn't understand the nature and consequences of the charges against her? If so, that's what the competency hearing is for. If she's judged incompetent, she goes back to the mental ward at Bellevue and then to an upstate locked mental institution until such time as she's deemed competent."

"Uh, no, actually I was referring to any criminal trial, and the fact that she's crazy and probably belongs in a mental institution, not a prison," Kern replied. "I mean, she thinks God told her to murder her children. She 'hears' God talking to her like I'm talking to you."

Karp liked Kern. She was everything he wanted in the leader of the sex crimes unit—a unit his wife, Marlene, had created and run for a while—tough, committed, and thorough. But like many women who worked sex crimes, she was likely to take the woman's side automatically. He looked over at Kenny Katz. "That's certain to be the defense argument. You want to respond?"

Some of the old hands leaned forward in anticipation. It could be fun when the boss started stirring the pot.

Kenny pursed his lips. "Sure." He turned to Kern and shrugged. "No argument, Jessica Campbell is nuts, bonkers, cuckoo for Cocoa Puffs. However, that doesn't mean that she is not criminally responsible for her actions."

"Wait a second, you just said she's crazy."

"The legal question isn't whether we—as in so-called normal people—consider what she did to be crazy. Of course it's crazy to murder your children because you think God told you to do it. But it's also crazy to rob a liquor store, stick a shotgun in some poor Korean's face, and blow his brains all over the wall just because you need money for your heroin addiction.

Different people answer to different gods. So, do we not prosecute the guy with the shotgun?"

"Of course," Kern said with disdain. "But I'll bet the shrink will say that Jessica Campbell suffers from a mental defect. The guy with the shotgun is a drug addict."

"And probably a sociopath—at least 80 percent of everybody in prison has anti-social personality disorder," Katz argued. "That's a mental defect, too. In fact, Ted Bundy had a mental defect—he was a psycho—but they still fried his ass. Maybe he should have been put in a mental hospital, too."

"But she did whatever she did because she has a mental illness," Kern replied, though her resolve seemed to be weakening. "She likely suffers from postpartum depression, which can be pretty heavy-duty. A lot of people with it commit suicide."

"Yes, many women suffer from postpartum depression," Katz noted. "But very few murder their children. Jessica Campbell didn't commit suicide, she acted out a violent impulse."

"Under orders from God," Kern shot back.

"But God's not on trial here. The legal question is whether Jessica Campbell understood the nature and consequences of her actions, and did she know that what she did was wrong."

Kern was silent, so Karp used the moment to call off the dog. "Okay, okay," he interjected. "I think we've heard from both sides. Thank you, Mrs. Kern and Mr. Katz. Let's move on so we can spend some time throwing bad guys in the pokey."

Next in line was the homicide bureau chief, who reported on the status of sundry shootings, stabbings, stranglings, bludgeonings, and deaths by other methods. He ended on what for a homicide prosecutor was a bright note. A murder mystery. A skull had been found on the shore at the north end of Manhattan Island by a turbulent stretch of water where the Hudson and East rivers met called Spuyten Duyvil. As he intended when he said the name—"In Spite of the Devil" in old Dutch—everyone in the room swiveled to look at him.

Andrew Kane, the former mayoral candidate who turned out to be a murderous sociopath, had tried to escape capture by diving into those waters. But he'd been followed by David Grale, the "mad monk" who lived with his army of Mole People in the tunnels and caves beneath the city, hunting "evil" men. Grale had told Karp that the two had fought with knives beneath the surface and that he thought he'd given Kane a mortal wound. However, the body had never been recovered.

Now, the homicide chief held up his hand. "Sorry, no it's not *that* person's skull," he said. "For one thing it's more recent. There was still some skin left, including enough to see that '777' had been carved into the forehead. Might be a gang or cult thing. We haven't been able to identify the owner yet, but we have enough from the dental record to know it's not Andrew Kane."

"Kane had his face altered with plastic surgery," Murrow pointed out. "Maybe he had dental work done, too."

"We thought of that," Karp said. "So we talked to Charlotte Gates—she's a forensic anthropologist with our Baker Street Irregular friends—and she was able to extract 'tooth pulp' from inside one of the molars of the deceased. She checked it against Kane's DNA. Negative. She wants to do more tests, but she's pretty sure the skull belongs to a Caucasian or Hispanic male, late twenties."

The Case of the Mysterious 777 Skull wrapped up the presentation for the homicide bureau, and Murrow quickly moved through the rest of the meeting. After they finished scrutinizing all the armed robberies, rapes, burglaries, and other types of mayhem on the agenda, everybody began gathering their papers to leave, but stopped when Karp cleared his throat. He looked at V. T. Newbury, who had not spoken or shown any interest in the proceedings.

"There is one final item," Karp said. "It is with great regret that I'm forced to announce that our own Vinson Talcott Newbury has tendered his resignation. He's off to greener pastures, and maybe he'll stop by soon and give us a ride in the new Mercedes."

"I own an Aston Martin," Newbury said. "Not enough room for much of anyone else." He scooped up his papers and stalked out of the room as the others watched in embarrassed silence.

Two minutes later, Karp nearly bumped into Mrs. Milquetost in the hall. "Oh, pardon me," she exclaimed. "I was just coming to find you. Your wife called. She wants you to call immediately." The receptionist and Marlene did not get along, and it was clear from her tone that she didn't think the missus should be ordering the boss to do anything "immediately."

Karp thanked her and walked into his office where he sat down with a sigh. He never knew what he was going to hear when he called Marlene—it could be anything from asking him to pick up a loaf of bread on the way home to the twins causing a riot on the block. "Call immediately" didn't sound like an errand to the baker, so it was with great trepidation that he dialed her cell number.

Marlene answered at the first ring. "Oh Butch, thanks for calling," she said, obviously frightened, which took a lot when it came to his wife. He immediately thought of the kids, but this time the trouble lay with a different generation.

"Dad's missing," she said, her voice cracking. "I can't find him anywhere."

8

Marlene had arrived that morning at her father's small brick house in Queens with a knot in her stomach. She had been raised there, and after she had moved away it had been such a sanctuary to her, a place where she could go home and feel like a child again, even after she became a mother herself. But that had been while her own mother, Concetta Ciampi, had still been her mom, before Alzheimer's took her mind and left her body behind like an empty suitcase.

For more than sixty years, Concetta had been the rock upon which the family's foundation had rested. Once the disease set in, that foundation had crumbled quickly. Before Concetta's death, she believed that her husband, whom she'd met as a teenager on the boat coming over from Sicily, had been replaced by a stranger who lived in his body. She had only rarely recognized Marlene, more often confusing her with a sister who'd died many years before.

It had been tough on Marlene but pure hell for her father. Where was the woman he'd married? His lover, his friend, the mother of his children? He was dealing with the onset of senior dementia himself—becoming forgetful and apt to get lost if he got turned around—so the rapid deterioration of the woman he'd counted on all those years frightened him. He'd become easily irritated, angry—not at all the gentle, humorous man Marlene adored.

After her mother's death the previous year, Marlene—already predisposed toward a guilty conscience by her Catholic upbringing—had beat herself up for thinking of her mother's physical death as a blessing instead of a curse. And she assumed it was her own guilt that made her wonder if her father had finally cracked and put a pillow over his wife's sleeping face to end the torment. Her father had guessed what she was thinking and wept that she would ever think he would kill the woman he'd promised to love and cherish "*fino alla morte facciali parte.*"

His tears had shamed Marlene. Still, when she'd been granted a private audience with the pope following the hostage situation at St. Patrick's Cathedral a year earlier, in which she'd played no small role in thwarting the terrorists, she'd asked forgiveness for both herself and her father. The pontiff had given them both his blessing, and Marlene her penance, but said that if Mariano Ciampi had sins to confess, he would have to do so to a priest in person, not by proxy.

Ever since, Mariano's mind had continued to deteriorate. He insisted that Concetta's ghost still wandered the rooms of the house they'd shared for so many years. "She's waiting for me," he claimed. He wasn't frightened of his wife's spirit, and he looked forward to spending eternity in her company. He told his daughter that he was in no hurry to join Concetta, but in some ways, he was already gone.

Alzheimer's had destroyed Concetta's mind in a fast, merciless attack. With Mariano, it was more like he was saying goodbye; taking his time, but leaving just the same.

Marlene had all the proof she needed of that when she drove up to the house that morning. Mariano and Concetta had taken great pride in the appearance of their home and yard. By unspoken agreement, he cared for the lawn and trees, made sure the house got painted when it needed a fresh coat, and took care of the cars. She worked in her gardens, especially among her beloved roses, and kept the interior of the house spotless, yet as warm and comforting as the loaves of foccacia bread she pulled fresh out of her oven several times a week.

Now, the property looked as if the owners of the house had moved out and left no caretaker. The lawn, littered with leaves and bits of trash, was shaggy and brown, and in some spots nothing more than dirt. Even sadder to Marlene were her mother's once proud flower gardens, now patches of weeds. The gardens had been abandoned for years because her mother had quit going outside. The world beyond the front door confused and frightened her.

It was the thought of the state of the garden that brought Marlene to the house that morning dressed in work clothes. She had a dozen new rose bushes in the back of her truck. She'd spend a few hours weeding and planting, then rake up the leaves and pick up the trash, and she intended at some point to get out to the garage and find out if the old lawnmower would still fire up.

As she got out of her truck, she saw that the front door was open. She searched both inside and out, but there was no sign of her father. An open can of Budweiser on the table next to his favorite chair was still cool to the touch.

Further investigation led her back outside, where she saw the next-door neighbor—a young black woman—picking weeds from her flower garden with an infant in a backpack. "Hi, I'm Marlene," she said, walking over to shake the woman's hand. "I used to live here . . . with my parents. In fact, I just came over to see my father, and he's not here. I don't suppose you saw him leave and head off in any particular direction?"

"Hi, I'm Lakeesha," the woman replied. "But no, I'm sorry, I didn't notice him leaving. In fact, we hardly ever see him. . . . I . . . I didn't even know he had a daughter."

Marlene knew the other woman had not meant to make her feel guiltier than she already did, but that was the effect of the comment. *I should have introduced myself to the neighbors long before this*, she thought. *Then if Pops needed something, they might notice and call me*. Her father was notorious for refusing to ask for help or directions. "I'm not incompetent," he'd railed at her the last time she'd been over. "I can take care of myself."

Ever since her mother had died, Marlene had been trying to get him to consider moving to an assisted-living community. It was pricey, practically a country club for the elderly, but she had plenty of money—having made millions when a high-profile VIP security firm she'd helped found went public on the New York Stock Exchange. He refused, and the more she brought it up, the louder he continued to refuse. He'd always been independent and his house was his joy. "I'll leave when I'm dead," he stated flatly. "Put me in an old folk's home and you might as well shoot me. Guess it wouldn't matter, I'm no use to anyone anymore."

Part of the issue was that the neighborhood had changed so much. All of his former neighbors, those who'd raised their families next to his, were dead or had moved to Florida. They'd been replaced by new young couples, including, as her father had noted, "a lot of colored folks." She'd never heard him make remarks about race in the past, but it was clear that he was uncomfortable with the changing demographics and didn't know how to deal with it.

So she told him about an article she'd read recently that reported that blacks in Queens, most of whom were immigrants from the Caribbean, had a higher educational level and income than American-born blacks living else-where in the Five Boroughs or in his old blue-collar neighborhood. The point was that this new, upwardly mobile class was a good thing for the neighborhood; their pride in ownership in their neatly kept properties was evident.

"Which can only help your property values, too, Pops," she'd said. "I bet you'd find that they're great neighbors, if you just gave them a chance." But he'd responded that he didn't want to "bother anyone . . . and what would they want from an old man anyway?"

Marlene walked back to her truck thinking about where her father might have gone. He'd lost his driver's license after a fender-bender accident that he'd caused a year earlier and rarely went anywhere on foot, unless it was to the VFW a few blocks away. It was the best place she could think of to start.

———

A few minutes later, she pulled into the parking lot of the hall and stopped in front of the two flagpoles, one flying the American flag and the other the black and white flag for MIA-POWs. Both flags were as tattered and tired as the building itself, which had all the architectural appeal of a cereal box laid on its face. It desperately needed new paint, if not a bulldozer.

Still, it had been home away from home for several generations of veterans—from men who'd stormed the beaches at Normandy and Guadalcanal, or, like her father, fought their way up the Italian peninsula, to those who'd fought the Chinese in Korea, or the Vietnamese in Hue, to the newcomers, those whose tours had taken them to Kabul and Baghdad. Whatever their age difference, inside the hall, they'd all found brothers who knew what it was like to be "over there," wherever "there" had been.

There were only two other cars in the parking lot. Marlene got out of her truck and walked into the building. She stood for a moment in the poorly lit interior to let her eyes adjust, and saw that two old men—neither of them her father—sat at the bar in their peaked VFW caps, the smoke from their cigarettes swirling around them like winter fog over New York Harbor. Behind the bar, a familiar figure leaned back against the mirror and blew smoke rings of his own at the low-hung ceiling.

Despite her worries, Marlene smiled. It had been many years since she'd last been in the bar. But she would have sworn that the same two old geezers had been sitting on the same stools then, and that the same half-played game of eight-ball was waiting for the next shooter on the worn pool table.

Just as familiar was the smell of ancient tobacco smoke, spilled beer, bodies of hard-working men who could have used more time around soap and water, and the astringent aroma of the little blue tablets placed in the urinals of the men's bathrooms. She'd spent plenty of time in the hall herself, either accompanying her father or sent by her mother to retrieve him for dinner.

"Tell him to finish his beer and whatever lie he's telling for the hundredth time quick and hurry home if he doesn't want the malocchio *from his adoring wife,"* Concetta would say, but with a laugh that assured her daughter that her father was in no real danger from "the evil eye."

"Well, I'll be damned, if it ain't the lovely Marlene Ciampi!"

Marlene was jolted from her thoughts by the voice of the heavyset, middle-aged man behind the bar. "Hi Bert," she responded. "Still holding down the fort, I see, and still in need of glasses . . . lovely, my eye."

Bert the Bartender wiped a spot on the bar in front of one of the stools and invited her to take a seat. He glared at the two old men sitting at the bar. "Atten-hut!" he ordered. "There's a lady present."

One of the old men did his best to hop down from his bar stool and snap to attention, but he had to grab the bar to keep himself from falling over.

The other remained in his seat, his head nodding as he mumbled something about a girl he'd met in Rome long ago. A few words at a time came out between draws on the Chesterfield pinched between his forefinger and thumb.

"A little early for a classy broad like you to be making the rounds, ain't it?" Bert the Bartender asked.

Marlene laughed at the teasing from an old friend. Bert had been one of the neighborhood guys when she was growing up, destined from birth to be a borough rat all his life. In fact, he would have probably never made it any farther abroad than the Jersey Turnpike, except he'd been drafted in '68 and sent to Vietnam, where he'd lost a leg to a landmine. He came home to a job at the VFW, where he'd been handing out drinks and cleaning up spills and vomit for more than thirty years.

"What can I get ya?" Bert asked, moving a lock of greasy hair out of his eyes. "A Shirley Temple? Maybe a Manhattan? Or does Marlene 'Just One of the Boys' Ciampi want to have a beer with an old friend whose heart she broke before he went away to fight for his country?"

Marlene laughed. "If I remember right, you were two years older, the untouchable Captain of the Football Team, and wouldn't even give me a second look as long as Betty Schneider and her 36-Ds were around."

Bert chuckled. "Well, you have to admit that Betty was built like a brick shithouse. . . . Heard she's living over in Yonkers now, pushing 250 pounds and on her third husband. But you're looking mighty fine, Ms. Ciampi. You still married to that lawyer?"

"If you mean the District Attorney of New York City, yes. But sorry, I'll have to take a rain check on that drink. I'm looking for Pops and was wondering if he's been in today?"

Bert's heavy brow furrowed. "Tell you the truth, I ain't seen him in here in months. In fact, I don't know that I seen him since . . . well, you know, your mom died, God rest her soul. . . . Anyway, he's missing? There something I can do?"

Marlene shook her head. "Nah, that's okay. I stopped by the house to see him, but he wasn't there and the door was wide open. He's getting a little forgetful these days and probably just didn't shut it well when he went out for a walk."

"No evidence of foul play?" Bert asked. Ever since Marlene had known him, he'd dreamed of joining the thin blue line of the New York Police Department. Vietnam had shattered that possibility, and he compensated for that by watching too many television cop shows.

"No, just an open door and an empty house. I'm sure it's not a big deal. I just thought that he might have headed this way. He always loved it here, you know."

Marlene grabbed a cocktail napkin and pen to write down a number. "This is my cell. If he shows up, be a pal and call me please, so I can call off the search party. Don't lose it, okay?"

Bert folded the napkin and put it in his pocket. "Lose it? I've been trying to get your phone number for years. I'm going to get this framed."

"Oh Bert, a guy like you is too good for the likes of me. But call if Pops shows up, would ya?"

"Will do," he answered. "I'm sure he's okay. Probably just visiting old friends."

"You're probably right. I'm not panicking . . . yet."

An hour later, however, and she was ready to revise that into definitely panicked. She'd checked with every old friend of his in the neighborhood she could find, but many of his friends no longer lived in their former homes. She went back to his house to see if he'd returned; finding nothing, she took a photograph of him so that she could canvas area businesses. No one had seen the man in the picture.

She decided it was time to call Butch. Ever since they'd been young prosecutors at the DAO, he'd been the steadiest man she'd ever known, and the most competent. Shortly after they'd started dating, she had opened a letter bomb intended for him—jealous that it might be from his ex-wife—and lost an eye and several fingers. But he had stuck by her, and in fact had married her "scarred for life" and all, though she remained always stunningly attractive.

He'd even hung in there over the past couple of years when—having left the DAO to work as a security consultant—she'd had a crisis of faith in the legal system. To deal with it, she'd turned to vigilante justice, which in turn threatened to consume her soul in a world of violence and gray moral choices. Although the poster boy for the rule of law and order, he wouldn't let her go when she tried to push him and the kids away because she felt she was somehow tainted and also a danger to them. It was because of his love and faith in her—along with the spiritual guidance of John Jojola—that she was at least most of the way back.

She felt guilty about calling him. As the head of one of the busiest DAOs in the country, he didn't really have time to be bothered with her search for an old man who'd probably just gone out for a walk and would turn up on his own shortly. But Butch Karp was also a man who had his priorities straight; if his wife or kids needed him, there was no power on Earth that could stop him from dropping whatever he was doing and flying to their aid.

As expected, he responded by insisting that he come help her look. "And I'll get Clay to let the cops know to be watching for some crazy old Italian wandering around Queens."

"Well," she laughed in spite of her anxiety, "that will narrow it down to a mere few thousand."

———

Karp got off the phone with his wife and called Fulton to explain what was going on. He asked him to get a "Be On the Lookout" alert to the cops in Queens and mentioned that he was going to take a taxi to the area, but Clay had other ideas. "I have some time. Why don't I take you over in my car and we can canvass the neighborhood and check out the hospitals . . . that sort of thing?"

When Karp hesitated, Fulton insisted. After all, he said, one of his jobs was providing security for the district attorney, and there were parts of Queens where it wasn't safe for him to be wandering around.

A few minutes later, they were heading for the Queens Midtown Tunnel when Karp received a call from Mrs. Milquetost. "Yes, Darla?"

"A Mr. Moishe Sobelman called from a bakery on Third Avenue and 29th Street. Apparently, your father-in-law is there but confused as to how he got there. Mr. Sobelman left a telephone number. Have you got a pen?"

"Yes, thank you, go ahead." As Fulton headed for Third and 29th, Karp called the number.

"Il Buon Pane bakery, Moishe Sobelman speaking," a man with a heavy accent answered.

"Yes, hello, this is Butch Karp . . ."

"Ah yes, Mr. Karp, thank you for calling me back. I believe you are related to one Mariano Ciampi?"

"He's my father-in-law. I was told that he might be there."

"He is indeed. He walked in an hour ago and wanted a piece of my cherry cheese coffee-cake. But he couldn't find his wallet—not that I cared, I gave him the coffee cake on credit—and then he couldn't remember how he got here or what he was supposed to be doing. He told me his name and that he lives with Concetta in Queens, but not much else. I didn't want him to wander away, so I asked him a few questions. He remembered that his daughter, Marlene, was married to the district attorney of New York. So I called your office."

"Thank you so much for all your trouble," Karp said, thinking how well Mr. Sobelman exemplified the ability New Yorkers had shown after 9/11 to come through for each other in tough times.

"It's been my pleasure. Mariano is good company, and we have traded old stories over coffee cake and cappuccino. I think he knew the former owner and that's why he came here. Besides, you and I have a mutual acquaintance."

"Oh? Who is that?"

"Vladimir Karchovski. I believe this is one of those 'small world' sort of things, no?"

Karp was silent for a moment. Vladimir Karchovski was his great uncle, the brother of his grandfather on his father's side. He was also connected with the Russian mob over in the Brighton Beach area of Brooklyn. "Uh, yes, it is a small world," he replied and changed the subject; it was not one he was comfortable discussing, especially with a stranger. "I'd really appreciate it if you could keep my father-in-law there until I show up. We're five minutes away."

"No rush," Sobelman replied. "We're enjoying our cappuccinos."

"Again, thank you," Karp said. "I better get off now and let my wife—Mariano's daughter—know that he's safe. And maybe I can get her to join us for a piece of the cherry cheese coffee-cake."

"The best in the Five Boroughs," Sobelman said with a laugh. "I make it from the family recipe I inherited from Mariano's old friend. I have some baking right now so it will be fresh and warm when you arrive."

Karp hung up and looked at the cell phone for a moment without speaking. When Sobelman had mentioned that Karchovski was a mutual acquaintance, he'd wondered if there was something sinister afoot. Perhaps Mariano had been kidnapped, and this was part of an elaborate blackmail plot. Karp had never publicly disclosed his family connection to an organized-crime boss, and in fact had taken great pains to keep his distance.

As gangsters went, the Karchovski clan was rather benign. They didn't deal in drugs or guns or prostitution. They made their living off of gambling and smuggling illegal immigrants—especially from Russia and former Soviet Bloc countries—into the United States while smuggling goods into Russia for the black market. That didn't make them Boy Scouts either; there'd been times when Vladimir Karchovski and his son, Ivgeny, had had their people resort to violence to protect their territory and themselves from rival gangs.

Karp quickly dismissed the idea that Sobelman had intended his remark as a threat. The fact of the matter was that Ivgeny Karchovski, a former colonel in the Red Army who'd been seriously wounded fighting in Afghanistan, had proved a valuable ally in recent run-ins with Islamic terrorists and Nadya Malovo, a former Soviet KGB agent turned hired gun for certain government and crime interests in Russia. That past spring Ivgeny had also helped him expose Jon Ellis as a double agent and a traitor.

Karp decided that Sobelman meant the comment as no more than it had seemed, acknowledgment of a mutual acquaintance. He opened the cell phone again and dialed Marlene's number. "I'm on my way to meet your father," he said when she answered, "who is relaxing over coffee cake and cappuccino at the Il Buon Pane bakery on Third Avenue and 29th."

"Il Buon Pane bakery?" Marlene exclaimed. "His friend, Alfredo Turrisi used to own the place. They met on the boat coming over from Sicily, but he's been dead for twenty years. What's Pops doing there? And what the hell is he doing scaring me half to death?"

"Beats me. We can take him back to the loft, sit him down under a 100-watt bulb, and hit him with a hose until he talks. But I was promised a piece of cherry cheese coffee-cake, so the interrogation will have to wait until I've finished."

"Cherry cheese coffee-cake, eh? So much for the diet, big boy. Well, it better be good if Pops had to jump across the river to get it."

"I'm assured it's the best in the Five Boroughs, which would have to mean the best in the world," Karp said. "But I'll let you be the judge of that if you'd care to join us there."

"I'm on my way."

Fulton let Karp out in front of the bakery but declined to come in. "I have a few things I want to check out on a case," he said, "and Marlene has her truck, right? Good. She can drop you off downtown. Catch you later."

Il Buon Pane was located on the southwest corner of the busy intersection—one of those precious holdovers from another era when New York City, for all its skyscrapers and asphalt, was still the land of promise for immigrants. As in the past, its large windows were filled with many-tiered wedding cakes, pastries, and breads of every imaginable type. Even out on the sidewalk, the smell of the fresh-baked delights drifted by so that few who walked past could resist turning their heads and at least wishing they could stop and sample.

Above the store was an apartment with a menorah in the window, which Karp assumed belonged to the baker. It was another reminder of the days when New Yorkers lived and worked in their neighborhoods. He pulled the door open to the tinkling of bells.

A gnomish man with a big nose and ears that jutted out beneath a tall baker's hat looked up from behind the counter, where he'd been helping an equally tiny woman with red hair that fell about her face in ringlets. "I'll be right with you," the man said.

Karp recognized the voice as belonging to Moishe Sobelman. "Take your time. I see my appointment," he said, pointing toward the back of the store. Two small tables with chairs occupied what little space there was, and sitting at one of them, hunched over a game of checkers, was his father-in-law, who looked up as he approached and seemed surprised to see him.

"Butch!" Mariano Ciampi shouted. "What the hell are you doing here? Not more than five minutes ago—five minutes I tell you—me and my friend Alfredo were talking about you."

The man behind the counter wiped flour-covered hands on his apron. "Moishe Sobelman," he said, extending a hand to Karp. "I'm afraid my new friend Mariano has me confused with the former owner."

Mariano looked confused for a moment, but then he smiled sheepishly. "That's right. That's right. All this talk about old times, I got mixed up. Alfredo has been dead many years. This is Moishe's place now, and it's just as good as it ever was. He kept the name you know, Il Buon Pane, 'The Good Bread' bakery."

Sobelman waved Karp to the seat across the table from his father-in-law. He pointed to the woman behind the counter. "And that's my boss, Goldie Sobelman. She doesn't speak, but she understands more than all of us put together."

Karp nodded to the woman, who smiled and headed back to the kitchen. He turned in time to see Moishe's look as he watched her go. He looked like a proud man who'd just introduced his beautiful young bride to the neighbors, though both Sobelmans were only a little younger than Mariano. "Did you know the former owner, Alfredo Turrisi?" Karp asked.

"Yes, I have worked here since 1959," he replied. "I was new to this country when our mutual friend Vladimir Karchovski introduced me, and Mr. Turrisi gave me a job. I believe I remember Mariano coming into the shop to see his friend, but it has been many years."

"Nonsense," Mariano chimed in from his seat. "I remember you well. You always had flour on your cheeks and hardly spoke a word of English. In fact, you reminded me of myself when I came over from the Old Country. We were good friends with Alfredo and his wife, Helen—though not so good that he would ever tell me the secret to making his delicious cherry cheese coffee-cake."

Karp smiled and patted his father-in-law on the shoulder. Whether Mariano truly remembered young Moishe with flour on his cheeks didn't matter; it was a fine memory now.

"I was sworn to maintain that secrecy when Alfredo sold me the business and the apartment above. That was when he got sick and could no longer work," Sobelman said. He winked at Karp. "But I'm forgetting my manners. I believe I promised you a piece of that same cherry cheese coffee-cake."

"It's to die for," Mariano Ciampi assured his son-in-law.

Sobelman moved quickly for a man his age and disappeared into the kitchen. A minute later, he returned with an enormous piece of coffee cake oozing cherries and cream cheese. As he placed the delicacy on the table, the shirtsleeve covering Sobelman's forearm slipped back, revealing an old blue-green tattoo of a number. Karp had seen many such numbers before on older Jewish men and women, their permanent reminder of time spent in Nazi concentration camps.

Sobelman pulled the sleeve back to cover the tattoo. "Long story," he said quietly. "Perhaps I'll tell it to you someday since it has a happy ending, because of my friend Vladimir."

"Vladimir? Who the hell is Vladimir?" Mariano asked.

"Just an old friend," Karp assured his father-in-law.

Karp had just finished his coffee cake and was contemplating the calories he'd have to work off if he asked for a second piece when Marlene marched in through the door. She wasted little time letting her father know she wasn't happy.

"So Pops . . . how'd you get here?"

"The subway, what else?" Mariano rolled his eyes at the men present. "I took the Seven to Grand Central Terminal, then the Green Line to the 23rd Street station. I walked the rest of the way."

"Okay," Marlene said. "But why? You scared me to death. I show up at the place and the door is wide open but no Pops around."

Mariano frowned. "I thought your mother would close it," he said. "After all, she's the one who suggested that I come see my old friend Alfredo." He stopped and looked at Sobelman. "But of course, Alfredo is dead and this is Moishe's bakery. I don't know why she'd forget something like that."

The comment was followed by an embarrassed silence until Sobelman spoke. "I know why," he said. "It was so that I could meet a new friend—or perhaps an old friend—as well as your beautiful daughter and her fine husband. And such a treat for me, a rare beauty and the district attorney of New York in my humble little bakery."

Everyone laughed, grateful for the out. "You're right," Mariano agreed. "God works in mysterious ways, and He must have guided my feet today."

"Yes, God has His own way of doing things, and His own reasons," Sobelman agreed. "I hope you'll come often. Now, wait a minute so that I can get a photograph of my new friends so that I can prove to my old friends that such a thing really did happen."

Sobelman nipped behind the counter again and reemerged with a digital camera, which he used to snap several photographs. A few minutes later, as Marlene and her father stuffed their faces with more coffee cake, the little baker quietly pulled Karp aside. "Is there anything you can tell me about whoever was behind the bombing of our synagogue?"

Surprised, Karp asked, "You belong to that synagogue?"

"Yes, for many years. And I noticed on the message board that you teach a bar mitzvah class. You are also a scholar of the Torah, as well as U.S. law?"

Karp shook his head. "Unfortunately, I'm not," he said. "It's more of a class about modern issues."

"There are no modern issues," Sobelman responded. "Just old issues with new names. But forget my question, it was rude to put you on the spot."

"Don't worry about it," Karp said. "There's really not much I can say that you probably haven't heard. The investigation is being handled by federal agencies."

"I see."

"Did you lose any friends?"

Sobelman studied Karp's face before speaking. "I have lost many friends over many years to acts of evil," he said quietly. "And yes I lost friends this time, too. But I was asking because I was there when the bomb exploded, and I constantly wonder why God continues to spare me and not others."

Karp was still thinking about that last conversation with Sobelman when Marlene pulled up in front of the Criminal Courts building to drop him off. He kissed her and was about to get out of the truck when Mariano, who was riding in the jumpseat, suddenly covered his face and wailed. "Oh God," he cried. "I'm such an old fool. I'm no use to anyone and just cause trouble."

Marlene turned in her seat and reached back to put her hand on her father's face. "Don't say that Pops. You're not useless. You're just a little forgetful sometimes, but who isn't? And we do need you. The kids need you, and I need you. Do you understand that?"

Mariano nodded and wiped away the tears on his cheeks. But when Karp again started to get out of the car, he suddenly reached forward and gripped his son-in-law's arm. "Just hope you die before you get old, Butch. Losing your mind isn't a lot of fun."

9

Kenny Katz looked at his watch as his taxi pulled up in front of Bellevue Hospital. *Good, I'm early*, he thought. Because of the media attention on the Campbell case, he'd been told by the judge's clerk that it would be handled first on the docket that morning.

Be there on time, if you know what's good for you. This judge does not like to be kept waiting.

As he got out of the cab, he noticed a tall, unkempt man in a faded army field jacket standing in front of an older couple. He had his right hand and one long crooked finger raised in the air; his left arm was outstretched toward them. In a way, with his wild shocks of wiry, graying brown hair and his righteous, somewhat insane-looking, wildly rolling eyes, he reminded Katz of a painting he'd once seen by nineteenth-century artist Jacob Lawrence of the old abolitionist John Brown. If he hadn't known any better, he would have thought that the man had just been released from the hospital's psychiatric ward.

However, they'd been introduced the first day he'd started working on the Campbell case with Karp. According to legend at the DAO, Edward Treacher had once been a respected professor of religious studies at NYCU. But apparently he'd swallowed too many tabs of LSD in the late 1960s with his friend Timothy Leary and there'd been a disconnect in his brain. That had earned him his first stint at Bellevue. He seemed to think fondly of the place, for he occasionally returned for a sabbatical in a straitjacket. Otherwise he lived on the streets, following his new calling as an apocalyptic preacher known around the courts building for his dire biblical warnings and odd sense of humor.

Katz had asked Karp about Treacher one day when the boss invited him to lunch at one of the vending carts across the street. As Karp washed a bite of his potato knish down with an orange soda, he noted the quizzical triumvirate of street people who regularly hung out around 100 Centre Street— The Walking Booger, Dirty Warren, and Edward Treacher.

Kenny Katz had grown up on some pretty tough streets in Queens and had known plenty of street people. Some were no better than sociopaths and criminals who preyed on law-abiding citizens—and each other— if they got the chance. However, others, he learned over time, had little control over the illnesses and addictions that had taken over their minds and lives.

Most were gentle, living in a frightening world whose "normal" citizens looked away, not caring to see them. They ranged from the mentally challenged to people with brilliant minds that were still whirring away inside, but with gears that did not quite mesh.

There was something different about the Centre Street gang.

"It's almost like they consider hanging around the courts building as their jobs," Kenny remarked, watching Treacher chase down a couple of Japanese tourists. They turned and stood politely while he railed at them about "The End of Days," and then just as politely handed over their spare change.

"Yeah, to be honest, I've thought that myself about those characters," Karp said, surprising Katz with the almost affectionate tone in his voice. "For one thing, they keep showing up at the most unusual, and often perfect, times. Sometimes, I even wonder if they're spying on me and my family, but if so, it's like they're trying to watch out for us. My daughter thinks they're actually guardian angels sent to protect us."

"Guardian angels? The Walking Booger?"

Karp just shrugged and polished off the remains of his knish. "I don't know," he said. "But there's a lot more going on behind those rolling eyes than is readily apparent."

———

Katz knew that Treacher was basically harmless, despite the thundering voice and bits of spittle that flew from his mouth as he spoke. However, it was clear that he was frightening the older couple trying to get around him to the hospital entrance. The preacher kept anticipating their moves and stepping in the way.

"AND BEHOLD," Treacher shouted, "A WOMAN OF CANAAN CRIED UNTO HIM, SAYING, 'HAVE MERCY ON ME, O LORD, THOU SON OF DAVID; MY DAUGHTER IS GRIEVOUSLY VEXED WITH A DEVIL!'"

"Please, let us pass," the man pleaded. "This is hard enough."

Treacher peered suspiciously at the man as if he hadn't considered that he might actually be disturbing someone. Kenny used the moment to step between him and the couple.

"Hello, Mr. Treacher," he said, extending his hand as he waited for the electric blue eyes to stop rolling around like dice on a craps table. "I don't know if you remember me. I'm Ken Katz, an assistant district attorney. Mr. Karp introduced us."

Treacher scratched at his beard in confusion; Katz pretended not to notice that several items fell out of the tangled mess and landed on the ancient Grateful Dead T-shirt beneath the field jacket. Then the man smiled. "But, of course, my good man," he said pumping Katz's hand enthusiastically. "You're Butch Karp's young protégé."

"Yes, that would be me," Katz replied. "Anyway, I think these people are in a hurry to get into the hospital this morning. Would you mind letting them get past you?"

Treacher glanced back at the couple, who were huddled as if preparing for flight in case the madman did something dangerous. But the madman only looked at them as if the question itself was ludicrous.

"But of course," Treacher said and bowed dramatically, as his free hand swept magnanimously toward the entrance. "I wouldn't dream of delaying them. I just thought that considering who they are, they might be interested in that little passage from Matthew 15:22. It's a story about a woman whose daughter was inhabited by a demon until Jesus came along and cast it out. Sometimes the demons hopped into the bodies of pigs and then jumped in the ocean and drowned. Quite the scene I'm sure. But perhaps they could ask Jesus to do the same for their daughter. . . . Haven't seen any pigs around though, unless you count the local gendarme?" He nodded his head toward a uniformed NYPD officer.

"Yes, I do," Katz said, retrieving his hand. "I'm not real familiar with the Jesus story, but now might not be the right moment to hear more." He turned to the couple and held out his hand again. "Ken Katz with the District Attorney's Office. I believe that you're free to proceed."

The man started to raise his hand but his wife stopped him. Her eyes were angry, but her voice was frightened as she said, "We know who you are. You're the Nazi who's trying to put our daughter in prison. She's a sick woman and suffering—as are we. That should be punishment enough, Mister Katz, but no, you feel the need to torture sick people who need help, not to be locked away in a prison cell. She still has a lot to offer society . . . certainly more than some two-bit power-hungry lawyer like you."

Katz let his hand drop. He now recognized Benjamin and Liza Gupperstein, whom he'd seen in newspaper photographs accompanying articles about Jessica Campbell's case. The articles invariably quoted people saying that Karp was essentially a new version of Heinrich Himmler, and Katz a willing member of the neo-SS. The woman's remarks hurt, but as his boss had said, suffering the slings and arrows of outrageous criticism came with the territory.

"I'm sorry for your loss," he said, stepping aside to let the Guppersteins pass, which they did without looking at him again—one out of anger and the other out of embarrassment.

Katz gathered himself to walk in through the door when he felt a hand on his shoulder and smelled an odor like Manhattan during a summer garbage strike. He'd forgotten about Edward Treacher, who was behind him. He turned and looked into a pair of blue eyes that were no longer wild but kind and sympathetic.

"When justice is done," Treacher said quietly, "it brings joy to the righteous but terror to evildoers . . . Proverbs 21:15. You're here to see that justice is done for those three innocent little babies, Mr. Katz, just remember that."

"Thanks, Mr. Treacher. I appreciate the sentiment."

"Please, let's not stand on formalities; it's Edward."

"Okay, thanks Edward, and it's Kenny to my friends." Katz began to turn, then paused. "See you around."

"Without a doubt, Kenny," the former professor of religious studies replied. "Without a doubt." The big man gave him a wink and then whirled, sending several new arrivals outside the hospital scurrying. "STAND AGAINST THE DEVIL, AND THE DEVIL WILL RUN FROM YOU! JAMES 4:7. And by the way, would any of you kind folks have any spare change to help feed the hungry, the hungry being me?"

Inside the hospital, Katz was directed to the psychiatric ward dayroom where the weekly competency hearings were held for those accused of crimes when their mental capacity to stand trial was at question. He looked at his watch again as he opened the door. Five minutes to spare, even after the affair at the front door.

He'd been warned—twice—about being late, first by the clerk and then by Karp, who had told Kenny that the judges who had the rotating competency-hearings duty liked to finish them in the morning so they could take the rest of the day off on the taxpayers' dime. "And there may be fifty cases to get through, so they need to run things tight if they want to make their afternoon tee time at Bamm Hollow Country Club in Jersey."

The first person Katz saw was defense attorney Linda Lewis, who was sitting at a table near the front. She gave him the sort of look one generally reserves for bad smells. He'd heard that she was a heck of a lawyer, but she was also supposed to be willing to bend whatever rule she needed to win.

A tiny blonde woman with large pink-rimmed glasses sat next to Lewis. She appeared to be meditating. Her eyes were shut and her index fingers and thumbs were closed in small circles, resting on the table. *The defense psychiatrist*, he realized.

As Katz walked up to the table set aside for the prosecution, he glanced at the Guppersteins, who sat in the first row of chairs behind the defense table. They had not turned when he entered and made no effort to acknowledge his presence now.

Behind them and somewhat off to the side, as though to say "we're on the same team as my in-laws, but we don't like each other," Charlie Campbell sat with a man in an immaculately tailored suit, whom Katz pegged as Charlie's lawyer. Their heads tilted toward one another as they whispered.

Katz turned when the door of the dayroom opened and felt his stomach twist into a knot. The Boss, Butch Karp, had come to check on his "protégé."

The competency hearing was a "due process classic." The defendant had the right to a speedy trial; however, fairness, and due process, in these circumstances, required that the accused be aware of the charges and able to assist her lawyer in the proceedings against her. If the objective facts suggested this might not be the case, then a Bellevue-type competency hearing was an appropriate safeguard. The major focus would be the reports written by two Bellevue psychiatrists weighing in on whether the defendant was competent to stand trial.

As Katz had explained at the staff meeting, whether Campbell was competent to stand trial was an entirely separate issue from the insanity defense her attorney was expected to use at trial. There, the defense argument would be that Campbell was legally insane, and therefore not responsible, at the time of the murders.

Both sides already knew the content of the reports from the state psychiatrists, who had agreed that Campbell was competent. Their reports had been sent to the DAO, the court, and the defense team.

There was little chance that the judge would not accept the conclusions of the two psychiatrists. However, Lewis had indicated that she intended to bring in her own psychiatrist—the little blonde woman—to challenge the report. If she won that challenge, then Campbell would be sent to a psychiatric institution—probably somewhere more comfortable than Bellevue—until such time as she was deemed competent.

———

Karp noted the look of surprise on Katz's face when he entered the dayroom. He would have felt the same way if Garrahy had suddenly dropped in on him.

As the district attorney, he was responsible for the 600 assistant district attorneys who worked for the busiest DAO in the country. Although the papers had been reporting on the "amazing" drop in crime rates in New York City compared to other large American cities, dealing with the current volume still meant handling a yearly tally of 50,000 violent crimes, of which 500 or so would be murders, another 1,500 rapes, and the rest a smorgasbord of robberies and assaults. That didn't include the tens of thousands of other types of felony cases like burglary, larceny, and fraud, or vehicle code and misdemeanor offenses. Or even the several hundred cases on appeal that were Harry Kipman's bailiwick.

Most of the young ADAs would burn out within a few years from the heavy caseload, the psychological trauma of dealing with criminals and victims, and the low pay, at least compared to the going rate in private practice. Well-trained, courtroom-trial-tested, experienced prosecutors with the New York DAO were considered prime prospects by the city's white-shoe firms, which regularly scouted the criminal courts for likely candidates among the young attorneys.

Some lawyers put their time in at the DAO just to become competent trial lawyers with the hope of trading their trial expertise for a high-income job lawyering with the upper crust. On the other hand, there were the few bright stars who were not only exceptional prosecutors at every level, but who also eschewed the offers that came from private firms. Often, they chose to remain with the DAO because they were idealists committed to the cause of justice. Public servants in the most noble sense of the term, they enjoyed their role as good guys in the battle against the forces of evil.

Every generation seemed to produce just enough to make the New York District Attorney's Office one of the best. In their time, Karp and Marlene, until she'd opted out for other pursuits, as well as Ray Guma and V. T. Newbury, had all fit the bill as the new idealistic hotshots.

The current crop looked to be a good one, too, with Kenny Katz leading the way. No one knew whether they'd give in to the siren call of Fifth Avenue suites and six-figure salaries with perks, or whether they were tough enough and good enough to take on the worst of the city's worst. But Karp had a feeling that they would be.

Katz had come to Karp's attention several months earlier during the murder trial of a gang member who'd stabbed a rival to death in the parking lot of a shopping center. Just before Katz's star witness—another gang member who'd been present at the crime—was set to testify, the witness decided he wanted a better deal. He'd agreed to plead guilty to acting in concert with the defendant during the course of the murder and accept ten years in exchange for testifying against his homeboy. But now he and his attorney were demanding no prison time.

According to what Karp had been told by Fulton, who'd heard the story from the police detective assigned to the case, Katz had left the witness waiting room to think over the dilemma. Then he'd spotted a blank video-tape lying on a table. Thinking quickly, he'd borrowed a black felt-tip pen, which he used to scrawl in big block letters, "MURDER SCENE—PARK-ING LOT SURVEILLANCE TAPE" and the date of the murder. He then walked back into the waiting room and tossed the tape onto the table in front of the witness and his attorney.

"He didn't say anything about the tape," Fulton related. "Just, 'Forget it, I don't need you anymore. No deal of any sort. The next time I see you in court, you'll be sitting at the defense table.' He started to walk out but apparently the lawyer for this scumbag beat him to the door, babbling about how there'd been a big misunderstanding. His client was prepared to testify and the original deal was just fine with him. Dude testified and sent his homie upriver for life."

The witness's attorney had cried foul later when he discovered there was no real surveillance tape depicting the murder, but it didn't matter. Katz had never said there was anything on the tape. The lawyer and the witness had just been free to read into it what they wanted.

———

It was the sort of quick thinking on his feet and under pressure that Karp was looking for in someone to take under his wing and groom for the future as a possible bureau chief. So he'd called the young man in for an interview.

Before Katz arrived, Karp had checked out his file and suddenly won-dered if he'd made a mistake. It wasn't the growing up in Queens only a few blocks from where Marlene's parents' home was located, or his top-of-the-class grades he'd received at Columbia Law School, that caught his atten-tion. It was Katz's military record and how he'd behaved after returning from a tour of duty in Afghanistan.

According to the resume, in September 2001 Katz had been in his last year at Columbia when the terrorists destroyed the World Trade Center.

Two days later, he'd dropped out and enlisted in the army. After basic training, he'd asked to be assigned to Ranger school, one of the toughest units in the U.S. Armed Forces. He'd then been sent to Afghanistan, where he'd been wounded twice. He received the Silver Star for gallantry along with two Purple Hearts and an honorable discharge.

All of that impressed Karp, but then he'd come across a newspaper clipping that someone had seen in the *Times* and inserted in the file. It was actually just a photograph of Katz, looking the part of a college student with his kinky hair bushed out in what Karp thought of as a "Jew Fro," attending an anti-war rally. The photograph showed Katz tossing what the caption said were his medals on the fire, and that rankled Karp.

As a boy growing up in Brooklyn just after the end of World War II, Karp had often gone on walks around the neighborhood with his parents. He was probably seven or eight when he'd remarked about the gold stars he could see in the windows of some of the homes they passed.

"Those are for the boys who didn't come home from the war, Roger," his mother tearfully said. He'd never forgotten the sadness in her voice and the way she'd pulled him closer to her. *"That's where their parents live."*

They were the local boys—the high school athletes and bookworms, the sons of the local baker, the family who ran the candy store, and the guy who owned the car dealership—who'd become heroes of nearly mythic proportions.

"They were just boys," his mother noted, like those who played ball in the Avenue P Park between 4th and 5th streets below Ocean Parkway in Brooklyn.

While conceding to Katz his free-speech rights, Karp couldn't get past the feeling that burning the medals was a slap in the face to all those gold-star moms. The medals had nothing to do with the politics of the war. They were an acknowledgment of personal sacrifice. So his first inclination was to cancel the interview—that kind of cheap theatrics were for defense attorneys. But then his better angels prevailed, and he decided to go through with the interview and ask Katz to explain the photograph.

The young man had been surprised when Karp handed him the newspaper clipping. *"To be honest, I have another set of medals at home,"* the wise-cracking street kid from Queens joked. *"I was just trying to get laid by one of those hippie chicks. They really go for that sensitive-war-hero shit."*

Army Ranger and war hero or not, Karp was about to kick him out of his office and down to the traffic bureau when the young man realized that flippancy had been the wrong way to handle the question. *"Sorry,"* he'd said. *"I have a bad habit when I'm nervous of being a smart-ass."*

"Then relax and tell me the real story," Karp had replied. The answer had surprised him.

Katz said he'd had been raised in one of those intellectual Jewish households where all questions, statements, and firmly held beliefs were examined and debated.

His grandparents and father had fled Germany shortly after *Krystalnacht*, the night in 1938 when anti-Jew riots broke out in Germany and Austria. The Katz family arrived in Queens grateful for the sanctuary and ready to repay the debt. Katz's father, Jacob, had served two tours of duty in Vietnam.

Kenny Katz had been walking to class at Columbia University on the far north end of Manhattan Island that morning on September 11, 2001, when he saw the dark plume of smoke rising from the southern end. He'd run into the student center and made it to the television lounge just in time to see the second airliner crash into the tower, and he stayed to watch as it all came plummeting to the ground.

An overwhelming anger began to burn inside of him. He'd always planned on applying to the New York District Attorney's Office when he got out of law school, hoping to work in the homicide bureau putting away killers. Here was murder on a scale that no DAO or international court of law could ever fathom; it was going to take more than talk and law books to deal with the murderers of 9/11.

Even as U.S. lawmakers and the president were making plans to go after Al Qaeda and their hosts, the Taliban in Afghanistan, he'd walked into his counselor's office at the law school and announced that he would be taking a leave from law school to join the army. He just wanted to let the man know that he planned to return when he could to resume his studies.

Katz didn't know what sort of response he'd get, but it wasn't what he'd hoped. The man, a noted liberal scholar, had looked at him with a bemused smile on his face and shaken his head. "Look, Kenny," he said, his voice dripping with sarcasm, as if Katz had just told him he planned to run away and join the circus. "We're all upset about what happened, but let's not all go off half-cocked to 'save the world' from a few misguided Muslims. Besides, I have it from reputable sources that there's a good chance the Republicans—or maybe somebody even more sinister—was behind this as an excuse to go to war for oil."

"That's about the stupidest thing I ever heard," Katz heard himself say to the man who could easily derail his pursuit of a law degree. "You stay here until they come for you with their Qur'an and their bombs. Me, I'm off to put a stop to it if I can."

"Good luck with that," the counselor said scornfully. "I doubt Columbia will have a place for you when you get back."

"I doubt I'd want it if you did," he'd retorted.

During basic training and in Ranger School, Katz had spent his free time studying up on Islamic extremism and the road leading to the attack on the World Trade Center, and saw a nation that was slow to respond to an impending threat. Most of that was due to weak-willed politicians who hamstrung any attempts to stop a growing sense on the part of the terrorists that America was too cowardly to stand up to them. And it had been going on for a long time and through several administrations and congresses—from the 1983 attack on the Marine barracks in Beirut, killing 241 servicemen; to the 1988 bombing and the deaths of 259 passengers and crew aboard an airliner over Lockerbie, Scotland; the 1998 bombing of the U.S. embassy in Kenya; the attack in 2000 on the USS *Cole*; and finally the attack on the World Trade Center. All those lives had been lost, while America's elected officials slept and worried about their next election.

No more, he thought, as his company at last received their orders to deploy to Afghanistan, where they would be assigned to hunt bin Laden and his associates in the mountains around Tora Bora. *"We had him, too,"* Katz recalled for Karp. *"But once again, the politicians and the bureaucrats kept dicking around and let him get away because they didn't want to offend our supposed allies in Pakistan."*

He'd soon grown jaded to the fact that partisan politics mattered more than the lives of U.S. soldiers. His father had warned him that ever since Vietnam, the politicians, not the generals, had been in charge of the battlefield, and they were more worried about what the press would say than they were about an American son coming home in a body bag.

"All this crap you hear about we don't know who we're fighting . . . that it's not like a conventional war because the terrorists don't have a standing army, is just pure horse manure," Katz had said to Karp that day in his office. *"We know who they are. We know where they are. We know that during the night they're trying to kill U.S. troops, and then smiling and waving at us the next day. They hide in houses with women and children, and then when we shoot back and civilians are killed, they wring their hands and cry about the Americans for the press. We don't lack the ability to fight these guys, we lack the will to do what it will take to make Americans safe again."*

However, as much as he learned to despise politicians, Katz had a profound love for the men he fought with. *"We were from all over the place,"* he told Karp. *"Rich, poor, black, white, Jew, and even a couple of Muslim guys who hated these bastards more than we did because of what they were doing in the name of the Qur'an."*

One night his unit received information from Pakistani intelligence officers that a high-level Al Qaeda leader was hiding out in a nearby village. *"We didn't really trust those guys,"* he said of the Pakistanis. *"Half of them were Al Qaeda or willing to lie or run off if someone slipped them a few dollars, but this seemed like good intel so we went."*

They were making their way through a narrow ravine when they were ambushed. The two men on point went down in the first fusillade, while the rest of the company was pinned down in the rocks.

Sgt. Kenny Katz jumped from the relative safety of the rocks and sprinted for the wounded men. *"I don't remember making a conscious decision to do it,"* he said. *"I still don't think of it as heroic. My guys were hurt, and I wasn't going to leave them out there to die."* He made it to the first man and miraculously dragged him back to safety as the bullets rang off the rocks all around them. Then he went back for the second soldier.

"The next thing I knew, I was sitting on the ground feeling like somebody had punched me in the guts," he said. *"I looked down and could see I was bleeding on one side of my ribs. I was amazed that it didn't hurt, and only then realized that bullets were zinging all around me still."*

Instead of running back to cover, he went forward and retrieved the body of the second man, but he was dead. He was crawling back toward his company when a bullet struck his hip. *"Shattered the joint,"* Katz said. *"But I was lucky. I didn't lose my leg, just got me a new titanium hip joint and a small limp. Lots of guys got it worse."*

Katz was silent for a minute, looking down at the newspaper photograph in his hands. When he looked up there were tears in his eyes. "*Anyway, I was discharged and forced Columbia to let me pick up where I left off. They didn't want to but I had a good lawyer. I got out, went to work for you, and now here we sit.*"

Karp nodded at the photograph. "*I don't know if I have the right to ask,*" he said. "*But I take it you weren't there to pick up chicks.*"

Katz smiled. "*Well, not entirely,*" he laughed. "*No. To be honest, I didn't intend to be there at all. I was just finishing law school and in fact was moving out of my apartment near campus for the one I'm in now in the Lower East Side. You'll see the date, May 3, 2003. Ring a bell?*"

"No, not really," Karp replied.

"*That was the day after the president landed on the aircraft carrier off of Iraq and declared 'Mission Accomplished,'*" Katz said. "*I was angry. I'd just been e-mailing with a buddy who was still in, but now they were stationed in Anbar Province. The mission was anything but over. They were up to their necks in a guerrilla war. Nothing the boys couldn't've handled if they'd been given the right equipment and support, including enough troop strength to root out those motherfuckers. These insurgents are like cockroaches—doesn't do you any good to kill most of them, you've got to kill all of them or they'll lay eggs. In this case that means some asshole talking shit to a bunch of poor, ignorant locals until dying for Allah looks like a good deal. But my buddy was telling me they weren't getting the right equipment—no body armor, unless they bought it themselves, no armor for the frickin' Humvees, which were never meant to be fighting vehicles. But here's the president declaring 'Mission Accomplished.' What a bunch of crap.*"

Katz suddenly stopped talking. His face had grown red with anger. He tried to laugh it off. "*Look at me, giving an overlong closing argument when all you asked for was a simple answer to a simple question . . .*"

But Karp waved his hand. "*This wasn't a simple question, and it taught me a lesson about jumping to simple conclusions before learning all the facts. Please, finish your story.*"

"*Well, the long and short of all that was this mission wasn't going to be over for a long time, and not without a lot of guys dying before the politicians learned to quit trying to tell the military how to conduct wars,*" Katz said. "*We're going to have to accept that people will die who you wish did not have to die. But a lot fewer of those kinds of people will die if by their deaths the war and the killing stops, or in that part of the world, slows down to a trickle. And when you wage war, do so with a plan for what you're going to do when the initial round of shooting stops. Have a Marshall Plan on how to turn your former enemies into your grateful friends. But the politicians fucked this one up from the word go."*

Katz drew a deep breath and let it out in a long sigh. *"So that's my soapbox speech and brings me to crossing campus with a duffel bag full of my stuff, pissed off about 'Mission Accomplished,' and I find myself at this anti-war demonstration."*

"So that's why you threw your medals on the fire," Karp said.

Katz nodded. *"Yeah. The 'anything for peace' crowd are not exactly my people; if they get their way, it will eventually mean slavery and subjugation for the non-Muslim world. But I was thinking about my buddies fighting and dying while politicians did nothing to support them. So I pretty much walked up, tossed the medals on the fire, and walked away. Just so happened that a photographer was there to catch the moment. Then I made the mistake of giving the guy my name. So, anything else you need to know about me?"*

"Yeah," Karp said with a nod. *"How would you like to work in the homicide bureau full-time, only you'd have to put up with me kibitzing from time to time?"*

"That's an affirmative," Katz said and then shook his head. *"I thought when I saw that photograph you were going to fire my ass."*

"Nah," Karp lied, and they both knew it. *"I was just going to ask if it got you laid by one of those hippie chicks."*

"Don't I wish," Kenny replied. *"But no, I'm saving myself for marriage."*

"Yeah, I'll bet," Karp laughed. *"But now you don't have your medals to impress your future bride with."*

"Actually, I do," Katz said. *"As soon as I tossed them in the fire, I regretted it. I earned those suckers the hard way. So I wrote to the army and got a duplicate set. Got 'em framed and hanging on the wall of my apartment right below a photograph of me and my unit on top of the Khyber Pass."*

———

Months later, Karp turned when the door to the dayroom opened and Jessica Campbell, wearing red institutional "pajamas" special to the psychiatric ward, shuffled in, escorted by a guard. This mission was still not accomplished either.

10

Jessica Campbell glanced quickly around the dayroom and sat down next to her lawyer. She gave a slight trembling smile to her parents but then turned away and sat with her head bowed.

Lewis leaned over and whispered, "Charlie's here."

"I don't care about him."

"That's okay today, honey," Lewis replied, patting her arm. "But remember to smile at him during the trial. He's going to testify that it was all his fault, and we want the jury to sympathize with the two of you in your grief."

"I don't care."

In fact, she didn't care about much of anything now that the voice of God had abandoned her. Just like the voice had warned her—the mood stabilizers and anti-depressants had silenced the Divine in her.

———

Unfortunately, the drugs also helped her remember things she had tried to forget. Like how baby Benjamin had struggled as she held him under water. She was surprised that an infant was so strong and had not just gone meekly to meet his Maker, as she'd expected. But at last he stopped kicking, his whole body going rigid, his little fists clenched tight, and stayed that way.

He was as stiff as a plastic doll when she dressed him in the little white suit she'd bought for him. But she did the best she could, smoothed his fine fluffy hair to the side, and tried to close his wide, staring eyes. That she could still see a glint beneath the lids bothered her, but she was on a mission from God.

"*Time for Chelsea.*" The voice coaxed her back to her feet. She drifted back to her middle child's bedroom, picked up the sleeping child, and brought her back to the bathroom.

Rubbing her eyes as her mother undressed her, Chelsea saw her little brother lying on the towel. "Is Benny sleeping?"

"*He's with God,*" the voice said.

"He's with God now," Jessica told her daughter. "God will take care of him. Now get in the tub."

She washed the girl with lots of soap and shampooed her hair. She wanted her children to look their best when they arrived in heaven.

Chelsea looked up at her and smiled. Such trust. "*This is wrong,*" shouted the other voice. Jessica started to pick Chelsea up to remove her from the tub.

"*It's the only way,*" God replied.

Jessica's heart broke. She gently shoved Chelsea down in the water. "*Hineini,*" she whispered tearfully as the child thrashed and scratched at her arms. Again, the struggle seemed to last an eternity before her daughter's body went limp. She held the child under a minute longer just to be sure.

She was just lifting Chelsea out of the water to place her on her own special white towel, and then dress her in her special white dress, when a voice interrupted. But this one came from behind her.

"*What are you doing, Mommy?*" Hillary was standing in the doorway in her nightgown. The child's sleepy eyes took in the scene and clicked from puzzlement to fear.

"*Your brother and sister have gone to be with God,*" Jessica said. "*Would you like to be with Him, too?*"

"Yes," said the voice of God, "*send her to me.*"

"No," said the other voice. "*There's still time. Stop this madness!*"

"*Don't listen to her,*" said God. "*Obey me!*"

Hillary looked at her mother, her eyes growing wide in terror. *"No!"* she screamed, and she ran down the hallway.

"Catch her," warned the voice of God. *"If she gets away, she'll tell someone; her soul won't be saved, and you'll be caught and punished."*

Jessica followed her daughter to her room, but Hillary had locked the door.

"Silly girl," Jessica chided when she tried the knob. She removed a bobby pin from her hair and inserted it into the little hold in the knob. There was a satisfying click and the knob turned.

Hillary screamed when her wet and wild-eyed mother hopped into the room. *"Peek-a-boo!"*

"No, Mommy! No, Mommy!" Hillary pleaded.

Jessica lunged for her but the girl dodged to the side and tried to run past. Her mother caught one of her arms and began dragging Hillary toward the bathroom. The desperate child bit her on the arm.

Surprised by the sudden pain, Jessica let go of her daughter, who raced for the front door. She almost made it, but her mother caught her by the hair and pulled her back from the handle.

"Now you're being bad," Jessica snarled. *"Now you're being like your father, and he's the Devil. If you don't behave you'll go to hell and be with him instead of God."*

Hillary screamed and tried to bite her again. In a rage, Jessica picked her daughter up and slammed her down into the tub, banging her head on the porcelain rim. The girl went limp, and it was easy to push her beneath the waters. The voice exulted inside her head. *"Now I know you fear me, since you have not withheld even your children from me."*

"God's will be done," Jessica said.

When she felt enough time had passed, Jessica leaned over to lift Hillary out of the tub to lay her next to her siblings. But suddenly the child gasped and her frightened eyes flew open. Those eyes bored into Jessica, but she made no more attempts to get away. She just floated there, sucking in air . . . staring.

Jessica looked over at the bathroom vanity. There it was. The knife she had bought from the man at the sporting goods store, who told her it could cut through steel. She'd thought originally that she might have to use it as Abraham had intended with Isaac. But then she'd thought of drowning them . . . less messy. So much for that plan, she thought as she picked up the knife.

Hillary watched her raise it above her, and her eyes darted from her mother's face to the shining blade and back again. Then the fear faded; she just looked sad.

That was the memory that had really stuck with her, even before the drugs made her remember the rest. *Hineini. I am here*, she thought as she sat in the dayroom at Bellevue. But God didn't answer. She heard only the voice that she supposed was that of her conscience, the one that reminded her that she'd murdered her children and even suggested that she'd done it to get even with her husband.

The day before, when she had met with Dr. Nickles and her attorney, Linda, she'd thought about pleading guilty and taking her punishment. But the prospect of spending the rest of her life in prison terrified her. It was much easier to believe Linda and Dr. Nickles when they told her it wasn't her fault. She didn't know what she was doing. She didn't know it was wrong. She'd been crazy when she killed her kids.

It was a lie. A lie she wanted to believe. She was never going to see her kids again. If there was a heaven, that meant there had to be a hell, and that's where she was going. But she didn't want eternal damnation to start with the rest of her life in prison.

At least tell somebody where the children are, suggested the voice of her conscience. But Lewis had not asked, and that had given the impression that she didn't want to know. *So no, I'm not going to tell anybody*, she thought, *especially not Charlie. I don't want to give him the satisfaction of ever knowing.* She'd refused to tell him that night when he came home from his whoring, and he'd have to live with knowing that they died while he was screwing . . . but how? . . . where? That he'd never know.

Per the instructions of her attorney, she turned and gave Charlie a tiny smile. *Fornicator. Adulterer.* Jessica relaxed at the sound of the familiar voice. So God had not forsaken her after all; he was right there in her head.

———

Charlie Campbell acknowledged his wife's smile with his best tragic, yet supportive, smile of his own. Representatives of the press weren't allowed in the dayroom for the hearing, so it didn't count for anything, but he thought it would be good to practice for the trial.

There had been a brief chance to get a little ink and face time earlier. The press had been waiting outside the hospital when he arrived, clamoring like seals for a fish from the trainer. He pushed through them without a word and then paused, as if being reluctantly tugged back into their midst by an invisible beam.

"I'd just like to thank the people who have written or called to express their sympathy for this great tragedy that has befallen my family," he said, solemnly reading from a prepared statement he'd pulled from his breast pocket. "Before you today is a man grieving for the loss of his children, whose bodies have still not been recovered, and for that matter, the loss of the woman he fell in love with and married. I do not blame my wife for what has happened. I blame myself for missing the warning signs of mental illness."

"What about the district attorney putting your wife on trial for murder?" a shill asked.

Charlie hesitated, his handler placing a sympathetic hand on his shoulder. "I'd like to be able to say that I understand that Mr. Karp is just doing his job. But I don't understand it. It just shows that even in a great, enlightened country like ours, some people are still in the Dark Ages when it comes to understanding the ravages of mental illness. If he is watching this, I hope Mr. Karp will someday drop these charges so that my wife can get the medical help she needs."

Charlie spotted the man his handler had paid to ask the next question. "Yes sir," he said, pointing.

"Mr. Campbell, are you still planning to run for Congress next year?"

Charlie bowed his head. "Believe me, that's something I've thought long and hard about. For the longest time, my heart was too shattered to even think about more than just getting through the next day. But thanks to good friends, and to be honest, the voters who had urged me to press on, I think the only way out of this nightmare is to dedicate myself to working for the people of the 8th Congressional District." He paused to let the print reporters get the quote down accurately. "No firm decision has been made. Right now, my number one priority is to support my wife and do everything in my power to get her the help she needs. I can assure you, though, that if I do run for Congress and am elected, one of the planks in my platform will be to make sure we as a nation are doing everything we can to understand and combat mental illness. Now thank you for respecting my privacy. I need to go inside."

Inside, his handler shook his hand. "Well done," he said. "They ate it up." Charlie allowed himself a brief smile. There might just be a way out of this, he thought.

———

The media had been all over him since "that day" when he'd come home and found his wife in bed, hiding under the covers, and the children nowhere to be seen. He figured the nanny, Rebecca, had them until she called a half hour later to check in on the family. "I talked to the missus this morning," the nanny said. "And she sounded a little . . . strange. She told me not to come today because she was taking care of them alone."

Charlie ran into the master bedroom and pulled the covers off his wife. "Where are the kids, Jessica?"

Jessica tried to pull the covers back over her face, but when he wouldn't let her, she swore at him. "Fornicator!" she screamed. "Adulterer! Because of you our children's souls were doomed. But not anymore, Charlie Campbell. I saved them. They're with God!"

As the implication of what she'd said took hold, Charlie stood in stunned silence. He shook his head, trying to clear the white noise that had suddenly become a roar between his ears, and then took off, running madly throughout the brownstone calling the kids' names, afraid that he was about to stumble onto their bodies. But there was no sign of them, or of what might have happened to them. No blood. No mess. In fact, the house was extraordinarily clean, everything in its place.

Charlie's search took him to the garage, where he discovered that the family's Volvo station wagon was gone. He ran back into the house and grabbed Jessica by the shoulders. "Where are the kids?" he screamed. "What did you do with the car?"

"I told you," Jessica replied calmly. "The children are with God."

"The car, Jessica, where's the car?"

She shrugged. "That's between me and God."

Charlie sat down on the edge of the bed as Jessica wandered out of the room. He needed to collect his thoughts. This was going to be a disaster for his campaign. He called his lawyer, Bart Braxton, who told him he'd be right over.

"*I'm going to call Diane,*" Charlie said.

"*Don't you fucking dare,*" Braxton, a middle-weight partner with Newbury, Newbury and White, commanded. "*If they find out there's another woman involved, the press will crucify you. You're going to stay away from Diane until this blows over . . . if it blows over.*"

Braxton arrived and after a second search of the brownstone arranged to have an unresponsive Jessica transported to Bellevue Hospital. Only then did he notify the police that the Campbell children were missing. There was a chance, he added, that their mother, Jessica Campbell, was somehow involved, but as her husband's attorney, he was advising her not to speak unless he was present.

The police placed a criminal hold on Jessica, who'd been housed in a padded cell under suicide watch at the lawyer's insistence. The lawyer also prevented Jessica from talking to the police, so it didn't take long for them to complete the initial phase of their investigation and turn the case over to the District Attorney's Office.

The media storm broke with a vengeance. But between his attorney and the political spin machine the party ramped up, Charlie had weathered the worst of it. He was going to play the role of the victim. His wife was mentally ill, and she'd murdered their children. He was the romantically gallant public servant who was going to stand by her . . . at least until after the trial.

The party, with generous donations from the Guppersteins, had located the most prominent experts on postpartum depression in the country and paid them to make themselves available to the press. The media cooperated by rolling out multiple-part series and television specials dedicated to "the tragically misunderstood and deadly postpartum depression syndrome."

Charlie had played his part beautifully. He'd tearfully discussed how he and his "college sweetheart" had been battling her depression ever since the birth of their first child. "She was on medication and we thought we had it under control," he repeated at least two dozen times the first week after the murders. "But the experts got it wrong. Now, my children are gone, presumably dead, and my poor, sick wife is being charged with murder." Afterward, his lawyer hinted that a lawsuit might be forthcoming against those unnamed "experts."

Charlie ended every interview by thanking "the many well-wishers who've expressed their support in this time of need. I just ask that everyone say their prayers for our three little angels, and save one for Jessica."

———

My wife the murdering bitch, Charlie repeated to himself. He'd hoped that with Jessica in the looney bin and scheduled to go to trial, he'd get to spend time with Diane. But the lawyer and handler had nixed that. If the press caught on to his liaison, all the public sympathy they'd been nurturing would go down the toilet.

"Keep your cock in your pants a little while longer, Romeo," his attorney commiserated. "We'll get Jessica committed to a mental hospital and you into Congress. They won't be watching your every move in Washington, D.C., and then you can screw whoever you want. But in the meantime, if there's so much as a hint that you're fucking around while your children are dead and your crazy wife is on trial for her life, you might as well strap a bunch of dynamite around your dick and blow yourself up in a synagogue."

Charlie wondered why he didn't feel more grief at the death of his children. They'd been part of the big picture, but he'd had so little to do with their upbringing that it was like they'd been little strangers living in his house. He was sad that they were gone, but unless he was looking at a photograph, he had a hard time remembering their faces.

He looked over at Linda Lewis, who gave him the same look she'd given that curly-haired bastard with the DA's office. She was the wild card in all of this. His people had made overtures about him doing the grieving husband "should have seen the signs" thing. But so far she hadn't returned their phone calls.

The sooner Jessica was committed to a mental hospital, and he was in Congress, the sooner he could one day announce that it was with great regret that he had to divorce his wife so that they could both move on with their lives.

His reverie was interrupted when Judge Brooke Jackman entered the room and sat down behind a fold-up table.

———

Judge Jackman, a balding man who looked like he'd just eaten a sour pickle, lifted the first file on the table and glanced quickly through the pages. When he finished, he grunted once, then said, "In the matter of the State versus Jessica Campbell, I've read the reports of the state psychiatrists, who unanimously agree that the defendant is competent to stand trial." He looked at Lewis. "Do you have anything you'd like to present that contradicts that?"

Lewis rose quickly. "Yes, your honor," she said. "I'd like to call Dr. Niki Nickles."

Jackman scowled. It was going to be tough to get through the day's docket and still make it to the afternoon poker game in SoHo. "All right. Let's make it quick. Will the witness rise and be sworn in."

Nickles almost trotted to the witness chair. She was sworn in and turned quickly to Lewis as though to help the judge speed up the process.

"Dr. Nickles, have you seen the reports submitted to this court by the state's psychiatrists?" Lewis asked.

"Um . . . yes, I have, um, yes."

"And do you concur with their conclusions that the defendant, Jessica Campbell, is competent to stand trial?"

"No, I do not . . . um, yes . . . concur."

"Could you explain your reasons to the court, please?"

"Yes," Nickles said. "I have conducted . . . um hmmm . . . several hours' worth of interviews with Mrs. . . . hhhhmm aaah . . . Campbell and conclude that she does not understand the nature and consequences of the charges against her."

"And what do you base that on?"

"She believes that . . . uh, um . . . God told her to commit these acts and that . . . um, yes . . . therefore God will not let her be . . . ummm . . . punished."

"I see," Lewis said. "And doctor, the second question that we must address is: Do you believe she is capable of assisting with her defense?"

Nickles shook her head. "How could she? She . . . um . . . won't even divulge what she did with her children to her . . . aaahhh . . . attorney."

"That it?" the judge asked. "Jesus woman, it took you long enough to spit that out."

"Sorry your honor, she's got a speech impediment," Lewis pointed out.

"I figured that out on my own, counsel," Jackman growled. "But I get the idea. Mr. Assistant District Attorney, have you got anything to say?"

Katz rose, though more slowly. "No, your honor. We feel that the certified medical reports speak for themselves. I don't want to take up any more of your time."

The judge looked out from underneath his bushy eyebrows to see if the ADA was being a smart aleck. "All right then. I find the defendant competent to stand trial and order that a date be set. . . . Talk to my clerk about it. If there's nothing further, clear out."

11

S. P. Jaxon entered a courtyard leading to the entrance of the Al-Aqsa mosque in Harlem, his eyes rapidly flicking from place to place, face to face, constantly recording and assessing his surroundings. But he couldn't shake the feeling that something was out of place, or perhaps out of its place in time.

The building's entrance did not squarely face the street but instead was angled slightly off square, as if the builder had been dizzy. Having made himself a student of Islam for the past fifteen years, Jaxon knew that, as with mosques all over the world, the entrance and courtyard had been designed to face the Great Mosque in Mecca. Inside, the alter niche, or *mihrab*, was also aligned with Mecca, the holiest of cities in the Muslim world. In this particular case, the line ran from Manhattan at longitude 74°45' west and latitude 40°56' north to Mecca at longitude 39°49' east and latitude 21°27' north. It made for a peculiar angle in relation to the city's street grid.

Yet, it was more than the curious alignment that disturbed him. The simple, square building itself seemed out of place. Even something about the rounded dome and the towering minaret, from which he'd heard the *muezzin* call the faithful to prayers that morning as he waited to be admitted, made him uneasy. He'd always found Arabic to be a strange language, wild and harsh and unforgiving like the desert it sprang from.

Jaxon glanced up at the crescent moon symbols on top of the dome and minaret. The crescent moon was to Muslims what the cross was to Christians, or the Star of David to Jews. It was the symbol of Ramadan—Islam's holiest time of year when the words of Allah had been revealed to the Prophet Muhammad—which began in the ninth month with the first sighting of the young moon. He'd recently read a newspaper story saying that the Hayden Planetarium had already received hundreds of calls from worshipers asking what day they could first expect to see the symbol of their faith, though the event was still weeks away.

In any case, he observed, the mosque stood out like an igloo in this neighborhood, which consisted primarily of old red-brown brick and dingy gray cement tenements baking in the August heat. The walls that surrounded the property, as well as the mosque, minaret, and attendant buildings, were dazzlingly white.

Though simple in design, the complex had cost a lot of money to build, and the project had only become possible after a sudden turnabout in the mosque's fortunes. Up until 1998, the small group of Muslims who followed Imam Sharif Jabbar, mostly African Americans by birth and a few immigrants, had gathered for prayers at a former liquor store at 124th and Malcolm X Boulevard. After the liquor store was gutted by fire, the building had been converted into a prayer room. Then in 1999 there had been a sudden infusion of several million dollars from the governments of Saudi Arabia and Libya. The group used that money to purchase the new property, level the rat-infested tenement that stood on it, and build the mosque. They'd named it after the famous mosque in Jerusalem.

The generous funding from outside sources was not without precedent. Governments of Islamic countries, as well as their wealthy citizens, had been known to contribute large amounts to Muslim communities in the United States for such purposes before. This did not seem odd to Jaxon; after all, Christian groups in the United States often built churches and proselytized in other countries. As one Saudi VIP had noted at the opening of the mosque in 2000, such efforts were necessary to meet the spiritual needs on an ever-increasing population of Muslims in the United States, most of whom were recent immigrants. Estimates of that population varied widely, Jaxon had found, depending on the sources he consulted, but the most reliable put the number at between 3 million and 6 million people.

Jaxon had no problem with the proliferation of mosques in America or the people they served. Like immigrant populations before them, whether Irish or Italian or Chinese, the vast majority of immigrants from Muslim countries were peaceful, law-abiding members of their communities. Like those other immigrants, they struggled to reach their American dream and meanwhile concentrated on learning English, working menial jobs, like driving taxis in New York City, or perhaps starting their own businesses, while sending their kids off to school so that they could be more than their parents.

Yet, based on what he had seen as a federal agent, Jaxon believed there was a dangerous element in the Muslim population that no other immigrant group had brought with them, at least not to the same degree or as a stated purpose. There had been anarchists and social revolutionaries from the start—individuals who disembarked from the boats at Ellis Island or came on planes or across the border intending to cause trouble. And certainly there had been a few Japanese and German sympathizers among those ethnic groups during World War II—though that was no justification for the internment camps of that era. But the revolutionaries, spies, and saboteurs had been rare and the danger they represented minimal.

This group of immigrants was different. For most immigrant populations, the ultimate goal had been to assimilate and eventually become American citizens. Barring those few agitators and spies, their first loyalty had been to their adoptive country, and they had come seeking freedom, grateful for the chance to live in a democracy. For many Muslims coming from the Middle East, especially those who were poorly educated and already indoctrinated by extremists in their native lands, their first loyalty was to religious leaders and Allah. And if they believed that extremist views, like those of Mullah Omar Rahman, represented Allah's will, and that Allah's will demanded the destruction of the United States and Western culture, then *Inshallah*, God's will be done.

Even in the mosques whose imams preached assimilation into the mainstream community and whose congregations publicly denounced the violence of Islamic extremists, there had been no great effort to cooperate with law-enforcement agencies in identifying possible terrorists in their midst. And the denunciations always seemed to come with some caveat that the United States was a target because of its support for Israel. Some of the 9/11 hijackers had worshiped at such mosques and even let their extremist views be known to various members of the congregation. But the excuse when those hijackers, or others suspected of plotting terrorist acts, were later identified or apprehended was that the congregation "did not know" that they would actually act on their beliefs.

Jaxon believed that a more accurate assessment was that Muslim immigrants did not want to know—caught as they were between wanting to be good citizens and a kind of romantic image of jihadis fighting for Muslims everywhere, even if they didn't agree with the tactics. He suspected that many of them felt that their non-Muslim neighbors, who weren't always welcoming or friendly, had some of it coming to them.

And then there were mosques like Al-Aqsa and imams like Jabbar, an American-born black who had changed his name from DeWayne Wallace. Jabbar had converted to Islam while serving time in Attica for murder and armed robbery. His sermons were often inflammatory—anti-Semitic, anti–United States, anti-white, and bordering on criminal incitement. However, with the help of good lawyers, he'd hidden behind his constitutional guarantees of freedom of speech and decried how he was being persecuted.

When still "officially" with the FBI, and even while heading up counterterrorism efforts in New York City, Jaxon knew that many of the "guest speakers" invited to the mosque from Muslim countries were little more than bagmen for Islamic extremist movements. There was actually a circuit such speakers traveled around the country, and they went not only to mosques known to be fundamentalist but also to many of the so-called "moderate" mosques, raising money for various Islamic "charities." The funds actually went to support terrorist organizations like Al Qaeda, Hamas, and Islamic Jihad, but there was little law-enforcement agencies could do except try to follow the money through various channels and link it to outlawed organizations.

"My, aren't we on a soapbox this morning," Jaxon muttered, noting that the men gathered in the courtyard stopped talking and followed him with unfriendly eyes as he made his way to the entrance.

"What was that, Espey?"

Jaxon looked over at the young woman walking by his side who had spoken. "What? Oh, it wasn't important . . . Marie," he replied, placing special emphasis on the name. "I was just preaching to the choir."

Lucy Karp, otherwise known as Marie Smith, smiled. "I do a lot of that, too," she said in a hushed tone. "But aren't you worried that people will think you're crazy if you talk to yourself?"

"They'd be crazy not to," he replied with a grin.

Lucy laughed. Though she'd known "Uncle Espey" most of her life, he'd often been assigned to other parts of the country, so it was only recently that she had really gotten to know him. *And boy didn't that work out well,* she thought.

Late that past fall, he'd come to New Mexico, where she was living while working on the Taos Indian Pueblo reservation. He had needed help translating a taped conversation in an unknown language, and she'd correctly identified the language as Manx, the nearly extinct language of the Isle of Man. But it was not one of the dozens of languages she was familiar with, so she'd turned for help to a friend, Cian Magee, a master of Celtic languages, of which Manx was one.

A reclusive hermit who essentially lived his life in his below-street apartment/Celtic bookstore on the Lower East Side, Magee had interpreted the tape, which had included a coded message as well as what turned out to be the motto of a shadowy syndicate called the Sons of Man. *Myr shegin dy ve, bee eh.* What must be, will be.

Magee had then received a rare book, an apparently unauthorized history of the Sons of Man, which he told Lucy had been written sometime around 1930. The book described how the Sons of Man were descendants of smugglers who'd left the Isle of Man with their families near the end of the eighteenth century to escape the British Navy. According to the book, the original enterprise of smuggling—everything from guns to rum—which had continued in America, evolved into a sophisticated means of financing a powerful organization that had infiltrated all areas of American life.

Before Magee was able to say much about who the descendants of the families were—if he knew—both he and the book perished in a fire that started in his apartment. Who had sent him the book remained a mystery. But Lucy felt sure it contained a secret that was so important that the Sons of Man had been willing to commit murder to keep it hidden.

It was small consolation that Magee did not die in vain. His translation of the tape helped Lucy—aided by her boyfriend, Ned, as well as Jojola and Tran—to foil a plot by the Sons of Man to assassinate U.S. Senator Tom

McCullum. A critic of the Patriot Act, which he believed overreached the intent of the original bill as a weapon in the War on Terrorism to become a tool for domestic spying, McCullum was also calling for congressional investigations into a series of attacks by Islamic terrorists acting in collusion with certain interests in the Russian government and mob—and, Jaxon now believed, the Sons of Man.

Magee's murder, as well as the sinister aims of the Sons of Man, had moved Lucy to volunteer, over her father's objections, to join Jaxon's team. Her first assignment was to serve as interpreter for Prince Esra bin Afraan Al-Saud, who preferred to speak French, though some of the members of his entourage spoke only Arabic. She would go by the name of Marie Smith for this job.

Marie Smith had been a real woman of about the same age who'd died some years before in a traffic accident in Ohio. Whoever did such macabre research had done a good job of finding someone believable. Marie had been a foreign languages student at Ohio State who was fluent in four languages. Lucy could handle seventeen times that many. She had spoken French like a native by the time she was six and Arabic by the time she was twelve.

Jaxon had told her that he didn't expect that her language talents would be necessary at the mosque immediately. The prince was in Washington, D.C., where he would be attending a state dinner at the White House and addressing Congress before arriving in New York. While in the capital, the prince's security would be the responsibility of the U.S. Secret Service; he'd requested that Jaxon take over once he got to Manhattan.

However, the prince had sent an advance team who might be at the mosque and need an Arabic interpreter. "And you never know when you might overhear an unguarded conversation of interest," Jaxon noted.

Jaxon had also told Lucy that he was counting on her adding to his knowledge of Muslim culture. As a student of languages, Lucy had always made it a point to learn what she could about the people who spoke them, as it gave her context to add meaning to the language. For instance, she told him, Esra bin Afraan Al-Saud meant Esra, son of Afraan of the Saud family. "The part at the end identifies which tribe they belong to, which is very important in Saudi Arabia," she noted.

Many of the two dozen or so men in the courtyard were dressed in traditional robes. Others wore everyday clothing indistinguishable from anyone on the other side of the white walls. They all had on the small, round *kufie* prayer caps, but there was nothing of particular note about that; even non-Muslim blacks in America had adopted the look as a fashion statement.

The few women present were dressed as they would have been in any conservative Muslim country. All of them wore traditional loose-fitting robes, and their heads were covered by the *hajib* scarf; several of them also wore the *niqab*, or face veil, as well.

The veil was often associated with *Salafism*, the puritanical version of Islam known for its extremist views. Its proponents claimed this was the "pure" Islam and made it their goal to remain undiluted by contact with other cultures and religions—especially modern and Western influences. Sometimes called Wahabism, especially in Saudi Arabia, it was the brand of Islam that promoted what other branches of the faith sometimes considered twisted interpretations of the Qur'an from which terrorist organizations like Al Qaeda had sprung.

The Wahabi sect was known for labeling anyone who did not adhere to their narrow views, including other Muslims, as *takfir*, or apostate, which meant that Salafists were within their rights, even obligated, to kill them. They sometimes issued *fatwas* to excuse such behaviors as killing other Muslims, seeking the violent overthrow of Muslim governments, making war on women and children, and suicide, though they avoided the word "suicide" in favor of "martyrdom."

The women's dress did not necessarily mean the members of the mosque were Salafists, however; the robes and head scarves could have merely reflected the conservative nature of the mosque's community. Lucy knew that oftentimes, new converts—whether they were Protestants in Catholic Mexico or Muslims in Baptist Harlem—were more conservative than their native counterparts, as if out to prove that they belonged.

Nor was wearing the *hajib* or even the *niqab* necessarily a symbol of oppression of women by Islam. Lucy had several female Muslim friends in New York who, although modern in most other ways, wore the *hajib* as a sign of their faith and out of respect for their culture. They even defended their attire as a sort of equalizer between men and women in the workplace.

"At least in my robes, they're not checking out my body," Fatima had explained to her. "And with my hair and part of my face covered, men don't look at me as if they're judging my looks. They have to judge me by my abilities, and what I have to say."

Out of respect, Lucy had herself worn a *hajib* that morning. As she crossed the courtyard with Jaxon, some of the men and women glanced at her head covering and nodded with approval.

The pair reached the door of the mosque where an immense black man stood barring their way. He hardly gave her a glance before addressing Jaxon.

———

"Identification," the guard demanded, holding out a hand the size of a baseball mitt.

Jaxon handed over his PrimeTech Security Corporation identification card. It did not have the same effect he'd received when he'd flashed his Federal Bureau of Investigation credentials, but it seemed to work well enough.

"The woman, too," said the guard.

Any arguments her friend had made about gender equality in Muslim society vaporized for Lucy. In this world, a woman was the responsibility and property of the man she was with. But she wasn't there to argue feminism, so she reached into her purse to hand over her Marie Smith identification card.

The guard hardly looked at the card before handing it back to Jaxon. "Follow me," he said, pushing open the door leading into the mosque.

They found themselves in the spacious interior sanctuary, where the ceiling rose to the shell of the dome. The beautiful marbled floors remained clear of any benches in favor of the prayer rugs of worshipers. Shadowed and cool, a respite from the gathering heat outside, Lucy felt at once its purpose as a place to worship the Divine. Unlike a Christian church, the mosque had no statues, paintings, stained-glass murals, or other decorations that might distract the faithful from devoting all of their attention to Allah.

Only after passing through the sanctuary and reaching a hallway did they reenter the modern world. Lucy paused to read the postings on a bulletin board. Most were similar to those she'd expect to see in any church: times for various classes to study the Qur'an, a schedule for the next seminar in

"What It Means to Be Muslim in America," a sign-up sheet to work at the mosque's soup kitchen, and a newsletter listing the accomplishments of various members of the congregation. But then there were also newspaper clippings decrying the actions of "Israeli Terrorists" and "Zionist Murderers" who'd stormed the Al-Aqsa Mosque in Jerusalem during a "peaceful demonstration in support of Palestinian freedom fighters." The article was accompanied by a notice that Dr. Amin Hussein, a member of the government of Palestine, would be speaking at the mosque in October to raise money for refugee camps. "Suggested donation $10," the notice said.

Jaxon knew that in Muslim countries, a mosque was used only for worship. However, in Western countries, mosques included schools and meeting rooms and often became centers for political and community activism. In the United States, most served to help assimilate immigrants into mainstream society. In England, some mosques went even further, becoming recruiting stations for radical Islamic clerics who openly encouraged disaffected Muslim youth to join jihad. The London bus bombing and various other plots that had been broken up by British MI-5 anti-terrorism squads had all been traced back to these rogue mosques.

Jaxon worried that the same sort of "homegrown" terrorists were being recruited in the decaying urban centers of the United States among poor, undereducated blacks as well as among immigrants from Muslim countries. By demonizing whites, Jews, and the government as the cause of their poverty, an imam like Jabbar could offer young black men something to belong to that was more powerful than even the lure of gangs.

———

Jaxon realized by now that he need look no further than Rondell James to find proof that his worries were on target. The Department of Homeland Security was still keeping his name under wraps, despite the howls of the press and their legal motions. But even the department didn't seem to know about his other name, Muhammad Jamal Khalifa, much less his connection to the Al-Aqsa mosque. For the time being, Jaxon was playing dumb, too, and had asked for the audience with Jabbar merely to discuss security for the prince's visit.

Karp's crumpled food-stamp certificate had proved to be a godsend. It had been issued to a Jamal Khalifa, who'd given his address as 173 E. 117th Street, Apartment D.

A week ago, while Jojola and Tran stood watch, Jaxon had picked the lock to the apartment to go inside with his men from the bureau. Ray Guma and Clay Fulton from the DAO had been with them as well. The interior of the apartment told the story of a lonely man who'd given up on the world. The few dishes he'd owned were washed and stacked neatly next to the kitchen sink, from which a few brave cockroaches reluctantly retreated at their approach. A worn toothbrush and a solitary, threadbare towel were the only evidence of habitation in the bathroom.

In the corner room was a stained twin mattress covered with a few moth-eaten blankets. On the ground next to the mattress was a lamp with a 60-watt bulb but no lampshade, a worn English translation of the Qur'an, and a small framed photograph of a young black woman in a *hajib*, a shy smile playing across her lips as she held a happy young boy. Jaxon picked it up and placed it in an evidence bag; his employer had secretly obtained a special search warrant for him so that someday, if they needed to use what they found in court, it would be legal.

If Jaxon didn't know what Khalifa had done, the meager furnishings and the photograph might have led him to feel sorry for the young man. The living room, however, while just as Spartan in furnishings, was chilling. In a corner away from the window and any prying eyes from neighboring buildings, a folding chair stood next to an old desk on which lay a needle, scissors and thread, bits and pieces of material, some electrical wires, a package for a Hewlett-Packard Series 2100 pager, and packaging that had once held plastic explosives, marked USMC. A box on the ground bearing the logo and address of the "Mechanic's Choice Ballbearing Co." still contained a half dozen or so of the bright, marble-sized, stainless-steel balls. A *half-dozen . . . why not use all of them?* Jaxon wondered.

Even the evidence of the killer's bomb-making wasn't as striking as the green symbols that had been written on the otherwise dingy white wall, however. He couldn't read the writing, but he'd seen similar calligraphy written on banners hung behind suicide bombers in the Middle East as they videotaped their last will and testament before going out to slaughter innocent people in the name of Islam.

As one of his agents took photographs of the writing, Jaxon, Guma, and Fulton inspected the last two objects in the room. Pointed at the inscription was an old video camera on a tripod. Jaxon walked over to a small television set with a built-in VCR player and pressed the "Eject" button. A tape popped out, which he pocketed, and with a nod to the other men, they slipped out of the apartment.

Jaxon had hoped that the tape would reveal Khalifa's motives behind his attack on the synagogue and perhaps say whether it was part of some greater conspiracy. He was therefore somewhat disappointed to find out it was a family tape, mostly of the young boy and the woman in the photograph. In the segments that included Khalifa, the family looked happy, and Jaxon wondered how the man in those scenes could be the same man who created the horrific scene at the Third Avenue synagogue.

"I'm betting he videotaped his little martyrdom speech," Jaxon said as they drove away. "I wonder where it is?"

"It will probably show up on Al Jazeera in a few days," Guma replied. "A real public relations coup for Al Qaeda, a black American Islamic 'martyr.' I don't know why we don't plant a cruise missile up Al Jazeera's ass just like we took out Saddam's Ministry of Misinformation for supplying aid and comfort to the enemy."

Jaxon figured that Guma was probably right about the destination of the tape. The "unknown martyr" who'd attacked the Zionists in New York City had been hailed as a hero in the Middle East. The United States had been put on red alert, fearing that his actions would spur others to commit similar atrocities. It would be as easy as downloading "The Belt of Martyrdom," a twenty-five-minute instructional DVD for making personal suicide bombs, which noted that would-be perpetrators didn't have to use C-4; commercially available dynamite would do.

At the same time, Jaxon wondered why someone in the U.S. government had requested him specifically to head up security for the prince. Was it to get him out of the way of some bigger plan? It wasn't out of the realm of possibilities that it was all innocent, either; he'd had some dealings with the Saudi intelligence and counter-terrorism agencies during his career in the FBI.

The sophistication of Khalifa's vest was enough to convince Jaxon that he'd had some sort of assistance. It did not appear that he had acted on his own, but it was still not certain that his action was part of a larger plot, either. Even if Khalifa had help, Jabbar could have been nothing more than the inspiration that set Khalifa down the road that led to the attack.

Nor did Khalifa's attack or affiliation with the mosque mean there was any threat to Prince Esra bin Afraan in the offing. But good detectives don't believe in coincidences until everything else has been checked out, and that was why he was at the mosque this morning.

After the synagogue attack, the New York media had interviewed various Muslim religious and community leaders in Manhattan. Most vehemently denounced the attack and expressed fears that it would engender retaliatory attacks. Only a couple noted that it was "bound to happen," as young Muslim men felt marginalized by U.S. society. But Jabbar had been unusually quiet. Asked to comment, one of Jabbar's spokesmen said only that the imam was unavailable to comment and would remain so after Ramadan.

The guard led them from the hallway to a modern reception area outside an office. The room lacked any artwork, but two photographs were hanging on one wall. One was the picture of a man Jaxon recognized as Sayyid Qutb, the godfather of the radical Islamist movement; the other was Sheik Omar Abdul Rahman, the blind sheik imprisoned in Colorado for terrorism. *A curious pair of photographs*, he thought.

Behind the receptionist's desk sat a young woman with a pretty, oval face the color of dark chocolate. As he and Lucy approached, she picked up the telephone, said something quietly into the receiver, and hung up. "You may go inside," she told the visitors.

Their escort turned to Jaxon. "She stays here," he said, without bothering to look at Lucy. "And I need to search you before you go in."

"Is that really necessary?" Jaxon said. "We're all friends here, aren't we?"

"The enemies of Islam are many. As are the enemies of Imam Jabbar. No one goes in without being searched."

Lucy sat down on a chair across from the receptionist's desk as Jaxon was patted down. She saw a bulge underneath the back of the guard's tunic that she knew was a gun.

Satisfied, he rapped on the door, eliciting a muffled reply. The man motioned to Jaxon to step past him into the room. He remained outside and closed the door.

Lucy was trying to ignore the big man, who stood in front of the door with his arms crossed, when she caught the tune that the receptionist was humming. It was a Kenyan lullaby.

"*Jambo*," she said quietly, a friendly greeting in Swahili.

"*Sjambo*," the young woman replied.

The guard barked. "No talking!" He scowled at the receptionist, who dipped her head. But a minute later, with a quick glance to make sure he wasn't watching, she flashed Lucy a smile.

Inside the office, Jaxon quickly looked around as he walked over to where two men waited, one sitting behind a desk and the other in a chair to one side. Again, there was nothing on the walls, no books or magazines on shelves or tabletops. Just a large English version of the Qur'an on a pedestal off to the side of the main desk.

Jaxon recognized the man behind the desk from photographs he'd seen in the newspapers. Imam Jabbar sat expressionless, watching Jaxon with his oddly bulging eyes, his purple lips drawn in a taut line across his face.

The other man was something of a surprise. He was white, older—maybe in his late seventies—and wearing a business suit that probably would have cost Jaxon most of a month's salary at the bureau.

"Agent S. P. Jaxon, I presume?" the man said, getting up from his seat to cross the room and shake hands. "Dean Newbury. I represent the imam's legal interests. I apologize that your colleague was asked to wait in the outer office. It's a matter of some cultural sensitivity."

Newbury had a firmer grip than one might have expected for a man his age. "Her name is Marie Smith," Jaxon said. "She works for our firm as a translator—English, French, and Arabic. We were told that Prince Esra and his people needed a translator and . . ."

"We were expecting a man," Jabbar interrupted. "A woman's presence would not be appropriate."

Jaxon frowned. "The prince's people made no specific request, and it's our understanding that the prince considers himself *modern* in regards to his views on women." He knew that the word modern, much less the emphasis he'd placed on it, would irritate a conservative such as Jabbar. He watched Jabbar's face tighten. "She is our only translator at the moment with the requisite language skills—and she is familiar with business terminology, which will be of great assistance to the prince and his people when it comes to the financial issues he'll be conducting."

Releasing his gaze from the imam, whose eyes had begun to waver—from anger or a loss of confidence it was difficult to tell—Jaxon turned back to Newbury. "However, for the purpose of this meeting, it's obvious we won't need the services of a translator, so there is no need to apologize for Miss Smith's absence. The reason for my request to meet with Mr. Jabbar . . ."

"*Imam* Jabbar," Newbury insisted.

"My apologies," Jaxon said, trying to sound like he meant it. "Imam Jabbar . . . is to discuss security issues regarding Prince Esra's visit to the Al-Aqsa mosque. As I'm sure you know, there are elements within the Muslim population that are antagonistic toward the Saudi royal family. There have been threats of assassination in the past from terrorist organizations, and I just wanted to discuss with Imam Jabbar if he had concerns about any members of the mosque who might present a security problem. We're especially sensitive, given last month's bombing of the synagogue."

"We're Muslim, so I'm sure we're all guilty," Jabbar sneered.

"What my client means to say is that he, and his congregation, grow tired of these implications that all Muslims are terrorists," Newbury explained. "It's the same thing from the press, the public, and even law-enforcement officers who are sworn to protect *all* citizens equally. The old crime of 'driving while black' has now evolved to 'driving while black and Muslim.' Really, it's quite a civil liberties issue."

Jaxon bit his tongue on the reply he wanted to make. "I understand," he replied evenly. "And my company certainly does not want to harass anyone or abridge their civil liberties. I was merely asking if there was anybody he thought we should be aware of; after all, this is a big mosque with a lot of people from all sorts of places. He can't be expected to control everyone who might harbor violent urges."

"I am aware of no such person," Jabbar replied. "We, of course, abhor what occurred at the synagogue. Then again, violence begets violence, something the United States government might want to consider the next time it drops a bomb on an Iraqi street, or an Israeli tank demolishes a Palestinian's home."

"Not here to argue politics, or who's right and who's wrong," Jaxon responded. "I put in my time working for the government. Right now, I'm just trying to make enough to pay for my kids' college and maybe retire someday. But that means doing my job, and that job is making sure nothing happens to the prince. So I need to cover all my bases." He stood up and laid a business card on Jabbar's desk. "Give me a call if something comes up. And I'd like to speak to whoever runs security at the mosque—it's my understanding that you have your own team—so that we can coordinate."

The imam started to speak but Newbury silenced him with a look. *Who's the boss here?* Jaxon wondered.

"We understand," Newbury replied. "It is a big responsibility and a dangerous world out there. But the imam assures you he knows of no one in his congregation who would want to harm Prince Esra bin Affaan Al-Saud. Quite the contrary, they are all excited about the visit and his gift that will help them build a fine, new school on the grounds. What happened was a horrible tragedy, but certainly had nothing to do with the Al-Aqsa Mosque. By the way, have they released the bomber's name yet?"

Jaxon was looking at Jabbar, who looked at him as Newbury made his remark. It seemed clear that the only "horrible tragedy" about the bombing in the mind of the imam was that more Jews weren't killed. "That's good to know," the agent said. "And I haven't heard about the name. Then again, I don't have access to all that information anymore."

"Well, then," Newbury said, escorting Jaxon to the door, "you'll have our full cooperation regarding the prince's visit. I'm quite sure that it will all go without incident. In the meantime, if you'd like to talk to Imam Jabbar again, please call me at my office, and we'll see what we can do to accommodate you."

———

A few minutes later, Jaxon and Lucy were back out on the street and on their way to the waiting car. "That was fast," she said.

"Yeah, I've been bum-rushed by bar bouncers who were more subtle about wanting me off the premises."

Lucy laughed. "Really? You'll have to tell me the story, or stories. My Uncle Espey battling bar bouncers."

Jaxon grinned. "If I told you, your dad wouldn't let you come out to play anymore."

"I'd sneak out." Her face grew serious as she told him about the possibility of Salafist leanings at the mosque. "And, Mr. Super Agent, I'll bet there's something I know that you don't."

"I'm quite sure there's a lot you know that I don't know. But what is this particular bit of intel?"

"Did you get a good look at the receptionist?"

Jaxon tried to recall the woman's face. Pretty eyes, dark skin . . . but the hajib made it difficult to remember details. "Not really."

"She's the woman in the photograph," Lucy replied.

"What photograph?"

"The one you guys found in Khalifa's apartment, the woman holding the little boy. That's the thing about the hajib; it really does distract men. I didn't recognize her at first, either, until I saw her smile."

"Her smile?" Jaxon replied. "You're sure?"

"Positive. And she speaks Swahili, so I'm guessing she's an immigrant from East Africa. . . . I couldn't quite pick up which part—we only said one word each. But I'm guessing that she's Kikuyu from Kenya."

Jaxon shook his head. "You would make a hell of an FBI agent, Niece Lucy."

"Why, thank you." Lucy looked into the rearview mirror and saw that the driver was watching her and smiling. He has nice eyes, she thought, before hurriedly reminding herself that Ned had nice eyes, too. "I did think it was a rather nice catch."

12

The old men leaned back in their seats, soaking up the morning sunshine outside The Kitchenette. Soon they'd have to either retreat inside or head home to their wives and the air-conditioning. August in New York City could be pretty intimidating.

"Hey, you old farts gonna' sit here all day taking up space I could use for payin' customers, or what?" The forty-something waitress managed to spit the words out in classic Bronx vernacular and chomp gum noisily at the same time. She placed her hands on her hips, which caused her already tight blouse to strain against its buttons.

Ever hopeful for a miracle, the old men focused on her bustline. "What are you geezers lookin' at?" she snapped.

"I was trying to read your name tag," quipped Bill Florence.

"The name's Marjorie, which you've known for, oh, I don't know . . . How long you geezers been hangin' around here ogling the goods? Eight years? So get a camera and take a picture, it'll last longer."

"A thing of beauty is a joy forever. John Keats must have been thinking about you when he wrote that."

Marjorie the Waitress's jaw stopped in mid chew, and then she laughed and shook her head. "Well, put it like that, Geoffrey, and *you* can look all you want," she said to the group's resident artist. "The rest of you mugs

153

could learn a thing or two from Mr. Gilbert here about how to talk to a lady. If it's not too late to teach ancient dogs new tricks."

The reference to dogs caused several members of the group to start howling as Marjorie rolled her eyes and waited for the clamor to die down. It was all in good fun, the Sons of Liberty Breakfast Club, as they called themselves, were loyal customers and her most ardent fans.

"What do you say, gentlemen, another round of orange juice?" asked Murray Epstein, the round-faced former defense attorney.

"I dare say we could use the Vitamin C," replied Dennis Hall, the envy of the group because his boyishly curly hair was still full and more brown than gray. "Helps stave off colds and even avian flu, I've heard."

"Vitamin C, my sweet ass," Marjorie scoffed. "I know all about that little flask you senior citizens pass around to spike your juice. You're usually half-potted by the time you totter out of here. I don't want none of you getting your wrinkly old derrieres run over by a cab and then have to listen to your wives blaming me for contributing to your sudden departure from the planet. . . . Though I expect half of them would thank me."

When Marjorie left, Saul Silverstein leaned forward to get back to the conversation they'd been having before the short siesta in the sun. A big, heavyset man with thick features, he was the oldest member of the group. "So where were we?"

"I believe in the process of trying to figure out how to locate and destroy the Sons of Man without being wiped off the face of the Earth like so many pesky gnats," said Gilbert, who understandably tended to be the most dramatic of the Breakfast Club members, as well as its only confirmed bachelor, though his friends carefully avoided discussing the reason why.

Father Jim Sunderland, who had stayed out of the waitress-ogling and sat quietly thinking while the others were having their fun, replied, "I think we need to take a chance and reach out to Vince Newbury's boy." He looked from face to face. "If what we suspect is true—that our friend and V. T. Newbury's father was murdered by Vince's own brother . . . that scoundrel Dean Newbury . . ."

"I still can't believe that V. T. and Butch Karp have had a falling-out and that he's gone over to the enemy's camp," Hall said.

Florence shrugged. "Well, that's the word from my source in the DAO. She overheard several arguments that were anything but friendly. When

Karp announced V. T.'s resignation, there were no 'best of luck' wishes. More like 'don't let the door hit you in the ass on the way out.'"

"V. T. may not be aware of the Sons of Man or his uncle's connection," Epstein noted. "Not unless he's been a mole at the DAO for what? Thirty-plus years? Is he that good of an actor . . . or spy, and now he's being brought in from the cold? Maybe this is just a midlife crisis, and he's decided he'd better go for the money while there's still the opportunity, now that his dad is dead."

"What if he is being groomed as Dean Newbury's heir apparent—not just at the firm but with the Sons of Manly Bitches?" Florence asked. "How do we know we can trust him not to just turn us over for summary execution? It wouldn't be the first time that money and power meant more than the death of a blood relative. What do you think, Frank?"

The judge rubbed his neck. "I think this reversal is completely out of character for young Mr. Newbury," he said at last. "I don't think he's been faking it all these years. He's been as able a prosecutor as the DAO has ever had, and until this apparent falling-out, I would have bet that he was cut from the same ethical cloth as our Mr. Karp."

"What about their arguing?" Florence asked.

"Troubling, I agree," Plaut said. "We've also heard that the beating he took left him a changed man. He also wouldn't be the first victim to let anger and fear change him."

"It might in some ways," Sunderland agreed. "But I don't think he'd have anything to do with someone who murdered his father. We all know those two loved each other."

"Perhaps," Hall said. "But we have no proof that Vince was murdered. According to the family doc, it was a massive heart attack . . ."

"Yeah," Gilbert scoffed, "an hour after having dinner with his brother Dean."

"The medical examiner's findings concurred with the original diagnosis," Epstein noted.

"Maybe the ME didn't look much beyond a trusted physician's assessment," Hall replied.

"Which brings us back to the fact that we have no proof to back up going to V. T. Newbury and telling him, 'We think your father was murdered by your uncle because he stumbled upon a massive criminal syndicate that plans to take over the country . . . and maybe the world.' Who is going to believe that without at least an offer of proof?" Hall said. "Not to mention, other than Dean Newbury, we have no idea who else might be involved with the Sons of Man. All we know is that they're one secretive, powerful, ruthless group of sons of bitches who'd stomp us into the ground without a second thought."

"All the more reason to think long and hard about telling V. T.," Gilbert suggested. "Even if we went to the authorities and the press, too, we'd just be the latest bunch of conspiracy nuts. Then when no one was watching anymore, they could bump us off one at a time. A half-dozen more 'massive heart attacks' or 'traffic accidents' or 'victims of random violent crime,' and who'd bother to look into it?"

"So what's the alternative?" the former Marine, Silverstein, argued. "Our friend Vince dies getting us that book on the Sons of Man, thinking we might know what to do with it. We send the tape to Jaxon, who brings in Lucy, who brings in Cian Magee, and it gets that poor fellow burned to death. But we're worried that someone might find out that we're on to them and take the last few years we have left away from us? What's the matter, you guys want to live forever?"

"I was considering the possibility," Gilbert quipped. They all laughed but grew somber when Gilbert spotted Butch Karp approaching from down the block.

———

"So gentlemen, what's the topic of conversation this morning?" Karp asked, pulling up a chair at the table. With a daughter playing spy with a real spy and infiltrating a mosque that might be affiliated with a suicide bomber, he'd decided that a trip to The Kitchenette was in order to distract him.

"Ah, we were just discussing our colleague Dennis Hall's appearance on the *Off the Hook Show with Barry Queen*," Gilbert replied.

"I heard something about that," Karp said. "You discussed the Duke Lacrosse Team rape case, right?"

"I really feel for those kids who were charged," Dennis Hall mused, "and the torment that the prosecutor put their families through."

"I agree. From Day One at the DAO," Karp replied, "Garrahy drilled into us that the worst thing law enforcement could do was convict the un-justly accused."

The group was silent for a moment, then Gilbert blurted out, "We hear that you've been asked to appear on the *Off the Hook Show* regarding the Jessica Campbell case."

As usual, Karp was surprised that the group seemed to know so much about what was going on—often behind closed doors—in his office. It was only the night before that his aide-de-camp, Gilbert Murrow, had left a message on his cell phone saying that the show's producer had called and asked for him to be a guest. He'd heard the hopeful tone in Murrow's voice—the little man spent a lot more time worrying about Karp's public image than he did. But Murrow no doubt also knew what Karp's reaction would be, and that was probably why he had left the message on Karp's cell phone, which he rarely answered after he left work, rather than calling him at home.

"Might ask where you heard that?" he asked the Breakfast Club.

"You'll never get it from me, copper," Florence retorted.

"Actually, I overheard that they were going to ask you on the show last night," Hall said.

"So you going to do it?" Sunderland asked quickly.

"I wouldn't count on it. I don't believe in trying cases in public." Karp didn't mean to lecture these men, all of them smart and well-respected in their own right, so he smiled to let them know that it was okay that they asked. "Besides, I've been told that I have a face meant for radio, not television."

The others applauded. "Come now, gentlemen," Judge Plaut said. "I think we all know that OUR district attorney, unlike others elsewhere, will not be pandering to the press, or even answering our questions regarding an ongoing case."

"If I was going to talk to anyone," Karp said, "it would be my friends with the Sons of Liberty Breakfast Club. If I can't trust you, who can I trust?"

"Absolutely, hear, hear," they cheered, clinking their glasses of spiked orange juice.

"However," Plaut said, "we were discussing something earlier that I believe has some relevance to our last discussion on Muslim complaints about their portrayal in the media. Bill, perhaps you could bring Mr. Karp up to speed?"

Florence nodded and picked up the *Times*, thumbing through until he found the article he was looking for. "This is a story out of Colorado. Apparently, law-enforcement authorities in Denver arrested and charged a wealthy Saudi Arabian citizen and his wife for their treatment of an Indonesian maid they'd brought with them into the country. According to the story, they treated her as a slave, confiscated her passport so that she couldn't travel, or escape, and kept her locked in the basement when she wasn't toiling away in their house in an upper-crust neighborhood. They generously paid her all of $2 a day, which she rarely saw, and it seems the man of the house regularly sexually assaulted her."

"Nice folks," Karp responded.

"It gets worse," Florence said. "The wife pleaded guilty to unlawful detention and kidnapping and was deported. The husband was charged with the same crimes, as well as sexual assault. Apparently, this guy had the best lawyers money could buy. He immediately posted a half-million-dollar bail—all of it paid for by the Saudi government. According to the story, the man's family has a great deal of influence in Saudi Arabia, especially with an important imam, who has a lot of clout with the state-run press over there. But here's the rub . . . during his trial, the man and his lawyers raised a big stink about how he was being persecuted because he was Muslim."

"The fact that he was keeping someone as a slave and sexually assaulting her had nothing to do with it," Karp scoffed.

"Yeah, right," Florence nodded. "Anyway, the jury didn't buy it and convicted him of the charges, which carried a sentence of twenty years to life. But rather than apologize and throw himself on the mercy of the court at his sentencing hearing, this arrogant joker contended that he shouldn't be penalized for, and I quote, 'traditional Muslim behaviors.'"

"So there you have it," Sunderland interjected. "We now have it on authority that slavery, kidnapping, and sexual assault on housemaids are all traditional Muslim behaviors."

"You'd think Muslims would object to that," Gilbert noted.

"Well, yes, you'd think so, but then you'd be wrong, at least overseas," Florence said. "Apparently, the man's conviction set off quite the international furor in Muslim countries, including Saudi Arabia . . . the usual angry protests outside U.S. embassies and flag burnings. But the Muslim reaction isn't the worst of it. According to the story, the U.S. State Department called the Colorado attorney general and asked him to go to Saudi Arabia to 'explain the American justice system,' as if rape and slavery being crimes need an explanation."

"What a bunch of hooey," Silverstein snorted with disgust. "Now these jokers are 'summoning' our law enforcement to explain why we prosecute criminals. I would have sent them a telegram saying, 'Go fuck yourself'— pardon my French—'but despite what we hear about certain Muslim countries, we haven't allowed people to keep slaves in this country since the Emancipation Proclamation. Oh, and by the way, rape was never legal.'"

"Now, now, Saul," Plaut replied. "We have to be understanding. After all, slavery has only been outlawed in Saudi Arabia since 1962, and according to a human rights organization that I have some association with, there are apparently quite a number of slaves still kept in the countryside and behind closed doors, most of them women. Big surprise there."

"Oh, but wait," Gilbert protested. "I thought the United States was the Great Satan who oppressed poor people?"

Hall scoffed. "You've been watching too much CNN. They agree with whatever criticism is leveled at this country without question."

"Unfair, we're a sitting duck on this one," Epstein protested.

"More fair than CNN and her sister station Al Jazeera," Hall retorted. "The liberal press's double standards when it comes to reporting on Muslim countries is laughable. Osama bin Laden and his ilk rail about modern Crusaders, and CNN does a thirty-minute special on the history of Muslim anger at the Western world. But does anybody note that the Prophet Muhammad himself fought some seventy wars of aggression to spread the Muslim faith? Or that the slaughter went on for hundreds of years until Islam had been crammed down the throats—often throats without heads—of people from Spain to China? The number of people murdered in the name of Allah makes the Crusaders look like Girl Scouts. But, of course, that fact of history is ignored by the press and never tossed back at these Islamic extremists and their idiotic pronouncements."

"Well said," Plaut agreed. "Bill, wasn't there more to that story? Didn't the Colorado attorney general actually respond to the State Department request by spending taxpayer dollars to fly to Saudi Arabia?"

"Yes," Florence replied and found his place on the page. "According to the article, he first met with members of what I assume is the equivalent of the bar association in Saudi Arabia, where these so-called lawyers, and this is another quote, 'couldn't believe that a jury would actually believe the word of a mere Indonesian maid over a rich Saudi businessman.' I guess in Saudi Arabia only wealthy rapists are to be believed."

"No surprise there, either," Gilbert noted. "The women's rights movement hasn't exactly set up shop in the desert. They have to be covered from head to toe, they're not allowed to drive, or vote, or even leave the country without the written permission of a male relative. The punishment for violating any of these rules is public lashing or even stoning."

Silverstein slammed a big fist on the table, making the others jump. "What I don't get is why our government continues to act like these Saudi Arabian assholes are our friends," he said. "It's the Saudi government that supports these madrasah schools that teach a sick, twisted version of Islam and preach jihad. Hell, the Saudi government even sponsors telethons to raise money for terrorists like Hamas. But our State Department asks the Colorado attorney general to go hat in hand, or better yet, on his hands and knees, and apologize for putting a rapist in prison."

"But we need their oil and military bases so we can fight the War on Terror," Epstein said facetiously.

"Yeah, yeah, even though the worst of the terrorists are from Saudi Arabia and get a lot of their money from Saudi Arabians in and out of the government," Silverstein growled. "Doesn't anybody ever get tired of our government substituting political expediency for moral convictions?"

The priest, Sunderland, turned to Karp. "What about you, Mr. District Attorney? We know better than to ask you about the Campbell case. But what is your response to someone who says that he has a right to commit certain crimes because they are part of his cultural or religious beliefs?"

"Then they can commit them in their own countries," Karp replied. "There are no fatwas here that allow someone to break our laws."

The Breakfast Club applauded and raised their orange juice glasses. "Down with fatwas," Gilbert said.

"What I want you to put down are your glasses before you hurt someone," Marjorie said as she appeared with a plate of pancakes. "Here you go, Butch. Can I bring you some syrup or maybe a little special honey?"

The Breakfast Club howled again with delight.

———

Thirty minutes later, as they watched Karp walk off down West Broadway, Plaut said, "We have to be more careful about things we hear out of his office. We don't want to jeopardize our Deep Throat, do we, Bill?"

"Not if we want to keep her employed," the newspaperman replied. "She's already uncomfortable with the spying, even though she knows it's for the greater good."

"I still don't know why we don't just tell him about our suspicions about what happened to Vince and what we know about the Sons of Man," Gilbert said.

"Tell him what about Vince? We're in the same boat with Butch as we are with V. T. There's no proof. Just a bunch of old fogies who stumbled on something bigger than they know what to do with."

"Don't you think Jaxon already told him about the Sons of Man?" Sunderland said. "Surely he's been told about the book, and his daughter, Lucy, was the last one who talked to Cian Magee."

"The book was written in 1930," Hall said. "There's nothing we have that proves the group still exists—if it ever did, for that matter. What's to say it wasn't a work of fiction?"

"What about the attempt on Senator McCullum's life?" Gilbert pointed out.

"The official version is that the former police officer who fired the shots was actually trying to hit the police chief because he'd been released from the force," Hall noted. "We only suspect that he was after McCullum. As you know, the assassin was killed by John Jojola before he could talk."

"Mr. Karp isn't about to take us into his confidence on what he does or doesn't know about the Sons of Man," Plaut said. "And we do suspect that there are other spies in the DAO. We cannot afford to be exposed, or the truth may never come out. But I think we need to do something."

"Which means we find a way to talk to V. T. Newbury without revealing our identities?" Florence asked.

"That's my opinion. But this club is a democracy, so let's put it to a vote. All in favor say 'aye.'"

Marjorie the Waitress reappeared just as the men voted in favor. "What's with these 'ayes'? You sound like a bunch of ancient mariners," she said.

"Oooh, good one," Gilbert laughed. "We were just voting."

"What for? Whether it's time to take a nap or drink more prune juice?" Epstein grinned wickedly. "Nah, just whether those tits are real or fake."

Marjorie rolled her eyes. "No wonder your wives kick you out of the house first thing in the morning. What's with men? From the moment they're born to the second they die, they're fixated on a couple of specialized sweat glands."

Epstein made a face. "Ugh, talk like that and I might forget to stare at yours."

The waitress laughed. "Sorry, I didn't mean to wreck your fantasies. I know that's about all you have left."

"Were we right or wrong?" Florence asked.

"How many voted for: 'Those puppies are real?'" Marjorie asked.

"All of us," Gilbert replied.

"Then you're not as senile as you look."

13

Inside the mosque office, Dean Newbury and Imam Jabbar watched a security monitor as Jaxon and the interpreter, Marie Smith, left the grounds. The men were soon joined by a tall blonde woman and a short man who looked like he was from the Middle East. He had droopy brown eyes and an oversized eagle's beak for a nose.

"Do you think he knows about Khalifa?" the woman asked.

Newbury thought about it for a moment. "It's difficult to tell, Ajmaani," he said, using the name the woman assumed to pass herself off as an Islamic extremist from Chechnya. Her real name was Nadya Malovo, and she worked for Russian employers, who for the time being had told her to cooperate with Dean Newbury in this project.

"It's a federal case, and my people were able to delete any cross-reference to the name Muhammad Jamal Khalifa on the national crime computer. They're keeping the name Rondell James away from the press," Newbury continued. "There's no way for the NYPD or the District Attorney's Office to track him down with what they've got. I think we're okay, but it really is quite unfortunate that this incident took place. It could have ruined everything." He shot Jabbar and Malovo a hard look.

"I had nothing to do with his training," Jabbar protested.

"You vouched for him," Malovo hissed. "And then didn't keep track of what he was up to after you kicked him out. He should have been eliminated."

"That might have been worse," Jabbar insisted. "His father-in-law is respected in the mosque. He might have asked a lot of questions."

"Isn't he asking questions now?" Newbury asked.

Jabbar shook his head. "Nobody knows that Khalifa was the bomber. The story is that after he and his wife fought, he left to go on jihad to Pakistan. The family's been told that if the authorities find out, they'll be deported to Kenya. They're in the country illegally, and I've hinted that our brothers in Nairobi might not appreciate the Jumas helping the infidels identify an American jihadi."

"In my opinion, leaving them alive is a risk," Malovo said. "What if they figure out that Khalifa was the bomber? They might go to the authorities and connect him to the mosque."

Jabbar ignored her. Malovo was dangerous, but Newbury and the other man in the room were calling the shots. "Killing them would raise more questions," Jabbar replied. "We're keeping an eye on them. The father spends most of his free time here. We insisted that Khalifa's wife, Miriam, take a job as our receptionist. She is the woman sitting outside the door now. We made it clear this was not a request . . . not if she wanted to stay away from the immigration officers."

Newbury thought about it for a moment. "You'll excuse us for a few minutes, please," he said to Jabbar.

The imam cleared his throat. He didn't like it when these people cut him out of the inner circle. He'd performed as requested and was an important figure in the events that were about to change the world. But the other three were clearly waiting for him to depart. "It is almost time for prayers," he said. "I should go."

When he was gone, Malovo spoke first. "How do we know for certain that Jaxon is not playing at this new role?"

"We don't," Newbury replied. "But my sources tell me that the 'defection' to private enterprise is real. His former colleagues at the FBI are angry with him, especially because he took several other agents with him. We've also discovered that Jaxon apparently has money problems, which got him into trouble with the Italian mob. He's been paying them back in cash and with favors that neither a federal salary nor his FBI badge could cover.

Also, we have a source within the District Attorney's Office who's over-heard conversations between him and Karp that would corroborate that he is persona non grata with the federal agencies."

"Is this the same source who tells us that the split between Karp and your nephew is real?" Malovo queried.

Newbury caught the hint of sarcasm and didn't like it. He wasn't used to being challenged—as the most senior and ruthless member of the Sons of Man Council, he wasn't about to tolerate insubordination from a mere as-sassin now. Who did this woman think she was talking to? If she kept it up, he'd send her tongue back to her Russian bosses. "My sources are my own, Ajmaani," he replied coldly. "And I will be the judge of my nephew's role."

Malovo wasn't easily cowed. "I think this is a dangerous game you play," she said. "Jaxon is nobody to be trifled with and neither is your nephew. They're not idiots, and we've had quite enough interference from their Jew friend Karp."

Newbury felt the anger flush his cheeks, but he said nothing. He was well aware that he was taking a chance with V. T., but he was doing so in the hopes that his nephew would "see the light" and someday replace him on the council. He wanted the Newbury name to continue on, since his own son, Quilliam, had rejected his birthright, enlisted in the Marines, and died in Vietnam.

Not that family could always be trusted. His brother, Vincent, had spied on him and betrayed the brotherhood when he took the rare copy of the Sons of Man book from Dean's office, which found its way to that Celtic bookstore owner. The bookseller, Cian Magee, had begun to tell Lucy Karp, the bitch daughter of his enemy the district attorney, about their organiza-tion. But fortunately, he'd been killed and the book destroyed before too much was revealed.

Dean had also murdered his brother by ordering his chef to lace Vin-cent's dinner with foxglove, the natural source of digitalis, a heart medica-tion his brother was taking. However, in large amounts, digitalis had the opposite effect, and his brother had died of a massive heart attack, which the family doctor had ruled "natural causes."

Dean Newbury felt no remorse for killing his brother, nor would he feel any if it turned out that his nephew couldn't be persuaded that the only hope for Western civilization was the iron-willed leadership of the Sons of

Man. It was just an old man's hope that he would be around to initiate the new world order and that his DNA, if not his direct heir, would remain to guide the council in the centuries to come.

"I'm watching my nephew carefully," Newbury replied evenly. "And as we all know, his test is coming, which he will either pass or fail with fatal implications. As for keeping Jaxon close, that was at the direct request of our friend, The Sheik, here." He turned to the other man, who'd been quietly listening to the debate.

When that man now spoke it was in French. "Enough of this argument, I wanted this infidel Jaxon pulled into our web. The reasons are twofold. One, he is a dangerous opponent, especially when we do not know where he is or what he is up to. There is an old Arabic saying that it is good to draw your enemy's attention to the horizon, so that when he realizes the danger comes from within his own tent, the dagger will already be in his back. The second reason is personal. I am not prepared to say why at this moment, but just know that I want the blood of this man. I want him to know that he failed to stop the new era."

Newbury looked at Malovo and shrugged as if to say that the matter was closed. *Because I allow it to be closed,* he thought. He would use this "Sheik" for his own purposes. He thought the man acted like a child and was too blinded by pride to see why the very idea of Muslim world domination was a joke. The extremists were living in the fifteenth century. They couldn't agree on a common purpose, or who would lead them, without starting a hundred-year feud and spending more time killing each other than they did their enemies in the West.

Dangerous, yes, Newbury thought as he looked at The Sheik, in the way that a crocodile is dangerous when you don't know where he is, but no more than raw material for boots and purses when you do. They made good bogeyman, too, and could be used to frighten the American public into placing the reins of power into the hands of anyone who could protect them.

The Sheik had come to them because he needed assistance to pull off a plan that was brilliant in design. The man could not use his real name, due to his current position in Saudi Arabia, but his idea was much more subtle than that of men like bin Laden. If it worked, the world would be changed forever.

The amusing part was that The Sheik, for all his brilliance, believed that would mean a worldwide caliphate, in which a single Islamic leader would rule. Once the Sons of Man were in power in the United States, these Middle Eastern bandits with their minds stuck in the fifteenth century would learn the difference between a nation that had the means to destroy them and one that would actually use those means. The terms would be simple. Disobey once, and Medina, the second holiest city in the Muslim world, would disappear. Another infraction and the remains of Mecca would smolder and glow for a thousand years. There would be no hiding in the mountains of Pakistan from weary U.S. soldiers, because those mountains would be turned into a nuclear wasteland, the mouths of their caves melted shut. There would be none of this "reasoned response" or any effort to minimize civilian deaths—*kill them all and let their Allah sort them out*.

"Speak English," Malovo scowled. Her French was worse than Newbury's, though she was fluent in Arabic, which he was not. "It's easier for all of us."

The Sheik answered in French. "It is bad enough that I have to play any part other than conqueror in the land of my enemies. But I will not speak their filthy language, and Mr. Newbury does not speak the language of The Prophet."

"But France is a Western nation," Newbury noted, not that he really cared about what language they spoke. But he was a student of what motivated people, which was a way to determine their weaknesses.

"It will be an Islamic nation soon," The Sheik smirked. "Even without our project, they would soon be overrun with millions of poor, angry Muslim immigrants, and there will be yet another bloody French revolution. If their history is any indication, once our goals are achieved, the infidels in France will surrender. The blood of unbelievers will flow nonetheless in rivers beneath the Arc de Triomphe."

"And what about your 'partners,' like myself and Ms. Ajmaani?" Newbury asked lightly. *Such poetic idiots these sand niggers*, he thought, *blood in rivers indeed*. "Beneath which of our monuments do you plan to spread the red deluge?"

The Sheik pulled back from what he really wanted to say. "We are not greedy," he replied. "We will be content with our former empire, plus perhaps a bit more of Europe, where so many of our oppressed people await the day of liberation." He inclined his head toward Malovo. "Of course, we may need to . . . negotiate . . . with our friends, the Russians, regarding Muslim territory in Chechnya."

"Non-negotiable," Malovo smiled back, also not saying what she wanted to say. "The access to warm-water ports and oil is a national security issue."

"Friends . . . there will be time to work out the details," Newbury interjected. "We need to keep our minds on the immediate task as we take these first steps toward . . . " he paused, knowing both of the others were thinking the exact words he was—the final struggle—but for now he only clasped his hands in front of him and added " . . . those future negotiations."

Newbury steered the conversation to business. The Sheik's plan was brilliant, but it was also complex and would require precise timing and total commitment. "When is the package from the Philippines due?" he asked.

"Three days before the plan goes forward," Malovo responded.

"Is that enough time?"

"It will be enough. His role is simple, though obviously extremely important from both a tactical and strategic standpoint. We don't want him to arrive too soon and risk him being identified by the federal agencies who are not part of our plan."

"What about Jabbar and his people?" Newbury asked.

"They'll do," Malovo replied. "We need foot soldiers who are totally committed and don't expect to survive. Where else do you find that, except among those who believe that they're paving their way to Paradise? Amazing what the promise of virgins will do for a man."

The Sheik scowled. "I don't like your sarcasm. The mujahideen all over the world will rise up when they hear what has happened here."

"True, there will be plenty more willing to die for Allah," Malovo replied. "More than enough."

14

Leaving the Breakfast Club members to their discussions, Karp walked south on West Broadway until he got to Chambers and then headed east toward the impressive array of buildings that made up Civic Center, City Hall, and Federal Plaza. His kids would have thought it corny, but he loved looking up and reading the inscriptions carved into their stone facades. The Federal Courthouse quoted a line from Thomas Jefferson's first inaugural address: "Equal and Exact Justice To All Men of Whatever Station or Persuasion." Meanwhile, the inscription on City Hall affirmed that "The True Administration of Justice Is The Firmest Pillar of Good Government."

Karp wondered how many of the several hundred people now walking in the shadows of those buildings on their way to work that morning ever looked up at those inscriptions and believed in what they said. Most were probably too busy hoping the central air-conditioning was working right because the day was going to be another hot one. He turned left and walked swiftly north on Centre until reaching the park at Foley Square across from the Criminal Courts building. A knot of people had gathered in front of the building and were passing out protest signs.

A young boy and his mother, apparently on the way to school, walked in front of him. The child was wearing a New York Yankees cap and replica pinstripe jersey with the name "Jeter" stenciled on the back. It reminded

Karp of how much he'd enjoyed this time of year when he was that age. Soon it would be September and the Yankees would be in the thick of a pennant race. But back then, the name he would have had on his jersey would have been Mantle or Maris.

Karp sighed for the days before terrorists blew themselves up for God in public places or rammed airplanes into buildings, the days before kids went on shooting rampages in their high schools. He knew that to say it was a more innocent time was clichéd and inaccurate, though. That era had had its own fears and problems, such as the ever-present threat of nuclear war, and Jim Crow laws. But for a kid from Brooklyn who loved his parents, his country, playing basketball, and the Yankees, in that order, it was a special childhood.

Karp looked up at the massive Criminal Courts building, with its four front towers of limestone and granite. It squatted in the very heart of what during the nineteenth century had been the notorious Five Points district, a disease- and crime-ridden slum where gangs like the Pug Uglies and the Bowery Bums preyed upon poor immigrants and helpless citizens. But they were gone, replaced by that monument to the legal system.

Glancing back down, Karp noted that the protesters were forming up. According to their signs, they represented NOF, the National Organization of Feminists, as well as several mental-health advocacy groups. They were there to protest the upcoming trial of Jessica Campbell, which had been set for early September.

"DA Hates Women," read one sign. "Kave Man Karp," stated another. Further down the row he saw "Help Not Hate" and "Free Jessica Campbell."

Using Dirty Warren's newsstand across the street for cover, he crossed. "Mother fucker shit . . . Karp," the little man swore, taking off his thick glasses and trying futilely to clean them on his equally filthy apron. He nodded at the protesters. "Looks like . . . ahhhh crap piss . . . you're making new friends as usual."

"Morning Warren," Karp replied, buying a copy of the *Times*. "Yeah, looks like my popularity is soaring. So any good movie trivia?"

"Yeah, yeah . . . whoo boy . . . been saving this one," Warren said, the tic in his left eye causing him to wink several times in a row. "Son of a bitch . . . it's got several parts though, and you have to get them all or I win."

"Okay, but does that mean that if I answer them all correctly, I've beaten you that many more times, or just once?" Karp asked. "Not that it matters, since I lost track somewhere around ten thousand for me and zero for you."

"Screw you, Karp." Dirty Warren shifted back and forth from one foot to the other like a little boy needing to use the restroom. "Okay, here goes. Everybody knows that in *The Wizard of Oz*, Frank Morgan played Professor Marvel AND the Wizard. But how many other parts did he play and what were they?"

The question wasn't very difficult for Karp. The Wizard of Oz had been a favorite of his, and he and his mother had seen it at least a dozen times. But he liked to lead Dirty Warren on. "Boy, this is going to be tough," he said. "Let's see. Professor Marvel. The Wizard. And . . . hmmmm . . . I believe there were three other roles . . . "

Dirty Warren's grin turned into a frown. He pulled his stocking cap, which he wore no matter what the temperature was, down over his ears. A bead of sweat trickled down the bridge of his narrow, pointed nose, hesitated for a moment, then fell with a splat on a stack of newspapers. "You have to be exact, no partial answers."

"Let's see, in the Emerald City, he was also . . . the cabbie who drove the Horse-of-a-Different-Color, the guard at the entrance to the Wizard's palace, and . . . hmmmm . . ."

"What, piss, shit, mother whore Christ on a stick?" Warren snarled.

"And the doorman at the palace."

"Crap! Crap! Dammit Karp, if you spent half as much time putting scumbags in prison as you do reading movie trivia magazines, there'd be . . . whoo boy, fuck me naked . . . no crime in this goddamned city."

"Why, thank you, Warren. Good to know I can count on your vote in the next election." Then he saw a sly smile creep onto the news vendor's face. "Okay, Warren, where's the zinger?"

Dirty Warren hopped on a foot. "All right, wiseguy. Where'd they get the coat Morgan wore as Professor Marvel, and whose was it originally? And I want the full story or you're out of here."

Karp knitted his brow. There were many myths surrounding the making of *The Wizard of Oz*, such as that one of the male Munchkins hanged himself on the set after his amorous advances were rejected by a female Munchkin. According to legend, his dangling body could be seen in the film when Dorothy, the Scarecrow, and the Tin Man set off on the road to see the Wizard. The truth was that the dark, fuzzy image moving in the background was a real crane borrowed from the Los Angeles Zoo to help create a fantasyland, and the bird chose that moment to flap its wings. However, the story Dirty Warren was referring to was real.

"Now that's a really good question," Karp said.

"You bet your ass it is."

Karp let him enjoy his moment of anticipated triumph. There was such hope in those weak and watery blue eyes, he considered letting the man win one. *But that wouldn't be right.*

It was too late to let him win anyway. Dirty Warren had seen the smile on Karp's face and knew that he was beaten again. "Lousy . . . shit piss fuck . . . cheater," he said.

"The coat came from a second-hand store where it was chosen by Morgan to be part of Professor Marvel's wardrobe."

"Oooh boy oooh boy," his opponent cried.

"And, this is the strange-but-true part," Karp continued, stretching out his answer to allow Dirty Warren to boil in oil a bit longer. "One day Morgan happened to look on the inside sleeve of the coat, and low and behold if he didn't discover the initials L. F. B. stitched there. The coat, it so happened, had originally been owned by . . . drumroll please . . ."

"Scratch my balls Jewboy . . . whoo boy . . . whoo boy."

"Not exactly the drum roll I had in mind, Warren, but it will do," Karp replied and then put the man out of his misery. "L. Frank Baum, the author of *The Wonderful Wizard of Oz.* The coat was even identified by the tailor who made it and verified by Baum's widow."

"You slimy toad-sucking whore," Dirty Warren howled. "You do this to torment me, Karp! Just once, I'd like to . . . penis poop . . . win!"

"Now Warren, you wouldn't want me to let you win. That wouldn't be ethical," Karp chided. "And on that note, better luck next time. I'm out of here."

"I hope they tear you a new one, asshole," Dirty Warren shouted after him.

Karp waved without turning back around. He'd chosen a moment when the apparent leaders of the protest were being interviewed for the morning news down the block from the entrance. He was almost to the door before one of the other protesters spotted him.

"There he is," she shrieked. At first her companions seemed confused, but they looked around to see where she was pointing and saw him. They yelled, enraged that they were missing their golden opportunity to get on television while accosting the district attorney. But he was through the door and into the lobby before they could catch up.

———

Kenny Katz was waiting by the elevator. "We still on for this morning?"

Karp looked at his watch. "Yeah, the main meeting room in about fifteen minutes."

Mrs. Milquetost looked up from her desk when he walked in. *Damn, the woman must sleep here,* he thought.

"Your wife and the others are here," Milquetost sniffed. "She said they'd wait for you in the meeting room." Her tone implied that she felt the boss's wife was taking liberties.

Karp wasn't about to engage her on that subject, so he just nodded and said "Good morning, Darla." He started past her desk when he noticed a long-stemmed red rose in a vase next to her computer. "Don't tell me I've forgotten your birthday?"

Darla Milquetost looked at the rose and blushed. "Oh, that . . . it's from my friend Bill. . . . A young man delivered it this morning as I arrived at the door." Suddenly, she looked chagrined. "I'm sorry. He shouldn't have sent it to my place of business."

"Nonsense," Karp said. "It brightens up the room. And it's nice to see that someone appreciates a lovely woman." He lingered a moment to see if he could get his receptionist to turn the same shade as the rose. *Darla's got a boyfriend. Darla's got a boyfriend.* He hoped Ray Guma didn't find out or he'd be on her like a hyena scenting blood.

Mrs. Milquetost remembered something. "Oh, I almost forgot. Mr. Murrow is waiting for you in your office," she said. Gilbert Murrow was another of her favorites, and therefore she'd granted him access to Karp's office without question.

"Good morning, Gilbert," Karp said, entering the office. "What's up?" He knew perfectly well that Murrow wanted to talk about his appearing on the *Off the Hook Show*, but he was feeling ornery so he was going to make the man squirm.

Indeed, Murrow was already nervously fiddling with his bow tie. "Just hear me out on this," Murrow began. "I left you a message on this but the producer from the *Off the Hook Show* called and they'd like you to appear to discuss the Campbell case."

"No way in hell," Karp said calmly. "We don't try our cases on television."

Murrow winced, but he wasn't about to stop. Karp had learned a long time ago that his aide had the tenacity and courage of a bulldog.

He would have to or no way would he last five minutes with Ariadne Stupenagel, Karp thought. It was one of the great wonders of the world to him that his aide had taken up with the abrasive reporter. Personally, Karp had always had a love-hate relationship with the woman, made more challenging by the fact that she had been Marlene's college roommate. The two women were still good friends, and Karp had to admit that as journalists went, she was honest, ethical, and accurate—though not above stretching the truth—as well as fearless in pursuit of a story. She was also pretty good looking in a big, brassy sort of way.

Still, when Murrow started dating her, Karp had laughed it off, sure that such a mismatch couldn't last. For one thing, the woman was several inches taller and forty pounds heavier than Gilbert, who was bookish and given to classical music and quiet evenings at home. At least that's what Karp thought. Only lately had he learned that Murrow and Stupenagel were both fans of punk rock, Sinatra, and just about everything in between and around. Even more surprising was Murrow's assertion that Stupenagel was just as likely as he was to want to stay home and curl up at night with a good book and her "Murry."

"Yeah, I knew you'd say that, and hey, I agree wholeheartedly," Murrow replied. "But I was thinking that if you avoided—refused, I mean—talking about the details of the case and discussed more general questions about the legal definitions of insanity, it would be a good public service. I don't know if you saw those protesters outside, but there's a lot of misconceptions about the insanity defense."

Karp started to grouse that he didn't care about the protesters, but Murrow, who could speak faster than any human being he'd ever heard outside of a rap artist, made one last pitch. "The producer said that Linda Lewis and Charlie Campbell have already agreed to do the show."

"All the more reason for me to avoid it," Karp responded. When it came to most defense lawyers, Karp had no major issues. He recognized that the system was set up in such a way that a defense attorney's job was to be an advocate for his or her clients and "zealously" protect their rights. However, some attorneys took "zealous" too far.

As far as he was concerned, Linda Lewis was one of those. She was perfectly comfortable using the media to sway the court of public opinion, as well as potential jurors. And Karp believed that like some other defense attorneys, Lewis used the "abuse excuse" disingenuously. Killing someone due to an imminent threat to one's life was self-defense plain and simple. However, he drew the line with those who planned a murder, sometimes for hours or days, or even weeks and months, and then carried it out. In his view, they could have gone to a safehouse or asked for police protection. The law simply did not, as far as he was concerned, allow someone to plan and then commit murder, even of abusive bullies.

It had not surprised him that Lewis had latched onto the Campbell case within hours of her "hospital arrest" at Bellevue. Nor was it unexpected that she'd immediately started launching media salvos denouncing the "insensitive male district attorney, who heads the male-dominated DAO." Of course, the "chauvinist pig would consider criminal charges against a woman who was obviously suffering from serious mental disease, literally wallowing in insanity."

Apparently, not all men were cave-dwellers. At least initially, Lewis had lauded Jessica's husband, Charlie, for "his understanding and compassion in the midst of an enormous family tragedy" and for his promise to seek funding to combat "the hidden epidemic of postpartum depression" if elected to Congress.

Interestingly, Karp noted that Lewis's more recent interviews with the press had left Charlie out, and he wondered what it meant. *Perhaps we'll learn from the show*, he thought. But he looked at Murrow's hopeful face and shook his head. "Sorry Gilbert," he said. "This is the sort of grandstanding that taints jury pools."

"Exactly," Murrow responded, "which would balance what Lewis is hoping to accomplish."

"We're not in the business of balancing public opinion because of what some defense lawyer wants to say on television."

Murrow made one last effort. "We're taking some real hits in the opinion polls on this."

Karp was well aware of what his aide was referring to. According to a recent poll taken by the *New York Times*, most New Yorkers thought that Jessica Campbell fit the definition of legally insane. Most respondents said that sending her to a mental institution was "more appropriate than criminal prosecution." Karp assumed that many would also agree with a statement made by the president of NOF labeling him a "misogynist pig" whose mental intelligence ranked right up there with Neanderthals.

Stone Age imagery again, he thought. "This isn't a popularity contest, Gilbert," Karp replied. "Besides, I thought I had at least another three years before we had to start worrying about what people thought of me."

"It's never too early," Murrow pouted. "Even bald-faced lies, if allowed to go unchallenged, can stay in the voters' minds long after they've been proven false."

"I'll take it under advisement," Karp replied, then noticed Gilbert's slumping shoulders. "And Gilbert, I may not always express it properly, but I really do appreciate the efforts you make to portray this office in a good light. But let's keep to the high road no matter what; I think the public is smart enough to understand when someone is pandering or lying."

Murrow looked up with wet eyes and smiled. "Thanks . . . I do my best. And really, I'm proud to be working for maybe the last public official in the country who does what's right and not what's politically expedient or necessarily very smart for his political longevity and the public's perception of him."

"Nice try, Gilbert," Karp laughed. "You just don't give up."

Murrow chuckled. "All right, all right. Just don't blame me if those protesters turn into an ugly mob after the show."

———

When Karp walked into the meeting room, the first people he saw were Marlene and Fulton laughing at something a short, older man was saying.

The man had always reminded Karp of Santa Claus. His snow-white hair fell to his shoulders and matched the full beard that covered nearly all of his face except his round rosy cheeks, red button nose (*and up the chimney he rose*) and cupid-bow lips. The man's merry Aqua Velva–colored eyes twinkled as he delivered the punch line of whatever joke he was telling before turning to give Karp a wink.

However, Jack Swanburg was a lot more than a right jolly old elf. He had been a forensic pathologist by trade, and after his retirement a decade or so before, he'd help found and develop the 221b Baker Street Irregulars.

With him this day were two other members of the group, Charlotte Gates, one of the leading forensic anthropologists in the country, whose responsibility at crime-scene investigations was the meticulous recovery and identification of human remains and, if possible, determination of the cause of death. Karp estimated the petite Gates to be in her early fifties, though her age was difficult to gauge because her tan face and agile movements from a lifetime spent outdoors made her seem young. With other members of the Irregulars, she'd already assisted his office with several cases, but in her "real job" she was one of the first people the authorities called upon to respond to mass fatalities. She had assisted in the aftermath of the World Trade Center attacks and in many other tragic situations.

"How do you do it?" Karp had asked her shortly after she'd helped Marlene solve a murder case in Idaho that past spring. "How do you cope with all that hands-on experience with violent death?"

"The honest answer is that I don't always cope with it—at least not very well," she'd replied. "There are plenty of sleepless nights and nightmares. But pretty early on in my career, I started making it a point to know as much about the victims when they were alive as I could. I'd ask to see photographs of them with their families and enjoying themselves; I'd ask the people who knew them what they were like, what were their dreams . . . that sort of thing." She'd pointed to her head. "I put them up here in a village I've created, so that when I'm working with their remains, I'm seeing real people."

Gates and Swanburg had been accompanied from Denver, where the group was headquartered, to New York by geologist James Reedy, whose tough grizzled face and wiry reddish beard reminded Karp of a miner in a western film. In reality, he was a Ph.D. who taught at the Colorado School of Mines. He, too, had been instrumental in the recovery of the murder victim's body in Idaho.

Karp was shaking hands with Reedy when Kenny Katz walked into the room. "Sorry, I hope I'm not late."

"Not at all," Marlene said. "This group usually arrives early so we can catch up."

"It comes from some of us having nothing better to do than exercise our gums," Swanburg said, sticking out his pudgy hand. "Jack Swanburg, damn glad to meet you."

"Speak for yourself about flapping gums, old man," Reedy replied. "Some of us aren't leading the life of leisure on the government dole."

"Well-earned retirement, you mean, you young whippersnapper," Swanburg retorted and turned back to Katz. "I assume of the three beautiful women in the room, you know your boss's wife, Marlene Ciampi, and the even shorter one there is Charlotte Gates, one of the founding members of the Baker Street Irregulars."

"*The* Charlotte Gates?" Katz asked, surprised. "I spent a lot of time when I was in the Rangers studying the Lockerbie airliner bombing. You really worked wonders putting that together."

"Well, I'm flattered," Gates responded, offering a handshake that was surprisingly strong for such a small woman. "But handsome young men, even Rangers, ought to spend less of their time studying mass fatalities and more on young women. Got a girlfriend?" The anthropologist wiggled her eyebrows suggestively.

As Katz blushed, Swanburg turned his attention to the last female in the room, an attractive black woman in her thirties. "I'm afraid no one has introduced me to this lovely young lady," he said.

"My bad," Fulton apologized. "My manners go to hell if my wife isn't around to remind me I'm supposed to have some. Anyway, this is Detective Marj Cobing of the NYPD homicide division. She's the detective assigned to the Campbell case."

The introductions over, Karp motioned for everyone to take a seat. "I don't plan on running this meeting," he said. "We're here to discuss the Campbell case and, in particular, what efforts we can make to locate the bodies of the three Campbell children. And since I've worked with the 221b Baker Street Irregulars, as has my wife, Marlene, I thought I'd start by vouching for their abilities and their integrity."

Karp summarized the obstacles facing the prosecution of a "bodiless homicide." As with any murder case, the prosecution needed to be able to provide jurors with admissible evidence that proved beyond a reasonable doubt that the defendant murdered the victim or victims. In a case in which the bodies could not be found, the first major obstacle was proving beyond a reasonable doubt that the victim or victims were in fact dead, and hadn't simply run off or been kidnapped.

"In the Campbell case, I don't think we're going to have much of a problem there," Karp said. "We have three young children who have been missing for nearly six months, and their mother telling her husband that she 'sent them to God.' However, the defense attorney in this case is likely to try anything, including bringing up the possibility that an intruder took the children and that's what caused Mrs. Campbell to become delusional, as she believed the intruder was actually an 'Angel of the Lord.'"

Kenny Katz looked shocked. "Where'd that come from?"

Karp shrugged. "Actually, I read it in a *National Enquirer* article at the dentist's office a month ago. It was completely made up—no named sources—but I wouldn't put it past Lewis to give it a try. But in fact, we don't know where Campbell killed them—which could be a jurisdictional problem, if, say, she actually did it in New Jersey—nor do we know how. It's that second one that concerns me."

"How do you mean?" Gates asked.

"With an insanity defense, we're going to have to prove that Jessica Campbell was aware of the nature and consequences of her actions," Karp said. "Shoot somebody in the head, and the law assumes that you meant to kill them. But how about if she put the kids in a rowboat and shoved them out into the Atlantic so that God could pick them up? Or maybe she took them into the woods and left them in the car for God to find. Could it then be argued that she didn't actually intend for her children to die, but thought she was just leaving them in the hands of an Almighty babysitter? And would she therefore not have realized the nature and consequences of her actions, making her legally insane at the time?"

"I assume the house was gone over meticulously, including testing for blood?" Swanburg asked.

"Detective Cobing, you want to handle that?" Fulton said, looking to the young woman.

Cobing had been listening politely, but with her arms crossed in the manner of detectives who don't like other people tottering around in their cases. "Crime-scene guys didn't find a thing," she said. "They practically painted the place with Luminol, which as you probably know reacts with material that has iron in it, like blood. Even the tiniest amounts will show up under a black light."

"Nothing at all?" Swanburg asked.

"Nothing significant. A few flecks on the bathroom floor, but that's not unusual. Kids get cuts and people nick themselves shaving. Nor was it a significant amount. We even tested all the knives in the house, including the steak knives. Sometimes a killer will use a knife and then run it through the dishwasher, but we'll still find blood up under the handle. In this case, nothing. The car's still missing, too, so no telling what we'd find there."

"Even if the jury accepts that the children are dead and buys that their mother knew what she was doing when she murdered them," Karp noted, "we still have to show that she knew that what she was doing was wrong. I'm betting the defense attorney plans to use the 'sent them to God' statement to show that Mrs. Campbell, in her delusional state, didn't know that killing for God was against the law. So discovering evidence that she went to some lengths to hide the crime would go a long way toward countering that."

"Let's start with finding the car," Reedy said. "I'm sure you've all checked with the chop shops. Sorry if that sounds like Detective Class 101, but you'd be surprised how some of the best cops overlook the easy answer."

"We checked," Cobing said. "No Volvo station wagons have turned up. We have the VIN on the National Crime Computer just in case God drove the car to Ohio or somewhere, but no hits yet."

Gates looked at Reedy. "You're thinking the car was used as the coffin, like in Idaho?"

The geologist shrugged. "Maybe, but in Idaho, the killers had access to heavy machinery and buried the car in a gravel pit. Unless Mrs. Campbell had help, and it doesn't sound like it unless she's part of a cult or something, we're talking about one woman getting rid of a car with her kids' bodies in it. I doubt she has a backhoe and knows how to use it. But it's worth checking out." He turned to Cobing. "So she leaves the house and takes the kids somewhere—alive or dead we don't know—and then comes back home without kids or car? Do we know what sort of a window of time she had to do this?"

Cobing opened her notebook. "According to the records of the cab company, Mr. Campbell was picked up at 7:15 in the morning. She then called the nanny and told her not to come to work. Mr. Campbell returned at 6 P.M. that evening; the children were gone and his wife was in bed sleeping. That gave her a window of about ten hours, a long time."

"If I remember right," Gates interjected, "it's possible to get from the home to the garage without being seen?

Cobing nodded. "Yes. This particular brownstone has an enclosed three-car garage off the alley. Why?"

"It has to do with the psychology of murderers," Gates replied. "If she intends to 'sacrifice' her children to God, I don't think she is going to take a chance on being detected and stopped. Yet she does this in the middle of the day in March. We checked with the National Weather Service, and it was actually an unseasonably warm day, so one might expect other people to be about. I also remember something from the police report saying there were signs that Mrs. Campbell had been in a struggle?"

"Yes, scratch marks on her arms and a pretty good bite mark."

"And I assume the bite wound was matched to the dental records of the children?" Gates asked.

The detective paused and gave her a funny look. "You know," she said, "I'm not sure about that. It's a good question though."

"It would definitely indicate which child bit her, and prove that she struggled with at least one of them. My guess is that the children were killed in the home and then taken somewhere."

"How do you think she did it?" asked Cobing, who seemed to be gaining respect for the "amateurs" as the questioning went on. "There's too much blood to clean it up that well if she used a gun, plus the bullet will often go through a victim and we'd be able to find it or evidence of it. There's also a lot of blood with a knife."

"But the house was spotless?" Swanburg asked.

"Immaculate. And you can't just clean blood out of the carpet or even grout. Even if you can't see it, the Luminol will find it."

"Unless the blood was contained somehow," Swanburg said.

"The bathtub," Fulton said. "If she kills them in the bathtub, it's easy enough to wash any blood down the drain."

"I think that's a good place to look further, detectives," Swanburg said. "There's a chance she drowned them. I saw the photographs of Mrs. Campbell's arms, and she did have some pretty good scratches—so one or more of those kids put up a prolonged fight. But forcibly drowning someone is tougher to do than you'd think, even with kids, so it would have taken a while for them to die. One of them may have put up a fight, and that fight may have occurred in or around the tub. There may or may not be any blood left there at this point, but it's worth checking."

"Those poor babies," Marlene said.

Karp put his hand on his wife's arm. She was as tough as they came and had been involved in her share of violent episodes, including a few where she'd been the avenging angel. But the tears were now coursing down her cheeks.

"Sorry," she said. "I just got this image of those little children and the terror they must have felt."

Swanburg looked back at Cobing. "Can you get a second warrant to search the house?"

"Sure we can," said the detective, who was much more attentive now. "But what can you do that we haven't already done?"

"I want to take apart that bathtub, get down into the drain, and see what Luminol finds. And there's one place that crime-scene techies sometimes forget to check in the tub—the plumbing—but it'll depend on just how good a job Mrs. Campbell did of cleaning."

Katz summed up the discussion: "So we're working on the premise that Mrs. Campbell kills the kids in the house, makes quite the effort to clean up all the evidence, lugs the bodies down to the garage and puts them in the Volvo, and then drives them somewhere . . ."

"Sounds like she didn't want to get caught," Karp said.

"Which shows that she understood that it was wrong," Marlene added.

"And the consequences."

"So she finds someplace to dump the car with the bodies," Fulton said. "And then gets back home before her husband shows up."

"Anybody call the taxi companies to see if somebody dropped her off?" Marlene asked.

"That we did do," Cobing replied. "No record of anyone fitting Jessica Campbell's description being dropped off in the neighborhood."

"So she takes some other sort of transportation to get back," Reedy said.

"Grand Central Terminal," Karp suggested. "She drives the car somewhere and then catches a train back to Grand Central and walks the rest of the way home. That's quite a ways, but again, demonstrates that she's thinking clearly enough to not take a cab and risk being tied to the brownstone."

"But where'd she go?" Marlene asked, posing the big question. "How do you kill three kids, clean up the evidence, then drive the car and the bodies somewhere, bury the car so that it hasn't been found in six months, and still get back home in time?"

"Well," Reedy said with a grin. "You don't bury it, you submerge it. Takes no time to cover a car with water. So, anyone think we can find a place where Mrs. Campbell could roll the family station wagon into the water and then catch a ride home?"

"Maybe you didn't notice, Sherlock," Swanburg said, "but Manhattan is an island. You know, surrounded by water."

"Very funny, my dear Watson," Reedy said. "But remember, this is the middle of the day and Manhattan is a very busy island crowded with people. Somebody's going to notice if Jessica rolled the Volvo off the Brooklyn Bridge. What I need is a map."

"Be right back," Fulton said, leaving the room. He returned with a large rolled-up map of New York State, which he pinned up on the wall.

Twenty minutes later, they all stood back and looked at the map and their handiwork. There were so many colored dots indicating possible locations where Jessica Campbell might have left her car and the bodies of her children that the map appeared to have come down with some sort of disease. The ten-hour time frame left too much of the area to cover, but there were other criteria for narrowing down the possibilities: The place where Jessica did her work had to be a body of water deep enough to submerge a car, either from some sort of platform, such as a bridge or dock, or from the shore; it had to be close enough to a rail or bus line that Jessica could have used to get home; and it had to be out of sight from possible witnesses.

"Shit," Marlene swore, looking at the dots, which ranged from New Jersey and Connecticut to upstate New York and Vermont. "That's still a lot of ground to cover."

"Well, let's try to narrow it down further," Swanburg said. Addressing Cobing, he asked, "Is there anything we know about her past that might point us in the right direction? Someplace she might feel comfortable; psychological profiles show that killers who hide their victims usually pick a spot they know or one that resembles a place they once felt comfortable in."

Cobing told him what she knew. Jessica was raised in Harlem and later moved to SoHo with her wealthy parents. Then there was college in Poughkeepsie, graduate school at Columbia . . .

"Poughkeepsie?" Swanburg said, peering at the map. "I remember seeing the name."

"Yes, Vassar College." Cobing pointed to the place on the map.

"Up north, eh?" Swanburg said. "And damn close to the Hudson River." He looked at the others. "Might need another one of those dots."

Cobing relaxed. "I think I'll see what her friends—not that she has many—and family have to say. So far I haven't had much luck with them, but who knows, maybe an innocent discussion about old favorite places for family picnics along the Hudson would break the ice."

15

"Look at this crap," Dean Newbury swore as he walked into the office of his nephew, V. T., tossing the Saturday edition of the *New York Times* on his desk.

V. T. picked up the paper and scanned the front page. "Which article are you talking about, or is it all crap?" he said with a smile. "My guess is it's the story about the Yankees being five games back from the Red Sox?"

The old man cackled. "Good one," he said. "Damn Yankees . . . no pun intended." Then his face returned to its usual blend of constipation and anger. "But you're right. It's all a bunch of left-wing drivel. There was a time when that rag, even as liberal as its editorial board has always been—bunch of Jews and faggots—at least kept most of the opinion stuff on the editorial pages. Now it permeates every single page like mold in bread. The only decent things in that old fish-wrapper are the crossword puzzle and the Sudoku."

"I didn't know you were a fan of puzzles," V. T. replied. Such an innocent pastime seemed out of character for his no-nonsense uncle.

"Since I was a kid," the old man snorted. "But that's not important." Dean Newbury stomped around the desk and stabbed a bony finger at the paper. "That's what I'm talking about," he said, bending over to read it out loud. "Listen to this from that goddamned pinko senator McCullum. He's

185

constantly attacking the Patriot Act. *'The means of defense against foreign danger historically have become the instruments of tyranny at home.'* What kind of bullshit is that?"

"Actually, I think he's quoting James Madison," V. T. pointed out. "I think Madison also said, *'If Tyranny and Oppression come to this land, it will be in the guise of fighting a foreign enemy.'*"

"Just because the quotations are old doesn't make them right," Dean Newbury said icily. "That might have been fine to say at the end of the eighteenth century; they didn't have a bunch of religious zealots blowing themselves up in public places and flying airplanes into buildings. I guess they might have had a few beheadings over in France, but it's a different world now. New problems require new measures."

"Of course, of course," V. T. said, holding up his hands. "I wasn't trying to defend the remarks. Just recalling an old history lesson. New measures, indeed."

The old man glared at his nephew. It was times like this when he had to admit that the others on the council were probably right. His nephew was never going to "get it." He was just like his father.

He had no fond memories of his brother Vincent, V. T.'s father, not even from childhood. The truth was, he'd never liked him and all his whining about playing fair.

Once, he'd witnessed his brother get into a schoolyard fight at the private academy to which they, like all the Newburys before them, had been sent. To his surprise, his mild-mannered little brother had prevailed against an older bully, bloodying the boy's nose, which pretty much ended the fight.

Dean was furious that Vincent didn't press home his advantage. So he'd rushed in and kicked the other boy in the stomach, knocking him to the ground, and then continued to kick him again and again until someone shouted that the headmaster was coming.

After they were released from the headmaster's office with a stern lecture—there were not about to be any real consequences for one of the Newbury boys—Dean had turned on his brother and berated him. "Never show mercy," he snarled. "Your enemies will only perceive it as weakness. Once you get him down, you keep him down so that he fears you and never dares to oppose you again."

"But all I wanted was for him to stop picking on me. He gave up. You didn't have to hurt him so bad. You heard what the headmaster said; they took him to the hospital with a broken arm and cracked ribs."

"Good, I hope he dies."

"You don't really mean that."

Dean had whirled and grabbed his brother by the front of his shirt. "Don't you ever believe that," he spat. "I mean everything I ever say."

They'd both become attorneys in the family firm, though Vincent had never been trusted. Although a first-rate lawyer, he was too squeamish about doing whatever was necessary for their more challenging clients. They'd also argued frequently about Vincent's insistence on taking pro bono cases, especially when he went up against corporations or wealthy people who might have otherwise someday become clients.

Vincent had never been taken into their father's confidence or been privy to the family's secrets, especially its place as one of the founding families of the Sons of Man. "It happens," their father, a cold, one-eyed pirate, believed. "Some just don't have the stomach for greatness."

Dean, on the other hand, was his father's boy, groomed from childhood to take over the firm as well as the old man's seat on the Sons of Man Council. It had not earned him any more love from his father—the old man was incapable of such a worthless emotion—but it had earned him something he considered vastly more important. It earned him respect, and eventually the old man's chair.

Good thing, too, as the Sons of Man needed the iron will of a Newbury at this critical time in their history. They had always prospered the most during times of strife and war. And they'd never been afraid of growth. Gun runners during the American Revolution and the Civil War, they were now international arms dealers, selling to whoever had the money. They'd smuggled alcohol during Prohibition, and drugs—heroin, cocaine, marijuana, you name it—while Nancy Reagan was urging everybody to "just say no."

Their main money-maker at the beginning of the twenty-first century was dealing in black-market oil. With the complicity of officials at the United Nations, the Sons of Man had made hundreds of millions off of the "Food for Oil" program, under which Saddam Hussein's government had been allowed to sell oil in order to pay for food for the Iraqi people. Of course, very little food ever made it to anyone's table, and most of the oil had been shipped off to the black market.

The Iraq War closed that nice little money pot but provided other avenues, including siphoning off oil and then having "insurgents"—actually mercenaries—blow up pipelines and refineries to disguise the theft. The war had also provided its own bump in the arms trade; the real insurgents needed weapons, too.

The organization that the Sons of Man had created and maintained over so many centuries was no mere crime syndicate. Early on, the leaders had realized that in order to obtain real power and protect their interests, they needed to divest. Their sons and nephews were steered into legitimate business interests, especially banking and finance, as well as careers in law, politics, the military, and journalism—after all, the public needed to be told what to believe.

They moved in the best circles of society, model citizens with roots in the community and a history of public service—so long as it served the council's aims. In New York, they belonged to the finest clubs, contributed to conservative politicians, especially those in the family, and for more than two centuries attended old Trinity Church at Broadway and Wall Street in Lower Downtown. In fact, a number of Newburys and their relatives had been buried in the ancient graveyard there along with John Jacob Astor and Alexander Hamilton. Since 1842, when the old cemetery ran out of room, family members had had to settle for a mausoleum at the second Trinity cemetery at the Chapel of the Intercession at 155th Street and Broadway.

As the families' influence grew, so did their ambitions—and their intolerance for weak-willed liberals, who, in their view, kowtowed to anybody who wasn't white. The Sons of Man were going to save the United States for white people, at least those who deserved it and were willing to leave the Sons in power. But it wasn't so much a matter of patriotism—Newbury could have given a fig about the Constitution. It was self-interest, fueled by racism and xenophobia, that motivated them.

To Dean and the other members of the council, the country was being overrun with "mud people"—all the brown, yellow, semi-literate scum of the Earth. The thought of welcoming the world's "huddled masses yearning to breathe free" was pure stupidity. But that would all change when the

Sons of Man wrested control of the economy from the hands of legitimate authorities and ran the government of the most powerful nation on Earth.

And the best tool for that was fear. The American people needed to be frightened into giving up their so-called liberties and hand the reins of power over to the Sons of Man for the sake of "security." The Patriot Act had been a good start, especially as a means of keeping tabs on the American people under the ruse of fighting terrorism. That's why McCullum's harping and insistence on more stringent limits and increased oversight by Congress had been particularly irritating.

Tyranny and oppression, my ass, Dean Newbury thought. *Leadership and security. Get 'em scared enough, and the American public couldn't care less about privacy and the loss of a few liberties they don't need or use anyway. Too bad our guy messed up at the St. Patrick's Day parade and didn't kill Senator McCullum, that big, dumb bastard. We'll have to remedy that some other time.*

Soon Americans would welcome strong men with a clear vision who would protect them from themselves and all their altruistic intentions. Someday the border would be closed and the mud people—the niggers and the spics and the gooks and the Arabs, and toss in the Jews—would be kept out or pay the penalty in slave labor and death camps.

In the meantime, keeping on track meant striking a deal with the devil, this so-called Sheik. It also meant putting his nephew to the test. Would he pass and take his place on the council? Dean Newbury hoped so. He wasted no energy on emotions like love and compassion: Even the death of his own son, Quilliam—who died in combat, a decorated hero—had only made him angry because he had disobeyed him. But he did believe in the family legacy, and unless V. T. assumed his seat, the name Newbury would disappear from the council, replaced by the name of some lesser family.

Yet he would do his duty. If V. T. failed the test, Dean wouldn't mourn his death any more than he had his brother's. *Myr shegin dy ve, bee eh,* he thought. What must be, will be!

"I'll tell you right now," Dean Newbury said to V. T., scowling as he walked toward the door of the office, which had been his brother's, "idiots in Congress like Tom McCullum will get us all killed. All this whining about losing civil liberties is nice to chat about in the halls of Congress, but we're in a war, and wars sometimes call for extreme measures."

The old man saw that his nephew was looking out the window. "Enjoying the view?" He tried to make his voice sound friendly. Seeing him there with New York spread out below him, he thought there had to still be a chance that V. T. would grasp the benefits of money and power. *Yes, he thought, all the little people of the world are living out there below you.*

V. T. turned toward him. "I was just remembering how my dad would stand here for the longest time looking at Central Park."

"Ah, yes, Vincent was always one to watch the leaves grow on trees," Dean Newbury said. He caught the look of pain that crossed his nephew's face. "That didn't come out the way I meant it. I was just trying to say that he knew how to stop and smell the roses. Sometimes I envied him for that." *Like hell I did.*

"I understood what you meant," V. T. answered. "And anyway, you're right in both cases. Dad would have probably preferred to be a gardener more than a lawyer; watching leaves grow and smelling roses would have agreed with him, especially after Mom died. But that doesn't mean you and I have to get our hands dirty. Right?"

Dean Newbury uttered what he hoped sounded like a proud-uncle laugh. *That's more like it. There might be hope yet.* "Right you are, my boy. To each his own, which is why I asked you to come in on a Saturday to meet a very important new client whom I'd like you to take on. We're going to meet him right now. So if you're done watching leaves grow . . . ha ha . . . let's go do a little business."

"Let's," V. T. replied. "I've been admiring a certain little BMW, and I could use the cash."

"Good, good . . . plenty for that," Dean Newbury chuckled. "Oh, by the way, how's your French?"

"Je parle français comme un indigene."

"Like a native, eh? *Très bon.*"

Dean led the way down the hall and through a set of frosted double doors, bringing them to a small anteroom outside another elevator door, which V. T. understood led to a private underground parking level for VIP clients who did not wish to be seen. In front of them was another door, but this one was stainless steel and looked more like the entry to a vault than a meeting room. Dean Newbury pressed the palm of his hand against a panel and the door slid open.

V. T. recognized one of the three men in the room. "Well, this is a surprise, Espey Jaxon," he said. "I'd heard you quit the agency and were working private security."

"And it would seem that what I heard was true, too; you left the DAO," Jaxon said, crossing the room to shake V. T.'s hand. "Who would have thought that would happen?"

"For either of us," V. T. agreed. "But I guess at some point public service salaries and hours lose their glamour."

"Amen to that," Dean Newbury interjected. "You both did your part for the unappreciative public. There's nothing wrong with looking out for yourselves now."

"Nothing wrong at all," Jaxon agreed. He turned to the two other men who'd remained talking over by the window. They both appeared to be of Middle Eastern descent, but after that, they could not have been more different.

The first man, obviously the one in charge, was tall and built like an athlete, with wavy black hair oiled back in jetsetter style. His face was tan, rather than swarthy, and a perfect smile radiated beneath the hooked nose and pencil-thin mustache and above a neatly trimmed goatee. His clothes were obviously expensive and perfectly tailored, accentuated by gold cufflinks with diamonds and a diamond stickpin in his tie.

"V. T. Newbury, I'd like you to meet Prince Esra bin Afraan Al-Saud," Jaxon said in French. "And his administrative assistant and chief financial officer, Amir Al-Sistani."

Al-Sistani gave V. T. an odd, appraising look and then bowed slightly. He was a small, slightly built man, dressed modestly in an off-the-rack business suit and thick, black-rimmed glasses that gave him the air of an accountant. He wore a *ghutra*, the all-white version of the traditional Arabic *keffiyeh* headdress.

"Ah, Mr. V. T.," said the prince, crossing the room with his hand extended and a wide smile, the same one he probably employed at the net following the defeat of a tennis opponent. "I've heard so much about you from your uncle. I am pleased to make your acquaintance and trust that our time together will be mutually beneficial to myself and your law firm. I hope you do not mind that we speak French rather than English?"

"Not at all," V. T. responded. "I rather enjoy the language and get so little opportunity to practice it."

"Well, you speak it very well, and I'm afraid my English is poor. My associate, Mr. Al-Sistani, does not speak it at all," he said. "And unfortunately, I don't believe that any of you speak Arabic. Nor is our lovely translator, Marie Smith, able to be with us this morning."

V. T. got the impression that the prince was not at all happy that the "lovely translator" was absent. He came off as another oil-kingdom playboy who probably wasn't entirely happy unless young women were fawning around him.

"I'm afraid Mr. Al-Sistani also lacks some of the usual social graces," the prince added, nodding at his CFO. "However, he is an excellent money manager, and I couldn't do what I do without him."

Al-Sistani inclined his head at the compliment. *"Merci,"* he mumbled, looking back up at the prince like a dog hoping for a bit of praise.

"Social graces are fine, but this is a business meeting, so perhaps it's just as well," Dean Newbury said and invited the others to sit down at the large circular table.

This was the second time V. T. had been in the room—the first had been to meet a dozen or so of his uncle's "friends and trusted advisers"—and he noted again the unusual gold inlay work in the wooden table. The symbol matched the one on his ring, or more accurately, the ring Quilliam had once worn that his uncle had given to him as a "family heirloom."

After they were seated, Dean Newbury turned to his nephew. "Prince Esra is essentially here for two reasons, in addition to a little nightlife," he said with a chuckle. "One is to present a $1.3 million check to build a religious school on the grounds of a mosque in Harlem. A very commendable thing to do. However, he is also the president and chief executive officer of Kingdom Investments, Inc., one of the largest hedge-fund companies in the world. I assume you are aware of what a hedge fund is?"

"My understanding is that hedge funds allow more aggressive strategies than, say, a mutual fund, and aren't as regulated," V. T. answered, "and because they only allow a maximum of a hundred investors, the minimum buy-in can be in the millions."

"Exactly," Dean Newbury said. "Prince Esra's company is one of the top five hedge funds in the world. As such they have billions of dollars invested, but perhaps more importantly, that money allows them to leverage many times that. . . . We're talking hundreds of billions."

V. T. looked properly impressed as he glanced over at the prince, who was studying his own immaculately manicured fingernails. When he looked, however, at Al-Sistani, the little man was staring at him. *As you'd expect of the man who actually has to look after all that money,* he thought.

"Anyway, to date, Prince Esra has been content to deal with the banks and trading firms he uses from afar. However, now he's decided to meet with them and actually get them to compete against one another for his business. I'm afraid there's some concern that they've been taking him for granted," Dean Newbury continued. "As you might imagine, there are enormous commissions in these transactions; we're talking millions in a single trade. So the incentive to compete is strong, and the prince wants to meet face to face with them and hear who's going to put the best plan together."

"Sounds logical," V. T. said.

"We've agreed that you will be chief counsel for the prince while he's in this country."

"Well, I'm flattered," V. T. replied. "But I'm afraid that my experience as a business lawyer is negligible. I'm sure the firm has more qualified people."

"Perhaps for the detail work and for drawing up contracts," Dean agreed. "But as I've explained to the prince, you have considerable background in ferreting out and prosecuting white-collar criminals. He doesn't want to run afoul of the Securities and Exchange Commission, and very much wants us—you—to protect his interests from unscrupulous bankers and stockbrokers."

Dean Newbury waited for a beat. "Besides, a lot of this business will transpire in a social setting. These people will wine and dine the prince and his entourage. I know that you're not unfamiliar with this set, and I think you're the man to guide the prince through these shark-infested waters. You'll act as the lead representative of our firm, and we can have some of the associates worry about the nitty-gritty paperwork."

V. T. thought about the offer for a moment. "Sounds exciting. I'm in," he said. "And I'll do my best on both counts."

Prince Esra smiled broadly. "Good . . . excellent. You'll keep an eye on those criminal bankers and stockbrokers for me. Mr. Al-Sistani will give you my itinerary and plan on joining us as we are 'wined and dined,' and," he winked, "perhaps there will be time for exploring a city that never sleeps at night."

"I'll try to keep up," said V. T.

"Well then, that settles it, 'Myr *shegin dy ve, bee eh,*'" Dean Newbury said.

"I'm afraid I do not understand," the prince said.

"It's something we like to say around here," Dean replied. "It's Manx . . . from the Isle of Man, which is where our family originated. It means, 'What must be, will be.'"

"Ah," the prince replied. "We Muslims have a similar sentiment, '*Inshallah.*' It means, 'as God wills.'"

16

Karp left the family loft and emerged from the five-story brick building on Crosby Street. Stopping on the sidewalk, he sniffed the air suspiciously and then smiled. That air actually smelled clean and lacked the usual *odeur de la ville*. A cool breeze had blown in from the harbor during the night, one of the first harbingers of the coming fall.

It was Saturday and he was considering which way to head for a morning walk. Marlene and the twins were already gone; the boys were staying with her father for the weekend, and she was off with the Baker Street Irregulars, plus Kenny Katz and Fulton. Her alarm had gone off before dawn, after which she'd expertly eluded his wandering hands as he tried to pull her back beneath the sheets.

"Should have thought of that last night, Lover Boy, but you were snoring before your head hit the pillow. The others are going to be here in a half hour. I don't have time for your nonsense."

Defeated, Karp had fallen back asleep until half-awakened by the presence of a warm body crawling into bed with him. Groggily hoping that Marlene had changed her mind, he turned and was shocked wide awake when the tongue that licked his lips was not hers but that of Gilgamesh, Marlene's 150-pound Presa Canario guard dog. Gilgamesh was her "baby"—trained to immediately obey both hand and voice commands, and capable of instantaneous violence, but otherwise a great big slobbery puppy.

"Guck!" Karp complained and wiped his mouth with the sleeve of his nightshirt. Giving up on more sleep, he got out of bed to read the newspaper over a cup of coffee. His eyes went first to a story about the Yankees trying to catch the Red Sox, which meant something wasn't right with the world. Then he read the story about Senator McCullum criticizing the Patriot Act again. He'd met the man, heard him speak on the post-9/11 erosion of civil liberties, and respected him.

"*The means of defense against foreign danger historically have become the instruments of tyranny at home,*" Karp read aloud. Now, there was someone whose politics he also liked, James Madison. The man had been absolutely devoted to the creation of a Constitution that would protect the individual from an intrusive government.

Got another quote for you, Tom, he thought. *Dad liked the one from Abraham Lincoln. 'America will never be destroyed from the outside. If we falter and lose our freedoms, it will be because we destroyed ourselves.' I think we do well to think on that one a while, too.*

When he finished the paper, Karp climbed into one of the sweatsuits he favored on weekends and went outside. He was still recovering from the gunshot wounds, especially the one to his right leg, which he blamed for the pounds he'd gained over the past year and was now determined to lose.

It didn't help that Marlene had learned to cook from her Sicilian immigrant mother, the acknowledged neighborhood queen of meatballs in marinara sauce served over linguini. Nor did it help that he was battling an addiction to the hot pastrami–corned beef combo sandwiches, served with old Coney Island curly fries and an assortment of dill pickles, at the Carnegie Deli on 54th and Seventh Avenue.

Karp salivated like Gilgamesh at the thought of the sandwich, but that was a bit far to hike—all the way on the north end of Times Square. He could have taken a subway, but he'd promised his physical therapist and his waistline that today he'd walk. If he then deserved sustenance of some sort that he found along the way, at least he would have earned it.

He allowed himself a moment to gaze north up Crosby. He loved that street, but sometimes life got so busy that he hardly noticed it anymore.

Considering the value of real estate in lower Manhattan, it was amazing that the little street, with its old, low-rise brick buildings, small shops, and loft apartments, could survive, surrounded as it was by mountains of high-rise concrete, steel, and reflective glass.

Crosby was still paved with cobblestones, and steel fire escapes clung to the red brick like giant rust-colored insects. Except for those brief moments around midday, the sun rarely found its way into the shadows of the north-south-running lane, and the lack of direct sunlight added to the long-ago feel of the place. The buildings pressed so close from either side of the street—two vehicles couldn't pass without one going up on the sidewalk—that it almost seemed like you could jump from one rooftop to another across the way, with a running start and a stiff breeze at your back.

Even the businesses in the lane seemed part of a different, older New York. Although the original Madame Celeste, for whom the street-level Madame Celeste's Tarot Parlor and Piercing Studio had been named, was no longer on this side of the spirit world, she'd been replaced by a new, thirty-something Madame Celeste named Cindy.

Anthony's Best Shoe Repair in the walk-down shop across the street was still manned by hunchbacked gnome Giuseppe Cumino, who swore that some quiet nights when he was closing shop he could hear voices of long-ago immigrants shouting and laughing in Italian, Polish, and Yiddish. "They were happy here, and their souls don't want to leave," he once told Karp.

Ready to begin his walk, Karp opted for the morning sunlight and turned south for Grand Avenue. He then headed east into Little Italy, where sleepy busboys swept the sidewalks in front of the restaurants or carefully wrote the day's lunch specials on chalkboards next to the door.

His stomach growled as he read the selections, especially one that promised "New York's best cheese coffee-cake." *No disrespect, friend*, he thought, *but I know where the real best cheese coffee-cake is in New York, especially cherry cheese coffee-cake.*

Now he knew where he was going and turned north on Bowery and followed it until it merged with Third Avenue. He enjoyed the city's streets on weekend mornings. The sidewalks weren't as busy as they were week-days, and the people who were out and about weren't in as much of a rush to get wherever they were going. Most seemed to be enjoying a stroll, like himself, or heading toward a favorite sidewalk café or park bench.

Karp wondered how things were going up north on the Hudson with Marlene and the Baker Street Irregulars. He'd also picked up a message from his homicide bureau chief about another body found in the park near Spuyten Duyvil, this one with the numeral 777 carved into the chest.

"Three sevens again, huh?" Karp asked when he called. "What's that, the Devil plus one hundred and eleven?"

"Don't know," the bureau chief said. "The cops say they're hearing about some new gang out of Harlem calling itself the Rollin' 7s, but they're not sure there's a connection yet. Just letting you know that it's now a double homicide."

By the time he reached Il Buon Pane on 29th Street, Karp's wounded leg was aching from the exertion. Thus it was a bitter disappointment to see that the lights of the bakery were off and a sign in the door read "Closed." Only then did he remember that Moishe Sobelman was an Orthodox Jew and that "baking" was one of the prohibited labors on the Sabbath. He was considering whether to take a taxi back to Little Italy for what could have been at most the second-best cheese coffee-cake in the world when he heard a voice behind him.

"Well, if it isn't my friend, the district attorney, come to visit. Shalom. Shalom."

Karp turned and saw the little baker approaching from the north. "Shalom," he replied. "I was indeed hoping for a piece of cherry cheese coffee-cake and some conversation, but I forgot that you'd be closed on the Sabbath."

"A Jew who forgets the Sabbath? I don't mean to lecture, my friend, but there are some things Jews must never forget, and that this is a day for resting from our labors and counting our blessing is one of them." The baker said it with such a twinkle in his eye that Karp knew no offense had been intended. "But come, come, visiting friends is a 'mitzvah,' a good thing, on the Sabbath," Sobelman added, unlocking the door to the bakery.

The way Sobelman carried his keys was another reminder to Karp that there are Jews and then there are Jews. Attaching one's keys to the outside of a piece of clothing, rather than, say, putting them in a pocket, allowed one to avoid violating the prohibition against "carrying useful items" on the Sabbath because the item—be it a set of keys or a piece of jewelry—was then worn and not carried. There were thirty-nine categories of work prohibited by the Talmud, the book of Jewish law. But Jewish scholars had pored over the letter of the laws and found "workarounds" for most categories.

"You sure?" Karp asked, stepping into the bakery and inhaling the intoxicating aroma of bread and pastries. "I shouldn't disturb your Sabbath."

"Nonsense," Sobelman exclaimed. "Like I said, we are supposed to visit with friends and family on the Sabbath—so long as you walk. . . . You did walk?"

"Uh, yes, I walked," Karp replied, thinking that when he left, he was going to have to wait until Sobelman was out of sight if he planned to hail a taxi.

"Good, good," Sobelman replied, "though I would not have held it against you. I keep the Sabbath as I think it works for me, but I leave it for every Jew to find his or her own way. I was just returning from the synagogue. The reading of the *Sefer Torah* was particularly long today. Ever since the bombing, the services have grown longer and longer. But I am starving. You will join my wife and me for *shalosh seudot?*"

Karp's stomach growled its acceptance but he shook his head. "No, thanks. I couldn't impose like that."

"Please, it's been a long time since we last had you under our roof," Sobelman said, "and we would consider it an honor. I observe the Sabbath more for the enjoyable aspects—the eating and conversations with one's friends and family—than because I like not doing anything."

Thinking that he would, indeed, enjoy spending time in this man's company, Karp let himself be persuaded. "Well, then I accept."

Sobelman led the way through the bakery to the back of the store, where stairs led to the apartment above.

Karp found himself in an entryway surrounded on both sides by what appeared to be old family photographs. Most of them looked to have been taken many years before and reminded him of photographs in the Ellis Island museum of immigrants from Eastern Europe. The men wore stiff black coats and wide-brimmed hats, or *kippah,* while the women dressed conservatively. He noticed a more recent photograph of a smiling young man in a suit next to a beautiful young woman in a wedding dress. It took him a moment to realize that the couple was Moishe Sobelman and his wife, Goldie.

"Welcome to our humble home," Sobelman said as his wife appeared, surprised to see a guest. "Ah, my bride. Look, my love, who came to visit on the Sabbath, our friend, Butch Karp."

Goldie Sobelman smiled shyly and then signed her response to her husband, who translated for Karp. "After scolding me for not giving her more warning, she said that you are most welcome. And she's off to set another place at the table," he said.

"You are both too kind," Karp said. He pointed to the older photographs. "Are these your families?"

The baker looked fondly at the photographs. "Yes, these are the only photographs we were able to find after the war. The people in them are all dead—none survived the camps. Only Goldie and I from both of our families."

Karp bowed his head. "I'm sorry. I can't imagine that kind of loss."

"Neither could I until it happened," Sobelman said quietly. "But that was a long time ago, and the Talmud forbids us to discuss unpleasant things on the Sabbath. This is a day for pleasant conversations."

The baker led Karp into the dining room, where the latter noted the double candlestick holder on the table, with long white candles that were already lit. Karp's own parents were non-observant Jews, ignoring most customs except for Passover and Chanukah, which they'd often spent with his grandparents. And then there was his bar mitzvah, of course. However, he knew that the two candles symbolized the two admonitions: to observe the Sabbath by refraining from forbidden activity, and to remember their heritage in their words, thoughts, and actions. The candles would have been lit shortly before sunset on Friday and would be extinguished at sundown Saturday.

Suddenly, Karp felt naked. "I apologize," he said. "My head isn't covered."

Sobelman, who was still wearing his *kippah* from the synagogue services, reached up to the top of a wooden vanity and found another, which he offered to Karp. "I keep a spare for such occasions."

Insisting that Karp sit in what was obviously his own favored chair, Sobelman then took a seat between it and where his wife would sit. "So what brings the district attorney to my little bakery? Surely not just the cherry cheese coffee-cake?"

"And why not?" Karp said. "It's the best in the Five Boroughs. It's hard to find the best of anything, so I better enjoy it while it lasts."

Sobelman's face fell into an expression of mock horror. "What? You have some word that I will not be here much longer?"

Karp chuckled. "No, nothing like that. I was actually out to get exercise and thought that I might reward myself." He explained how his political rival, Rachman, had tried to shoot her way to the post he now held.

Sobelman wagged his head. "I remember reading the newspaper accounts of the shooting. Such a thing to happen in America, but politics is a dirty business, so I'm told."

Goldie appeared with a plate of boiled chicken and then sat down. "But again, such a topic is not for this day," her husband said. "Instead, let us break *challah* bread together."

———

The three were soon eating and laughing like old friends. Goldie was as much a part of the conversation as Moishe and Karp; she simply signed whatever she wanted to say, and then her husband relayed her contribution to Karp. When they finished the main course, she "found" three pieces of cherry cheese coffee-cake, which she served with strong black coffee. Finishing, she stood and started clearing the dishes, pushing Karp down by his shoulders when he tried to rise up to help her. She signaled to her husband.

"She said, 'It's my kitchen, and I won't have a man lumbering around in it and breaking my china.' Don't worry, my friend, I've tried for more than fifty years, but she'll have none of it."

As Goldie left the room, Karp again noted how Moishe followed her with his eyes until he could no longer see her. "A wonderful woman, your wife," he said.

"The best," Moishe nodded, "meaning no disrespect to your lovely wife or anybody else's. But she has been through more than any person should have ever had to face, much less someone with such a gentle soul. . . . She was just a girl when she and her entire family—father, mother, two brothers, and sister—were taken to Auschwitz. They were all murdered, but she survived because the Nazi 'doctors' used her for experimental surgery they were trying on pre-pubescent girls."

Sobelman stopped a moment to gather himself. "It is the reason we could not have children. It is also the reason she does not speak. There is nothing physically wrong with her voice; she simply has chosen not to speak. She once told me with sign language that it was because, if she opened her mouth to speak, all she would be able to do is scream."

"Where did you meet?"

"Ah, this is where you and I could both say what a small world it is," he said. "As the war was ending, I joined up with Jewish partisans in Poland when we came upon right-wing Polish Nationalists who were preparing to murder a group of Jews, all former prisoners at Auschwitz. She was among them. We killed the murdering pigs and took the survivors who could walk with us. Goldie was young, and beautiful even though she weighed no more than a child half her age. For some reason, she refused to leave my side, though I assure you there was no physical relationship between us—that would take many years of gaining her trust and love."

Sobelman recalled how his band of resistance fighters and the people they'd saved had fled west, hoping to avoid the approaching Russians, who had no more love for Jews than the Nazis did. They made it to the American sector in Austria. However, there they were among the millions of other people displaced by the war. Some of the Jews they were with took the first opportunity to leave for Palestine, where, rumor had it, there was going to be a Jewish state. But as a boy growing up in Poland, he'd seen a photograph of the Statue of Liberty with the New York skyline in the background, and he dreamed of going to America, where even Jews were safe.

"We had no money, but we had hope," Sobelman recalled. "One day in the refugee camp I saw an important man—I could tell he was important because his clothes had no patches or holes and his shoes were new. He was looking for someone, and I was able to help. He asked me about myself and Goldie, who clung to me like a child. I told him our stories, and when I finished, he cried . . . not much or loudly, but like a strong man cries when he hears of injustice. Then this man, this good man, put us on a boat to America, where we were given papers, and I was given a job working for the second-kindest man I ever met, Alfredo Turrisi, who owned this bakery. I believe, though, that you know the man who saved us, no?"

Karp was silent for a moment, feeling guilty about his earlier worries that this kind little baker might have been considering blackmail. "My guess is that he would be Vladimir Karchovski."

"Yes, your great-uncle, Mr. Karchovski," Sobelman confirmed. "I know that in your position, you must be careful regarding your association with a man like him, who has broken the law. But as someone who shares the same blood, you should be very proud of the man he really is. When I had some money, I happily offered to pay him for all he had done for us, but he wouldn't take a cent. He said the world owed us and he would not charge us until that debt was paid. I do not agree; the world doesn't owe me or Goldie. The ones responsible for what they did to us, yes, they owe a debt that cannot be repaid. But most of them are dead, so I give them little thought."

Vladimir Karchovski had also paid for the wedding of Goldie Klarsfeld and Moishe Sobelman, including the dress Karp had seen in the wedding photograph. "For that he has never asked one cent," Sobelman said. "Nor would he accept anything more than some of my cheese coffee-cakes—he prefers blueberry—which I have delivered to his home every Friday before the Shabbat for all these years. I am proud that he accepts even that much."

The two men sat quietly for a minute, sipping their coffee. Karp wanted to ask about the tattooed number on Moishe's forearm and how he came to be a partisan fighting in the woods of Poland. And about his experience with the bombing of the synagogue on Third Avenue. But he knew that there'd already been too much talk of dark things for the Sabbath. Sobelman seemed to sense this, too, and so for the rest of his visit they steered clear of anything troubling.

When Karp announced it was time for him to leave, Sobelman said, "I'll walk part of the way with you. I'm supposed to be resting after such a good meal, but I'm reluctant to part with such good company. Besides, God did not 'rest' on the seventh day of creation—that is a misinterpretation of the Torah. After all, why would an all-powerful God need to rest? The real translation is that on the seventh day, God 'ceased,' meaning He ceased His work and then stepped back to survey what He had done. Like any great artist who is pleased with a work and considers it finished, He stopped and enjoyed the accomplishment. So while I have ceased my work, a walk with a friend is something to be enjoyed."

Moishe kissed his wife and promised to return soon so that they could celebrate the end of Sabbath together. She then handed Karp a paper bag from which the smell of warm coffee cake emanated. *I can always diet tomorrow,* he thought after thanking her.

Sobelman locked the door of the bakery, and they set off down Third Avenue. They didn't say much for the first couple of blocks, just remarks about the meal and their respective wives. Then the baker glanced up at Karp and cleared his throat. "I'm sorry if this constitutes work, but something has been troubling me."

"What's that, Moishe?"

"I have been following this case of the woman who murdered her children. I do not understand these people who say she was not responsible for her actions. I was watching the *Off the Hook Show* the other night when the defense attorney, I believe her name was Lewis, was interviewed, and that's what she says. Did you see the show?"

"I saw some of it," Karp acknowledged.

In fact, he'd watched because it might give him an indication of Lewis's strategy at trial. The trial judge, Timothy Dermondy, had imposed a gag order, meaning neither side was supposed to discuss details of the case with the media, but Lewis had simply ignored it. Nothing unusual about that, but Karp had not expected Lewis to point at Charlie Campbell, who was also a guest, and blame him for the deaths of the children and her client's mental deterioration.

"If anybody should have been charged in this case, it is the man sitting right there," Lewis said as Campbell's mouth dropped open. He looked to someone off-screen in a silent but easily understood cry for help.

"What do you mean?" Barry Queen, the host of the show, asked.

Karp realized right away that it was a setup. He knew she was going to make the accusation before she did it. *Better step out of the batter's box, Charlie, they're about to throw one high and tight.* . . . *A little chin music,* he thought.

"What I mean is that shortly after the birth of their second child, Jessica Campbell considered killing her child and herself."

Queen looked shocked. "I don't understand."

"As a result, the Campbells consulted a psychiatrist."

"Any particular reason?"

There's the setup pitch, Karp thought.

"I really must protest," Charlie stammered. "This was a family matter, and I'd appreciate it if you'd respect our privacy."

Steeee-rike One!

"I'm sure you would, Mr. Campbell, but I don't represent you," Lewis spat. "We have the sworn deposition of Dr. Harry Winkler, one of the most respected experts in postpartum depression in the world, who at that time diagnosed my client with severe postpartum depression. I will leave the details for the trial, but the long and short of it is that Dr. Winkler strongly advised the Campbells against having more children, as the condition could be expected to worsen after each childbirth. Charlie Campbell, in particular, was warned that another pregnancy posed a great risk to Jessica and the children."

"This really is a mischaracterization of the truth . . ." Charlie squeaked, trying to recall some verbiage from his unused law degree.

Steeee-rike Two!

"Hardly," Lewis sneered. "But like I said, this will all come out at trial. I don't want to taint the jury pool by arguing the evidence on television."

Like hell you don't, Karp scoffed.

"However, we'll be able to prove that Charlie Campbell, despite this dire warning, insisted that Jessica bear a third child. He wanted a boy in order to further his political career."

"Are you saying . . . ?" Queen ventured.

" . . . that he used his penis as a weapon that destroyed the mental health of Jessica Campbell until she actually believed that God was ordering her to kill their three children to save their souls. . . . In the state she was in, impregnating her was no different from putting a gun in her hands and telling her to pull the trigger."

Of course, the network had bleeped the word "penis," but the whole television world knew what she had said. The camera panned back so that it now included Charlie Campbell, who sat staring straight ahead, blinking like a windshield wiper set on intermittent.

"So, Mr. Campbell, pretty heavy stuff. Do you have any comment?" Queen asked.

Blink. Blink. Blink.

At home in front of the television, Karp had to laugh. *Oooooh, beaned him with a pitch! He's out cold. Would somebody please pinch-run for Mr. Campbell?*

"So that's what I meant," Lewis said, as if she'd merely been answering an innocent question, "when I said that if the district attorney of New York wants to prosecute somebody for the deaths of the Campbell children, it should be the one who couldn't keep his *BLEEP* in his pants."

"Well, that's about all the time we have tonight. I'd like to thank my guests Linda Lewis and Charlie Campbell . . ." The lawyer dipped her head a smidge. Charlie's lower lip quivered; it appeared he might cry as soon as the camera went black.

Karp shed no tears for Charlie Campbell. But he'd picked up a few useful hints about Lewis's approach to the insanity defense.

Kenny Katz had also seen the show and called him at home. To counter the defense's psychiatric testimony, he wanted to bring in a psychiatrist he'd found who thought the whole "postpartum depression syndrome" was a bunch of bullshit.

"We're not going to need him," Karp responded.

"But they're going to be piling it on with this Winkler and that other shrink, Nickles," the younger man complained. "They'll spend hours telling the jury the same psycho-babble."

"Let 'em. We'll counter with the facts."

"But we need someone who can speak the language and cut through the crap," Kenny contended.

"We don't if we don't get into it," Karp replied and left it at that.

———————

It's driving Katz batty, Karp thought as he and Sobelman reached 14th Street, where the old man pulled up and said that he needed to get back to Goldie.

"So do you think Mrs. Campbell should be prosecuted for a crime?"

Sobelman looked troubled. "I'm not an expert on law. I suppose anyone who would murder another human being is crazy. But if I understand correctly, the legal issue is whether she knew what she was doing was wrong?

And do we differentiate between murder committed in a fit of rage, or for money, or because a person was told to kill by someone in a position of authority?"

"What if that someone was God or if they believed it to be God?" Karp asked.

Sobelman scoffed and brushed away the idea with a wave of his hand. "That's right. Blame it on God. . . . God is on their side . . . God told them to commit murder in His name. . . . God hates non-believers and Jews and innocent children and wants them all dead. Can't people hear the voice of Evil and understand it's not God's fault?"

The little baker shook his head sadly. "I'm sorry, Mr. Karp, I've had quite enough of human beings blaming their own evil behavior on 'higher authorities,' whether it's God, or the Führer, or Osama bin Laden. We are each responsible for our actions. We can refuse to do evil in some other name, or we are just as guilty. Unless we are so incapable of reasoning that we are no more than a beast in the fields that does not know that killing the farmer's sheep is wrong, then we are responsible. And those of us who watch the slaughter are just as guilty if we do nothing to make them accountable."

"We are each guilty of the good we did not do," Karp said, recalling a similar conversation with his daughter.

"Voltaire," said Sobelman. He held out his hand to say goodbye, exposing the old tattoo on his forearm. He noticed Karp's eyes drift to the mark. "Do you know where your family came from . . . in the old country?" he asked Karp.

Karp nodded. "Yes, Poland."

"Indeed, and have you ever heard of a place called Sobibor?"

"It sounds familiar," Karp replied, "but I couldn't tell you why."

"Perhaps, then, someday I will tell you why you should know the name," Sobelman said. "But it is a long story, and I've already disturbed the Sabbath."

"No, not at all," Karp replied. "You are kind and too generous. Please, give my thanks again to Goldie. We'll have to have you to our home when this trial is over."

"We'd enjoy that," Sobelman said. "Now, my bride awaits and I must be off."

Karp turned for his own home and, he hoped, his bride. He was disappointed that neither she nor the twins were home, the latter mostly because he wanted their help with the Internet.

An admitted computer caveman, and somewhat proud of the distinction, he at last located a search engine and looked up Sobibor. After reading for an hour, he glanced at the clock. He wanted to call Moishe Sobelman but knew he would not pick up the phone on the Sabbath until after sundown.

So he occupied his time feeding Gilgamesh and then took the dog out for another walk around the block. They got back as the sun was setting, so he placed his call.

"Shalom," Moishe Sobelman answered.

"Shalom," Karp replied. "This is Butch Karp. I just wanted to thank you again for today."

"We both enjoyed it. And I hope it won't be so long before our next meeting."

"Actually, that was another reason I called," Karp said. "I spent a little time when I got home researching Sobibor." There was silence on the other end as the baker waited for him to go on. "I think this is a story that my bar mitzvah class should hear and, if it's not too much trouble, I was going to ask if you'd be willing to discuss it with them."

"It is not a pleasant story, Butch. I cannot tell it without expressing the horror of that time. Their parents will complain that I've given their children nightmares."

"I'll make sure their parents are present," Karp replied. "And if they should have trouble sleeping, it's better than ignorance, especially after what happened in July."

"Then let me know the time, and I will be there."

Karp had barely hung up when the telephone rang. The Caller ID indicated it was from Marlene's cell phone. "Hi babe."

"Well, hey good-looking," answered a male voice.

"Oh, uh, hey Jack," Karp laughed. "What have you done with my wife?"

"That's for me to know and you to never find out," Swanburg replied.

"Uh-oh, now I'm sure she's been ruined for any other man," Karp said. "But the kids still need her so if you could send her home when you're through with her, we'd all appreciate it."

"No problem. 'Old love 'em and leave 'em Swanburg' can't be tied down to any one woman, no matter how good looking. And besides, my wife would cut my heart out with a spoon if she found out."

"Ouch. Now that we've settled that, was there a reason you stole my wife's phone and called me?"

"Oh, yeah, that. We thought you might like to know that we found the Volvo station wagon. Marlene's down at the river while they haul it out. She asked me to give you a call."

"That's great news!" Karp exclaimed. "How'd you do it?"

"As the Great Detective would say, it was elementary."

17

Earlier that morning, Marlene had gazed appreciatively at the forests of elm, beech, spruce, and oak trees that lined both sides of the Taconic State Parkway. "Beautiful, isn't it?"

"'Tis indeed," remarked Swanburg, who sat in the passenger seat next to her.

Her other passenger, the forensic anthropologist Charlotte Gates, who was riding in the club cab of her truck, didn't answer.

They'd taken Cross Bronx Expressway out of Manhattan and merged onto Interstate 95 heading north. Their destination was a small hamlet on the Hudson River called Staatsburg, based on what some people might have called an educated guess, and others pure deductive logic. It didn't matter so long as they located the Campbell family's station wagon and its tragic crew of three small bodies.

Gates had fallen silent by the time they hit the Major Deegan Expressway and stayed quiet when they turned onto the parkway. Marlene thought she might have been sleeping, but when she looked in the mirror she saw that Gates was staring out the window. *It has to be tough on her,* Marlene thought. *She's the one who has the most contact with the dead.*

In front of her, Fulton drove the DAO Lincoln with Kenny Katz and Detective Marj Cobing on board. Behind her was an NYPD van marked

"NYPD Dive Team," towing a rubber-pontoon Zodiac. Inside the van were four members of the dive team and geologist James Reedy, who was explaining how they were going to go about locating a small car in a big, muddy river.

After the meeting with the 221b Baker Street Irregulars, the next step had been for Detective Cobing to speak to Jessica Campbell's parents at their loft in SoHo. Although gracious enough on the telephone when the detective called to arrange an interview, Liza Gupperstein had been hostile when Cobing arrived.

"Why should we talk to you?" she said after inviting Cobing into her living room. "Our daughter is sick and needs help. But that Nazi Karp wants to put her in prison. Can't he see that she's already suffered enough?"

"I avoided saying what I was thinking—that those three children had suffered worse," Cobing told the search team that morning. "Instead, I told her, 'Look, I know you're hurting. And I understand where you're coming from. I have a child myself, and I'd do anything to protect her. But I don't make the decisions on whether to prosecute someone or not. I just try to gather all the facts I can, and then give them to the district attorney, who makes the decision on how to handle the case.'"

"That still doesn't give us a reason to talk to you," Liza had told her.

"Then she started crying," Cobing recalled. "So I said, 'Look, I don't need you to talk about Jessica. What I'm trying to do now is find your grandchildren. We know they're dead; it's time to bring their bodies home and put them to rest.'"

"A stranger could have taken them," Liza had blurted out. "One of Charlie's political enemies . . . or one of these right-wing nuts who doesn't like Jessica's politics. He could be holding them for ransom, or . . ."

"I didn't know how to respond," Cobing said. "She just wasn't dealing with reality. But her husband touched her arm, real gentle like, and told her, 'Please, Liza, enough. We have to face this.' Then his voice cracked and he said, 'The babies are gone. And the cold, hard truth is that our daughter, their mother, took their lives.'"

Ben Gupperstein had turned back to the detective. "Ask your questions," he'd said. "We will say nothing that might help the DA send our daughter to prison, but we want our grandchildren—their bodies—returned to us. They deserve a decent burial in a place where the people who loved them can mourn properly."

Cobing wiped at her eyes. "I tell you, that was as tough an interview as I've ever done, emotionally speaking. I kept looking at my notebook, but I was on the verge of tears myself. Finally, I asked him if there was any place in particular where the family had gone when Jessica was a child—someplace she would have been happy and would feel comfortable. Near a large body of water."

Benjamin Gupperstein mentioned a beach house they'd once owned on Long Island when their kids were young. But Liza interrupted him. "She loved our little summer cottage on the Hudson River near Staatsburg, just north of Hyde Park," she had said.

"That's right," Benjamin had agreed. "It's about a hundred miles north of here. We'd canoe and picnic in the summers. And sometimes we'd even head up in the winter to go sledding on a big hill in Mills Memorial State Park."

"Jessica never wanted to come back to the city," Liza added. "She would have stayed there, and that's really why she attended Vassar College in Poughkeepsie for her bachelor's degree."

After her interview, Cobing called Swanburg, and they'd agreed that Staatsburg was their best shot. It was in range; the railroad ran right through town; and the killer was familiar with the territory and felt comfortable there.

———

Marlene had followed Fulton when he turned off the Taconic State Parkway onto New York Highway 9-G and from there to North Cross Road into Staatsburg. The trip had taken a little more than two hours.

The convoy met up with Sgt. Larry Washington of the Duchess County Sheriff's Office at Mills Mansion State Park. The search team and police officers congregated around Washington's car, where he had a large map laid out on the hood.

As arranged, Washington, a large black man with salt-and-pepper hair and a belly that hung over his belt, brought detailed U.S. Geological Survey maps that showed the Hudson River and east shoreline. He pointed out the park where they were meeting and then to a road. "This is Highway 9, better known around here as the Albany Post Road, which was originally constructed a couple hundred years ago to connect New York City to Albany in order to deliver the mail, or 'post.' As you can see, it goes right through town and pretty much parallels the river." He pointed to another line on the map that ran along the bank. "That's the Hudson River Railroad, serves Amtrak and commuter trains."

Washington turned to Reedy, who'd been introduced as the Irregular who would do the searching with the dive team. "If I understood the two detectives correctly, you're interested in places where your suspect could have run her car into the river in the middle of the day and then hopped the train back to the city." He cocked his head and waited for someone to tell him differently.

When no one did, he shrugged. "I think that rules out the park itself. Although it's pretty damn big and there's access to the river, including boat ramps and such, it's a busy place, and chances of someone noticing a car go into the river would have been pretty high. But as you can see from the map, there are any number of small roads—some of them paved, others just a couple of ruts through the underbrush—leading to the river. The foliage is dense along the Hudson, and some of the boat ramps are secluded and hidden, unless you're actually out on the water looking toward shore. There are a few places somebody could roll a car into the river without being seen and still easily walk back to Staatsburg to catch the train."

When the police sergeant was finished, Reedy positioned himself in front of the map with a ruler and pencil and began to make grids along the shoreline, starting with an access point north of town that seemed about as far as Jessica Campbell would have been willing to walk. "The trick will be determining how far from a ramp a car would move downriver," he said. "Last March, the river was a few feet higher than it is right now—flowing a lot faster with spring runoff and flooding. There's a good chance that a car could have been carried a ways downstream from the entry point."

The searchers got back in their cars and drove north on the Albany Post Road and then turned toward the river on a small offshoot called South

Mill Road. They'd chosen for their new command post one of the access roads leading to a boat ramp about halfway between the northernmost point of the grid and the town.

As the Baker Street and dive teams began to unload and check their equipment, the Duchess County sergeant and his deputy cordoned off the area to prevent the public from wandering in. "Marj and I are going back to town," Fulton said as he and Cobing stood watching with Marlene and Kenny Katz. "We'll start at the train station and see if anybody recalls seeing Jessica Campbell up here last March. We've checked her credit card purchases. There's nothing for a train or bus ticket, but she could have paid in cash."

"Which would be interesting from the trial standpoint," Kenny said, pulling out a small pad to write himself a note. "Indicates someone who is making a conscious decision to avoid detection, wouldn't you say, Marlene?"

"Seems a logical conclusion," she agreed. "I guess God told her to visit an ATM first."

Surrounded by a rapt audience, Swanburg explained how the Baker Street Irregulars approached locating clandestine graves: "by combining science, the powers of observation, and, admittedly, a bit of luck and intuition."

"We've done our homework," he said. "One of the first assignments was calling the New York district of the U.S. Army Corps of Engineers, which is responsible for the maintenance of navigation channels on U.S. rivers. The Corps keeps the Hudson channel clear to a minimum of 32 feet—not necessarily in all parts or along the banks, but the main shipping channel. It's also deeper, much deeper in parts, so hopefully our car didn't get too far out into the current before it sank. Here's Jim. He can tell you more about how they're going to search for what we cannot see."

Swanburg waved to the geologist, who wore a floppy, wide-brimmed fly-fisherman's hat and an aloha shirt. "Hey Jim, got a moment to explain your gadgets?"

"Sure, the dive team's still got to get the Zodiac off the trailer and into the water," Reedy said. "We first considered using a type of sonar equipment typically used to map the bottom of large bodies of water—the ocean, big lakes. It's useful when looking for certain geological formations that might indicate mineral deposits and potential drilling sites, or searching for lost equipment, and even sunken vessels and aircraft. Essentially it takes 'photographs' of what's below, sort of like satellite imagery, only these images are created by bouncing sound waves off of objects. That data is fed into a computer that translates it into an image that mirrors the geography—like rock formations or crevices. Sometimes it's clear enough to detect the silhouette of manmade objects, like a car. Some of that depends on what objects are next to it and what angle it may have come to rest at on the bottom."

However, he'd decided against sonar. "The river's not deep enough," he explained. "Just like with aerial photography or satellite imagery, you have to be a good distance above the object to understand what you are looking at. Too close and it's all just a blur."

Instead, he'd decided on using a magnetometer. "As you'll remember from our excursion in Idaho when we were searching for a buried car in a gravel pit, the Earth is a big magnet that generates magnetic fields running north and south. Also, objects made of ferrous materials—like iron and steel—have their own magnetic fields. Now the Earth's magnetic field has a certain measurable intensity, but place an object made of iron or steel—such as a Volvo station wagon—and it will ramp up the intensity at that particular spot. The magnetometer detects these changes. As we pass a magnetometer over a certain area, it takes readings and feeds them back into our computer. The result looks like a topographic map, only these lines denote magnetic intensity rather than elevation. Large variations in this topography are what we call 'anomalies,' and that's what we're looking for here."

"How would you know that you're looking at a car, rather than, say, a steel drum?"

"Good question, Sergeant Washington. That's where knowing what we're looking for, and if possible, the amount of ferrous materials used to create it, becomes important. A 1,500-pound car made of steel is going to give off a much more intense reading than a 50-pound steel drum."

"Where's the magnetometer?" Katz asked, looking over at the Baker Street equipment. Nothing looked particularly sexy. Just some machines with graph paper and dials and knobs.

"That gadget sitting in the inner tube over there," Reedy said, pointing. "And we're going to be towing it behind us so that it doesn't get thrown off by being close to the boat's motor."

"Because it's noisy?"

"Well, that's part of it, but really it's because the engine is made of steel and has a magnetic field," Reedy explained. "In fact, that's part of the reason we're using a Zodiac, which is predominantly made out of rubber and has no electromagnetic field."

Swanburg explained that he'd contacted the Volvo manufacturer, and after being "passed from one confused engineer to another" he'd been put in touch with someone who could actually give him the weight of the steel in the car, as well as the percentage of iron in that steel. "It really helps us calibrate the instrument," he said. "In fact, the Volvo guy was a big help all around."

"You know how Volvo is always boasting in their ads about how safety-conscious they are?" Reedy said. "Well, those guys have actually performed tests on how long their cars float if they go into the water. They've even done them with the windows up and with the windows down, which obviously makes the car sink faster. Along with the flowcharts we got from the Corps of Engineers, the 'float times' give us an idea of how far down from each access point we should be concentrating. At least to start."

When the dive team had the boat in the water, Reedy and Gates got in along with the police officer who would be manning the helm. Reedy would be monitoring the magnetometer, while Gates used Global Positioning System equipment to record the exact location of any anomalies he saw. "I'd like to go," Swanburg said, "but these old knees can't take sitting in a cramped boat all day."

"What about them?" Katz asked. He pointed to the dive team, who, after getting their scuba equipment, ropes, and other items out of the van and launching the boat, were settling into lawn chairs.

"They'll only go in if there's something worth checking out," Swanburg said. "The river looks calm. But you'd be surprised how powerful that current is. The Hudson is greatly affected by the Atlantic Ocean's tides, which can push brackish water as far north as Poughkeepsie, and when the tide goes the other way, it's like a vacuum cleaner sucking the water down. It can be dangerous, plus you never know what's moving down the current beneath the surface, like submerged logs, and there isn't much visibility. It's risky business, even for guys who know what they're doing."

Reedy shoved the boat from shore and hopped aboard. The boat roared off into the river and headed north.

Marlene watched until it disappeared around a bend in the river. She knew that once they reached the farthest access road on their search pattern, they would begin the tedious process of going back and forth from one bank to the shipping channel, working their way downstream through the first grid. When they finished the first grid, they would begin the next—back and forth, one run slightly overlapping the last so as not to miss anything, moving below access points with the current.

Marlene started to turn away from the river just as an Amtrak train appeared from the same direction, riding a rail above the water and twenty-five yards from the shore. As the train passed, she could see curious faces pressed against the window as they spotted the police cars and curious gathering on the shore. A child waved to her and she raised a hand to reply before the little face was gone. It reminded her of the photographs she'd seen of the three children, who waited . . . she was sure of this . . . out there beneath the murky waters.

In the meantime, there wasn't much for her to do except go into town to pick up some food for lunch. Cobing and Fulton had already headed for town, so she invited Katz and Swanburg, but they'd settled into chairs and were telling "old war stories." Without any other company to keep her occupied, she decided to call Giancarlo to see how he and his brother were faring with her dad.

"Great!" he replied. "We're going to Coney Island for a Nathan's hot dog and the roller coaster."

Marlene laughed. "Maybe you ought to reverse the order and do the roller coaster before the hot dog . . . if you know what I mean. . . . Anyway, remind me to call my cousin Eric when I get back to confirm our field trip to the New York Stock Exchange."

Giancarlo, who was much more likely to remember than his brother, promised he would. The boys were required to write up a report after spending a day at a New York City landmark for a civics class, and they'd chosen the Exchange. In the past, that would have been easy enough to arrange, as the NYSE had been open to the public. Before 9/11, its viewing gallery had always been brimming with tourists and schoolchildren who had come to learn about the financial center of the American economy. However, after that it was much tougher to get in. Visitors had to be sponsored by someone who already had security clearance . . . such as her cousin Enrique "Eric" Eliaso, who was a floor manager for one of the big trading banks.

"Sure, no problem, be good to see you and those juvenile delinquents you been raising," he'd assured her just that past week. But Eric liked to party and there was a good chance he'd forget to get her and the twins on the list to get in unless she stayed on him.

After leaving the Staatsburg grocery store, Marlene followed the Lincoln back to the encampment. She could tell by the way Fulton bounced out of the car and called to Katz and Swanburg that the hunting trip had been a success.

"You look like the cat that swallowed the canary," she said as she brought the groceries over to the table, where the rest of the group was gathering around Fulton. "What's up . . . or, as the twins' might say . . . 'sup?"

"Word," Fulton replied, miming gang posturing and cracking open a bottle of beer. "I'll let Detective Marj fill you all in. After all, she was the one who sweet-talked the station master into cooperating with Johnny Law."

Cobing gave Fulton a smile. "The station master is exactly what you'd expect in a small town—crotchety and suspicious. He was 'too busy' to want to look at a photo lineup we brought along that includes a head shot of Jessica Campbell. But I turned on the charm, asked a few questions about trains, and that warmed him right up. The man positively loves trains, especially the Hudson Railway trains. I now know more about narrow-gauge and standard-gauge tracks than this city girl ever wanted to know. But he also agreed to look at our photo lineup."

Staatsburg had a population of less than a thousand and for the most part served a few regular commuters—people willing to spend the time to live in the country when their jobs were in the big city. Otherwise, the station didn't do a lot of business, and its staff almost never saw strangers who walked in from nowhere and bought a one-way ticket to Grand Central Terminal. Certainly no one like the woman who'd obviously been wearing a bad wig and cheap, oversized sunglasses.

"This 'stranger' paid cash," Cobing said, "which is apparently unusual and something the station master noted. And he picked her out of the photo lineup."

"So she was wearing a disguise," Marlene said.

Kenny made more notes in his pad. "Let's hope we can find her car," he said. They all turned to look at the river as they heard the Zodiac approaching.

Marlene laid out the lunch materials as the others waited for the boat team to stow their gear and walk to the table. "So anything interesting?" she asked when they arrived.

"Yeah, we've come across several anomalies worth checking out," Reedy said, fishing a cold beer out of the cooler and taking a swig. "Oh man that's good. It's flippin' hot out there with that sun beating on you from above and reflecting back up at you from the water. . . . Anyway, there's one right off that first boat ramp. It's in shallow water, but it isn't a real strong signal—my guess is somebody lost their boat trailer. However, there are several other anomalies with pretty intense magnetic fields that seemed to be about the distance a car might drift after rolling in from the access point. In fact, let's go over the map, and we'll plot them right now."

Using the GPS coordinates Gates had written down, Reedy marked the location of the anomalies on the Corps of Engineers maps. When he finished, he pointed to one near the first access point. "If she rolled the car in there, she would have had to walk nearly four miles back into town."

"Or hitchhike," Washington said. "Folks around here would pick up a woman and give her a lift."

Reedy pointed to two dots on the map. "Nothing much here. However, when we got to the grid right above here, we hooked into a couple of good ones." He pointed to first one and then a second dot on the map. "The readings were so intense, I thought something had to have been wrong. So I recalibrated the machine and we tried again. Same thing." The geologist stopped talking and looked down at his feet.

"You got a hunch," Marlene said. "Give it up, Jim."

Reedy shook his head. "I'm a scientist, we don't believe in hunches."

"Bullshit," Gates snorted. "What's scientific theory except somebody's educated hunch that if such and such happens, this will be the result?"

"Okay, okay," Reedy laughed. "Yeah, if I had to pick a spot right now, my hunch is that's a submerged car," he said, pointing to the second dot. "Doesn't make it our submerged car, but you asked. If we're doing this right, though, we ought to check out the next two grids, at least down to Staatsburg."

"I vote for intuition," Marlene said. "If this hunch doesn't pan out, then we check out the next two grids. Come on, Jim, live a little dangerously."

Reedy scratched under his hat. "It's completely against the scientist's code, but okay," he said with a grin. "Let's do it."

A dozen willing hands pushed the Zodiac back into the current and cheered again as it roared off upriver.

The small Zodiac was soon joined by a much larger boat owned by the Duchess County Sheriff's Office. The big boat was carrying several large anchors with cables attached that were in turn attached to buoys.

With Reedy directing, the sheriff's boat maneuvered into position just upstream of the first of the two anomalies he'd noted. He wasn't willing to completely abandon scientific practice and just go with his hunch, so he'd decided they'd check out the closer of the two first.

The first attempt to drop an anchor misjudged the current; the anchor ended up too far downriver and had to be hauled back to the surface. The second attempt was nearly a bull's-eye.

As Reedy reported their progress like a play-by-play announcer for those on shore, the divers clipped their safety ropes to the cable running down to the anchor and went over the edge. They didn't wear fins, since they weren't going to be able to swim against the current. Instead, they wore extra weight to help them get to the bottom and explore on foot. As they sank beneath the surface, those in the boat and on the shore were glued to their tinny-sounding accounts from their headset radios.

"Jesus, Mary, and Joseph, I can't see my hand in front of my face," said the first diver.

"It is a might murky," replied the second. "Uh, Houston, the Eagles have landed. We're going to walk around a bit on the dark side of the moon here if we can. That's one small step for a man . . ."

The radios were silent for several minutes when the excited voice of one of the divers broke in. "Found it," he shouted. "It's definitely the bumper of a car. Let me work my way around to the side . . ."

A few moments later, the voice reported in again. "What we got here is a genuine Ford Econoline van, circa 1970s."

"Might as well look inside," said the second diver. "Maybe we'll solve some other murder."

"Yeah, a two-fer," said the first. "Hold on, the side door is open. . . . HOLY SHIT!"

The next few moments were filled with sounds of panic. Then a laugh. "Sorry about that folks. I poked my head in the side door of this baby and nearly got run over by one big fuckin' ass sturgeon. Damn thing was the size of a shark!"

"Oh, come on, O'Donnell, I've got goldfish bigger than that," his partner laughed. "I've never see you move that fast on dry land."

"Fuck you, Clanahan. But there's a bunch of crap in the back of this van. Might be worth hauling out of the water someday, but it ain't no Volvo and it's been here awhile."

The divers pulled themselves hand over hand to the surface and climbed back inside the Zodiac. The sheriff's boat then hauled the anchor, cable, and weights back up and the two craft headed for the next anomaly, where the process was repeated.

Once again, those in the boat and on shore could only wait as the two divers sank into the gloom to the river bed, bantering as they went. But within moments O'Donnell's voice came across the radio, sounding excited. "Houston, we practically landed on top of the target," he said. "And we, in fact, have another car, resting partly on its side. I do believe it's a station wagon. Let me see if I can find something to identify it."

The radios were silent again until Fulton grabbed one of the radios from a dive team member on shore. "Goddam it," he swore. "What kind of car is it?"

"Hold your horses, son," Clanahan replied. "Let me see if I can detach the license plate. . . . Got it! I'm coming up."

On shore, Swanburg opened the three-ring binder he'd brought with specifics from the case, including the license-plate number of the Campbell station wagon. He found the right page just as Reedy's voice came over the radio.

"I see an arm coming out of the water, holding a license plate," he shouted. "Hey, I can't see it, face this way. . . . Okay . . . New York plate, A . . . C . . . X . . . 75 . . . 18."

"BINGO!" Swanburg shouted into the microphone. "Ladies and gentle-men, I do believe we've found our Volvo!"

On the river and the shore of the Hudson, an odd assortment of police officers, scientists, investigators, an assistant district attorney, and Marlene Ciampi jumped like children and cheered as they clapped each other on the back. After a minute, Marlene suddenly noticed that Charlotte Gates was still sitting in her chair, with her head between her hands.

"Are you all right?" she asked, regretting that their success at finding a car was only part of the battle. The worst, at least for this woman who was death's constant companion, was yet to come.

Looking up, Gates had tears in her eyes. "Yeah," she said. "I'll take a look at those family shots of the kids before I look in the car. But even then, I'll be okay. I'm here to take them home now, and that will get me through this."

Swanburg came up and patted Marlene and Gates on the shoulder. "I need to get a couple of things for the exhumation. If you want, I'll call Butch and let him know we found the car."

"Yes, please," Marlene said, not wanting to leave the other woman. "Here, take my cell phone."

The team spent the next hour moving their headquarters to the river access point closest to the submerged vehicle. Meanwhile, the second set of divers went back down to the car to seal the doors and hatchback with large rubber bands and hooks. This would prevent the contents of the car from slipping out as the Volvo was pulled to the surface.

A sheriff's office tow truck arrived and extended a cable that could be attached to other cables hooked to the car. Then, with a great whirring of its winch and belching of diesel smoke as the driver revved the engine, the cable was slowly retrieved along with its prize catch.

As the car was gently pulled from its resting spot, Reedy described watching the diver's arm come out of the water with the license plate. "It was like the Lady in the Lake holding up Excalibur," he said. "I was too excited to remember the correct number. But I knew we had it."

"A hunch, eh?" Gates teased.

"Male intuition," Reedy replied. "So much more refined than female intuition. We just don't like to talk about it like girls do."

"Uh-huh," Marlene, Cobing, and Gates all replied.

"Good thing we went with your hunch," O'Donnell said. "I wouldn't have wanted to check out every single flippin' dot on the chart. I mean, it was dark and cold and nasty down there. Something bumped into me— probably just a log or piece of trash—but it scared the piss out of me."

They all gathered on the bank of the river as the car slowly emerged from the water until it sat on the boat ramp, water draining from the interior. Gates directed the tow-truck driver to pull it a little farther to a flat paved spot.

The windows of the car were partly rolled up to about three inches from the top, and the interior was invisible to those outside. "Think we're going to have to cut our way into it?" Washington asked Gates, who circled the car like a boxer looking for an opening.

Gates walked to the driver's side door and pulled the handle. To everyone's amazement, the door opened and water poured out in a torrent that included several small fish, along with sand and mud. "Be careful," she said, stepping around the pile of debris created outside the door. We're going to want to sift through all of that to make sure we don't miss anything."

The tiny anthropologist and her Baker Street Irregular colleagues began the meticulous process of excavating the interior of the car. Bit by bit, Gates removed the silt and debris using a garden trowel and placed it in a bucket, which was taken to a large wood-framed screen to be sifted and examined for evidence.

When they'd finished the front seat compartment, Gates got out of the car to allow Swanburg, the group's photographer, to take shots of the interior. She spoke into a mini tape recorder. "Keys still in the ignition and turned on. The transmission is in 'Drive,' and a stick is wedged between the gas pedal and the seat, depressing it nearly to the floor."

Gates spoke to Cobing. "That engine would have been screaming when she leaned in and pulled it into 'Drive.' She would have had to jump back or roll away from the car. Was there any evidence on her body of something like that happening?"

The detective nodded. "Yeah, we've been wondering about that. In addition to the scratches that had obviously been made by the kids' fingernails, she had abrasions on her knees, the palms of her hands, and one of her elbows . . . like I got when I was a kid playing stickball in the street and fell. That's damn good detective work. What else you got?"

"I'll take that as a hell of a compliment coming from an NYPD detective," Gates replied. She looked back into the interior of the car. "We are going to have to excavate the entire car; you never know what you might otherwise miss. But from here I can see a large footlocker in the luggage area."

Nobody spoke. Nobody moved, until Gates walked around to the back of the car. "It doesn't really matter what order we do the rest of it," she said, "we might as well answer the big question."

The hatchback opened as easily as the front door had, with another gush of water and river muck. With a sigh, the anthropologist and her colleagues began to dig out the footlocker.

"Would some of you strong gentlemen lift the trunk out and place it on the pavement please?" Gates asked.

Several members of the dive team, as well as Washington and his deputy, delivered it to the ground, where the anthropologist bent over to examine the lock. She straightened and walked over to the table that had been set up for evidence gathered during the excavation of the front compartment. All of the objects of potential value had been laid out neatly so they could be photographed and cataloged.

Gates quickly scanned the objects, then picked up a red laminated tag attached to a small plastic bag that bore the name "O'Hara's Hardware." She read the tag then returned to the footlocker, where she knelt and began to turn the combination on the stainless-steel lock.

Speaking into the tape recorder in her shirt pocket as well as for her audience, Gates said, "I'm using a combination written on the tag for a combination lock found in the glovebox of the Volvo station wagon. I'm turning right to 26, back around left to 5, and to the right to 13." She gave the lock a little tug and it fell open.

The anthropologist looked back, her eyes meeting Marlene's, who nodded encouragement.

"She left the combination in the bag from the store where she bought the lock," Gates said. "I guess, she thought God might need the numbers to find the kids."

The sun was dipping low as the search team gathered in a semi-circle around a small, tough woman, who placed her hand on the footlocker and paused. They weren't close enough to see inside when she took a deep breath, flipped up the latch, and opened the lid. But they could tell from the way her shoulders sagged and she slowly lowered the lid again that they'd found what they'd come looking for.

Gates stood up and faced the others. "I'd like to ask everyone for a moment of silence to reflect on the loss of these poor, innocent children."

Without thinking about it, those gathered there next to the Hudson River reached for each other's hands and stood quietly. Up north, a train whistled.

When she was ready to continue, Gates spoke to the others. "I want you to know that there's no shame in sitting this part out. And Sergeant Washington . . ."

"Yes, ma'am," the sergeant responded.

"Now would be a good time to call the coroner."

18

The Sheik struggled to keep the asinine smile on his face as the fat banker hovered in front of him like a big pink sausage stuffed in an expensive but overburdened suit. He wanted desperately to wipe the pig's sweat off after their handshake. *Or, better yet,* he thought, *I want to wipe his blood off of my knife after holding his head up for Al Jazeera television.*

That image was the only way he could keep smiling at the piggy little blue eyes and the small, upturned nose. The top of the man's nearly bald head—a few strands of blond hair bent over like palm trees in a hurricane—shone with sweat.

It was amusing to see how all the other bankers and brokerage-firm bigwigs kept shooting envious looks in their direction while trying to maneuver for a little "face time" themselves. It was the only reason they'd accepted the invitation to attend the Saturday night reception at the administration building on the grounds of the mosque in Harlem for the presentation of the $1.3 million check to build a new madrasah. Otherwise, they wouldn't have come within shooting distance of the heart of Harlem. The fact that it was a Muslim event at a mosque only made them sweat around the starched collars of their button-down Reuben Alexander shirts that much more profusely.

Some of the banks and brokerages had sent a black representative in an effort to demonstrate their support for multiculturalism; they were not any

more comfortable than their white counterparts, having never stepped foot
into Harlem unless it was for a concert at the Apollo. There were no
women, as the competitors had been told that it would not be appropriate
to send female reps. Even the PrimeTech Security Corporation translator,
Marie Smith, who was at least somewhat modest in her dress and had
wisely adopted the use of the hajib when at the mosque, had been asked to
remain outside the room where the men were gathered.

Not one of them wants to be here, The Sheik thought with anger. He could
gauge how uncomfortable each man was—surrounded by dark-skinned
members of the mosque as well as the Saudi contingent—by the number of
times they told him what "a wonderful thing" the donation was for Harlem's
youth, and how they were really all one big ecumenical family: Jews, Christians, Muslims. But, of course, that was the money talking; they didn't believe it any more than he did. *Or they're bigger fools than I thought.*

Over the past week, they'd tripped all over themselves to impress the visitors. They'd been treated to dinner at the best restaurants in town, complete
with lovely female companions in low-cut blouses and dresses immodestly
displaying their breasts and necks. Even their hosts' wives and daughters, introduced at the dinner parties, were dressed like whores, from his perspective. And there'd been many late nights touring the city's discothèques
where the decadence of this depraved culture was on fleshy, gyrating display.

Each banker and trading firm fought to set itself apart from its competitors. There'd been elegant black-tie affairs in lavish penthouse suites off
Park Avenue, and even a "genuine American barbeque" at the beachside
home on Long Island of the president of one of the largest brokerages—who
just happened to "hail," whatever that meant, from Texas. Too bad no one
told the man until it was too late that serving pig to Muslims was a major af-
front. The oaf looked like he'd swallowed his profane tongue when told why
the Saudis were suddenly exiting the party with angry looks and gestures.

Of course, The Sheik had worked that faux pas to his advantage.
Through urgent telephone calls, gift baskets, box seats at Yankee Stadium,
and groveling visits from intermediaries, the man had practically offered
himself up to be raped by a herd of camels not to lose out on a share of the
hedge-fund transactions. Now there was nothing the man would question
and nothing he wouldn't do for, as he called it, "a piece of the pie."

Nothing, The Sheik thought with immense satisfaction. There were two things you could count on with American businesspeople and politicians. First, they had no idea how to deal with men from other cultures. They thought that everybody thought as they did. But despite their best intentions, they were constantly stepping in dung—take their miscalculation of the insurgency in Iraq.

The second was greed. Especially the men in that room; they'd do anything for a few million dollars. *Or do nothing, if that's what the situation calls for.*

And those two things would be the undoing of the United States. Not bombs. Not suicidal jihadis. Not mass fatalities, although they would play a role. But unlike some of his predecessors, who thought that if they punched America in the nose, its people would back down, he thought the opposite. They'd absorbed the 9/11 attacks, and rather than grovel like the French or Spanish, they'd stormed back, even demonstrating a potent willingness to pay for revenge in blood.

No, the key to ultimate victory over the Americans, and by default the rest of Western culture, would be the very thing that made them such a formidable enemy, their economy. *And I am the one who, thanks be to Allah for His blessings, knows how to use their own strength against them to drive a stake through the heart of The Great Satan.*

The fat banker started talking in terrible French punctuated by English translations. "*C'est une chose merveilleuse que vous faites ici.* . . . It's a wonderful thing you're doing here. . . . I'm a Christian myself. . . . *Je suis un chrétien moi-même.* . . . But the important thing is that we are all men of faith and believe in God, and it's the same God. Uh . . . *Mais la chose importante est que nous sommes tous les hommes de la foi et croyons en Dieu, et c'est même Dieu.* So, really, we're all just people of faith. . . . *Tellement, vraiment, nous sommes tous les personnes justes de la foi.* . . . It's wonderful, really, just wonderful. . . . *Il est merveilleux et simplement.*" The pig beamed like he'd just recited a difficult lesson for his high school French teacher.

Idiot, the Sheik thought. *Of course it's not the same God. You are infidels and don't know Allah. If there was ever a time when the roots of your misbegotten religions were intertwined with those of Islam, you long ago deviated from the One True Path. You worship false prophets who bastardized the Word of God as it was revealed again to the Prophet Muhammad, may Allah be pleased with him. Idolaters. You are fools not to recognize the supremacy of Islam. But it requires patience; the day is not yet here.*

"*Pas encore,*" he said aloud.

The banker furrowed his brow. "*Pas encore?* Not yet?" He shook his head. "I'm sorry, I don't understand. . . . *Je suis désolé, je ne comprends pas.*"

"*Il n'était rien,*" The Sheik replied. *It was nothing. Only that Jews, Christians, Buddhists, Hindi, and all other non-believers will all be put to the sword or pay the blood price to keep your heads. And only if it pleases us.*

"It was nothing?" the banker repeated in English. A light went off in his head, and he chuckled like he finally got a complicated joke. "Oh hey, happens to me, too. I forget what I'm saying all the time. . . . *J'oublie ce que je dis toute l'heure.* Ha ha." He took a quick look around at the faces of his competitors, then whispered to The Sheik, "*Avez-vous pris plus d'en considération notre offre? Je battrai n'importe quoi que mes concurrents vous donnent.*"

No I have not given your offer any consideration, you swine, The Sheik thought. *And I'm certain you will do what it takes to beat the best offers of your competitors. Now I will teach you a lesson.* He replied quietly but with a definite edge. "*N'est pas maintenant l'heure de discuter des affaires.*"

"Now is not the time to discuss business," the banker translated aloud. The blood drained from his face. His voice trembled and his jowls shook as he back-pedaled. "Of course not, forgive me. . . . *Naturellement pas, pardonnez-moi.*" He glanced back at his competitors, whose faces had as one creased with smiles as they realized from the look on his face that he'd made some major blunder. "*Je ne sais pas ce qui m'a rendu si grossier.*"

You don't know what caused you to be so rude? The Sheik translated in his head. *That's easy. Greed.* Having put the man in his place, he reeled him back in. "*Oui, oui, ce n'est pas un problème. Nous parlerons plus tard,*" The Sheik said, patting the banker man on his rounded shoulder.

The banker nearly wet his pants at the reprieve. In fact, he did heed the call of nature and excused himself, remembering to give his competition a triumphant look on the way out. Surely they'd seen the affectionate tap on his shoulder. *New house in the Hamptons, here I come.*

Pissing all over himself like a dog getting his belly scratched by his Master, thought The Sheik as the president of a trading firm sidled up to him. He longed for the day when he wouldn't have to play these games with men whose very existence he detested. Soon, though, his public persona would disappear from the face of the Earth and he would be reborn as simply The Sheik, the nameless, faceless Scourge of the Great Satan, Defender of the One True Faith. And as an added bonus, he would be avenged for his older brother's death.

In theory, he'd agreed with his friend Osama bin Laden's strategy, which was designed to engage the United States by acts of terrorism so vicious that the Americans would be certain to react violently and without much thought. In addition to overextending its military and taxing its economy, the United States would be certain to increase its military and cultural presence in the Middle East, which bin Laden and his advisers believed would cause a general uprising in even "moderate" Muslim countries.

The desired result would be an Islamic revolution that would lead to the reestablishment of the caliphate, the combination of religion and state under the rule of one supreme cleric, the Caliph, in all Muslim lands. And as the Qur'an foretold, eventually Islam would hold dominion over the entire world until the end of days.

However, bin Laden had not been prepared for the speed or massiveness of the U.S. response after the World Trade Center fell, or the failure of any general uprising to materialize. Now, the Taliban was reduced to banditry and roadside bombs, having been hunted like dogs through the mountains of Afghanistan and Pakistan, while Al Qaeda's leadership cowered in caves and made videotapes of their useless threats.

During a recent counsel with Al Qaeda and Abu Sayyaf, an Islamic militant group in Southeast Asia and Indonesia, to make arrangements for implementing The Sheik's plan, he had listened to their argument that the attacks on the World Trade Center had also led the United States into a quagmire in Iraq. But they'd grown silent when he pointed out that while Muslim killed Muslim in Iraq, the United States was more powerful than ever, with an even larger presence in the Middle East.

"It was a glorious blow for Allah, all praise to Him, and struck fear into the hearts of infidels all over the world," The Sheik had said, not wanting to alienate his co-conspirators. "But if we want to finish them, we must stop giving glancing blows to the skin of the beast and hurt him internally."

Part of the plan was to support this madrasah in the heart of New York City, and there were more being created in the ghettos of other U.S. cities. Those who hated the United States would use its own protections for free speech and freedom of religion to act like a worm in an apple. Recruiters would find in Harlem, and Chicago's South Side, Dearborn, and Watts the same sort of "martyrs" they did in Kabul, Cairo, Sanaa, Peshawar, Fallujah, Dubai, and Ahmedabad. Poor, disenfranchised, marginalized young men looking for a purpose, as well as a better life in the next world than they'd found in this one, would become their tools in this new kind of war.

As the trading-firm president jockeyed into position for a "little private talk," The Sheik saw Dean Newbury cut through the crowd toward him. *Now here is the more dangerous enemy,* he thought. *He's as ruthless as I am and in control of a wealthy, determined group of infidels with their own delusions of world dominion.*

The Sheik knew that the current arrangement was one of convenience. He was well aware that Newbury's group had no intention of allowing a caliphate to exist, except, perhaps, as a puppet regime to keep the Muslim countries in line and producing cheap oil. Someday they, too, would clash, but he believed that by then, the outcome, with Allah's help, would favor Islam. *Which reminds me, I need to make another donation to Iran's uranium enrichment program.*

The Sheik held out his hand as the old man walked up. "*Bonsoir, mon ami,* Newbury," he said.

"*Bonsoir,*" Dean Newbury replied. "Do I understand correctly that our guest's arrival is on schedule? The great day is fast approaching."

"*Oui,*" The Sheik replied. He pulled an envelope with the mosque's crescent moon logo out of his breast pocket and handed it to Newbury. "He arrives next Wednesday. Here is the information you need. I trust you will make the arrangements so that he is not disturbed."

"We'll do our part. After that, you must do yours, or not only will the plan fail, but my people will experience tremendous losses."

"*Bonsoir, messieurs.*" The voice of V. T. Newbury caught his uncle and the Saudi Arabian by surprise.

Dean Newbury hurriedly jammed the envelope into his suit. "Oh, *bonsoir,* V. T. We were chatting about what a wonderful reception this is . . . truly

232   ROBERT K. TANENBAUM

historic." *And the beginning of the Thousand Year Reign of the Sons of Man. Myr shegin dy ve, bee eh!*

As Jaxon patrolled the reception room where the men gathered, Lucy stood against a wall in a large room reserved for the women attending the night's event. The space was dark, lit mostly by candles and dimmed lighting.

Most of the women in the room huddled off in small clusters and ignored her. When they did look at her, however, it was with curiosity, not hostility. Only once had she felt uncomfortable. That was shortly after she'd arrived, when suddenly she felt the hair on the back of her neck stand on end and a chill run up her spine, as if something evil was watching her. She turned quickly but there was no one looking in her direction. *A little jumpy for a spy, aren't you?* she'd chided herself.

Right now, she was trying to keep an eye on a young black woman, the receptionist she'd seen outside Imam Jabbar's office. She'd been trying to figure out how to approach the widow of Jamal Khalifa without revealing that she was anything more than a translator for a security company. If there was some connection between the suicide bombing, the mosque, and Prince Esra bin Afraan's visit, and she was part of it, Lucy couldn't afford to expose herself. However, the widow might also be their best bet in the quest to learn if there was a wider conspiracy.

If she could just talk to the woman, she might get some hint as to her involvement. Unfortunately, the opportunity to speak to her had not come up. So Lucy passed the time rehearsing what she might say to introduce herself. A glance told her that the widow was talking to another woman dressed in conservative Muslim clothing.

"You should just go talk to her," said the voice in her head.

"I will as soon as she gets through talking to the other woman," Lucy replied. "And why are you speaking Spanish?"

"Because as you know, I was from Castile," said the voice, which came from the shadow of a woman standing next to her. "And what other woman?"

St. Teresa appeared to her as she would have looked in her day—a large but pretty woman dressed in the dark robes and white coif of a Spanish nun. Lucy turned to the . . . well, what was she . . . an imaginary friend? . . . A ghost? . . . A figment of her imagination? *Perhaps,* she thought, *a hallucination brought on by some particular as-yet-undiagnosed psychosis?*

Her friend and human spiritual guide, John Jojola, thought that St. Teresa of Avila was her spirit guide. He often talked about the village of spirits who didn't just live in his head, but all around him in waking life. There were good ones who helped people, he said, and bad ones who caused problems. As St. Teresa usually showed up in times of danger and stress to help or console Lucy, he figured she was good. "Don't be afraid to accept her," he had said. "It is good to have spirit allies."

Lucy looked back at the widow. The figure of her companion wavered and seemed part of the shadows behind her, a common occurrence when she looked at St. Teresa. *I'm just tired,* she thought. The past week had been a blur of parties, business meetings, and expensive meals—any one of which cost more than a year's salary working for the Catholic diocese at the Taos Pueblo—not that she would have traded the latter for the jet-set life. If she never went to another black-tie event again it would be too soon.

Still, the week had its moments. It was sort of funny watching Jaxon "work security" for the prince at discothèques. She wished she could have seen him do the same at the "gentlemen's clubs" they visited, but she had been made to wait in the limousine while the men watched the strippers.

The prince could be charming enough in a vapid playboy sort of way. But she wasn't his type, unless his type—buxom, giggly, and willing—wasn't around, which rarely happened after business hours were over and party time began.

However, there was another side to him, a mean, spoiled side that she supposed came with the territory. He enjoyed watching the supposed Wall Street Masters of the Universe grovel at his feet, and he also liked asking anxious bank and trading-firm presidents to run small errands and favors for him like low-level flunkies. At times she almost felt embarrassed for them, but mostly she felt sad that her country depended on such spineless, money-grubbing sycophants.

Nor was the prince any better to his own people, whom he treated as slaves and retainers. He was cruelest to Amir al-Sistani, his chief financial officer and whipping boy. While he would brag about al-Sistani's abilities with finances, he more often treated him like a trained dog. He constantly dressed the man down for his "lack of style" and loudly told the women that he suspected that Amir was either "a virgin or a homosexual."

"Either way, he's too busy for sex," the prince smirked. "Always counting my money or praying. That's about all he's good for. Isn't that right, Amir?"

Lucy wanted al-Sistani to stand up for himself, but all he would do was adjust his keffiyeh headdress and mumble in French. *"Oui, mon prince."*

"The prince sometimes calls him *al-Iraqii*, which means 'son of, or native of, Iraq,'" Lucy had told Jaxon before the reception.

"Is that a problem?"

"Well, in some places it doesn't mean much more than identifying where someone comes from. But used by a member of the Saudi royal family, it's meant as an insult. There are a lot of highly placed Iraqis in Saudi Arabia, some of whom enjoy a nice life. But to be referred to as *'al-Iraqii'* is to be reminded that they will never belong to upper society. They may have wealth and prestige, but when it comes to the social strata of Arabians, they are lower than a shop owner."

"Sounds like the sort of person who might have a reason to dislike the prince?"

"Probably. Though he seems too timid to do anything about it."

They'd agreed that al-Sistani bore watching as a potential threat. In the meantime, Lucy was supposed to try to get a feel for the widow of a man who'd blown himself up in a synagogue. She'd been about to walk over, only now there was a second apparition, which was startling in itself. Even more surprising was the fact that the widow seemed to be talking to the shadow person.

Then again, it was a relief to know that someone else saw ghosts, which made up her mind for her. She crossed the room to speak to the woman . . . or women.

"Jambo," Lucy greeted the widow, who had her back to her. *"U hali gani?"*

"Sjambo," the woman replied, startled.

You don't look fine, Lucy thought. *You look frightened and tired.* "So you see them, too?" she asked in Swahili.

The woman gave her a funny look and tried to walk away. But Lucy stepped in front of her and nodded to where St. Teresa now stood next to the other spirit. "Mine was a nun in Spain about four hundred years ago.

Her name was Teresa. I see her when there is danger or I'm stressed out. She told me to talk to you."

The woman hesitated, then laughed as if Lucy had told her a joke. But her voice was serious. "Her name is Hazrat Fatemeh Masumeh, a blessed and divine lady of the Prophet's household. She was martyred more than 1,200 years ago. I, too, see her when I am in danger, which may be because we are being watched. . . . Careful, don't say anything."

As if on cue, another woman approached, a Caucasian. She also looked familiar, but with the hajib she wore, it was difficult to say why.

"You must be the translator," the woman said in English. "I heard you and Miriam speaking and didn't recognize the language."

"It was Swahili," Lucy replied. "Yes, I'm the translator." She held out her hand. "Marie Smith. . . . I heard . . . Miriam, was it? . . . I heard her talking and recognized the language, though I've only picked up a few words of Swahili here and there."

"Quite a talent," the woman said. "So many languages in one head. Do I understand you also speak French and Arabic?"

"Those I can speak fluently. Unfortunately, my Swahili is rather rudimentary," Lucy replied. A quick glance told her that St. Teresa and Hazrat Fatemeh Masumeh were gone or had faded back into the shadows. "I'm sure I butchered the few words I know."

"No, actually, you speak my language like a native," Miriam said in Swahili, lightly tapping Lucy on the shoulder as if teasing her before continuing in English. "Oh no, not too bad for a beginner."

Lucy laughed, too. *Thanks for picking up on the cue,* she thought. "You're too kind," she said and then turned to the strange woman. "That accent. You're from?"

"Chechnya," the woman replied. "I am *hekharna konsultant,* a um . . . training consultant . . . for an oil consortium that does business with Prince bin Afraan. He owns several oil fields in my country, and I'm here with a team to negotiate a contract to provide drilling expertise and technology."

"Ah Chechen," Lucy said. *"As-salaamu alaikum!"*

The woman looked surprised. She repeated the Chechen Muslim greeting. *"As-salaamu alaikum."*

"Ha tse hu yu?" Lucy asked the woman her name.

"Humma dats," was the curt reply.

It doesn't matter, huh? Lucy thought, *then why is a Russian pretending to be a Chechen?* She welcomed the woman to the United States. *"Marsha yooghill Amerika!"*

The woman bowed slightly but with a look of disdain. *"Barkalla,"* she replied before switching back to English. "Thank you. It was a pleasure to meet you and, I must say, a surprise to find someone who also speaks Arabic, French, and a few words of Swahili and is so fluent in Chechen. Such a unique gift."

Lucy wished she had not been so revealing. It was like she'd been showing off, and now this woman was suspicious. However, the woman wished them a good evening, *"De dika doila,"* and walked away.

When she was out of earshot, Miriam let her breath out in a hiss. "I do not like that one," she said in Swahili. "She watches me constantly. She claims to be Muslim, but I am not so sure."

"Is there a reason she watches you?"

Instead of answering, Miriam asked her own question. "You are more than who you say you are."

"Yes."

"The divine lady says that I should trust you."

"I guess that makes two spirits who think we should chat."

This time the woman's laugh was not faked. "I am so happy that someone else sees ghosts. It means I am not the only crazy one."

"I know what you mean." She looked across the room and saw that the "Chechen" woman was watching them. "Our friend isn't happy about our talking, and I don't want to make trouble for you."

"Thanks to Allah, I am not afraid," Miriam replied.

"Well, it could still be dangerous, so we should be careful. I will leave a card with a telephone number underneath the box of tissues in the women's restroom. Call me if you'd like to talk."

19

V. T. Newbury was about to enter his uncle's office when he caught the sound of Dean's voice and hesitated outside the door. The old man was obviously irritated and, as if speaking to someone whose intelligence was less than adequate, fumbled between English and what sounded like Russian.

"Listen close you idiot. . . . S . . . T . . . M . . . 17 and Number 13," he snarled. "Pay whoever you need to pay, but no one is to inspect the contents or bother the visitors! Не докучайте пассажирам! You are to keep guards on duty around the clock. Do you understand? Вы понимаете?"

Dean Newbury listened. When he spoke again, he seemed satisfied with the answer. "Good. Good. Хорошо. Хорошо."

V. T. knocked and walked in. His uncle was sitting in his chair with his back to him, facing the window that looked south over midtown Manhattan. Although V. T. preferred the same view his father had enjoyed looking north to Central Park, he had to admit that at night the skyline from fifty stories up was beautiful and awe-inspiring. The old man swiveled in his seat to face his visitor with a scowl on his face. When he saw that it was V. T., he smiled and motioned for him to sit.

As V. T. took a seat in front of the massive granite desk, his uncle tossed a small sheet of paper that he'd been holding in his hand onto it. The paper landed on an envelope that had been torn open, the same envelope V. T. had seen his uncle pocket during the reception at the mosque earlier that evening. He glanced at the sheet of paper, which was blank except for the few letters and numbers he'd heard his uncle relay over the telephone.

Dean Newbury saw his nephew's eyes go to the piece of paper and quickly picked it back up off his desk and fed it into a paper shredder on the floor. "UPS tracking number."

"I didn't know you spoke Russian," V. T. said.

Dean Newbury shrugged. "A little," he said. "We have clients who have business interests in Russia, so I've picked up a smattering of the language . . . mostly things like 'Do you understand?' Which, by the way, they always say that they do; but they'll figure out how to screw it up somehow unless you stay after them. The Russians we deal with are not the most reliable people in the world. However, as far as their language goes, if there's anything more difficult than the few words I've absorbed, I have to use a translator."

The old man hopped up from his chair with surprising agility and walked swiftly over to the chrome and black-granite bar that set a small kitchen off from the rest of the office. "Fix you something?"

"I'll take a brandy if you have it."

"I do indeed, an excellent choice for a man of means and taste. How would a 1960 Hine cognac suit you?"

"Lovely. A vintage cognac . . . rare and expensive."

"As with anything worth having," Dean agreed as he handed V. T. a snifter of the dark amber-colored liquid.

When V. T. held up his hand for the drink, his uncle noted the ring on his finger. "Looks good on you," he said, holding up an exact copy on his own hand. "The triskele. Three golden spiral legs joined in the middle against a field of black. Symbol of the Isle of Man." He held his ring out as if to study it from a distance. "It's really a stylized version of three human legs joined in the middle and running, an ancient symbol that shows up in ancient art from Celtic ruins to Spain and Sicily. 'Quocunque jeceris stabit.'"

"Wherever you will throw it, it stands," V. T. translated, raising his glass to his nose to inhale the aroma of leather and spices.

"Ah yes, you were the Latin scholar in boarding school," Dean Newbury recalled. "It's appropriate, too, as the motto of our families for more than two hundred years." He gestured to the skyline. "Hard to believe from this lofty perch that it hasn't always been easy for us. There have been a lot of hard decisions and many obstacles, as well as enemies who wanted us to fail, but we've always been able to prosper."

"If that's the family motto," V. T. asked, confused, "then what's *Myr shegin dy ve, bee eh?*"

"What must be, will be. It's more of an invocation, a statement of purpose . . . that in this family, we determine our own fate."

"A good outlook," V. T. acknowledged, feeling the rush of the alcohol.

"If you have purpose, you can change the world," Dean Newbury continued. "Make it better."

"To a better world," V. T. toasted. *"Myr shegin dy ve, bee eh."*

Dean Newbury's eyes sparkled. *"Myr shegin dy ve, bee eh,* indeed." He put his glass down and leaned forward to study his nephew's face. "So, what did you think of the little soiree this evening?"

V. T. shrugged. "What am I supposed to think? I don't really do anything for the client, except get him from business meeting to party to business meeting to nightclub. All the paperwork has been handled by Mr. White."

"Ah yes, William, the best business-law attorney we have. The son of our other senior partner. He's not much in the courtroom, but he can write a contract so tight God couldn't break it. If anything ever happens to me, and you take over, rely on him."

"Good to know. But I trust you're not going anywhere. I'd prefer not to lose my father and my only uncle in the same year."

"Why thanks, nephew. I appreciate the sentiment. But no fears." He tapped on his bony chest. "Healthy as an ox. . . . So, this evening's festivities."

"I've attended more black-tie dinners and shaken more hands in a week than a presidential candidate two days before the election, and may I never have to enter another discothèque."

Dean Newbury chortled. "Sorry about that, I'm sure it was an auditory challenge, if not a legal one. But everything I've heard from our client is that you've represented the firm well and that the prince and his people are comfortable with you. They know that people like our Mr. White are foot soldiers, so it's been important to them that we also presented them a general."

"That's quite the promotion from the junior lieutenant I was at the DAO," V. T. replied. "I'm not sure that I did much other than exercise my inherited ability for small talk, but I'm glad I could be of service."

"Yes, leading from behind takes some getting used to," Dean said. "The further up the chain of command we move, the less we're on the chess board where the action is. Still, we're the guys moving the pieces into the right places. However, somebody has to do that well enough, or we'll find ourselves in checkmate."

He looked over at the wall above his shelf of books and pointed to a row of portraits hanging beneath three paintings of sailing ships. "Those men knew how to play the game."

V. T. knew that the portraits were of the Newbury ancestors who'd headed the firm over the past two hundred years. And, as his uncle had once explained, the sailing ships were a reminder of the family's early beginnings "as seagoing men."

"I don't think I need to remind you—not after the way those two niggers beat you bloody and still haven't been caught—that this world is going to hell in a handbasket," Dean said.

The remark caught V. T. by surprise. He felt tears rise up in his eyes, and walked over to the bar where he poured himself another glass of cognac, bringing the bottle over to refresh his uncle's glass.

"The justice system can't deal with the numbers anymore," his uncle continued. "Which leaves the scum of the Earth to terrorize good, hard-working people. In the meantime, illegal immigrants flood across our borders, taking jobs, living off taxpayers, committing crimes with little to fear in consequences. They're like a bunch of cockroaches, hiding from the light, spreading pestilence, reproducing more vermin."

The old man stood up and started to pace. "In Washington, D.C., weak-willed administrations and do-nothing Congresses pussy-foot around the threat of Islamic extremism and rogue nuclear states. They're either so busy appeasing these criminals so that our so-called 'allies' don't get their panties in a bunch, or they blunder about like drunk cowboys, shooting every which way but never really going for the kill. They don't have the balls to do what's necessary to make the world safe for the next generation of white Americans."

V. T. joined him at the window. "So what are a couple of aging attorneys to do about it?" he asked and took another sip of the cognac. His brain felt like someone had turned a fog machine on inside it.

When his uncle turned to face him, V. T. was reminded of the fierce predatory look of eagles and hawks. "We do what we can," he said firmly. "We are in a war, and sometimes in war it's necessary to do things that are unpleasant, sometimes even repugnant. But we keep our eyes on the future and understand that sometimes the ends do justify the means if the cause is a good one."

"There's precedent for the government to usurp civil liberties on a temporary basis in times of war," V. T. noted. "Sometimes liberty must be tempered by realism."

"Exactly. But then the left-wing liberal dogs start whining about their precious liberties; they just don't understand that unless the realities are taken care of, there won't be any civil liberties to lose."

"I get your point."

"I've hoped you would. You've already met my associates and know that they care deeply about where this country is headed. Once you've earned their trust, you can trust them yourself as no other. They're men who are ready to act to save this country, and Western civilization."

As Dean Newbury spoke, his breathing grew faster and more labored. He had to put a hand against the glass window to steady himself.

V. T. shot out a hand to hold him by the elbow. "Are you all right?"

Dean Newbury took a sip of cognac. "Ah, yes, thank you, my boy, quite all right. Afraid I get myself a little worked up. For two hundred years this family and others have worked to build something great here, and we won't see it overrun by the immigrant horde, unchecked criminality, and Islamic extremists."

"I'm with you on that."

The old man reached over and gripped his arm so hard it hurt. "You may be called upon to make a hard decision soon," he said. "And at first, the right answer might not seem clear. But your family and your country need you to make the correct choice. *Myr shegin dy ve, bee eh.*"

V. T. patted his uncle's hand to loosen the grip on his arm. "I hope I'm up to the task when the time comes," he said.

The old man's face looked predatory again when he answered. "So do I, my boy, so do I."

A half hour later, V. T. was still thinking about the conversation when he got out of the taxicab in front of his walkup apartment on Minetta Lane down in the Village. On the outside, it was a modest brick building, constructed well over a hundred years earlier; no one would know by looking at it that he'd purchased the entire top floor and completely remodeled the interior.

V. T. had more money than he knew what to do with from the inheritance he had received from his mother, a New England blueblood whose family went back to the Mayflower and whose fortune originated with the spice trade. His father had quietly amassed a personal fortune as well, through judicious investing of his large salary from the firm.

V. T. had indulged himself with his apartment, which among other things featured the best entertainment system to listen to his beloved jazz. He also drove an Aston Martin, but other than that was not ostentatious with his toys or lifestyle. True, there was the place in the Vermont countryside, and the family beach house in Martha's Vineyard; a painting of himself as a child, picnicking on the sands there with his mother and father, hung in his office. The thought of it now made him nostalgic, which is why his self-preservation radar didn't pick up the four men who had followed him up the steps. When he opened the door, they shoved him roughly inside.

They were dressed in black, including the ski masks that covered their faces. One of them pointed a gun at his head. "Don't move, Mr. Newbury. We only want to talk to you."

Apparently, the gunman was nervous, because his finger touched the button that released the bullet clip from the gun and it clattered to the floor. The gunman bent over to retrieve the clip, knocking his head against the head of one of his comrades who'd been doing the same thing. They remained crouched over, rubbing their heads and cursing one another.

"Whoever you are," V. T. said, not sure if he should laugh or fight while they were occupied, "you're really not very good at this. I suggest that you let me go before this gets out of hand."

"Shaddup punk," the shortest of the men snarled like a movie gangster. He waved a canister of pepper spray at V. T.'s face. "Don't make me get rough."

The fourth man, who had a gray ponytail peeking out from under his ski mask, sighed. "Excuse the theatrics, Mr. Newbury," he said in a low voice obviously meant to disguise his real one. "I wouldn't blame you for thinking that this is some sort of joke. You're right, we're not very good at this. But what we want to talk to you about is very serious."

"Then why don't you take off the ridiculous masks, put away the gun— by the way, I can see that there's no bullet in the clip—and get your friend here doing the James Cagney imitation to take his finger off the pepper spray. And then we can talk like civilized people."

The four men shook their heads. "We can't do that," said the fourth man. "Whatever you may think of our drama here, it's not meant to be a comedy. People have already died, and we can't risk that you're not the man we think you are . . . or were. But you should know that this concerns your father and how he was killed."

The partial smile disappeared from V. T.'s face. "What do you mean 'killed'? My father died of a heart attack. If this is some sort of looney theory, I don't appreciate it."

"I can assure you this is not a looney anything," said the heavyset man who'd pulled the gun, which now dangled absently in his hand. "Nor would we go to this extreme—as you've correctly noted, this isn't our usual line of work—if we didn't think this was important."

The portly man added, "Say that we knew your father . . . for a long time . . . and we liked him very much."

"Then stop acting like the Keystone Kops and talk," V. T. said.

"We have our reasons for the disguises," the man with the ponytail said. "Please, have a seat, and I'm afraid we're going to have to tie you up."

"Oh, come on," Newbury said. "It's really not necessary. And besides, your gun doesn't work."

"Yeah, but this does," the short man said, waving the pepper spray.

The portly man pulled a Taser stun gun from his pocket. "And so does this. I'd rather not use it, but I will if I have to."

Newbury sat down. The big man put his gun in his pocket and produced a roll of duct tape that he used to secure him.

"All right, now I'm no danger to you," V. T. said angrily. "So what is it that is so important you'd commit a half-dozen major felonies to say it?"

The fourth man with the ponytail spoke. "Like I said, what I'm about to tell you, you may already know, and if so, and you've done nothing about it, then you are not your father's son, and we will have kept our identity a secret for a good reason. Mr. Newbury, what do you know about the Sons of Man?"

"Sons of who?"

The four masked men looked at each other. "The Sons of Man," said the ponytailed man. "It's a long story, but we have a few minutes."

He began by telling V. T. how they'd met his father at law school. "We were young and idealistic," he said. "We didn't always agree with each other, but we swore that we'd always defend the Constitution and what it stands for."

According to his captors, they'd lost touch with Vincent Newbury over the years. He went into the family law firm, and they'd gone on to their own careers. Then suddenly one day, Vincent got back in touch with them. He said he'd stumbled on a Newbury family connection to a secretive cabal of powerful men. "He believed that their ultimate goal was the destruction of the Constitution and the government," the ponytailed man said.

To get proof, he'd taped a conversation between Dean Newbury and a man named Jamys Kellagh. "Who we believe was actually Jon Ellis, an assistant director with the Department of Homeland Security."

"A spook," said the little man with the pepper spray.

"The discussion was conducted in an ancient language called Manx," the ponytailed man said. "Anyway, they were discussing a plan to assassinate a U.S. Senator, Tom McCullum."

"My uncle? Dean Newberry? An assassination? That's crazy."

"Maybe so," the ponytailed man replied. "But would-be dictators have done crazier things for power. We're not exactly sure why McCullum was targeted, except that he's made a number of enemies on the Right with his attacks on the Patriot Act. We think it also has something to do with the senator's upcoming congressional hearings on recent terrorist activities that seem to implicate people in the Russian and U.S. governments, as well as business and crime syndicate leaders."

"I'm sure this would all make a good movie, but what proof do you have?" V. T. demanded.

"You mean other than the attempt on McCullum's life at the St. Patrick's Day Parade?"

"I believe the current theory is that the assassin was after the mayor or the police chief. The shooter was a former cop who'd been fired. What you're saying sounds like more conspiracy theory bullshit."

"We know it's hard to accept," the ponytailed man continued. "At one time, we had more proof—a book that your father took from your uncle's bookshelf. A book about the Sons of Man."

"So my uncle killed his brother, my dad, because he took this book. Please!"

"We think that book could have exposed the entire organization if the right people had it and traced the genealogy," the portly man said. "So yes, we think Dean Newbury killed Vincent because he took the book . . . and taped that conversation."

"Where's the book now?" V. T. asked.

"Gone. Along with the man to whom we sent it, hoping that he'd be able to get the information into the right hands. Unfortunately, he was murdered and the book destroyed."

"Let me get this straight," V. T. said. "My uncle is part of a secret organization, one that was behind at least these two murders. But your only proof is gone. Sounds far-fetched, don't you think? Now, how is it you think my father was murdered?"

"Are you sure his heart attack was not induced?" the ponytailed man asked.

"Could have been. But if so, it appears that it might have been an accidental overdose of his digitalis medicine."

"Accidental?" the heavyset man scoffed. "He had dinner with your uncle that night and suddenly keels over because he took an accidental overdose of prescription medicine. Was he that senile he couldn't remember taking his pills?"

"He was old," V. T. responded. "His memory wasn't as sharp as it once was. . . . Maybe he took his pill, forgot, and took another."

"Was that the level of digitalis in his bloodstream?" the ponytailed man asked. "One extra pill? Or did he take a dozen extra? Enough to stop his heart?"

"Have you seen the medical reports?" asked the short man. "What was the level of digitalis?"

"I only saw the certificate of death," V. T. acknowledged. "It said natural causes."

"Maybe you didn't care to know the truth," said the short man.

V. T. glared at him. "I loved my father. Say that again, and I'll forget that you're a bunch of old men playing James Bond."

But the short man wasn't backing down. "Then prove it. All I see is a guy who sold out for money and is working for the man who I think killed his father. If that's true, I'll cut you out of that chair and kick your ass myself . . . old man or not."

Before V. T. could respond, the man with the ponytail held up his hand. "Enough," he said, using his normal voice, a voice used to commanding and being obeyed. "Handsome is as handsome does, Mr. Newbury. In the meantime, I'd point out that the ring you wear bears the symbol of the Sons of Man, which makes you suspect in our eyes."

V. T. glanced at his ring. "I'm hardly the one in this group to be called a suspect. If you're so sure of all of this, why haven't you gone to the police?"

"You pointed it out yourself," the portly man said. "We have no proof."

"But," the ponytailed man continued, "given Mr. Ellis's position with the Department of Homeland Security, we're also convinced that it's tough to trust some of our law-enforcement agencies with this information."

"What makes you so sure that I won't go straight to my uncle and have you all wiped out?"

The other men were quiet. "We aren't, Mr. Newbury," the ponytailed man said at last. "You're right, we're old and for us the world seems to have gone crazy. Old values like faith and loyalty seem to be in short supply. But we thought that if there was one thing that we might still be able to count on, that would be the love of a son for his father."

With that he leaned forward and started to place a piece of duct tape over Newbury's mouth. "That's not necessary," V. T. said. "I'll count to a thousand before I yell for help."

"Sorry," the ponytailed man said, and applied the tape. "We can't take that chance. We'd like to trust you, Mr. Newbury, for your father's sake. However, that ring gives us cause to wonder. Sit tight for twenty minutes and someone will come to release you."

With that the short man turned on the television, which to all of their surprise was set on MTV. They shrugged and turned up the volume. But Newbury shouted a muffled protest. He was obviously in such distress that the man with the ponytail pulled back the tape from his mouth. "What is it?" he asked.

"There are laws against torture," Newbury replied. "The housekeeper must have been here today and turned the channel to MTV. Please, twenty minutes of that and I'll be stark raving mad."

The ponytailed man looked over at the television and laughed. "You're quite right," he said, replacing the duct tape but also nodding to the short man, who picked up the remote and turned to a Nature Channel special on dinosaurs. The men started to leave, but then the short man turned around and pointed a stubby finger at V. T. "We'll be watching, punk."

The four men removed their masks before leaving the walkup. Outside, Geoffrey Gilbert, who'd been leaning against a wall, "minding my own business," whistled and waved. Down the block, a car turned on its lights, which flashed twice before rolling forward.

When it was even with the apartment building, the four men rushed forward to get into the doors, while Gilbert hopped in from the other side. "Hello, Father Jim," Judge Plaut, the ponytailed fourth man, said to the driver next to him.

"Hi Frank. Was the mission a success?" the priest asked as he pulled onto Sixth Avenue.

"Well, if you mean did we discuss our concerns with Mr. Newbury without revealing our identities, then yes," Plaut replied. "Though I'd like to ask Mr. Florence about some of the more dramatic dialogue." He turned to the short former newspaper editor. "What was with the 'Shaddup punk. Don't make me get rough' speech? You sounded like you were in a B-grade gangster movie."

"Hey, I got a little carried away," Florence pouted. "I was just trying to get the point across that we meant business, while that other yahoo dropped his gun. If he'd decided to resist, he probably would have kicked all of our asses, even with the pepper spray. I was just trying to head him off at the pass. And besides, Saul, what's with the gun falling apart?"

"Hey, I've had it since Dubya-Dubya Two," Silverstein growled. "What'd you expect? Something that actually shoots?"

Sunderland laughed. "I see I missed some great theater."

"Well, to be honest, I kind of liked it," Murray Epstein said. "I kept waiting for Bill to drop a 'you dirty rat' on him."

The men laughed. "You think it will do any good?" Sunderland asked.

"I don't know," Plaut said. "I know he wears that triskele ring. But he was also listening when we talked about the Sons of Man. I've been reading lawyers' faces in courtrooms for a long time, and I think I know when they're actually paying attention."

"He could have been trying to find out what we actually know," Epstein pointed out. "Which isn't much more than we told him."

"The worst scenario is that we warned the Sons of Bitches that someone out here—a crack team of secret agents—is aware of their existence," Gilbert said.

"That can be a dangerous thing," Sunderland pointed out. "Two men are already dead . . . at least."

"Well, we had to take the risk," Plaut said. "And what's done's done. So, Bill, do you have that telephone number?"

"Yeah," Florence replied. "I have to say, I'm a little uneasy about using my 'informant' in the DA's office for getting me this sort of information. Sooner or later, they're going to figure out that there's a leak."

"I'd say sooner," Plaut replied. "Our Mr. Karp is pretty sharp. I'd be very surprised if he wasn't aware of it already."

"All the more reason for her to lay low," Florence replied, dialing the telephone number he'd been given.

20

As promised, twenty minutes after his kidnappers left, V. T. heard some-one fiddling with the lock on his apartment door. That was followed by a moment of silence, and then a crash. A moment later, an enormous man with a face that looked like a gargoyle on a European church rushed into the room with a gun.

The big man was followed by Ray Guma, who took one look at his friend and started to laugh. "You can put the heat away, Gino," he said between fits of mirth. "I think Mr. Newbury is alone." He walked over and pulled the duct tape from V. T.'s mouth.

"Ouch, dammit! Guma, you enjoyed that," V. T. complained. "Gino" moved around behind the chair, flipped open a switchblade, and cut through the tape binding him to the seat.

Guma shrugged. "I was worried you couldn't breathe," he said. "But if you're going to whine, see if I ever come to your rescue again. And by the way, you're going to need a carpenter to fix your door. Gino tried his hand at picking the lock, but he doesn't have a great deal of patience. He sort of kicked it in."

"How'd you know to come find me?"

"Beats me," Guma replied. "There I was, minding my own business, play-ing chess with my cousin here when I get a call on my cell phone—a very

249

private and unlisted number mind you—that says you're tied up in your apartment. This goomba warns me not to call the cops 'or else.' So here I am, and there you were . . . tied up and gagged, just like the man says."

V. T. rubbed his wrists to regain circulation. "Well, thanks. Say Gino, have we met before? You look familiar."

"I wouldn't know nuttin' about dat," Cousin Gino replied, glancing at Guma and then turning to leave the room. "I'll be waitin' in the car. And just so you remember, ya rat, it's my move when we get back to da apartment."

"*Sulla vostra estremità!*" Guma shouted after his cousin.

"What's that mean?" V. T. asked, stretching his legs.

"Up your ass. It's a Sicilian term of endearment."

"He isn't one of the guys who . . ."

Guma held up his hand. "As my cousin would say, 'I wouldn't know nuttin' about dat,' and leave it at that. So what's with the bondage scene? You got a kinky girlfriend you haven't introduced me to?"

"I have plenty of girlfriends I haven't introduced you to," V. T. said. "Which is why they remain my friends." He told Guma the story of his capture.

Guma chuckled. "So a gang of senior citizens got the drop on V. T. Newbury, the scourge of the New York mob. Can't wait to tell the gang back at the office."

"If you do, I'll wring your guinea neck."

"You wouldn't dare. You want I should call my cousin back?" They both laughed, and then Guma turned serious. "So what's next?"

Newbury thought about it for a moment. "I think it's time to have a face-to-face with the boss."

"Tonight?"

"Yeah. Whatever's going on, it seems to be moving rather quickly. Can you make the call for me from your place . . . just in case?"

"Sure," Guma replied. "What do I tell him?"

"Just that Lewis Carroll would like to have a word with him at the usual spot. Say in about an hour."

———

At the appointed time, V. T. arrived by taxi at Fifth Avenue and the Central Park side of East 76th Street. There were only a few people about on the sidewalk. A middle-aged, raggedly dressed woman raided a trash can for anything of value—cans, bottles, half-eaten sandwiches—while two well-heeled couples, decked out in a few thousand dollars' worth of evening wear, passed by laughing loudly while averting their eyes.

The bag lady suddenly looked up at V. T., and her eyes narrowed. "What are you lookin' at, Fancy Pants?" she snarled, but then smiled when she added. "Maybe you want a blow job in the bushes? Twenty bucks and worth every penny."

"Um, no thanks," V. T. replied.

"Suit yourself. You look like the type who likes boys anyway."

He entered the park and hurried down the path to the statue of a little girl sitting on a mushroom flanked by the March Hare and the Mad Hatter. Even in the yellow glow of streetlights, the bronze patina of Lewis Carroll's heroine, Alice, shone, thanks to the polishing of millions of small hands who had climbed about on its surface. The famous 1959 statue was abandoned at this time of night; no one was in sight except for a large bum who appeared to be nodding off on one of the nearby benches. V. T. walked over to the bum. "Mind if I have a seat?"

"Free country," the bum replied, then leaned toward V. T. and held out a hand. "A big-shot, white-shoe lawyer like you wouldn't have any spare change on him would you?"

V. T. reached for his wallet. "What's the matter? The County of New York bankrupt and failing to meet its payroll obligations?"

The bum, Butch Karp, accepted the bill V. T. handed him. "A dollar? Hell, I can't buy a hot dog at Nathan's anymore for a buck."

"Beggars can't be choosers, right?"

"I guess not. I hope that you have something more than a George Washington to drag me away from hearth and home."

V. T. frowned. "I'm not sure. Meaning, I'm not sure what it all means. But something's in the works that, when considered with other recent events, convinced me that you and I should chat. Besides, I could use another set of eyes and a brain; it's been enough for my simple mind to stay 'in character' when I loathe this role."

"I know it's not easy, V. T." Karp kept his head down, as if "the bum" no longer cared about his bench-warming companion, in case anybody was watching.

Picking up his cue, V. T. stared straight ahead at Alice and her friends. "Okay to talk here?"

"I think so. Clay's got some of his folks running interference. They'll notice anybody who seems too interested. You might have seen Detective Barb DiBiasi on the sidewalk. . . . She makes a great homeless woman."

V. T. chuckled. "Yeah, I think we met. She called me Fancy Pants and asked if I wanted a blow job for twenty bucks."

"Hey, she told me it was twenty-five!"

"I guess some of us have it, and some of us don't."

"Yeah, I guess. But seriously, I know it's got to be wearing you down."

"It's okay; I need to do this . . . for my dad, if nothing else, but maybe a whole lot of other people, too. I'm a regular Scaramouche, you know, 'born with a gift of laughter and a sense that the world is mad.' I'll be okay."

Karp stole a glance at V. T. *He looks older,* he thought. *Even in this lighting, it's obvious that the lines around his eyes and mouth are deeper.*

"So how's Uncle Dean?" Karp asked.

V. T. snorted. "Practically a father to me," he said sarcastically. "Heck, he's even insisted on taking me to a firing range with him so that I can pack a pistol for the next time 'some niggers try to jump you'—his words not mine. A real bonding experience, let me tell you. Nothing says love like a warm gun."

The "falling-out" between Karp and V. T. had been a ruse. After the double-agent Jon Ellis tried to kill Karp in April, Lucy had seen the triskele-emblem ring on V. T.'s finger. "Where'd you get that?" she'd asked, horrified, as she knew it was the symbol for the Sons of Man, who'd murdered Cian Magee.

V. T. had explained that the ring had belonged to his cousin, Quilliam, and had been given to him by his uncle, Dean Newbury, who wore a similar ring, as did a group of his business associates.

It wasn't proof that they were the Sons of Man, but it was certainly a smoking gun. So they'd come up with a plan to get V. T. in with his uncle, who'd already been making overtures regarding him joining the family firm after his father's death. The first step had been coming up with a powerful enough reason for V. T. to change from public servant to Fifth Avenue lawyer.

Guma had happily arranged to have "a couple of associates" rough up V. T. They'd been told to make it look good, but maybe relished a little too much the free pass to put it to an assistant district attorney. The broken nose and ribs, as well as the rest of his beat, went a long way toward convincing Dean of the reasons behind his nephew's change of heart. The fair-minded V. T. had felt guilty about laying the rap on "two black guys," but it was a matter of playing to his uncle's worldview. The man was a racist, and the image of black muggers conformed to what he believed the world to be like. That had been followed by the public "falling-out" between Karp and V. T.

They'd recognized early on that Dean Newbury had at least one spy in the DAO, and they were sure the loud arguments, the insults, and the erosion of respect would get back to him. But Karp had seen to it that they'd also taken their time to set the trap. Instead of V. T. leaving the hospital after the assault and joining the family law firm, he suggested that V. T. waver, as if torn by the decision.

"Let's force the old man to woo you into the fold, rather than you jumping in," Karp had said in a meeting with V. T., Guma, and Jaxon—the only people except Marlene from whom there were no secrets. "Then it's all his idea. Just be increasingly receptive. In the meantime, you and I are going to go through a nasty divorce."

However, from the beginning there'd been little more than the triskele rings to connect Dean Newbury to the Sons of Man. The first indication of a possible link to anything unusual had actually come from Guma, when he noted that Khalifa had been represented by William White in the assault case. Karp had written it down on his notepad to bring up with V. T. during one of their "angry" meetings that so upset Mrs. Milquetost.

It did seem unusual that Newbury, Newbury and White—a firm not exactly known for its pro bono work, especially after V. T.'s father, Vincent, died—had represented a black Muslim with no resources. But it had since become clear that Khalifa had been working as a bodyguard for Imam Jabbar and that Jabbar and the Al-Aqsa mosque had plenty of Saudi money for engaging a high-priced law firm.

As V. T. had pointed out during that meeting, it still did not draw a line between Dean Newbury's role with the Sons of Man and any plots connected to Khalifa's bombing of the Third Avenue Synagogue. "Still, something's fishy," V. T. pointed out. "The country's supposedly foremost federal anti-terrorism agencies . . . apparently . . . haven't discovered that Rondell James changed his name, or that the man also known as Muhammad Jamal

Khalifa was a member of a mosque founded by a radical anti-American cleric. It's either gross ineptitude, a cover-up, or someone with powerful enough connections to keep it quiet."

Later, Jaxon told Karp about The Sheik and the possibility of terrorist activity, perhaps involving Prince Esra bin Afraan Al-Saud, and the prince's intended visit to the Al-Aqsa mosque. Again, Karp had made notations on his legal pad and then discussed the information with V. T. and Guma after the bureau chiefs meeting in which he'd announced V. T.'s resignation.

When V. T. was introduced to his new client, Prince Esra, they wondered if he might now learn something of importance to the investigation. But again, there was nothing to link Dean Newbury or the Sons of Man to any illegal plots or the synagogue bombing. Even V. T.'s wine-and-dine responsibilities with the prince had all been aboveboard, if boring and distasteful.

Not until that night, when V. T. saw his uncle accept the envelope at the reception, and then later when he saw the envelope and the note with "STM-17" written on it, did he think he was on to something. "I didn't even know he could speak Russian," he said to Karp. "What do you make of it?"

Karp pretended to be nodding off, letting his head sag onto his chest. "To be honest, I don't know," he responded quietly. "It could be innocent . . . though I'm like you . . . your uncle gets this secret envelope with some sort of coded message which he passes on to someone speaking Russian. What grabs my attention is his demand that whoever he's talking to prevent anyone from inspecting 'the contents' or bothering 'the visitors.' What contents and what visitors?"

"He didn't like it that I saw that note. I could tell. The guy normally radiates suspicion, but tonight it was oozing out of him."

Karp thought about it. "I think this is something I should pass on to our Russian friends in Brooklyn. Maybe it'll make sense to them."

V. T. knew about Karp's great-uncle and cousin, the Karchovskis, but it was not one of those things they brought up. "Good idea."

Changing the subject, Karp asked, "What's this I heard about you being kidnapped tonight? Guma told me a little, but it seemed a bit strange."

"You're telling me. Essentially, I was tied up by a squad of geriatric gangsters. They kind of bumbled around, but I think they were telling the truth—at least as far as they know it."

V. T. explained what had happened from start to finish. Karp had to stop himself from chuckling. But the kidnappers had confirmed what Karp and Jaxon already believed—that the Celtic bookstore owner, Cian Magee, had been murdered by the Sons of Man to destroy the book about the group and prevent Magee from discussing it more with Lucy.

Of course, there was another murder they had implicated Dean Newbury with . . . the fratricide of Vincent Newbury. "Do you think they're right about that, too?" Karp asked.

"I think there's a good chance."

"Any ideas on how to prove it?"

V. T. twisted the triskele ring around on his finger. "I'm not sure. Who do you know at the medical examiner's office who owes you a favor and can be trusted to keep a secret?"

"I have a few chits I can call in. What should they be looking for?"

"Anything in the medical report that's out of order, but I'd particularly like to know about the levels of digitalis in his system. If this doesn't work, we may have to exhume his body, but as that would certainly tip my uncle off, I want to keep it quiet for now."

"You bet," Karp said, stifling a real yawn behind his hand. "Anything else?"

"Any idea on who the Senior Avengers are and how they're involved in all this?"

"I have a hunch," Karp replied. "I'll check it out and let you know. . . . You want to leave first?"

"Sure, I'm about wiped out and want to be home asleep." With that V. T. got up and walked over to the statue where he patted the Mad Hatter on his hat. "'Yes,'" he whispered. "'You can always take more than nothing.'"

21

The blonde woman sitting in the window booth of the Khartoum Restaurant across the street from the Al-Aqsa mosque ignored the dark looks she was getting from the mostly Muslim male patrons and staff. She was the only white person in the crowded café—famous for its *shorba*, a puree of lamb, served with warm *kisra* bread—as well as the only female not wearing a hajib.

In fact, she was dressed in tight, black leather pants, a form-fitting white T-shirt, a black leather coat and beret, and large, white-framed sunglasses, despite the early evening. She wore the outfit for three reasons: to deliver a slap in the face to the locals, whom she regarded with contempt; to drive her "date" crazy with lust later that night; and, as she'd explained to her black male companion, to disguise her identity from someone who had only seen her wearing loose-fitting robes and a head covering.

When they walked into the restaurant, the owner insisted to her accomplice, a homegrown jihadi named Ali Hazzan, that she leave. Hazzan had explained that she was a "special guest" of Imam Jabbar's and not to be trifled with. The owner glared at her for a moment, but then retreated to the kitchen. The patrons overheard the reference to the imam and did not express their displeasure either—the imam's inner circle of bodyguards played rough.

Nadya Malovo could not have cared less what they thought. Even her companion was beginning to irritate her. She certainly didn't need his protection—she could have killed him and several more like him without much trouble—but he knew his way around the city and its subways; otherwise she would have acted alone.

Hazzan and the others she had been training at the "Phase Two" site in Vermont called her "Ajmaani" and thought she was Chechen, fighting to establish an Islamic state in the former southern state of the Soviet Union. They'd heard about the Beslan school massacre that she'd helped to engineer, and they'd seen enough of her violent personality on a firsthand basis to be scared to death of her.

Malovo was actually a former KGB agent, recruited as a teenager off the streets of Moscow and trained as an assassin, and she'd first plied her trade in Afghanistan during and after the Soviet invasion. When the USSR crumbled, she'd gone into private practice, working for a coalition of crooked politicians, mob bosses, and corrupt military men.

Her orders in Chechnya and other former satellite states on the southern border were to carry out "Islamic terrorist" actions to discredit legitimate nationalist movements by Muslims. By publicly aligning herself with the nationalists, who didn't want her help, she gave the Russians a reason to send in troops to quash the "Islamic extremists." Of course, Russia's real purpose was to keep the area's oil resources, as well as unfettered access to warm-water ports on the Black Sea. The true Islamic extremists, mostly foreigners fighting to establish Islamic fundamentalist states ruled by religious law, didn't know her true purpose and welcomed her as one of their own. And as it turned out, her employers saw the value of allying themselves with the group represented by Dean Newbury.

Without saying anything to Hazzan, Malovo got up from the table. Across the street, the woman she'd been waiting for left the Al-Aqsa mosque and began walking west on 124th. She hesitated by the door, as Hazzan paid the bill, to allow the young woman to get far enough ahead, and then left the restaurant and began to follow.

Although the day had been warm, there was a bite to the air now that the sun had gone down, leaving the city bathed in a soft blue-gray light.

Miriam Khalifa looked up at the sky, hoping to see above the surrounding buildings her first glimpse of the new crescent moon signaling the start of Ramadan. The exact time of its appearance had been the subject of much spirited debate at the mosque—some relied on the Hayden observatory, while others eschewed "modern" means and preferred to try to work it out with the old Arabic formulas.

"Any night now," her father, Mahmoud Juma, would say with a laugh as he had every year of her life in the days before Ramadan. "We must be ready." A simple fisherman in their native Kenya, he was a devout Muslim and cherished this time of year as the most important to his faith.

Miriam pulled the edges of her lime-green hajib close around her face to ward off the chill and hurried along the sidewalk until she reached the corner of Frederick Douglass Boulevard, where she turned right and headed north. She was filled with trepidation.

The night before she'd been visited again by the spirit of Hazrat Fatemeh Masumeh, a Muslim saint. The Aalimah, or "learned lady," had been with her since her childhood in a tiny village on the shores of the Indian Ocean, usually in times of danger or uncertainty. She'd been appearing more often of late.

The first time she'd seen her had been when she was about nine years old and waiting on the beach for her father and brother to return from the sea in the family fishing boat. They were overdue, having been expected the day before. That in itself was not unusual; sometimes if the catch was particularly bountiful they would stay until the boat couldn't hold any more. But the other fishermen who had returned spoke of a sudden squall that had nearly swamped their boats, and she had a feeling that something was just not right.

"Please Aalimah, if it pleases Allah, bring my father and brother back," she prayed. "My mother is not well and my sisters and I are afraid."

A devout Muslim like her father, she loved hearing stories about the heroes of Islam. Of these, her favorite had always been Hazrat Fatemeh Masumeh, who had been related to the Prophet and was taught the Islamic sciences by the most important imams of her time. Miriam liked that in their male-dominated culture, her heroine was respected and revered for her intelligence, piety, and knowledge as well as her scholarship of the *Ahadith*, the traditions passed down directly from Allah's messenger,

Muhammad. Masumeh was devout, kind, and gracious—said to have performed many miracles—some of which Miriam's father would describe in stories told by the family fire. She was loved by her people in her own time as well as by the millions of pilgrims who had visited her shrine in Qom, the city where she'd died as a martyr in a.d. 780.

Hazrat Fatemeh Masumeh was said to fulfill the rightful wishes of believers and heal incurable diseases. When nothing happened in response to Miriam's prayer—not a sail on the horizon—she was disappointed. She was as devout a little girl as there was in her entire village. She had not asked for riches, or anything for herself, only the safe return of her father and brother.

At that moment, she'd looked down the white sands of the beach and spied a dark figure walking toward her—a woman by her robes and scarves that fluttered in a breeze that had suddenly come from the ocean. She expected the woman, who was a stranger—and oddly, not African—to pass by, but instead she approached and spoke to her.

"*Jambo*, Miriam," the woman had said in the traditional Swahili greeting. "Why do you wait?"

"I wait for my father and brother to return from the sea," Miriam said. "I am worried that a storm has taken them." She could not see much of the woman, but she appeared to be Arabian. Miriam knew even then that the Arabs were a people who had visited that coast for thousands of years, bringing trade and Islam. The woman had olive skin and light brown eyes, and it seemed to Miriam that she could smell rose petals in her presence.

"Why worry? If all things are in the hands of Allah, then we believers must accept that things will turn out as they are intended," the woman said.

"But if I pray to Allah, then He may answer my prayers and what is intended will be the return of my father and brother," Miriam replied.

The woman smiled with her eyes. "And that by definition is God, with whom all things are possible." As she spoke the woman turned to look out to sea and sniffed at the stiffening wind.

Miriam followed her gaze with her own eyes and out of the blinding sun a dark shape appeared on the horizon. "It sails oddly," she said excitedly as she stood and shaded her eyes with a hand. "But it is my father's boat." With tears in her eyes, she turned to the woman. "Are you Hazrat Fatemeh Masumeh?"

The woman caressed her face. "I am who you need me to be," she said. "And I will be with you when you need me."

Miriam ran forward as her father brought his boat onto the beach, where her brother jumped off to secure it with a rope. "I am so glad you are home," she said. "I would like you to meet my friend, Hazrat Fatemeh Masumeh."

Her brother had looked at her with surprise and then burst out laughing. "What are you talking about, little nut?" he teased. "Have you been sitting in the sun too long?"

Miriam whirled around expecting to see the woman, but the beach was empty. "But she was here," she insisted. "I prayed to Allah that you would come home safely, and Aalimah granted my wish."

Her brother started to tease Miriam more, but her father had stopped him. "It is not important whether Aalimah was here in body," he said. "What is important is that you believed that with God all things are possible, and if you are devout and ask, your wish may be granted. Tonight, this family will say an extra prayer of thanks for Hazrat Fatemeh Masumeh, may Allah bless her and give her peace."

Miriam had never loved her father more than she did at that moment. But neither had she ever loved him less since. His faith was the Islam she knew—full of wonder at the greatness and compassion of God. Through His Prophet, He had given mankind rules so that they could live in peace with one another while worshiping God, not out of fear, but out of praise for all He had created for them. A God of the family hearth. A God who brought fish to the nets of her father. A God who would give them a place in Paradise someday, if they just followed the teachings of the Prophet.

As it turned out, the squall had snapped off the mast of her father's boat and hurled it away. Adrift, surrounded by sharks, they were sure to die in the blazing sun when their water ran out unless discovered by another fishing boat, but that would have taken a miracle on so great an ocean. And yet, even at their bleakest hour, there was no fear.

"We placed our lives in the hands of Allah, the merciful, and were content to die if it was His will," her father recalled. But that morning a breeze had started blowing from the east—a good thing—but with no way to take advantage of it, they could not hope to be blown to the shore. Then Miriam's brother had spotted something in the water.

"It was our mast with the sail still attached," her brother explained. "A miracle."

They'd retrieved the mast and rigged it the best they could. Progress had been slow, but the wind remained steady and blew them home.

At bedtime that night her father sat with her until her eyes grew heavy, and then bent over to kiss her on her forehead. "Thank you for your prayers, little Miriam," he whispered. "I believe they saved us."

———

After that, Hazrat Fatemeh Masumeh had appeared to Miriam often. One day she had showed up in time to push her away from the strike of a giant cobra. She did not answer all of the girl's prayers, such as those she'd repeated over and over while her mother and one of her sisters lay dying of malaria. However, the saint had stood by her side as she grieved at their gravesides and assured her that they would wait for her in Paradise.

In 1998, the Juma family traveled to Nairobi, where they hoped to get work visas that would allow them to emigrate to the United States. Following the death of his wife, Mahmoud Juma had lost his heart for fishing and their life in the tiny village. But his son, Miriam's brother, had already immigrated and was working as a taxi driver in New York City. His letters back home had been filled with fabulous stories about his new home, as well as the money he was making and the dreams he had of starting his own fish market some day. He urged his father and sister to join him, and with nothing left for him on the shores of the Indian Ocean, Mahmoud had agreed to give it a try.

The sisters were delighted. They'd heard that women in America were treated more as equals than in Muslim Kenya, and that their opportunities were nearly limitless.

"I hear any woman can attend university and have a career," said her older sister, Ayaan.

"I don't believe it," the shocked Miriam had whispered as they slept on the floor at the home of a family friend that first night in Nairobi.

"It's true," Ayaan giggled. "And you can even pick the man you marry!"

"Papa would never allow it," fourteen-year-old Miriam scolded. "It wouldn't be proper for a Muslim woman."

"Maybe not," Ayaan, then fifteen, laughed before dropping her voice again. "But it would be more fun."

They rose the next morning before dawn to go to the U.S. Embassy, where they had to spend hours waiting in line. When their father was out of hearing range, they at first passed the time scandalizing each other with the things they would do in America. Nearly eight hours later, they had tired of that game and silently fanned themselves in the merciless sun.

Miriam was wishing she could have a drink of water when Hazrat Fatemeh Masumeh appeared behind her in line. There was real fear in the woman's eyes.

"You must leave here," she cried in Miriam's mind. "There is great evil afoot. Oh, the poor people . . ."

The thought of leaving after getting so close to the gate, now only fifty feet away, made Miriam want to weep. "But we've been standing here all day in the hot sun," she replied in her thoughts. "Can't we get our visas first?"

"No!" The Aalimah was more insistent than she had ever been. "You must take your father and sister and go away from here as fast as you can."

Miriam thought about ignoring the spirit. But Hazrat Fatemeh Masumeh had never lied to her. "We have to leave," she said to her father and sister.

The others had looked at her incredulously. "Why should we go?" Ayaan demanded to know.

"I don't know why," she replied. "I just know that we must."

"But we will have to start over tomorrow," Ayaan complained.

Mahmoud Juma, however, looked thoughtfully at his daughter and then asked, "Has she spoken to you?" He knew his daughter seemed to have a special relationship with the Aalimah, may Allah bless and keep her.

"Yes," Miriam replied. "And she says that we must go away from here as fast as we can. There are *shayteen*, little demons, present, and they intend to hurt people."

Her father wasted no more time. "Then we leave," he said, stepping out of line. "Quickly!"

With Ayaan still complaining, the family moved as fast as they could away from the gate. As they walked, a large truck drove by them going in the other direction; when it had passed, Miriam looked across the street and saw Hazrat Fatemeh Masumeh staring after the truck with a hand covering her veiled mouth.

A moment later, there was a blinding flash of light, followed by an ear-shattering blast and wave of heat as the truck bomb exploded in front of the U.S. Embassy. They were knocked to the ground as debris the size of cars, and, in fact, cars, flew and crashed around them.

When the destructive moment had passed, the Jumas looked back in horror. The area where they had been standing was now a huge smoking crater littered with human remains and the burning hulks of cars. The entire front of the building they'd hoped to enter was gone; it looked as if someone had taken a giant cleaver and hacked it down the middle. The air that the moment before had been rent by the blast was now filled with screams and yells and, after a bit, the far-off sirens responding.

Al Qaeda claimed responsibility for the bombing of the U.S. Embassy in Nairobi, which took 291 lives, most of the victims Muslim. It was not the Islam that Miriam knew. But it was her first experience with Islamic extremism and murder committed in the name of Allah.

In her village before the blast, the elders had talked about the troubling brand of Islamic militancy growing in the Middle East and hoped in their prayers that such a thing would not come to Kenya. But some of the young men had come back from their travels and talked about how one group in particular, Al Qaeda, wanted to create a world through jihad that would be ruled by Islamic law. A world in which Muslims were the ascendant people and all others subservient. The elders had rolled their eyes and then lectured the young men.

"The Qur'an prohibits making war except in self-defense," they pointed out, reading from the appropriate places in their sacred book. "There are no excuses for making war on innocent people, especially women and children. And killing other Muslims? That is a sure road to the fiery pits of hell."

At one discussion she'd overheard, it was her father who quoted from the Qur'an. He was warning a young man about views he'd picked up while on hajj in Mecca. "'And there are among us Muslims and others who deviate from justice. As for those who deviate, they will be firewood for the Hellfire,'" he had said.

After the bombing in Nairobi, Miriam felt guilty because Hazrat Fatemeh Masumeh had warned her, but she in turn had not warned the 291 others who had perished. She was grateful, she told the saint later in her prayers, but she didn't understand why she had been spared.

"You have nothing to feel guilty about," Masumeh answered. "It was the will of Allah that you listened to the voice of his messenger. What happened, and what will happen in the future, has already been written. Don't be in such a hurry to die. You may yet be asked to martyr yourself for your faith, as was I."

———

Lying in her bed at her father's apartment in Harlem the night before, Miriam had recalled that conversation with a spirit in Kenya. She was lonely, and in spite of everything, she missed Jamal. But she knew he was not in Pakistan; she knew he was the murderer who blew himself up in the synagogue. She knew because he'd told her, though not in the usual way.

What he had done shamed her. She blamed the imam and those who came to the mosque from other countries to preach Islam as a religion of hate. Good men like her father tried to mitigate the damage and argued the true path of the Qur'an. But young men who had so little, sometimes not even their pride, would always listen to men who promised to give them the world. Even if it was in exchange for their blood.

What she had not done shamed her even more, and she'd decided to act. And the Aalimah had been there—a shadow in her bedroom that had materialized into a form—to talk with her through the night, brush the tears from her face, and promise that everything would be all right in the end. *Inshallah*.

In the morning, she borrowed a neighbor's cell phone and called the number on the card she'd found beneath the box of tissues in the mosque's ladies room. "*Jambo*," she said when the other woman answered.

There was a slight hesitation and then the reply. "*Sjambo*."

"I have something that I need to give to you," Miriam said. "It has to do with the bombing of the synagogue."

Another pause and then a reply. "Do you want to send it to me? Would that be safer?"

"No, there are things I must tell you in person."

"Let me call you back in just a minute," the woman named Marie said. She then did as she'd promised, giving Miriam a set of specific instructions on how to find her. "Please follow these exactly. We will have people watching for you along the way who may be able to help if you need it."

Miriam hesitated when she reached the corner of 125th Street and Frederick Douglass Boulevard; the hair on the back of her neck was standing on end. She glanced behind her. There were many people on the street, but her eyes went to the couple who were looking in the window of Hue-Man Bookstore & Café. The man was black and looked familiar; the woman was white, and she was sure she'd never seen anyone who dressed like that before.

Clutching her large handbag with its damning evidence against her chest, she walked quickly on. What would be had already been written. All she could do was follow the path laid out before her.

Hurrying across the boulevard, Malovo just barely caught a glimpse of her quarry heading down the stairs of the subway entrance at St. Nicholas Avenue. "Run," she ordered her companion and sprinted ahead for the entrance, taking the stairs two at a time.

She pulled up at the bottom of the stairs when she spotted Miriam standing on the platform. She was alone, minding her business as only New Yorkers, even new New Yorkers, can. Eyes averted. Deep in thought, or the appearance of thought. Every so often, those closest to the edge of the platform would step forward and look down the line, trying to spot the light of an approaching train as if by doing so they could speed up the process.

Only one thing wrong here, Malovo thought: Miriam Khalifa didn't need to take a subway to the apartment she now shared with her father and sister a few blocks from the mosque. It was the first time Miriam had deviated from her habit of going straight home after work since Malovo started having her watched following the reception. *Who are you going to meet, my little Muslim flower?*

Miriam shot a glance up the platform in her direction. Malovo turned to her shocked companion and embraced him. "Hug me, fool," she hissed, turning away from the other woman's sight. "Remember, I'm your girlfriend."

Hazzan nearly fainted at the demand. He'd been watching two large rats on the tracks below fighting viciously over the remains of a donut when he glanced up and saw a young man of about his own age also watching. The man was with a group of Orthodox Jews in their broad-brimmed black hats.

Until recently Hazzan had never really thought much about Jews one way or the other, except for fantasizing, like every other small-time criminal, about robbing one of the Hasidic diamond dealers who were known to carry the gems on their person. But it had remained only a fantasy; everybody knew that robbing one of those guys would get you one of two things, an ass-kicking and arrest by the NYPD, or, if the Jewish mob got to you first, dead in some alleyway. Still, he hadn't hated them, or their nation of Israel, for that matter, until joining the mosque. That's when he learned that it was the Jews who controlled the white man, who was keeping the black man down.

"What is she doing?" Malovo asked.

"She is watching for the train," he responded. "She looked at us but didn't seem to care."

Malovo broke off the embrace as the B train slid into the station. She and Hazzan hopped on the car behind the one Miriam stepped into and rode it to Fifth Avenue where Miriam got off. They followed her onto the platform, where she remained, apparently waiting for the F train, which was scheduled to arrive next.

The glow from the light of the train had just appeared far down the track when a tall, filthy man with wiry hair and a wild beard stepped in between Malovo and her line of sight. "Say friends, got any spare change for the hungry . . . the hungry being me?" the man asked, though it was difficult to see his mouth for all the hair around it.

Malovo scowled and stepped to the side, but the man moved with her. "Get out of my way, disgusting scum," she snarled.

Instead of shuffling away, the beggar rose up to his full height, his eyes suddenly ablaze with righteousness, and waved a nearly black finger in Malovo's face.

"'HE'—or in this case, SHE—'WHO MOCKS THE POOR SHOWS CONTEMPT FOR THEIR MAKER,'" he shouted. Heads turned, wary of what might be happening. "And I expect this probably applies to you, 'WHOEVER GLOATS OVER DISASTER WILL NOT GO UNPUNISHED.' . . . That's Proverbs 17:5!"

The F train rumbled to a stop. Peering around the lunatic, Malovo saw Miriam dash inside a car.

"Get out of my way!" Malovo shouted and connected a foot with his groin. She dodged around him as he sank to the ground with a groan and got on the car, with her companion scrambling to make it just behind her.

As the train rumbled out of the station, the beggar pulled himself to his feet and stumbled through the toll gates to a pay phone. He picked up the receiver and punched in a code that only linemen with the New York City phone company were supposed to know. When he got the right tone, he dialed a number. "She's being followed," he said. "White woman dressed like a skunk—can't miss her, and a black dude . . . tall, skinny."

Edward Treacher doubled over as a fresh wave of nausea emanated from his testicles to his mouth. "I hope you know I sacrificed the family jewels for the cause," he gasped into the receiver. He listened and in spite of the pain, chuckled. "Very funny, but it doesn't mean I enjoy getting them kicked up into my stomach."

22

"We have a special guest with us this evening," Karp told the class. "His name is Moishe Sobelman, and he owns a bakery on 29th and Third that makes the best cherry cheese coffee-cake in the world."

Three dozen pairs of eyes glanced longingly at the tray on a table off to the side from which the smell of warm coffee cake rose. Karp was pleased that not one of his students was absent, and most of their parents, whom he'd made a special effort to invite, were with them.

The death of Rabbi Romberg had been a blow to the congregation, especially the children and the youth groups whom the rabbi mentored. Karp had seen many of his students at the funeral, the devastation written all over their faces. And yet here they were, ready to move on with their lives.

Maybe some of that has to do with knowing that the idea for this class was his, Karp thought. "As you know, this class was created by Rabbi Romberg to introduce you to role models in the Jewish community, and I don't think you'll find a better one than Mr. Sobelman. Tonight, I've asked him to speak to you about his experiences at a place called Sobibor during World War II. I'll warn you now, it isn't a pleasant story. If it gets to be too much for you, you may excuse yourself. However, I think it's a story that is relevant today, and one I believe that we all should know."

Sobelman got up from his chair and walked to the front of the classroom. He looked at the students for a moment, a sad look passing across his face. "Who can tell me about the Holocaust?"

Elisa Robyn's hand shot up. "The Holocaust refers to Nazi Germany's efforts to remove Jews and other 'undesirables' from Europe by putting them in death camps.

"About 6 million Jews, and another 6 million other people, like Gypsies, Slavs, Communists, and even Catholics, were murdered."

"Very good, Miss . . . ?" Sobelman replied.

"Robyn, Elisa Robyn," the girl replied, turning to bat her eyes at Giancarlo, who responded with a "well done" nod.

"Nice to meet you, Miss Robyn, Elisa Robyn," Sobelman said with a little bow. "Can anybody here tell me about Krystalnacht?"

Elisa's hand shot up again. But Sobelman called on a boy with Woody Allen glasses and demeanor. "Yes, what is your name?"

"Aaron Spellman," the boy replied. "Krystalnacht means 'Night of Broken Glass' because so many windows of Jewish homes and businesses were destroyed during anti-Jewish riots in Germany. It was November 9, 1938 . . . at the beginning of the Holocaust."

"Yes, yes . . . the beginning," Sobelman replied as if the words themselves haunted him. "Though at the time, many did not see it as a warning of what was to come. After all, only 100 Jews were killed and 30,000 sent to the 'work camps' that were beginning to spring up in the German countryside. Of course, that doesn't account for the 7,000 shops and 1,500 synagogues that were also damaged or destroyed, or similar attacks that took place in Vienna at the same time. Some Jews saw the writing on the wall and fled Germany and Europe before it was too late, but most just thought it was those crazy Nazi bullies blowing off steam and that soon the German people would rein them in."

Sobelman straightened his shoulders as he looked at his audience. "We as a people underestimated the power of propaganda and hate. There was a worldwide depression, jobs were scarce. In order to rise to power, the Nazis needed someone to blame it on—a scapegoat. And Jews were convenient as they always had been, though in truth Germany had historically treated Jews better than many other European countries. They were an integral part of the community, respected and liked . . . good businessmen." He paused. "By the way, who knows the historic reason that Jews are said to be money-grubbers?"

Giancarlo raised his hand. "It started in the Middle Ages. Christians were not supposed to charge other Christians usury, meaning interest, if they loaned money. Of course, that meant no Christian was going to loan money. But Jews could loan money and charge interest, so they were sort of the first bankers."

"Yes, yes, very good," Sobelman nodded. "A fine young man who knows his history."

"Ass kisser," Zak whispered, though not quietly enough.

"And you, young man," the baker asked Zak, "what do you know of pogroms?"

"Uh, that would be when the other people in the community attacked Jews without reason," Zak answered. If it had to do with bloodshed and fighting, he was all over it.

"Oh they had reasons, perhaps not legitimate ones, but they had reasons," Sobelman replied. "During feudal times, nobles were required to supply the local king with military help in times of war in exchange for titles and lands. But it cost a lot of money to keep up a castle as well as an armed force. The nobles often had to borrow money against their crops or lands, and the only place they could do that was their local Jewish merchant. They racked up quite a lot of debt that way. And during the Crusades, it was even worse. Galloping off with your men to the Holy Land was expensive business, and they had to borrow even more money until they were so far in debt, they really didn't own their own horse, much less their land."

Sobelman shrugged. "Of course, one way to get out of paying one's debts is to murder the person you owe. They couldn't say it like that, so they came up with 'reasons,' often with the approval of their local churchmen. One reason they invented was that Jews murdered Christian babies to use their blood for Satanic rituals; that was why the harvest was poor, or the plague was back inside the castle. But it was sometimes hard to look upon the kindly old Jewish moneylender as a monster. So they used propaganda to depict Jews as hiding their real faces behind their big noses and smiles, when everybody knew they really looked a lot like Satan, complete with horns and fangs. And that is how it starts . . . first you destroy the idea of your enemy as a human being, and then you can destroy their lives without the guilt."

"What's that have to do with Krystalnacht?" Zak asked.

"Because that was how the Holocaust started, and we should have been aware that history was repeating itself on a grand scale. There were actually Nazi cartoons that showed big-nosed Jews with horns. It was the Jews who controlled the money, according to the Nazi propaganda machine; Jews who stopped good Aryan men from being able to put bread on the table for their families. Convince a man that someone is attacking his family, and he will gladly break the windows of that man's business and his home . . . and then it is not such a far leap to break his bones and smash his teeth. Such a man will go along with those who say they have a plan, then try to pretend he doesn't know what is happening . . . or, as so many did, join in and be part of the solution, the Final Solution."

Moishe Sobelman sighed. "Your teacher, Mr. Karp, asked me to speak to you tonight about my experiences when I was not so much older than you. In fact, it all began shortly after my bar mitzvah in Amsterdam."

"You're from Holland?" Giancarlo asked.

Sobelman nodded. Yes, he was from Holland, or more officially, the Netherlands, where Jews had long been an important part of the community. The Christian Dutch had struggled for many years for their own religious freedom and so were tolerant of others; indeed, they'd welcomed 25,000 German Jews who fled their native land ahead of the coming storm in the late 1930s.

"We lived in a small town outside of Amsterdam where my father was also a baker," Sobelman said, smiling at Karp. "He was not so famous for his cherry cheese coffee-cake, but his strudel was the best in Holland. People would drive out from the city just to get it when it was hot from the ovens. He was a good man and had many friends, Jews and Gentiles."

The Jews in Holland watched the growing power of Hitler and the Nazi Party with concern, but they thought his rise would be a short-lived aberration. "Then came the news of Krystalnacht," Sobelman recalled. "Our parents thought that would be the last straw before the German people would come to their senses and throw the criminals in prison."

The next thing they knew, Sobelman continued, Hitler had invaded Poland, and then France fell, and finally the Netherlands capitulated.

What frightened Amsterdam's Jews were the stories that other Jews were being rounded up in Germany and the occupied countries and shipped off. . . . Where, no one knew, only that they did not come back again and there was no word of their fate. "Oh, occasionally someone heard from somebody who'd heard from a relative of a person who said that these Jews were being murdered in massive numbers," he said. "But the rumors were too horrible to believe."

For a time, the Jews in Holland believed that they were safe. The country was occupied by the Germans, but their fellow Dutch would never let them be singled out for extermination. Then in 1943, the Germans announced that the Dutch Jews would be "relocated." Sobelman paused and shook his head before looking back at his audience. "And you know what is the strangest part of all? We didn't resist; we went along like so many sheep to the slaughter. People acted as if we were all going on vacation together. Families packed suitcases and dressed in their best traveling clothes. The vacation would last until the war was over, our parents told each other, and then we would all go home."

Moishe Sobelman, his parents, Ibrahim and Sarah, and his four-year-old sister, Rebecca, were sent to a relocation camp near the Polish village and rail station for which it would be named. A quiet place in the country called Sobibor, surrounded by forests and swamps; a lightly populated area, but strategically placed near the large Jewish populations in the Chelm and Lublin districts.

Construction of the Sobibor camp had begun in March 1942, and the project was a model of German efficiency—a large rectangle of land, 400 by 600 meters in size, was cleared and then surrounded by triple lines of barbed-wire fence, each three meters high and under the watchful shadows of strategically placed guard towers. Tree branches were intertwined in the fences so that the casual passerby wouldn't know what he or she was looking at.

The camp itself was divided into three areas, each also surrounded by barbed-wire fencing and guard towers. The first, the administrative area, was placed close to the railroad station, which had a platform that could accommodate twenty freight cars at a time. "It could have been a train station like any other in Europe," Sobelman said. "We were told it was merely a transit point and that we would be moving on shortly. Only they would not say where we were going."

This area also included the living quarters for the guards, "SS soldiers and Ukrainians who were forced to work in concentration camps, though in truth many of them enjoyed their work; after all, their people had a long history of murdering Jews." The first area was also where the guards housed the Jewish prisoners that were used as the camp's labor force.

The second area, called Camp II, was where the arriving Jews were marched to be separated from their belongings and each other. "The young children went with the women," Sobelman said quietly. "That was the last time I saw my mother and sister. They and the others were taken to a building where they were forced to undress before going into a special hut to have their heads shaved so that the Germans could make use of their hair. I can remember to this day a woman who started screaming hysterically as she was led away, 'It's impossible! It's impossible! It cannot be!'"

Most of those who arrived on the train soon passed from Camp II to Camp III through a walkway two or three meters wide, surrounded on both sides by barbed wire. It was covered with branches so that the prisoners could not see out or be seen by those outside. "The Tube," as it was called, ran for 150 meters—"that would be more than one and a half American football fields"—toward a group of trees.

"Behind the trees was a large, ugly brick building containing three rooms—each about twelve feet by twelve feet," Sobelman said. "Into these rooms naked, frightened Jews were driven—as many as 160 people, sometimes more, at a time, all crammed together and unable to move as they listened to the sound of diesel engines starting outside and then smelled the exhaust being pumped into the rooms."

Sobelman looked around the room. He had their complete, undivided attention. "Now imagine that you are in one of those rooms. You cannot sit down. You cannot smell the carbon monoxide in the fumes, but you know it is there. So you and the others begin to panic. You fight and claw and climb over one another's naked bodies, looking for an escape. But there is none, and all you can do before you die is scream or pray."

Sobelman closed his eyes. "Ach, I still can hear the voices of the Hassidic women shouting the Shema Israel." His voice suddenly grew so loud that the audience sat up and their eyes flew open wide. "SHEMA YISRAEL ADONAI ELOHEINU ADONAI ECHAD! HEAR O ISRAEL, THE LORD IS OUR GOD, THE LORD IS ONE!"

Then Sobelman was quiet again. His voice wavered. "But they did not shout very long . . . not long at all. In fact, from the time most of us arrived at the rail station until those final moments in the gas chambers, it was only two or three hours. That's all it took to process and murder four or five hundred people at a time. . . . Men, women, children, they spared no one."

Zak raised his hand and kept it up until the old man nodded to him. "How . . . how come you're alive?"

Sobelman laughed, though the sound was free of humor. "How many times have I asked myself that question, and still I have no answers. I was with my father when we were forced to strip and then herded toward those gas chambers past the SS guards and Ukranians, who laughed and hit us with sticks to make us keep moving. We had just about reached the building when a German officer grabbed me by the arm. . . . I wanted to stay with my father and held onto his hand, but he pulled away and said, 'Do not forget.' And then he was gone into the building, and I never saw him again."

The class remained silent as the old man in front of them broke down and wept. Karp walked over with a glass of water and placed a hand on Sobelman's shoulder. "Would you prefer to continue some other time?"

Sobelman gratefully accepted the water and drank. "No, I will finish my story. My father told me to never forget because justice needs a witness." He patted Karp on his shoulder. "Thank you, my friend, for your concern, but telling a story such as this is not as hard as living it."

Sobelman turned his attention back to the audience. Many of their faces were pale, and most had tears in their eyes, even the adults.

"I was spared not through some kindness, but because the Germans and their Ukranian dogs did not want to do the dirty work," he said. "They kept several hundred Jewish slave laborers for that. . . . We worked in teams. Some cleaned out the killing rooms, the bodies so tightly packed that even when they were dead, there was no room to fall down. Rail tracks ran up to the back of the building; bodies were hauled out the rear doors and loaded on trolleys to be taken to pits, where other prisoners stacked them like cordwood for efficiency, then burned and buried them."

Sobelman sighed and then continued. "There were many jobs in the camp. Some gathered the hair in the shaving hut and sorted it by color and quality—most going to stuff mattresses though the best was used for wigs. Other slaves gathered bodies in the camp of laborers who had been killed by guards or died of starvation simply because they had no wish to live any longer. My job was to remove gold fillings from the teeth of the corpses before they were placed on the trolleys for the burial pits."

"Oh my God," cried one of the mothers as she placed a hand over her mouth. She looked in desperation at her husband as if hoping he might take her and their child out of the room. But he just took her hand in his and nodded toward Sobelman, which allowed her to gather herself and face the old man, too.

"Oh my God," Sobelman repeated. "How many times, in how many languages, did I hear some Jew on the way to the gas chambers ask, 'My God, how can this happen?' But this was not a place where God answered many prayers . . . why, I do not know . . . but in this place, evil reigned supreme."

The first commandant at Sobibor was a man named Franz Stangl. He was an Austrian and had been a master weaver and then a police detective before the war. "During his tenure from when the camp opened for business in May 1942 until July 1942, approximately 100,000 Jews were murdered at Sobibor," Sobelman said. "Most came from Lublin, as well as Czechoslovkia, Germany, and Austria."

In late summer 1942, the mass killings stopped as repairs were made to the main rail line and the number of gas chambers doubled to six. "Operations resumed in October. Only now they could rob, strip, murder, and dispose of 1,200 innocent people at a time."

By the spring of 1943, more than a quarter million Jews had been killed. "Mostly from Galicia, Poland, Germany, and Slavic lands. Then in March, the first trainloads of French Jews arrived and were exterminated, followed by 35,000 Jews from Holland, including myself and my family. Jews were being drained from the population of Europe like water from a bathtub."

"Even children?" another of the mothers cried out.

"Yes, my dear," Sobelman replied heavily. "Even the children. I remember especially one of the trains from Holland had so many children that it was impossible to process them quickly. They were separated from their mothers and formed into a spiraling line in one of the yards. They were beautiful children—little blondes in sailor suits and pigtails with round, red cheeks, all dressed up as if going on holiday. Hour after hour they waited in the line with their little suitcases and bags. Some knelt to play in the sand, while others cried for their mothers. But they were good children and did as they were told and waited even when the Ukrainians made a game of trying to frighten them. All day long, from morning until night, that line uncoiled as the children were slowly led into a building where their clothes and baggage were taken from them. Then they were herded like little animals up The Tube where their parents had already gone, and into the brick building. Then the engines would start and a few minutes later, the doors at the back of the building would open and out they would fall like potatoes from a truck."

Even being a slave laborer was no guarantee of staying alive. "I was spared because of my father's occupation," Sobelman said. "One day, a German officer named Johann Klier, who had owned his own bakery before the war and ran the camp's, sought me out. Other prisoners who had known my father told Herr Klier that I was an experienced baker. So I went from pulling the teeth of corpses to baking bread. Oh, and Herr Klier also was in charge of collecting the shoes from prisoners. He once told me that he estimated 45,000 pairs of shoes in his inventory."

"Was Klier as bad as the others?" Zak asked.

"I guess you could say that on a scale of lesser evils, he was more humane than some of the others, though he knew what was going on in the camp, and did nothing about it. He was also not above beating prisoners for the slightest infraction. But there were those who enjoyed the brutality more than others."

There were some like Paul Bredow, a former police officer from Silesia. He would wait on the train platform to weed out the invalids or those too weakened from the strain of the trip to make the journey to Camp II. Instead, he would have other prisoners take them to "the chapel" where, he assured them, they would be taken care of. However, it was just a building where he practiced what he called his "hobby," which was target shooting, with Jews as his targets. "He set himself a daily quota of fifty."

Others enjoyed raping young girls and their mothers in front of each other. Or making new prisoners haul out the bodies of their family members and take them to the pits where they were forced to watch the bodies burn before they were shot and kicked into the pits as well."

"They were monsters!" Giancarlo exclaimed. "You'd have to be crazy to do something so horrible."

Sobelman shook his head. "Monsters? Crazy? Perhaps you could say that their deeds were monstrous and crazy, but to let them blame it on some mass psychosis that overtook the German race is to give them an excuse for deliberately murdering 12 million people."

Elisa Robyn's mother raised her hand. "What about people who say the Holocaust never happened?" she asked. "The president of Iran says it was a hoax. And so do some people in this country."

Sobelman's eyes glittered with anger. "Some hoax." He rolled up the sleeve on his right arm and held up the tattoo for all to see. "I'm sure you've all heard about these numbers," he said. "Well, do you know why they numbered us? It was so they could keep track of how many they killed. So how do we know it was not a hoax? Well, for starters, while they did their best to kill all the Jews in their camps, they did not succeed. So I suppose all those survivors were just lying? And what about the confessions of those who worked as guards and staff at the camps? I suppose they are lying, too, to make themselves look bad? Or perhaps their confessions were beat out of them the way they used to beat their prisoners? Of course, if you listened to those guards and officers, it was always someone else who did the killing; they always worked in some other part of the camp and had nothing to do with it."

As he continued to speak, Sobelman began pacing back and forth. "And what of the photographs the Germans took of the stacked bodies or the piles of bodies simply thrown into pits? And how about the photographs taken by the Allied soldiers who liberated the camps? I suppose they are all part of this grand hoax as well."

Sobelman stopped pacing. "But how do we really know for sure? Where did we come up with these outrageous figures of 6 million dead Jews for this hoax? Why, from the murderers themselves!"

He tapped the number on his forearm. "The Germans are a very meticulous people; they take great pride in it, and in this case, they kept detailed records. Remember all those personal belongings we surrendered when we arrived at the camps? They cataloged and tagged it all. . . . they even gave us receipts, though that was probably to lull us into a false sense of security."

"I think they were evil," said the woman who'd cried out earlier.

"I guess if you define an evil person as someone who commits evil deeds, then yes," Sobelman agreed, but then frowned. "However, if you're saying that by being evil they were not human—that they grew horns or spoke in gibberish—then again, you are making an excuse for their behavior. You're saying that they were evil and therefore could not help themselves, as if evil were a form of insanity."

Sobelman shook his head. "The acts were evil, but the actors were just humans. Most were ordinary people before the war. It's true that most of the SS and camp guards, and even the officers, weren't well-educated; they'd been factory workers, bakers, weavers, salesmen, and shop workers, just like their fathers had been before them. Many of them were married and had children."

"How could they do this then?" Zak complained.

"How could they, indeed. After the war, those who were put on trial said they were just following orders. It is always this way when men are held accountable for crimes: They blame someone else—a Führer, a king, an imam, their government, the other soldier. They even blame God. But all the while they know what they are doing is wrong, and that's what makes them guilty."

"How did you escape?" Giancarlo asked.

Sobelman looked at Karp. "Do we have time?"

Karp glanced at his watch. "Yes, but I do hear that cherry cheese coffee-cake calling my name."

Sobelman smiled. "Then we should answer. But perhaps this last story will be a good way to end such a horrible tale. For you see, those intent on evil can break our bones and knock out our teeth; they can murder us in gas chambers and blow themselves up in our synagogues. But there is one thing no one can do to you unless you let them . . . "

The friendly little old baker suddenly straightened his back, and his eyes grew fierce as he pointed a finger at his audience. "They cannot take your soul, and in the end, we did not let them take ours."

23

As the F train rumbled south, Malovo and Hazzan stayed near the door, ready to get off quickly. Malovo nearly lost her balance and had to reach out and grab her companion's arm as the train swung around a sudden bend in the rail line. He started to laugh—having ridden the subway system since childhood, he knew how to keep his footing the way a cowboy knows how to stay on a bucking horse. But since he'd known her, he'd never seen Ajmaani lose her composure, or her balance, and it seemed comical until he caught the look in her eye.

When the train reached the Delancey Street station, the woman they were following waited until the last moment and then stepped out as the doors were about to close. Malovo wondered if Miriam was on to them. But the younger woman never turned to look back. Instead, she stood for a moment to study the subway station signs and then headed for the exit she wanted, her two trackers following.

The sky had darkened considerably by the time they walked onto Delancey Street in the Lower East Side. The sidewalks were in transition, with some people heading home and others walking to the area's restaurants, which were doing a brisk table business as people enjoyed one of the last warm evenings of August.

It took Malovo a moment to spot the back of the lime-green hajib, but then she spotted Miriam heading into Sarah Roosevelt Park. The younger woman cut through the park onto Chrystie Street, which she followed north until she reached Rivington. Suddenly she stopped and wheeled.

This time Malovo anticipated the move by stooping to inspect the wares of a sidewalk purse vendor, who tried to sell her a knock-off Prada. Meanwhile, Hazzan pointed to a framed photograph of the World Trade Center as it had appeared at night from the art vendor seated next door. Their target just seemed to be trying to get her bearings before crossing Chrystie to Rivington, where she was set upon by two bums looking for change.

With Miriam distracted, Malovo crossed Chrystie and hid in a doorway. She was tired of this game. *We should have just killed her after her idiot husband blew himself up,* she thought. At the time, she'd argued that they had no idea what Jamal might have told his wife about the plan—maybe enough that someone could piece some of it together. "I'll make it look like just another violent crime for which New York is reputed," she had said to Jabbar.

Malovo suspected that the imam had his eyes on the Widow Khalifa, although he was twice her age and reminded the Russian of a lizard with his bulgy eyes and the way his pink tongue constantly wet his thin lips. He'd argued that if something happened to her, Mahmoud Juma, the old man, might raise enough of a stink that the NYPD might start asking questions. The attorney, Dean Newbury, had agreed. "So far, according to my sources, the federal agencies haven't linked her husband to the mosque," he said. "We dodged a bullet, which we might not do a second time if the police come snooping around here for a murder investigation."

So Malovo had allowed herself to be persuaded that the threat of deportation—as well as an unfriendly reception in Nairobi should her family return—would be enough to force Miriam's silence. But she wasn't so sure anymore. A feeling of unease had been growing ever since she overhead Miriam Khalifa talking to the security-firm translator, Marie Smith, at the reception.

PrimeTech Security Corporation charged a lot of money, and they could no doubt hire the best of the best. Espey Jaxon was a prime example. As an FBI agent he'd caused her and others, like Andrew Kane, a lot of trouble. Finding out that Jaxon had a gambling problem had been a real surprise—but it seemed to check out with her mob sources.

She was just as sure that the firm's translators would also be high-priced and more than competent. Still, one who could speak French, English, Arabic, Chechen, and "a few words of Swahili," not to mention any languages she had failed to mention, was, as she'd said, unique. What else this "Marie" might be capable of if she started talking to Miriam Khalifa wasn't something Malovo wanted to leave to chance.

Malovo had tried to have Smith followed after the reception. But the mujahideen assigned to the task had lost her after she arrived back at the security firm's headquarters in New Jersey. The firm was guarded about the living arrangements of its personnel, and when a half-dozen sedans with dark-tinted windows left an hour later, the mujahideen didn't know which one to follow.

So Malovo decided she would have Miriam Khalifa watched instead. The men assigned to the task, however, reported nothing out of the ordinary. Each weekday morning, the woman brought her son to the mosque school, went to work at the reception desk until school was out, and then picked him up and walked him home to the apartment she shared with her father and sister. On weekends, she spent most of her time at Marcus Garvey or Central Park with her family.

This morning, the routine changed. Miriam had arrived at the mosque without her son. When one of the watchers reported this, Malovo had checked with the teacher and was told that the boy's mother said he wasn't feeling well and had stayed home with her father. But Malovo had several opportunities during the day to observe the younger woman without being seen, and she thought she seemed nervous and preoccupied. She kept talking to some unseen person, which made her wonder if the woman was wired for sound.

So Malovo dismissed one of the men assigned to keep an eye on Miriam and took a seat herself at the Khartoum Restaurant and then followed her to Rivington Street. She peeked around the edge of the doorway. Miriam was searching her purse for something to give the beggars.

The question was whether or not to kill the woman now. The last piece of the puzzle would arrive in a few days, and then the plan would go forward. They could not afford to arouse the suspicions of the police, whether they were looking into a murder or following up on anything Miriam Khalifa might tell them. But which was the more likely scenario?

Malovo looked at her watch. Whatever she was going to do, it would have to be done soon—a difficult proposition on a busy side street. She was supposed to meet her "lover" in a little more than an hour in Brooklyn. The idea of it made her stomach lurch, but he, too, was necessary to the plan. She would have to tolerate his grunting and groaning, while fantasizing what it was going to be like to kill him. Now, that was enough to give a girl an orgasm.

She peeked and saw that Miriam was walking away from the beggars, moving out of sight down Rivington. "Let's go," she told Hazzan.

———

When the smaller of the two beggars approached, Miriam had recoiled at his foul language more than his odd looks and the muscle spasms in his face. It took her a moment to realize he was trying to pass on a message.

"You're being . . . piss fuck me . . . followed," the man said, staring at her through dirty glasses that magnified his watery blue eye. "The woman in the black leather . . . what a whore crap . . . with the black boyfriend. No, don't turn. Pretend to give me and Booger here a . . . oh boy oh boy bitch . . . a couple of bucks."

A gigantic man-beast, who appeared to be covered from head to toe in fur, hovered behind him. She gasped as she caught the full effect of the big man's odiferous body; he smelled like he'd been rolling around on bags of garbage left for a week in the sun.

"What is the password?" Miriam remembered to ask. She'd seen the woman, too, on the subway station platform and again near the park, and intuition had already told her she was being watched. Still, these two street people weren't the sort of people she'd expected to be looking out for her.

"God is . . . fucking . . . great," said the little man as his face went through a series of grimaces.

Miriam wanted to tell the man not to blaspheme, but she finally understood that he had no control over his language or the facial tics. Allah had made him as he was, and that meant Allah had a purpose for the afflictions. She reached into her purse and found two dollar bills.

"Thanks," the little man said, accepting the bills and handing one back to the one he'd called Booger. "Now, walk up the block and go . . . damn

damn oh boy crap . . . down the alley. You'll meet a . . . whore vagina oh boy . . . man in there. He'll help. Don't be . . . hold my penis . . . afraid."

Miriam reached the alley on the north side of the street but hesitated. The streetlights had come on, but they did little to illuminate more than a few feet of the graffiti-covered alley.

She considered walking on, getting back on the subway, and going home to her family. If she truly was being followed, then they suspected her, and she might be in danger, or worse, she might be endangering her son.

Imam Jabbar had pulled her aside a few days earlier and told her that Jamal was "missing in action" fighting against NATO troops in Afghanistan. He said that as the widow of a martyr, she would be entitled to a monetary stipend provided by "certain friends of the mosque in the Middle East." In order to receive these benefits, however, it was necessary for her to keep her mouth shut and say nothing of her husband, especially if the authorities nosed around.

If that happened, not only would she lose the "martyr's wife" stipend, she and her family would be deported. "And I would not be able to protect you in Kenya," he said, placing a hand on her shoulder in an inappropriately familiar way. She'd removed his hand but nodded that she understood both the offer and the implied threat.

Maybe I should take Jabbar up on it, she thought. Whatever the Americans made of the information she carried in her handbag and in her head, she would still be the widow of a mass murderer. And an illegal immigrant. Surely they would make her and her family leave the country.

The whole reason her father had been willing to entertain the possibility of marriage between herself and Jamal when the imam inquired was that it might make obtaining permanent residence status easier for Miriam. Jabbar had pointed out that it might even help Mahmoud and Ayaan remain in the country legally.

Miriam had wanted very much to remain in America. Maybe if she had never known anything more than the simple fishing village on the coast of Kenya, she would have been content there. She would have married a local boy, and they would have raised their children to be good Muslims as her people had been for nearly twelve centuries.

However, she did know more than that village. There was a world of possibilities for her in America that she could have never pursued in Kenya.

Here she could still be a good Muslim and go to college and have a career. She could even enjoy art and music in the more liberal Islamic community of the United States.

Jamal Khalifa wasn't exactly the man of her dreams. She didn't care for his pockmarked face, or worse, that he worked for the imam as one of his "security team." However, after they were formally introduced, he seemed nice enough, so she agreed to go for a chaperoned walk with him to see if they got along. "As long as I don't have to marry him if I don't like him," she told her father.

"I would rather return to Kenya and fish for the rest of my days than for you to be unhappily married," Mahmoud replied.

So she and Jamal went for a stroll in Central Park as one of the older women from the mosque stood in for Miriam's mother and followed at a discreet, but visible, distance. Jamal was shy because of his scarred face, but she thought he had pretty eyes and a nice smile. It went better after he started telling her about his dream of maybe owning a business, or even studying to become an imam of his own mosque.

After the first meeting, she'd agreed to see him again, and after a time the older woman had deemed the escort unnecessary; everyone could see that the couple were growing closer. They were walking one early summer evening in 2002 through the neighborhood where he'd grown up, so that she could visualize a game of stickball or kick-the-can, when he stopped. "Listen," he said. "Do you hear that?"

At first, she heard nothing, but then in the distance, she heard the first few notes of tinny, happy music, which soon grew louder. "What is it?" she asked.

"A miracle," he replied with a sly smile. "Look!"

At first all she saw was a city street at the end of a hot day, but then a white truck appeared with a loudspeaker playing music above the windshield. Yelling with delight, children came running from the stoops and out of the buildings, abandoning their games and rope-skipping to swarm around the truck.

Laughing like a little boy, Jamal Khalifa pulled her by the hand until they stood at the side of the truck. "Choose one," he insisted, pointing up at the pictures of the various treats.

At first she demurred, but he wouldn't order for himself until she did. So she pointed to one, mostly because it was pink and pretty. "Strawberry

Shortcake and a Drumstick," Jamal told the man inside the truck. He then proudly handed her the ice cream bar.

It was the most delicious treat she'd ever eaten. By the time she got home that evening, she had made up her mind to marry Jamal. She still didn't like his politicizing of Islam or defense of extremists who talked about jihad. When he tried to defend the attack on the World Trade Center as an act of war, she'd told him about the bombing of the U.S. Embassy in Nairobi.

"Even if it had been a military target, and it was not," she argued, "it killed more Muslims than anyone else, and that is certainly against the teachings of the Qur'an. It was an act by cowards who were picking and choosing and misinterpreting the Qur'an to achieve their own selfish, evil ends. I don't want to marry a martyr; I want a good Muslim husband and good father for my children."

Occasionally, Jamal had put his foot down as the man of the house, such as when she wanted to send Abdullah to public school and he insisted that he attend the madrasah. But that was his right in accordance with the Qur'an. And he at least had not said no when she mentioned that she might want to attend night classes to get her G.E.D. and possibly even go to college "so that I can help contribute to our family's prosperity."

However, that might have been because he was struggling to make ends meet. His felony record and lack of education weighed heavily against him. Bankers just laughed at him when he went in to ask for a business loan; they laughed at him again when he asked for a loan to go back to school.

Over the years since their marriage and the birth of their son, Jamal had grown increasingly bitter. He started spending more time at the mosque, which meant less time looking for a job. That past spring he had begun taking the imam's night classes, and she had welcomed that at first because he told her they were special religious classes. But later she grew suspicious and started asking questions, especially after he started talking about going on jihad. When she noted that his "classmates" were the young radicals from the mosque, he became more secretive. And then there was the night he came home drunk.

Stumbling in the door, he'd started raving about how "one little mistake" had spoiled everything. He wasn't going to be allowed to participate in some "big plan." As he carried on, he took swigs from a bottle he kept in a brown paper bag. When she tried to take it away from him, he pushed her down. The fight frightened Abdullah, who started crying, but that only seemed to make Jamal angrier. When she got back up and tried to get the bottle again, he hit her.

When his rage was spent, he fell asleep. Miriam then packed a few belongings and, with Abdullah, left for her father's apartment.

Mahmoud listened to what had happened and became angry. He grabbed a knife and said he was going to go over to her apartment and slit his son-in-law's throat. Only her pleas stopped him.

"Perhaps, he has become possessed by jinn," her sister, Ayaan, suggested as she rubbed ice on Miriam's bruised ribs. Jinn were evil spirits who loved to cause problems for humans.

"No, he is possessed by the hatred of those who corrupt the teaching of the Prophet," her father answered.

When Jamal arrived at the apartment the next day to speak to her, Mahmoud stood in the doorway and wouldn't let him pass. Tearfully, Jamal tried to apologize, but her father would not listen. "Go tell it to Jabbar; he is the one who set you on this road."

Then came the terrible day in July when she dropped Abdullah off at school. The mosque was buzzing with fear and questions. A suicide bomber had blown himself up in a synagogue on Third Avenue. No one knew who had done it. "But we'll all be blamed," one woman wailed in the courtyard. "Life was hard enough without this!"

Miriam was talking to several of the other women when one of Jabbar's bodyguards pulled her aside. "The imam needs to see you," he said, but he offered no other information as he led the way to Jabbar's office.

Inside the office, Jabbar asked her to take a seat. He said he had important news. "We have learned that Jamal has gone on hajj," he said. "He will be gone for several months, maybe longer."

"Hajj?" she asked. "Where would he get the money for that?"

"A scholarship fund established by our friends in Saudi Arabia," Jabbar explained. "A sort of educational fund to help poor Muslims in America take the pilgrimage. It is a great honor, and since the two of you have . . . separated . . . he felt this was a good time to go."

"Why didn't he say anything to me?" she asked. "Or say goodbye at least to his son?"

"Apparently, you haven't been willing to talk to him," Jabbar said. "And it is probably for the best. I believe that after Mecca, he may be seeking martyrdom as a jihadi in Afghanistan or Iraq."

Miriam didn't know what to say. He had talked about going on jihad, and now he had. She felt tears well up in her eyes but willed them to stay put. She didn't want to cry in front of this bad man.

"In the meantime, Jamal asked that we look after you, so we have decided that you will be the new receptionist for the mosque," Jabbar said, smiling as if he'd just given her unbelievably good news.

"I don't want the job," Miriam said flatly. "I think you're an evil man, and this is because of you."

Jabbar looked at her for a moment with his big bug-eyes blinking angrily, but then he smiled again. "I'm sorry but I really must insist," he said.

Miriam knew a threat when it was stuck in her face. It made her mad, but she also had to consider her father, son, and sister, who was getting married in September after Ramadan. "As you wish," she hissed.

Jabbar's smile widened. "A wise choice," he said. "I'm sure we'll get along well together. . . . And by the way, not a word of this. . . . Jamal has gone on hajj. . . . You're not sure when he'll be returning."

Then I learned the truth, Miriam thought as she stood outside the dark alley off of Rivington. She felt for the package in her handbag. *And now I have to do something about it.*

As she peered into the shadows, she became so frightened that she thought her bladder might empty. But a quick glance down Rivington and the sight of the woman and man who had been following her convinced her that she had no choice. She stepped in and was swallowed by the shadows.

When Miriam disappeared from sight down Rivington, Malovo sprang forward, worried that she'd lose track of her. She rounded the corner and ran into the enormous belly of the panhandler she'd seen begging from Miriam.

He was well over six foot, and, she guessed, at least 300 pounds, but even if the man's size hadn't been intimidating, the odor wafting off his body and the multiple layers of filthy clothing would have been more than enough to repulse her. In fact, his whole appearance resembled that of a large, bedraggled bear. The parts of his face that were not covered with hair were dark with grime, and two small, beady eyes completed the metaphor. He held out one enormous paw, while the other supported the hot-dog-sized finger inserted up one nostril.

"Can u 'pare um change?" the giant mumbled. "Booger 'ongry."

Malovo's stomach heaved when the finger left his nose and was inserted into his mouth with a loud sucking noise. "Ugh, what's he saying?" she asked Hazzan, trying to sidestep the monster so that she could see Miriam.

"I think he's asking for money," Hazzan replied. "He says he's hungry." He began to reach inside his pants pocket.

"What are you doing?" Malovo demanded.

"The Qur'an teaches us to be kind to beggars. Did not the Prophet, peace and blessings to his name, say, 'Therefore the orphan oppress not; therefore the beggar drive not away?'"

Malovo's instinct was to poke the idiot in the eye. But she had to rely on him and his ignorant comrades to provide the cannon fodder for the plan, so she held off. "Then give him something and hurry up. Our friend just went into the alley."

The beast lurched in front of her again. "Come on 'ady, 'pare um change? Booger 'ongry."

"Get away from me, you filthy animal."

"Hey! . . . Fuck shit . . . don't talk to my . . . crap piss . . . friend like that," said a voice. The smaller beggar appeared at the other one's side.

"Get away from me," she repeated.

"Fuh-fuh-fuh-foreigner, eh?" the little man stammered. "Well . . . bitch mother fucker oh boy . . . there's no need to talk to people like that; he's just hungry . . . eat my ass oh boy."

Malovo's mouth dropped open and stayed that way. In her career, she'd tortured and killed many men who had screamed profanities in their torment, but she had never heard (or smelled) anything quite like this.

Her companion came to the rescue. "Here," he said, holding out two dollar bills. "Now let us pass in the name of Allah, the most merciful."

"Allah eh?" the little man eyed the bills suspiciously.

"'lah eh?" repeated the hairy man, who reached out and snatched the money before it could be withdrawn, saying "'ank you." He and his friend let them pass.

Malovo cursed under her breath as she moved quickly to the alley. "I don't understand why garbage like that is allowed to live. Hopefully, they won't in the new world."

"Blessed be the . . ."

"Shut up," she snarled. "Or I'll cut your tongue out and take it back to that animal for his dinner."

Hazzan swallowed hard and nodded at the alley. "She went in there?"

Malovo didn't answer as she stared into the gloom. The alley might as well have been a mineshaft it was so dark.

"Go after her," she ordered. "I'll circle around the block and intercept her on the other end."

Hazzan licked his lips nervously. "Why don't we both just go around and pick her up on the other side?"

Malovo glared at him. "Are you disobeying me?"

Hazzan glanced at her and shook his head. Whatever might be in the alley, he figured it couldn't be any more dangerous than Ajmaani. He put his hand up under his sweatshirt and grasped the handgun in his waistband. It made him feel a whole lot braver. "What should I do if I find her?"

Malovo thought about the question for a moment. She had no proof that the woman was doing anything to betray them; for all she knew, Miriam Khalifa was whoring herself in back alleys to make extra cash. But with only a few days to go, she didn't want to worry about it anymore. "Kill her. But make it look like she was robbed. If you want to rape her that's okay, too."

Hazzan looked shocked. Bombs and guns and knives were part of jihad. But rape? However, he was not about to question Ajmaani any further. He pulled the gun out and walked into the alley.

Malovo watched for a minute and then turned to walk around the block. But she hadn't gone far before she heard Hazzan shout something. There was a gunshot followed by a scream. A man's scream.

Almost immediately upon entering the alley Miriam had regretted it. The darkness and the smell had enveloped her like a grave. She jumped when a voice whispered in her ear. "It's all right, child, I am here."

"Aalimah?" Miriam asked the dark. Although there was no reply, she was comforted knowing she wasn't alone.

She walked what she estimated to be halfway down the alley. Something scurried in the dark. *Rats*, she thought. She looked back in the direction she had come and saw two people, a man and a woman, standing at the entrance, then the man entered.

Miriam turned to run but a hand went over her mouth and an arm around her waist. Her assailant didn't hurt her, but neither was she able to resist his strength. He pulled her back into what was apparently a back entrance to one of the buildings. *Allah, help me*, she prayed. *I'm going to be raped and murdered.*

The man released his grip around her waist but kept his hand on her mouth, moving around until he was in front of her. She couldn't see his face, though she could tell he was wearing a hood. She started to cry, but when he spoke, his voice was kind and soothing.

"Hush, sister," he whispered. "You've been followed by an evil woman and her companion. They mean to do you harm. But in case there is any doubt as to who your friends are, God is great."

Miriam relaxed. Yet another strange character had given the password.

"Stay here," he said, "while I deal with our visitor. If I don't return, remain in the shadows of this doorway and someone will come for you soon."

She reached out and caught his sleeve. Odd, but she now thought of him as her protector.

"I'll be back," he whispered and disappeared into the gloom.

Miriam thought she saw shadows moving. There was a shout, a flash followed by the loud report of a gun, then a scream.

She waited until her protector appeared in front of her again. "It is finished. We are safe for the moment."

Her protector led her farther into the alley until they reached a handrail. "Careful, these are steps leading down," he said. "Don't be afraid, friends are waiting for you. When you reach the bottom, knock three times on the door."

The man turned to leave but was overcome by a fit of coughing—a heavy, wet sound. "Are you all right?" she asked, as he caught his breath and appeared to wipe his mouth on his sleeve.

"'The earth is suffocating. Swear to make them cut me open, so that I won't be buried alive,'" he replied, then coughed again so hard that she could tell his whole body shook.

"I don't understand."

The man barked a laugh. "Neither do I, Miriam," he said. "But never mind. It was just something Frederic Chopin said about a similar medical condition. But I must leave the rest of this conversation to another time. Please, go to the bottom of the stairs—watch your step—you'll find a door there. Knock three times."

"Wait," she said. "You know my name. What is yours?"

"David."

"Thank you, David," she said, but he was already gone.

Miriam felt her way to the bottom of the stairwell until she found the door. She knocked three times.

There was a grating sound as a deadbolt was pulled back from its rusty berth and then the sound of a latch being lifted. She braced herself for some new fright, but was pleasantly surprised when the door creaked open, bathing her in the soft light of the interior, and she was greeted by the smiling face of the translator, Marie Smith.

———

At the sound of the scream, Malovo had run back to the alley as other pedestrians who'd been passing by or were near at hand gathered at the entrance.

"Did you hear that?" a young woman asked. "It sounded like a gunshot!"

"Yeah, and how about that scream?" her male companion said. "I about shit."

"Somebody should call the cops," said an older man who was out walking his dachshund.

"I already did."

"It's too late for whoever was screaming," said a teenager with a skateboard under one arm. "That was sick, dude."

Malovo waited to see if Hazzan would return. When he didn't, she considered going in herself, but something about the scream had unnerved her. It was a feeling she'd never experienced before in her murderous career.

At the sound of the police car siren, she backed away. She didn't know what had happened to Hazzan, but if she ever saw Miriam Khalifa again, she'd torture her until she found out.

"Jambo," Marie Smith said.

"Sjambo," Miriam replied. They entered a comfortable, if plain and apparently windowless, basement room. Standing in front of a chair was the man she'd seen from the security firm. He held out his hand. "Espey Jaxon. Thanks for coming. I'm sorry about the trouble. Please, have a seat."

Miriam gratefully accepted the tea Marie had prepared on a tiny stove in the corner of the room.

"I think you know that you were followed by someone from the mosque," Marie said. "If one of the people, a woman, is who we think, you are in great danger."

Miriam nodded. "I know," she said.

"What about your son and the rest of your family?"

"My son is with my father, who has made arrangements to go visit friends after the start of Ramadan. My sister will stay with the man she intends to marry. They are very modern."

The thought made her want to cry. That morning, she had told her father the truth about Jamal and what she intended to do. He hadn't tried to argue with her until she asked him to take their son and go visit a friend who lived in Chicago. "I need to be here to protect you," he said.

"You cannot protect me, father. My fate is in the hands of Allah now."

Mahmoud Juma stood silently for a minute. "Have you spoken to her again?"

They both knew who he meant. Hazrat Fatemeh Masumeh, the Aalimah. "Yes, now please make arrangements for your trip," she said.

Marie Smith asked her a question. "You said you had something you wanted to give us?"

"Yes." Miriam reached into her bag and removed a large mustard-colored mailing envelope, which she handed to Jaxon.

Jaxon looked inside and then back at Miriam. "Have you looked at it?"

Miriam nodded. She started to speak but the words got caught in her mouth. She passed a hand over her eyes and wiped the tears away.

"What is it?" Lucy asked.

Miriam sighed. "It is the last will and testament of the murderer Muhammad Jamal Khalifa. . . . May Allah have mercy on his soul . . . he was my husband."

24

Just after noon on Wednesday, the first day of the Jessica Campbell murder trial, Butch Karp stood inside the area cordoned off by the police in front of the Criminal Courts building watching the circus that had come to town. A mob of tourists gathered to snap photographs of the competing circles of protesters and gawkers on display for the latest "Trial of the Century." Meanwhile, street vendors were hawking "Free Jessica, Jail God" T-shirts and "God's Calling" caps.

Out in front of his newsstand, Dirty Warren was capitalizing on the spectacle, too. "Get your . . . fu-fu-fuck it . . . *Special Edition New York* . . . oh boy oh boy shit crap . . . *Post*," he shouted. "Eight-page blowout on the Campbell Kid Killings trial . . . eat me whoop whoop . . . with shocking, never seen before, photographs!"

Most of the photos were nothing more than mugshots of Jessica's family. But some lowlife—Marlene suspected an employee at the coroner's or sheriff's office—had supplied two more grisly photographs, one of the inside of the Volvo, and another of the children's bodies lying on a white sheet next to the footlocker. The photographs were blurry, apparently taken quickly with a cell-phone camera, and details were hard to distinguish, but still . . .

The National Organization of Feminists protesters kept trying to set up someplace where they could get away from Edward Treacher. But every time they moved their signs, Treacher got down from his milk crate, calmly picked it up, and followed them to the next spot.

Obviously the protesters were upset with him, but it wasn't clear whether Treacher was trying to irritate them more or merely thought he was one of them. "ACQUITTING THE GUILTY AND CONDEMNING THE INNOCENT—THE LORD DETESTS THEM BOTH!" he shouted above the women's requests that he quit stalking them. "That's Proverbs 17:15 folks. Say, can you spare something for the hungry?"

One of the women from NOF reached up to hand Treacher several dollars and pointed across the street, where she evidently thought he might want to move. But he just pocketed the money and continued to preach.

The woman then stomped over to a nearby police officer and angrily gestured at Treacher. But the officer just shrugged and said something—Karp imagined it was the usual "free country, free speech" reply, which when translated meant "don't bother me with piddly crap"—and looked away.

The woman marched back to her group, where she made a series of rude hand gestures toward the officer and Treacher. Then, as if playing a game of musical chairs, the group suddenly picked up their signs, ran to the other side of the cordoned area, and began to reassemble.

Treacher stopped shouting and gazed after them, swaying on top of his crate as if blown about by the non-existent wind. Sighing, he stepped down, stooped for his crate, and shuffled over to the group. They saw him coming and formed into a tight circle, like a herd of buffalo protecting itself from a wolf. Smiling at his new "friends," he placed his crate back on the ground and stepped up with his arms raised above his head.

"WHEN JUSTICE IS DONE," he shouted, then paused for a moment to nod to the protesters, who glared back at him. "IT BRINGS JOY TO THE RIGHTEOUS BUT TERROR TO EVILDOERS!"

The woman who had talked to the police officer fluttered her hands at Treacher and then gave up. She organized the protesters into a circle and handed them picket signs and cardboard megaphones. She then pulled a bullhorn out of a backpack and began trying to outshout Treacher.

"Justice for Jessica Campbell," she yelled, waving her hand like an orchestra conductor to encourage her supporters, who replied in quasi-unison, "Justice for Jessica!"

Several of the placards were directed at Karp. He'd been called a lot of names in thirty years of public service; now, there were signs labeling him a Nazi, and he was reminded of Sobelman's recollections of Sobibor: "There is one thing no one can do to you unless you let them. They cannot take your soul, and in the end, we did not let them take ours."

By the late summer of 1943, more than 250,000 people had been murdered at Sobibor, their bodies burned and buried. But it became apparent that the Nazis were stepping up their operations.

Those prisoners who had so far been spared to work as laborers knew that the end was coming and so, led by a man named Leon Feldhendler, some of them planned to escape rather than wait for death. The idea gained momentum in mid-September when a trainload of Soviet prisoners of war, most of them Jews, arrived at the camp for disposal.

Among them was a young Jew still wearing his Red Army lieutenant's uniform. His name was Alexander "Sasha" Pechorsky, and the escape committee soon put him in command, with Feldhendler as his deputy.

On the morning of October 14, only a small percentage of the prisoners in the camp knew what was about to happen; they did not want to take the chance that spies mixed in with the camp population, or cowards who might be willing to sell out their fellow prisoners for a piece of bread or a few more days of living, would find out. The day progressed with business as usual—the brutish Ukrainian guards manned the towers with their machine guns or herded, kicked, and pummeled prisoners bound for the gas chamber.

A little before noon, the eleven SS guards in the camp were called to the workshops. When they arrived, the prisoners killed them. According to plan, electricity and telephone lines were cut and rifles were taken from the armory, all without the Ukrainian guards being aware that anything was amiss.

When the Ukrainians ordered the prisoners to line up for roll call, the prisoners killed them with axes. Only then did the guards in the towers realize what was happening, and they opened fire. The prisoners with rifles returned fire, killing several.

Inside the fences, prisoners ran and dodged to avoid being struck by bullets, as well as to escape. Those in the know, including the Soviet prisoners of war, broke for the gate and fences. Those who made it through the gate ran for the nearby woods. Others got through a fence only to run into a minefield, where many were soon killed or maimed; those who followed after them, stepping over and sometimes on their fallen comrades, were luckier, as the mines had already been tripped.

"There were 600 of us in the camp that day," Sobelman told Karp's class. "About 150 were killed by the guards or the mines. Three hundred of us escaped; those who didn't were shot the following day when the SS returned."

The Germans and their thugs pursued the escapees relentlessly. Not only were they worried that the Jews would join with the partisans fighting a guerrilla war from the forests, they wanted to prevent them from telling the outside world about the exterminations at Sobibor. Already the German high command and government officials were concerned about what would happen if they lost the war and were held accountable for war crimes.

"I escaped with Pechorsky," Sobelman said. "We numbered about 75. But we broke into smaller groups to avoid detection. Myself and a handful of comrades wandered the Parczew forest northwest of Sobibor for weeks. We were lucky and met up with Yehiel Grynszpan's Jewish partisans, who welcomed us like heroes, though it was hard to feel we deserved the accolades with so many of our friends and families dead. I think today the psychologists call this 'survivor's guilt,' and believe me, it would last all the rest of our lives."

In the week following the escape, 100 of the 300 escapees were recaptured or killed. "Two hundred of us survived to tell the story," Sobelman recalled. "But of them, only about fifty survived the war. Even after the day of liberation, some were killed, including Feldhendler, by right-wing Polish National Army troops, who were actively hunting down Jews. You see, it was not just Germans or Nazis, or their servants, who murdered Jews."

"Didn't the Germans know that what they were doing was wrong?" Zak asked.

"Of course, they knew. And if I was a brilliant district attorney like Mr. Karp, I could prove it in court. You want evidence? Here's some. At the beginning of the genocide, they tried mass killings of Jews by having them shot down by regular German Army troops, but German officers complained that the face-to-face killing of unarmed civilians was having a severely negative psychological impact on their soldiers. So the Nazis decided to pursue more mechanical methods, such as the gas chambers at Sobibor and the other extermination camps, and use the sort of people who could handle the work of murder. So yes, they knew it was wrong, because their soldiers told them it was. But you want more evidence?"

Three days after the revolt, the Nazis had tried to erase any evidence that the camp had even existed. The buildings were dismantled, the land ploughed up, and trees planted to disguise the site as a farm.

"It was as if by doing so, they could deny that the evil they had done was real. Those at the top also realized that any witnesses left alive could implicate them. So even their own SS guards were sent to dangerous positions on the front lines where it was hoped that they would be killed. But some of them lived, and though they tried to hide, they were found by Nazi-hunters after the war, who heard what had happened from those of us who survived.

"When you believe that what you are doing is right, you do not try to hide or deny it," he said. "Oh, they knew it was wrong, but they did it anyway."

Karp turned away from the circus outside the Criminal Courts building and went inside. After a week of jury selection, opening statements were finally set to begin at 1:30 before Judge Tim Dermondy.

When he got off the elevator, the first person he saw was Darla Milquetost poking her head out of the office door. "Oh there you are," she said. "Mr. Newbury just called and left a message. Shall I call him back for you?"

"What'd he want?" Karp growled.

"Oh, well," stammered Mrs. Milquetost, the hope for an imminent happy reunion fading from her face like a sunset. She picked up her notepad. "He was calling to remind you that the file for the Black Sea Café bombing is still in his office under the suspect's name, Stanislas Tomas Meyerhoff. He said to remind you that he's a minor, seventeen years old, and from Brooklyn. He believes that the arraignment is tomorrow, Wednesday, and that the Russian authorities should be contacted." She held the note out to Karp. "Shall I get that file from his office for you?"

"No, Mrs. Milquetost," he replied, taking the note and crumpling it in his hand. "I'm quite sure that Mr. Newbury's replacement has it covered."

Karp went into his office and shut the door. He walked over to his desk, picked up the telephone, and dialed. When it was answered he spoke quickly. "I believe the contents and visitors will be arriving in Brooklyn to-morrow. That's all I have." He listened to the reply and hung up without saying anything more just as Mrs. Milquetost called to say that Kenny Katz had arrived.

They spent the next thirty minutes going over for the umpteenth time the outline for the case. When they were through, Karp's young colleague remained in his seat with his head down.

"You okay with this case?" Karp asked. "I don't want you participating if you don't believe in it. If you have any qualms, I understand. I can try the case on my own if I need to."

Katz looked up, surprised. "No way, I guess I was spacing and wondering what God thinks about everybody trying to pin all these murders on Him. 'God told me to kill Jews. God told me to kill Palestinians. God told me to kill my neighbors, my wife, my children.' I'm tired of it, and I'm pretty sure God is, too. I saw enough people killed in the name of Allah on 9/11 and in Afghanistan, and if I was God or Allah I'd be pretty fucking ticked off that they're saying it's what I want."

The young man wandered over to the window. "You know, last night I was thinking about Campbell's statements to her husband about sending her children to God. I remembered this patrol I was on in Kabul. We were moving through an outdoor market and suddenly we see this kid walking down the middle of everybody, just staring at us sort of glassy-eyed. He was maybe fourteen, tops, probably younger, but he opened up his coat and showed us that he had a suicide vest on. Then he shouted, '*Allah-u-Akbar*. God is great.' As if God had anything to do with what he was doing."

"That's rough," Karp commiserated. "What'd you do?"

"Me?" Kenny asked as if there was any question. "I shot him between the eyes before he could pull the cord."

"Hard to imagine having to do something like that," Karp said quietly.

"No problems," Kenny replied. "I did what I had to do. And eventually, I was able to come to terms with the fact that I wasn't the one who talked that kid into putting on a vest full of dynamite and nails, or told him that God wanted him to kill. But it took a while before I quit dreaming of that kid's face in my rifle sight. . . . I'm just tired of God getting the bad rap and sometimes wish He'd do something about it."

Mrs. Milquetost buzzed in on the intercom. "Mr. Karp, the press is here and asking for a comment."

"Tell them there will be no comment. And make them wait in the hall or the courtroom. That's where I'll be doing all the talking that I intend to do in this case." He gave his ADA a chance to collect himself, then asked, "You ready?"

Katz gave him a wink. "As I'll ever be."

———

A few minutes later, Karp opened the door to the reception area and caught Mrs. Milquetost in mid-gossip with a young female assistant district attorney. "I just wish they would get over themselves and make up," Milquetost was saying. "Who knows? Maybe V. T. . . . ."

The receptionist looked up when he cleared his throat. She blushed as she tried desperately to cover her tracks. "I, uh . . . um . . . good luck in the trial."

"Thank you," Karp said. He opened the door, which had the effect of setting off a half-dozen camera flashes and a jumble of voices all asking for him to say something pithy. The only reason he and Katz could move into the hall at all was because Gilbert Murrow held them all at bay in a semi-circle with commands of "stand back" and "give us some room." The aide then led the way to the elevators, occasionally using a stiff-arm worthy of a Heisman Trophy running back.

Karp answered none of the questions yelled out to him, but he smiled and wished a "good morning" to those in the media horde he knew. When the elevator door opened, several members of the press stepped forward in an attempt to get on with the prosecution team, but Murrow pushed them back. "Sorry, we're full."

In a demonstration of complete impartiality, he didn't let his girlfriend Stupenagel aboard either. "Sorry babe, join the rest of the vultures."

"Yeah? Well, maybe we'll see who's sleeping with the pigeons when you get home tonight, buster," she yelled as the doors slid shut.

"You're going to pay for that one," Karp told his aide, who pressed the button for the twelfth floor.

"Just remember who took the bullet for you," Murrow replied sadly. Obviously, he'd had bigger plans than sleeping on the roof that evening. He perked up though when the doors slid open again to a whole new gaggle of journalists, all elbowing each other and shouting the same questions.

The press followed Karp and Katz into the courtroom, scurrying like rats in a maze to find the few remaining seats in the pews on either side of the aisle. A shouting match ensued when the unlucky ones were told they would have to watch the trial on a monitor in another room. Those who had seats looked smug.

A low buzz permeated the air of the courtroom, over a hundred people speaking quietly but excitedly to each other—a sort of white noise that increased in volume anytime someone of note, such as the prosecutors, entered.

As Karp and Katz made their way to the prosecution table, Karp saw that the defendant and her lawyer were already seated at the defense table. Over the objection of her attorney, Linda Lewis, who never minded a little press, Karp had won a motion to have Jessica Campbell brought to the courtroom early to avoid the crush of reporters and the off-chance that some nut-job in the crowd would try to hurt her.

Lewis had been busy filing last-minute motions, including one to have the case thrown out, and another to have witnesses excluded. One she had not filed was to allow Campbell to dress in civilian clothes for the trial instead of the jumpsuit worn by psychiatric patients at Bellevue. Normally, a defense attorney worried that jail garb would make their client look guilty in the eyes of the jurors, but Lewis wanted Campbell clearly identified as a psych patient.

Another trick of the defense trade was to clean up the appearance of defendants. That's why murderers who'd previously dressed like Hell's Angels bikers appeared at trial in sweater vests and horn-rimmed glasses with their hair cut and looking like frat boys. For the same reason, a female defendant arrested in a bikini top and shorts exposing her butt cheeks would most likely be brought to court in a dress so conservative that she would look like a turn-of-the-twentieth-century missionary to Africa.

Here again, Lewis had opted for a different strategy. Campbell's hair, which at a pre-trial hearing only a week before had been long and neatly trimmed, now looked like someone had hacked at it with a dull knife. She was pale as milk, which was to be somewhat expected, as she had spent nearly all of her time indoors, but the lack of color was emphasized by the dark circles under her eyes.

Karp wondered if Lewis had used makeup to enhance the bedraggled appearance or had simply told her client to avoid getting any sleep. The look certainly fit the stereotype of a "crazy woman."

Campbell glanced over at him, but her eyes filled with tears; she looked back down at a large sketch pad on which she was drawing with a pencil. But Lewis was watching him.

He'd expected her to be more flamboyant in dress, having seen her in action before; however, she looked like an assistant district attorney in her off-the-rack gray dress suit. She gave Karp a curt nod—the sort an antagonist might use before choosing a dueling pistol, then turned her back to him to say something to her client.

Karp turned in his seat to look at the spectator section of the court. Sitting directly behind the defense table were Liza and Benjamin Gupperstein. On the other side of Ben Gupperstein, but a world apart otherwise, was Charlie Campbell. After the *Off the Hook Show*, his ranking in the polls had fallen like the New Year's Eve globe at Times Square and he'd disappeared from public view for a while.

When he reappeared, he was back in the defense camp, apparently having worked out a deal. Publicly and frequently, he blamed himself "for not taking the psychiatrist's warning seriously enough." At the same time, Lewis stopped demanding that he be prosecuted for conspiracy to commit murder. His poll numbers had since stabilized, a trend Karp figured would continue as long as Charlie behaved.

The president of NOF and a phalanx of angry women sat in the row directly behind Charlie. A couple of token men sat near the president, too, but they had the look of worker drones attending to a queen bee.

Karp had heard from the court security chief that many of the spectators had shown up outside the building during the night and slept on the sidewalk to assure themselves a seat in the courtroom. "It's like a damn rock concert," the man had complained. Those who outfought the media for a seat were now eagerly waiting for the show to begin; several apparently even brought snacks.

The crowding in the courtroom prevented spectators and the press from "choosing sides" the way they often did when attending a trial—that is, sitting behind either the prosecution table or the defense table. He'd even seen people switch from one side to the other during the course of a trial as their opinions changed. This morning, however, they'd taken seats wherever they could find them, and he noticed that some of the women sitting on the prosecution side of the aisle looked uncomfortable. One in particular was shooting him dirty looks and mouthing something that he didn't care to translate.

The Jessica Campbell murder trial had become a national story. The *Off the Hook Show* had been the first to latch on to it, but it hadn't been the last. Every major network had done a piece along the lines of "Moms Who Kill," with special emphasis on the "growing phenomena" of postpartum depression as a cause of homicide.

Karp began to say something to Katz when there was a sudden commotion behind him. The woman who had been glaring at him and mouthing slurs apparently couldn't take it anymore. She stood up and tried to spit on him.

Fortunately for Karp—but not for a well-known television newscaster two rows in front of her—the lubricious projectile lacked sufficient velocity and trajectory. It struck the man in the forehead as he turned to see what the fuss was about. He screamed shrilly, as if her spit consisted of hydrochloric acid. The woman pointed at Karp and shouted. "Satan! Get thee gone! How dare you persecute a woman who hears and obeys the word of God. Who are you to judge her, except one of those accursed people who killed Jesus!"

Security guards rushed down the aisle and into the row to grab her. She kicked and screamed and tried to sit back down; the guards tugged from one direction and her friends held on in the other. All three women were eventually pulled from the courtroom and their seats filled with the next three in line.

"I'll never question the need for metal detectors at the front doors again," Kenny said in a low voice.

Karp chuckled. "All in a day's work." He'd been worried that the distractions would have an effect on his protégé, but Katz was handling the scene like a seasoned veteran.

Glancing at his legal pad, Karp recalled his discussion with Katz about how to begin the trial. "I'm just going to lay it out—simply, clearly. I'll leave the theatrics for the other side. If we let them make this a trial based on emotions, we'll lose."

"I hear what you're saying," Katz had responded, "but isn't that kind of tough? Every time I see a photograph of those kids' bodies and think about what they went through, I just want to snap that woman's neck."

"Precisely my point," Karp had replied. "You've looked at the evidence, and the evidence told you that Jessica Campbell knew what she was doing and deserves to be punished. So what makes you think the jury won't have the same reaction when they see what you've seen, heard what you've heard, and know what you know? This has got to be about the vicious, off-the-charts brutal acts of murder committed against these defenseless children by their caretaker-in-chief, and not about the defendant's mental defect."

Voices fell silent and everyone scrambled to their feet when the court clerk announced the arrival of New York Supreme Court Judge Timothy Dermondy. Unlike almost all other state supreme courts, the New York Supreme Court is not the highest appellate court in the state judicial system; instead, it is the actual trial court. This anomaly has a tendency to drive first-year law students to drink when they make the mistake of believing they have appellate precedent when they cite a decision by a New York Supreme Court judge.

Five foot ten, slim, and balding, Dermondy had graduated at the top of his class from Fordham Law School and then joined the New York DAO, where he served for many years before becoming a judge. At the time he had joined the staff, the DAO was headed by Francis Garrahy, and Karp wasn't even out of high school.

The Dermondy family had a long history of serving the citizens of Manhattan. His dad and uncles had been big-time brass with the NYPD, and Timothy had become Garrahy's top ADA, the eventual chief of the homicide bureau and one of the top trial lawyers ever to walk into a New York City courtroom. On the bench, he was considered by attorneys on both sides of the aisle to be fair-minded and even-handed; but he did not suffer well any ADA who was not prepared. Painstaking, thorough preparation was the bedrock of success. Karp considered himself fortunate to have been mentored by Dermondy, just as he was now tutoring Katz.

Dermondy left everybody standing while he looked out at them like a loving father whose unruly children were beginning to try his patience. "Now, good people," he said firmly. "I've been told by my clerk that there has already been an unseemly outburst. I must let you know right now that I won't tolerate another. You'll conduct yourselves in a manner both respectful and orderly, or you will be taken to The Tombs and left there to contemplate the error of your ways. This goes for lawyers, spectators, and the media. Am I clear?"

The crowd nodded as one. "All right then," the judge said, "you may take your seats."

Judge Dermondy asked that the jury be brought in and seated, and once they were in place he made a short speech about the history of the jury system in the United States. "It is a sacred duty," he warned the jurors. "And you must do nothing that abridges that duty, including talking to the media or discussing the case with anyone until I have given you leave to do so. Am I clear?"

This time it was the jurors' turn to nod. "Good," the judge said. "I'm sure we'll get along famously, and thank you for taking on this very important task." He looked at the prosecution team. "Are you ready with your opening statement?"

"Yes, your honor," Karp said, rising.

"Then let's have it, Mr. Karp."

Karp approached the podium, which was placed between and slightly ahead of the defense and prosecution tables, and put down his legal pad. He took a final look at what he'd written.

"On the morning of March 17, Jessica Campbell went to the below-street-level parking garage of her home on Central Park West to run a few errands. She got in the family's Volvo station wagon and left the garage, driving south until she reached the Holland Tunnel, which she took to New Jersey. In Newark, Mrs. Campbell drove to the O'Hara's Hardware Store on London Road, where she purchased a large footlocker and a stainless steel combination padlock. She then drove 3.8 miles farther to Bucky's Sporting Goods, where she purchased an Old Timer hunting knife with a nine-inch blade. Any of these same items could have been bought much closer to home, but Jessica Campbell didn't want to be recognized. Why? Because she knew what she intended to use these items for."

On the morning of the murders, Karp told the jurors, Jessica Campbell rose from her bed, fixed her husband a large breakfast, "which he did not eat and left on the counter," and then waited for him to leave for a meeting. "A meeting, he told her, which might last well into the evening," he added.

Karp paused to emphasize his next point. "Not until after he left, and could ask no questions, did Mrs. Campbell then call the nanny, Rebecca, and tell her not to come to work that day. As Rebecca will testify, her boss said she was going to 'take care of the children herself.' Mrs. Campbell then proceeded to the main floor bathroom of the family brownstone and filled the tub with water.

"We will learn from the evidence that Jessica Campbell brought her children into the bathroom and placed them in the tub. But she wasn't there to bathe them, or play with them; she put them there in order to kill them."

Karp walked over to the side of the prosecution table where he picked out a poster-sized photograph of the Campbell family fixed to a Styrofoam board. He crossed the floor and placed the photograph on an easel near the jury box, and went back to the podium.

"This was the Campbell family in January of this year," Karp continued. "That's Charlie Campbell on the left and Jessica Campbell on the right holding the infant, Benjamin, who was only a few weeks old; standing in front of them is seven-year-old Hillary and her four-year-old sister, Chelsea."

Karp paused to let the jurors get a good look at the photograph before he resumed. "The Campbell children did not go easily. The evidence will show that it took several minutes to drown each child as they kicked, scratched, and fought with their mother, the defendant, to stay alive."

A sudden sob broke the stillness of the courtroom. All heads turned to the source of the sound, Jessica Campbell, and waited to see what she would do next. But she kept her head down and returned to drawing on her sketch pad.

"In fact, one of the children, Hillary, fought bravely. She scratched and even managed to bite her mother hard enough to leave a clear set of teeth marks on Jessica Campbell's arm. She struggled to stay alive so hard that when drowning failed to kill her, Jessica Campbell had to resort to Plan B, the hunting knife she purchased at Bucky's. You will hear testimony that she plunged that knife into her daughter's body at least six times, each time painful and brutal, until the life bled out of Hillary into the waters of that bathtub."

Karp looked down at his pad and then back to the jurors. "When the defendant accomplished the deed she'd planned so carefully, Jessica Campbell moved on to the next phase. She retrieved the footlocker and placed the bodies of her three children in it, dragged it through the house—we will show you a photograph in which you can see the scratches the footlocker caused on the hardwood floors—to the family's Volvo station wagon. The locker had to be heavy, about 150 pounds, but she managed to lift it up and into the car's cargo space in the back.

"After Mrs. Campbell's arrest, crime-scene technicians went over the entire house and discovered that everything was clean and in seemingly perfect order. In fact, we will learn from the evidence that the main floor bathroom was so clean that it was nearly impossible to get even one clear fingerprint. Imagine that—two adults, three children, and not a single fingerprint. . . . There was certainly no blood, and in fact, the bathroom was so spotless that it was difficult to imagine that it was the place where the defendant had ruthlessly snuffed out the lives of her three trusting children. The defendant, Jessica Campbell, had gone to great lengths to clean the scene of the murders, and she went to these lengths to hide what she had done, aware of the enormity of what had happened. As a further part of her premeditated plan to cover up the murders, Jessica Campbell drove the Volvo north to the little town of Staatsburg, a village on the Hudson River she'd known growing up, and rolled the car, containing the trunk with her children's bodies stuffed inside, into the river."

Over the next half hour, Karp outlined how "a unique and effective group of forensic investigators" had figured out how to find the car and what its contents had revealed. "It showed that this was no spur-of-the-moment decision. No bolt out of the blue," he said. "These murders were well-planned, well-executed crimes committed by a person who had plenty of time to consider the nature and consequences of what she was doing and who took elaborate, diabolical steps to avoid detection. Even months after she committed these crimes, she refused to tell anyone where the bodies of her children were hidden, not even to allow them to be brought home to be buried decently."

The courtroom was still, the loudest sound the soft crying of Liza Gupperstein. Karp used the moment to check his notecards and then strolled to the front of the jury box, his arms folded across his chest.

"You're going to hear a lot of talk about mental illness and psychological terms like 'postpartum depression' and 'psychosis.' The defense will be trying to tell you that Jessica Campbell was legally insane at the time of these crimes and therefore not responsible for her actions. I think we can all agree that acting purposefully and intentionally killing another human being, except in self-defense or in the defense of others, may be just plain crazy," Karp said. "At least in our everyday use of the word. But that's not how the law defines insanity. With the law, it's all about responsibility. And to determine if the defendant is responsible or not, the law asks you to hear and see the evidence and then answer two questions: Did the defendant know the nature and consequences of her actions? And did she know that it was wrong?"

Karp rocked on his heels as he looked at the jurors, making eye contact with several of them. "And when you have answered these questions, and have come to the inevitable conclusion that the defendant knew the nature and consequences of her acts and knew what she did was wrong, I will ask you, in the name of the People of the State of New York, to find the defendant, Jessica Campbell, guilty of the murder of baby Benjamin, guilty of the murder of his four-year-old sister, Chelsea, and guilty of the murder of seven-year-old Hillary."

———

Karp returned to his seat and stole a glance around the courtroom. Jessica sat furiously drawing on the sketch pad as if her art mattered more to her than the proceedings.

Charlie Campbell sat turned slightly away from his in-laws, who were ignoring his existence. Ben Gupperstein had his arm around his wife, who leaned her head against his chest, her eyes closed.

Linda Lewis rose from her seat, flipped through several pages on a legal pad she had on the table, and then walked to the lectern, where she stopped for a moment with her head down, as if listening to an inner voice.

"What if God was one of us?" she asked, then smiled. "Yes, I know, those are the words of a Joan Osborne song, but what if God really *was* one of us? In human form, walking around, talking to us, asking us . . . no, telling us . . . what He wanted us to do? How would we recognize Him? Or what if God simply spoke to us in our minds? How could we distinguish that from a mental illness?"

Lewis walked behind Jessica Campbell and rested her hands on the shoulders of her client. "And if we believed, we really and truly believed, that God was speaking to us, would we not listen? And if God, or what we believed to be God, told us that in order to save our children's souls, we would have to sacrifice them, would we do it?"

She shook her head. "Only if we were insane." She looked over at Karp and Katz. "The chief prosecutor just told you that murder is an act of insanity, and maybe it is, but there are different degrees of insanity. Shooting somebody over a drug deal or even raping and murdering a college coed, as heinous as those crimes might be, do not rise to the level of insanity of a good and caring mother taking the lives of her three children because she believes that's what God has ordered her to do."

Lewis kept her eyes on Karp. "It's easy for the prosecution to dismiss mental illness as a 'bad excuse.' But that sort of thinking belongs in the Dark Ages, when we used to throw mentally ill people into dungeons or burn them at the stake. Fortunately, right-thinking people today understand that mental illness is just that—an illness that can be treated. It is not something that the patient brought upon herself. And just as other serious illnesses can sometimes be cured, and the patient can return to a normal life, so can the mentally ill be cured and returned to a productive, normal life."

Lewis went into a "layman's explanation" of the role of chemicals in the brain and their effect on postpartum depression before addressing some of Karp's opening statement. "Why did Jessica drive to Newark to purchase the footlocker and other items?" she asked. "Yes, it was to avoid detection. But not for the reason the prosecution said. She wanted to make sure that no one could stop her from obeying God's commandments. Not the police, nor her husband, Charlie Campbell. You will learn that Charlie Campbell ignored a psychiatrist's very strongly worded advice against Jessica having more children and instead pressured her to conceive again because of his own selfish political motives."

Everyone turned to Charlie Campbell, who bravely lifted his chin for the press, a man ready to accept his punishment and throw himself on the court of public opinion. Lewis threw him a bone.

"Most of us don't really understand how the brain works," she said. "How could Charlie Campbell, who went to school to be an attorney, be expected to give credence to this warning when the district attorney's office, which deals with mentally ill people every day, still doesn't get it? If Charlie erred in his judgment, then surely the DA is erring in prosecuting Jessica Campbell for something she could not control, and that she cannot even remember."

The courtroom stirred at the contention that Jessica had amnesia about the killings. This was new.

"Yes, that's right," Lewis said. "If you listened to Mr. Karp, you would think there was no explanation for why Jessica would not help them find her children except that she was trying to get away with something. But in reality, it's because she didn't know where they were. As a matter of fact, Dr. Niki Nickles, one of the country's leading psychiatrists, will testify that Jessica Campbell experienced a disassociative episode where, for all intents and purposes, she wasn't in control of her mind. One moment, she's watching her husband leave for his meeting, battling the voice in her head that is urging her to save her children's souls, and the next thing she knows, it's twelve hours later and she's lying in bed, her children are nowhere to be found, and all she can remember is that she sent them to be with God."

Lewis went back to her place behind Jessica Campbell but this time placed only one hand lightly on her shoulder. "Imagine how she feels now that with the aid of modern medicine and counseling, she knows what she did back then," the attorney said softly. "Her babies are dead, and she killed them. If you don't think that's a punishment that will last for the rest of her life, then it's because you haven't watched her deal with her grief as I have over these past months. But you must remember that while she may remember now, even if it's in bits and pieces, at the time of this horrible tragedy she could not help herself. And we will ask you to return a verdict of not guilty by reason of insanity. Thank you."

The opening statements were concluded by late afternoon, and Judge Dermondy sent the jury home. Karp excused himself from Katz and Guma, who'd showed up to watch. "I have to make a few calls," he said and quickly made his way back to his office.

Mrs. Milquetost was gone, having left a Post-It note on his desk reminding him that he'd said she could get off early that day to meet her "friend" for a black-tie opening at the Guggenheim Museum. *Good timing,* he thought as he walked into the inner office to find Jaxon waiting for him.

"Were you able to contact the Russian authorities?" Karp asked.

"I was indeed. In fact, we're going to meet later tonight. In the meantime, would you like to go to dinner?"

"Sounds great," Karp replied. "My gang's all over at Grandpa Ciampi's for a few days, and I'm starving. Where do you want to go?"

"How about Chinese?"

25

The bum shuffled along the sidewalk, passing in and out of the shadows of the 200 block of Bowery Street. He was only a few blocks from the expensive bars, art galleries, and restaurants of Little Italy and SoHo, but this wasn't that part of the Lower East Side. This was its dark heart where the tourists didn't venture after sundown—at least not if they had any sense.

Even the streetlights had stopped working on this particular block. The corners of buildings and stairwells reeked of urine and vomit. Here and there in the semi-dark, knots of tattered men and a few lost women stood talking and smoking, or leaned against the big brick building that stretched along the east side of the street. A few were in wheelchairs or balanced on crutches—casualties of alcohol-induced diabetes and untreated wounds.

They tended to be segregated by race; apparently the common obstacles of poverty and addiction did not make them brothers. And they kept a wary eye on each other and sized up newcomers—or the occasional stragglers from the nicer part of town who hurried along, even crossing Bowery to avoid contact.

The bum glanced up at the small sign that glowed red in the dark above the only lit doorway: Bowery Mission. Something of a New York City history buff, he knew that the mission had been founded in 1879 and was the third-oldest Gospel Mission in the United States. It still served three meals and a dose of religion daily to the city's homeless, who could also get a shower up to three times a week, free medical attention, the occasional clean change of clothes, and a bed if he or she got there early enough and was sober.

This bum wasn't looking for a bed or a bath. He was searching for one person, but it wasn't until the other man lurched up to him like a sailboat tacking in the wind that he recognized him. "Hey, buddy, can you spare a dime?"

The bum, Espey Jaxon, did a double-take at the rugged facial features and the long black hair beneath a battered New York Yankees cap. "A dime won't buy much these days," he replied in the pre-arranged greeting. "Jesus, John, nice getup. I didn't recognize you."

John Jojola grinned, then held a hand up to listen to the radio transmitter he had plugged into one ear. Satisfied with what he heard, he looked back at the agent. "Yeah, nobody wants to know a drunken Indian. We can be damned dangerous. But you don't look like an upstanding member of the community yourself. And by the way, Tran just confirmed we're in the clear. If you had a tail you lost him."

Jaxon relaxed. He'd gone to dinner with Karp and then wandered around aimlessly in Chinatown for an hour before suddenly slipping into the Shanghai Emporium, a tourist shop owned by Tran, who used it as a front for his other "business activities."

Led to the back office, Jaxon changed into his "bum disguise" and was then shown the door to an alley. He spent another hour following a set of directions that would take him past various members of Tran's gang, who of course blended in with the rest of the Chinatown population, not so easy for anyone else who might be following the city's newest panhandler. He never knew which of the characters he passed on the sidewalk were Tran's men. It could be any one of the shop owners tugging at the arms of tourists on the sidewalk, urging them inside for the "best prices anywhere," or a tough-looking teen in a Mohawk and metal-studded leather clothing.

The instructions gradually took him over to Bowery, which he'd followed north to the mission to meet Jojola. If the Indian had asked him for a dollar, Jaxon would have moved on. Asking for a dime meant the coast was clear.

"Busy night," Jaxon noted, nodding toward the men queuing up in front of the mission door.

"Hoping for a bed, a hot meal, and maybe a hot shower," Jojola replied. His eyes suddenly shifted to something over Jaxon's shoulder.

A large young black man approached, having decided that the old bums looked like easy marks. "Hey, muthafuckas, got any money or grass on you?" he demanded. He gave them his best 'I might be crazy' glare, which generally was enough to get what he wanted.

"Get lost," Jojola replied.

"What'd you say?" the young man snarled. "I'm gonna fuck you up . . ."

The young man's voice trailed off as he felt a sharp jab in his ample stomach. He looked down at the biggest knife he'd ever seen.

"I said, 'Get lost.' Now, what part of that didn't you understand?"

"Easy, old man," the thug said. "I was just messin' wif ya."

"Then I'm giving you this opportunity to leave before I cut off your nuts and stuff them in your mouth," the "old man" replied. "I've been watching you shaking down these guys all night, and I don't like it. If you're still on this block when I come back, I'm going to let the knife drink deep. *Comprende?*"

"No . . . no . . . no problem," the young man stammered. "I got to be getting on anyway." He backed away and then ran off into the night.

"That was easy," Jojola said. "Guess he prefers picking on drunks." He looked over at the derelicts next to the building. "I was one of them for a while after I got back from 'Nam. It's hard enough losing your pride without some asshole taking your last dollar, too. . . . What?"

"I didn't say anything," Jaxon replied. "I was just thinking about the times when that pig-sticker of yours would come in handy in an interrogation room."

"Can't say I ever used it at the pueblo for police work," Jojola replied. "Been tempted a time or two, but I'm sure the ACLU would have bitched about any confessions 'volunteered' under such circumstances. However, there might have been once or twice where I made sure it was lying around in plain sight."

Jaxon laughed. He knew the history of the knife—bone handled with a razor-sharp nine-inch blade—which had been handed down from generation to generation and finally to Jojola from his grandfather just before he shipped off to Vietnam in '68 as a U.S. Army commando. The Jojolas belonged to a Taos Pueblo warrior clan whose traditions went back until before the first European arrived in the area in the late 1500s.

As quickly as the knife had appeared, it was again sheathed and hidden beneath the old army jacket Jojola wore. The Indian set off for the end of the building, which led to a narrow passageway and a set of stairs up to a side door, above which hung a sign that said "Emergency Exit Only."

"For an Indian from the desert, you seem to be adapting well to city life," Jaxon noted.

Jojola grunted. "I learned a long time ago that you adapt to your surroundings or you don't live long. I don't like it though. I always feel dirty here, even when I'm not playing a bum. I can't seem to get the smell of the city off of my skin. Next time I talk to my boss, I'm going to ask for a little time to get back to the res' for some R&R. I feel the need of a sweat lodge to get the junk out of my pores and out of my mind for a bit."

"Let's finish saving the world," Jaxon replied, patting his friend on the shoulder. "And then you're free to sweat all you want."

"Thanks, chief." He moved up the steps and knocked on the door with Jaxon close behind him.

The door opened into a dark hallway. A flashlight beam blinded them. "How you . . . fuck me oh boy oh boy . . . doing, Mr. Jaxon?" asked the voice on the other end of the light.

"Fine, Warren, thanks for asking. How are you?" Before the little man answered, the agent caught a whiff of something pungent. "And you, too, Booger."

"Ooooh crap . . . I'm good."

"'ood, 'ank you."

The men shut the door. A light came on revealing that they were in a long hallway with Dirty Warren and Booger, who'd been manning the switch. Dirty Warren led the way to a door, where he knocked "shave and a haircut, two bits" and opened the door. He motioned for Jaxon and Jojola to go in and closed the door behind them.

The room was apparently used at the mission as a library; a vast array of books, both paperback and hardback, lined a shelf, inviting the visitor to stay and read in one of the tattered but comfortable chairs. A tall, thin man in a friar's robe sat in one of them reading Joseph Conrad's *Heart of Darkness*, which he put down with a sigh before rising to shake their hands.

The man was even thinner and paler than the last time they'd seen him. He started to say something, but his hand went quickly to cover his mouth as he tried to suppress a cough. "My apologies," he said softly when the fit was over. "Agent Jaxon, John, good to meet you again, though I often see you more than you see me."

"No doubt," Jaxon replied. "How are you, David?"

Of all the odd characters who seemed to have gravitated into Jaxon's life over the past couple of years, David Grale, a former Catholic social worker, was the most unlikely. Jaxon had spent a good deal of his career with the FBI chasing after killers and psychopaths, yet here in front of him was a mass-murderer extraordinaire. It shouldn't have mattered that his victims were themselves murderers, thugs, and terrorists; there was nothing in the oath Jaxon had sworn to uphold that allowed for vigilante justice. But such were the times that he found himself allied with a killer, and besides, he liked the guy and wasn't losing a lot of sleep over his victims.

"How am I?" Grale repeated. "I'm in the same condition that all men are from the day we're born. In other words, I'm dying. But thank you for asking."

"I know a few docs who work for the government and . . ."

"Thanks again," Grale said, "but God will call me home in his time. Meanwhile, I have my work to do, which seems to be coinciding with the work of others."

As though on cue, there was another knock on the door. "Come in," Grale answered. He smiled when he saw Lucy Karp enter the room. He'd first met Lucy when she was a young teenager volunteering at the soup kitchen he ran for the church. That was before she, and her parents, had learned that though he was a social worker by day, he spent his nights killing men who'd been murdering homeless people. His crusade had since expanded to hunting other "evil men," who he believed were actually demons inhabiting human bodies. He hid from his enemies and the authorities in his underground "kingdom" of sewers, tunnels, and natural caverns beneath the city's streets with his ragtag army of Mole People, other homeless, forgotten people.

Lucy was followed by a tall man wearing a black eye-patch. The side of his face was scarred and had the waxy, melted look of skin that has been exposed to intense heat. But except for the physical disfigurement, Ivgeny Karchovski could have been mistaken for his cousin, Butch Karp.

Now, here's as odd a band of patriots as any that ever existed, Jaxon thought. *A religious psychopath, a Russian mob boss, a language-savant-slash-daughter of the New York DA, an Indian police chief and former commando from New Mex-*

ico, and a G-man pretending to be a Rent-a-Cop. His musing was interrupted when Tran entered. . . . *Oh yeah, let's not forget the former schoolteacher, turned VC guerrilla, turned restaurateur, who now makes his living as the head of a Vietnamese crime syndicate.*

The new arrivals took seats or, like Jaxon, remained standing according to their preference. Grale sat back down and nodded to Jaxon. "I believe that you were the one who called this august council together?"

Jaxon nodded and began to brief the others on Miriam Khalifa's story, starting with the night her husband came home drunk. "He was talking about some 'big plan' that was being cooked up at the Al-Aqsa mosque. Then he started babbling about blowing up 'the Metro,' though she thought there was more to the name than that. Have I got it right so far, Lucy?"

"Yep. She also said that her husband had been attending these late-night 'classes' with other men from the mosque. These guys tended to be young and liked to talk about 'jihad,' inspired by Imam Jabbar. After her husband's suicide, this group stopped coming to the mosque. At first she thought they were simply avoiding the place so as not to be implicated in the attack on the synagogue."

"You said, 'at first.' What does she think now?" Tran asked.

"You noticed that, huh? Well, the feds and the NYPD never showed, but these guys still didn't return. She didn't make much of that until a couple of weeks ago when they started drifting back into the mosque community, two or three at a time. It was obvious that they were trying to blend in again. Then she heard through the mosque grapevine that those same men weren't just skipping prayers, they weren't in the city."

"Off somewhere training?" Jojola asked.

"Maybe." Jaxon took up the story again. "Of particular interest to me was that he mentioned a character who calls himself The Sheik. There's a lot of concern in D.C. about what this guy might be up to."

"Jamal also talked about Ajmaani," Lucy noted, looking at her uncle.

"My old friend, Nadya Malovo," Karchovski growled. They'd been lovers when he was with the Soviet Army in Afghanistan and Malovo had been assigned there with the KGB. More recently, though, it had been a relationship based on who would kill the other first.

"Yes," Jaxon replied. "And when you have Malovo, The Sheik, and a dozen young men who believe they are working for Allah, including one who already killed himself and others in a suicide bombing, it adds up to something big."

"What about Prince Esra?" Lucy asked. "Where does he fit in?"

"The timing and the 'coincidence' of Khalifa belonging to the very mosque to which the prince was giving a lot of money can't be ignored," Jaxon replied. "But is the prince part of a plot, or is he the target?"

"Why kill the prince?" Tran asked. "What would that accomplish?"

"It would certainly be a major blow against the Saudi royal family," Jaxon said. "If it happened here, it would strain U.S.-Saudi relations. One of the primary objectives of Islamic extremism is not just to remove U.S. troops from the Middle East, but to establish a religious dictatorship, the caliphate, throughout the Muslim world and beyond . . . starting with Saudi Arabia. And that means getting rid of the royal family. It wouldn't take much to ignite a popular uprising, and we'll be viewed as having supported an oppressive government. I think we're all old enough to remember— well, maybe not Lucy—but the U.S. supported the Shah in Iran when the people revolted, and look how that turned out. We're the Great Satan and the extremists are viewed as the good guys."

"You think killing the prince in the United States gets the revolution rolling?" Jojola asked.

"Could be at least part of it. But his death could also be damaging to the economy. He runs one of the world's biggest hedge funds, which means he controls hundreds of billions of dollars. Kill him and it could really shake up the market."

"You also said that Khalifa was ranting about blowing up the Metro," Tran pointed out. "So does that mean they're going to assassinate the prince by blowing up a subway car when he's on it? I didn't know guys like him rode the subway."

"They don't," Lucy said. "At least not this one. I've spent the past two weeks or so with him, and it's limos all the way."

Grale asked, "What happened to Miriam?"

"She's very brave," Lucy replied. "I was worried about her going back, but she insisted. Otherwise, she thought that the others might change the plan and we wouldn't know as much as we do now. So we worked out a lit- tle play. The next day she asked to see the imam, who apparently has a thing for her. She burst into tears and 'confessed' that the day before she'd gone to meet a lover who lives in a back-alley walkdown in the Lower East Side. Some man had apparently tried to rape her in an alley but was stopped and killed by her lover."

"They believe her? Malovo isn't easy to fool," Karchovski said.

"Apparently," Lucy giggled. "Of course, we helped the story along. Today she left the mosque in the early afternoon to meet her 'lover,' our own John Jojola, though considerably cleaned up from his current appearance. She was, of course, followed, but this time we made sure her trackers saw her embracing John at the entrance to the alley. They then scooted off to John's pad for a couple hours of carnal knowledge."

"I taught her the basics of chess," Jojola said.

"Very basic if you taught them," Tran laughed.

"And the imam's reaction to her confession?" Grale asked.

"Anger," Jojola said. "He told her that as the wife of a martyr for Allah she was disgraced and that in any decent country, she would be stoned to death for her transgression. However, she remains as the receptionist for the time being."

"Did Khalifa blurt out anything about where this attack on the prince is supposed to take place?" Jojola asked. "Or when?"

Jaxon reached inside his coat and pulled out a VCR tape. "Not much. But I do have this, and maybe we can put our collective heads together after we see it."

"What is it?" Tran asked.

"This is an Al Jazeera news special starring Muhammad Jamal Khalifa shortly before the attack on the Third Avenue synagogue. It was inside a package mailed to Imam Jabbar at the mosque. Miriam had just started her new job as the receptionist and was bringing in the mail when she recognized her husband's handwriting on the envelope. She took a considerable risk to keep the package and its contents, and then an even greater one to get it to us. I tried to tell her that the United States owed her. But she said, 'No, I owed it to my faith.'"

"The only thing she asked is that if it helps, she and her family be allowed to remain in the country," Lucy said. "Seems like a small enough request."

Jaxon crossed the room to a VCR player and television. He inserted the tape and turned on the set, which blinked to life, showing a white wall covered with green writing.

"What's it say, Lucy?" Jojola asked.

"The writing is Arabic. A few of the characters aren't quite right but it's a pretty common invocation, roughly equivalent to 'In the name of Allah, the most gracious, the most merciful.'"

A young black man with a scarred face appeared on-screen. He took a few self-conscious moments to arrange himself, and then bent over to pick up something out of the camera's view. When he stood up it was to strap himself into a heavy vest.

"Greetings my brothers in jihad," Jamal Khalifa said, reading from a note before looking up and into the camera. "I am Muhammad Jamal Khalifa and today, with the blessings of Allah, with whom all things are possible, I will offer myself in jihad against the Zionists. It was my wish to join my mujahideen brothers on the day the gates of Paradise open. I was to take part in the great plan with Tatay, while The Sheik accomplished the fatal blow to the Enemy of God, may Allah be pleased with them. It is my hope that with Allah's help, we would change the world for the glory of Allah. However, because of my own weakness, I will no longer be with you, may my brothers in jihad forgive me."

Jamal barely got through the last sentence before his voice cracked. He quit talking before letting out a long sigh and resuming his speech. "I atone for my sins through this action against the Zionists, committed in the name of Allah and His messenger Muhammad, peace and blessings of Allah be upon him, in order to inspire you to complete your tasks."

Khalifa looked into the camera and shouted, "Warriors of Islam, *Sayick* awaits you. Slay the infidels! Destroy the Metro. Slay the Great Satan! God is great! *Allah-u-Akbar!* I will wait for you at the gates of Paradise! *Allah-u-Akbar!*"

Khalifa started to move out of the picture but remembered something. Gone was the anger, replaced by sadness. "I leave you with no regrets, but I want to say 'I love you,' to my wife, Miriam, and my son, Abdullah, may Allah watch over them both." His head dropped and he walked out of the picture frame, then the tape went dark.

Jaxon ejected the tape before turning back to the others. "Any thoughts?"

"Chilling," Lucy said. "But I guess it means that Khalifa's attack on the synagogue was his idea—that somewhere along the line he messed up and got cut out of the main event."

"Main events," Tran noted. "It sounded to me like there's something with this Tatay, but the 'great blow' will come from The Sheik."

"There's the other guys who were training with Khalifa," Lucy pointed out. "Maybe they're all preparing to put on vests and blow themselves up in different places?"

"Maybe," Jojola said. "But hard as it is to imagine, I think I agree with Tran . . ."

" . . . uh-oh, well, scratch that theory; if Jojola's for it, it's got to be wrong," Tran teased.

" . . . as I was saying before the Worthy Oriental Gentleman . . ."

" . . . Watch it Pocahontas . . ."

" . . . interrupted me, it even sounds like this Tatay, The Sheik, and maybe Ajmaani are intending to go to Paradise, too."

"Ajmaani-Malovo would never kill herself," Karchovski interjected. "She's no coward, but she also doesn't believe anything is worth dying for . . . except maybe money."

"Then just Tatay and The Sheik?" Jojola said. He looked at Jaxon. "What do you think?"

"That's been troubling me, too," Jaxon said. "My information is that this sheik isn't about to blow himself up either. He's into ruling on Earth, not being fed grapes by virgins in heaven. But I don't know about this man Tatay."

"It's not actually a name," Lucy said.

"What?"

"I guess it could mean something else to these people, but *Tatay* means 'Father' in Tagalog, one of the main languages of the Philippines. I think it's somebody's nickname."

"That somebody is Azahari Mujahid." All heads swiveled to look at Ivgeny Karchovski.

"The Caller?" Jaxon asked.

"That's what he's sometimes called by intelligence agencies," the Russian acknowledged. "But his followers refer to him as 'Tatay,' or, as Lucy said, 'Father.' And now that message about STM-17 that my cousin passed on makes sense."

"Okay, now I'm really confused," Lucy said.

"It would not mean much to most people," Karchovski said, "but because of my family's . . . business . . . I recognized it as Russian ship registration.

STM-17 is also called the *Star of Vladivostok*, which is also known to me. It is 243-ton cargo vessel that belongs to one of our main . . . competitors, the Tazamov family, who use it for smuggling. We had heard that they were forming a partnership with Islamic extremist groups, and this confirms it."

"Terrorists are buying ships?" Jojola asked.

"There is nothing they are not buying if it fits their aims," Karchovski said. "But they are careful that ownership cannot easily be traced to them. In the business, it is called 'ship laundering,' which is similar to money laundering in that they use a series of false companies to disguise the true ownership. This ship still flies the Russian flag, and its captain answers to the Tazamovs, but apparently they are in on this plan."

"How does this relate to Tatay?" Tran asked.

Ivgeny laughed. "Are you accusing a Russian of milking a story for all it is worth?" he said. "I am offended."

"That was not my intention, my friend. Do continue at whatever pace you desire. I am a Buddhist, you know, and we have great patience, even if it takes all night."

"I get a hint," Karchovski said with a laugh. "I will speed up my talking. Since receiving this information, I put a full effort into tracking the whereabouts of this ship. Two weeks ago, the *Star of Vladivostok* left Hong Kong bound for New York. Friends in Manila report that the ship made an unexpected visit to the Philippines, where it put into port barely long enough to dock . . . or pick up a passenger . . . before putting back to sea."

"You think this Tatay, or Azahari Mujahid, is on his way to the United States to take part in this attack?" Lucy asked.

"Makes sense," Jaxon said thoughtfully. "The Philippines is a hotbed for Islamic extremists linked to Al Qaeda, especially new converts."

"Converts?" Jojola asked. "I thought the Philippines were Catholic?"

"Yeah. Generally speaking, the Philippines are heavily Roman Catholic. However, we've been noting a phenomenon that's been growing among Catholic migrant workers who leave the Philippines to work in the Middle East. A lot of them return home as Muslim converts. For some, it's just a way of increasing their job prospects in countries like Saudi Arabia, where employers legally discriminate against Christians. But quite a few have responded to the imams who point out that the Philippines was a Muslim country for centuries before the Spanish colonialists took over in the sixteenth century and forced Filipinos to convert to Christianity or be put to the sword. It's the same rhetoric that is finding a place with some African Americans, like Jamal. Christianity is the religion of their oppressors, and Islam is their native faith."

"Which is only half true," Lucy said. "Muslims practiced slavery long after it was abolished in the West, and it still exists today in places like the Sudan and, though hidden, Saudi Arabia."

"Nevertheless, Islam resonates strongly in the Philippine migrant community," Jaxon continued. "The Spanish were never able to completely eradicate it in the Philippines. I believe the latest figures for native Muslims are somewhere around 8 million. But about a quarter million more are converts, and most of these worked as migrant laborers in the Middle East and got their brand of Islam from the more militant imams at the madrasahs. They also tend to be more zealous than native Muslims in an effort to 'prove' themselves. Groups like Abu Sayyaf, which has been responsible for terrorist bombings and murders in the Philippines, sprang from that ideology."

"And Azahari Mujahid is one of these?" Jojola asked.

"As a matter of fact, he worked for many years in Saudi Arabia," Karchovski replied. "When he returned to the Philippines, it was as a convert and agitator who started his own group, mostly to protest the presence of the U.S. military in the Philippines."

"They locked him up for a while," Jaxon added. "And Philippine prisons are not nice places. Treat a dog bad enough for long enough and it will turn mean. When Azahari Mujahid got out of prison, he was ready to ramp it up a few notches, especially after he merged with Abu Sayyaf. You might remember a few years back when a ferry was blown up; several hundred people died. And then there was the Regent Hotel bombing in Manila."

"Leveled the place," Tran said. "He and his pals took over a floor, killed everyone working there, and then planted his bomb against the ceiling and supporting structures to bring the whole thing down, one floor pancaking down on the floor beneath it. Hundreds of people were crushed. And the sick bastard stayed around to watch it happen. He actually uses a telephone pager as the trigger device—dials the number from his cell phone and 'boom.' That's where he gets his other nickname, 'The Caller.'"

"You seem to know a lot about him," Lucy said. "You an admirer?"

Tran swore at her in Vietnamese. "Hardly. I owned that hotel. I owe this bastard."

"If he's made a name for himself in the Philippines, why come here?" Jojola asked.

"We wondered the same thing," Karchovski said. "My people in Manila say that the rumor on the streets is that he's been ill; in fact, he disappeared for a while, presumably to get medical treatment."

"Gee, that's too bad."

"Yes, a shame. A few more calls to certain friends in the Russian Embassy revealed that they believe he's left the Philippines again. They'd presumed for more medical treatments, but now I think he doesn't plan on getting well."

"Maybe he's dying and now he's on a kamikaze mission," Jojola said. "Do we know what this guy looks like?"

Jaxon shook his head. "As far as we know, there aren't any photographs of him, not even from his time in the Philippine prison system. All we know is that he's ethnically Malaysian."

"Where's the ship now?"

Karchovski looked at his watch. "It's 11 p.m. The *Star of Vladivostok* is due to dock in approximately six hours."

"Where?" Jaxon asked.

"Brooklyn shipyards," Karchovski spat out angrily. "At a dock controlled by the Tazamov family. Apparently the word is out—no one is to inspect this ship or inquire about the passengers."

"Confirms a message your cousin got from a little birdie at the mosque," Jaxon said. "Wednesday and Brooklyn."

"Maybe we should pay this ship a visit when it puts in to port," Jojola suggested.

"Maybe. But we need to be careful. As you've already pointed out, there may be two or more 'main events.' We might get Azahari Mujahid, but we don't know what else is planned, and we don't want to tip the others off until we do."

"It sounds like they're at least going to attack the subway system," Jojola said. "But where? I read a tourist brochure that said there are about 700 miles of track; that's a lot of ground to cover."

"And when are the main events to go down?" Jaxon mused.

"I think I know," Lucy replied. "Khalifa gave it away when he referred to the gates of Paradise being open."

"Don't all of these guys think that when they die for Allah, they go straight to heaven?" Jojola asked.

Lucy shook her head. "The gates of heaven aren't always open. According to the Prophet, 'When Ramadan comes, the gates of Paradise are opened and the gates of Hell are closed, and the devils are put in chains.' I think that's the clue."

"Ramadan lasts for a month," Jaxon pointed out.

"Yes, and maybe I'm taking Khalifa too literally, but he said he will be there waiting for his mujahideen brothers when the gates open. They open the first day of Ramadan, which begins the day after the crescent moon appears in the sky."

"When's that?" Jojola asked.

"Monday night," Jaxon said, "according to the Hayden Planetarium." He pulled out an electronic day-timer and checked the calendar. "Busy day for me. The prince is scheduled to ring the opening bell at the New York Stock Exchange."

"Does the subway run close enough to the exchange that a bomb on one of the trains might bring the building down?" Tran asked.

"A couple of lines run right under it," Grale interjected. "But I venture to guess that it would have to be a really, really big bomb, which would be tough to get on a train unnoticed. And there's no guarantee it would kill the prince, or even bring down the Exchange, which is a pretty tough old building."

"Not a very soft target, which is what terrorists prefer," Jaxon agreed. "There are cops and security people all over the place. However, there's one other possibility—a very soft target—with connections to the Metro and the prince's schedule. After the stock exchange, the prince is scheduled to cut the ribbon at a Saudi Arabian cultural display in one of the exhibition halls at Grand Central Terminal. Security was going to be a nightmare even before we knew about this. A dozen guys in suicide vests could kill a lot of regular folks, as well as one spoiled Saudi prince."

"Shouldn't we ask the mayor or the feds to close the Metro?" Lucy asked.

"Shut down the city? A million-plus people depend on the subway every day."

"Better than thousands of deaths," Lucy pointed out.

"I agree. But what if we're wrong about the day? And we have no idea where along those 700 miles of track the attack will take place—other than an educated guess that it may be Grand Central Terminal. If we tip our hand, what's to prevent these people from waiting for the heat to die down and trying again, only we won't know when?"

"Maybe we raid the mosque," Lucy said. "Lock everybody up. Somebody will talk."

"What grounds do you use for the search warrant? Khalifa didn't name the mosque or Jabbar in his video. We have his wife's word that he attended these classes—so what?—and we know he talked about blowing up the Metro. If we did get into the mosque, and we didn't find anything, who do we lock up? Jabbar, I guess, but who else? The rest of his congregation? If the planning and operations are being handled elsewhere, we'll have let the bad guys know that we're on to them."

"Not to change the subject, but what is Sayick?" Jojola asked.

"There is a town in Uzbekistan called Sayek that has a reputation for breeding Islamic extremists," Karchovski noted. "It was part of southern former Soviet Union, and has a Muslim population, like Chechnya. Same troubles there—nationalists want republic, extremists want a religious state, gangsters want the opium trade, and Russia wants the oil. If Malovo is part of this, it might make sense. But how, I don't know."

"Sayek is also the pronoun 'I' in Tagalog," Lucy said. "Maybe it was Khalifa's way of trying to relate to Tatay. Maybe he was saying, 'I await you,' as in at the pearly gates."

"All possibilities," Jaxon agreed, "but which one, or is it something else entirely?"

"If we're not going to ask the mayor to shut down the subway system," Lucy said, "what are we going to do?"

Jaxon thought about it. "We'll make sure the warning gets to the proper authorities. They can step up security all along the Metro without raising too many flags, especially at Grand Central. Otherwise, I think we need to find a way to get inside. Any ideas?"

The group remained quiet for several minutes. Finally, Jojola spoke. "Espey, if I remember right, you said there are no photographs of this guy Azahari Mujahid, but he's ethnically Malaysian."

"Right, so what do you have in mind?"

"A Trojan horse," Jojola laughed.

"I take it you're not talking about condoms," Tran replied.

Jojola laughed, walked around behind his Vietnamese friend, and rubbed his shoulders. "I'd like you to meet Tatay Two," he said.

26

"All rise! Put down your papers . . ."

Like a church congregation stirred out of their post-sermon doldrums, those in the courtroom rose as one when the court clerk—a rotund Irishman named Edmund Farley—announced the entrance of Judge Dermondy.

"Oye oye oye," Farley continued, "all those who have business before Part 36 of the Supreme Court, State of New York, New York County, draw near and ye shall be heard. The honorable Supreme Court Justice Timothy Dermondy presiding. The case on trial, The People of the State of New York versus Jessica Campbell."

Like a fight announcer, Farley introduced the opponents in their respective corners. "Representing the People, the honorable District Attorney Roger Karp and assistant district attorney Kenny Katz; representing the defendant, Ms. Linda Lewis."

With a final glance around the courtroom, Farley turned to Dermondy. "Your honor, all of the jurors are present and accounted for . . . counsel and the defendant are present. . . . The case on trial is ready to continue." Dermondy nodded and his court clerk concluded, "Please be seated!"

"Thank you, Mr. Farley," Dermondy said. "Good morning, counsel, Ms. Campbell, and especially you jurors. I trust we are ready to proceed. Mr. Karp?"

Rising to his feet, Karp smiled. "Yes, Your Honor, thank you. The people call Detective Marj Cobing to the stand."

As he waited for the detective to enter the courtroom, Karp reflected on the scene outside the Criminal Courts building that morning. Many of the same cast of characters had lined up on the sidewalks. Only now, instead of a circus, they'd settled into a sort of organized encampment. They even seemed to be operating under a loose set of rules meant to keep the peace among natural enemies.

Karp had watched from Dirty Warren's newsstand as one of the NOF organizers showed up with a bagel and coffee for Edward Treacher. She handed it to the street preacher with a little bow, but didn't say a word. However, he picked up his milk crate and moved it to the other side of the police cordon from the NOF protest line, where he ate and drank with relish. He was still within shouting range when he resumed his perch on top of his crate; but he maintained his distance, and the two sides even took turns drowning each other out.

Meanwhile, little bands of tourists and curiosity-seekers, as well as the vendors and pickpockets who preyed on them, scurried up and down the sidewalk, or crossed the street haphazardly, hurrying to wherever there seemed to be a bit of action. One middle-aged mom from Wisconsin was struck by a taxi when she sprinted across the street to purchase the second "*Special* . . . fu-fu-fucking bullshit . . . *Edition*" of the *New York Post* from the nasty little man at the newsstand.

Every once in a while, some young man would sprint through the crowd, snatch a purse, and take off running with cops in hot pursuit. Otherwise, most of the activity occurred whenever the television cameras whirred into action, which would cause the protesters to start shouting and waving their signs.

Twelve floors above the commotion outside, Karp looked at his watch. Nine-thirty. They'd already wasted a half hour in Dermondy's office that morning on Linda Lewis's objection to Cobing taking the stand.

"If the prosecution insists on calling her, and you allow it," Lewis told Dermondy, "I especially object to her discussing statements allegedly made by Jessica Campbell to her husband."

"On what grounds?" Dermondy asked.

"On the grounds that the statement will be taken out of context and un-fairly prejudicial to the defendant."

"Your honor, that's nonsense," Karp argued. "Obviously, the law won't allow us to force Mr. Campbell to testify against his wife. However, there's nothing to prevent the detective from testifying as to what Mr. Campbell said of his own free will to police officers regarding relevant facts having everything to do with this case."

"Well, Miss Lewis, I'm going to overrule you on this," the judge said. "We'll just have to leave it to you to put the statements into context."

Cobing took the stand, where Karp led her through the police investiga-tion. "How was it that the NYPD located the defendant, Jessica Campbell?"

"We were called by her attorney and told that there was a possibility that the defendant had 'lost' her children, and that they might possibly be deceased."

"Were you able to speak to the defendant's husband, Charles Campbell?"

"Yes, I did get to speak to Mr. Campbell."

"Please tell us what, if anything, he said."

"He told me that when he came home that night, he couldn't locate his children, and that his wife was lying in bed."

"Did Mr. Campbell tell you anything the defendant said to him about the children?"

"Yes, he said she told him that she'd sent the children to be with God in order to save their souls from Satan."

"Thereafter, what did you do in furtherance of this investigation?"

"After speaking to Mr. Campbell, we believed that we had a homicide case, so we asked for a court order to obtain blood, tissue, and hair samples from Mrs. Campbell, as well as photographs of marks on her body."

"What sorts of marks?"

"Scratches on her arms and a bite mark on her forearm, as well as abra-sions and contusions on her arms, knees, and back."

"By abrasions and contusions, you mean scrapes and bruises."

"Yes, sir. Those would be the layman's terms."

Using photographs introduced into evidence to illustrate the detective's testimony, Karp had the detective point out the marks on Jessica Campbell. "Detective Cobing, did you learn when the defendant was injured?"

ESCAPE 331

"That day," she replied. "The physician who treated her at Bellevue said the injuries were less than twenty-four hours old. Also, Mr. Campbell told me that he didn't believe she'd had those marks on her body earlier that morning. But he wasn't certain with respect to the injuries on her back."

"And why was that?" Karp asked.

"Because Mr. Campbell said that he and his wife were not sleeping or dressing in each other's presence."

The answer caused a stir in the courtroom. One of the supermarket tabloids had run a story alleging that Charlie Campbell had been seen kissing another woman about the same time his wife was killing their kids.

Now, Charlie Campbell kept his head pointed straight forward. His wife stopped her drawing for a moment, then resumed again without looking up.

"However, she had been wearing a short-sleeved shirt and a skirt the previous evening when he got home," Cobing continued, "and was dressed similarly the morning he left her. He could not recall seeing any of the marks on her legs or arms."

"Detective, do you recall talking to a Mr. Homer Paris in Staatsburg?"

"Yes. He's the station master at the Staatsburg train station."

"And Staatsburg is a small town about one hundred miles north of Manhattan on the Hudson River, is that true?"

"Yes."

"What were you doing at the train station in Staatsburg?"

"I was attempting to locate anyone who might have seen Jessica Campbell there in March . . . around the time of the murders."

"How were you attempting to do this?"

"I had several photographs of women with me, including one of Jessica Campbell taken from the New York City University yearbook. I was asking people at the station if they, first, had been at the station in March, and if so, did they recognize any of the women in the photographs."

"And did you find such a person?"

"Yes, I found Mr. Paris."

"And who did Mr. Paris identify, if anyone?"

"He picked the photograph of Jessica Campbell. But he said she was wearing a disguise when he saw her in March."

"A disguise?"

"Yes, a wig—he described it as a bad wig—and big sunglasses."

"Yet, he recognized her."

"Yes, he said he recognized her big ears and her chin."

"What about her chin?"

"Well, the shape."

"What shape?"

"He said it looked like 'a little butt' because of the dimple in her chin."

The spectators burst into laughter. Judge Dermondy banged his gavel. "People, please," he drawled. "I'll ask you to remember we're here in a Supreme Court setting, which requires all of us to act like adults and respect the dignity of these proceedings." Smiles disappeared. "Now, let's all just pay attention and save our levity for when we have adjourned. Mr. Karp, let's proceed."

"Thank you, Your Honor," said Karp, who had always admired the way Dermondy controlled a courtroom whether as a prosecutor or a jurist. "Detective Cobing, can you recall any instance in which the defendant, Jessica Campbell, told anyone else where or how she murdered her three children?"

"No, not to my knowledge."

"Did she tell anyone where she hid their bodies?"

"Not to my knowledge."

"Are you aware of her ever telling anyone that she couldn't remember where she left their bodies?"

"No. To my knowledge, she simply refused to answer that question."

Karp kept his examination of the detective short. But Lewis's cross-examination was even briefer.

"Detective," she said, without bothering to move from behind the defense table, "do you know of any instance in which Jessica Campbell said that she had 'murdered' her children?"

"According to Mr. Campbell, she said she sent them to be with God."

"But she did not use the word 'murder' or even 'killed,' did she?"

"No."

"Because it's not what she believed, was it?" Lewis asked.

"I wouldn't know."

"No, you wouldn't. But detective, do you know of a single instance in which Jessica Campbell told anyone that she 'hid' the bodies of her children?"

"No."

"Thank you, no further questions."

Karp jumped up for redirect like a bantam rooster ready to fight. "Detective, when someone kills someone else—and it's not in self-defense, an accident, or a soldier at war—what is the word for it?"

"Murder."

"And when someone puts bodies in a car and then submerges that car into a river, is it fair to say that person tried to hide the bodies?"

"Absolutely."

_____

The rest of the morning had been taken up by the first police officers on the scene at the Campbell house, who testified that there'd been no sign of the children and no evidence that a crime had been committed.

"Did you notice anything in particular about the kitchen?" Karp asked.

"Not really," one of the officers testified. "It was a mess. There was a breakfast on the counter that looked like it hadn't been touched and dirty dishes here and there. But nothing unusual."

After the lunch break, Lewis objected again when Karp called the lead NYPD crime-scene investigator, Officer Bob Watts, to the stand—on, as she put it, "the same grounds, that the expected testimony will be taken out of context and will be unfairly prejudicial." Again the judge overruled the objection, and Watts entered the courtroom.

Referred to by his colleagues as "the Walrus," Watts fit the name, with thick reddish-brown hair cut short; a long mustache of the same color, which hung down on either side of his mouth like tusks; and a body built for surviving the frigid waters of the Arctic. He was also a consummate professional—affable and polite under the most heated cross-examination; jurors liked and believed him, which also made him a favorite of the DAO.

Under Karp's questioning, Watts explained that this case was unusual because when the police began their investigation, they believed that a crime had occurred—the murder of the Campbell children—but no one knew how or where it happened. "So we started with the defendant's residence and went over it with a fine-toothed comb," he said. "We didn't find much. Nothing unusual or indicating a crime—no blood or other physical evidence—not until we got to the main floor bathroom."

"And what did you find there?"

"Well, it was more of what we didn't find that was unusual," the investigator replied with just a touch of mystery.

"Could you explain what you mean by that?" Karp said, pitching the softball question.

"There were no fingerprints."

"No fingerprints? Do you mean only a few fingerprints?"

"No, I mean 'N-O' fingerprints. None. Zip. Nada."

"And why is that unusual?"

"In a house with three kids?" Watts scoffed and rolled his eyes. "I don't know about your kids, but when mine were growing up, they put their grimy little mitts on just about everything in our house. I would have expected the same of the Campbell kids. And as a matter of fact, they did leave fingerprints on just about every surface of that house—except for the main floor bathroom."

"Couldn't that be explained by a good housekeeper cleaning the bathroom?"

"Maybe Super Maid, but I doubt it. Fingerprints aren't necessarily visible to the naked eye, at least not the ones that aren't left by some goo- or dirt-covered hands. In my professional experience of twenty-five years as a crime-scene investigator, the only time a scene is that clean is when it has been wiped down specifically to remove fingerprints. It's the sort of thing I'd expect at the scene of a mob hit, and even then the suspects rarely get them all."

"So, Mr. Watts," Karp continued. "You are saying that it would be extremely unusual to NOT find any fingerprints in the main floor bathroom of a home occupied by two adults and three young children?"

"Especially where the children were bathed," Watts replied. "There were Sesame Street bath toys and a little boat on the edge of the tub."

"And why is it especially unusual in a bathroom?"

"Lots of smooth, hard surfaces—like metal, tile, and porcelain—all of which lend themselves to leaving latent fingerprints."

"And there were none?" Karp repeated for effect.

"Not a one. The place had been wiped clean as a whistle."

After Karp finished with the direct examination, Dermondy decided that it was a good time to take the afternoon break. When the trial resumed, Watts returned to the stand to be cross-examined by Linda Lewis. Again she kept it short.

"Mr. Watts, do you know why that bathroom was so spotless?"

"I believe I do now."

"Do you know who cleaned it?"

"I believe I do."

"Well, essentially all you really told this jury is that you didn't find anything at the Campbell residence to indicate a crime had been committed there, isn't that true?"

"Yes, ma'am. We didn't find any evidence that a crime had been committed."

"No further questions."

After Watts stepped down from the stand, Karp called his last witness of the day, Homer Paris, the station master from Staatsburg. The door at the back of the courtroom opened, and an old man—bent over at about mid-chest level like a candy cane—hobbled into the courtroom and stopped, looking around at the spectators with suspicion.

"What the hell you people looking at?" he snarled.

"Don't let them bother you, Mr. Paris," Judge Dermondy said, amused. "Please, come take a seat so that we can swear you in and these fine lawyers can ask you a few questions."

"Well, make it snappy," Paris replied. "I need to get back to my station."

"We'll do our best."

Homer Paris had not wanted to appear at the trial. "Waste of my time," he complained when Clay Fulton drove to Staatsburg to serve him with a subpoena. "Who's going to keep the trains running on time if I'm not here, huh? Answer me that."

Fulton had pointed out that the subpoena required him to appear in court or be held in contempt, "and possibly jailed or fined." He added that Detective Cobing would be there, too.

"Oh that cute little black cop is going to be there?" Paris replied. "Well, I suppose I can make it. She's a fine-looking woman."

When the station master spotted Cobing sitting in the pew behind the prosecution table, he stopped and winked. She smiled and nodded toward the witness stand. He gave her a little salute, then straightened his back as best he could and hobbled to the stand to be sworn in.

As requested, the attorneys kept it snappy. Essentially, Paris was asked to relate the story of the day that past March when the woman in the cheap wig and big sunglasses had walked into his station and asked for a one-way ticket to Grand Central Terminal. "Paid cash," he recalled. "Nobody pays cash anymore."

"Is that woman in the courtroom today?" Karp asked.

"You bet your ass, sonny," Paris replied and pointed at Jessica Campbell.

"The record should reflect that the witness, Mr. Paris, pointed to the defendant, Jessica Campbell," Karp noted. "How is it that you're so certain?"

"She's got big ears and her chin looks like a butt."

Before anyone could laugh, Dermondy cleared his throat, having anticipated the answer. "Please, don't," he warned those in the courtroom.

"Don't what?" Paris scowled. "Can I go now?"

Dermondy raised an eyebrow. "Mr. Karp?"

"No further questions."

"Miss Lewis?"

"No questions, your honor."

"Well then, Mr. Paris, thank you for your time. You may step down and return to your station," Dermondy said.

"Well la-di-da." The old man climbed down from the stand. "Brought me all the hell the way down here for that? Waste of my time, that's what it was."

Apparently not a complete waste, however, as he stopped again next to the pew and gave Cobing another wink. "Now that's a fine-looking woman," he announced. This time, Dermondy didn't bother to bang his gavel and laughed along with everyone else.

———

The irascible station master left the room with a few choice words for a couple of reporters who dared ask how to spell his last name. Dermondy shook his head and asked the attorneys if there was anything else. "As you know, we're going to call it a little early tonight. I got invited to a gig with Woody's group down at Michael's Pub."

"Nothing from us," Karp said. "We expect to finish our case in chief tomorrow."

"Miss Lewis?"

Lewis, who'd also stood and was waiting for Karp to finish, held up a sheaf of papers. "Yes, actually, there is, your honor. I'm making a motion for a mistrial due to my earlier objections to the testimony of Detective Cobing and Officer Watts."

Judge Dermondy stared at Lewis for a long time, as if doing so would make her go away, but when she didn't, he turned to the jury. "I'm going to excuse you now while we discuss some legal issues that are not part of the evidence. Refrain from watching television newscasts, listening to radio news reports, or reading newspaper stories about this case. You are not to talk about it with anyone—not your family, not your friends, not your priest or rabbi, not even the television set. If someone—including any one of these rascals in the press—approaches you, please report it to the court clerk, and I will deal with them as harshly as the law allows. Have a good night, eat something healthy, and sleep well. Remember, this is a marathon, not a sprint."

The jurors filed out of the courtroom. "Okay, counsel," Dermondy said, "what are your grounds for dismissal based on?"

"Judicial error. You should not have allowed that testimony."

"I'm inclined to let the appellate courts decide if you're correct," Judge Dermondy said. "I have little doubt that you'll not succeed there either. But for the record, let's hear your reasoning."

"I already said—the testimony was out of context and unfairly prejudicial to my client receiving a fair trial," Lewis retorted.

"Now Miss Lewis, isn't it a matter of record from your opening statements, and your cross-examination of the witnesses, that you intend to use some of these very same statements in your case to demonstrate that your client was mentally ill?"

"Yes, your honor, but as I said, it's a matter of context. The prosecution presented these witnesses' statements in an erroneous context as a 'confession' by my client, in essence telling the jury that she was aware that she was murdering her children. And the so-called 'evidence' that the bathroom was meticulously cleaned was meant to be perceived as an admission by my client that she knew that what she was doing was wrong. However, if presented in the proper context with a medically appropriate understanding of her mental state, it becomes apparent that the statements regarding sending her children to be with God were not confessions to murder at all, but proof of a mental illness that rendered her incapable of understanding what she had actually done."

"And what about cleaning the bathroom?"

"Again, in context it's clear that she was in a disassociative state where she thought she was simply being a good housewife and cleaning up a mess she'd made."

Karp jumped to his feet. "Your honor, how long do we have to listen to this nonsense? 'Cleaning up the mess she'd made' is an awfully cavalier description for drowning and butchering children."

As the courtroom spectators gasped and Jessica Campbell gave a muffled cry, Dermondy responded in his usual measured drawl. "Mr. Karp, you know that you and counsel, Miss Lewis, will have ample opportunity to argue the facts to the jury at the appropriate time. I recognize that competent counsel may, from time to time, engage in a partisan spin of facts. But both sides should trust in my ability to see it clearly and to rule impartially. So Miss Lewis, let me get this straight. You believe that you should be able to use these statements made by the defendant, so long as they are in what you deem the proper context, but the prosecution can't? Well, that's a particularly self-serving argument, and, without meaning to insult you, Miss Lewis, has the legal impact of a feather. Long ago, I'm sure, we all heard the old saw: 'What's good for the goose is good for the gander.' I'll let the jury decide how to interpret the evidence. Your motion to dismiss, most respectfully, is denied."

Karp expected Lewis to take her lumps and sit. But instead, she said, "Then I'd like to make an objection right now to the appearance of tomorrow's prosecution witnesses."

"Can't you do that tomorrow, Miss Lewis?"

Despite not liking her tactics or her personally, Karp had to grudgingly respect how hard the woman fought for her client. She was going to throw everything she could against the wall, hoping something would stick, and she was willing to piss off the judge to do it.

Finding the bodies of the Campbell children had been a real blow to the defense. No longer could it be argued or inferred that Jessica had simply left them somewhere—something along the lines of sticking them in a boat and shoving them out to sea to be found by God, an act that unfortunately resulted in their deaths. Sinking the car in the river, when combined with her efforts to clean any fingerprints and bloodstains in the bathroom, clearly came off as someone who knew that what she had done was wrong, trying to hide evidence. And Lewis knew that the forensic examination of the bodies by Gates and Swanburg was going to hurt her chances of convincing the jury that Jessica Campbell didn't know what she was doing when she murdered her children.

As expected in pre-trial hearings, Lewis had demanded that the evidence located in the Hudson River be suppressed due to what she said was "misconduct by law enforcement," chiefly several violations of constitutional protections against search and seizure. Part of her contention was that Detective Cobing had questioned Jessica's parents "under the pretext of simply wanting to find the children so that they could be properly buried, when the real motivation was to create probable cause for a judge to issue a search warrant."

But Dermondy hadn't bought it. "Miss Lewis, I don't believe that Mr. and Mrs. Gupperstein were forced to talk to Detective Cobing. No one sat them in a hot little room with a bright bulb over their heads . . . no rubber hoses . . . not even the threat of arrest. This 'interrogation,' as you call it, was non-custodial and in fact occurred in their home. They talked voluntarily under their own free will. Motion denied."

"Then I object to any testimony about what was inside the car, again for unlawful search and seizure. These investigators in essence broke into private property by searching the Campbells' car without their permission or a search warrant."

That had been a month ago. Now Dermondy smiled and shook his head. "I respect the vigor with which you defend your client, Miss Lewis," he said. "But your arguments stretch the bounds of common sense, much less the sensibilities of the law. For the record, all these search and seizure issues were fully litigated by the defense before, during, and after the evidentiary fact-finding hearings prior to trial before this court. Essentially, I ruled that the car and its contents were abandoned, leaving the authorities rightfully to seize all of it for evidentiary purposes. So, Miss Lewis, I denied your motions to dismiss then, as I do presently. Unless you have newly discovered evidence, or new facts, please do not repeat the same motions previously litigated. Now, there being no further business before this court, we will remain in recess until 9 a.m."

———

That evening after work, Karp slipped out of the loft with Gilgamesh and headed down the street, where he tied the dog to a railing outside the Housing Works Used Bookstore. He went inside and back to the coffee shop, where he sat down at a table already occupied by Jaxon, who told him about the meeting the night before.

"I've already spoken to the mayor and the chief of police. They agree that we can't shut down the entire Metro system without more specifics. But they're going to pump up the number of uniformed officers throughout the line, especially at Grand Central, as well as triple the number of plainclothes cops. The cops will be instructed to search a lot more backpacks and keep an eye out for the possibility of suicide vests under coats. They're to err on the side of caution, even if it means racial and ethnic profiling."

"What are you doing about this Tatay?" Karp asked.

Jaxon smiled. "Why, pay him a little visit, and welcome him to these golden shores."

27

The guard standing duty at the bottom of the gangplank leading from the dock to the deck of the *Star of Vladisvostok* lit a cigarette and took a deep drag. *Nothing like American tobacco,* he thought, savoring the flavor, *not like that cow dung we have in Russia.*

He glanced up at the ship he was guarding. It was a tramp steamer built in the 1960s, commanded by an owner-captain who was not particular about what sort of cargo he was transporting. Nor did his crew care so long as they got paid and had plenty of shore leave on which to spend their earnings.

The guard didn't know many details, but he was aware that the captain mainly worked for the Tazamov gang running drugs and weapons, as well as getting people in and out of countries secretly. He'd been told that the Tazamovs were relatively new to the *Russkaya Mafiya.* The Russian mob was centered in the Brighton Beach community of Brooklyn, known to the locals as Little Odessa because of its large Russian population. However, he knew that the Tazamov family wasn't new to organized crime.

They were a brutally bloody legend back in his hometown of St. Petersburg. Unlike most of the Russian gangs, which were run by ex–Soviet Army and ex-KGB agents who'd lost their jobs at the end of the Cold War, the Tazamovs had been involved in crime since the days of the tsars.

The gang's most notorious contribution to the colorful pantheon of Russian mobsters was Viktor "the Butcher" Tazamov. Legend had it that he'd doubled the family's considerable fortune by selling "long pork" to his starving fellow citizens during the German seige of Leningrad in the winter of 1943.

Of course, there were no pigs in the city at that time. No, the Butcher's herd had walked on two legs until starvation, cold, or German munitions killed them, though rumor had it that some were not dead when Viktor sent them to hang in his meat locker. It could have been merely legend, but supposedly he'd joked after the war that he'd spent December 1943 "having my competition over for dinner."

Small wonder that the U.S. offshoot of the gang arrived in the 1990s with few, if any, scruples as to what they would and would not do for money. In that way, the ship's captain fit right in with the Tazamovs.

This particular dock was considered Tazamov territory. The longshore-men and dock security personnel had been bribed to ignore the ships that docked there and not to pay too much attention to whatever cargo was lifted, or walked, on and off the vessels.

What the guard, an able-bodied seaman who knew a thing or two about the seamy side of the world, wondered was why U.S. federal agents weren't all over this place, given the heightened threat of terrorism. But after the first couple of trips went smoothly, he'd decided to believe the captain's as-surances that this was a milk run. It didn't hurt that the crew had received generous bonuses, as well as plenty of time to partake of New York's bars and sexual street vendors.

Somebody is paying somebody else a lot of money, he thought. *I wish I had that kind of dough.* His pay seemed to be predicated on the degree of risk. This time the bonus had been twice as big as any other, which made him a little nervous. But the only downside so far had been that the crew was for-bidden to go into the city—instead a small bar with several prostitutes available had been set up in a nearby warehouse—and it was to be a short trip, two nights in port and that was all.

They don't want one of us getting drunk and saying the wrong thing to the wrong person, he thought as he looked up at the moonless night sky. *Our passengers must be very important.*

Not that they cared, but the crew had been told to stay away from the men they'd picked up on an equally short, and disappointing, stop in Manila. The guard had only seen the guests once and didn't want to know them any better; they looked hard and tough. Physically he would have pegged them as Southeast Asian, maybe Chinese. It appeared that they were Muslim, however, as various crew members had seen or heard them at their prayers on the passage over.

Whatever the passengers were up to in New York City, the guard knew that it was not sightseeing. But what they did was none of his business. It was a screwed-up world, and if the people in it wanted to kill each other, so be it, as long as he had a bottle of vodka, American cigarettes, and the occasional prostitute.

As if in answer to his prayers, the guard saw someone walking down the dock toward him. His hand went to the opening of his jacket, where he carried a gun in a shoulder holster, but then he relaxed. All he could see was a silhouette because of the lights from a warehouse behind her, but the figure was definitely that of a woman, and apparently a drunk woman by the way she wobbled. He licked his lips, hoping his comrades had sent one of the hookers over to offer their lonely shipmate a quick bang.

Just don't look at her face, he reminded himself with a grin. There were always a few working girls servicing the men who worked the dockyards or the sailors who didn't have shore leave. But they were usually past their prime—if they'd ever had a prime—if not downright old enough to be his grandmother or with faces ravaged by diseases and just poor genetics.

As the woman drew closer, he could tell she was a lot younger than the usual dock whores and a whole lot better looking, even if her nose was a little too big for his tastes. True, there wasn't much meat on her, not for a sailor who liked plenty of cushion; but she was wearing a mini-skirt that showed off nice legs, and he was more than willing to pay top dollar for such a treat. He wondered if he had enough money in his wallet.

"Hi baby," the woman purred. "You look lonely. Want a date?"

"Sure, what is price?" he replied in broken English.

"I speak Russian, honey," the young woman replied, switching languages. "The price depends on what you want. Fifty dollars for a suck, one hundred for anything else."

Must be my lucky day, he thought. *I'm going to have sex with a classy young bitch with legs that look like they could go around me twice.* He didn't have that kind of money on him, but he figured that she would just have to give him a discount.

"I want it all," the guard said, reaching for her. But she dodged his hand.

"Not here, you fool," she smiled coyly. "Do you think I want to be a show for others on the ship? That would cost extra."

The guard scowled. He'd been told not to abandon his post on pain of being thrown overboard once they were back at sea. "Where?"

The woman nodded toward a stack of shipping containers. "It's dark over there," she said. "I cost a little more money, but you can do anything . . . anything you want and you won't have to hurry. I'm new at this and a little shy."

The guard bit his lip. *I shouldn't have to guard this old rust bucket,* he thought. *I don't even like carrying a gun. People with guns get shot.* He looked again at the girl, who was turned sideways, giving him a good look at the profile of her breasts. *Not large, but perky,* he thought. *And if she's not lying, practically a virgin!* The thought of anything he might want was too much to resist. She wouldn't get paid after it was over, as punishment for making him take this risk, but what the hell could she do about it? Report him to the police?

"Let's go," she said and hooked her arm in his, leading him back toward the containers like they were on a high school date.

They had just reached the shadows when another figure loomed in front of them. The guard's first instinct was to go for his gun, but he couldn't move his arm because the girl tightened her grip and held it fast. A third person grabbed him from behind, an arm going around his neck in a figure-four headlock. *I wish I'd had sex first,* he thought just before he passed out.

———

"Oh my God, if I never wear high heels and a mini-skirt again, it will be too soon," Lucy said as John Jojola let the man slump to the ground. "I thought I was going to break my ankle out there. I probably looked drunk." She glanced down at the sailor. "Is he dead?"

"No, it's just an old jujitsu choke-hold, *hadaka shime*; cuts off the blood supply to the brain. The victim goes out in a few seconds, but after you let go, most people wake up on their own in a matter of minutes."

"Most people? What about the others?"

Jojola shrugged. "They don't wake up without being revived. That's why most police departments have stopped using the 'sleeper hold.' But I'm not particularly worried about whether this dirtbag wakes up."

The man on the ground took a deep breath and groaned. "See, he's okay," Jojola said as other figures emerged from the dark, led by a tall man with an eye-patch.

"What do we do with this one, Mr. Karchovski?" asked one of the men. "A bullet and over the side? He works for those scum, the Tazamovs."

Ivgeny Karchovski toed the fallen man, whose eyes fluttered open. "We will have words with the Tazamovs soon enough," he said, but in such a way that Lucy was sure that more than words would be exchanged. "But no, this one is just stupid Russian sailor who fell for cute girl; he wasn't the first and won't be the last. Just take his clothes and tie him up; we'll figure out what to do with him and his comrades later."

Two men soon had the prisoner stripped of his pants, coat, and hat. They were joined by Tran, Jaxon, and several of his FBI agents. "The bar's secure," Jaxon said. "We had to shoot the bartender, who apparently worked for the local mob, present company excluded. But the others gave up easily enough; they're just sailors, though I know some people who'll be interested in talking to them about this ship's travels and cargoes."

Karchovski's men quickly settled on who among them most closely resembled the prisoner, and that man donned the confiscated pants, coat, and hat. He offered his arm to Lucy. "Wait for my signal," he said.

"And make sure my little cousin is clear before we go," Karchovski added.

Lucy and her escort walked out of the shadows. She clung to his arm, laughing and staggering—not entirely on purpose. As they drew near the gangplank they stopped, and the faux sailor handed her money.

"Was worth every ruble," he laughed, flashing a much nicer smile than his predecessor.

Ned better get back soon from Navy SEAL training, Lucy thought. *A young woman only has so much willpower.* "Next time it's free," she said, loud enough for any observers to hear.

Lucy reached the shadows, where Ivgeny met her first. "You're one fine actress," he said. "Though I suspect that if my cousin, Butch, your father, knew I'd dressed you up like prostitute and sent you to meet Russian sailors and terrorists, he would find a way to prosecute me in Brooklyn and send me to prison for life."

"Probably. He still thinks I'm in junior high and need protecting." She could see her escort pacing at the bottom of the gangplank. "What's the signal?" she asked.

"When he lights his cigarette," Ivgeny replied.

———

Azahari Mujahid paused at the rail outside his berth. He'd come out to look at the night sky. In a few days, the crescent moon would rise, signaling the start of Ramadan. *And,* he thought, *with Allah's blessing, the start of a new world of Islam.*

The moment was tarnished when he saw the filthy infidel sailor and the *pokpok* emerge from the shadows by the containers. He gave the man who was standing outside the passenger cabins as a sentry a disgusted look, which the man answered by spitting in the direction of the Russian guard.

Mujahid was fifty years old and originally from the Philippine island of Panay, where his Malaysian ancestors had immigrated hundreds of years before. Almost thirty of those years he'd been a Muslim after converting during his years as a migrant laborer in Saudi Arabia. Born Emil Santos, he considered himself lucky to have been befriended by the imam of a Medina mosque. He'd gone there one day to learn more about his host country's religion, which he'd been told had been usurped from the Filipino people by the Spanish colonialists. Shortly thereafter, he committed his life to the worship of Allah and the promotion of Islam, taking the name Azahari Mujahid.

When he returned to the Philippines after nearly fifteen years abroad, he discovered that his wife and daughter were westernized. They'd spent his hard-earned money on shopping trips to buy indecent clothing. He tried to persuade them to convert to Islam, but his wife had no intentions of abandoning her Catholic upbringing, and his daughter just laughed in his face when he suggested that she wear a scarf to cover her hair.

One day, fed up with her insolence, he wrapped his hands, strong as vises, around her neck and squeezed. His wife had returned from a trip in time to see him choke the last bit of life out of their daughter. She screamed and tried to run, but he caught her and dragged her back into the house, where he beat her to death with a tire iron.

Mujahid fled, arriving on the island of Mindanao where the main population of Filipino Muslims lived. He felt little remorse over the murders of his wife and daughter, believing the imam who said that he'd only acted in accordance with the Qur'an.

Like other recent converts, he felt that the local Muslims were too permissive and didn't follow the teachings of the Prophet. Worse, they were content to be ostracized and discriminated against by the Roman Catholic majority in other parts of the Philippines. The entire country had been cowed into accepting the presence of the U.S. military, much as those who ruled Saudi Arabia were submissive to the infidel troops trampling holy Arabian soil.

Mujahid dedicated himself to returning the Philippines to a Muslim state and ridding it of all Western influences. He'd traveled to Africa and Pakistan, where Islamic fundamentalists were organizing and training to defeat the West. Soon he was specializing in making bombs—little bombs like the ones used in suicide vests and big bombs capable of leveling multistoried buildings. Soon his car bombs were exploding outside of U.S. military bases and inside busy Manila shopping malls.

In the 90s, he'd merged his group with Abu Sayyaf, the militant Philippine Islamic organization loosely affiliated with Al Qaeda and Indonesia's Jemaah Islamiah. He'd become part of the upper command of the group where he was known by his nom de guerre, Tatay

Mujahid thought of himself as a team player. He'd sent a message of congratulations to Osama bin Laden and the Taliban after the September 11, 2001, attack and celebrated the victory by blowing up a Manila discotheque frequented by American soldiers. Nearly 300 people had died while he sat in a car a block away and dialed the telephone number of the pager he'd used as a detonator.

He'd used a similar device to tear a hole in a ferry carrying nearly a thousand people between the islands of Mindanao and Samar. Two vans packed with plastic explosives and driven aboard the ferry had been sufficient to sink the vessel in the shark-infested waters. Afterward, he'd cruised slowly through the flaming debris, shooting survivors as they struggled in the water begging for help.

The greatest feat accomplished so far had been the Regent Hotel bombing. Even he had been surprised at how thoroughly the building could be destroyed from the inside, as opposed to a truck bomb on the outside.

Now his career was coming to an end. He'd lost many of his fellow Filipino mujahideen, but always he'd stayed a step ahead of the U.S. Special Forces and the Philippine army commandos who had tracked and killed them in the jungle. He attributed his longevity to two things: Allah's will, and the fact that he never allowed himself to be photographed and rarely met with anyone outside of his inner circle. Even around other mujahideen, his men were instructed not to defer to him, call him by name, or treat him any different from the way they would treat one another. That way, when the inevitable traitors reported to the Americans, they could not say for sure that Tatay had been among them.

However, Allah had decided it was time for him to enter the gates of Paradise, sending him a clear message by giving him the cancer that was eating its way through his guts. At first, he'd resisted the will of Allah by secretly checking into an Egyptian hospital, where he had undergone both surgery and chemotherapy. When that did not stop the gnawing pain, he accepted that his time on Earth was up. He wondered how best to end his life, what final gesture of jihad he could make that would be greater than anything he had done in the past.

Then a messenger of Allah came to him with a suggestion. He was still in the Egyptian hospital, growing strong enough to travel following the last bout with chemotherapy, when late one night he received a visit from a representative of a very special man, the one his benefactors called The Sheik.

Mujahid knew The Sheik only by reputation as a financier of terrorist groups, including Abu Sayyaf. But recently he'd seemed to be making his move to assume the power vacuum created by the absence of any real leadership from Al Qaeda. The bombing of a secret police barracks in Saudi Arabia and renewed vigor of the insurgency in Iraq were attributed to him, and many were heeding his calls for unity among the world's Islamic militant groups.

When The Sheik's representative appeared at the hospital, he handed Mujahid a letter from his master, as well as one from the old imam from

Medina, who vouched for the messenger. After reading them, Mujahid asked, "What can I do for The Sheik in the time I have left?"

The man explained that The Sheik wanted Mujahid to help him strike a mortal blow to the United States. "It will be more devastating than the World Trade Center attack, which the Enemy of God absorbed as an elephant absorbs an arrow in its side," he said. "Yes, the elephant was hurt, but it became angry and trampled everything in its path. All it ended up accomplishing in the end was giving the Enemy of God an excuse to deomonstrate its military strength in Afghanistan and Iraq while the hoped-for uprising did not come."

Mujahid knew only in general terms what might be accomplished by The Sheik's plan. Even of his own part, he knew very little. He did not know where the attack would take place or who else would be involved. The messenger had told him only that he would need to create a special bomb.

When he had asked for more information, The Sheik's man had refused to answer his questions. "You will learn everything else when you arrive in New York," he had said. "This way, if something goes wrong, Allah forbid, and you are captured, the plan will go on. What you have to know is that together we will not shoot an arrow into the beast, we will cut its hamstrings so that it stumbles and falls, allowing us to finish it off at our leisure, Allah be praised."

Although somewhat annoyed that the younger man would think that he would ever talk if captured—*not even if I was being consumed by the fires of hell*—Mujahid recognized the wisdom of the other man's words. It was enough that if the plan worked, his name would be remembered as one of the great Islamic warriors of modern times.

Over the past few months, maps and blueprints had been delivered to Mujahid with descriptions of the obstacles he would face. He had replied with a list of supplies. He left the selection and training of the jihadis who would accompany him to others. But three of his own men had volunteered to enter the gates of Paradise with him.

Traveling to America tried his patience and offended his sensibilities. The ship was filthy, its crew of Russian sailors a bunch of degenerates, as demonstrated by the so-called guard below who'd abandoned his post to fornicate like a dog in the shadows. He would inform the captain of the transgression before disembarking the ship the next morning.

As the man below lit another cigarette, Mujahid started to turn back to his cabin. Just then, the lights along the dock flickered and went out. Mujahid shouted a warning to his men, who swarmed on deck with assault rifles at the ready. After perhaps thirty seconds, the lights went back on.

Below them, the Russian guard was still at his post, although he now had his gun drawn and was peering up and down the dock while nervously puffing on his cigarette. Someone on one of the decks below yelled a question in Russian, and the guard answered and then holstered his gun.

"Did you see anything before the lights went out?" Mujahid asked his sentry.

"No, Tatay, just the man and the *pokpok*."

"False alarm," Mujahid told the rest of his men. "Apparently, the Americans still haven't figured out electricity." The men laughed and headed back to their bunks.

Mujahid took another deep breath. *Ugh*, he thought as he left the rail for his cabin. *I can't wait to get off this ship in the morning.*

When the cigarette was lit, one of Karchovski's men cut the power, while four others—former elite Russian commandos—sprinted across the dock in padded shoes and up the gangplank to cover the deck, with infrared scopes mounted on their rifles. Following more slowly were Jojola, Tran, Jaxon, and Ivgeny and his men; despite her protests, Lucy had been left behind until the ship could be secured.

Once all the men were aboard and the lights were back on, Jaxon's men headed for the ship's communications center and the crew's quarters. Meanwhile, Karchovski's commandos raced up the ladders to the deck outside the passenger cabins. The first man up shot the surprised guard. The others took up positions to cover the cabin doors.

Jojola, Tran, Jaxon, and Karchovski moved quickly to locate the ship's captain. Startled awake, the captain tried to roll his fat body over to grab a gun that lay on a nightstand next to the bed. He stopped short with Jojola's knife against his throat.

Karchovski snarled something in Russian to the ship's capitan, who turned fearful, glaring with red-rimmed eyes at Jojola. The odor of urine filled the cabin.

Jojola looked at Karchovski. "You just scared the piss out of him. What did you say?"

"I said, 'Do not move, dumb shit,'" Karchovski laughed. "And that the man with the knife is an American Indian, and Indians, as we all know, are savages and expert with sharp blades."

"You've seen too many movies," Tran interjected. "He's lucky if he doesn't cut himself with that knife."

Karchovski addressed the captain, this time in English. "Stand up, asshole. We need your help to capture your passenger, Azahari Mujahid."

"I don't know who you are talking about," the captain said. "We are innocent cargo ship hauling electronic goods from China. Check the manifest."

Karchovski gave Jojola a look. The knife flashed upward followed by the captain looking down at his feet with his mouth open as though he couldn't quite grasp what his left ear was doing lying on the deck. Only then did he feel the pain and clamp his hand over the bleeding hole on the side of his head. He started to scream but stopped when Jojola moved toward him again with the knife.

"I warned you about Indians; they've been known to remove the hair from their still-living victims," Karchovski pointed out. "So far you have only lost one ear. I cannot say what he will do next. Now, I suggest you take me to Mujahid."

"I don't know their names," the captain cried, moving as far back from Jojola as he could get.

"He would be the leader of the pieces of shit you picked up in Manila And in case you plan to betray us, just remember that your life is already forfeit for working for those scumbags the Tazamovs, so consider yourself on parole. If you'd like to extend your days, no tricks, or my friend will make sure that this night is your last."

"But his men are always on guard," the captain complained. "You will never get past them."

"We shall see. Now here is what I want you to do." Karchovski looked at one of his men, a former Red Army medic. "Let's patch his head as best we can. He can listen with his other ear."

A few minutes later, the captain knocked on the door of Azahari Mujahid's cabin, which was opened by one of his men. "What do you want?" the man at the door demanded.

"I need to talk to my passenger," the captain replied. "I need to leave early tomorrow. I want to know what time that will be possible."

"You've been paid," the man in the doorway sneered. "You will leave when we say you can." He stepped a little farther out of the room. "What happened to your head?"

"An accident," the captain replied. "I banged my head on a shelf."

The man turned back to the room. "He is saying his final prayers for the night and cannot be disturbed." He was about to close the door when the captain noticed that a small red dot had appeared on the man's forehead. There was no sound of a gunshot, just a buzzing as the bullet went past, and then the top of the man's head disappeared in a spray of blood and gore.

As the captain backed away, the men in the adjoining rooms rushed out to see what had caused the sudden end to the conversation. They died instantly, slain by Karchovski's men, who had been out of sight around the corners and now tossed a flash-bang grenade into Mujahid's room.

They found Mujahid lying in a fetal position on his prayer rug with small trickles of blood coming out of his ears. The medic rushed to his side.

"Is he hurt bad?" Karchovski asked.

The medic shook his head. "Only stunned. He'll be all right in a minute; maybe a little deaf."

Mujahid was hauled roughly to his feet. He glared at the men around him.

"Azahari Mujahid," Jaxon said, stepping in front of the prisoner.

"I don't know that name. My name is Emil Santos. I am a citizen of the Philippines and . . ."

"Enough," Jaxon replied. "I don't have time to play games." He nodded to Karchovski's men. "Let's take him to meet his jailer."

———————

The assault team reassembled with their prisoner in the warehouse that had been used as a bar. The prostitutes were long gone, though Karchovski's men had hung the bartender up by his heels from a rafter. "As a little warning for the Tazamovs."

Mujahid stood sullenly as Jaxon approached him for a second time. "I want to know why you're here," he asked.

"Ask whatever you want, you will get no answers from me," Mujahid replied.

"I would suggest you answer my questions, or . . ."

Mujahid smirked. "Or what? I will be killed? I welcome martyrdom. Or perhaps you will send me to Guantanamo, where I will be welcomed by my fellow holy warriors."

"No, where you're going would be much worse than Guantanamo," Jaxon replied.

"Worse? The federal penitentiary in Denver? Perhaps you could arrange a room next to Sheik Rahman. I would enjoy spending my remaining days in the company of such a great man."

"Well, no," Jaxon said. "I'm afraid you'll be spending your remaining days, however long they last, in the presence of a truly great man . . . not that ugly piece of crap Rahman." He looked over his shoulder into the shadows of the back part of the warehouse. "David, are you here?"

As Mujahid turned to look, a tall, pale man in a robe stepped into the light. "So this is my executioner?" he asked and laughed.

"No," Grale replied. "Merely your host and inquisitor on behalf of God. But you will beg me to kill you long before death comes in my home beneath the city, away from the light of the sun, where your only roommates will be the rats and those things that crawl in the dark places."

"What nonsense is this?" Mujahid scoffed. "A stupid trick to frighten me as you would a child."

Grale turned to Jaxon. "I will relieve you now of your prisoner. I'm sure that I can learn what you need to know very quickly. Savage Indians . . ." he added with a smile to Jojola and Karchovski, " . . . are not the only experts with a knife."

Jaxon looked at the prisoner. "Last chance, but I really don't think you want to go where Mr. Grale and his friends are going to take you."

When Mujahid looked up and saw Grale's "friends" emerge from the shadows, he quailed. While some of the Mole People looked no worse than the average street person, others had been driven from even that community by their deformities—cancerous growths and skin diseases, missing limbs and eyes and noses. Some seemed half mad.

"*Shayteen,*" Mujahid whispered in spite of himself.

Grale laughed. "Demons? No . . . though perhaps these soldiers of God would appear to be devils to an evil man. A matter of perspective, I suppose. But as they and rats will be your only companions in the long days ahead, I would suggest that you treat them with respect. They tend to hold grudges."

Grale's men stepped forward, bound the terrorist's wrists, and placed a loop over his neck, cinching it tight. "Where are you taking me?" Mujahid cried, now clearly frightened. "I demand a lawyer!"

A dozen men around him laughed as if he'd told a great joke. "A lawyer? You've obviously been watching too many American television shows," Grale said with a smile. "These men believe that you are an incarnation of evil, and you will be afforded the same rights as any demon."

One of the men, who appeared to be missing his nose, held up a bag. "Last chance, asshole," he cackled. "Hope you got a good look up there on the ship because you ain't never going to see the stars again."

It was too much. Mujahid would gladly have died in a shootout with the police, or by blowing himself up with as many infidels as he could kill. But his doctors had told him he could live as long as six months, and he knew he would go insane living as the prisoner of these men. And when his long, painful death came, he would be too far gone into madness to testify that "There is no God but God, and Muhammad is the Messenger of God" and be admitted to Paradise.

"I will want medical attention for my cancer," he demanded. "And incarceration in the federal penitentiary."

"Tell me why you're here," Jaxon repeated.

An hour later, Mujahid finished telling his captors what he knew of The Sheik's plan. It wasn't as much as they'd hoped for.

"Where is the attack taking place?" Jaxon demanded.

"I don't know."

Grale took a step forward.

"I swear it," Mujahid swore. "I was not told on purpose . . . for just this reason."

Jaxon looked long and hard at the terrorist. "I think he's telling the truth," he said. "Makes sense that this Sheik wouldn't divulge the entire plan."

"So what do we know?" Jojola said. "This character's here to make a special bomb, but he won't know what it is until he meets with whoever."

"And this meeting's in," Jaxon looked at his watch, "a little more than twenty-four hours. That leaves us with the question of whether to go forward with our plan."

"I don't like it," Lucy spoke for the first time. "I think it's too dangerous to ask Tran to do this. What if somebody knows Mujahid?"

"From what we know and have been told, it's unlikely," Jojola pointed out.

"I am touched by your concern, child," Tran said. "But we've been over this before. We need to get someone on the inside of the operation. So now we have twenty-four hours for me to brush up on my bomb-making, as well as take a crash course in Islam."

Grale approached Mujahid. "Is there anything you haven't told us?"

"That is all I know."

"There is no password for the people you are expected to meet?"

"Oh, yes, I forgot," Mujahid said. "It is a passage from the Qur'an. The challenge will be, 'In the name of Allah, Most Gracious, Most Merciful.'"

"So the response is: 'Praise be to Allah, the Cherisher and Sustainer of the worlds,'" Lucy replied.

"That is correct," Mujahid said, nodding his head emphatically.

Grale placed his hand under Mujahid's chin and lifted until the man had to look him in the eyes. "I don't believe you," he said. "But just so you know, if you betray my friends, the six months you have left will feel like sixty years."

The mad monk nodded to his men, who began to drag Mujahid back to the shadows. "Wait!" Mujahid screamed to Jaxon. "You agreed to give me medical treatment and the federal penitentiary."

"You demanded, but I agreed to nothing," Jaxon replied. "If you are telling the truth, and we are able to stop this plan, then I will ask my friend Mr. Grale and his comrades to release you to the care of the United States government. Until then, I hope you enjoy the dark."

Mujahid's eyes grew wide. He grabbed Jaxon's arm. "It just comes to me that what I told you is not the correct password," he said. "In fact, it is what I would use to warn the others that something is not right."

One of the Mole People raised a curved linoleum knife to Mujahid's neck. "Stop!" Grale shouted. "A quick death is what he seeks. We'll take him below and see what else he has lied about."

Panicked, Mujahid turned to Lucy. "The correct passage comes from the Qur'an, Surah 9:29. 'Fight against such of those who have been given the Scripture as believe not in Allah nor the Last Day, and forbid not that which Allah hath forbidden by His messenger, and follow not the Religion of Truth . . .'" He stopped.

Lucy finished the passage, "'. . . until they pay the tribute readily, being brought low.'" She looked at her companions. "It's a popular passage for Muslims who believe that Islam should reign supreme. Essentially, in their world, we will all have to convert to Islam or pay a tax to stay alive."

"Is that the correct passage?" Grale demanded.

Mujahid quivered. "That is the truth."

Again, at Grale's signal, one of the Mole People slipped a bag over Mujahid's head and the others began to drag the terrorist away. He pleaded through the cloth. "Take me to jail. In Allah's name be merciful."

Grale held up his hand and his men stopped. "Don't use God's name in front of me again. You are a murderer and a demon in a man's body. There is nothing in the Qur'an that excuses the taking of innocent lives. You are apostate and doomed to hell. All you can hope is that my friends survive the next few days, or your hell will begin while you are still alive."

With Mujahid's muffled pleas receding, Jaxon turned to Tran. "We better get back on board the ship and start teaching you to be a Filipino terrorist."

"You sure you want to go through with this?" Lucy asked. "There has to be another way."

"If you can think of it in the next twenty-four hours, I'm all ears, which is more than you can say for the captain of the *Star of Vladivostock*."

"Don't worry," Jojola added. "He's not going alone. Tonto needs to make sure the Lone VC Ranger doesn't fuck this up. I'm going, too."

"Like hell you are," Tran shot back. "That's not part of the plan."

"It is now," Jojola replied. "The real Mujahid had bodyguards. I think it would look funny if the fake Tatay didn't have even one."

28

Under the headline "Crazed Cabbie Nearly Kills Woman at Campbell Trial!" the *London World Herald's* New York correspondent, J. Luffington Nottingham-Tinsdale IV, scooped the rest of the media by getting an exclusive interview with the woman who'd been struck the day before as she ran across Centre Street after buying a paper from Dirty Warren.

"On the way back to her family, Deb Hurley, of 15239 Evergreen St., Milwaukee, thought (correctly) that the cab driver (a refugee from Kosovo named Annan) saw her (affirmative), had plenty of time to stop (easily) and would therefore hit the brakes to avoid hitting her (not a chance in the world)," Nottingham-Tinsdale IV wrote.

"The unfortunate woman was taken to Bellevue Hospital with two broken legs and a healthier understanding of the ruthless nature it takes to pilot a Yellow Cab in big, bad Gotham City."

Nottingham-Tinsdale IV's article concluded by quoting Hurley and her new attorney as "exploring the possibility" of suing New York City, the Taxi and Limousine Commission, and the driver, as well as Dirty Warren and his newsstand, which, ironically, the lawyer called an "attractive nuisance, having lured Mrs. Hurley across a dangerous street."

"Crazed Cabbie!" was a big seller for Dirty Warren, who was enjoying his little piece of public notoriety. "Read all about it. . . . I'm a . . . piss off motherfuckers . . . attractive nuisance," the little man shouted above the roar of his friend Treacher, who was making a little extra money by wearing a sandwich board for "Rico's Bail Bonds Service, Inc."

The news vendor and Treacher had been arguing all morning over who had a bigger coup as a media celebrity: Warren because of the threatened lawsuit, or Treacher, who had been quoted in the *Times* as saying that Jessica Campbell "gives crazy people a bad name."

An editorial in the same edition of the *Times* noted that so far the prosecution case lacked "much pop . . . or for that matter, anything that would lead us to conclude that Jessica Campbell belongs someplace other than a psychiatric ward." The editor concluded, "Perhaps District Attorney Roger Karp's budget has grown so large he feels that he can waste taxpayer money on a case such as this, which to us smacks more of a political maneuver, to be seen as the DAO being willing to prosecute an educated, white woman, than a legitimate pursuit of justice."

Karp was made aware of the editorial that morning before court when Murrow marched into his office and slammed a copy on his desk. "The rat bastards have really crossed the line this time!"

"Rat bastards? Have you been watching *The Sopranos* again?" Karp asked mildly.

"Every episode. But it's true, they really are rat bastards."

Karp read the editorial aloud to Guma, who'd walked in just in time for Murrow's "rat bastards" comment. "Catering to minorities again, eh?" Guma chuckled.

"It's not funny," Murrow sulked. "One unfair portrayal in the minds of the voters can haunt you politically for the rest of your career. Look what happened to McGovern. The man was a war hero for chrissake! But a couple of tears over Vietnam and he never shook the 'pansy' image."

"I don't think we have to worry about that right now," Karp said. "And I do believe it's time to head to the courtroom."

"I'll go run interference," Murrow said glumly. "Maybe I'll see somebody with the *Times* and shove him down the elevator shaft."

Before bringing in the jury, Dermondy announced that he'd ruled on Lewis's motion to exclude the Baker Street Irregulars from testifying. "I've looked at the resumes, as well as read the impressive and impassioned accolades given by law-enforcement officials, and find that the witnesses are more than qualified to speak to this court," he stated. "Therefore, defense counsel's objection is overruled. Mr. Farley, please bring in the jury."

As the jury took their seats, Karp did his usual quick scan of the courtroom. Jessica Campbell continued to work on her drawing while Lewis sat next to her staring straight ahead. Benjamin Gupperstein sat in the first row behind the defense table but without his wife. Karp had asked Detective Cobing to warn Jessica's parents that today's testimony was going to be graphic, and they might want to skip it. Apparently, Liza Gupperstein had decided to do that.

Geologist James Reedy was the first up. He explained how with the help of the DA's office and the NYPD, the Baker Street grave-hunters had gone about determining where to look for the Campbell's station wagon, and then he described the technology he'd used to locate it. "But really, the credit goes to those NYPD divers," he said. "That took real guts. . . . And when I saw that hand come up out of the water with that license plate, it sent a chill up my spine. It was like the King Arthur story where the Lady of the Lake holds up . . ."

"Objection," Lewis said. "What's with the fairy-tale imagery and the apparent 'characterization virus' running amok among the prosecution witnesses?"

Dermondy held up a hand. "Just a moment, Miss Lewis. Mr. Reedy, please finish your analogy."

"Well, Your Honor, it reminded me of the King Arthur tale where the Lady of the Lake raises up Excalibur. All you see is her arm rising out of the water, holding up the sword."

"Thank you, Mr. Reedy," Dermondy said. "Miss Lewis, your objection is overruled." He turned to the jurors. "Ladies and gentlemen, I find the imagery enlightening, but you, of course, will base your findings solely on the evidence. Let's proceed."

Charlotte Gates was next. Of the three, she had the most experience on the witness stand, having testified in dozens of murder cases where the identity of the victims was a potential obstacle for the prosecution.

She began by describing how the dive team secured the car before it was pulled from the bottom of the river "so that no evidence would be lost." Then she described the initial phase of her excavation of the car, beginning with the front seating area.

"Would you please describe the items found in the glovebox?" Karp asked.

"In addition to common items such as the car registration and proof of insurance, I found a plastic bag marked 'O'Hara's Hardware' on the outside and containing a receipt from that store for a footlocker and a padlock, as well as the packaging and combination tag for that padlock."

"Miss Gates, in your examination of the vehicle, did you note the position of the door windows?"

"Yes, they were all rolled down approximately three inches."

Karp's questions shifted to the stick found holding the accelerator down. "Was this something that could have happened by accident? For instance, could the stick have floated into the car through one of the three-inch gaps in a window and become lodged there?"

Gates thought about the question for a moment. "I suppose anything is possible. But this stick had been broken off on one end and was exactly the right size to be jammed into position so that it held the accelerator pedal all the way to the floorboard. It would have taken pretty good force to mash it in there; it certainly took pretty good force to dislodge it."

"With respect to the car's transmission, please tell us what position you observed it to be in," Karp asked.

"It was in the 'Drive' position," Gates answered. "And the key switched to the 'On' position."

"Thank you. The key is in the 'On' position, the accelerator to the floor. So that engine was probably pretty revved up when she leaned in and pulled the transmission shifter into 'Drive.'" As he spoke, he acted out the steps.

"Yes."

"That car must have taken off fairly quickly?"

"Yes, with the accelerator down and the key switched to 'On,' it would have moved quite swiftly."

"Fast enough to bruise Jessica Campbell's back and knock her to the ground?"

Lewis was on her feet. "Objection, Your Honor! Calls for speculation."

"Sustained. You know better, Mr. Karp."

Gates testified that the combination found on the card in the glovebox opened the padlock that held the footlocker's clasp shut.

"What did you find in the footlocker, Miss Gates?" Those in the courtroom held their breath for the expected answer.

"Inside the footlocker were . . . were the remains of three young children."

Karp caught the hitch in her voice and poured her a glass of water. For all of her supposed scientific detachment, he remembered the account of how, after she'd finished exhuming the bodies that night, she'd gone to the river with Marlene, where the two women stood with their arms around each other's shoulders and cried.

When Gates appeared ready to go on, Karp continued. "Miss Gates, was there something unusual about the condition of these remains?"

"Yes, or at least unexpected." She turned to the jury and spoke directly to them. "The children had been dead since March. This was July, so they had been in the footlocker for four months. I would have expected that bodies that had been submerged in water and subject to microorganisms in that water for that long would have been severely decomposed. However, this was a nearly watertight footlocker with rubber seals around the edges. Also, the car was found at a depth of about twenty-five feet in relatively cold water. So the bodies were very well preserved, considering."

Karp walked over to the prosecution table where he searched among several photographs and selected one which he asked be marked for identification, and with the court's permission he handed it to the anthropologist. "Does this photograph fairly and accurately depict what you observed when you opened the footlocker?"

Gates glanced at it. "Yes, that was taken within a minute of my opening the footlocker."

"Tell us what you observed."

"The bodies of the three Campbell children—Hillary, Chelsea, and Benjamin."

Karp held up the photograph for the defense to see. "The People ask that this photograph be received in evidence, Your Honor."

Jessica Campbell had immediately looked away, but Lewis studied the photograph carefully as though expecting some sort of trick. She made a notation on a legal pad. "My previous objection," she said. At a pre-trial hearing she had tried to prevent the prosecution from using photographs of the bodies as "unnecessarily gruesome and likely to unfairly sway the jury against my client," but the judge had overruled her then and did so again now.

"Miss Gates, were you able to identify the remains of the three children found in the footlocker through some scientific means?" Karp asked.

"Yes. We were able to identify the children through DNA testing that matched to a high degree of scientific certainty to their parents, as well as dental records for the two girls. The development of the skeletal remains also matched the known ages of the children."

"Now, Miss Gates, if I understand correctly, you don't deal with the so-called 'soft-tissue' remains."

"That's correct. I mostly work with hard structures—bones and teeth. Mr. Swanburg is a pathologist, which is a field that deals with the soft-tissue remains."

"So your examination followed Mr. Swanburg's examination of the soft-tissue remains," Karp said, "and after those remains were completely removed from the bones?"

"Yes. The skeletal remains were cleaned of any soft tissues."

"Why did you do that?"

"To determine if any wounds would be evident on the bones," Gates replied. "Mr. Swanburg had noted what appeared to be several incisions, or lacerations, on the body of the eldest child, Hillary."

"And could you verify that by looking at the skeleton?"

"Yes, there were marks on the bones from at least a half-dozen blows to her chest caused by a sharp instrument."

"Any idea what sort of sharp instrument that would have been?"

"Something with a sharp point, a very sharp blade, but a wider back, likely a large knife."

Karp walked over to the prosecution table, picked up a plastic evidence bag containing a hunting knife, removed it, and brought it to the witness stand. "I believe you've had the opportunity to examine this knife. Do you recognize it?"

"Yes, it was found in the footlocker."

"Your Honor, the People ask that this knife, previously marked People's Exhibit 19 for identification, be received in evidence," Karp said, holding up the knife so that everyone in the courtroom could see it.

Lewis didn't even look up from her notepad. "No objection."

Karp placed the knife on the evidence table. "Miss Gates," he continued, "as you just testified, you've had a chance to examine the knife. Is
there some conclusion you've been able to draw from that?"

"Yes, it's likely to a reasonable degree of scientific certainty to be the
weapon that caused the wounds on Hillary's chest."

"How do you know that?"

"Well, to start, it fits the marks, both in the soft tissue examined by
Mr. Swanburg and on the skeletal remains. Several of the blows pierced all
the way through the child's rib cage, leaving a perfectly delineated entry
wound into which this knife fit exactly."

"And?"

"Although it had been wiped clean of most of the blood, there were still
small particles imbedded where the blade fit into the hilt. It was Hillary's
blood."

"Was there anything else you learned by examining the bones?"

Gates nodded, but as she started to speak, her voice cracked and she had
to take a moment to pull herself together. "Yes, when I examined the hands
of the middle child, Chelsea, I noted that several of her fingers were broken."

"Could you tell how that happened?"

"It's the sort of injury we see when someone is gripping something very
hard, so hard that the bones break before the grip can be loosened."

The already still courtroom grew quieter. Campbell stopped drawing, her
pencil hovering above the pad; but she did not raise her head and after a
moment started to draw again. Across the room on the witness stand, Gates
closed her eyes, but a tear still managed to slip out.

"Thank you, Miss Gates," Karp said softly. "No more questions."

When Jack Swanburg took the witness stand after the mid-morning
break, he seemed reluctant to be there. He'd seen his share of violent
death, too, but as he'd told Karp that morning, there was always something
different about the murder of a child.

"Especially when the killer is someone they know and trust. I just keep
thinking that the last thing those children saw was the face of their mother.

That's tough to deal with, really tough. Connie and I were never able to have kids, and . . . well, this was a tough one."

Now he sighed heavily as he sat down with his head resting on his chest, thumbs hooked into his trademark suspenders—a tired old man, tired of death and violence. Yet when he began his testimony he was the picture of scientific objectivity, carefully explaining how DNA testing worked, his role as a pathologist, and finally, his examination of the children's bodies.

"Mr. Swanburg, how did the Campbell children die?"

"The two youngest were drowned."

"How did you determine the cause of death?"

"Well, the bodies were remarkably well preserved," Swanburg said. "There was some decomposition, but I was able to remove the internal organs and compare them to what we should see if the deaths were from natural causes. The organs of the Campbell children were what we call waterlogged."

"Waterlogged? How so?"

"When a person is forcibly drowned, they often struggle violently for a long time, which actually forces fluid into their internal organs, especially the brain; the scientific term for this excess fluid is 'edema.' In particular, the brains of the Campbell children were significantly heavy due to edema; in fact, they were nearly the size and weight of adult brains."

"And what does that indicate to you?"

"That they fought under water for several minutes. It was a slow, agonizing death."

"Objection," Lewis said. "Relevance."

"Relevance, Miss Lewis?" Dermondy asked.

"Yes, relevance. What does it matter if the deaths were slow or fast, agonizing or painless? The point of this trial is only whether Jessica Campbell knew what she was doing and if she knew that it was wrong."

Karp glared at his counterpart. "Your Honor, the witness's testimony unequivocally makes it crystal clear beyond any and all doubt that each of these precious, defenseless children underwent a vicious, merciless execution and that the defendant knew exactly what she was doing."

"MISTRIAL!" Lewis shouted.

Dermondy raised his hand to silence her. "Miss Lewis, your initial comment about relevance was ill-advised. If the witness Swanburg's testimony was not relevant I would have so ruled *sua sponte*. Moreover, you must have known that your outburst was going to illicit a response from the highly experienced district attorney, whose rhetorical flourish clearly explained the People's position. But . . ." he raised his voice and looked at Karp, " . . . it should have been saved for final summation. So, let's get back to our trial. Your objection regarding relevance, Miss Lewis, is duly noted and overruled."

"Mr. Swanburg, you stated that the cause of death for the two younger children was drowning," Karp said. "Can you tell us what caused the death of the eldest child, Hillary?"

Swanburg held up a hand, which he waggled to indicate uncertainty. "That's a little dicier. But it was one of three things. She was either drowned, or she bled to death from the stab wounds, or it was a combination of the two—in other words, it's possible that she was being held under water as she was being stabbed."

One of the women jurors failed to stifle a tiny cry of horror by covering her mouth.

"Are you all right?" Dermondy asked her. She nodded but pulled a tissue from a box provided by the court clerk and dabbed at her eyes. The outburst seemed to set off a chorus of other small cries and sniffles in the courtroom, including from Ben Gupperstein, who sat weeping with his head bowed.

Dermondy noted the wet eyes and faces drained of color. He looked at the clock and said, "I think we can all use a break about now, if that's all right, Mr. Karp?"

"That would be fine, Your Honor."

"Thank you," the judge said and then addressed the jury. "We'll take our noon break. I'd urge you to get yourselves something to eat and drink. These trials can be physically as well as emotionally draining. I do understand the enormous strain this places on you, and you are to be commended for doing your duty as citizens. But I know saying that doesn't make this easier. We'll reconvene in a half hour; please refrain from talking about this amongst yourselves and certainly not with anyone else."

When the jurors left the room, the judge looked at Karp. "I'm not trying to rush you, but how much more will there be along these lines?"

Karp considered his notes. "I'd say about a half hour."

The judge bit his lip. "Okay, you do what you feel you need to do. But remember, this can be pretty hard on civilians."

———

A half hour later, the jurors returned to the courtroom and Swanburg was called back to the stand.

"When court recessed, we were talking about the stab wounds to Hillary Campbell," Karp said. "These stab wounds were to her chest, correct?"

"Yes, to the chest area, mostly centered in the middle."

"Would these be the sort of wounds that someone would inflict to cause death?"

"If you mean that the wounds were not haphazard, as though made without reason—for instance, slashing wounds to the arms or legs—but instead directed at an area of the body that would be expected to have serious consequences," Swanburg replied, "then yes. Four wounds in particular would have been fatal without immediate medical attention. One sliced through the left ventricle of her heart. Two punctured her lungs. And one severed the aorta leading to the heart."

"But you testified that Hillary also had edema consistent with being forcibly drowned. Could you tell which occurred first, the drowning or the wounds from the knife?"

"Because the wounds to the heart and aorta would have caused her to 'bleed out' and lose consciousness in a short amount of time, and because the severity of the edema indicated that she struggled under water for several minutes, my best guess is that the defendant was forcibly drowning her and then stabbed her repeatedly at some point after that process began."

Karp let the last image hang in the air. When he again addressed the witness, it was to change to another topic. "Mr. Swanburg, yesterday, crime-scene investigator Bob Watts testified that during his investigation, no evidence of blood was found in the Campbell home, and particularly none in a bathroom that he described as having been wiped clean. Is that consistent with your own examination of the home and bathroom?"

"No. But that's not a reflection on Mr. Watts or the NYPD crime-scene folks; they're as good as it gets. When they first arrived at what I believe proves to be the actual murder scene at the Campbell residence, they didn't know what they were looking for; they had some missing kids and that was about it. They had no clues about the manner of death. For that matter, they couldn't be sure that a murder had taken place. The kids could have been abducted or visiting a relative for all they knew, because other than comments, such as that she had sent them to God, the defendant wasn't saying much, nor were . . ."

Swanburg stopped talking and glanced over at Lewis, who was beginning to rise from her seat. One of the earlier pre-trial motions she had won was that prosecution witnesses would not be allowed to testify that Jessica Campbell had "lawyered up" and had not been allowed to speak to police. Jurors sometimes looked at the right to remain silent as an admission of guilt, Lewis had argued, "and in this case, they might not understand that my client was not in a position mentally to be talking to the police."

Swanburg had almost stepped across that line, but caught himself. " . . . nor were there any indications in the house about what might have happened. . . . Mr. Watts and his team were suspicious about the lack of fingerprints in the bathroom . . ."

"I object, the witness is now testifying about what other people were thinking," said Lewis, who'd remained standing.

"The witness has reviewed the police reports and crime-scene notes," Karp replied, "which is very much in line with his long experience as a pathologist. Pathologists rely on such documentation to determine such issues as time, manner, and cause of death."

"Overruled, you may sit Miss Lewis," the judge said.

"Anyway, in his report," Swanburg continued, "Mr. Watts noted that the main floor bathroom was devoid of fingerprints and that he found this to be, and I quote, 'highly unlikely,' end of quote. There were no positive results for blood. Now remember, that was back in March. When we found the bodies in July we were able to ascertain that Hillary had been stabbed repeatedly in the chest, which would have resulted in a lot of blood. However, if the crime had occurred in the house—as we believed—the blood had somehow been contained. Just like it was unusual not to find fingerprints, it's nearly impossible to stab someone in the manner that this little girl was stabbed and not leave some blood evidence, even if it is minuscule."

Swanburg adjusted his suspenders and clasped his hands on his round belly. "We've all had our blood pressure tested, right?" He waited for the jurors to nod. "So we know that blood in the body is under pressure. When someone is shot or stabbed, blood sprays or gushes or splatters—sometimes quite a distance from the victim. Tiny droplets will fall from the blade of a knife or be released in a fine mist, with some ending up on a wall or a piece of furniture. We can find even the tiniest amounts using a substance called Luminol, which reacts with iron in the blood and will glow under a black light. But what if we know there was a stabbing but there's no blood?"

Swanburg looked from juror to juror as if expecting one of them to raise a hand to answer like children in a classroom. "The blood must have been contained somehow."

Guy's frickin' brilliant, Karp thought.

"And we have the bodies of three children who were violently drowned, which is no easy task even for an adult, so better to do it away from prying eyes," Swanburg said. "That's when we put two and two and two together— the evidence of drownings, the ultra-clean bathroom, and the lack of blood—and came up with the bathtub."

The NYPD investigators had already tested the bathtub with Luminol, Swanburg noted. "They tried the drain and around the edges. But they did miss one thing. Remember that old television commercial? 'Ring around the bathtub'? Well, that's what they missed. As any homemaker can tell you, one of the most difficult cleaning jobs is trying to get rid of that ring, a residue of soap, hard minerals, and biological material such as dead skin cells and body oils. The stuff is miserable to get out, right? Anyway, we tested the ring with Luminol, and that's where we discovered a ring of blood around the tub, indistinguishable from the rest of the residue except that it glowed in a black light."

"Was it a lot of blood?" Karp asked. "Perhaps one of the children had a cut or a bloody nose in the past."

"The amount was pretty consistent through the ring," Swanburg said, "instead of being stronger at one place and more diluted at another, which in my opinion meant there was quite a bit of blood that had diffused throughout the water in the tub."

"Were you able to tell whose blood it was?"

"Unfortunately, it was so mixed in with the rest of the residue that we couldn't get a clean enough sample to test for DNA."

Swanburg testified that he had called in a plumber, who knocked out a wall and took apart the drain apparatus beneath the tub. "Again, as any of us home plumbers know, particularly one living in a house with women, a lot of hair and junk gets stuck in there, and more junk settles into the bottom of the drain pipe. That's where we also found a significant amount of blood caught up in this gooey mess of hair and whatever, enough that we were able to test it."

"And what was the result?"

"The blood was that of Hillary Campbell."

"And your conclusion as to how it got there?"

"I believe she was stabbed in the bathtub, which also made it the likely site of the drownings."

Karp glanced at the jurors, who were beginning to look worried that they were going to be dragged back into the horror. It was one thing to listen to kindly old Jack Swanburg lecture about forensic technique, quite another when the testimony turned to the details involved in the brutal murder of three young children.

"Mr. Swanburg, you've already testified that in your opinion, based upon the evidence, the Campbell children fought to stay alive. Is there anything else that you learned during your investigation that supports that conclusion?"

"Yes. During the autopsy, I examined the hands of the three children, looking for defensive wounds. I saw nothing of note with Benjamin. However, with the two older children, Hillary and Chelsea, many of their fingernails were missing. Now some of that was due to decomposition. But under a magnifying lens, several of their nailbeds showed evidence of their fingernails having been torn out. Also, from beneath two of Hillary's nails that were still in place, and three of Chelsea's, I was able to extract a small amount of skin tissue."

"Were you able to ascertain where the tissue came from?"

"I was able to compare it to skin samples taken by court order from Jessica Campbell. They were a match for the skin tissue beneath the fingernails of the two girls."

Karp leafed through the photographs and selected a half-dozen of them, which he walked over to the witness. "Your Honor, with the court's permission,

I would like the witness to review these six photographs, previously marked for identification People's Exhibits 21–26."

Dermondy nodded, so Karp continued. "Have you seen these photographs before?"

"Yes. These were taken by a New York police photographer the night the defendant was taken to Bellevue; they are of the defendant's arms, legs, and one of her back."

"Mr. Swanburg, first, do these photographs fairly and accurately depict the wounds on the arms of the defendant?"

"Yes, the long red marks."

"Do you have an opinion on what caused them?"

"Yes, given the skin residue beneath the fingernails of Hillary and Chelsea, the wounds are consistent with the children having scratched at their assailant."

"Are there any other wounds or marks depicted by the photographs?" Karp asked as he crossed over to the jury box.

"Yes, there are scrapes and bruises on the defendant's elbows and knees, as well as a large bruise on her back," Swanburg replied.

"And again, do you have an opinion as to what caused these wounds?"

"Not specifically as to the exact cause. But the scrapes and bruises on her arms and legs are consistent with a fall. The bruise on her back is consistent with having been struck by a hard object that caused bruising over a fairly wide area on her ribs."

"And Mr. Swanburg, is there one more wound on one of the defendant's arms that we haven't discussed yet?" Karp picked up one more photograph from the prosecution table, which he kept hidden from view.

"Yes, there was a bite mark on her arm," Swanburg said.

"Were you able to determine who bit her?"

"Yes, Hillary was missing her two front incisors. Pretty common for someone her age."

"Does one of these photographs demonstrate what you are talking about?" Karp asked.

"Yes. A purple bite mark is clearly evident—except there was a space in the front where Hillary's two front teeth would have been.

Karp now held up his last photograph, taken of Hillary that year for her class photograph. The little girl smiled out at the jurors, completely oblivious to the missing teeth. Several of the jurors shook their heads sadly and then looked over at Jessica, who just kept drawing.

Time to finish, Karp told himself. He'd gone over this moment a dozen times in his head getting ready for the trial. *Allow enough time to let the photograph sink in with the jury,* he'd told himself. He looked down at his legal pad and made notations with his pen, checking off his questions. Only then did he lift his head and look at Swanburg.

"I won't keep you much longer," Karp said and thought he heard, or felt, a sigh of relief from the jurors. "I'd just like to sum this up so that I have it all straight. So far you've testified that all three Campbell children were forcibly drowned—causing death in two of them, and possibly the third, though it's possible that she might have died from wounds caused by a hunting knife."

"That's correct."

"And you further testified that they fought so violently that their internal organs swelled with fluid, that two of them managed to scratch their attacker, and that each murder took several minutes . . ."

"At least . . ."

" . . . thank you, several minutes at least. And that theirs was a slow death."

"Yes. A slow, agonizing death."

Karp nodded as he walked slowly over to stand near the jury box. "If I asked your opinion on whether the defendant intended to cause the death of her children and knew what she was doing . . ."

"Objection! Calls for giving a psychological opinion that the witness is not qualified to render."

"Mr. Karp?" asked the judge.

"Once again, Your Honor, as a pathologist, Mr. Swanburg is asked not only to render opinions on the medical cause of death, but also whether that death was accidental, the result of a reckless but unintended act, or a homicide—in all of its various shades from manslaughter to deliberate, premeditated murder."

The judge thought about it, then nodded. "I believe the witness is qualified to answer the question. Overruled."

"You can answer the question, Mr. Swanburg," Karp said.

Swanburg let out a sigh; he'd never quite developed skin thick enough to pretend that it was all just about science. "I know, just give me a moment to collect my thoughts," he said, looking at the jurors, taking in each face, some of them in tears, others set grimly, all of them just wishing it could be over.

"Yes," he answered at last. "The person who did these things to these children intended to kill them. And despite how hard they fought to stay alive, this person held them under water or stabbed them until they were dead. The person who did this knew what she was doing."

29

Since parking on the street across from the docks before dawn Saturday morning, Suleiman Abdalla had kept his eye on the *Star of Vladivostok* as instructed. He was to report anything that seemed amiss, but other than the guard smoking and pacing beneath the weak yellow light at the bottom of the gangplank, there'd hardly been any activity at all.

To keep himself from dozing, he listened to a taped English-language version of Sayyid Qutb's book *Social Justice in Islam*. And when that threatened to put him to sleep, he turned on a flashlight to read a newspaper that he'd found lying on a bus-stop bench. The newspaper had a story about a "crazed cabbie" who had run over a woman outside of the building where Jessica Campbell was on trial.

Small world, he thought. He'd met Campbell years ago as a student at NYCU before getting kicked out for bad grades. Now there she was on trial for murder, claiming that God had told her to kill her children. Ironically, he, too, would soon kill for God.

In a few days, the world would forget all about Jessica Campbell and instead be talking about Suleiman Abdalla and the other members of the Al-Aqsa Brigade. Instead of a courtroom artist's watercolor depiction of his former professor sitting at the defense table drawing on a sketch pad, he himself would be immortalized on the front pages. His photograph would appear for years to come in newspapers and magazines, and used in the background for television specials about terrorism in the United States. There'd be hundreds, maybe thousands, of stories written about the "Ramadan Martyrs," he liked to fantasize; and every year on the anniversary of their deaths, the stories would be regurgitated, along with pious commentary about what had been learned . . . or not.

Family members and friends, not that he'd had many, would talk about him—how he'd been a "normal kid" and an "excellent student" and how none of them had "seen this coming." They'd blame "his affliction" for his actions.

They don't understand what it means to give yourself up to the will of Allah . . . to hear His voice and understand His plans for you, Abdalla thought as he turned the pages to follow the story of the woman struck by the taxi, who, according to the story, was going to sue even the newsstand vendor because she had been stupid enough to run out into the street.

"This country deserves whatever Allah, to whom all thanks are due, and The Sheik have in mind," he muttered. "Americans are the ones with the affliction."

———————

Suleiman Abdalla was a short, wiry, twenty-five-year-old African American with *vitiligo.* As a doctor had explained to his horrified parents when he was a kid, vitiligo is a skin disorder in which the body attacks its own melanocytes, the skin cells that produce melanin, the substance that determines the amount of pigmentation in the skin.

Christened as Justin Rhodes Jr. at Cathedral Church of St. John the Divine on Columbus Avenue, he'd grown up with all the advantages. His father, Justin Rhodes Sr., was an internationally known oncologist at Memorial Sloan-Kettering Cancer Center, and his mother, the former Beatrice Little, had once been Miss Black New York City. With those kinds of genes and financing, he should have had it made.

Early life meant English nannies, piano lessons from a semi-famous Russian composer, a French tutor for French lessons, and a Japanese monk for Buddhism and karate instruction. There'd been summer camp in the Poconos and, beginning in third grade, attendance at a small private school in

New Jersey. Most weekends he had come home to his parents' four-bedroom suite in the Helmsley Carlton House on Madison to be spoiled rotten, and at the end of every visit he was shipped back across the Hudson with the admonition to "study hard so that you can be a doctor like daddy."

In the sixth grade, while showering after gym class, one of his older classmates saw the patch of white skin that had started to spread across his genitals. "What'd you do, rub it off?" the boy had shouted, pointing with derision.

Having recently discovered masturbation, and concerned that there might be some truth to his tormentor's comment, Justin was reluctant to tell any adult. He avoided the shower for the rest of the semester—until, during one visit home, his mother took note of the white spaces on his hands and a spot on his nose. He'd been taken to see the best skin specialists in New York. But there was nothing they could do except inform the Rhodes family that the condition was not dangerous. Their boy would simply lose the pigmentation in his skin until it either stopped on its own accord or he was as white as Casper the Ghost.

During the summers, he would return to Manhattan to live with his parents, though within two weeks he always sensed that he was overstaying his welcome. So to get out of the apartment during the summer between his junior and senior years, he'd responded to an ad in the newspaper for a part-time "baker's apprentice."

When he arrived at the Il Buon Pane bakery on Third Avenue, he hesitated, afraid that the owner would look at his skin and be repulsed. But the little old man who owned the place saw him looking in the window and waved him in.

"Hello, my friend," Moishe Sobelman had greeted him, as he would every weekday morning until Justin had to go back to school. The baker had made him sit down and try his cherry cheese coffee-cake, "the best in the world," and only then had they talked about the job.

The job requirements were to show up for work on time, do what he was asked, and treat the customers like they were his friends. "Can you do that, Mr. Rhodes?"

"Yes, Mr. Sobelman, but aren't you worried that your customers won't like how I look?"

The old Jew sat there for a moment and then rolled up the sleeve of his shirt, exposing a faded purple number. "You see this," he said. "A long time ago, evil men put this here; I did not let it dictate the type of person I would become. God made you as you are, which means you were made perfect; do not let what others think or do dictate the type of person you will become."

Justin smiled. "When can I start?"

It was the best summer of his life. He worked hard and learned how to be a baker from Mr. Sobelman, as well as how to treat other people. The old man's wife, Goldie, had always greeted him with a hug, and several times on Friday afternoons he'd stayed for a dinner of boiled chicken after the shop shut down for Shabbat. Then he could hardly wait for it to open again on Monday, often showing up before Mr. Sobelman had even come downstairs.

Then summer ended and it was time to go back to school. "I don't want to go," he told the old man on his last day of work. "I want to stay and work for you. I want to be a baker."

The old man patted him on the back but shook his head. "School is important," he said. "You need to finish so that you keep your options open. There will always be a place for you here if you decide that working for an old baker is what you want to do with your life. Perhaps we'll see you next summer, eh?"

Justin never went back. During his senior year, the vitiligo spread quickly across his face until he looked like a mime. Except for a few faint freckles on his cheeks and nose, his soft brown eyes, and his dark hair, he had no color left. Nor did he have friends. The few blacks at the school shunned him, as if he might be contagious, and the whites avoided him as "a freak." Even weekends at home were uncomfortable; it was obvious that his parents were embarrassed by his appearance and happy when he returned to school.

Trying to regain some measure of blackness, Justin started "slumming" after school and on weekends, riding the bus to Harlem where he hung out on the streets. He had a lot of spending cash, so after shaking him down the first couple of times, a local gang decided it was more lucrative to let him buy his way into their company. But no matter how much he paid or complained, he was the brunt of their jokes and given derogatory nicknames such as "Whitey" and "Snowball."

After high school, he left the gang and walked into the neighborhood office of the Nation of Islam, located at the corner of 112th and St. Nicholas Avenue on the north end of Central Park. The man sitting at the reception desk with his feet propped up was watching a video of Nation of Islam leader Louis Farrakhan railing about the Jews. The man handed him some literature and said he was welcome to stay and watch. "This goes back a few years when Minister Farrakhan was speaking at the Maryam Mosque in Chicago," the man explained.

More out of politeness than because he wanted to watch some guy in a bow tie yelling into a microphone, Justin sat down.

"German Jews financed Hitler right here in America," shouted Farrakhan. "International bankers financed Hitler, and poor Jews died while big Jews were at the root of what you call the Holocaust. Little Jews died while big Jews made money. Little Jews were being turned into soap while big Jews washed themselves with it. Jews were playing violin, Jews were playing music, while other Jews were marching into the gas chambers."

"That's Allah's truth right there," the man told Justin, who nodded but wasn't sure what to make of it.

He thought about Moishe Sobelman, obviously a little Jew who'd blamed the Nazis for the Holocaust. *Perhaps he didn't realize that it was the big Jews who were responsible for Sobibor.*

Justin joined the Nation of Islam. If his welcome wasn't warm and he occasionally had to field the question "what the hell happened to your skin, brother?" at least no one called him names. He learned a lot from the local leaders, a whole different truth from what he'd been taught in schools.

Late at night in his bedroom at his parent's apartment, he'd devoured the *Autobiography of Malcolm X* and various tracts written by Farrakhan, from which he learned to hate Jews, Israel, homosexuals, and all white people. Even outwardly nice Jews, like the Sobelmans, were only disguising their true natures and using him to further their own financial gains. Nor were whites to be looked up to; they were, Farrakhan pointed out, only "potential human beings . . . who have not evolved yet." And, of course, Christianity was the religion of his oppressors; Islam was the true religion for the African man.

The more he learned, the more he argued with his parents about what he was learning from the Nation of Islam. When he came home for the weekends, they seemed to spend a lot of the time elsewhere; if they hosted a

dinner party, he was welcome only "so long as you leave that Nation of Islam crap at the door." The fall after he graduated, his parents were only too
happy to rent a small apartment for him in the East Village so that he could
attend New York City University. He became a sociology major in the
African American Studies program.

One of his professors was Jessica Campbell, who wasn't all bad for a
white bitch. She was the one who'd told him and the other blacks in the
auditorium attending a round-table discussion of her essay "A Feminist
View of the Criminality of White Males in American Politics" to "rise up
against the man." But when he learned that she was a Jew, he'd dropped her
class. Pretty soon he stopped going to all of his classes, and when he failed
every course, he was expelled.

As a member of the Nation of Islam he felt he finally had a place where
he belonged. Then one day he'd arrived early for an appointment, hoping
to learn that he'd been awarded a paid internship to work with underprivi-
leged kids in Harlem at an NOI-sponsored summer camp. No one was at
the reception desk, so he'd wandered back until he heard voices coming
from the director's office.

"So who gets the internship?" asked a voice he recognized as belonging
to the director.

"Well, Justin probably deserves it," said another voice, which belonged
to the youth minister. "He's been here the longest and done the most volunteer work. The other candidate, Kasheena Johnson, is only here to meet
boys, and she's damn lazy."

"Yeah, but her daddy is a doorman at the Apollo and can get us free tickets," the director noted. The two men laughed. "Besides, that half-albino
mother fucker gives me the creeps; it's like some sort of white fungus is eating away his blackness."

Again the men had laughed as Justin felt the blood rush to his "albino"
face and tears sprang to his eyes. "A fungus among us," chortled the youth
minister.

Justin rushed from the office not caring if the men heard him slam the
door behind him; he was never going back. He told himself he was relieved
to be away from the Nation of Islam. The way he saw it, they weren't really
Muslims. Few of the leaders he'd met had ever read the Qur'an; most of

what they knew they'd heard from others, and a lot of that seemed to have been made up as they went along. If he was going to dedicate his life to Allah, he'd find a real mosque.

———

A fungus among us, Abdalla repeated softy, aware that a soft light was beginning to grow in the east. He could even make out some details of the ship and the docks.

Like his friend Muhammad Jamal Khalifa, he had been both horrified and excited by the events of September 11, 2001. It was staggering to imagine so much death and destruction from a couple of airplanes. But it was good that people of color had hit back at the whites and Jews who ran the country, and he was proud that fellow Muslims had taken the initiative.

He was standing only a few feet away from Khalifa that day on the street corner listening to Imam Jabbar, and he, too, had been invited back to the mosque for prayers. He knew that night he'd found a home. This was the real Islam. At the Al-Aqsa Mosque, men prayed five times a day and studied the Qur'an. Sometimes a visiting imam from the Middle East, in New York to raise money for Islamic charities, would read the Word of Allah, which made it even more real.

A year or so after he joined, he found himself among the select few invited to special classes with the imam to hear stories about jihad and the martyrs who were fighting the Enemies of Islam to expel them from the Middle East. Like the martyrs of 9/11, they had been willing to die to bring about a world governed by the laws of Islam and now enjoyed the fruits of Paradise. Even some of the enemy recognized the rightness of their cause, the imam had said, posting the article "What Goes Around, Comes Around" by Jessica Campbell on the mosque bulletin board.

On the night that Justin Rhodes declared to the imam that he would die for Allah, he was given a new name, Suleiman Abdalla. And this time it was not meant as an insult.

"The Suleiman Abdalla for whom you are named is a modern warrior of Islam," Jabbar explained at the ceremony. "He is currently imprisoned in Colorado for the brave attack on the U.S. Embassy in Kenya. He would be proud if his namesake carried on the jihad he could no longer wage from prison."

I wonder what Paradise will be like, Abdalla thought as he neatly folded the *London World Herald* and placed it next to him on the seat of the car. He was thinking about the nubile virgins who would be his reward for martyrdom. He'd never been with a woman, or even had a girlfriend.

Thinking about it dredged up the old feelings of hatred and anger. Soon they would all regret it—his parents, his classmates, the whores, and the gang members. And when the crescent moon signaled the start of Ramadan, he'd show those big-talking blowhards with the Nation of Islam what it meant to be a true believer.

As he prayed at the mosque for the will to perform jihad, he knew that he was doing as Allah intended. A part of him tried to tell him that killing people, especially women and children, was wrong. But the other part argued that it wasn't wrong if it was Allah's will, and if the victims were truly innocent, they would enter the gates of Paradise, too. *Inshallah . . .* God's will be done.

Khalifa could have ruined it for all of them. It was bad enough that he was too weak to stay away from alcohol and got kicked out of the brigade. But then he'd selfishly jeopardized the plan by blowing himself up at the synagogue.

The others in the Al-Aqsa Brigade had been told about Khalifa's "martyrdom." The imam and the Chechen woman, Ajmaani, had explained that while they understood the desire to sacrifice themselves for Islam, such unilateral actions risked exposing "the spectacular event" envisioned by The Sheik before it could be accomplished.

Khalifa's death hurt, too, because he and a heavy boy named Abdul Raouf had been Abdalla's only friends at the mosque. They'd all received their Muslim names on the same night and often talked about going on jihad to Afghanistan together.

Perhaps because his own face was scarred from smallpox, Khalifa never commented on Abdalla's vitiligo and had often had him over to his home for dinner. In honesty, Suleiman had a crush on Khalifa's wife, Miriam, the most beautiful woman in the world, he thought; she didn't look at his skin when she talked to him but into his eyes. He'd honored her as the wife of his best friend but kept his feelings to himself, even after Khalifa killed himself.

Abdalla had only seen his friend once after he'd been kicked out of the brigade. He was living in his tiny new apartment, and they talked for a long time about how much Khalifa missed his wife and son. As Abdalla was leaving, Khalifa had handed him a book of food-stamp certificates. "I won't need these," he said. But when Abdalla inquired as to why, Khalifa just shrugged and said he had a new job.

Abdalla had kept the food stamps in his wallet, too embarrassed to actually use them. However, recently while scouting out an "escape route" that The Sheik would be using after the great plan had been implemented, an enormous panhandler had approached him.

"'ooger 'ongry," the filthy giant complained, holding out a large, dirt-encrusted hand. "Can u 'pare um change?"

Suleiman had been thinking about putting the food stamps in the charity box at the mosque on Ramadan, when good deeds earned special rewards. *But I might not get the chance,* he thought, fishing his wallet out of his pocket.

"Here you go," he'd said, handing the hungry giant the certificates. "*Salaam.*"

The beggar had looked at the stamps suspiciously but then brightened. "'ank you, 'ery much," he said and shuffled off.

After the synagogue bombing, Abdalla had felt a twinge of envy when he had read all the newspaper accounts of Khalifa's martyrdom. But then he realized that his friend had not accomplished what he had hoped. Khalifa had always complained that he was a "nobody." Now he still was. . . . No one knew—except, apparently, his former comrades at Al-Aqsa—that he was the martyr. It seemed a cruel trick of fate, or perhaps it was a punishment from Allah for putting himself above the greater good.

You are still a nobody, Jamal, Abdalla thought. *But soon I will be somebody.*

———

Shortly after Khalifa's death, Abdalla and the others had been told to pack a few days' worth of clothing and bring it to the mosque that night. Once there, they were told to board a bus driven by one of the imam's body-guards. It left the mosque grounds and Abdalla soon fell asleep; later he awoke to the sound of the bus's tires crunching on gravel just before they came to a halt.

The driver ordered them to collect their things, get off the bus, and form into two lines outside. They'd done as they were told, trying to make out their new surroundings in the darkness. They were obviously not in the city anymore.

Nearly all the jihadis had been born and raised in Harlem, and the closest they'd ever come to The Great Outdoors had been Central Park. Even Abdalla, who had attended summer camp as a youth, was disconcerted. All he could tell was that they were out in the country on what appeared to be some sort of farm surrounded by a dark forest.

The two lines were quickly marched off to a long low building with only one door and no windows. The interior was non-descript, just a row of bunk beds on either wall, and had a strange musty smell to it.

"Get some sleep," the bodyguard had ordered. "Tomorrow, you begin the road to jihad. *Allah-u-Akbar!*"

"*Allah-u-Akbar,*" the young men responded as the driver left. They then chose their beds and gratefully turned in.

The first morning, they were rousted before dawn by Ajmaani.

"Where are we?" one of the sleepy men asked after roll call.

"That's not important," Ajmaani had replied. "You are not to ask questions unless it is to review what you will be taught. All that you need to know is that you have sworn your lives to jihad and that you have been specially selected to, God willing, carry out a very important martyr mission that will strike a crippling blow to your oppressor, your enslaver, the United States of America. Are you ready to become holy warriors of Islam?"

The young men of the Al-Aqsa Brigade had done their best to snap to attention as they shouted: "*Allah-u-Akbar! Allah-u-Akbar!*" Nobody back home had ever treated them with much respect, but now they were holy warriors of Islam, specially chosen.

They spent the next few weeks getting physically fit. Only one of the men—Abdalla's other friend, Abdul Raouf, a large, overweight young man—couldn't make it. It was difficult for him to shed the pounds and get in better shape.

Then one day, Raouf quit halfway through the obstacle course as he bent over and threw up. Seeing this, Ajmaani screamed for the others to halt and gather around the heaving man. "Are you quitting?" she shouted at him.

"Fuck this, I just need to catch my breath a minute," Raouf gasped.

The woman appeared not to hear him, or care. "You quit," she sneered. "What if your objective required you to cover that distance quickly or the entire mission would be a failure?"

"I'm doing my best," Raouf replied sullenly. "Maybe I'm just not cut out for this."

Ajmaani turned to the others. "What is the penalty for quitting?" she demanded.

No one answered. They'd all been told that the only way out of the brigade was death.

Realizing what she'd said, Raouf stood up with fear in his eyes. "I can go on now," he said and started to lumber off.

"You have two minutes to complete the obstacle course," Ajmaani shouted after him.

The big man stopped short. "Ain't no way," he complained. "Ain't nobody could do that."

The other members of the brigade looked at each other; the fastest, most able among them would have had difficulty completing the task. But Ajmaani held out her hand to one of the bodyguards, who handed her his 9 mm Glock semi-automatic. She leveled it at Raouf. "You now have less than two minutes," she said quietly.

With a cry of terror, Raouf took off running. He reached the far end of the course and started back, fear and desperation keeping his heavy legs moving. They could hear his breathing—big, ragged gulps that whistled in and out of his mouth—as he drew close and finally collapsed across the finish line. His fellow mujahideen smiled; Raouf was one of the friendlier members of the brigade, a dedicated student of the Qur'an and always willing to help the others with their studies.

Then Ajmaani looked at her watch and announced. "You were twenty seconds late," she snarled, crossing the few yards and kicking him as hard as she could in the ribs. Raouf screamed and rolled over on his back, blinking in the sun.

Ajmaani pointed the gun at his head. "Because this man quit, you were all killed by the Enemies of God," she shouted. "But worse than that, your mission failed and there is no place in Paradise for you. You are not martyrs, you are all failures."

Raouf began to cry. "I'm sorry," he apologized. "I'm sorry my brothers. I'll try harder."

"Try harder?" Ajmaani scoffed, her green eyes blazing. "Is that what you'll say the next time you quit and your 'brothers' die for nothing?" She turned back to the main group and held up the handgun. "Who will kill this quitter for me?"

The men looked at her in shocked silence, shifting back and forth from one foot to the other. She scowled as she looked from face to face.

"Is there no one who will strike this betrayer down for Allah?" Ajmaani demanded. She chose Suleiman. "You, Abdalla, you shoot him."

"I couldn't. He's my friend."

"Your friend just betrayed his oath to Allah," Ajmaani snarled. "Who do you choose, this fat pig or Allah? Shoot him for Allah!"

Abdalla stepped forward and accepted the weapon from her. It seemed so heavy; his hand fell to his side.

"Do it!" Ajmaani commanded.

Abdalla walked over to where Raouf had risen to his elbows and now begged for his life. "Sule," he cried. "We're friends. Please, I want to die as a martyr for God, not like this!"

"Kill him," Ajmaani hissed in his ear as she stepped up behind Abdalla. "*Inshallah* . . . it's God's will."

Abdalla sighted down the barrel at the blubbering face of Raouf. "Kill him!" Ajmaani suddenly screamed in his ear. He pulled the trigger. Nothing happened. The gun didn't fire.

Ajmaani smiled. "I see it is time to begin weapons training," she announced as if it had only been a test. "You must first release the safety." She sidled up behind him, placing a hand on his shoulder while her other hand snaked along his arm that held the gun until her hand covered his. She pressed a little lever on the side of the gun. "The safety," she said softly in his ear. "Now, pull the trigger, Suleiman."

All Abdalla could think about was the pressure of her breasts against his back and her hips against his buttocks. It was easy to forget that he was

pointing a gun at the head of a man pleading for his life. He only remembered when Ajmaani squeezed his finger and the gun roared.

In that moment, everything came back into focus. A neat dark hole appeared in Raouf's forehead at the same time blood and gore blew out the
back of his skull.

Abdalla remained frozen in place, his arm extended, pointing the gun as
a wisp of smoke escaped the barrel. Patting him on the shoulder, Ajmaani
gently removed the weapon. She held the gun aloft and pointed her other
hand at him.

"Behold, Suleiman Abdalla, a true warrior of Islam!" she shouted.
"Without hesitation, he strikes down the Enemies of God. He has killed a
man who would have failed you and prevented you from fulfilling your
sworn duty to Allah! Blessing of Allah to Suleiman."

As he looked into the smiling eyes of the woman, Suleiman Abdalla believed that he had reached the defining moment of his life. He was no
longer Justin Rhodes with a skin disease; he was Suleiman Abdalla, a warrior of God, and the new favorite of the beautiful Ajmaani.

As promised, Ajmaani began teaching them to use weapons—assault rifles,
handguns, grenades, and knives. After just a few weeks, she told them
they'd become an elite fighting force capable of taking on and defeating
any enemy.

During a visit to the camp, Imam Jabbar had congratulated them for becoming the vanguard of a militant American Islamic movement that would
someday reach millions of young men in America's urban centers who'd
been oppressed by whites and Jews for far too long. Inspired by the legend
of the Al-Aqsa Mosque Brigade, they would rise, "an Army of Allah," and
with their brothers-in-jihad overseas defeat the West's decadence and bring
about a new era.

At inspirational night meetings, they swore on the Qur'an to die for each
other and the glory of Allah. *And for Ajmaani,* Suleiman would add to himself.

So he was terribly disappointed when the brigade was divided into two
groups, each with a separate mission, and he was assigned to the group that
would be lead by The Sheik, not Ajmaani. When he complained, she

rubbed his shoulder and said she understood, but he should look at it as a reward.

"Because you have been true," she said, "you have been given the greater honor of going on jihad with The Sheik." She'd looked around to make sure none of the others were in hearing range before confiding that of the two missions, his was the more important. "It may well be that the success of the entire plan may ultimately depend on you."

Abdalla blushed with pride but said he would still rather die with her. It was the closest he'd ever come to expressing feelings for a woman, and as soon as he said it he cringed, fearing that she would laugh.

However, Ajmaani smiled. "We will die together," she promised. "But in two different places. Now can you do that for me, Suleiman?"

He nodded his head and murmured "*Inshallah*," thinking that he sounded romantically fatalistic.

"Yes," she responded. "As God wills."

Toward the end of their stay in camp, they received a visit from the man they were told to call The Sheik. He delivered a brief inspirational speech in which he told them that their sacrifice would "change the world." In such a world, men of color and faith would rule, and whites and Jews would be their slaves.

Abdalla was thrilled to be introduced to The Sheik. But then he felt like someone had punched him in the stomach when the man looked at him with distaste. "What is the matter with your skin?" he asked bluntly.

"It is a disorder of the skin that he cannot help," Imam Jabbar explained. "Ajmaani says that he is the most apt of the jihadis."

That Ajmaani spoke so highly of him to such important people made Abdalla dismiss what The Sheik said. He didn't care what this Arab thought so long as Ajmaani considered him her most apt pupil.

However, Abdalla's jealousy reared its head when he heard that Ajmaani's team would be joined by the great Azahari Mujahid. They'd been told about his achievements while working on the suicide vests that he'd designed.

"Why can't I be in your group?" Abdalla whined when he had a moment alone with Ajmaani one evening. "I want to die with you and Tatay."

This time, instead of offering a smile and reassurance, she struck him. And not a mere slap from a woman, but a powerful backhand that knocked him to the floor.

"There is no more time to coddle you, Abdalla," she hissed. "Do as you are told and do not complain again."

Abdalla nodded and waited until she left the room to get back up. He no longer hoped that one of his virgins would look like Ajmaani.

In mid-August they'd been loaded back on the bus and driven back to Harlem, again arriving late at night. As the men filtered back into the community, they answered questions about where they'd been as vaguely as possible. Some simply shrugged and said they'd been around, just busy. Others said they'd been working out of state. A few said they'd been on a spiritual retreat with other young Muslims.

Many of the congregation thought that wherever they'd been, these young men had grown and matured. They noted that the young men never missed their prayers and seemed content to let others argue about politics, declining even to enter debates over Israel and Palestine. Nor did they speak any longer of jihad.

A *passing fancy*, their families thought with relief. The elders at the mosque nodded in satisfaction; perhaps the late-night meetings studying the Qur'an had been a good thing after all.

Several days before he began his vigil at the dock, Abdalla had gone home to see his parents. They'd been estranged ever since he'd joined the mosque and changed his name, so he wasn't sure what he was hoping for or the reception he would get.

Dinner started off tensely when he refused a glass of red wine, saying it was against the teaching of the Qur'an. His father rolled his eyes, and they hardly spoke during the meal. Afterward, his mother had patted him twice on the head and then gone to bed complaining of a headache even though it was barely six o'clock.

At his father's request, Abdalla had followed him into his study, where the older man sat in his leather chair with a snifter full of cognac while his son sipped at a glass of water. "So," his father began, slapping the arms of his chair as if to start an unpleasant but necessary negotiation. "When do you expect to be done with this nonsense?"

"What do you mean?"

Dr. Rhodes shrugged. "I mean you're getting older and this constant 'finding yourself' is getting tiresome. You spend all of your time with ghetto niggers who don't even belong to the same church you were born into. They're not part of the culture your mother and I raised you in."

"My culture?" Abdalla scowled. "You mean the culture that was crammed down my ancestors' throats after they were torn from Africa in chains and their religion taken from them?"

The doctor scoffed. "Ah yes, the evils of slavery," he snorted. "Well, hate to tell you—and I'm not condoning it—but the end result was that this family isn't running around in the jungle, trying to avoid genocidal warfare, most of it propagated by Muslims, on that dark and benighted continent. We're Christians in this family, and have been for over two hundred years."

"There is no God but God, and Muhammad is his messenger," Abdalla retorted.

Abdalla's father looked at him for a minute and then sighed. "Whatever . . . I don't really care what religion you ascribe to—cut the heads off of chickens and paint yourself with their blood for all I care. However, I do think it's time you thought about your future. It's not too late to finish college and get into med school. Who knows? Perhaps you could be the one who cures your affliction."

Somewhere in Abdalla's mind he knew that his father, however insensitive, had meant that in a positive way. But he didn't have to like it. "Allah made me this way," he said, standing up. "And that means I am perfect because Allah does not create imperfection."

Dr. Rhodes furrowed his brow. "So did Allah create cancer?" he asked. "And does that mean cancer is perfect and that I should not try to save people from it? And if God created vitiligo, was it because He wanted to make your life miserable . . . to have you spend it as some sort of freak?"

As soon as he said it, Dr. Rhodes regretted it. But there was no opportunity to take it back. His boy blinked back the tears and walked out.

"Wait, son," the father called out. It was too late; his son was gone.

Abdalla ran out of the building and took off south on Madison Avenue, wiping at the tears and cursing anyone whose eyes met his. "What are you looking at?" he screamed at one woman who asked if he was all right. "I'm not some helpless freak." He finally ran out of steam when he reached 29th

Street. Realizing where he was, he veered left until he found himself standing outside Il Buon Pane.

It was late, well past closing time, but as he looked in the window, he saw Moishe Sobelman emerging from the back wiping flour off of his hands. The old man looked up at the window and squinted, as if trying to see who stood there in the dark outside. He started to smile, but then Abdalla took off running.

He caught a taxi back to the mosque where he had a cot in the basement. *This is where I belong*, he thought as he fell asleep. *This is where God is telling me to be.*

Despite the backhand from Ajmaani, she apparently still trusted him more than she trusted the others. He'd been given the honor of picking up Azahari Mujahid from the ship and bringing him back to the mosque.

"The car you drive won't attract attention," Ajmaani assured him. "The license plates are valid and all the lights work. Just follow the traffic laws and don't get pulled over. If you do, wait for the police officer to approach, and if he seems suspicious, detonate your vest of martyrdom."

Abdalla looked over at the cumbersome vest that lay on the seat next to him and then at his watch. It was 6 a.m. The vest was uncomfortable to wear, but he decided that he should put it on now, as the call he was waiting for could come at any moment.

In fact, he'd barely slipped into the vest, fastened it, and then slipped on a sweatshirt when the cell phone rang and he flipped it open to answer.

"Most Gracious, Most Merciful; Master of the Day of Judgment," said an accented male voice.

"Thee do we worship," he replied, "and Thine aid we seek." He closed the cell phone. It was the signal to pick up his passenger.

As he pulled up to the gate, a tall, well-tanned man appeared and let him in. The man pointed him in the right direction, and he drove forward and down the docks until reaching the *Star of Vladivostok*, where the guard signaled for him to stop. He didn't have to wait long before two men hurried down the gangplank and jumped into the backseat.

"*Salaam, Assalamu Alikum,*" Abdalla greeted the men.

"*Assalamu Alikum Wa Rahmatulah Wa Barakatuh*," said one. Abdalla assumed he was Azahari Mujahid by the way the other deferred to him.

"Are you the only ones?" Abdalla asked. "I thought there'd be more."

Mujahid met his eyes in the rearview mirror. "How many do you think I need?"

Now that's the face of a stone-cold killer, Abdalla thought and asked no further questions.

Crossing the Manhattan Bridge, they'd reached Third Avenue and turned north when a police car suddenly pulled in behind them, lights flashing. Abdalla's hand slipped beneath his sweatshirt and felt for the pager that was attached to his martyr's vest. But as he slowed to pull over, the police car swerved around him and went on.

Still sweating the close call, Abdalla was happy to pull through the security gate at the mosque and drive into the underground parking structure. There they were met by Imam Jabbar and his bodyguards, who led them to one of the basement rooms.

As they entered, Ajmaani stood and said, "*Salaam*. Fight against such of those who have been given the Scripture as believe not in Allah nor the Last Day . . ."

"And forbid not that which Allah hath forbidden by His messenger, and follow not the Religion of Truth," Mujahid said.

Ajmaani appeared to relax. "Praise be to Allah," she said, "the Cherisher and Sustainer of the worlds."

Mujahid turned to his companion and said something in a language that Abdalla didn't know. Faster than his eye was able to follow it, the second man struck one of Imam Jabbar's bodyguards in the throat. He pulled the man's gun from its shoulder holster before he even hit the ground. In the next instant, he had the gun trained on Ajmaani while the other bodyguards were still fumbling for their weapons.

"That was not the correct response," Mujahid snarled. "We have been betrayed!"

Abdalla didn't know what to do and thought it was all going to end badly. But then Ajmaani held up her hands and smiled. "Please forgive me, Sheik Mujahid. I apologize for the deception, but I am under orders to be extremely careful and test repeatedly to make sure our friends are who they say they are. The response you're looking for is, of course, the completion of the verse from the Qur'an. I should have said, 'Until they pay the tribute readily, being brought low.'"

Mujahid's eyes narrowed. "That was a dangerous game. My friend, Abu Samar, might have shot you."

"Perhaps, but not with that gun. There are no bullets."

Mujahid said something to Samar, who squeezed the trigger. The gun clicked, empty, but still Ajmaani's face had drained of color for a moment. She recovered quickly, however, and glared at where the wounded body-guard gasped and struggled for air.

"His larynx is crushed," Mujahid said. "It will continue to swell until it cuts off all air. If he is to live, he needs a doctor."

Ajmaani stood, revealing a handgun she'd been hiding beneath the table. She walked over to the injured man and studied his desperate face. "*Inshallah*," she said and ended the man's torment.

Signaling for the other guards to remove the body, Ajmaani then walked over to look Samar in the eye. "Your friend," she said to Mujahid. "Where is he from?"

"He is Malay," Mujahid replied. "We have been in jihad for many years together."

"Does he speak English?"

"No, only Malay and some Tagalog from living in the Philippines."

Ajmaani turned back to Mujahid. "You are looking well," she said. "I understand that you are ill with cancer?"

"Appearances can be deceiving. The pain medication, thanks be to Allah, allows me to continue to do His work, though some days are better than others. However, there isn't much time, so if you are finished with the games, may we proceed?"

"Yes, we must move on. Come with me; I want to show you how we've been preparing for your arrival."

The woman led the others out of the room and down a hallway. She arrived at another room, swung open the steel door that guarded the dark interior, and invited the others to enter ahead of her. As Mujahid and Samar walked in, the recessed lights in the ceiling gradually became brighter, revealing the contents of the room.

An overhead projector sat in the middle of the room facing a screen. On a large table next to the projector was a roll of blueprints, and on shelves lining a wall hundreds of rectangular packages marked "Danger. Explosive. C-4" were piled.

"What do you think?" Ajmaani asked, nodding at the explosives.

Mujahid turned to her. "I could attack a fortress with this amount," he replied.

Ajmaani smiled even wider and gave a little bow. "Exactly," she said.

30

"Ah, Mr. Karp, just the man we wanted to see." Former U.S. Attorney Dennis Hall stood up and motioned for Karp to take the seat next to him. "We prosecutors need to stick together on this," he explained. "Mr. Epstein and I were just debating what I call the insanity of the insanity defense. Would you care to weigh in?"

It was 6:30 on Monday morning, and The Breakfast Club was already at it. There was a definite nip in the September air that hadn't been there just that past week, but they were still sitting outside wearing sweaters, jackets, and caps.

"Afraid I'm going to have to pass," Karp replied. "I still have a trial going on, and the walls have ears. I thought I'd stop by for the pancakes and to listen to better minds than mine. The defense starts its case this morning. So if you don't mind, I'll just be part of the peanut gallery."

"I hardly think that's the case," Bill Florence, the former newspaper editor and Breakfast Club trivia expert, said. "'Peanut gallery' refers to the people sitting in the uppermost, cheapest seats in a theater during the nineteenth century. If they didn't like the show, they threw peanuts at the stage and those seated below them. Today, of course, it refers to people whose opinions are considered unimportant, which is certainly not you."

Hall turned to Epstein. "Where were we? Oh yes . . . the insanity defense as it stands now is a farce. It's just an escape mechanism for violent criminal misconduct. In this particular case, it's clear that the defense thinks that a mass murderer, Jessica Campbell, should escape justice because she was suffering from a delusional belief—i.e., a direct pipeline to God—that created irrational motivations—saving her children's souls—which compelled her to act out violently."

"So there's no such thing as 'not guilty due to mental defect'?" Epstein retorted. "Just lock them all up and throw away the key, even if they're completely out of touch with reality."

"Nonsense, nobody's saying that, but how like a defense attorney to immediately jump to an extreme scenario."

"As opposed to simply hanging people for jaywalking," Epstein shot back. "But do go on."

"Thank you, I think I shall. Obviously, we don't want to be incarcerating—or executing, my overly dramatic friend—someone who is truly insane. Doesn't know what planet they're on. Thinks they're shooting giant lizards from Venus, not people . . ."

"Believes that God told her to kill her kids . . ."

"No, because then she's aware that she is committing murder," Hall replied. "But perhaps, if she truly believed God told her that pushing them off the Brooklyn Bridge would turn them into angels and they could then fly to heaven, there'd be a difference. In other words, someone who, based upon a mental disease or defect, did not know or appreciate the nature and consequences of her acts . . . or know that those acts were wrong."

"But isn't it obvious that Campbell has some sort of mental defect?" Gilbert asked.

"Something like half of everybody in prison now qualifies as a sociopath," Plaut replied. "The rest are schizophrenic or narcissistic or obsessive-compulsive. If having a mental defect is your criterion for not being responsible for committing crimes, then there's no point trying to lock anybody up. They're all mentally ill."

"What if that defect meant she couldn't control herself?"

"Isn't one of the major purposes of the criminal justice system to incarcerate those violent criminals who cannot control their violent impulses but instead act them out?" Hall countered.

The old men argued on for another half hour and then gave it up just as Karp finished his pancakes and stood to leave. "Oh, I meant to ask you all a question," he said.

The Breakfast Club members stopped talking and glanced at each other like little boys who'd hit a baseball through a neighbor's window and now were going to be brought to task for it. "Go ahead," Gilbert said.

"It's probably not something you can help with. But I thought that given your activities in the senior community, perhaps you might have heard something about a group of older gentlemen running around kidnapping private citizens and making wild accusations."

"It's a big city," Saul Silverstein replied. "Lots of us old geezers roaming the streets. Why do you think we'd know them?"

Karp shrugged. "I don't know. Just a hunch."

"Are the police looking for them?" Gilbert asked.

"Good question. They did commit several major felonies. But I don't think the victim is pressing charges . . . for the time being."

"That's good," Father Sunderland noted.

Karp gave him a funny look. "Why, Father, are you condoning this sort of behavior?"

The priest shook his head. "No, that's not what I meant. I was just thinking that perhaps these men would have learned their lesson and won't be repeating it."

"My hope as well. If I could speak to them, I'd warn them that they're treading in dangerous waters. Apparently they passed on valuable information; however, it's time for them to let others handle the situation, unless, of course, they have something else to say of import."

"No, they don't," Gilbert replied. "I mean, I would think they would have said all that needed to be said and will probably just lay low now."

"That's all I needed to hear. Thanks. And if you do happen to run into these nefarious gentlemen, please convey my message."

"We certainly will, Mr. Karp," Hall promised.

Karp looked at his watch. "Oops, 7:15, sorry to eat and run, gentlemen. Thanks for the conversations, they have been . . . most illuminating."

As he got out of the taxi across from the Criminal Courts building, Karp heard the roar of a subway train passing beneath the street. He immediately felt guilty. Tonight the new crescent moon would appear in the sky, signaling the start of Ramadan. If Jaxon was right, terrorists were plotting to attack the subway system tomorrow. But they'd all agreed that they couldn't shut down the city's main transportation system without causing mass panic.

Of course, that will be nothing if people die, he thought. But they didn't know how, where, or when these guys were going to strike. *If they shut the city down this time, and nothing happens, what do they do the next time someone makes a threat?*

Karp wondered where Lucy was in all of this. Jaxon had told him that she was working undercover. "She's safe, I have guys who watch her 24/7," he said. "But it wouldn't be good if she stopped by the loft and the bad guys put two and two together. I don't have the manpower to watch the whole Karp-Ciampi clan."

It had been a lonely weekend on Crosby. Marlene and the twins were staying in Queens to spend a little time with her dad; the boys had a long weekend off from school and were hoping Grandpa could be persuaded to go with them to Coney Island. Then on Tuesday, they were all going on a field trip to the New York Stock Exchange. So he was a bachelor until Tuesday night.

The protesters in front of the courthouse hardly acknowledged his arrival. *Monday morning blues, I guess.* Even Treacher seemed worn out. He merely waved from Dirty Warren's stand, where he and the newspaper vendor were playing chess.

Kenny Katz was waiting for him in his office. "I want to make one last pitch to put on our own psychiatrist to counter the crap the jury is going to hear today," he said.

"We don't need 'em," Karp replied. "It's only playing into the defense's hands to make this a showdown between shrinks."

Karp had kept the state psychiatrists, and even the hired gun Katz had located, on the witness list. But that was to keep Lewis guessing. Meanwhile, he stayed with the game plan of playing it straight and simple. Even the small touches of emotion from the Baker Street gang had come off as genuine precisely because he hadn't tried to squeeze it out of them.

"Look, Kenny, first of all, I think prosecutors make a big mistake by trying to 'out-shrink' the shrinks. When you start trying to play psychologist, using their language, you're in their territory, which puts you at a disadvantage."

"Which is why we call someone who speaks the language and can explain their bullshit to the jury," Kenny countered.

"Why give it that much credibility? The defense wants this to be a trial about how crazy Jessica Campbell is. We want this to be a trial about whether she knew what she was doing and was aware that it was wrong. That's all we want to prove, and we don't need a shrink to do it."

Kenny's shoulders sagged, and Karp knew why. The kid had poured his heart and soul into the case—engaged in all the painstaking preparations and pre-trial hearings. Now he thought that Karp might lose the case if the defense's expert witnesses confused the jury; all it would take was one unsure juror and Campbell was off to the funny farm instead of prison.

"You've done a great job with this case," Karp said. "I gave you the ball and you ran with it. But I want you to think long and hard about what I'm saying now. You did it without resorting to fifty-cent words or cheap theatrics; this has been strictly about the evidence, no smoke and mirrors, no confusing the jury with fancy phrases and psychobabble. You've heard me talk about my mentor, Francis Garrahy. Well, he used to constantly remind me that this job isn't just about prosecuting criminals and throwing them in jail. The DAO is supposed to stand for something; it's supposed to stand for the truth, and the truth doesn't need to be embellished or danced around."

Karp wondered if he was getting through. He knew this went against everything taught in law school. "I hope you'll see that these parades of expert witnesses are mostly meant to confuse the issue, not illuminate it. Each side calls upon its paid witnesses to reach ironclad, but totally divergent, opinions on the defendant's state of mind. It's at best conjecture."

Psychologists and psychiatrists could not testify "with the degree of scientific certainty that someone like a ballistics expert could," Karp went on. "And this reliance on pseudoscience betrays the purpose of a criminal trial, which is the search for truth guided by the rules of evidence, and the meting out of justice. For Lewis and all those lawyers like her, it's all just a game in which, if they win, criminally violent and unpredictable individuals are exonerated, not because they provided a legitimate defense—like self-defense—but because their hired-gun psychiatrist was more convincing than the state's hired-gun psychiatrist."

Karp looked at his watch. "We're on in ten minutes. Don't look so glum, Sergeant Katz. We're going to win this on the facts and the evidence. Now, are you with me?"

Kenny heaved a sigh. "Yeah, I'm with you. Lock and load, let's go rest our case."

Like the crowd outside the courts building, the spectators inside the courtroom seemed to also be suffering from the Monday malaise. There were even a few empty seats as Karp and Katz entered and made their way to the front.

After the jury was seated, Dermondy looked at the prosecution table. "I believe we are still on the People's case in chief. Please call your next witness."

Karp rose to his feet. "The People, Your Honor, have concluded our presentation."

"What?" Lewis demanded, jumping to her feet. "What about your psychiatric expert?"

Kenny shot Karp a look. It was almost a plea, but the boss shook his head. "Not going to call him."

Lewis's face turned red. "Your Honor, may we approach the bench?"

"Please do. I'm as curious about this turn of events as you are," Dermondy replied.

When the lawyers reached the judge, Lewis angrily insisted that the prosecution was trying to pull a fast one. "This is a case about the mental condition of the defendant," she hissed.

"I beg to differ," Karp said. "This is a murder case. You're claiming the defendant has a mental health excuse . . ."

"Illness."

"Excuse," Karp repeated. "We're saying she doesn't, so we don't need to confuse the issue with more psychologists and psychiatrists."

"But we read the report by Dr. Drummond, and we're prepared to rebut it with our own witnesses," Lewis complained.

"Now you won't have to do that," Karp replied mildly, enjoying how the coloration of her face kept changing with her emotions. "It will save your client money." *Ooooh, nice shade of purple.*

Dermondy shrugged. "Sorry, Miss Lewis, but I can't force the People to call a witness. We're going to have to muddle along with whomever you call to the stand to explain the psychological issues. Are you prepared to call your first witness?"

"No, I'm not," Lewis snapped. "My witnesses are not scheduled to show up until after the noon break. As Mr. Karp so blithely noted, these people are expensive and charge by the hour. We expected this examination and cross to last most of the morning, and then I intended to file several motions to dismiss."

"Well, then, Miss Lewis, I suggest you file the motions, and we'll see what time we have before the noon hour," he said. "In the meantime, I suggest you have an assistant get on the telephone to see if you can get your witnesses here sooner."

When the jury was gone, Lewis made two motions asking that the case be dismissed. The first asserted that the judge had erred at the competency hearing when he had ruled that Jessica Campbell was competent to stand trial. This motion was a routine effort to preserve the record for appeal, and Karp knew Lewis did not expect a favorable ruling. Dermondy noted that she had not offered any new evidence to support her position. The second motion was also routine. She argued that the People had not made out a prima facie case and that therefore there was no reason for the defense to present a case.

"As you know, Your Honor, in an insanity trial the state must prove not only that the defendant killed the victims, which we concede, but also that she was aware of the nature and consequences of what she was doing and that she knew it was wrong," she said. "As I've said all along—to no avail—these witnesses and the manipulated so-called evidence presented by the state does not prove their case, but rather reinforces our contention that Jessica Campbell was legally insane at the time of these unfortunate and tragic deaths. Every point they made had a better explanation as proof of extreme mental illness.

"One, Mrs. Campbell believes that she was talking to God and that she was 'sacrificing' their lives to send them to God in order to save their souls. Does that sound like a mentally responsible person to you? Two, cleaning the bathroom to such an extreme is certainly the obsessive-compulsive behavior we often see with psychoses; certainly no rational person would think that such 'housework' would prevent them from being caught and punished. It all points to the fact that Jessica Campbell, who was suffering from an extreme case of postpartum depression, was a very sick woman and needs a hospital, not a prison cell."

Judge Dermondy looked over at Karp. "Your Honor, just two quick points," Karp said. "First, based upon the substantial credible evidence in the record offered during the People's case in chief, we have more than satisfied our legal burden of presenting to the court and jury a prima facie case. So the People's case will suffice unless contradicted and overcome by other evidence that the defense now has the opportunity to present. Secondly, Your Honor, as Miss Lewis knows, there is in law a presumption of sanity, meaning responsibility, which the defense seeks to rebut. Similarly, the law provides that an individual is presumed to intend the natural and probable consequences of her acts. No clear and convincing evidence has been presented to rebut these presumptions. So unless Miss Lewis has a crystal ball and is determined that the jury will see the case her way only, her motion is devoid of legal impact."

"I have to agree with Mr. Karp's basic premise," Dermondy responded. "The presumptions have not been rebutted, Miss Lewis. Moreover, the People have presented more than sufficient evidence in the record to permit this jury to render a verdict. Your motion, Miss Lewis, is denied."

The judge looked up at the clock on the wall. "Well, we've managed to use up all of an hour. I'm going to send the jury to lunch early, and we'll start at noon. I suggest you get a witness here, Miss Lewis."

With that, court was adjourned. Lewis got up and started to leave, but then turned back to the prosecution table. "That was low," she said.

"No, it was right down the middle, about belt high, a perfect strike," Karp replied. Watching her stomp from the courtroom, he turned back to Katz and gave him a wink.

"Nice work," Katz chuckled. "Couldn't have said it better myself."

As promised, Dermondy called the court to session at noon. "You ready?" he asked Lewis.

"Yes, sir, Your Honor. Let's go."

The jurors were seated, and Lewis called her first witness. "Dr. E. Humphrey Splotz."

She'd found Splotz, a pathologist, in South Carolina and contacted him about the case. He'd read her synopsis of what happened, took a glance at the medical examiner's report, skimmed the lengthier treatise by the Baker Street Irregulars, and said he would testify that the deaths of the Campbell children had been relatively quick. "My fee is $500 an hour, $600 if you want me to look at photographs and render an opinion. My secretary will contact your secretary for billing information."

A small man who resembled a bowling pin with Donald Trump's hair, Splotz sat down in the witness stand and started to rock slightly back and forth as if he needed to use the restroom. However, he got through presenting his resume without any mishaps, and Lewis began her questioning.

"Dr. Splotz, have you examined the evidence in this case?"

"I have."

"And have you reached any conclusions about the manner and cause of death in regard to the Campbell children?"

"I have."

"Doctor . . . the jury has heard testimony that these deaths were particularly slow and agonizing. . . . Would you agree with that conclusion?"

"No."

"And why not?"

"It's not accurate."

Oh my God, thought Karp, *this guy is going to bore the jury to death. He must bill by the hour.*

"How so?"

Splotz looked up in the air and then out at the spectators. "Well, for one thing, it was considerably quicker than many instances of fatalities caused by gunshot or, say, a knife. Those victims may live for hours, even days, in horrible pain."

"So drowning is faster in many instances?"

"Yes."

"Is it more agonizing?"

"Actually, no."

"Why not?"

Splotz squinted over at the jurors as if he were trying to bring them into better focus. "I call it the 'mind-body death disconnect.'"

"The 'mind-body death disconnect'?"

"Yes."

"Can you tell us about it?"

"Well, yes, I've written a book about it called The *Mind-Body Death Disconnect*. Oh, and by the way, the term 'mind-body death disconnect' is copyrighted; my agent says I'm supposed to say that whenever I talk about the book," Splotz grinned smugly.

"And what do you mean by the 'mind-body death disconnect'?" Lewis asked.

"Well, when an animal recognizes that it is about to die in a violent way, there is a sort of 'disconnect.' The animal goes into a sort of shock that takes over the entire physiological system, shutting down the body's pain mechanisms and conscious thought. Animal biologists have noted this 'mind-body death disconnect,' for instance, when a lion brings down a ze-bra and begins to feed. It's obvious from the kicking legs and such that the zebra is still physically alive, but its mind is in a state of shock, essentially functioning on autopilot until physical death."

"So in effect, even if it took several minutes for the Campbell children to physically die, you believe that the 'mind-body death disconnect' has shut down their ability to feel pain or think consciously?"

"Yes."

"And when you say 'think consciously,' you mean . . . ?"

"They would no longer be aware of what was happening to them."

"Would they feel fear?"

"Perhaps for a few seconds before they recognize—unconsciously, of course—that they are about to die. Then their minds would have discon-nected . . ." Splotz snapped his fingers once for emphasis. " . . . from their bodies. The mind goes on autopilot; the body goes through the throes of physical death."

"Thank you, doctor. No further questions."

Judge Dermondy looked at the prosecution table. "Mr. Karp?"

"Thank you, your honor. Dr. Splotz, have you seen the photographs of the defendant's arm after she murdered her children?"

Splotz sat back as though he'd been assaulted. "Well, yes, I've examined them." he said.

"So you've seen the scratches and the bite mark on the defendant's arms?"

"Yes."

"But you don't think the children were fighting for their lives?"

"Well, perhaps at first, but then as the reality of death set in there would have been a 'mind-body death disconnect.'"

"And this happened quickly?"

"Yes . . . in less than thirty seconds I believe."

"Oh, really? How do you know? Have you ever timed this phenomenon?"

"Well, no. It's an educated guess."

"Based on what?"

"Well, based on that people tend to pass out after about thirty seconds without air . . . and those animal studies I cited. You know, the zebra has been taken down and it just sort of lays there, looking off into the distance while the lions feed."

Nice going, Sherlock, Karp thought. *Just reminded the jury of another lioness with bloody mouth and paws.* "Dr. Splotz, have you ever been held under water either on purpose or accidentally?"

"Well, no."

"Really? I'd think that nearly everyone in this courtroom, maybe as a kid at the pool, has experienced not being able to get a breath of air. But you haven't?"

"No."

"What about choked on something? I mean really choked to where you couldn't breathe?"

"Oh, well, sure, I suppose."

"And how did that feel?"

"What do you mean?"

"What sort of emotions did you experience? Panic?"

"Probably."

"Fear?"

"Undoubtedly.

"For how long?"

"What?"

"For how long? How long did you experience panic and fear?"

"I suppose until I could breathe again."

Karp smiled. *This is like shooting fish in a barrel, not that I know what that's like.* "Until you could breathe again," he repeated for emphasis. "Dr. Splotz, have you ever been stabbed with a nine-inch hunting knife right here?" Karp touched himself in the center of his chest.

"No."

"How about here? Or here? Or here?"

"No."

"Can you imagine how that would feel?"

Splotz looked at the jury, then out at the spectators, and finally at the ceiling.

"Dr. Splotz, I asked you a question."

"I get what you're trying to do. Yes, it would hurt and cause fear. But only until the 'mind-body death disconnect' kicked in."

"Which takes how long when you're being stabbed and drowned?"

"I can't say exactly."

"No you can't, can you?" Karp shook his head in disgust. It was exactly what he'd tried to explain to Kenny. People like Splotz made a mockery of the justice system.

"Dr. Splotz, have you ever been chased by a lioness, pulled down with her claws, and ripped open and then smothered when her teeth clamped down around your throat?"

"I object, Your Honor. Counsel is being ridiculous," Lewis countered. "What's he supposed to say? 'Yes, I was ripped open by a lion, but I got better'?"

"The witness is the one who drew the comparison, Your Honor. I was merely improving it."

"Overruled. It was the witness's analogy, Miss Lewis. The witness may answer the question."

Splotz looked disappointed but shook his head. "No, I've never been chased, clawed, or ripped open by a lioness."

"Then how in the hell would you know what it feels like? Or how long it takes before the 'mind-body death disconnect,' if there is such a thing, kicks in?"

The courtroom was silent. Splotz looked at the banister in front of him and traced along the wood with a finger. He shrugged.

"No further questions."

———

Lewis called psychiatrist Harry Winkler to the stand. He testified that Charlie Campbell had brought his wife to him suffering from severe postpartum depression after the birth of their second child. "She had just attempted suicide by swallowing an overdose of Prozac, which followed homicidal ideation toward her second child, Chelsea."

"Doctor, when you're talking about 'depression,' do you mean someone is feeling bluesy or sad?" Lewis asked.

"Those can be symptoms of depression. But we all have down moments that we might call bluesy or sad. Usually it has something to do with a recent experience, such as the death of a family member or the loss of a job. When we're talking about clinical depression, we're talking about symptoms caused by a chemical imbalance in our brains. When there's a proper mix of this, let's call it a chemical soup, we may feel a little up one day and a little down another, but generally we're pretty evenly keeled. Neither up nor down—especially down—lasts very long. And it doesn't interfere with functioning in our daily lives. However, if these chemicals are out of balance the effect can be devastating. These bluesy or sad feelings can be magnified into black depths of utter hopelessness and despair. The patient may not get out of bed for days, and may even feel physically in pain. They can't function, go to work, go to school, or carry on normal activities or conversations. The patient may feel like there is no way out; so suicidal ideation is common, as is actual successful suicide."

"Can depression get worse?"

"Depression in general has a tendency, if untreated, to get worse. Many people respond to treatment, both medication and counseling. However, there are some in whom the disease continues to progress; they don't respond to medication and give up on counseling."

"In the defendant's case, you believed that her depressive episodes were brought on by giving birth?"

"She probably already had some issues with depression. However, yes, postpartum depression is not uncommon. Pregnancy and birthing can both get a woman's hormones out of whack. It may manifest itself as crying for no reason, or even little fits of anger. But usually, this isn't serious and, given time, tends to fix itself."

"What happened to Jessica Campbell after the birth of her daughter, Chelsea?"

"She experienced severe postpartum depression to the point that she actually considered harming her child and then did attempt to harm herself."

"Doctor, have you seen or heard of cases where a new mother might experience postpartum depression and then have it go away, either on its own or through medication, only to have it return after another birth, only this time it's even more severe?"

"Absolutely. We're not sure of all the mechanisms, and it could be that in some cases, the mother never completely regains her chemical balance after the first episode. So when another child is born, the patient may already be predisposed to the condition, and when combined with the new episode, it's worse."

"Doctor, were you made aware that Jessica Campbell may have suffered a postpartum depression episode after her first child, Hillary, was born?"

"Yes. And I concur with the diagnosis."

"So two children, two episodes of postpartum depression?"

"Yes."

"After you diagnosed Jessica Campbell as suffering from severe postpartum depression, did you make a recommendation to the Campbells regarding having any more children?"

All eyes in the courtroom shifted to Charlie, who kept his eyes on Lewis. "Yes, I warned them that it was likely that the depression would return and also that the next episode could be worse."

"And did you, in fact, warn both Charlie and Jessica Campbell that a third pregnancy could pose a danger to both the infant and the mother?"

"Yes. That was my concern."

Karp wasted little time going for the counterattack. "Dr. Winkler, do you have reason to believe that Charlie Campbell raped his wife and impregnated her?"

Although nearly every mouth in the courtroom had dropped open in unison, not a sound came out of any of them.

"No, of course, not," Winkler replied. "However, it's my understanding that he gave her an ultimatum . . ."

Karp held up his hand and the psychologist stopped mid-sentence. "I didn't ask you what you may have heard from some other party. I asked if you, personally, had reason to believe that Jessica Campbell was forced to have sex against her will and therefore had no choice when deciding whether to conceive a third child?"

"No."

"So then it stands to reason that Jessica Campbell was at least partly responsible for this conception? In other words, half the DNA in little Benjamin, as well as his two sisters, was Jessica's."

"As far as I know."

"And therefore, half the responsibility for ignoring your recommendation was Jessica Campbell's."

Winkler glanced over at Lewis but got no help. "I suppose she had something to do with it."

Karp pressed on. "You testified that postpartum depression is not uncommon, is that correct?"

"It is."

"Do you have any idea what percentage of new mothers have postpartum depression?"

"No, I've never seen a figure for that."

"But quite a few?"

"Yes . . . enough anyway that those of us who treat it consider it prevalent in the population."

"So if there are about 4 million births a year in the United States, would it be safe to say that thousands of those women would experience postpartum depression?"

"Yes, based on anecdotal evidence and a few studies I've seen, that's probably a low number."

"Thousands might be a low number," Karp agreed. "And of those thousands, maybe more, how many of those women hold their children under water while they scratch and fight for their lives until they're dead, or stab them in the chest until they bleed to death?"

"Objection," Lewis said. "Counsel is giving another speech. How is the witness supposed to know the answer to that?"

"Your Honor, the witness has testified that within his profession it is a known fact that postpartum depression is not uncommon," Karp said. "He has also testified that he treats quite a number of women for this affliction. I'm asking if he has personal or professional knowledge of how many women have committed these acts upon their children."

"Overruled. The witness may answer the question."

Winkler shrugged. "Not many."

"Not many? Do you know of any others in, say, the past six months since this happened, which would be about 2 million births?"

"No."

"How about the past year, two years? How far back are we going to have to go?"

"I don't know of any specifically. However, I do know there have been other cases of women suffering from postpartum depression who have harmed their children."

"But you can't name one. Let's assume such instances are rare. In how many of these rare instances would the mother NOT have realized that holding her children under water or stabbing them would injure or kill them?"

"Objection," Lewis said. "The witness has already said he doesn't know of any other cases. And besides, we're talking about one specific case here, not any others."

"Okay, I withdraw the question," Karp responded. "Instead, I'd like to ask the witness if he knows whether Jessica Campbell was aware that holding her children under water for a long period of time, or stabbing one of them in the chest six times, would injure or kill them."

Winkler waited for Lewis to object again, but when she didn't he had to answer. "I haven't examined Mrs. Campbell since this happened. I don't know what she thought or realized."

"I understand. But if I remember correctly, she did tell you she considered placing a pillow over Chelsea's head. But she knew that would harm or kill the child."

"Yes, that's what she told me."

"So even though she was suffering from severe postpartum depression like thousands of other women at that time, she knew then that smothering her child would harm or kill the child?"

"I suppose that's correct."

"Well, if she knew that smothering her child was likely to cause harm or death then, do you have reason to believe that she had no idea in March of this year that drowning her children, or stabbing one of them six times in the chest, was going to cause harm or death?"

The psychologist frowned. "I haven't spoken to Jessica about this unfortunate affair, so I don't know if something changed in her thinking."

"I see. Again, if I remember correctly, the reason Jessica did not smother her second child was because she knew that it was wrong. In fact, her suicide attempt was to prevent herself from harming her child because mothers aren't supposed to kill their children."

"I object to the overly dramatic characterization here," Lewis said. "There hasn't been any testimony about what mothers are or aren't supposed to do . . . another attempt by Mr. Karp to give a little speech."

"Perhaps a bit less dramatic, Mr. Karp," Dermondy said. "Sustained. Try and sharpen the focus of your question."

"My apologies, Your Honor and counsel. So, Dr. Winkler, Jessica Campbell told you she didn't kill her second child four years ago because she knew that it was wrong. Am I correct?"

"That's what she told me."

"So even though she was suffering from postpartum depression like thousands of other women at that time, she knew it was wrong to harm her child back then?"

"Asked and answered," Lewis said.

"Sustained."

"Well, then, Dr. Winkler, do you have reason to believe that she did not know it was wrong in March of this year to kill all three children?"

"Like I said. I haven't spoken to her. I don't know what she was thinking."

"That's correct," Karp replied. "You don't know what she was thinking."

Winkler didn't respond. He had the look of a man who desperately wanted to be someplace else, but Karp wasn't through with him. "Do you know of any women with postpartum depression who injured or killed their children and then took elaborate steps to hide the evidence, including removing the bodies and refusing to say what happened?"

"Objection. As the prosecution witnesses noted, Jessica Campbell did say what happened. . . . She sent the children to be with God."

"Let me rephrase that last part. I should have said 'refused to say what actually happened.'"

Winkler wasn't about to get into another scrap with Karp on his own. "I don't know of any."

"Would it be fair to say that as a psychologist you are a student of human behavior?"

"That's an apt description of one aspect of my profession, yes."

"As a student of human behavior, if you knew of someone who had killed someone else, then cleaned up the murder scene, including hiding the bodies, and then refused to discuss what she had done or where the bodies might be found, how would you describe that behavior?"

Winkler again looked at the defense table, but Lewis was looking down at her notes. *Well, if that's the way she's going to be.* He didn't have a dog in this fight and would get paid the same amount whatever happened. "In some cases it would be an indication of guilty behavior."

"Guilty behavior because they understood that what they had done was wrong?"

"Or would be considered wrong by others."

Karp let the answer hang in the air. "Thank you, no further questions."

As Karp sat down, Kenny Katz leaned over and whispered, "Like I said, who needs a shrink?"

31

Tran and Jojola strolled the grounds of Al-Aqsa wearing traditional tunics and *kufie* hats to blend in. They'd been told, politely, to stay within the walls surrounding the mosque; two of the mujahideen walked behind them "for your protection."

The guards had wanted to walk with them. One, their driver from the docks, who'd introduced himself as "Suleiman Abdalla," said it would be an honor to speak with two such highly regarded jihadis. But "Azahari Mujahid" insisted on his space, so they'd backed off out of earshot.

Still, they spoke in near whispers. Jojola had picked up a smattering of Vietnamese when he was "in country" back in the late '60s—what Tran referred to as Americanamese. "Good for picking up prostitutes, ordering beer, and pushing Vietnamese peasants around," he joked. It would serve to communicate basic information, and their "hosts" wouldn't know it from Tagalog, but to carry on a conversation they had to speak in English.

"It's a good thing you didn't blow her head off," Tran said. "This is bigger than Nadya Malovo. We'd be dead and the plan would go forward."

"I knew there weren't any bullets in the gun when I held it. It was too light."

"There could have been one in the chamber. After you pulled the trigger, I could tell she was thinking about that possibility, too."

"Yeah," Jojola grinned. "She turned white as a ghost, sort of like that twerp behind us, though I sort of feel sorry for that guy. It must have been rough growing up looking like that."

"Maybe, but I kept thinking about that bulge under his sweatshirt when the cop came up behind us. I'm betting it was a bomb, and if something had gone wrong, he was supposed to incinerate himself and us."

"You're right. The sympathy train grinds to a halt though when I think of what one of his buddies did in the synagogue. It's tough to keep remembering the big picture here. There was something pleasurable about looking down the barrel at Malovo's face and pulling the trigger."

"Hopefully, you'll get another chance tomorrow," Tran said. "But not until we know what they're up to."

After their arrival Saturday morning, Malovo had started right in explaining the plan—at least their part in it. The blueprints on the table were for an unidentified building. However, it was clear that the attack was at least two-pronged—"timing and coordination are essential," Malovo said. "That is, in part, why your experience and skill were requested."

They'd been told by the real Azahari Mujahid that The Sheik had recruited him not only for his expertise with explosives, but also as a display of solidarity between Islamic extremists in the Middle East and those in Asia. He'd been told that there would be other powers at play, powers that could manipulate and confuse U.S. law-enforcement and anti-terrorism agencies.

"Your martyrdom will inspire millions of new mujahideen," Malovo told Tran during a break in the planning. "There will be a global uprising. The United States will be weakened and isolated. Its allies in Europe, without U.S. support, will be forced to submit to Muslim rule. With Allah's blessing it will be a glorious new day!"

Mujahid's experience with the Regent Hotel was particularly helpful, Malovo explained, because this would be another "inside job." The target building, she said, was nearly impossible to attack from the outside. "Our objective is a single floor that must be destroyed at the proper moment in order for the plan to work."

"How do we reach this objective?" Tran asked.

Malovo unrolled one of the blueprints of a floor plan. As impervious as the building was to attack from the outside, with reinforced steel and concrete outer walls and nearly impenetrable polycarbonate windows, the interior of the building structure was nothing out of the ordinary.

Tran had looked at the plan, grateful that as a former Viet Cong guerrilla, he had experience making bombs and had been updated by one of Jaxon's agents on board the ship in Mujahid's particular style. He did what he hoped was a passable job of indicating where he would plant the charges against the ceiling's support beams in order to destroy the floor above. What he and Jojola found interesting was that their part in the plan wasn't to cause massive casualties. Malovo had even shrugged when Tran noted that explosives alone might not bring the building down.

To accomplish his part of the mission, Tran would have Jojola and two members of the Al-Aqsa Brigade, who had been training in explosives, at his disposal. Malovo and the others assigned to this part of the mission would be responsible for securing the floor and holding off any counterattacks by law-enforcement and security forces.

After finalizing the plan that morning, Tran and Jojola helped supervise the loading of explosives and weapons into two vans. They were ready to go.

"So where is this building?" Tran asked.

Malovo gave him a funny look. "It is not necessary for you to know yet. This is not to insult you, but for the success of the mission. If any of us are captured or betrayed, no one person—except for myself and The Sheik— will know the entire plan. That is why we don't even have the name of the building on the blueprints."

"And what if you're captured or betrayed?"

Malovo smiled, but only so that she could point to one of her molars. "This is a false tooth. It takes considerable force to break it—so that there are no accidents—but it can be done, releasing a poison so powerful that I would be dead before I blinked."

"I would like to know at some point what I will be destroying," Tran said. "I can picture the New York skyline in my mind. I have imagined it ever since the great attack of September 2001. I had hoped to subtract from that skyline myself. Now, my final legacy is to be one floor of a building?"

"It would do you no good to imagine any single structure," she said. "And besides, the target is not in Manhattan, but across the river in Brooklyn. It is not the building that is important. If you need to imagine something as your final legacy, then imagine a map of the United States going up in flames."

Tran smiled and spoke to Jojola in Vietnamese. "Laugh and smile, stupid American dog," he said to his friend, who gave him a hard look but then did as he was told.

Tran bowed and said in English, "We think that is a very good image. Thank you for this opportunity, Ajmaani."

With nothing else to do but wait, Tran and Jojola went outside hoping to talk privately. As they drew close to the back security gate of the compound, they could hear a man outside the walls shouting. Looking through the bars of the gate, they saw Edward Treacher standing on his milk crate.

"Who is this fool?" Tran asked, moving closer to the gate.

A guard shrugged. "Just some filthy street preacher." The guard then shouted at Treacher, saying, "Go on, this is a place for good Muslims, not infidel beggars and human garbage."

Outside the gate, Treacher glared at his detractor and pointed at him, his eyes rolling wildly around beneath his bushy brows. "WHEN HE BROKE OPEN THE FIFTH SEAL, I SAW UNDERNEATH THE ALTAR THE SOULS OF THOSE WHO HAD BEEN SLAUGHTERED BECAUSE OF THE WITNESS THEY BORE TO THE WORD OF GOD! THEY CRIED OUT IN A LOUD VOICE, 'HOW LONG WILL IT BE, HOLY AND TRUE MASTER, BEFORE YOU SIT IN JUDGMENT AND AVENGE OUR BLOOD ON THE INHABITANTS OF THE EARTH?'"

Treacher stood with his finger still raised as though he might conjure up a bolt of lightning with which to strike the guard down. Then he hopped down off the milk crate to the sidewalk. "That was Revelations 6:9–10, friends. I don't suppose you fellow travelers have any spare change with which to feed the hungry . . . the hungry being yours truly?"

"Go on, get away," the guard shouted, moving his hand beneath his tunic as if to draw the gun he obviously had strapped beneath his arm. "Or I'll come out there and shoot your non-believer ass."

Treacher screwed up his face as if contemplating a biblical retort to put the guard in his place, but then thought better of it and turned to leave.

"Wait," Tran commanded. He pointed up to the darkening sky where the tiniest sliver of the new moon hung like an earring. "Tonight begins Ramadan, the month blessed by Allah as the most sacred. Good acts bring a greater reward during this month than at any other time of the year."

Tran pulled a dollar bill and a pen from the pocket of the pants he wore beneath his tunic. He wrote a few words on the bill, then balled it up and tossed it through the bars of the gate before the guards could react.

"What did you write?" the guard demanded. He had been told by Ajmaani that the two visitors were not to have any outside contact. But now the little Asian had passed some sort of message to the bum. Ajmaani would not be happy if she knew.

"A message to save his soul—'There is no God but God, and Muhammad is His messenger'—not that I think this infidel dog has the brains to understand," Tran responded testily, thankful for his lesson in Islam from Lucy. "But if it is possible, then this is the month when non-believers may best be persuaded to submit to the One True Faith before it is too late."

"He's right," said the guard named Suleiman. "It's in the Qur'an. 'Whomsoever God desires to guide, He expands his breast to Islam.'"

Outside the gate, Treacher picked up the crumpled bill, which was blowing down the sidewalk in the slight breeze. He paid no attention to any message written on it and simply stuffed it in his pocket. "Thank you, kind sirs," he shouted back at the men inside the gate. "But a dollar doesn't go far in these troubled times. I don't suppose the rest of you would care to contribute to my ministry?"

When no one responded, Treacher shrugged and shuffled off down the street. "Merry Ramadan," he shouted over his shoulder. "Or whatever it is you folks wish each other."

———

As they turned away from the gate, Suleiman received a cell-phone call. He listened for a moment and then motioned his charges back inside the mosque. "The imam would like to speak to you," he said.

They'd turned to head for the entrance when they heard the sound of the security gate opening behind them. Tran and Jojola looked back and saw a long black limousine pull in and then head down into the underground parking structure.

Inside the mosque, Tran and Jojola were led past the sanctuary, where dozens of people were talking about where they'd been when they looked up and saw the new moon. The congregation had been told that the two visitors were imams from Indonesia in the United States to raise money for Muslim organizations caring for the victims of the December 2005 tsunami.

It was a generous congregation. In fact, the dollar bill Tran had given to Treacher had been pressed into his hands that afternoon by an older man who'd introduced himself as Mahmoud Juma, a native of Kenya.

"I don't have much, and I will not be here tonight for Ramadan service," the old man apologized. "I am going on a trip with my grandson. But I wanted to help."

Reaching the reception area outside of Jabbar's office, Jojola noted the absence of Miriam Khalifa. His biggest concern in joining Tran as Abu Samar had been that she might accidentally give him away if she saw him at the mosque. The test had come after they arrived Saturday morning and were introduced to the mosque community. Miriam had been there and he'd seen her eyes widen with recognition, but she'd quickly put her head down as befitted a modest Muslim woman and no one seemed to notice.

Ushered into the office, Tran and Jojola saw Jabbar sitting in his chair, engaged in an animated conversation with Malovo, who stood near the window. Whatever they were discussing, it came to a halt when they entered.

Moments later, they learned who had been in the limousine when an older white man and a younger Arab entered the room. "Salaam," Jabbar said, rising to introduce the newcomers to Tran and Jojola. "Sheik Mujahid and Sheik Samar, this is Mr. Dean Newbury and The Sheik."

Jabbar licked his thin eggplant-colored lips. The plan was nearly ready and not a moment too soon; Jabbar was sure that he'd developed an ulcer, and his sleep was restless and full of frightening dreams. Tonight he would sleep one last time in his bed, and tomorrow he would be on his way to Sudan, where his benefactors had arranged a comfortable "retirement" as a reward for his services. He would be given a new identity, though when the time was right and his enemies vanquished, he'd emerge as one of the heroes who had helped to bring about the new Islamic caliphate. Perhaps then he'd return to the mosque in Harlem to lord it over the weak-willed members of the congregation—people like Mahmoud Juma. *Too bad his daughter, the lovely Miriam, will not be present,* he thought as he smiled at The Sheik, *but everyone has to make sacrifices.*

Disgusting, thought The Sheik as he nodded back at Jabbar. *He looks like one of the lizards my brother and I used to chase in the al Zubair desert.* The thought of his brother brought a twinge of pain. *Don't worry, Anan, soon I will avenge your death, and the world we envisioned will be a reality.*

In the meantime, he needed Jabbar and the scum that he'd recruited as jihadis. They weren't much different from the illiterate, gullible mujahideen plucked from the slums of the Middle East and Asia; all of them were willing to die for a taste of Paradise. As for himself, tomorrow his public persona would "die," but The Sheik would rise from the ashes and the world would tremble.

The call of the *muezzin* signaled the start of the evening *Taraweeh* prayers that would be said every night throughout Ramadan. "I should go to lead the congregation," Jabbar said and looked at Tran and Jojola. "Would you do us the honor of joining us in preparation for your martyrdom?"

Tran and Jojola wanted to stay to hear what The Sheik and Dean Newbury, who had been a surprise, were going to talk about. But it was clear that they were expected to leave.

After they'd gone, The Sheik turned to Dean Newbury. "So have all arrangements been made for my 'escape' tomorrow?"

"Yes. One of the men who will be with you—the odd-looking nigger with the skin problem—will show you the exit, and my man will be waiting on the other end to take you to the airfield in New Jersey."

"And will your nephew still be with us?"

"He will, indeed," Newbury replied. Tomorrow was a big day in many respects. The start of the era of the Sons of Man and, he hoped, the day his nephew would prove that he could be trusted as his heir on the council. *Or he will die.*

"My knees are killing me," Jojola complained after prayer services. "I'm used to standing, or walking, or even sitting for long periods of time, but all that getting up and down, kneeling and bowing . . ."

"You need to do Kuntao Silat with me," Tran said, referring to the martial arts style he practiced daily. "It will keep even you limber."

"I'm plenty limber, and I can walk you into the ground any day of the week, Little Sister," Jojola replied. "Silat is for wussies who can't do jujitsu."

"Spoken like a true idiot," Tran laughed. He started to call Jojola a traditional Vietnamese expression for a man copulating with farm animals but suddenly dropped his voice. "Here comes Malovo."

"Come with me, please," she said and turned without waiting for a response.

The two men were surprised. It had been their understanding that they had a few more hours before the mission would start. Indeed, they'd been told to relax and make their peace with Allah. Apparently that had changed.

They followed Malovo down into the basement of the mosque to a door. Malovo opened it and gestured for them to enter.

They found themselves in another large room, featuring a full multimedia setup with several rows of seats facing a platform and wall at the far end of the room. A video camera on a tripod stood in the middle aisle facing the wall, on which hung a banner with writing similar to what Tran and Jojola had seen in the videotape made by Jamal Khalifa.

They were not alone either. More than a dozen men stood talking among themselves, or sitting quietly lost in thought.

The two friends recognized about half of the men as those who would be with them on their part of the mission. Many of the young men had been friendly and talkative about their backgrounds, and it was hard to believe that they were training for a suicide mission. Harder still for Tran and Jojola to think that they would have to kill them.

The young men in the room nudged each other and nodded in their direction when Ajmaani entered. "*Allah-u-Akbar! Allah-u-Akbar! Allah-u-Akbar!*" they cheered, led by Suleiman Abdalla.

Malovo clapped her hands. "Line up as you were told." The men, some of them carrying AK-47 assault rifles, gathered at the end of the room facing the camera, with Malovo prodding like a teacher lining up her students for a school photograph. Those with the guns practiced holding them aloft, while those without postured with their arms crossed over their chests.

Placing Tran and Jojola at the front of the group, Malovo handed a rifle to Jojola. She went back to the camera to look through the lens. With a few last commands of "get closer" or "stop smiling," she was at last satisfied and returned to stand next to Tran, whom she handed a piece of paper.

"What's this?" he scowled.

"Something I wrote for you. A last will and testament that will be sent to Al Jazeera and broadcast to millions of Muslims throughout the world. . . . You are free to change it if you like, but there is only a little time."

Tran looked over the document. "It will do."

Malovo looked at the cameraman and nodded. He pressed a button and a green light came on. "That means go," she whispered to Tran.

Glancing one more time at the paper, Tran looked into the camera. "All thanks are due to Allah. We ask for His help and guidance, and we ask His forgiveness for any sins we commit. I am Azahari Mujahid and stand today with my brothers of the Al-Aqsa Brigade, knowing that tomorrow, if it is Allah's will, we will be martyrs. This is our free decision, and I urge all of you to follow us in jihad."

Most of the rest of the speech contained fragments of verse from the Qur'an. A paragraph extolling the virtues of jihad was followed by another request that God forgive their sins. "We have made *bayt al-ridwan*," Tran said, noting the oath made on the Qur'an in which the jihadi promises not to waver in his mission. The term was also a reference to a special garden in Paradise reserved for the prophets and martyrs. The speech ended with the refrain they'd heard so many times since arriving at the mosque: "*Allah-u-Akbar!*"

Ajmaani clapped him on the shoulder. "May Allah be with you. May Allah give you success so that you achieve Paradise."

There was an awkward pause until he realized that she was waiting for a response. He hurriedly looked down at the note and read, "Turn back to the camera."

"No, no," Malovo whispered and leaned forward to point to what he was supposed to say.

"Oh, yes, of course," Tran replied, trying not to laugh for having blown his lines. This all seemed like a school play. "*Inshallah,* we will meet in Paradise."

Malovo nodded and started to turn to the cameraman, but Tran interrupted with a short speech in Vietnamese. He finished and glanced at the double agent. Angrily, she signaled the cameraman to turn off the machine.

"What did you say?" she demanded.

"The same thing, only in Tagalog, for my people in the Philippines. Many do not speak English."

"That was not authorized."

Tran decided that it was time for the great Tatay the Terrorist to show his stripes. "Mind your place, woman!" he spat. "I am not here for your little plays or insolence. Tomorrow I die in the name of Allah, and it is not for you to tell me how to speak."

Malovo's eyes flashed, but she bowed her head. "I did not mean to offend you."

Tran grunted his acceptance of her apology as the men behind them stood wide-eyed, wondering what to do next. They had never seen Ajmaani humiliated, and they half expected her to kill the little Asian. When she did not, they shrugged and began to leave their spots, but stopped when she snarled at them.

"Remain in your places," she spat. "We have a special send-off for your martyrdom." She nodded to a guard at the back of the room, who opened the door and led a bound and hooded woman into the room.

The woman's hands were oddly clenched and bloody, and blood stained the front of her robe. Her movements were stiff and she was obviously in pain, but she didn't cry out when she was shoved roughly to her knees in front of Jojola.

Malovo pulled the hood from the woman, revealing the blood-stained face of Miriam Khalifa.

————

When Miriam had left her father's apartment that evening, her heart had felt light—lighter than it had since the day her husband committed suicide. As light as that evening when Jamal had bought her the strawberry ice cream and she knew she would marry him.

She attributed the feeling to the sliver of moon that hung above the city, as if Allah had taken a sharp knife and cut a little slit in the fading blue of the sky to reveal a glimpse of Paradise beyond. It was Ramadan, the month in which the Qur'an was revealed to the Prophet Muhammad.

Ramadan was not a holiday like Christmas with presents and feasting. Muslims were expected to exercise self-control in all areas, including food and drink, sleeping, sex, and even the use of time. For the next thirty days, Muslims around the world would fast from dawn to dusk; the fasting, called *sawm*, was meant to encourage a feeling of closeness to God as their minds focused on giving thanks, atoning for past sins, and giving alms to the needy.

However, Ramadan had its rewards. To stand in prayer on *Lailat ul Qadr*, the actual night that the Qur'an was given to Muhammad by Allah, was said to be better than a thousand months of worship. And acts of charity and kindness would be rewarded on Earth and in Paradise.

Miriam had learned her love for Ramadan from her father, who looked forward to the month like a child waiting for a sweet after dinner. To him, Ramadan was more than the holiest month in Islam; it was the month when Muslims sought *tawhid*, unification with other Muslims, a coming together of their community.

"When Ramadan comes, the gates of Paradise are opened and the gates of Hell are closed, and the devils are put in chains," her father had reminded her that afternoon before he left for the mosque. "Therefore it is easier to do good in this month because the devils are chained in Hell and can't tempt believers."

"But what about Muslims who behave badly during Ramadan?" she'd asked.

"Any evil that men do during Ramadan comes from within; they cannot blame it on Satan or his demons."

This Ramadan, however, had not been a happy one. He would be leaving on the bus that evening with her son for Chicago. "Until the danger has passed," she had said when pleading with him to leave the city.

The old man had started to cry, but she reminded him that as good Muslims they had nothing to fear. "Whatever happens here, we will meet again soon in Paradise."

He'd wiped away the tears. "Look at who is telling me to place my trust in Allah."

While her dad packed, Miriam had gone into her son's bedroom and lay down beside him for a few minutes while he napped. She listened to his heart beating and then put her face into his curly hair. He smelled like a little boy should in the summertime . . . warm and dusty with a pinch of bitter sweat and sweet Good Humor ice cream.

She kissed Abdullah's face until he woke up. "Be a good boy, remember your prayers, read the Qur'an every day, and give praise to Allah," she whispered. "Now get up . . . You and grandfather Mahmoud are going on an exciting trip!"

When her father arrived back at the apartment, they'd said their goodbyes and she left for the mosque. As she glanced up again at the moon, she became aware of the presence beside her, as well as the scent of roses. "Aalimah," she said with a smile.

"*Salaam*, my child," Hazrat Fatemeh Masumeh greeted her, but with a tinge of sadness in her voice that sent a chill up Miriam's spine.

"What is it, Hazrat? What have you come to tell me?"

"Nothing you do not already know." The rustling of the saint's robes sounded like the leaves in the trees, stirred by a gentle breeze. "You will soon be tested . . . your courage and your faith. So I came to be with you and to bring you peace. . . . *Salaam*, my child, *salaam*."

Miriam bowed her head and her pace slowed as hot tears sprang to her eyes. She thought about the life she had wanted to lead—attending college, caring for her father into his old age, raising her son, and bouncing grandchildren on her knees. "My son, Abdullah, he is so young."

"He will be safe with your father and sister. But you are being called upon by Allah to protect the faith. The message of the Prophet is being corrupted by evil men who bring dishonor and a black stain on Islam. Will you answer this call?"

"*Inshallah*."

"Yes, child, as God wills," Masumeh agreed. "But don't be afraid. I will be with you always, and when the darkness comes, I will be there to take you by the hand and lead you to *bayt al-ridwan*, where you will sit with me among the prophets and wait for your loved ones to join us."

The two women walked the rest of the way to the mosque in silence. Those who passed saw only Miriam, though she walked as if holding the hand of someone unseen.

When Miriam reached the mosque, one of the imam's bodyguards intercepted her. "The imam wants to see you downstairs." He tried to look her in the eyes but could not hold her gaze.

"I know the way." She went ahead with the guard trailing silently behind.

When she came to a door, she looked back at the guard, a question on her face. He nodded and she entered.

It was a small room, bare except for a steel chair, to which the guard bound her wrists and ankles. "Forgive me," he said.

"I would," she said quietly, "but it is Allah from whom you must ask forgiveness."

The door opened and the woman whom Lucy had called Nadya Malovo entered. "Miriam Khalifa," the woman said.

"Here I am."

―――――――――

Before Malovo was finished, the nails had been torn from Miriam's fingers, which had been broken one at a time with pliers; her teeth had been knocked out and the socket around her right eye crushed by a hammer. She'd been burned with an iron and had her hair pulled out by the handful.

Yet Miriam experienced the pain as if from a distance. She heard herself scream, though it seemed another was using her voice. In the company of Hazrat Fatemeh Masumeh, she watched as Malovo demanded to know what Jamal had told her of any plans, and who she might have told. But she admitted to nothing more than enjoying carnal pleasures with her "lover" and witnessing a murder that she had not reported to the police.

At last, her tormentor left her in the dark, but not alone. The Aalimah knelt next to her and caressed her battered face. Then the guards came for her, pulling her to her feet and placing the hood over her head. Her injured body begged for release, but her mind knew no pain or fear as she was shoved to her knees and the hood was pulled from her head.

Miriam found herself looking up into the kind brown eyes of the man she knew as John. She saw his eyes harden and realized that he was going to fight for her. *Stop him,* she prayed to Masumeh. *Tell him that I am prepared to be martyred for my faith, but he must live to stop these people.*

―――――――――

"Who is she?" Tran demanded.

"Who?" Malovo repeated for the others. "This is the widow of the martyr Muhammad Jamal Khalifa. She has disgraced his memory by consorting with another man, an infidel she mated with in back alleys like a common whore. Her blood is forfeit and will bring Allah's blessing on our plans tomorrow."

The men murmured as Ajmaani spoke and then drew a large knife from beneath her robe. "Silence! The Sheik has approved this sacrifice."

She nodded to the cameraman to begin filming. "Tonight we slaughter the harlot wife of the martyr Muhammad Jamal Khalifa, may Allah be pleased with him, as tomorrow the martyrs of the Al-Aqsa Brigade will slaughter the enemies of Islam."

Jojola looked into the eyes of Miriam Khalifa and prepared to die. He knew by the weight of the AK-47 he held that, like the handgun, there were no bullets in the clip. Still, he thought he could kill Malovo with a blow to the head before the guards cut him down with their guns.

Then a voice entered his head, asking him to stop. A spiritual man who, in the way of his people, believed that spirits inhabited the world, he paid attention. As a child he had learned that some spirits who spoke to people were bad, but many helped the living. Sometimes they appeared as animals, or *kachina* spirits. Now, the image of a woman dressed in robes, her hair covered by a hajib, her face veiled, came to his mind.

Salaam, *John Jojola,* the woman said in a language he did not know but understood. *Miriam asks you to let her go without fighting. She is prepared for martyrdom in the hope that her one death may prevent thousands, even millions, done in the name of Allah, but not with his blessing.*

I can't do that, Jojola replied. *I won't see her butchered without a fight.*

Please, this is how it must be. She asks that you remember the lessons you taught her from chess. That sometimes one piece must be sacrificed for the good of the many. This is her last request, and she asks that you honor it so that you will live to do as you must tomorrow.

Jojola bowed his head, but then sensed Tran tensing for a fight to the death. "Do nothing," he said in Vietnamese. "This is as it should be."

Tran looked at him, his eyes angry, but after a moment he nodded.

"Is there a problem?" Malovo asked, signaling for the cameraman to stop filming.

"Jihad is not slaughtering helpless women in a basement," Tran replied.

Malovo laughed. "You? The man who sank a ferry full of helpless women and children and then shot them in the water?"

"It was an attack done in front of the world."

Malovo looked at him with scorn. "You have your reasons. I have mine." She signaled the cameraman, who pressed the button; the green light came back on.

Malovo pulled Miriam's head back, exposing her throat. She expected to see fear and waited to hear the young woman beg for her life. But instead, Miriam smiled at her.

"*La ilaha illal lah!* There is no God but God," Miriam testified calmly, looking into the dark, beautiful eyes of Hazrat Fatemeh Masumeh, "and Muhammad is the Messenger of God."

The response enraged Malovo. *No one should face such a hideous death so easily. But she'll scream when she feels my knife,* the assassin assured herself, and with a quick, violent motion drew the blade across her victim's throat, pleased to feel the hot blood spurt across her hand. But there was no scream, no desperate gurgling as the woman drowned in her blood.

Suddenly afraid, Malovo pushed Miriam forward to die. "*Allah-u-Akbar,*" she cried out, raising the bloody knife over her head. But there was no response from the others.

Miriam felt a burning sensation in her neck. *Where are you, Aalimah? I am afraid.*

Here I am, child, here I am. The scent of roses filled the air.

Hazrat! It is dark, and I am lost!

Take my hand, Miriam. There . . . can you see? It is Ramadan and the gates of Paradise are open!

Yes, yes, now I see. I am not afraid. Allah-u-Akbar . . . God is Great!

32

Nadya Malovo looked at the clock radio on the desk, which belonged to her now-former lover. Seven a.m. Another hour before most of the employees who worked in the building would arrive. Plenty of time to get done what she had to do.

She looked out the window onto the immense office complex. Comprising nine main buildings, it covered eighteen acres—about ten city blocks—and had cost a billion dollars to build. The most secure, technologically advanced structures in the world, the buildings had been designed with one purpose in mind: to draw big-money companies from Manhattan into Brooklyn.

It was considered the Fort Knox of office complexes. The entire facility could be cut off from public utilities for weeks and still be fully operational, and its designers believed it could withstand Oklahoma City–style truck bombs. After September 11, 2001, engineers had even determined that, with a certain amount of impact damage and casualties, it could hold up against a direct hit from an airliner. Those who had moved out of Manhattan and into the complex for financial or space reasons prior to 9/11 considered themselves lucky.

It was the home of Brooklyn Polytechnic University, an advanced engineering school, as well as a number of major financial institutions and businesses including Bear Stearns, JP Morgan Chase, Empire Blue Cross/Blue Shield, and the Securities Industries Information Corporation. In one of the buildings, the leaders of the financial world would gather in the event of a worldwide disaster. And in fact, on December 31, 1999, they had met there to see if the predictions of the Y2K catastrophe would come to fruition.

However, it was more than an educational and financial nexus. The building in which Malovo stood on Tuesday morning housed several of the most important nerve centers for New York City. These included the headquarters for the New York Fire Department and the New York Police Department 911 call center—every cop car dispatched in the city got the call from that building in Brooklyn.

When The Sheik had first suggested his plan, the biggest obstacle to carrying it out had been a company called Specialized Applications Integrated Corporation (SAIC). A rather benign-sounding name, Malovo thought, for a high-tech security and surveillance company so advanced that it was responsible for the security and surveillance requirements of the Department of Homeland Security, as well as a variety of other government agencies and financial giants.

It had been clear that the potential impact of The Sheik's plan was tremendous. Nothing like it had ever happened before. However, it could only be implemented if Malovo was able to figure out a way around, or through, SAIC, and that presented a huge problem.

The first issue had been solving the problem in time for The Sheik's artificial deadline of the first day of Ramadan. She had argued that the plan should go into effect when it was ready, not a date set months ahead of time for what she considered silly reasons. But The Sheik had insisted that the propaganda benefits of striking on that date were too great to pass up.

She had started by looking for weaknesses in the building's security. Dean Newbury was able to help by providing the architect's blueprints for the building, which were supposed to have been in a safe and inaccessible, as well as names and personal data on SAIC personnel who might have the security clearances she needed.

However, her attempts to breach the corporation had been fruitless. She knew that she was getting a little older and the lines in her face a bit more pronounced, but she liked to think that, given time, no man, and few women, could resist her charms. But time was not something she had a lot of, and the corporation selected its people with care, putting them through rigorous security clearances and keeping them under surveillance. They were real pros with the best technology in the spy and security business; just trying to get close to one of them might have raised suspicions and exposed the plan.

Next, Malovo looked into the building's janitorial services company, a business owned by a Russian immigrant on Atlantic Boulevard near Coney Island. After dating the owner for two weeks, she realized he didn't have the security clearances she needed, so she dropped him.

It looked like they'd have to try a direct assault. Perhaps commandeering an airliner, or a ground attack to force entry. Either one, she told Dean Newbury, was likely to end in failure. "We would need to reach the twentieth floor—up the stairwell or the elevator, all in view of security cameras, I'm sure, and then fight our way past a well-armed, well-trained security force, which would have every advantage."

"What about a missile attack from the outside?" Newbury had suggested.

She had dismissed that idea. "We'd have to get into another building just as well-protected to shoot directly across," she said. "And, of course, the target has to be destroyed at the exact right moment, or the plan will not work. No, the only way to do this is to gain access to the interior."

Malovo was just about to reconsider renewing her affair with the janitorial services owner—at least he could get her inside the building and perhaps buy her enough time to take the security forces by surprise—when Newbury provided the key to the castle. His people had discovered that although SAIC took care of security for the specific floor that she was targeting, a good, but less sophisticated firm handled security for the rest of the building.

———

Newbury's information had led her to the security manager for the day shift. Leonard "Leo" Sipowitz was a fifty-year-old ex-Marine trapped in a— as he described it to her on their first date—"passionless marriage." Newbury's source told her what bar Sipowitz liked to stop in for a drink on the way home to Yonkers and pointed him out to her as he was leaving the building. She'd wandered into the bar one day, apparently on the verge of tears, and made sure she was close to where he was sitting when she whimpered that she had a flat tire and didn't know how to fix it.

As expected, the ex-Marine was the sort to come to the rescue of a damsel in distress, especially if she was wearing a short skirt and a tight blouse. "Where are you from?" Sipowitz asked as he finished changing the tire.

"Brighton Beach," she replied, applying the accent that American men found irresistible.

Sipowitz laughed. "I meant originally."

"Oh, forgive me, my English is not so good. I am from Chechnya. You know of it?"

"Sure," he replied. "Part of the old Soviet Union. I didn't know there were such beautiful women in Chechnya."

"And I did not know that American men could be so charming," she said, blushing prettily. "Or so handsome."

Soon they were carrying on a torrid affair, meeting in hotel rooms, parks, and the back seats of cars all over the Five Boroughs. As far as Sipowitz was concerned, she was the perfect mistress. She told him that she had just gotten out of a mail-order bride marriage to an ugly older man "who beat me and made me perform unnatural acts." However, she was willing to give some of those acts a "second chance" because of her love for Sipowitz. The failed marriage had turned her off from starting anything permanent; she didn't want him to leave his wife, nor was she demanding in respect to expensive gifts. She was, indeed, perfect.

At first, he wouldn't talk much about his work. He said only that he was a "muckity-muck" with a security firm with "a lot of very important clients." She said she found his line of work very sexy. "It makes me hot," she purred and demonstrated what she meant.

That was how Sipowitz learned that "Natalie" had this thing for making love in unusual places, and that the chance of getting caught turned her on. Soon a ride in an elevator was an excuse for a quickie, supplemented by hand-jobs beneath the tablecloth at expensive restaurants. She'd even managed fellatio on the Ferris wheel at Coney Island, after which he confessed that she was the most exciting woman he'd ever met.

Of course, the very thought of his pale, hairy body, which at one time could have been "a lean mean fighting machine" but had since gone to seed, made her ill. Preferring women for sex anyway, she considered her encounters with "Leo" among her finest acting jobs as she pretended to have multiple orgasms during his rather weak performances.

Then came the night she'd been waiting for when, after letting him do one of the "unnatural acts," he told her that he loved her. It didn't mean he could leave his wife just yet, "but maybe someday, when the kids are grown, you and I can think about making a life together."

Malovo began to cry. "It is a nice dream. But how can you speak of making a life together when there are so many secrets between us still?"

"What do you mean, darling?"

"Secrets . . . like, I don't even really know what you do for a living. . . . You could be a . . . an insurance salesman," she cried, the implication being that an insurance salesman would have never been allowed to do what they had just done.

Sipowitz chuckled and ran his hand down her naked back. "I ain't no insurance salesman," he said, but it didn't stop her from burying her head in a pillow and sobbing.

Sipowitz weighed what he should do. He'd been a good Marine—fought for his country—and had been highly recruited by the firm that put him in charge of day security. They paid him more than five times what he'd made in the Marines, plus benefits and perks worth another year's salary.

However, his boss, and a square-jawed Cro-Magnon from SAIC, had emphasized when he was hired that he couldn't tell anyone except his wife where he worked. "It leaves you open to espionage," Mr. Cro-Magnon explained.

Sipowitz had followed the rules like a good Marine. Not even his parents or siblings, or any of his buddies from the Corps who dropped in from time to time, knew anything more than that he had a high-level job with a security firm. They all assumed he did secret government work and left it at that.

"You must promise to keep this a secret," he'd told the sobbing Natalie. "I'd lose my job if they knew I told you." The sobbing stopped. "You know the MetroTech buildings in Brooklyn?" Her beautiful blonde head nodded. "I work in one of those. In fact, I'm in charge of security at the most important one."

Natalie had flipped over onto her back, exposing the magnificent breasts that seemed impervious to gravity even after her nearly forty years on the planet. "That is exciting," she exclaimed, letting her hand drift to the in-side of his thigh. "Is very James Bond, no?"

"Well, I guess in a manner of speaking. Now, is that better?"

"Can I see this place?" Her hand stopped wandering.

He thought about it and then nodded. "I can probably get you a tour, say you're a possible new hire," he said. "But there will be a quick security check, my guys will run your fingerprints and . . . What is it, darling?"

At the mention of the word "fingerprints," Natalie smiled sadly and shook her head. "That is okay, my love," she said, using the "L" word for the first time. "It is not possible."

Sipowitz had pressed her to know what the problem was. "If it's the back-ground check . . . that's not much of anything," he said. "Just covers my butt if the bosses ask about you. I'd still probably get in trouble, but my guys will cover for me. They're mostly ex-Corps, too. That is, unless you're a ter-rorist or something." He'd laughed at the joke until she turned over on her stomach and started crying again.

Finally, after much pleading, Natalie confessed that she was in the country illegally. After her marriage fell apart, her mean old husband had reported her to the Immigration and Naturalization Service to get her deported. If his men ran her fingerprints, they'd learn that there was a deportation order out for her arrest; they'd have her on the next plane back to Chechnya.

"So you see, I am not to visit your place of work, my love," she sniffled. "And you should probably have nothing more to do with me. I am a bad person."

"No, no you're not." Sipowitz hugged her. "The immigration laws are all screwy." He thought for a moment. "You know what, there's another way." At his clearance level, he was allowed to bring his wife on the premises so long as he was with her at all times.

All it had taken was to steal his wife's driver's license and talk her into giving him a set of her fingerprints on a card. "They're doing background checks on all family members," he'd explained to his wife, who long ago had stopped caring about what he did for a living.

Then it had been easy to slip Natalie's photograph into his wife's license, bring her to the building, and substitute his wife's fingerprint card for Na-talie's. Of course, his crew knew that the good-looking "cougar," their term for a beautiful, "mature" woman, wasn't the boss's wife. But the guy was a bona-fide war hero who'd done his tours in the first Gulf War and Afghanistan; everyone knew his wife was a shrew. So if he was getting a little on the side, then *Semper Fi*, they weren't going to raise a ruckus.

Sipowitz was glad he had thought of the old switcheroo. Once he got Natalie into the building, she couldn't keep her hands off of him. Suddenly she wanted to "do it" everywhere—from a stall in the executive washroom of Bears Stearn to the desk of the chairman of JP Morgan early in the morning before he came to work. His crew cooperated by turning off the security cameras whenever the boss and his girl wanted to get busy in some new location.

There were a few floors, he told her, where he couldn't get her in. "Mostly just a bunch of computers anyway," he explained. "But they're kind of sensitive, so they have their own private security guys who know about that high-tech stuff." He and his crew and the other guys worked together in the sense that they'd report anything suspicious to each other, but otherwise their activities were autonomous.

Natalie's favorite place to visit during their trysts was the security firm's main office, which occupied the top floor of the thirty-story building, a location that allowed his firm to provide complete security for anyone landing on the helicopter pad. But what occupied most of his crew's time was what went on inside the building, from the top on down to the men stationed at the front desk. Natalie was fascinated by the security cameras they used to monitor the building and its environs, such as the bomb-proof underground garage. And sex in Sipowitz's office was particularly exciting.

———

Early that morning, she'd met Sipowitz at the parking lot near "the Metro," which is what he called the complex. He drove as fast as he could to the parking garage, and as fast as the elevator could move, they were on the top floor. "Um, Mrs. Sipowitz has something important she needs to share with me privately," he had said to the four guys monitoring the security cameras.

"Sure boss, no problem," one of the four said, as the others tried not to laugh. "We'll let you know if anything comes up. You do the same, eh?"

Sipowitz pulled Natalie back to his office. He closed the door and locked it. "Go ahead, yell all you want," he laughed as he started to unzip his pants. "Nobody will be able to hear you."

Ten minutes later, Malovo pulled her pants back on and looked down at the half-naked body of Leonard Sipowitz. A letter opener protruded from his left ear. She'd been on top and waited for the moment of his orgasm before shoving the blade into his brain, twisting the handle in several violent circles. She'd thought it was sexually exciting that he'd bucked so hard at first and then died in a series of convulsions. *I'll have to try that again sometime*, she thought as she looked at the clock radio. It was 7 a.m. . . . . Plenty of time to do everything that needed to be done.

Malovo opened her cell phone and dialed a number. "Where are you?" she asked. "Good. Are you prepared? Yes, *Allah-u-Akbar*. Now wait for my signal."

She pulled the gun from the shoulder-holster of her former lover. Even with her "wife's" visitor card, she had still had to pass through a metal detector. The fact that he always wore a Colt .45 to work made getting a firearm into the building that much easier.

She tucked the gun into the back of her waistband and walked into the monitoring room. The four young men watching the screens looked up, then went back to their duties. Sometimes the boss took a nap to recover from one of his little morning workouts.

Malovo wasted no time. The control center was also soundproofed, so she wasn't worried about the roar of the .45 as she shot first one, then the next, and then a third young man. The fourth she kept alive.

"Shhhhh, Billy." She pointed the gun at his head. "This is a robbery. Nothing worth losing your life about, am I not correct?"

"Yes, ma'am," Billy replied. He was the youngest and, she'd guessed correctly, the easiest to manipulate.

"Then do exactly as I say. First, clean the blood off those other monitors. I can't see a thing in them."

When Billy finished, Malovo had him handcuff himself to his desk with a telephone next to him. "If someone calls," she said, "you will answer as you would normally. Any attempt to give a warning, and I will shoot you in the balls and let you bleed to death. Your idiot boss told me the code words, so don't try anything stupid. Now be a good boy, and you will do better than your friends."

With Billy secured, Malovo flipped through the monitors to ascertain the whereabouts of the other security guards. The two at the front desk were chatting and drinking coffee; the other four on duty were making the early-morning rounds on various floors.

Satisfied that none were in problem areas, she dialed the telephone number of the man who had called earlier. "Okay, Car One, proceed." She turned to watch the monitor for the entrance to the underground garage until she saw the van turn in, and then switched to the garage camera.

The van pulled into a space and disgorged a half-dozen men armed with submachine guns and pistols. As they ran for the elevator, she checked the monitor and then spoke again into her telephone. "Fifth floor. He's in the hallway just to the right."

Malovo watched as the team burst from the elevator and took the guard by surprise. They incapacitated him with a stun gun and dragged him into the elevator.

"Second target, tenth floor."

Malovo's team captured the other patrolling security men in short order. They then transported their hostages to the nineteenth floor where, using a switch on the console, she unlocked the door into the office area. The four security guards were taken to a back office, forced to strip out of their uniforms, and executed.

Dressed in the dead men's uniforms, four members of the team took the elevator to the main floor, where they captured the two remaining guards. Two of Malovo's men remained at the front desk while the others took these guards back to the nineteenth floor to also be stripped and shot.

Except for the two on the front desk, the remaining members of the team returned to the garage. Malovo called a second number. "Car Two, proceed." She watched as the second van pulled into the garage and parked next to the first.

Another six men, including Azahari Mujahid and Abu Samar, got out of the van. Along with the first team, they now began loading dollies with C-4 explosives, which were transported along with wires and pager detonators to the nineteenth floor.

Once all of the explosives were transported, Malovo flipped on the audio switch that would allow her to broadcast to the nineteenth-floor, which housed the offices for a securities trading firm. The employees would have an unexpected and unpleasant surprise when they arrived for work.

"Congratulations, warriors of Islam," she said, winking at Billy. "You have completed Phase One. It is now 7:30, one-half hour before your next hostages will be arriving for work. You know what to do."

She picked out Mujahid, who with Samar was standing off a little to the side of the others. "Sheik Mujahid."

"Yes."

"My men will take care of any arrivals," she said. "You may proceed with your mission. *Allah-u-Akbar!*"

Malovo turned off the audio switch. "So Billy, where are you from?"

33

As the trial of Jessica Campbell resumed Tuesday morning, Dr. Louise "Niki" Nickles poked her head into the courtroom like an actor taking a peek at the audience before a performance, then stepped in. She adjusted a small pink beret on top of her Barbie-blonde hair, pushed the pink-tinted frames up on her nose, and marched to the witness stand.

Sitting down, she waved to the defendant. "Hello, Jessica," she said cheerily, as if they were old friends meeting for tea. Jessica looked up briefly but didn't return the smile as she went back to her drawing.

Lewis began by asking Nickles to brief the jury on her educational and professional background. The psychiatrist spent the next ten minutes reviewing her multiple degrees from an impressive slate of universities, the clinical trials she'd completed that had been funded through the National Institutes of Mental Health, her numerous awards, and a great many published works. At the conclusion of her speech, she smiled and nodded to the jurors as if expecting a round of applause. When none was forthcoming, she arched her eyebrows and frowned as she turned back to Lewis.

"Before we begin your analysis, Dr. Nickles," the attorney said, "you have an . . . unusual way of speaking, do you not?"

"Um, hmmm . . . yes. I have a speech impediment known as a . . . hmmm, ah . . . slackwater drawl, which causes me to sometimes . . . break my sentences into fragments at odd spots. However, it in no way affects the way my brain . . . mmm . . . functions." She looked at the jurors. "You just need to pay attention . . . hmmmm?"

"I'm sure we will. Doctor, have you had an opportunity to examine the defendant, Jessica Campbell?"

"Yes, on a number of occasions, for a total of about . . . ummm, ha . . . twenty hours."

Twenty hours at $250 an hour, Karp thought. Plus whatever time it took to think about it, discuss it, write it up, and discuss it some more. At least the taxpayers aren't footing the bill this time. And we're not paying anybody to refute her.

"And doctor, bearing in mind that another defense witness, Dr. Harry Winkler, has testified that when he saw Jessica Campbell four years ago, she was suffering from postpartum depression, are you able to confirm that diagnosis from your own examinations?"

"Actually . . . um, hmmm . . . no."

"No?" Lewis asked, looking over at the jurors as if surprised.

"No. While it is certainly true that Mrs. Campbell has . . . ah, yes . . . suffered from postpartum depression in the past, at the time of this, unfortunate occurrence, she was suffering from a much more severe illness called . . . mmm hmmm . . . postpartum psychosis."

"Postpartum psychosis?" Lewis repeated the words slowly.

"Yes, specifically, postpartum schizophrenia resulting in . . . ahem, mmm . . . delusions and a loss of touch with reality."

"I see. Now, doctor, I think most of us, when we hear the word 'schizophrenia,' think of 'split-personality'—that is, two or more 'personalities' inhabiting the same body."

Nickles rolled her eyes. "Ah yes, the television version of schizophrenia—Dr. Jekyll and Mr. Hyde, one good . . . hmmm . . . one monstrously bad."

Actually, the more proper term for the "split personality" condition was "multiple personalities," she explained. "But it has very little to do with . . . um . . . schizophrenia. In extreme cases . . . multiple personality disorder is where the individual seems to have . . . mmm . . . a different personality on different occasions. These personalities don't know about . . . each other; instead the individual . . . ah . . . acts as if they were two or more different people."

However, the sort of "split personality" that occasionally entered into part of a schizophrenia diagnosis wasn't "a case of more than one personality, each taking turns at being 'up front,' so to speak, but rather . . . mmm hmmm . . . the deterioration of the one 'original' personality into a second personality, with no going back and forth." Nickles paused. "Am I making myself . . . ah, yes, mmm . . . clear?"

Several of the jurors nodded their heads, but the others looked confused. Karp leaned over toward Kenny Katz. "This is what you think we need our own shrink for?"

"I already cried 'uncle,' what more do you want?"

Lewis, who was watching the jurors for their reaction, turned back to the psychiatrist. "So if this version of 'split or multiple personality' is only one of many components of schizophrenia, what then is schizophrenia?"

"Well, for that let us refer to the *Diagnostic and Statistical Manual of Mental Disorders*, or *DSM* for short, which . . . ummm, hmmm . . . is a handbook for *mental health professionals* listing various categories of *mental disorders* and the criteria for diagnosing them, according to the *American Psychiatric Association*, of which . . . ah, yes, umhmm . . . I was a past president."

Reciting from the *DSM*, Nickles defined schizophrenia as "a severe brain disease that . . . can make it difficult to know what is real and what is not. It can result in false perceptions and . . . hmm umm . . . expectations, in enormous difficulties in understanding reality, and in corresponding difficulties with language and expression."

"Doctor, we've already identified a variation of multiple personality disorder as one of the symptoms of schizophrenia. What are some of the others?" Lewis asked.

"Well, again referring to the *DSM*, the symptoms are quite wide ranging. They might include . . . umm mmm . . . psychotic manifestations, such as hearing voices, or assigning unusual meaning to an everyday event, or delusions, which are when a patient is convinced that . . . false personal beliefs are instead real."

"And doctor, how severe can these symptoms be?"

"Quite severe. They can totally impair . . . aha, yes . . . an individual's functioning in the world."

Lewis walked over to the defense table and stood next to Jessica. "So doctor, you testified that after more than twenty hours of examination, your diagnosis is that at the time of the . . . deaths of her children . . . Jessica Campbell suffered from postpartum psychosis, specifically postpartum schizophrenia."

"Um . . . hmm . . . that is correct."

"And how did you reach that conclusion?"

"Well, we may begin . . . with the auditory hallucinations. She heard a voice, or voices, commanding her to perform certain acts."

"A voice? Any particular voice?"

"Umm . . . yes, she believed that she was hearing the voice of God."

"The voice of God?"

"Yes, it was part of her delusions, which were also consistent with my diagnosis."

"And what was God asking her to do?"

"Commanding . . . God was commanding her to . . . ah, yes . . . 'send' her children to Him."

"Were there any other aspects to this delusional state?"

"Yes." Nickles looked at Charlie Campbell. "She believed that this was necessary to . . . mmmm hmmm . . . save their souls from Satan, as personified by her husband."

"Doctor, did this personification of Satan as Charlie Campbell have anything to do with your diagnosis?"

"Yes. This is one of those instances in which there was . . . a multiple-personality component . . . hmmm . . . of schizophrenia. I mean, here we had a well-regarded professor of political science at New York City University, active in political . . . and community activist circles, a good wife and . . . ah, yes . . . devoted mom, at least after treatment for postpartum depression following the . . . births of her children. And yet this illness got progressively worse with each birth. Her . . . mmm hmmm . . . 'original' personality began to disintegrate until . . . finally she was simply 'not herself.'"

"Not herself," Lewis repeated. "Doctor, in your opinion, when she was 'not herself,' was Jessica Campbell able to understand the nature and consequences of her actions that day?"

"No, I believe that . . . aha, yes, mmm . . . Jessica Campbell was lost in her delusions. She was now a religious zealot performing a ritual that would protect her children from evil and give them to God for safe-keeping. And while that may seem . . . um huh . . . insane and wrong to you and I, it made perfect, moral sense to her. She was doing as . . . ah, mmm, yes . . . God requested."

"Were her actions subsequent to the deaths of her children done to avoid punishment?" Lewis asked. "In other words, did she clean up the scene of the crime and hide the bodies because she knew that what she had done was wrong?"

"Not at all. She was complying with the wishes of a higher moral authority . . . God. And it's not as though she made rational choices to avoid . . . mmm . . . punishment."

"What do you mean by that?"

"Well, if she was really . . . hmmm ha . . . trying to 'get away with it,' she might have accused a stranger of breaking into the house and taking the children. Or said that she'd gone for a drive with the children and then . . . hmmm umm . . . somehow struck her head, developed amnesia and . . . ah, yes . . . couldn't remember what happened to the children. But instead, she told her husband . . . mmm hmm . . . that she'd sent the children to be with God, as if throwing it in his face. She'd thwarted his efforts to steal the souls of their children."

The psychiatrist, pretending to be Jessica Campbell, swatted at the man sitting in the pews. "Take that, Charlie Campbell! Begone, Satan!"

Jessica stopped drawing at the outburst. Lewis pointed to her. "Doctor, my client, as she sits here today, doesn't appear to be violent or dangerous. In fact, she doesn't seem to have anything wrong with her."

Nickles shrugged. "She is being treated for her mental illness. I believe . . . she has been taking quite large doses of . . . hmmm . . . lithium, as well as anti-psychotic medication."

"So is she cured?"

"No. Her mental defect is treatable so that the . . . umm, uh-huh . . . symptoms are not currently present, but she will never be 'cured' as we think of the word."

"Is she, in your medical opinion, a danger to herself and others?"

"Well, she has been through a . . . ha, yes . . . enormous trauma, and will need psychiatric counseling into the foreseeable future, as well as . . . medication to keep her stabilized. I believe that she still . . . hmmm . . . manifests some suicidal ideation and will have to be watched carefully. However, that is . . . related to the remorse she feels for what happened to her children now that she is able to understand . . . hmmm umm . . . that what she believed was real was actually delusional. But she does not represent a . . . hmmm . . . danger to others."

"The state would like to see her incarcerated," Lewis said, turning toward Karp and Katz. "Does Jessica Campbell belong in prison?"

Nickles shook her head so vehemently that she had to catch her glasses and push them back on her nose. "No, not at all. . . . That would be cruel and unusual . . . hmmm . . . As we all know, prisons have little help to . . . hmmm aha . . . offer the mentally ill. She would be at great risk for . . . mmmm mnnn . . . suicide and abuse by other prisoners. Jessica Campbell is a sick woman, not a criminal. Today she may seem fine, but in March, she had no idea what she was doing. She . . . was not responsible for her actions. And therefore, she . . . ha mmm . . . belongs in a secure hospital setting, not a . . . prison cell."

"Thank you, Dr. Nickles," Lewis said. "No further questions."

34

About the time Niki Nickles was testifying inside the Criminal Courts building at 100 Centre Street in Manhattan, Marlene arrived several blocks south with her father and the twins at the corner of Broad and Wall streets. A railing and half a dozen security guards stood between them and the entrance to the New York Stock Exchange. She approached one of the guards and gave their names. "We're supposed to meet Eric Eliaso. He's with Gotham City Bank."

The guard checked for their names on the clipboard, then used a cell phone to call Gotham City Bank's desk inside the building. "Yes, I have a Marlene Ciampi, Mariano Ciampi, and Isaac and Giancarlo Karp here for Mr. Eliaso. Thank you." He turned to Marlene. "He'll be right out. . . . As a reminder, cell phones are to be turned off and remain off in the building. No knives, pepper spray, or weapons of any kind are allowed, and you are to remain with your sponsor at all times."

As they waited for Marlene's cousin, Enrique "Eric" Eliaso, she noted the changes that had occurred since the last time she'd visited, which was well before 9/11. It started with the front of the neo-classical building. A huge American flag hung across the six massive Corinthian columns, a symbol of pride and resilience following the destruction of the World Trade Center. On the day of the attack, the building and those around it had been covered with a thick layer of gray ash. The flag said, *"You took your best shot and we're still here."* Yet there was no getting past the fact that the attack had changed the NYSE, like it had so many other "sensitive" institutions.

Prior to 9/11, the line of tourists would have stretched around the building as they waited to enter one of the most famous icons of American financial might. But the general public was no longer allowed inside to stand in the visitor's gallery above the trading floor. Now the only visitors were those with official business in the building, such as the representatives of traded companies, banks, or trading firms, or those sponsored by someone who worked there—all of whom had to pass security clearances.

Now tourists had to be content to snap their photographs from across Broad Street, which had been closed on that block to all traffic. Large cement flower planters and newly planted trees barricaded access to vehicles. Men in dark blue windbreakers with big yellow letters on the back spelling out "CANINE TEAM" cruised through the crowd outside the perimeter with their canine friends.

Bomb dogs, Marlene thought, *like the mastiff and Presa Canario pups we train at my farm on Long Island. Wonder if any of my former 'students' are working here?*

"Marlene! What's a hot babe like you doin' in a dump like this?" She turned at the sound of her name and smiled as her cousin Eric walked up to the security rail. He'd been quite the athlete "back in the day," a suave Italian quarterback with a full head of wavy black hair and the requisite good looks. He still had the smile that had charmed many a girl in their old Queens neighborhood, but there was scalp showing beneath the oiled-black hair and the six-pack belly had succumbed to pasta and red wine.

Eric never lost his thick-as-a-brick Queens accent created by waves of immigrants, each of which added its layer to the multilingual sandwich. Nor had he graduated high school, receiving his GED instead during a stint at the not-so-well-regarded Flushing Juvenile Detention Center, though he'd since made good at the Exchange and was now a floor manager, overseeing other traders for his bank.

The two cousins embraced, then Eric turned to Mariano. "Mr. Ciampi, how very good it is to see you."

"Enrique," Mariano replied coolly. He'd never forgiven his first cousin's son for a joyriding escapade with his daughter, Marlene, in high school that ended up with both of them in the pokey. "The wonder of that boy is that he's working for a bank," he'd said on the taxi ride over. "Instead of robbing them."

Eric didn't take the brush-off too hard. He figured the old man was probably right about him. He turned his attention to the twins. "Hey, look at you two wiseguys. Man, you're already almost as tall as me. You gonna play hoops like your old man?"

The twins beamed. Although they only saw him a few times a year, they liked "Cousin Eric." He could be counted on to keep up a constant monologue on women, parties, sports, and the joys of being a man. On occasion, out of their mother's hearing, he'd talk about mob hits and gang fights "like they was in the old day . . . none of this shooting each other shit. . . . Doesn't take a man to do that. . . . It was all about your fists, maybe a roll of quarters or the occasional knife. Guns are for removing problems, not earning respect."

Eric looked around. "Speaking of His Majesty the DA, where's Butch?"

"Couldn't be here," Marlene said. "He's in trial today."

"Oh right, the nutcase who drowned her kids. Ask me, and I don't go for these baloney excuses. So what if I think Jesus wants me to off my neighbor? Wouldn't that be a nice thing. 'Hey, scumbag, I got a hangover and Jesus don't like the way you're mowing your lawn too early on a Saturday morning. KABLOOIE, you're dead!' Hope she fries. I'd have done it myself if she killed one of mine."

"You don't have any kids, Enrique."

"That you know of," he said with a wink.

As they were walking up to the entrance, Eric stopped outside the building. "Okay, first off this area is the heart of the Financial District and is rich in history." He pointed to an old building diagonally across from the NYSE. "That there is the old Federal Building where in 1789, George Washington was sworn in as the first president of the United States. Those were the days when many thought that New York would be the nation's political home, instead of just its financial capital."

On the back side of the NYSE, he said, facing Broadway, was Trinity Church. Built in 1843, it was actually the third version. "The first having burned down in the Great New York Fire of 1776 after the British routed American troops from the southern part of the island, and the second succumbing to snowstorms in the 1840s."

The beautiful Episcopalian church, with its three immense bronze doors, Gothic revival flying buttresses, stained-glass windows, and vaulted ceilings, had literally stood in the shadow of the World Trade Center towers. "Yet it remained virtually unscathed as the skyscrapers crumbled. Its pipe organ filled with so much debris from the outside that it had to be replaced, but nothing much else happened to it. After the attack, the gates to the church were sort of an impromptu memorial where visitors left small notes and tokens in memory of the lives that was lost."

And for publicity-seekers like Jessica Campbell to get on a soapbox, Marlene thought with disgust.

"Okay, guys, take a look at the pediment on the Exchange," Eric said to the twins. "That's the triangular bit below the roof with the people carved in it. The scene is called 'Integrity Protecting the Works of Man.' The big-titted gal in the center is *Integrity* with her pals *Agriculture* and *Mining* to her left, and *Science, Industry,* and *Invention* over on her right. All of them together represent the sources of America's prosperity, and them waves on the sides are meant to show that the Exchange is important from coast to coast."

Eric led them to the security entrance where he flashed his security badge, which got them into the barricaded area. As they walked to the entrance of the Exchange, Marlene noted the new security measures outside and inside the building.

"Yeah, and it's too bad," her cousin replied. "We used to get a lot of visitors, which made it more exciting. Man, we'd get some high-class broads running around, wanting you to show them the 'real' Exchange." He sighed theatrically. "But 9/11 screwed that up. And those flower boxes you see all around the front? They ain't your mom's planters. No, sir, that's cement reinforced with heavy-duty steel bars, and the whole structure goes down eight feet below the street level. You couldn't go through one of them with a Sherman tank."

Inside the doors of the Exchange, the little entourage was required to pass through a metal detector and have their belongings X-rayed. They signed into the "guest book," and then stood on little taped marks on the floor to have their photographs taken for visitor cards.

As they gathered their belongings on the other end of the X-ray conveyor belt, Marlene watched as several police officers walked right through the metal detectors without bothering to remove their guns or other equipment.

They, of course, set off the alarms, which were ignored by the bored NYSE security guards.

Eric caught his cousin's look and chuckled. "Funny, ain't it?" he said under his breath as he led them to a door and down two flights of stairs. "All this big show of security, but then those guys just walk in, guns and all."

"So security isn't as tight as it seems?" Marlene noted.

"It depends. If you're some schmoe like me in a suit, you couldn't get past the front there with a bobby pin," he replied. "But there's two ways of getting in here without nobody sayin' nothin'. One is if you're a *dona bella* with a lot of cleavage showing, then them guys working security ain't lookin' at nuttin' but your bazoombas. You could walk in here with a flamethrower, as long as you got tits. The other way you just saw. If you're in an NYPD uniform, you can waltz right in with guns and whatever. And while it might look like there's a lot of cops patrolling around here, what most visitors don't know is that a lot of these guys aren't assigned to the stock exchange, they're just here for the free lunch."

"The free lunch?"

"Yeah, literally. The big-shots that run the Exchange think that having all these cops around makes it look like there's a ton of security; so they let New York's finest know that they're welcome to free lunch in the cafeteria. They don't even have to be from the local precinct. Hell, there's guys coming over on the Staten Island Ferry or taking the subway from Uptown. You'll see when we get to the cafeteria, it can look like the Policeman's Ball in there from 11 to 2 or later sometimes. Guess the criminals in this city take the noon hours off."

Marlene's cousin proved to be a jovial and informative guide, though some of his "insider" knowledge bordered on the pornographic. He started their tour in the farthest reaches of the basement, beginning with a large, otherwise non-descript room for office supplies—boxes and boxes of paper, notepads, pens, and whatever else the stock market required. Her cousin pointed out a couple of nooks and crannies out of the way of someone coming in the room just for supplies.

"Back in the day, guys would come in here to sleep one off after checking in upstairs," Eric said, then added with a wink at Mariano and the boys, "or he might bring a girl in here for a little of the old badda-boom badda-bing. You dig?"

As the "men" in the group laughed, Eric shook his head sadly. "But that was before all the new security. Now they got cameras everywhere," he said, nodding to one watching them from above the door sill.

Marlene pointed to a small grated door in the shadows toward the back of the room. It looked old and rusted. "Where's that go?" she asked.

Eric shrugged. "Not sure. I heard that it's an old coal tunnel for the original building that was here before they tore it down in 1901. In the old days, they used to have kids push wheelbarrows full of coal for the furnaces in the basements of a lot of the old buildings. Lots of Manhattan from Midtown on down is apparently honeycombed with these tunnels—some of which have been walled off, but others still open into the basement. I heard that when they built the Exchange, they kept some of the foundation and these basement rooms because they would have been too tough to remove."

Seeing that he had the full attention of the curious twins, Eric raised his eyebrows mysteriously and added, "Legend has it that the tunnel leads across the street to the crypts beneath Trinity Church." He leaned closer and looked around as if for prying eyes and ears, then whispered, "I heard that a few years ago, one of the floor managers came down here with his little doxie. They was lookin' for a little privacy, you know what I mean, and decided to try out the tunnel. Well, that's the last anybody ever heard from them."

"Is that true?" Giancarlo asked.

"No," Marlene replied.

"I don't know," Eric said. "But I hear that if you ask the right people over at Trinity, they'll tell you that about that same time, they heard screaming coming from down below the church. But when they got up the nerve to go look down in them crypts, they didn't find nothin' . . . except . . ." He paused, then moved swiftly to the little coal-tunnel door and paused as if listening. "Sorry, thought I heard somethin', probably just rats . . . mighty big rats though."

"Except what?" Zak demanded. "They didn't find nothin' . . ."

"They didn't find anything," his twin corrected.

"Screw you," Zak said, flipping off his brother before their mother could slap his hand. "So what did they not find? I mean, 'except' what? Dammit, Giancarlo, now you got me all confused!"

"That doesn't take much."

Eric looked through the grate of the door into the dark tunnel beyond. "They didn't find *anything*, except a sticky note left on one of the crypts."

"What'd it say?" asked Zak.

"It said 'Beware of the Coal Tunnel Ghost!'"

"Cool," the twins exclaimed. "Can we go in?"

"Not on your life," Marlene laughed. "Eric, you always did know how to spin a yarn."

They next arrived outside a glassed-in room that held row after row of tall black boxes with lines of blinking lights and digital readouts. A single table with a computer monitor and keyboard faced them.

"This is the brains of the stock exchange . . . at least when I'm not around. Ha ha," Eric joked. "This is the mainframe computer where every single transaction—no matter how big or small—is instantly recorded. And not just for the New York Stock Exchange. It keeps track of other exchanges all over the world. If somebody buys or sells a stock in Tokyo or Sydney, this baby knows as fast as they do it. And I mean that's millions and millions of little pieces of information every day."

"What happens if the computer crashes?" Giancarlo asked.

"Why, the end of the world as we know it, sport," Eric replied seriously, then leaned close to whisper again. "Now, this is top top secret; nobody's supposed to know this stuff—or at least they aren't very public with it—but there's a backup computer. It records everything this one does. Blow the shit out of this building and it ain't a good thing—don't get me wrong, there's a lot of money in these computers and the rest of the stuff—but all those transactions are still being recorded on the backup."

"Still, it seems like awfully important equipment to leave in a glass room," Marlene noted.

"Yeah, so it would seem," Eric replied. "But looks are deceiving. One of the security guys here told me that 'glass' is an inch thick, and made of multi-layered polycarbonate laminate. It can take the best shot from a high-powered rifle without a dent. He told me that it would even take a pretty good bomb to get through that stuff. That's a special door, too. Titanium frame and lock. No one gets in without a special code—mostly only the techies who take care of the brains. The room is kept at a constant temperature and humidity, dust-free too. That computer's got a nicer apartment than I do."

Eric led the group past the cafeteria, to the twins' disappointment. "Don't worry, we'll come back for lunch," he said. "They make a mean Hero Sandwich, and the brownies are to die for."

Back upstairs, he led them around the hardwood floor of the main trading area. "When they decided to replace the old exchange in 1901 and build this one here, the board of directors held a competition between the eight best architects in the city to see who could come up with the best design. The rules were simple: The trading floor needed to have a lot of space, a lot of light—that's a thirty-square-foot skylight in the ceiling—and be convenient and comfortable for transacting business. A guy named George B. Post won, and this is the result."

He continued the tour with obvious pride. "This building opened in 1903 and right away was recognized as one of the most magnificent structures in the entire country. The main trading room where we're standing is 109 feet by 140 feet, and those marble walls are 72 feet tall up to the ceiling."

"Wow, you really know your stuff," Marlene said.

"I used to date one of the tour guides when they let the public in here. She used to recite that stuff when we were . . ."

"Too much information," Marlene interjected.

Eric laughed and proceeded to lead them around the tall, vaguely figure-eight-shaped trading stations, talking and joking with many of the men and women who sat watching monitors as their fingers typed. "These guys are placing orders to buy and sell different stocks," he explained. "Some of them are general traders; they deal with whatever looks hot. Others specialize, like in oil futures or, say, airline stock. Most of them work for big banks and trading firms only doing really large transactions, like a million dollars or more. You used to have to buy a seat on the Exchange. Up to a few years ago, they were pretty pricey—the most expensive went for a little more than four million dollars."

Zak whistled. "Just to sit in front of those monitors?"

"Just to sit in front of those monitors and hopefully make a buttload of cash," Eric nodded.

"What's with all the people wearing the same color coats?" Zak asked. "I see blue, green, red."

"You mean like mine," Eric said, tugging on the blue jacket with Gotham City Bank stenciled on the back. "They identify who you work for and whether you belong here. They've been around since before 9/11, but now the security guys actually pay attention."

"What about the folks running around in the red hats?" Mariano asked.

"Those are people with companies that are being listed on the NYSE for the first time. They're here for a tour and the Opening Bell. It used to be a really big day for a company, and it still is to a degree, just not quite like it used to be."

Eric looked at his watch. "It's almost time for the Opening Bell now, and you guys will want to be there for that. Some bigshot Arab is ringing today."

In the gallery, Eric pointed to a small dais above the main trading floor. "Look, they're getting ready to ring the bell, which starts the trading day," he said. "The first bell was a Chinese gong; now they're brass bells."

The little group saw that a group of people had appeared on the dais. Several of them wore traditional Arab headdresses. There were also a few familiar faces in the crowd.

"Hey look, there's Lucy," Zak exclaimed.

"And V. T.," Giancarlo added.

Marlene frowned. *Where's Jaxon?*

Butch had called and told her about Jaxon's message that Lucy couldn't visit the loft for security reasons, so she hadn't expected her to show up in Queens. When the twins and her dad were otherwise occupied, they'd had a long talk about what she was doing, especially the meeting at the Bowery Mission and the Brooklyn dockyard.

"Just you and the twins stay out of the subway on Tuesday, and definitely don't go near Grand Central Terminal," Lucy had concluded. "I know it's selfish because I can't tell everybody, but I don't want to lose my family."

Lucy hadn't said anything about visiting the stock exchange, so this was a surprise. Especially because Jaxon was nowhere in sight. Maybe in another part of the building? . . . *Or where the danger is.*

"Can we go see Lucy?" Zak asked.

"No, she's working as a translator for some Saudi prince."

"That's some Saudi prince, all right," Eric said. "He's one of the richest men in the world. Just look at everybody pissing on themselves to get his attention."

Prince Esra bin Afraan al-Saud waved to a small crowd of photographers and reporters gathered on the floor below with an adoring crowd of stock-brokers. Next to him stood the president of the Exchange, who was beam-ing and waving as well. Some of the traders on the floor started applauding, and a few actually cheered.

"I take it this is a big deal," Marlene said.

"Yeah, if you're a whore," Eric scowled. "The guy has one of the biggest hedge-fund companies in the world, worth hundreds of millions of dollars, make that billions—he certainly controls that much anyway. It's a big deal when his people place an order. We're talking about millions of dollars' worth of stock in a single transaction, which means a hefty commission for the trader who places the order and for his bank. Ever since the prince got to New York, a lot of those guys down there have been bending over and taking it up the . . ."

"Uh, children present," Marlene interrupted, nodding at the twins.

"Oh, like we haven't heard that word before," Giancarlo laughed.

"Or what it means for someone to take it up the old . . ."

"ZAK! That's enough," Marlene exclaimed, shooting her cousin a dirty look. "Thank you very much for that imagery, Eric, but I believe we get your point. Prince Esra is worth a lot of money to a lot of people. So how come you're not down there groveling with the others?"

"I have my pride. Believe me, my bank has been brown-nosing with the best of them, though we're not one of the big players. But I'd rather deal with clients I know and trust, and who trust me. This business, as long as human beings are involved in the trades, is still based on that trust, and it's how I prefer to do business. Most of the people who work here at the Ex-change, I'd trust with my life, or at least the car keys to my BMW. We get the occasional joker who will stab you in the back—sell something out from under you after you've made a deal—some of them even make a good living. But nobody trusts them, and sooner or later they burn enough bridges and can't do any deals. By the same token, I don't trust these oil Arabs. They don't love us none, even the ones who pretend they do. Their granddaddies found black gold, and now they've got all this money and power, but they'd still like to stick it to us."

"You know the same sort of things have been said about Italians," Marlene pointed out. "We're all a bunch of gangsters and thieves. Dirty, illiterate WOPs . . . without papers. Can't trust us."

"Hey, don't I know it. We both have parents who came over on a boat and put up with that shit. But their whole goal was to assimilate as quickly as possible . . . to become Americans. Your dad and my dad, their first allegiance was to this country, not the Catholic Church. They dealt with a lot of prejudice, and some of them did become gangsters, but you didn't have home-grown Italian terrorists trying to take down the country on behalf of the Holy Ghost."

"That's a small percentage of them, Eric," Marlene said.

"Yeah, I know. But it's not just the Islamic terrorism thing. I'll admit that 9/11 created a lot of hard feelings toward anybody whose first allegiance is to Allah. But more than that . . . I think this guy, and other guys like him who run hedge funds, which are unregulated and unsupervised, are a real danger to the economy. And I'm talking the world economy. I don't like the idea of any one person, or company, having that much control over billions of dollars of stock. If something happened—say he got overextended or something bad happened to the company—it could cause a worldwide catastrophe."

"Like when the market crashed in 1929? I think it was called Black Friday," Giancarlo said.

"Yeah, you know about that, huh?" Eric replied.

"A little."

"Well, let me fill you in some more. In 1929, the U.S. economy was going gangbusters. World War I was over, the United States had emerged as a world power, and the stock market was through the roof. Everybody was investing in stocks. Banks were putting their entire portfolios into stocks, not hedging by keeping some assets spread around. Even regular folks were taking their entire retirement nesteggs and savings and putting them into stocks. A few economists kept warning that the market was going to correct itself, and it could be bad, but nobody wanted to listen. It was going to last forever."

Eric looked over at the dais where the prince was getting ready to ring the Opening Bell. He shook his head. "Then in late October 1929, some big companies started selling off their stock, taking their profit out of the market. Stock prices started to fall. Other people saw that and figured somethin' was up—they remembered what them economists were saying—and they started selling off, too. Suddenly, we got a panic on our hands. Everybody's selling and the market is crashing. All that stock was now worth pennies on the dollar; all those cash assets were gone like somebody put a torch to 'em. In one day, the United States lost more capital than it spent in all of World War I. Then banks collapsed; everything they had—all their customers' money—was gone. Ma and Pa Kettle ran down to their bank and demanded their money, even if it was run by smarter people who had diversified and weren't in serious trouble. So even the smart banks were wiped out. All those people—from bank presidents in New York to wheat farmers in Kansas—were left with nothin'. People was destitute. They lost their homes and businesses. Companies that had invested in the market closed; same with companies whose stock was now worthless. People were thrown out of work and couldn't pay their bills, closing more stores and companies. Guys was throwing themselves out of buildings, or shooting themselves."

"Wow, that really happened?" Zak asked.

"Damn straight it did. The problem is that nobody thinks something like that could happen again. They think they got all these protections and that people are smarter about putting all their eggs in one basket. But it could happen. This time, however, the danger is with these huge hedge funds that control so much of the capital invested in the market. In fact, there's already been one case where one went under and the U.S. government had to ask the World Bank to bail out the market, or there would have been a huge disaster. And that wasn't as bad as it could have been, or as bad as it would be now. We're talking about a lot more money, and a much bigger ripple effect on the world economy than happened on Black Friday."

"How serious could it be?" Giancarlo asked.

"Well, the market is all about consumer confidence. A stock has value only if people believe it does. If the market goes down, especially if it goes down suddenly and a lot of people start to panic, it's October 1929 all over again, times a million. And you know what? What happens to the U.S. economy affects the economies of countries all over the world. There'd be global panic—I'm talkin' riots in the streets, famine, unemployment, and even war."

ROBERT K. TANENBAUM

"And the prince could cause all that?" Marlene asked.

Eric shrugged. "What if he dies and the company gets torn apart by infighting or is mismanaged? Or the market takes a sudden downturn, devaluing a lot of the stock he has in the hedge fund, and he doesn't have the money to cover his transactions? Or maybe, something happens and he decides to sell what he has as fast as he can, and because he controls so much, it causes that panic we're all worried about?"

"Aren't there any safeguards?" Marlene asked.

"Sort of," Eric acknowledged. "Partly as a result of that other hedge fund running into trouble, and then 9/11, they put a supposedly fail-safe plan in place. It's called 'circuit breakers,' which operate like when an electronic device overloads and shuts down to prevent a fire. In the event of a sudden, drastic market decline, these circuit breakers shut down trading for certain periods of time."

"How do they know when to shut down?" Giancarlo asked.

"It's measured as a sudden decrease in the Dow Jones Industrial Average. There are three circuit-breaker thresholds—10 percent, 20 percent, and 30 percent. At 10 percent, the computer shuts the market down for an hour to see if that stabilizes things, and gives people a chance to stop panicking. But if necessary, they can shut it down for a day or more."

"Whew," Marlene said. "The way you were talking there for a moment I thought we were talking about the end of the world. Isn't that how you put it? Glad to know about those circuit breakers."

"Yeah? You really trust technology that much?" Eric gestured at the trading floor. "Just remember what I said about the loss of the human touch. It's a house of cards down there, Marlene."

As he said it, Prince Esra bin Afraan al-Saud rang the Opening Bell to cheers and laughter and high-fives all around. "It's a frickin' house of cards."

35

"Mr. Karp, are you prepared to cross-examine this witness?" Dermondy asked, having just called the court back in session following the morning break.

"I am, Your Honor," Karp said, standing but remaining at the table as if to say *this will be short and sweet.*

"Doctor, do you understand the law in regard to an insanity defense?"

"I have . . . umm . . . testified in more than . . ."

"That's not what I asked," Karp interrupted. "I asked if you understood the law."

Nickles tilted her head to the side and blinked. "Yes," she replied curtly. "In order to be found criminally . . . aah, umm . . . responsible, the defendant must have been aware of the nature . . . and . . . consequences of his or her actions, and whether . . . hmmm unnn . . . those actions were wrong."

"In other words, did the defendant know what she was doing and that she shouldn't do it."

"That's how the law reads . . . though, perhaps . . . ummm hmmm . . . there is room for revision."

"Well, we'll leave that for some other time, unless you want to instruct us on how the law should read and, perhaps, any others you don't care for."

The psychiatrist's mouth opened in surprise as Lewis jumped to her feet. "I object," said the attorney.

"So do . . . ummm . . . I," Nickles protested, pushing her glasses back up her nose.

"Counsel is being unnecessarily aggressive with the witness," Lewis continued, "for the sole purpose of casting her in a bad light with the jury!"

Dermondy looked at Karp. "How do you respond to that?"

"By apologizing, Your Honor. I'll try to be a kinder, gentler DA."

"I'd appreciate . . . mmm nnnh . . . that," Nickles sniffed.

Karp's smile disappeared. "Doctor, you're aware of the evidence that has been presented in this case?"

"I believe I've read . . . umm hmmm . . . just about everything in the defense files. Which I believe should include everything."

"Then you are aware that three days before the murders, Jessica Campbell drove her Volvo station wagon to Newark, where she purchased a footlocker and a padlock?"

"Yes, I am aware of . . . hmmm . . . that."

"And the purpose of the footlocker was to remove and store the bodies of her three dead children?"

"I don't know if that's what she . . . uh-huh . . . bought it for, but that's what she used it for."

"She bought it three days before she murdered her children."

"The word 'murdered' is pejorative in this context, as it implies that a criminal . . . hummm nnhh . . . act took place, when I . . . believe that this trial is about whether . . . aaah hmm . . . Jessica Campbell had the state of mind to form criminal intent."

Karp glanced down and gave Katz a "this is what I meant" look. "Then let's just say she bought the footlocker three days before she held her children under water and/or stabbed them until they were dead?"

"That's correct."

"And then used it to remove and hide their bodies."

"Again, Mr. Karp, the use of the word 'hide' implies that Mrs. Campbell was consciously trying . . . hhhmm mnnh . . . to avoid detection for fear . . . aaah . . . of punishment . . . aah mmm . . . as opposed to simply 'following orders' from above."

Karp leaned forward with his knuckles on the table. "Fine. She bought the footlocker several days before she held her children under water or stabbed them until they were dead, and then used the footlocker to remove their bodies, and then to store those bodies, inside a car, submerged in a river. Correct?"

"I believe that's . . . correct."

"Doctor, in arriving at your opinion that Jessica Campbell didn't know what she was doing, did you take into account that she purchased a footlocker and not a . . . oh, I don't know . . . say a large roll of toilet paper for this purpose?"

The unexpected turn in his line of questioning woke up the spectators. Lewis, however, scowled and objected. "There's no mention of any toilet paper in the testimony. Counsel is just being facetious . . . again."

"Mr. Karp?" Dermondy asked.

Karp held his hands out to the side. "There's nothing facetious about the question, Your Honor. We're talking about the defendant's state of mind—whether she knew what she was doing and why—and this witness has testified that the defendant was delusional and out of touch with reality. Therefore, why not wrap the bodies up in toilet paper and try to dispose of them that way, instead of in a sturdy footlocker?"

The judge considered. "I'll allow it." He looked at the witness and asked, "So I believe the question was, did you take all that into account?"

"Well, yes, I knew she purchased a footlocker . . . and not a roll of toilet paper . . . and used it to . . . ummm hmmm . . . remove and store the bodies."

Karp walked over to the evidence table. "And doctor, you are aware that on that same shopping trip, the defendant left the store where she purchased the footlocker and drove 3.8 miles farther down the road to a sporting goods store where she bought a hunting knife?" He picked up the weapon. "This knife."

"Yes. That is what she did, and I'll take your word for it that that is the knife."

"Thank you for that. And she bought this knife for the purpose of killing her children?"

"That is what she used it for in one case I believe."

"You'd be correct. So then, doctor, when you arrived at your opinion about her state of mind, did you take into account the fact that she purchased a hunting knife instead of, say, a banana with which to stab her child?"

Nickles looked over to see if Lewis was going to object. When no objection was forthcoming, Nickles answered peevishly. "I guess that . . . umm, yes, hmm . . . I knew that she used a knife to stab her daughter."

"And not a banana?"

"I don't see what bananas have to do with this?"

"Only that you've testified that the defendant was so delusional she didn't know what she was doing when she murdered her children. . . . So why not use a banana? . . . Or beat them with a head of lettuce?"

The spectators and even the jurors laughed. Lewis jumped to her feet, but the judge was already on it. "Mr. Karp, I believe counsel is about to object on the grounds that you are being argumentative. I'd have to concur. So I'll sustain the objection she was going to make."

Karp bowed. "Again, I apologize. But I'd just like a yes or no answer to my question." He turned again to Nickles. "In reaching your conclusion, did you take into account that Jessica Campbell used a knife, not a banana, to stab Hillary Campbell?"

Nickles blinked twice and worked her jaw. "Yes."

"Thank you so much. And did you take into account that the defendant filled the bathtub with a deadly weapon, in this case water, and not potato chips, for the purpose of drowning her children?"

Lewis didn't waste her breath with an objection, so Nickles answered. "Yes. She filled the bathtub with water, not potato chips."

"And, doctor, did you take into account the fact that the defendant waited until her husband had left their home before she began killing her children, instead of proceeding while he was there?"

"Yes."

"Why would you suppose she waited?"

"Objection," Lewis said. "Calls for conjecture. Dr. Nickles could not possibly know what Mrs. Campbell was thinking at that moment."

Karp took a step back as if surprised. "No? Her entire testimony has been about what was going on in the defendant's mind. This is merely another question along those same lines."

"You're quite correct, Mr. Karp," Dermondy ruled. "Dr. Nickles, please answer."

Nickles was beginning to look like an animal who sensed a trap but didn't know if leaping to the left or the right would increase her chances of falling in. "I suppose she thought he might . . . um, ah, yes . . . try to stop her. But again, she was in a disassociative state and was in a sense a . . . ummm . . . spectator watching this unfold."

"I see," Karp said in a manner that meant he didn't see it at all. "But I thought that you testified that with schizophrenia, there aren't really two personalities. There is the personality that exists first, and then a sort of deterioration into a different personality?"

"That is, basically, true."

"Well, then are you saying that the 'real' Jessica Campbell—who three days earlier had purchased a footlocker and a hunting knife—that morning fixed breakfast, carried on a normal conversation, kissed her husband goodbye, and only then slid downhill into a Mr. Hyde personality and murdered her children?"

"Well, uh . . . mmm hmmm . . . actually, she was probably schizophrenic and changing before then."

"So the new personality showed up sometime earlier?"

"Well, it's a gradual thing."

"I see. And did you take into account the fact that this new personality called the nanny and told her not to come in to work that day?"

"Yes."

"And in fact, the defendant came up with a logical reason for that. She was going to take care of the kids herself?"

"Yes."

"She didn't tell the nanny, 'I'm going to send the children to God now.'"

"No."

"And would it be fair to say that she wanted the nanny to stay home because the nanny might try to stop her from killing her children?"

"Yes, that . . . would be true, too."

"And the nanny and her husband would have stopped Jessica Campbell because . . ."

Nickles felt the jaws of the trap close, but there was nothing she could do. "Because it's wrong to . . . ummm hnn . . . kill other human beings."

"So she was aware that it was wrong?"

"Well, she thought that what . . . aah hnnnh . . . she was doing was morally right. She was trying to . . . hmmm mmm . . . save their souls."

"Would you agree, doctor, that at the time she submerged her children beneath the water, she appreciated that it would cause their deaths?"

"Appreciated?"

"In the 'understood' sense of the word. Did she believe that holding her children's heads under water—and in the case of Hillary, also stabbing her repeatedly in the chest—would cause their deaths?"

"Well, no, I don't think . . . mmm nnnn . . . that's how she saw it. She was 'sending them to God,' and this was how . . . she . . . was going to do that."

"Isn't 'send them to God' just a euphemism for murder?"

"No. It is a statement of reality such . . . hmmm nnnn . . . as she saw it."

Karp picked up one of the photographs taken of Jessica Campbell's scratched and bruised forearms. He showed it again to the jurors and then to the witness.

"Doctor, taking into account that the two older children, Hillary and Chelsea, fought to stay alive to the point of scratching their mother's arms, as this photograph demonstrates, was Mrs. Campbell so out of touch that she thought that they were playing a game?"

"I don't know what she thought . . . umm, uh-huh . . . they were doing. She was just complying with God's will . . . as she understood it."

"Just 'following orders,' right?"

"Yes, essentially."

"And when she pulled the first limp body out of the bathtub, did she realize then that she'd killed her child?"

"I . . . um ha . . . would assume that she thought she'd sent the child to God."

"The child was dead."

"Yes."

"Then she held the next child under water. Same result, right?"

"Yes."

"And then a third time. Same thing."

"Yes."

"Well then, doctor, please tell us at what point Jessica Campbell failed to know and appreciate the nature and consequences of her actions. After the first child? The second? The third?"

"I don't think she appreciated the nature and consequences of her actions at any time during this episode."

Karp's hand with the photograph dropped to his side. "Doctor, when you reached your conclusion that Jessica Campbell did not know that her actions were wrong, did you take into account that she purchased the foot-locker and knife in Newark rather than Manhattan?"

"Yes, I knew that."

"Did she do that to avoid being recognized?"

"She told me that," the psychiatrist admitted. "But once again it was . . . hmmm aaah . . . so that no one would prevent her from doing God's will."

Karp looked at the jurors and wondered if they thought this was as much bullshit as he did. They were certainly taking a lot of notes, whatever that meant.

"Doctor, did you take into account when rendering your opinion on whether Jessica Campbell understood the wrongfulness of her actions that the defendant cleaned the murder scene until it was spotless, placed the bodies in a footlocker, secured it with a padlock, placed the footlocker in her car, and drove the car one hundred miles to Staatsburg? There she care-fully wedged a stick between the seat and accelerator pedal, started the car, put it in drive, and watched it plunge into the Hudson River."

"I was . . . hmm . . . aware of all that."

"But if she didn't understand that what she had done was wrong, then why did she make such an effort to remove all trace that it occurred? Why not just leave the bodies in the bathroom and explain why it was all neces-sary when her husband got home?"

"Because God told her to do it."

"Oh, so it is God who knew that pushing these children under water and stabbing them would kill them, and since God knew it was wrong, He told Jessica to hide the evidence."

"In a sense, yes."

"Well, then excuse me. Your Honor, I'd like to move for a mistrial. We have the wrong person sitting at the defense table. It's God who should be sitting over there, not Jessica Campbell."

"Objection. Your Honor, would you instruct the district attorney to save the dramatics for his closing arguments?"

"Counsel, please save your dramatics for closing arguments," the judge repeated after Lewis.

"I withdraw the question and ask God's forgiveness." Karp turned his back to Nickles. "I have nothing further for this witness."

36

After the Opening Bell ceremony, Eric introduced the twins to various people around the stock exchange. As usual, their favorite place was with the guys who had the guns and fancy equipment—this time up in the security office, where the officer sitting in front of the monitors, a short, heavy Puerto Rican woman named Angela Flores, demonstrated how they could see into every corner of the building.

"Including the supply room, Mr. Eliaso," Flores laughed. "Yes, we see you trying to get away with shit down there. . . . Oh, 'scuse my language, boys. No more putting your coat over the camera, or I'm gonna come down there and take Poloroids of your white ass up to no good."

"I have no idea what you mean."

As they left the security office, the boys nearly bowled over two NYPD officers coming up the stairs. "Whoa, whoa, where's the fire?" one of the officers said, grabbing a rail with one hand and Zak with the other to keep them both from falling.

"Sorry, so sorry," Marlene apologized. "If you'd loan me your handcuffs, I'll see to it that they're brought under control. And maybe your pepper spray, too."

The officers laughed and continued on to the security office, while Marlene and all the boys headed down to the cafeteria for lunch. As Eric had promised, the room was full of NYPD officers enjoying free food, courtesy of the NYSE.

Marlene made sure that lunch was a leisurely affair. She'd noticed that Mariano wasn't talking much. *Too many stairs*, she thought. She decided that after lunch, she'd find a place to sit with him up in the visitor's gallery and let the boys follow Eric around.

She'd had to twist her father's arm to get him to come with them that morning. "I'll just be in the way," he groused. "And I'll slow you down."

"Ah, come on, Grandpa," Zak had insisted. "It's no fun when it's just Mom."

"Gee, thanks," Marlene had complained, giving her son a wink. Zak was a great kid no matter what his teachers, the neighbors, the mothers of teen-aged girls, and his brother said about him.

"Well, lived here most of my life, and I guess that's the one place I've never been," Mariano had said. "Tell you what, I'll go if you let me buy all of you cherry cheese coffee-cake at Il Buon Pane afterward. I haven't seen Alfredo in months!"

"Moishe, Pops, Moishe Sobelman owns it now."

"I know that. Well, maybe I forgot for a moment. Gee, can't I have a senior moment without somebody making a big deal?"

"Have all you want, Pops. You earned them. And we'll take you up on the cherry cheese coffee-cake."

Most of the crowd had cleared out of the cafeteria by the time Eric looked at his watch. "Okay, I still have a few minutes before I have to go make some money. So how much do you know about the history of the stock exchange?"

Giancarlo's hand shot up. "It started in 1792 when twenty-four stock-brokers met under a buttonwood tree to come up with a way to make it easier to buy and sell stock in companies. They signed the 'Buttonwood Agreement' to only trade with each other. And the first company listed was Bank of New York."

"That's right," Eric nodded. "This all started under a tree. Even when they started working out of a building, the traders would be up on a balcony yelling back and forth, making trades with people down on the street. That evolved into the scenario you guys have all seen in the movies, with guys frantically jumping around with pieces of paper, which are actually orders to buy or sell, yelling up at guys. We still have some days like that, but they're becoming fewer and further between."

"You've hinted that the Exchange is changing, maybe downsizing?" Marlene noted. "And I know it's been a while since I've been here, but there really doesn't seem to be as much activity as in the past."

"Yeah, to tell you the truth, the New York Stock Exchange as everybody pictures it may not exist much longer. In December 2005, the Exchange went public and electronic; you don't have to buy a seat on the Exchange to trade anymore. In fact, you don't have to be here at all."

"You mean like people who buy stock on the Internet?" Zak asked.

"Well, that has a little to do with it. But really, individuals who dabble online in the stock market don't account for much in the grand scheme of things. I'm talking about guys who buy and sell millions of shares at a time. They can do it instantaneously over the computer without going through a stockbroker."

"I guess if you can do it, it makes sense," Giancarlo said.

"Yeah, maybe. You don't have to pay some guy like me a commission. But I think that it will be a real shame when stock trading loses that human factor—some guy who can work a deal and get a better price for the buyer or seller. With a computer, the price is what it is. That's kind of sad for guys like me. It might surprise you, seeing as how I'm so smart and all, but a lot of us don't have much formal education. We're Italian and Irish kids from Brooklyn and Queens who started off working for the Exchange in the summer and on school holidays. We weren't too book smart, but we had street smarts and knew how to wheel and deal, which is really what the stock market is all about. We even manage to make a decent living . . . and there's always that really big deal out there just waiting to happen, like a pot of gold at the end of the rainbow. I love it; every day is different. Sometimes the market goes crazy, up or down, and it's like being on the rollercoaster at Coney Island, only you don't know what's coming around the next bend."

Eric took a sip of his coffee. "Remember those guys you saw sitting at the trading posts, looking up at the monitors? And how there wasn't even guys at some places? It wasn't too long ago when there'd be three or four queued up at every one of those seats, waiting to get on. There'd be a lot of pushing and shoving, and even the occasional fistfight. And tell you what . . . nothing but nothing stopped the trading."

"Not even some guy croaking?" Zak asked.

"Leave it to you to find some way to throw a little death into this," Marlene said.

"Actually, Zak's right." Eric lowered his voice. "They've had guys die in here and they fixed it so that the trading didn't stop, not even for a second. In fact, I was here a few winters ago when some guy who'd been shoveling snow at his house in Yonkers came to work and dropped dead at one of the monitors. Fell right off his seat onto the floor. But did that stop anybody? Hell no, other guys were stepping over him to get to his chair. They had some security guys drag him out the front door before the cops or ambulance could get here and interrupt business."

"Oh come on, that's an urban myth," Marlene scoffed.

"No, God's truth, cross my heart, hope to die, stick a needle in my guinea eye. If the cops had found him dead on the floor, they might have taped the area off and had a big investigation. But nothing shuts down the stock exchange if they can help it . . . except maybe blowing up the World Trade Center. That did it for four days, and the country lost more than a trillion dollars in capital."

Suddenly, Mariano stood up. "I need to find the restroom," he announced.

"Need me to go with you, Pops?" Marlene asked.

"What, you going to take me into the ladies room, or something?" he replied. "I'm perfectly capable of unzipping my own pants and washing my hands, thank you very much."

"You got two choices, Mr. Ciampi," Eric said. "You can go up the stairs and you'll find one. Or you can go back in the direction we came, and you'll find one just past the computer room."

As Mariano turned to go, Marlene nodded to the twins, who got the message and jumped up. "We need to go, too," Giancarlo said.

"Well, come on, you two," Mariano said. "At least we can use the same room. The Three Amigos pissing together, right?"

"Right."

Mariano started to leave, then seemed to remember something and turned back. "Don't be getting my daughter in no more trouble, Enrique!"

"No sir, I wouldn't dream of it." When the old man was out of range, he looked at his cousin. "Think he'll ever forgive me? That was thirty years ago, for chrissake."

"Sorry, Enrique. He can't remember where he lives half the time, but he will never, ever forgive you for getting me tossed in the slammer."

———

The three black NYPD officers sipped at their coffees as they waited for the noontime crowd to filter out of the stock exchange cafeteria. Finally, it got down to a couple of traders, a half-dozen food-service employees, a couple of other cops, and the woman and the guy with the Gotham City Bank jacket who'd been with the two boys and old guy they'd seen when they entered the building that morning.

The kids and the old man had been gone a while, and the woman was apparently getting agitated because they weren't back yet. She got up and walked past them to look out the door, then came back shaking her head and shrugging her shoulders. The guy in the jacket got up, and they left the cafeteria, heading for the stairs to the upper floors.

When the last of the other customers left, except for two other officers, the first set of officers got up and walked over to the table where the others were, apparently in no hurry to get back to their beat. "How ya doin'?" said one of the seated cops, a beefy Italian-looking guy about fifty years old with salt-and-pepper hair.

"About to head out," the leader of the three replied. "Just stopped in for the free lunch."

"Yeah? I ain't seen you guys around before. What precinct you with?" asked the other seated cop, a prototypical Irish officer with red hair and a round face covered with freckles.

"The 23rd."

"Shit . . . all the way down from Harlem just for cafeteria food?" the Italian officer laughed, rolling his eyes at his partner. "At least we're only from the First—Battery Park substation."

"Hey, I got a kid in college. If it's free, I'm there," the black officer laughed. Actually, he didn't have a kid and had never been married. He

had been a sergeant in the United States Army before he'd been dishonor-
ably discharged because he'd refused to fight against other Muslims in Iraq.

The Irish cop nodded. "I'm hearing you, brother," he said. "I got two in
school and another one living in my basement, no job, eats like a horse. But
whaddya gonna do? Old lady says he stays, or I'm sleeping on the couch."

"This is the best deal going," said the Italian cop. "It ain't like the old
days when my dad was walking a beat and could count on a free meal wherever he wanted. In them days, the restaurant owners liked having cops in
their joints. Kept the riffraff and robbers out. Even in Little Italy, all the
mobbed-up guys was the first to insist that you eat and drink as much as you
wanted. They knew that none of their competitors was going to shoot the
place up with a cop on the premises."

"Hell, Geno, half of them wiseguys was your dad's cousins anyway," the
Irish cop laughed.

"Yeah, what do you know, O'Toole, ya frickin' Mick," Geno replied. "I
heard your old man had a pint in every saloon on his beat."

"Man, were them the days," O'Toole sighed.

The black cop, whose name was Kareem Mousawi, smiled. "You got that
right . . . it ain't like the old days," he replied. *Nor will it ever be again,*
Inshallah.

The Italian cop looked at his watch. "Shit, running late. Eat up O'Toole,
we got to get back." He looked up at the three black cops, who didn't seem
to be going anywhere. "I guess you boys up in the Two-Three are pretty lax
about long lunch hours, eh?"

"Now that the temperatures have cooled some, the brothers are pretty
quiet," one of the younger black cops said.

"Well, we were just heading out," Mousawi added. With that he turned
and walked out the door followed by his two companions.

They'd just reached the hallway when two large Middle Eastern–looking
men in dark suits and dark glasses appeared from the direction of the stairs.
Advance security men for Prince Esra, they exchanged nods with the police officers as they passed by.

A few seconds later, the prince and his entourage arrived from the same
direction, escorted by a stock exchange official, who was giving a running
dialogue like a guide at a theme park. "This is the cafeteria, nothing too

exciting there, and I take it we all ate enough at that lovely luncheon upstairs. Just ahead are the 'brains' of our little endeavor."

The prince was accompanied by other Middle Eastern men, as well as two white guys in suits and a white woman. They all walked on down the hall and around the corner, headed for the computer room.

Mousawi adjusted his Kevlar vest. It was uncomfortable under the tight-fitting uniform shirt. Then again, beggars can't be choosers. It was hard enough to steal three NYPD uniforms and badges—five if you counted the two guys upstairs—much less get a perfect fit.

And you've been chowing pretty well lately, Mousawi, he thought. This was the third "free lunch" he and his companions had eaten over the past two weeks. The first two had been trial runs to see if it would be as easy to walk in with their weapons as their informant had told them. The first time, he'd braced for the worst and was prepared to run if the security guards so much as sniffed in his direction. But the guards had hardly given him a second glance, and the other cops ignored them, too, except to say hi.

Now, everything seemed to be moving right on schedule. "It's time," Mousawi said to the two officers accompanying him. "With Allah's blessing, tonight we enter Paradise as martyrs." He reached inside his vest for the silencer and unholstered the 9mm, while his accomplices did the same. When they were ready, he nodded in the direction the prince had come from. "Go to the end and set up. Make sure no one gets through," he said and then turned and reentered the cafeteria.

Without hesitation he walked up to the two police officers still lingering over their coffee. The Irish cop had his back to him, but the Italian cop saw him coming, first with a smile and then a frown when he saw the gun and silencer.

"What the fuh . . . " he shouted as he went for his gun. He died instantly when the bullet entered his brain through his left eye socket.

It took the Irish cop longer to realize that something wasn't right. Even then he didn't try to reach his gun until he saw his partner's brains hit the wall behind their table. He turned just in time for a bullet to blast away his jaw, slamming his head to the table; a second bullet in his temple finished him.

Mousawi looked up and saw a young Hispanic man standing twenty feet away holding a mop. He'd stopped in mid-swipe to watch the unusual event between the police officers, and realized too late that he was in danger. He shoved his mop handle in Mousawi's direction and turned to run. A moment later, he lay dying on the floor with two bullets in his back. *¿Cómo mi esposa y cabritos sobrevivirán?* he wondered as the third bullet crashed into his head.

The Jamaican woman replenishing the fruit offerings Mousawi shot twice in the chest. The bored Puerto Rican girl at the cash register managed to scream when she saw her co-worker drop an orange and fall to the ground with bright red flowers growing on the front of her white uniform shirt. But her scream was cut short by the bullet that struck her in the throat. She sat down on a stool that had been provided for her at her register and tried futilely to keep the blood from gushing out of the wound. She shook her head no when the killer aimed his gun at her, and thought maybe she'd won a reprieve when he pulled the trigger and there was only an empty click.

No matter, Mousawi thought. *I've got more.* He ejected the empty clip, slammed in a new one, and then shot the girl between the eyes. Walking back into the kitchen, he shot a short-order cook from the Dominican Republic and then the cook's brother and first cousin, who were washing dishes.

Mousawi bolted shut the Emergency Exit door that was to "remain open during business hours," and then went back out into the cafeteria. His two comrades, Ali and Farak, were dragging in the body of a fat man in a business suit and trader's jacket that read "Bank of America" on the back. "He wanted a cup of coffee and a donut, and refused to go back upstairs," Ali explained.

They left the cafeteria and stood looking down at the long smear of blood that trailed off down the hall. "*Inshallah,*" Mousawi shrugged. "No sense worrying about it now. Take up your new posts, and from now on, don't ask questions, just shoot."

The trio walked to the intersection with another hall. The two younger men turned right and took up positions behind filing cabinets moved there earlier, so they could get the drop on anyone who came down the hall. Ali reached into one of the filing cabinets and pulled out two martyr's vests.

Mousawi turned left in the direction of the brains of the New York Stock Exchange and The Sheik. *And my destiny,* he thought.

Behind him, the younger men put on their vests and shouted, "*Allah-u-Akbar! Allah-u-Akbar!*"

"*Allah-u-Akbar!*" he yelled back. "Tonight we will feast in the garden of *bayt al-ridwan!*"

———

Marlene guessed that her dad and the twins had gone upstairs. But Eric checked the bathrooms on the floors and then the visitor's gallery for her; they were nowhere in sight.

"They must have gone back down," Eric said.

"Sorry about that. I know they're supposed to stick close by."

"Don't sweat it. They're not getting out down there. I can hang for a few more minutes, then I got to get back to work."

As they waited, Marlene asked him about something that had been bugging her about their earlier conversation. "What if the market started to crash but something happened to the computer downstairs that prevented its circuit breakers from kicking in?"

"That's another reason for the backup system. It has its own set of circuit breakers, so if the main computer didn't shut the place down, the secondary computer would."

"What if somebody blew up both computers?"

"Geez, is this what you think about all day? Blowing shit up?"

"Sometimes," Marlene shrugged. "But humor me, what if terrorists blew up both computers?"

"Nice try, Osama," Eric said. "If they blew up the backup computer, of course nothing happens. This computer keeps whirring away, and if necessary its circuit breakers kick in. But if both computers suddenly go off-line—i.e., somebody blows them both up—there's no trading. Might as well have flipped the circuit breakers. Don't get me wrong, it would be a hell of a mess to pick up the pieces, which they'd have to do by reconstructing the data from those computers—by using data from computers with other stock exchanges—and of course, closing the stock exchange during trading hours hurts financially. But in the end, they couldn't keep the circuit breakers open and crash the market by blowing up both computers."

"So where's this backup computer?" Marlene asked. "Or is that a state secret?"

"Now I'm starting to get a little suspicious. We had a guy here from the Department of Homeland Security and he said to be wary of people who ask a lot of questions about blowing shit up."

"So it's a secret," Marlene said.

"Nah. They don't talk much about it, but it's not too hush-hush if I know about it. It's at MetroTech."

Marlene's eyes narrowed. "MetroTech? The urban renewal project in Brooklyn?"

"Yeah. A lot of the heavy hitters in the financial community have moved over there, like JP Morgan and Bear Stearns. Guess they figure Manhattan has a big target painted on it. That place is supposed to be a fortress—bomb-proof, high-tech security . . . the works."

"And that's where the backup system is located?"

"Yeah, same building where they put NYPD's dispatch center, so you know security's tighter than an Irishman on St. Patrick's Day. They even got some special company working security. Specialized Applications Integrated Corporation. I hear they do a lot of top-secret anti-terrorism stuff."

"Specialized Applications Integrated Corporation?" Marlene said. "Never heard of them. . . . Then again, I've been out of the security biz for a while."

"I hear them Say-ick guys are the real thing. Bet they get paid beaucoup bucks. . . . What? What did I say?"

Marlene's face had turned white. "What did you just call them?"

"Specialized Applications Integrated Corporation? Oh, you mean the acronym . . . S-A-I-C. . . . Everybody calls them 'Sayick.' Why? What's up?"

"I'm not sure. Maybe nothing. But please, do me a favor, go to the security office and ask if they see anything out of the ordinary. You might have them give SAIC a call and say there's been a credible terrorist threat and to take precautions."

Eric smirked. "You're kidding, right?"

"No. I'm hoping I'm wrong—considering everything you've said today about what would happen if the market suddenly crashed—and I don't know how they'd pull it off. But I'm not kidding. Just do this for me."

Her cousin looked at her for a moment. "What the fuck, why not? I don't mind being the boy who cried wolf. They'll just lock me up and take away my security badge for letting you talk me into this."

"Please."

"All right, all right, I said I'm going. What are you going to do in the meantime?"

"Go find my kids, what else?"

In the bowels of the New York Stock Exchange, Prince Esra bin Afraan Al-Saud paused politely outside the glassed-in computer room as the vice president in charge of technology for the stock exchange boasted about the Cray XT4, "one of the most powerful supercomputers in the world."

"If people are the heart of the New York Stock Exchange," recited the VP from a speech he'd given a thousand times before, "this is the brain, capable of tracking millions of transactions all over the world and adjusting market values faster than you can say 'blue chip.'"

"Blue chip," said the prince and laughed at his cleverness.

"Ha ha," the VP joined in. "Anyway, we keep this baby locked up in this airtight, temperature-controlled, and, I might add, bulletproof room."

"Je veux entrer. Je veux voir cet ordinateur 'superbe.'"

The vice president in charge of technology turned to Amir Al-Sistani, who'd spoken in French. The little man had a face that appeared to have been created from different animals—the eyes of a basset hound and an eagle's nose that might have fit better on a larger head. The VP had dismissed Al-Sistani as a flunky with his store-bought suit and Yassar Arafat headgear until he was informed that the little man was the hedge-fund manager.

In other words, he was the brains behind Kingdom Investments, Inc. Several years earlier, he'd earned the market's respect by purchasing $10 billion in U.S. government bonds and then using a little-known provision in bond regulations that allowed Kingdom Investments to borrow ten times that amount from the U.S. government. Al-Sistani had then sunk that $100 billion loan into unsecured equities.

It made NYSE and other stock-market administrators nervous because of the potential for disaster if Prince Esra's company failed. Like Marlene's cousin Eric Eliaso, the experts feared a situation where too many stocks were concentrated in a single entity. But hedge funds were unregulated, nobody was watching, and nobody dared say anything that might cause the prince—or his little manager—to take all that money and put it elsewhere.

"I'm sorry," the VP apologized. "My French is a bit rusty. No *parlez-vous*, eh?" He looked over at the young woman, Marie Smith.

"He asked if he can go in," she said. "He'd like to look at the supercomputer."

The VP shook his head. "I'm afraid we don't let anybody go in there except the techies. All the climate control and such. Isn't that right, Omar?"

Everybody looked at Omar Al-Hassan, who had been introduced when they'd arrived at the stock market that morning. He was somehow or another related to Al-Sistani, distant cousins or something, and worked at the stock exchange in technical support.

"Yes, that is usually correct," Al-Hassan said, "though we have occasionally allowed special guests."

Lucy Karp translated this, which caused Al-Sistani to complain to the prince in Arabic. "I'm sure that if we were some white American or European investors there would be no problem. But I guess we're just filthy brown Muslims."

"Oh, I'm sure that's not what he's saying," Prince Esra replied in Arabic. "I'm better dressed than he is. Why do you want to go look at boxes with blinking lights, anyway? It's not like you can see anything."

"Because I'm curious about this supercomputer. Maybe we should purchase one," Al-Sistani argued. "And also because we asked and they should do what we say. . . . Who is the one controlling one hundred billion American dollars?"

"Sometimes I wonder," the prince replied with an amused smile. "You or me? Huh, my little Iraqi pest?" The prince turned to Lucy and said, in French, "My chief financial officer wants to see the pretty machines up close. Tell this tiresome bureaucrat that we insist."

Lucy translated what had been said to the vice president, leaving out "tiresome bureaucrat." There were certainly more worrisome problems than whether some little techno-junkie money manager got close to a Cray supercomputer. Her concerns were fifty blocks to the north at Grand Central Terminal with S. P. Jaxon.

———

Jaxon had picked her up at her grandfather's house the night before. She thought he'd take her back to the "security firm's" office, which included apartments for Jaxon's team. But he got a call on his cell phone as they were crossing the Williamsburg Bridge and made a detour into East River Park.

"Let's take a walk," he'd said after parking. So they'd strolled along the riverfront path for twenty minutes talking about her family.

"Uh, Uncle Espey, is there any particular reason we're here?"

"Yeah." He pointed ahead, where the path dipped closer to the water's edge. "Him."

Lucy squinted into the dark. A crescent moon makes a nice symbol, she thought, but not much illumination to see by. All she could detect were shadows. Then one of the shadows separated itself from the others. There was only one man, who seemed more part of the shadow world than the world of light. He approached them.

"Hello, David."

"Good evening, Lucy. I have something I'd like you to decipher."

"What's that?"

"A message from Azahari Mujahid's better half," the mad monk replied. He held out his hand, which seemed unnaturally white beneath the sliver of moon, and gave her a piece of paper.

Jaxon turned on a small penlight to see by. "A dollar bill?"

"There's writing on it," David Grale said. "Our friend, Edward Treacher, was watching the Al-Aqsa mosque as requested, when he saw Tran and Jojola walking the grounds. Apparently they were accompanied by guards, so there was only time for Tran to write a quick message and toss it to the Reverend Treacher in the guise of giving alms to the poor. By the way, the reverend requests that we reimburse him the dollar."

Lucy looked at the thin handwriting on the top of the bill. "It's Vietnamese," she said. "Four words in sets of two, one alone. . . . 'Two attacks' . . . 'Stream line' . . . and the word for 'question.' What's it mean?"

"That there's more than one attack coming, which we'd guessed was a possibility from Khalifa's tape," Jaxon suggested. "But what's 'stream line'? . . . Is that a part of the Metro we haven't heard of before? Something to do with Grand Central?"

"Lucy, does that have to be 'stream'?" Grale asked.

"What do you mean?"

"Can it mean something similar, like 'creek' . . . or 'brook'?"

"Well, actually it translates to 'small running water' as opposed to 'large running water,' which translates to river. Why?"

"Brook . . . line," Grale said. "I'll bet there isn't a Vietnamese word for Brooklyn, and this was as close as he could get."

"Makes sense," Jaxon said. "So one attack will be in Brookline or Brooklyn, and the other . . ."

"Is a question," Lucy answered. "He doesn't know where the other will be."

"Maybe Grand Central is still on?"

"Maybe," Jaxon said. "It makes the most sense if the prince is still the target."

"Have you ever brought that up with Prince Esra?" Grale asked.

"Yeah, he pretty much brushed it off as yet another irritating fact of life. He's sort of oblivious to anything except money and blondes. But security's going to be tight. And we're going to keep the public well back from the exhibit while he's there. . . . Certainly nobody wearing bulky clothing or carrying a backpack is getting within sniffing distance. All we can do is pray we get whoever this is before they get frustrated and just decide to explode in a crowd."

"What's next?" Grale asked.

"I'm going to talk to the NYPD chief and let him know that Brooklyn's a likely target, maybe the Metro system over there," Jaxon answered. "Maybe it's a diversion, away from the prince. He can concentrate more forces that way. Plus I'll give our friends at the Russian Embassy in Brighton Beach a call and ask them to be on standby. Are you still willing to keep watch as agreed?"

Grale nodded. "Perhaps we'll catch the larger rat."

"Perhaps you will. Which is why I'll feel better if you and your people are on guard there. I think this covers the bases as best we can."

Jaxon had not wanted Lucy to go alone to the stock exchange. But he was going to have to stay on top of the situation at Grand Central, and because of Tran's note, he needed to be available for whatever might go down across the East River. "If I'm with the prince, it might be tough for me to break away quickly or very quietly if I had to. However, maybe you should call in sick," he suggested when he dropped her off that night. "It's just going to be a lot of hand-shaking, ass-kissing, ring the bell, have lunch while a bunch of bankers squirm and grovel, then a quick tour and they're out of there."

"Which is why I can handle it," she said. "If I'm not there, maybe somebody gets suspicious; or, if I'm not there, nobody else there knows about the rest of this stuff and we might miss something I'd catch. You said yourself that security at the Exchange is tight, lots of cops around, limited access. Besides, Uncle V. T. will be there—I saw his name on the prince's list."

Jaxon had given in. Just like the vice president of technology now gave in to Al-Sistani's request. He sighed and pulled out a key that had been hanging on a chain beneath his shirt.

"Like I said, we're careful about who gets near my baby," he said to the amused looks on the faces of nearly everyone in the entourage. He placed the key in a hole on the side of the door and a small panel slid open where a doorknob might have otherwise been to reveal a number pad. Shielding the pad from the others' eyes, he punched in a code. The door into the room sprang open with a slight hiss.

The VP invited his guests to enter the room. "After you, gentlemen . . . and lady. And please, don't touch anything."

The prince entered first and stood in front of the rows of boxes with his hands clasped behind his back, and Al-Sistani took a spot beside him. The rest followed—Lucy, the vice president, V. T., and Omar Al-Hassan.

The vice president was pointing out various knobs and readouts, occasionally asking Al-Hassan a technical question, when Lucy looked back toward the hall and saw three men approaching. One was dressed in a gray janitor's jumpsuit. At first she thought he was white; however, as he drew closer she saw that he was a black man who had lost much of the pigmentation in his face. The other two were the prince's security men who'd gone ahead to secure the route. The odd thing about the trio, however, was that they were all carrying guns.

Too late, she realized what the guns meant. She dashed for the door to slam it shut. In that split second, she realized that if she succeeded, they wouldn't be able to get in and would have to give up their plot. But when the one with the white face saw what she was doing, he moved that much faster and got a foot in the door. The other two hurried up behind him and slammed their bodies against the door and into her face, knocking her to the ground.

With the intruders' guns pointed at them, the others in the room had no choice but to raise their hands, and then react with surprise when Al-Sistani joined the gunmen, who handed him a 9mm. "Amir! What is the meaning of this?" shouted Prince Esra. "Have you gone mad?"

Al-Sistani turned slowly toward the prince and aimed the gun. "In the name of Allah, I sentence you to death," Al-Sistani shouted and extended his arm in a sudden violent jerk. "BANG!"

Prince Esra fell to the ground. It took him a moment to realize he had not been shot, but he had crapped in his favorite pair of Gucci stone-washed jeans. At the same time he noticed that his chief financial officer was laughing his ass off.

Al-Sistani pulled himself together and walked to where V. T. and Lucy stood, both of them with their hands still raised. He was about to say something when a large black police officer ran up to the door of the computer room. The hostages' hopes of a sudden rescue were dashed when he addressed Al-Sistani in English.

"All praise to Allah, my men are in position," Kareem Mousawi shouted.

"And the security cameras?" Al-Sistani asked.

"There's nobody there who cares anymore."

"Very well. Continue on to the supply room at the end of the next hall; make sure there's no one hiding back there. Kill anyone you find," Al-Sistani replied. Mousawi left.

"You speak English," Lucy said.

Al-Sistani smiled. "I prefer not to," he replied. "But pretending that I don't is handy around people who are not careful with their words. Though someday, sooner than later, the entire world will speak Arabic."

"You're insane."

"Insane? Hmmm . . . maybe a little. Aren't all great men? Nevertheless, I am as Allah made me, and therefore I am perfect . . . insane or not, eh Lucy Karp? . . . Ha, yes, I know who you are."

As the Iraqi took a step toward Lucy, V. T. stepped in front of her. "There's no reason to hurt her."

Al-Sistani looked at V. T. as if the idea of hurting Lucy had never crossed his mind. "Oh, I don't intend to. That I'll leave to you." He snapped his fingers and one of his men handed him a semiautomatic handgun, which he gave to V. T. "Kill her. Your uncle insists on it."

37

Like sparrows suddenly spotting a cat, the spectator gallery twittered when Lewis called Charlie Campbell to the stand after the lunch break. As he rose from his seat, the picture of the heartbroken family man, Karp thought, *Not bad for having been ridiculed, demeaned, and referred to as Satan.*

Of course that was the deal, Karp assumed, that Lewis had offered him after her tirade on the *Off the Hook Show with Barry Queen* where she'd accused him of coercing Jessica into having another child—thereby engaging in, as the ever non–politically correct Ray Guma called it, "criminal procreativity." He had to show up in court every day and accept whatever abuse was hurled his way with an expression that said, "*I support my psycho-killer wife no matter what.*"

In exchange, Lewis had issued a press release stating that Jessica Campbell hoped her husband would stay in the race for the 8th Congressional District and that the voters would continue to support him. "*Charlie is a good man,*" according to a statement attributed to Jessica. "*He made a mistake, and now we are all paying for it. Our dear children most of all. But he has learned from this experience a valuable lesson that will serve him well in Congress, where I know he will keep his word to seek funding for research into the misunderstood and deadly mental illness postpartum depression.*" The press release concluded by stating that Jessica would need years of treatment if she was to ever leave a secure hospital setting, and that she wanted Charlie to go on with his life *as your representative in the 8th Congressional District!*"

Charlie now testified about their visit to Dr. Winkler after Jessica's suicide attempt. "That's where I first learned that she'd considered harming our second child, Chelsea, too."

"Were you warned that this could happen again?"

"Yes," Charlie admitted, grabbing a tissue to blow his nose. "Excuse me . . . this is very hard. But yes, we were told not to have any more children because the next time Jessica's postpartum depression could get worse. And that it might put her life, even the children's lives, in great danger."

"And yet you insisted on impregnating Jessica again?"

Charlie nodded.

"I'm sorry, Mr. Campbell, but you're going to have to do more than nod."

"Yes, I wanted a boy."

"Mr. Campbell, do you blame yourself for your wife's mental illness and the deaths of your children?"

"Yes. I was selfish. I didn't take Dr. Winkler's warning seriously. And now my poor children . . . and poor Jessica. I've lost them all."

He started to cry as Lewis announced that she had no more questions.

———

"Your witness, Mr. Karp," Dermondy noted.

"Actually, Your Honor, my colleague, Mr. Katz, will be handling this cross."

"Ah, I was beginning to wonder if he spoke," Dermondy said, smiling.

Kenny Katz grinned as he stood. "I believe it was Mark Twain who said, 'It is better to keep your mouth closed and let people think you are a fool than to open it and remove all doubt.'"

"Apparently, you are ready to take that chance," Dermondy said.

"I am, Your Honor."

"Then, please, the witness is yours."

"Thank you." Katz turned to the witness stand. "Mr. Campbell, you testified a couple of minutes ago about the circumstance surrounding taking your wife to see Dr. Winkler?"

"Yes."

"And that was when you first heard that she had also wanted to harm Chelsea by smothering her with a pillow?"

"Yes, it was."

"And it's true that your wife told Dr. Winkler that the reason she attempted to commit suicide was to prevent herself from harming Chelsea and/or Hillary?"

"Well, yes."

"And that's because she knew it was wrong to harm her children?"

"At that time, she knew it was wrong to harm her children, and she—rather courageously, if you ask me—tried to prevent that by attempting suicide."

"Mr. Campbell, did your wife ever tell you that she was hearing a voice telling her to harm your children?"

"No, of course not. I would have sought medical attention for her."

"Really? But I thought your testimony was that you didn't heed Dr. Winkler's warning that having more children could have dangerous consequences?"

"Yes."

"But if Jessica had told you she was hearing voices, you would have taken that seriously."

"Well, that seems, you know, crazier."

"I see. And did your wife ever treat you in a manner that indicated she believed that you were Satan or were out to steal the children's souls?"

"No. She treated me pretty much like she always had."

"Which I take it was better than she would have treated Satan," Kenny said as light laughter rippled through the gallery.

"Yes, of course." Charlie scowled; he didn't like the way this was going.

"In the weeks or days leading up to the murders of your children, was there a time when you noticed that your wife's personality had changed?"

"Well, she was a little nicer," he replied, wincing when the gallery broke into laughter again. He glanced over at Jessica, whose mouth was set in a tight line as she drew more furiously than ever.

"As a matter of fact, she cooked you a big breakfast and kissed you good-bye that same morning that she drowned the children."

"Yes, she did."

"That you didn't eat."

"Um, no, I was in a hurry."

ROBERT K. TANENBAUM

"One last question, Mr. Campbell," Katz said, his hands on his hips facing the witness stand. "Why didn't your wife invite you to participate in her plan to send the children to God?"

Charlie made a face. "I guess she didn't want me to stop her?"

"Stop her from what?"

"Stop her from sending the children to God."

"Which meant?"

"Killing them."

"Because she knew that it was wrong, just like she knew before that it was wrong to smother Chelsea?"

"I don't know," Charlie responded. "The psychiatrists say . . ."

"I'm not interested in what the psychiatrists said," Kenny interrupted. "Do you think Jessica knew it was wrong to kill all of your children, just like she knew it was wrong to smother Chelsea?"

"I guess."

Kenny turned toward the jury box. "Mr. Campbell, you testified that you feel that you're to blame for your wife's mental illness and the deaths of your children."

"Yes."

"I think every one of us in this courtroom today understands the pain you're going through, but let's put the blame where blame belongs."

"I feel that I'm partly to blame."

"Okay, fine. We'll take into consideration that you wanted a son, and let's even say you coerced or badgered your wife into getting pregnant against the doctor's orders. Did you otherwise participate in the murders of your children?"

Charlie's face went blank. "What do you mean?"

"Did you plan to kill your kids?"

"No, of course not."

"Did you go shopping with your wife for the footlocker and knife three days before the murders?"

"No, I did not."

"In fact, had you ever seen that footlocker or knife until you entered this courtroom?"

"No, I hadn't."

"Did you call the nanny and tell her not to come to work?"

"No."

"Did you make sure there were no witnesses to the murders?"

"No."

"Did you hold Chelsea and Benjamin under water in the family bathtub until they were dead?"

"No. . . . Is this really necessary?" Charlie cried out.

"I'm afraid so, for just a little while longer, Mr. Campbell. Did you hold Hillary under water, and when she fought back, did you stab her six times in the chest with a large hunting knife? Did you stab her over and over again until she was dead?"

"No, I didn't! Obviously, I didn't do those things. Jessica did!"

"Yes. Jessica did those things. And then she put the bodies in the footlocker, cleaned up the mess, put the footlocker in the car, drove to Staatsburg, and dumped them into the Hudson River. Did you participate in any one or all of those things, Mr. Campbell?"

"No . . . no I didn't."

"Then, Mr. Campbell, are you responsible for the deaths of your children?"

"I shouldn't have . . ." his voice trailed off. "No, I didn't kill our kids."

"No, you didn't, Mr. Campbell, and therefore you are not guilty of murder." Katz looked at the judge. "I have no further questions."

Climbing down from the witness stand, Charlie Campbell no longer looked like the brave man bearing up under a terrible burden. He simply looked whipped. He didn't have to see the angry set to Lewis's face to know that all deals were off. He could kiss his political career goodbye . . . which meant he would never kiss the creamy breasts and soft lips of Diane Castrano again. She liked winners in politicians and boyfriends, and now he was a loser at both.

As he approached the space between the defense and prosecution tables, Jessica stopped drawing. Anticipating the drama of the moment, the courtroom was still, so that they all heard the two words she hissed.

"Adulterer . . . Fornicator."

Campbell paused as if considering a retort. But he bit his lip and walked quickly out of the courtroom, a flock of reporters trailing after him, barking his name like hounds after a bloodied rabbit.

38

"Hey, quit shoving!"

"Screw you, Zak; I can't see a damn thing!"

"Well, neither can I, dumbass."

"Up yours."

"Yours first."

The twins felt their way along the wall of the old coal tunnel. It wasn't much more than a small mine shaft carved out of the stone of Manhattan Island, rough walled with a ceiling low enough that they had to hold a hand in front of their faces to prevent themselves from hitting their heads.

They'd grown bored with listening to their mother and Uncle Eric talking about the good old days in Queens and had been only too happy to accompany their grandfather to the restroom.

"Aren't you boys coming in?" the old man had asked at the restroom door.

"Um, no, we don't have to go anymore," Zak replied.

"What? You go in your pants?"

"No, just walking did it, I guess," Giancarlo added.

"Hmmm . . . wouldn't be because you boys are planning on checking out that old coal tunnel?" their grandfather asked, giving them "the eye."

"Maybe just a little," Zak admitted.

"Well, make sure it's a little and then skedaddle back to your mom," Mariano ordered. "And don't get dirty, or your mom will kill me."

"What about you?"

"Knowing my prostate, this could take a while," the old man said. "I'll be along when I'm able. I'll meet you back in the visitor's gallery."

"You got it!" They raced off for the supply room, almost running into a janitor who was moving a filing cabinet onto a dolly.

"Hey you kids, you ain't supposed to be down here."

The twins stopped in surprise. The janitor had something wrong with his complexion; he was a black man, but it looked like the brown had been peeled from his face.

"Sorry sir, we were sent to get some supplies," said Zak, who was quicker at subterfuge.

"Uh, yeah . . . for the stockbrokers," Giancarlo added.

The janitor looked at his watch. "Okay, but get them and then get the hell out of here. I'm supposed to be cleaning that room, and I can't have kids messing up my floor."

"Sure, no problem," Giancarlo said. "We'll be in and out in a jiff."

"In a jiff?" Zak asked as they ran off. "What kind of dorky expression is that?"

"Dad says it all the time."

"Dad's a dinosaur, or haven't you noticed?"

The boys reached the supply room and the grated door that covered the tunnel entrance. "Look, the lock's jacked up," Zak pointed out.

Someone had sawed through one side of the rusted lock that held the gate closed. And recently enough that the metal filings were still on the ground below the lock.

Zak twisted the lock. "Hey, it'll come off," he said. "I'll bet somebody was sneaking down here so they could 'do it' in the tunnel where the camera couldn't watch."

"You don't know," Giancarlo replied skeptically, but curious nonetheless. "Let's go in."

Giancarlo looked around nervously. "Maybe we should be getting back. Grandpa's probably done and we'll catch hell if he gets back before we do."

"We'll just do what we always do and say we got lost. Come on, just a little ways." He slipped the lock off and tugged on the door. It swung open.

"I don't know, Zak. We could get in a lot of trouble with the stock exchange guys. You know we're supposed to stick close to Uncle Eric. He'll get in trouble too."

"Don't be a wimp. Where's your sense of adventure?" He went inside, followed by his reluctant brother. "Cool," he said, peering into the dark. "I bet these tunnels go all over the place. We could get into all kinds of buildings."

"You mean all kinds of trouble."

Just then they heard the sound of footsteps and voices coming from the hall outside the supply room. There wasn't time to get out of the tunnel, replace the lock, and pretend to be picking up supplies. Zak grabbed the door, tugging it shut, and pulled his brother farther back into the tunnel out of the light.

Two big men in dark suits and dark sunglasses entered the supply room. They quickly looked around, and satisfied that no one else was present, they walked over to a shelf and climbed up on a small stepladder to reach several large boxes on the top shelf marked "SEC—DO NOT OPEN."

As the twins watched from the shadows, the men placed the boxes on the ground and opened them. They began pulling out submachine guns and handguns.

"Uh, oh," Zak whispered. "Something's up."

"No shit, Sherlock. We need to warn Mom!"

"How you going to do that? Walk up to those guys and say, 'I want my mommy'?"

"What should we do?"

Zak looked down the dark tunnel. "Uncle Eric said these connect to other buildings . . ."

". . . and may be blocked off."

"He said he heard this one leads to Trinity Church, and there might be a way out there. That's only about a block."

"In the dark!"

"You got a better idea?"

Giancarlo was silent for a moment. "No. Let's go, Mom needs our help."

They stumbled along in the tunnel, splashing through unseen puddles, stepping over places where the roof had partially caved in. After what was probably about ten minutes, though it seemed much longer, Zak stopped. "Is that a light?"

"I think so. Maybe it's the way into the church."

The boys moved ahead as fast as they could. Suddenly, a dark figure appeared between them and the source of the light. *"Qui est là?"*

"The Coal Tunnel Ghost!" Zak yelled.

Giancarlo screamed.

Tran scratched at the incision under his arm where the miniature sensor had been inserted by one of Jaxon's men, apparently also a doctor, while they were waiting on the *Star of Vladivostok*. According to the agent who handled the team's high-tech gear, this was the latest such device and could actually monitor his body temperature and pulse while transmitting his whereabouts to a GPS satellite.

"All the data—body functions and location—are then transmitted to our ground station and from there to my Blackberry," Jaxon told him. "We'll be able to tell where you are to within a few yards."

"Why not stick it in him instead?" Tran groused, nodding at Jojola, who sat grinning off to the side. "He's the one getting lost all the time."

"If you two get separated, we need to know where 'the caller' is building his bomb. Besides, what if they decide he's expendable and send him on some suicide mission?"

"Ah, you're just trying to make me feel better," Tran complained. He looked at the agent who was feeding some information into Jaxon's Blackberry device. "Doesn't it need a battery? I'm not going to get electrocuted, am I?"

The agent shook his head. "Nope. It's powered electromechanically through muscle movement, and there's not enough juice in it to hurt a flea."

"So you've had lots of success with this, eh?" Jojola asked.

"Well, in a manner of speaking."

Tran's eyes narrowed. "What do you mean by that?"

"There's been lots of success tracking these," Jaxon explained. "But it's all been with dogs and cats. This technology was developed to help people find lost pets."

"How appropriate," Jojola laughed. "I don't suppose there's some hand-held gizmo I could have to zap him if he misbehaves?"

"Very funny," Tran snapped. "If this doesn't work you're up shit creek, too."

"But I'll be with my buddy."

"Yeah, some buddy."

Tran had no idea if the device was working inside the MetroTech build-ing, He'd thought the presence of the panhandler outside of the mosque was a good sign. They'd been told to watch out for bums who addressed them as "fellow travelers" and if possible to give them any messages they could. But the tattered madman didn't look like any federal agent he'd ever known; he could only hope that his message would get through and that Lucy or somebody would be able to read the Vietnamese.

"Is there a problem with your arm?"

The woman's voice startled him. Over the past few hours, Nadya Mal-ovo had been watching him carefully as he placed the explosive charges to destroy the floor above them.

"No, just an itch." Tran looked over her shoulder to where Jojola was staring at the back of her head with murder in his eye. *Easy, my friend,* he thought.

The night before, after Miriam's murder, they'd had a moment alone and Tran had asked why they had not acted. "Maybe if we'd killed Malovo and some of the others, it would have disrupted the plan enough," he whispered to his friend. "It was hard to watch that girl be butchered like that and do nothing."

"Believe me, I never wanted to kill somebody so bad in my life," Jojola answered. "But . . . and I know this sounds strange to you . . . but she told me, or her spirit guide did, to let her go. It was hard, but I know she was right. This is bigger than Malovo, and if I'd killed her, we would have all died and they would have still found a way to go through with the plan. But when the time is right, I'm going to cut that bitch so bad she'll arrive in the next world still screaming."

Tran wondered how long Jojola would have to wait for his revenge. "I don't even know what I'm blowing up," he complained to Malovo. "You didn't need me. You could have trained anyone for this."

"Not someone with your experience working from 'the inside' to destroy everything above," Malovo replied. "This is a special building. If the charges are not set correctly, the blast will not accomplish what must be done. And it must be destroyed at the exact moment. Not sooner, not later. Which is why your 'pager detonator' will be perfect; your martyrdom will arrive by telephone, by your own hand when I give you the signal. Besides, isn't it true that part of the reason you are here is that you are dying and wanted to strike one last blow against the Americans?"

"Yes, of course." Tran sensed a trap. "But what's so important on the floor above that I could not have achieved a more notable martyrdom, maybe destroying an entire building and killing thousands?"

Malovo sighed. These Islamic terrorists could be so tedious. It was all about bombs and body counts and making newspaper headlines. No well-thought-out, long-range plans. *Which is why my employers and Newbury's people will eventually exterminate them like a nest of poisonous snakes—dangerous if handled incorrectly, but easy enough to separate and kill with the proper mindset.* For now, Azahari Mujahid apparently needed a pep talk.

"On the floor above us is a very important computer system," she said. "Along with another such system, which The Sheik will take care of, they are the key to destroying the American economy. What you do here today will be greater than leveling all of the buildings in New York City. If you did that, they would rebuild. This, they will never recover from."

"Mujahid" appeared satisfied with the answer. "I understand. With Allah's blessings, it will be done."

"Are you almost finished?" Malovo asked.

"Yes." He'd hoped to be able to make it look good enough to fool Malovo but sabotage the setup in some way so that it would not work when the time came. But she apparently knew enough about bombs that she noted when he "made a mistake" and improperly wired the pager into the explosives. She'd watched him even more carefully after that.

"It is finished," he said and held up a cell phone. "When I receive your call, I will dial the number for the pager."

"And achieve your martyrdom."

"Yes, the gates of Paradise have opened," Tran said, looking at Jojola. "And tonight we will dine with the Prophet."

Malovo turned to leave. She and two of her men would wait in the security office on the top floor. Then, after the bomb went off, they would descend to make sure it had accomplished its purpose.

"You two," she said, pointing to the two more dependable members of the Al-Aqsa Brigade, "are to stand guard here at the detonator. From this point on, nobody but me is to approach it. Nobody."

Malovo looked at Tran to see if he'd complain. He said nothing, however, and went to have a seat at one of the cubicles across from the detonator, placing his cell phone on the desk.

The double agent looked around at the remaining six men who would stay behind. "Remember your oaths. You have given your lives into the hands of Allah. Fail him now and spend eternity in hell. Repel anyone who tries to take your martyrdom from you. *Allah-u-Akbar!*"

"*Allah-u-Akbar!*" the young men shouted. "*Allah-u-Akbar!*"

After Malovo left, Tran spoke to Jojola in a low voice. "So the question is, do we try to take weapons and shoot it out now, or do we wait and hope for reinforcements?"

Malovo had not seen fit to give them guns. "You're here to make a bomb," she'd said. "My men will do any necessary fighting."

All they had was Jojola's knife, which he'd insisted on keeping with him. "If we go now, we probably won't win," Tran said. "Plus we have these other people to worry about." As the folks with the securities trading firm had arrived for work that morning, they had been captured, relieved of their cell phones, and escorted to a back room. One of the mujahideen had manned the reception desk, telling all callers that they were having technical difficulties with the telephone service and to try back that afternoon.

"And we'd tip off the other half of these guys that something's gone wrong with their plan," Jojola added. "I think we have to wait and hope Jaxon gets to the other guys and that somebody comes to find their lost pet."

Tran scowled at the joke. "If you weren't such a lousy chess player at a dollar a game, I wouldn't have anything to do with you."

"Ah come on, Tran. You'd miss me if I were gone."

"Well, unless we figure something out, I might find out if that's true sooner than you or I wish."

———

Anybody else might have mistaken the red stain on the floor at the bottom of the stairs as a spilled lunch. But Marlene also spotted the blood spray pattern on the wall and knew it had been caused by a high-velocity projectile passing through a body. Worried, she wondered where Lucy, the twins, and her father were.

She surmised from the bits of brain matter and bone mixed in with the gore on the wall that the victim had been shot in the head and, with a guilty sigh of relief, that the victim must have been too tall to have been one of her boys. She reached into her purse and brought out her makeup compact, which she flipped open, using the mirror to look around the corner without exposing herself. There was no one in the hallways, just a trail of blood leading to the doors of the cafeteria.

She tried to call out on her cell phone but got no reception. *Okay, Marlene, the smart thing to do is wait for building security. They had to have seen something, and hopefully, Eric remembers to tell them not to shoot the Italian dona bella who just wants to find her kids.* She looked around the corner again with the compact. *Still nobody in the hall. But forget the smart thing; there's a killer on the loose around your kids. Cavalry's just going to have to catch up.*

Marlene slipped quietly down the hall in her bare feet until she stood outside the cafeteria, where she paused to listen. The room was silent except for the hum of the lights and vending machines patiently waiting for a customer.

Entering, she saw where the body from the hall had been laid for a minute and then dragged back toward the kitchen. She followed the trail, taking a stainless steel fork off of one of the tables. *Better than nothing, and if somebody's hurt one of my kids, this fork is going to be plenty.*

Marlene's heart sank when she reached the table where the two cops had been sitting. She'd known the Italian one from her old neighborhood—a good guy with a wife and a flock of kids. She could tell by the amount of blood that his wife was now a widow. She gripped the fork harder, hoping there would be somebody to stick it into.

The farther she went toward the kitchen, the more evidence of a massacre appeared: the cops' last meal; a red pool near a mop and bucket. Then she saw the two women behind the counter. Apparently, the killer or killers had given up trying to remove all the victims. There was plenty of blood beneath the swinging doors leading into the kitchen.

Steeling herself, Marlene went in. Saying a silent Our Father, she quickly moved to where the police officers had been laid side by side. She cursed when she saw that their service weapons had been removed from their holsters, then knelt down and felt around the calf of her former neighbor.

"Thanks, Joe," she whispered when she found what she'd hoped to. Like most "old school" cops, he carried a second gun in an ankle holster that the killer had failed to notice. It was a little .380, a regrettably small-caliber gun without much knock-down power in a shootout, but it felt a lot better in her hand than a fork. A pat-down discovered the other officer's second piece, also a .380.

Marlene walked out of the kitchen and back across the cafeteria. Whoever perpetrated the massacre obviously didn't care who he shot, and she was sure he wouldn't hesitate to kill two thirteen-year-old boys, a twenty-two-year-old woman, or an old man.

As she approached the door leading out of the cafeteria, she stopped. She could see a shadow creeping toward the door and flattened herself against the wall with the gun up, ready to blow the asshole to kingdom come.

Eric Eliaso came within a finger spasm of dying at his cousin's hand. "Jesus Christ, Marlene!"

"God dammit, Eric, don't you know enough not to sneak up on people? Did you alert security?"

"Hell no. I got up there and could see down the hall and poor Angela lying on the floor with blood all around her. I ducked back just as one of those cops we passed on the stairwell shut the door. He had his gun out but he didn't see me."

Marlene grabbed the mop that was lying on the floor and used it to knock a surveillance camera off its perch. "I think we can assume that the bad guys know we're here now. Did you tell any cops on the way down?"

"No, I didn't know who to trust after what I saw. I ran down here as fast as I could to warn you."

Marlene punched in a speed-dial number on her cell phone. "How far up do you have to get before you get reception?"

"Top of the stairs."

"Okay . . . take this and when you get there, hit this number. When the guy answers, tell him it's going down now at the stock exchange and the MetroTech. Tell him I'm down here and will try to stop it. He'll know what to do. Got it?"

"Yeah, stock exchange, MetroTech, Marlene's fighting the bad guys."

"Okay, get going," she said, then held out one of the guns. "You know how to use one of these?"

Eric looked insulted. "Hey, I grew up in Queens with the Gotti family. I knew how to use one of those before I knew how to ride a bike."

"Oh yeah, I almost forgot you were never an altar boy at Our Lady of the Roses," Marlene smiled.

"Not after I got caught drinking the Communion wine," he replied with a grin. "Better go."

"Watch out for those fake cops."

"Yeah, and you watch out for . . . whoever it is you have to watch out for."

39

Linda Lewis watched Charlie Campbell hurry out of the courtroom trailed by reporters and then turned to the judge. "Your Honor, the defense rests."

Karp glanced at the clock. Almost 1:30. He wondered how Marlene and the twins were doing at the stock exchange. *Hope they're having fun.* Apparently nothing was happening with Jaxon either; he'd asked Fulton to monitor the situation, but so far there'd been no word. Of course, the prince wasn't expected at Grand Central until 3, so it could be another hour and a half before something happened, whatever it was.

And we should be out of here by then. In the meantime, I need to focus on this trial. He wondered if that was the way of the future—where the potential for terrorism had to be factored into everyday life. *Like in Israel.*

Judge Dermondy explained to the jurors that since the prosecution had no rebuttal case, the trial would now move to the closing summations. "Once again, these are the lawyers' arguments, and should not be considered as evidence. It is up to each and every one of you to decide the case based on what you heard from the witness stand and learned from the exhibits received in evidence."

Karp watched the faces of the jurors. They looked tense, and some even appeared about to cry. They weren't supposed to discuss the case, even among themselves, until the judge sent them to deliberate, and their emotions already appeared about ready to boil over. He supposed the deliberations would be heated.

At the defense table, Linda Lewis sat with her eyes closed like a fighter summoning the energy for one last round. Meanwhile, Jessica Campbell seemed to be making finishing touches on whatever she'd been drawing. As far as he knew, no one had seen what it was except for Lewis, to whom she gave the sketch pad at the end of each day's proceedings.

When he looked at Jessica, Karp didn't see an evil person. Not like he did with some of the killers he'd prosecuted, or the sociopaths he'd tangled with, like Andrew Kane. But he did see someone who'd given in to violent impulses when she knew better and needed to take responsibility for her actions. He'd seen her tears splashing onto her drawing and recognized that she probably felt remorse. But for what? Most of the murderers he'd known were sorry they'd killed, even if it was only because it had gotten them into trouble. It didn't matter . . . in murder there were no take-backs, no second chances, no restitution.

Karp's glance went back to the Guppersteins sitting behind their daughter. He locked eyes with Ben Gupperstein; there didn't seem to be any recrimination in the other man's gaze, just profound sadness. His wife, who'd returned to her seat for the defense case, sat next to him with her head lying on his chest as if listening to his heartbeat.

Charlie had not returned. *The press is probably still picking at his bones,* Karp thought, turning around in his seat to face the back when he heard the courtroom door open. He smiled when he saw his guest and rose to get Moishe Sobelman's attention, pointing to the seat that he'd reserved for him in the first row behind the prosecution table in the gallery.

Sobelman waved and hurried to the proffered seat. Other spectators craned to see the little man who was getting such special attention from the district attorney. Was it Karp's dad? Maybe a surprise witness for the prosecution who was going to jump up and solve everything like in a Perry Mason movie?

"Sorry I was late," whispered Sobelman. "I had something to drop off."

"Not a problem. Glad you could make it."

"I wouldn't miss it for the world. . . . Justice needs witnesses."

"We're just about to hear the defense closing arguments."

"Ahhh, she is going to tell us what she wants the jury to believe."

"Yes, and then I'm going to tell the jury what's right."

"Miss Lewis, are you prepared to give your summation?"

The attorney rose, straightened her suit coat, and then placed a hand on Jessica's shoulder. "I am, your honor."

"Then proceed."

Lewis walked out in front of the jury box. She looked up at the ceiling as if asking for divine inspiration and then back at the jurors.

"Ladies and gentlemen of the jury, this is a case about what Jessica Campbell believed. Maybe not what was reality, or would make sense to you and me, but what made sense in her sick, delusional mind. Please remember that.

"On that fateful March morning, Jessica Campbell rose from her bed determined to complete an unpleasant task that she *believed* God had given her. She *believed* that by doing so, she would be saving their souls from Satan. So she cooked breakfast for her husband and sent him on his way so that Charlie Campbell would not stop her from accomplishing that mission. Not because she thought that what she was doing was wrong. How could it be wrong if God said it was right? But because she *believed* that Charlie, whom she *believed* to be an evil man, would try to stop her from accomplishing God's will.

"Then, when he was gone, she called the nanny and told her not to come to work. Again, not because she *believed* that what she was doing was wrong, but because she *believed* that the nanny wouldn't understand God's plan and also might try to stop her from saving her children."

Lewis spent about twenty minutes going over the testimony of Drs. Winkler and Nickles. "Remember, Dr. Winkler diagnosed her with severe postpartum depression, but four years later, Dr. Nickles believed that her mental illness had progressed—or regressed, perhaps we should say—probably exacerbated by the birth of Benjamin, until the diagnosis was now the much more serious postpartum psychosis, specifically schizophrenia. And that the symptoms which led her to this conclusion included psychotic manifestations, such as hearing voices, and delusions. These convinced her that her false personal beliefs—that God was talking to her and telling her to 'send her children' to Him to save their souls—were real. It's important to remember here what Dr. Nickles recited from the DSM handbook, that one of the hallmarks of schizophrenia is that it makes it difficult, if not impossible, to know what is real and what is not."

Lewis paused to look back at her client, who for the first time in the trial seemed to be paying attention. "We concede that Jessica Campbell ended the lives of her children. However, we contend that she didn't see it as such. No, in her psychotic, delusional state, she believed that she was freeing their souls from their physical bodies so that they could go to heaven."

Karp stood up. "Excuse me, Your Honor. There's been no testimony that the defendant thought any such thing."

"It's argument, your honor," Lewis contended. "I am trying to explain how the defendant's mind perceived her actions."

"I'll allow it," Dermondy said. "You, of course, are free to contradict defense counsel's arguments in your summation, Mr. Karp, and the jury is reminded, once again, to decide the case solely on the evidence."

Karp was not surprised by the judge's ruling. *But it doesn't hurt to alert the jury to what Lewis is doing,* he thought.

"Thank you, Your Honor." Lewis shot Karp an icy glare before facing the jury again. "You've heard a lot made of the fact that Jessica went through some efforts to 'cover up' this tragic event—that she cleaned the bathroom until it was spotless and, of course, placed the children in the footlocker, put it in her car, and ran it all into the river. And that she then refused to say where she had left the children's bodies. The prosecution offers this as proof that she knew that what she had done was wrong and that she was trying to avoid punishment.

"But surely, if she was thinking rationally, she could have come up with a better story than 'God told me to kill the kids and hide them.' But not if you understand how she was looking at it in her delusional state of mind. And in that state of mind, she believed that if Charlie or anybody else discovered the bodies, then the deal was off—their souls would not be safe.

"I know, it all sounds . . . well, crazy . . . but that's the point. We don't have to believe that Jessica Campbell heard the real voice of God. What matters is that Jessica *believes* that she did. And is there a higher moral authority than God?"

Walking slowly past the jury box, looking each juror in the eye, Lewis said, "I need you to be very honest with yourselves when you leave here to deliberate. I need every one of you to ask yourself a question. What if you truly believed that God had asked you to do something horrible—even something as terrible as sacrificing your children—and you were convinced that ultimately it was for a good reason, such as to save their souls from eternal damnation? Be honest, if you believed that this was true, what would you do? Tell God, 'No, I won't do it'? Could you say you would deny God?"

Lewis paused to look back at Jessica, who heaved a sigh but did not look up. "Jessica Campbell was a true believer."

She approached the bench. "Your Honor, I have a small slide presentation I'd like to show the jury. These are paintings and photographs of historical relevance to mental illness."

The judge looked at Karp. "Any objection?"

"None."

As the lights in the courtroom dimmed, the first slide appeared on a screen that had dropped from the ceiling. It was a black-and-white drawing of a medieval scene in which a screaming woman was tied to a post around which men in armor were lighting fires.

"So what should be done with Jessica Campbell?" asked Lewis as she changed to the next slide, another black-and-white drawing, this time of a wild-eyed, unkempt man being chased from a town by villagers throwing rocks and brandishing pitchforks. "In ancient times, people with mental illnesses were thought to be possessed by demons, or consorting with witches. Society dealt with them by stoning them to death, or burning them at the stake. Sick, delusional people who didn't know what was real and what was not were tortured into making confessions that they were in league with the Devil, and then eviscerated in public spectacles."

The slide was replaced by a painting Karp recognized as *Courtyard with Lunatics* by Francisco de Goya. Surrounded by a dark enclosure of stone, various characters crawled or writhed on the ground or huddled in fear. The focus was on two naked men who were wrestling while a third, clothed in dark apparel, beat them with a whip.

"Even when we evolved beyond murdering the mentally ill for a condition they could not help, our answer became 'lock them up.' . . . We continued to punish them for an illness we did not understand. They were housed in such deplorable conditions, beaten and abused—that in those days, prison might have been a better choice."

Lewis's last slide was a photograph taken at a modern facility that depicted happy people participating in what appeared to be a group therapy session in a clean, well-lit room. "Obviously, we've come a long way. Today, enlightened people recognize that mental defects are like any other illness. They're not the patient's fault and in most cases can be treated . . . just like we treat someone with cancer, or a heart condition."

As the lights came back up, Lewis turned toward the prosecution table. "We all recognize when someone is so stark raving mad that they need hospitalization. But what about those people whose suffering isn't so 'out there' or tangible? Unfortunately, even today, there are people who look at mental illness as something a person could just get over 'if they really wanted to.' These people look upon the severely depressed as being self-indulgent; the paranoid are 'just being silly,' and someone with delusional beliefs could just 'snap out of it' . . . if they really wanted to. But it's not as easy as that, is it? And fortunately the law is more enlightened than those people are. The law recognizes that mental illness can render a person incapable of forming the intent to commit a crime. And that's why it's up to the state to prove beyond a reasonable doubt that the defendant understood the nature and consequences of her action and also knew it was wrong. I submit to you that in the case of Jessica Campbell, the state has done neither."

Lewis walked back behind Jessica Campbell. "The task you have ahead of you is a hard one. You will look at the photographs of those poor, dead little children, and you will think about their terrible last moments here on Earth, and you will want revenge on their killer. But how do you punish a mental illness? Because, make no mistake, that is who the killer is, not Jessica Campbell. This thing inside of her mind is responsible, not their loving mother."

Lewis stood for a moment with her head down, then patted Jessica's shoulders. "We're not asking that you allow her to go free and resume her teaching career. She is still a very ill woman who will need hospitalization for a long time, especially as she comes to terms with what she did. Ladies and gentlemen of the jury, if you want retribution for those children, understand that Jessica Campbell is going to be punished for the rest of her life.

"We just ask you to remember that we're not in the Dark Ages anymore. We don't stone mentally ill people to death, we don't burn them at the stake . . . and we don't send them to prison where they can't get any help and will only get worse. We send criminals to prison, but we send ill people to hospitals. And for that reason we ask that you find Jessica Campbell not guilty by reason of insanity."

40

"Kill her. Your uncle insists on it."

V. T. scowled. "What are you talking about?"

Amir "The Sheik" Al-Sistani waved his gun at Lucy. "Call it a test. Your place in his . . . organization . . . rests on passing it. Your uncle said to remind you of a conversation you had about difficult times requiring difficult choices, and that this is one of those times. I myself wonder why you did not expose her. Surely you knew she was your former employer's daughter?"

V. T.'s voice was firm. "I've known her since she was a child, but I thought she was using an alias because of her work for the security firm. I wasn't privy to this little event and saw no reason to identify her by her real name."

"Understandable, I guess," Al-Sistani smirked. "However, I'm afraid that you will now need to kill her to prove your loyalty. Your uncle wants to know if you can be trusted—if so, you will have money and power beyond your wildest dreams."

"And if I won't do it?"

"Why, then you fail the test, of course. And you'll die with her."

"How do I know you're telling me the truth about my uncle's wishes?"

"Ah yes, your uncle also asked me to say 'Myr shegin dy ve, bee eh.' Now, what's your choice—pass or fail?"

V. T. thought about it for a moment, then faced Lucy. "I'm sorry. I don't see the point of this, but it comes down to your life, or saving our country from itself, and I have to choose for the greater good." He raised the gun and pointed it at her head.

"Uncle V. T.!" Lucy cried out.

V. T. stopped and looked strangely at the gun. He pulled the slide back and looked inside the chamber before turning to Al-Sistani. "What's with the fucking game? The gun's empty."

Al-Sistani seemed amused. "Did you think I was going to give a loaded gun to a man I didn't trust? What if you had decided to shoot me instead? But you've passed the test for now."

"What about her?"

"Oh, well, I guess I'll just shoot her myself," Al-Sistani replied, raising his gun toward Lucy. But V. T. jumped for him and grabbed his arm, fighting to wrest the gun from the terrorist.

"Don't just stand there, you idiots!" Al-Sistani shouted to his men. One of them stepped forward and clubbed V. T. with the butt of his gun, then struck him again until he fell to the floor.

"So, the tiger shows his true stripes," Al-Sistani snarled. "Your uncle won't be pleased; he had such high hopes for you. But I'm sure it will ease the pain when he hears that I've thrown you out of my jet at 30,000 feet."

"Why are you doing this?" Lucy cried.

"Why? Two reasons. The first is personal. Yes, I know, silly to mix business and pleasure, but you see, killing you—Miss Karp—is partial revenge for the death of my brother on New Year's Eve two years ago."

Lucy frowned. "Two years ago, we stopped a plot to blow up Times Square." She paused and then understood. "Al-Sistani. Your brother was Anan Al-Sistani? He was the one who organized the plot."

"It was a brilliant plan, though perhaps less subtle than what I have in mind. However, you and your ridiculous family, as well as Agent Jaxon, interfered, and my much-loved brother, the companion of my youth, died. We were very close, you know; we were going to rule the world together."

"He planned to murder thousands," Lucy said.

"People die in wars. It is the United States that is the aggressor in Muslim countries. Yet you complain when the battle is brought home to you. You can call it terrorism. I call it an act of war. The United States wants to spread democracy, which is antithetical to Islam; I am called upon by Allah to bring about a perfect, worldwide state of Islam.

"I had rather hoped that Agent Jaxon would be here today—he was supposed to be the first to die. But after Ajmaani figured out that a young woman who spoke so many languages had to be Lucy Karp, I thought this would be better. This way, your family will grieve, as I have grieved, before I eventually catch up to them all."

Al-Sistani nodded to one of his men, who placed Lucy against a support beam. He pulled her wrists behind her and around the beam, and bound her there with handcuffs.

"What are you planning to do?" asked the stock exchange vice president.

"What do I plan to do?" Al-Sistani said. "Oh yes, the business that I am mixing with my pleasure. Well, the short answer is 'destroy the world as you know it.' On my signal, a dozen banks and trading firms will start selling short our hedge fund's equities and government bonds—all of them. Of course, that will cause the market to crash, taking the U.S. economy and likely the world economy with it. The longer answer is a bit more complex, but that's the abbreviated version."

"They'll never do it," the vice president said. "A sudden order to bundle and sell that much and sell it short will raise red flags; they'll want to make sure it's legitimate, and even then, they'll talk to us first."

Al-Sistani looked amused. "Do you really believe that? I mean, I knew that I couldn't rely on just one bank or trading firm to sell off so much so quickly. And even now, I expect one or two might actually balk. Which is why we made arrangements with a dozen banks and trading firms to handle what they believe are the exclusive rights to our business. They're not aware that the others will be asked to do the same thing. And yes, with bundled orders this large, they really should question it, but if they do, my people will demand that they comply—unless they do not mind losing all of the prince's current and future business. Do you really think these greedy pigs will forgo multimillion-dollar commissions?"

"But Amir, this will ruin me," complained Prince Esra, who'd risen shakily to his feet.

"Really?" Al-Sistani said, looking genuinely concerned, until he laughed again. "That's all part of the . . . what is the saying? . . . Ah yes, the big picture. This will bankrupt you and a lot of other members of the al-Saud family and their supporters foolish enough to give control of so much of their assets to Kingdom Investments. They will, of course, have to make up for it by taking a larger share of the oil profits and burdening their people even more. The revolution is but a food riot away from your decadent palaces."

Al-Sistani raised the vice president's chin with the muzzle of the gun. "Ah, my faithful tour guide, perhaps you're thinking there's no need to worry, the 'circuit breakers' will kick in before my plan can do too much damage. However, my jihadi friend here, Omar Al-Hassan, will be disabling them."

The vice president shot Omar a look. "How could you?"

"Easy," Al-Sistani answered for Omar. "His family lives in a very dangerous part of Pakistan. People get killed there all of the time. You might say he has no choice, though if something were to befall him, he's been assured that his family will be taken care of as befits a martyr. Omar, are you ready to begin?"

Omar went over to the table with the monitor and keyboard and began typing.

"Oh, and one last thing," Al-Sistani said. "The backup computer you're expecting to save the day? The one at the MetroTech? It will be 'off-line' too. When the market starts to crash, there will be nothing to apply the brakes."

"I don't understand," Lucy said.

"Then let me explain," Al-Sistani replied. "I really am rather proud of this. I read some years ago how the failure of a large hedge fund nearly crashed the stock market. The World Bank actually had to come to the rescue of the United States economy. I came up with the idea of doing the same thing—only with a much larger hedge fund. A truly delicious irony is that I did it using U.S. Treasury bonds, which allow their owners to borrow up to ten times the amount owned. In effect, the United States will be paying for its own firing squad.

"The prince's original ten billion, I leveraged to one hundred billion, which I sank into unsecured equities. I'm going to 'dump' all of it on the market at low, low prices, which will crash the market. But that's only half of the game."

Al-Sistani began to pace as his men kept their weapons trained on the hostages. "Think of it as dominoes all lined up to fall in a pattern that reveals something that you can't quite see until it nears completion. I dump the stock and the first domino falls; the market starts to crash and U.S. Treasury bonds are devalued at the same time, that's dominoes two and three. The circuit breakers don't kick in at the stock exchange, and a timely explosion at MetroTech takes out the other computer."

As if lecturing students in a classroom, Al-Sistani looked around to make sure they were all absorbing his genius. "Remember, transactions happen now in the blink of an eye. The NYSE administrators will be watching the market plunge, expecting the circuit breakers to kick on at the first 10 percent drop. When they don't, there will be more hesitation, and by the time they realize that neither computer has closed out trading, the market is in free fall. In the end, the pattern becomes increasingly clear; the U.S. economy is imploding. Then, of course, nobody's paying any taxes; now not only are U.S. Treasury bonds worthless, but the government's revenue source is drying up. The U.S. can't pay its bills—not to other countries, not to its military—and U.S. support for its allies throughout the world, including Israel, dries up to nothing. Imagine . . . no more U.S. money to spend on food for Third World countries, no more U.S. money to support their economies, combat disease, educate their people. Imagine famine, riots, war."

"But how could this happen?" Lucy asked, looking at the vice president.

"Well, for one thing, I had great business professors at the University of Denver where I got my MBA," Al-Sistani said. "They used to play 'what if' with this particular scenario, and I listened closely. After that it was relatively simple. Even after the near-disaster, hedge funds were still not regulated or overseen by any agency—no rules, no one looking over your shoulder like there are for all other market transactions. Financial managers like me have absolute discretion in what we want to do with the funds. Given that and the U.S. government's hundred-billion-dollar loan, setting up the first domino was easy. It was more difficult to determine how to get past the circuit breakers; we were fortunate to locate Mr. Al-Hassan and then his family. But Mr. Dean Newbury has been extremely helpful as well, though of course for his own reasons."

The vice president closed his eyes. "It will be a worldwide disaster . . ."

"Yes," Al-Sistani agreed, "and from the ashes will rise the new caliphate and one world under Allah."

Enjoying the moment, Al-Sistani whirled to face V. T. "Your uncle has been quietly selling off hundreds of millions of dollars' worth of stocks for the past six months in anticipation of the market crashing. Over such a long period of time, and through many dummy accounts, no one really noticed. Then, when the market hits bottom, he plans to buy them for pennies on the dollar . . . at least those companies he believes will rebound. You could have been a very wealthy and powerful man, Mr. Newbury."

"I'd rather be dead," V. T. mumbled as he rose shakily to his feet.

"That will happen. By the way, did you know that your uncle poisoned your father?"

V. T. didn't answer. "I thought not," Al-Sistani smiled. "Happy to have been able to provide the news." His pacing brought him in front of Lucy. "And because I also want to make your family suffer personally, you're going to be here for the moment when the first domino falls."

"You're just another lousy terrorist," Lucy said and spat in his face.

Enraged, Al-Sistani stepped back and pointed the gun at Lucy, who didn't flinch. The terrorist gritted his teeth and looked like he would pull the trigger, but then gradually got himself under control. "No, not yet. I want you to watch the minutes and seconds to your death count off." He looked at Suleiman Abdalla, who stood with his gun trained on the hostages, not quite understanding what was going on. "Are you prepared for martyrdom?"

"Yes," Suleiman responded. He opened a backpack he'd brought from the boxes in the supply room, took out the suicide vest, and pulled it on. He fastened it and plugged in the wires to connect the detonator to the plastic explosives.

"I was hoping to use Azahari Mujahid's ingenious pager detonator so that I could send this brave jihadi to Paradise when I was well away from the explosion," Al-Sistani said, "so that I may lead the faithful to the ultimate victory of Allah. However, cell-phone service is poor down here, I'm told—so much for modern technology."

He patted Abdalla on the shoulder. "This vest is on a timer. When I punch in the code, even my brave martyr here would be unable to stop it if he chose. . . . Not that he would ever consider dishonoring his oath, would you, Suleiman?"

"No, Sheik. I am ready to die for Allah."

"What about me?" the prince cried. "Amir, haven't I always treated you well? Why would you want to do this to me?"

"Treated me well?" Al-Sistani scoffed. "You care for your hounds more than you cared for me. But it's all right, I forgive you. I've been using you, too, for your money and your connections, all these years as my plan came to fruition. But now, I need you for a public service announcement."

The prince looked confused as one of his former bodyguards brought out the video camera that until half an hour earlier had been used to record the prince's grand day at the stock exchange. At a nod from Al-Sistani, who put on a thin black mask he had pulled from his suit pocket, the guard began to film.

"Get on your knees al-Saud dog," Al-Sistani demanded, pointing his gun at the whimpering prince. Looking up at the camera, he delivered a quick message in Arabic and then in English. "Mujahideen, warriors of Islam, I . . . The Sheik . . . announce the end of the unholy dominance of the West and the beginning of a new era in which Islam will reign supreme. By my hand this day, The Great Satan has suffered a mortal wound. Rise up in jihad and deliver the fatal blow to the West. Overthrow the apostate governments who have been the lackeys of the United States and Israel. As proof of my vow to make their blood flow in rivers, I deliver to hell Prince Esra bin Afraan al-Saud. Death to the royal family! Death to the United States! Death to Israel! Death to all who do not acknowledge that there is no God but Allah, and the Prophet is his messenger!"

"No, don't!" the prince screamed, but his voice was drowned out by the gunshot. His body pitched forward and lay convulsing on the floor of the computer room. Al-Sistani aimed again and finished the job.

"That's it," Al-Sistani said to the cameraman. "Give me the tape."

The cameraman ejected the tape and handed it to Al-Sistani, who placed it in his pocket just as Mousawi returned. "The way out is clear," he said.

Al-Sistani turned to Omar Al-Hassan. "Why aren't you finished yet?"

"A couple more minutes," Al-Hassan replied. "I have to get past the firewalls."

"Do it quickly. They're waiting for my call in Brooklyn."

———

When the police officer was gone, Mariano Ciampi got down from his perch on top of the toilet tank. He'd started to leave the restroom a few

minutes earlier and happened to glance down the hall when the police officer shot a young woman who came out of the women's room.

The cop had his back to him so he'd been able to duck back inside the
men's room. Climbing on top of the toilet so that his feet wouldn't show
was a trick he'd once seen in a movie, and he was amazed it had worked.

Mariano hesitated by the door. Something bad was happening; a killer in
a police uniform was murdering people, but he didn't know what to do.
You're a worthless old man, he thought.

He froze at the sound of footsteps returning from the direction of the
supply room. They stopped outside the door, and he knew that if the police
officer came in, he'd die. He jumped when whoever was standing outside
the door suddenly spoke.

"What in Allah's name do you mean there's a woman with a gun down
here?" The man stopped talking to listen. "Get your asses down here. And
take out the woman!" The footsteps hurried on.

Maybe you should just stay here, said a voice in Mariano's head. He knew
the voice; he'd heard it more and more as he had grown older—warning
him about the blacks moving into the neighborhood, cautioning him to
take it easy, as he might hurt himself mowing the lawn or raking the leaves.
He was old. He was frail. The world was full of danger.

"What in the hell are you talking about, Ciampi," he chided himself.
"Your grandkids and your daughter are in danger, and you're in here hiding
like some pansy. You fought your way to Rome against a lot harder sons-of-
bitches than some coward in a cop uniform who shoots helpless women.
Get a grip on your bladder, old man."

He peeked out the door just in time to see the bad cop disappear around
a corner heading toward the computer room. Slipping out the door, he
walked quietly up to the woman on the ground; her pretty green eyes were
wide open, but they weren't seeing anything. "I'm sorry, honey," he whispered as he bent over to look in her purse for any kind of weapon. "I'll try
to get the guy who did this."

A moment later, Mariano stood up, armed and ready to go to war. The
young woman had found a way to get pepper spray in past the security desk,
as well as a pair of heavy-duty knitting needles. "Not exactly my old M-1,"
he said, "but it's going to have to do."

You don't have to do this, said the voice. "Yes I do," Mariano replied and began walking toward the computer room. "I wonder where Marlene is?"

———————

After Malovo left the nineteenth floor, she returned with two of her men to the security office, where Billy was trying to pick the lock on his handcuffs. She struck him across the face with her gun. "Is that how you repay my kindness for letting you live?"

"Go to hell," Billy answered.

Malovo looked at him for a moment. "You first," she said and shot him.

Her plan was to wait for the call from The Sheik, Amir Al-Sistani, saying that the circuit breaker for the main computer was down. She would watch the updated stock-market returns on her Blackberry, and when it approached the number for the circuit breakers in the backup computer to kick in, she'd call Mujahid and give him the honor of blowing himself and SAIC into oblivion. She and the remaining members of her team would go down the stairwell and ensure that the computers were destroyed, killing any survivors they found. Then she would effect her escape . . . and be once again in the good graces of her Russian bosses, having more than made up for her previous failures.

Her musings were cut short by a call on her cell phone from two of her men in the parking garage. "What is it?"

"The janitorial service people are here," one said. "They say they're supposed to clean on the nineteenth floor today. What should we do with them?"

Malovo walked over to Billy's monitor and shoved his body aside. She flipped to the right camera and could see the "Little Odessa Janitorial Services" van in the garage. It was her former lover's company, and she wondered if he was on the cleaning crew. *Now that would be a delicious irony.*

Right now, she needed to get the janitors out of the way without raising suspicions. "Accompany them to the nineteenth floor—tell them there's been a security breach and you're just taking precautions. Then lock them up with the others."

Malovo flipped through the other cameras. In most of the building, life went on as usual. She hoped Mujahid's experience and the building's structure would prevent the explosion from reaching as high as the thirtieth floor; her escape plan counted on it. Otherwise, everything was in place.

Marlene, in fact, was creeping down the hall, stopping every couple of feet to listen. She wanted to hurry, but it wasn't going to do anybody any good if she ran into a trap.

A couple of bad cops upstairs had control of the security room, so she had to assume that they'd spotted her and Eric and would be waiting. She just needed to figure out where . . . *then blast my way past them . . . take on whoever else there might be . . . no sweat . . . and with what? Are there eight bullets in one of these little babies?*

She prayed that the silence wasn't because everyone was already dead except the killer. . . . *Or killers*, she thought. Her mind flashed on the three black cops from the cafeteria. They were the only other ones with guns down here when she went upstairs. And there was something about them she'd noticed but didn't understand that had been bugging her until now. Call it a feeling, but she'd spent most of her life around cops . . . hell, there were a lot more cops in the extended family . . . and they all had a certain feel about them. Some were pretty good at undercover, but if you knew cops well, you could spot them, too. Maybe it was the way they carried themselves or looked at you in the eye, even when acting out a role as a panhandler, but especially in uniform they oozed that "don't fuck with me" attitude.

The older guy could have been, she thought, *at least ex-military. Straight back. Turns his head to look you straight in the eye. Assessing his surroundings and the people in it.* The other two had more of a feel of hoodrats. Slouching. Insolent. They watched everything, especially women, but always with a sideways glance. *That's what I'm up against . . . at least.* She didn't know what the killings had to do with the prince—or whether the bad cops were alone, or part of something bigger. Given her conversation with Lucy and her suspicions about MetroTech, she bet on the latter.

She was almost to the intersection when she heard low voices. She couldn't tell which direction they were coming from. Left went to the computer room, but she was trying to remember what lay to the right. Then something banged to the right . . . like furniture being pushed around.

She crossed to an old five-foot-tall filing cabinet that had been left against a wall partway down the hall, close enough so she could make out what they were saying.

"How much longer?"

"Al-Hassan has to get into the system," said another, "and they're waiting to hear from Ajmaani in Brooklyn to say that the bomb is ready, Allah be praised."

"I hope they try to rush us," said the first. "I want to go out with my martyr's belt. They say there's no pain. One second you're here, the next second . . . Paradise, man. I'm lookin' forward to getting me a couple of virgins and . . ."

"They're not for sex, Ali," the second chided. "They just serve you grapes and stuff, but you ain't allowed to touch them."

"Yeah? Well believe you me, that rule's off when I get there. Them sweet young thangs is going to be serving up a lot more than grapes."

The two men laughed. They were obviously young and looking forward to dying, but that didn't make them easy targets for Marlene. *They're set up in the hallway, probably behind something. The only way to come at them is to expose yourself,* she thought as she looked around. *What I need is a good smokescreen.*

Marlene ran back to the cafeteria and found the laundry cart she'd seen, full of dirty tablecloths and napkins. *Apparently, the bigwigs eat better than the peasants today—and off linen.* Dashing into the kitchen, she emerged with several large jugs of olive oil and a large tin of cayenne pepper, which she dumped into the laundry cart. She went back in and grabbed a large bucket of old fry grease next to the short-order grill. She hauled it back out to the cafeteria and nearly dropped it. "Jesus, Eric!" she yelled at her cousin, who was standing in the middle of the room. "You're going to have to stop doing that or I'm going to shoot you just on principle."

Eric flashed his trademark smile. "I called and the guy said to tell you that the cavalry's on the way but it could take a little time, which, by the way, we don't have much of. Those cops from the security room are on their way. I saw them coming across the trading floor; they'll be here in a minute."

Marlene poured half the frying grease in on top of the other ingredients. "Got a lighter?"

"Yeah, here, but don't lose it. It's my favorite Zippo."

"If we live, I'll give it back." She explained her plan. "Ready?"

"I was born ready, sister."

They left the cafeteria. Eric turned to the left with the remains of the fry grease, which he took to the end of the hall and sloshed across the landing at the bottom of the stairs. He then took up a position in a nook that would give him some cover while keeping the landing in his line of sight.

Marlene pushed her cart out into the hall and began walking it toward the intersection. *They hear me coming but will wait to ambush me, which will let me get close.* Ten feet from the intersection, she flipped open the Zippo and tossed it in the cart with a silent Hail Mary for lying to her cousin.

The fry grease caught, then the olive oil, and finally the whole cart erupted in flame and dense, oily smoke. The cayenne pepper made her eyes water as she pushed the cart just hard enough for it to roll in front of the hallway where the two men waited. She back-pedaled to the filing cabinet and then lay down on the floor to get below the smoke and draw a bead on anyone who emerged.

Behind her, she heard a gunshot. *Sounded like a .380. Game on.*

41

As Lewis took her seat, Karp could hear a few sniffles coming from the jury box as well as the spectator gallery. It was going to be a minefield, and he would have to pick his way carefully to get to the other side with the jury.

Karp placed his notepad on the lectern and leaned on it with his elbows as he looked at the jurors. He didn't care if the press, or the spectators—the activists and justice junkies and would-be true-crime authors—could hear him. He needed to have a conversation with the twelve jurors and four alternates in the box.

"Ladies and gentlemen," he began, "first I want to thank you for your service; this has been a tough case to hear and see. I know it doesn't make it any easier on you, but it was as difficult a case to prosecute as I, and certainly my young colleague, have ever had to take on. We understand that Jessica Campbell has a mental defect, but we also understand that mental defects don't excuse responsibility for criminal acts except in a very narrow definition of the law."

He moved out from behind the lectern, arms crossed and head down for a moment, as he carefully chose his words. "The tears that some of you have shed and I expect will shed again in the jury room, and again when this is all over and you go home, are a natural reaction to the horrors and the tragedy of what happened to the Campbell children last March. They're nothing to be ashamed of, nothing to be embarrassed by; indeed, you have my respect, because despite what you've been put through, there you sit."

Crossing to the exhibits table, he picked out a portrait photograph of the three children and placed it on the easel. "As a father and a husband, I understand those feelings. But let us not forget that those tears rightfully belong to Hillary, Chelsea, and Benjamin, not their mother. Let us remember that justice belongs to three small children who are not with us here today because of what the defendant knowingly, consciously, and wrongfully did. The only justice that belongs to the defendant is a guilty verdict."

Karp let his words sink in before going on. "When I say that this has been a tough case to prosecute, it isn't because I have any reservations about the charges being appropriate. Most of the time, it isn't difficult for me to summon righteous indignation when the person sitting where Mrs. Campbell now sits has taken the life of another human being. Sometimes I can understand when a murder happens in the heat of a moment, or through recklessness, but it still does not excuse the behavior. And there are times when I'm absolutely, positively sure that the defendant regrets his or her actions—is genuinely remorseful, and not just because they got caught. But that doesn't excuse the fact that they committed a crime or that it's the deceased who deserves justice and our tears."

Karp turned toward Lewis and Campbell. "Defense counsel has pointed to the defendant and told you that she is suffering and that this will affect her for the rest of her life. And I'm sure she's right. So how can we, as thoughtful, compassionate human beings, not feel sympathy for her? Well, it's okay to feel sympathy for Jessica Campbell, just like you might feel sympathy for an otherwise 'good guy,' a decent, hard-working family man, who has a few too many to drink, gets behind the wheel of a car, and kills somebody running a red light at an intersection. But having sympathy doesn't mean we excuse the behavior, especially when the defendant knew what she was doing, knew it was wrong, and did it anyway. If her life has been negatively impacted by her actions, think about the three other lives and the negative impact on them."

Returning to the lectern, Karp glanced at his notepad. "In all honesty, what we have going on here with defense counsel's arguments is what I call 'a cruel reversal of the facts.' And to explain what I mean, allow me to digress for a moment and tell you a story about a place called Sobibor . . . a concentration camp during World War II where Jews were shipped to be exterminated . . ."

"Objection!" Lewis rose from her seat with a scowl on her face. "What does this 'story' have to do with the facts of the case? Dredging up ghosts of Nazi concentration camps is hardly relevant to the trial of my client in New York City. It's an egregious attempt by the prosecutor to draw an imaginary line between Nazis and my client and sway the jury based on emotions, not evidence."

Judge Dermondy raised an eyebrow. "Mr. Karp?"

"Your Honor, I believe Miss Lewis was the one who started delving into history, complete with a slide show. In fact, your honor, I have a few slides I'd like to show the jury that are also of historical relevance."

"My argument was relevant in discussing mental illness," Lewis argued

"And mine is relevant in a discussion about mass murder. In fact, it deals with mass murder whose perpetrators often blamed it on a type of mass hysteria."

"Miss Lewis, I believe you opened the door for this," Dermondy decided. "I'm going to allow it, as well as the slides."

"Thank you, Your Honor." Karp handed the DVD to the court clerk, who inserted it into the courtroom's multi-media system. As the lights dimmed, a photograph depicting dead bodies neatly stacked like cordwood appeared on the screen.

"This is a photograph taken in 1943 at Sobibor. The bodies are stacked like that so that they will burn more efficiently." Karp changed to the next photograph. "And this is one of the gas chambers as bodies are being unloaded." Another photograph showed children standing in lines, many holding suitcases and toys. "These Dutch Jewish children are waiting to be undressed and sent to the gas chamber."

Thanking good timing for having ordered the DVD from the library to show the bar mitzvah class, Karp left the last photograph up on the screen. "I don't have time to tell you about all the horrors of Sobibor. Other than that 250,000 men, women, and children, most of them Jews, were murdered there. Stripped of everything they owned, including their modesty, herded into gas chambers, murdered, and then taken away to be burned and buried. This went on until a group of brave prisoners . . ." he stopped and looked at Sobelman, who sat with a hand over his eyes, " . . . escaped carrying the news of what had happened there. So the Germans killed those who still remained in the camp, then tore it down, plowed it under, and planted crops and trees to make it look like it had always been farmland. As far as they were concerned, the camp at Sobibor never existed."

Karp flipped through several more photographs, letting each linger just long enough for the horror to sink in, then settled on one that simply looked like a farm. "This was taken that next spring, where the concentration camp once stood. When some of the people who were responsible for Sobibor, and for the other concentration camps that together murdered an estimated 12 million people, were brought to trial for war crimes, many of them pleaded a sort of mass insanity—that they'd been brainwashed by Hitler and the Nazi Party, that they were just following orders, and were, in fact, also victims. They were good people, just lost their minds for a few years—I guess the DSM might even call it a mass schizophrenia—their "real" personalities devolved into monsters. But now that they were better, the world should forgive them. And that, ladies and gentlemen, is what I mean by a cruel reversal of the facts. They were not the victims; they knew what they were doing; they knew it was wrong; and they went ahead and did it anyway . . . and then they tried to cover it up, pretend that it never happened."

Karp pointed at Jessica Campbell. "Neither is she the victim here. She knew what she was doing; she knew that it was wrong; but she went ahead and did it anyway . . . and then she tried to cover it up. But because this particular mass murderer is the mother of the victims, instead of a stranger, we're now supposed to overlook all of that, feel sorry for her because she has suffered enough and will have to live with her crime? Ladies and gentlemen, that is truly a cruel reversal of the facts."

Karp allowed anger to creep into his voice. It was no act, and he had to remind himself to keep it in check. He walked to the prosecution table and poured himself a glass of water. His eyes met with Sobelman's, which were wet with tears. *Sometimes justice needs a witness.*

He turned back to the jury. "In her closing, defense counsel played fast and loose with what she said the evidence demonstrated in regard to what Jessica Campbell was supposedly thinking. I contend there was not one bit of evidence to support most of that. I will leave it for you to decide if she was telling the truth. But let's now review the real facts of the case."

Karp walked over to the easel, removed the photograph of the Campbell children, clipped a large sheet of blank paper to it, and picked up a black magic marker. "One, Jessica Campbell planned this murder," he said, and wrote the numeral "1" and "Planned the murder" on the paper. "Three days before the murders, she drove to Newark where she purchased a footlocker, a padlock, and a knife. These were not random items; she knew what she needed them for and they were very carefully selected. And why did she go to Newark, instead of shopping for the same items closer to home? I believe that the evidence suggests that it was to avoid being recognized. And we know why she should care about that: because she was planning to use these items in a murder."

Karp wrote the numeral "2" and "No witnesses/No stop." "Before drowning her children, the defendant waited for her husband to leave the house and then called to tell the nanny that she would not be needed. Why? So there would not be any witnesses, or anyone who would be able to stop her. If she's so delusional, why didn't she get up that morning and tell her husband, or the nanny, or her parents, or any one of a number of other people, 'God told me to kill my children today'?

"Three, she drew the bathwater knowing that it would be used as the means to execute her children. Four, she held her two youngest children's heads under water until they stopped moving, even though her middle child tried to fight and claw to stay alive. But that wasn't enough for Hillary, her oldest, who desperately wanted to live, so the defendant, her mother, also had to stab her six times in the chest."

Jurors and spectators alike wiped at their eyes, but Karp kept at it. "She did this because God told her to, she says. But did she leave her handiwork for the world to see? *Hineini* . . . the ancient Jewish promise to do God's work when called upon . . . 'Here I am, God! See, I have done what you have asked. Shout it from every mountaintop!'? . . . No, she cleaned up, loaded the bodies in the footlocker, drove them a hundred miles to the north, and dumped them in the river to hide what she'd done, just like the Nazis did at Sobibor. Then she put on a disguise, returned to Manhattan via train—paying in cash so that there'd be no record, and walked home more than twenty blocks rather than take a taxi that might have a driver who would remember picking her up."

Hands in his pockets, Karp strolled over to the jury box. "Still, she brutally murdered her own children because she thought God wanted her to. Isn't that crazy? Isn't she nuts? The answer is, 'Of course she is.' How else could thoughtful, compassionate people describe someone who would do such a thing? As I said, we know Jessica Campbell suffers from a mental defect. She suffered from delusions that impelled her to kill her children. But should our criminal justice system allow individuals with a delusional belief system that induces irrational motivations which result in violent, wrongful conduct to be exonerated? Isn't one of the major purposes of the criminal justice system to incarcerate those violent criminals who cannot control, and instead act upon, their violent impulses? I believe we heard testimony that a large percentage of those people currently incarcerated suffer from a variety of personality disorders—whether they are anti-social, narcissistic, or schizophrenic. But if we're not going to excuse their behavior, why would we consider excusing the behavior of Jessica Campbell?

"Defense counsel suggested that if the defendant knew that killing her children was wrong, but wanted to get away with it, she would have come up with a better plan. But I'd wager that every convicted killer wishes he or she had come up with a better plan. Heck, some didn't even try to hide their crimes, which doesn't make sense, but it also doesn't mean they were not responsible when they killed another human being."

Wrapping up, Karp analyzed the insanity defense: Was the defendant aware of the nature and consequences of her actions? And did she know it was wrong? "I don't know about you, but it offends my notion of common sense that the criminal justice system creates—by the misuse of the insanity defense—the very mechanism for violent offenders to avoid responsibility and escape punishment.

"How do we know Jessica Campbell intended to kill her children? She planned the crime, she bought the materials to commit it, and she carried out her plan—not with a banana or a bathtub full of potato chips, but with a knife and a tub full of water. She drowned them and stabbed them until they were dead—not unconscious, not wounded . . . dead. They fought back, surely a clue that killing them was wrong. I urge you to look at the photographs of Jessica's arms and think about what the last moments were like for those poor little kids. And then think about the efforts she made after they were dead—ask yourselves, Were those the actions of a person who was so out of her mind that she didn't know what she was doing, or were those the actions of someone who felt guilty, who was trying to hide what she had done because she didn't want to be caught and punished? It doesn't matter if it was a rational plan; our prisons are full of the creators of irrational plans."

Karp walked back over to the prosecution table and took another sip of water, not because he was thirsty but because he wanted the jury to have time to absorb what he'd said.

"The defense counsel asked you to consider what you would do if you truly believed that God asked you to do some horrible thing because there was some greater purpose. I don't believe that a great and compassionate God would ask such things of us. . . . But isn't that the same argument used by Islamic terrorists when they fly airplanes into office buildings, or massacre women and children on school buses, or blow themselves up in places of worship? Don't they say they are doing God's will?"

Karp let the image hang in the air like the pall that still hung over his city. "Ladies and gentlemen, if it's okay for Jessica Campbell to knowingly, wrongfully do what she did because she believed she was obeying God, then by that argument we cannot in good faith hold terrorists responsible for their actions either. They, too, believe that God told them to do it. So what's the difference?

"There is none. Pointing the finger at God, or Hitler, or Allah, or Osama bin Laden and saying, 'He told me to do it,' does not absolve anyone from personal responsibility for their actions. Ladies and gentlemen, save your tears for Hillary, Chelsea, and Benjamin. Save justice for Jessica Campbell. In the name of the People of the State of New York, I ask you to find her guilty of the murder of Hillary, guilty of the murder of Chelsea, and guilty of the murder of baby Benjamin."

With summations concluded, Dermondy instructed the jury on the law, sent them to deliberate, and adjourned the court. As he rose from his seat, there was a commotion at the back of the courtroom. The cause became clear when Clay Fulton pushed through the last of the spectators.

"Is there something we can help you with, Detective Fulton?" Dermondy asked.

"Forgive me, Your Honor," Fulton replied. "But I urgently need to speak to Mr. Karp about an entirely different matter."

"By all means, detective. Mr. Farley, will you see that the rest of these people clear the courtroom at once?"

"Yes, sir," Farley replied and turned to those spectators, mostly media types, who lingered to see what went on between Fulton and Karp. "All right, folks, show's over for today. Everybody clear the courtroom. Thank you . . . that's it, move along."

Fulton walked quickly to where Karp had moved near the witness stand and out of hearing range of the public. "Boss," said the big detective, "we've got a problem."

42

"I've done it!" Omar Al-Hassan shouted. "The circuit breakers are bypassed!"

Al-Sistani grinned. "Allah be praised and may he be happy with you, Omar Al-Hassan. Place the calls."

Picking up the land-line telephone next to the monitor, Al-Hassan quickly punched in a number. "There is no God but Allah, and the Prophet is his messenger," he said, reciting the *Shahada* to the person on the other end. Then he hung up and called another number.

Al-Sistani explained. "My people will now call the banks and trading firms, who will in turn place the orders to sell off Kingdom Investments. Omar is also calling our friend in Brooklyn. She will watch the Dow Jones Industrial Average; when it drops by 9 percent, they will blow up the backup computer in the MetroTech. The circuit breakers will not kick in, and by the time anyone reacts, it will be too late. Especially when this computer, too, is destroyed."

He pointed his gun at Omar. "I'm sorry, but you must now be martyred."

"But I don't understand! You said I would leave with you!"

"You will . . . just not the way you thought. Amir Al-Sistani is going to die with all of you. Other than my most faithful of retainers . . ." he pointed to the two former bodyguards of the former prince, " . . . I cannot trust anyone to know the true identity of The Sheik."

"I promise I won't . . ."

Omar's last words were cut off by the bullet that tore through his heart. He felt at his chest and tried to speak, but then sat back down at the computer table, shivered once, and died.

"Oh my God," the vice president cried. "Please, I want to live."

"I can't allow that either. If the police get here before Suleiman's bomb goes off, I can't have you telling them the pass code to get into the room."

The vice president ran for the door and was shot. Al-Sistani walked over to the body and ripped the chain with the key from his neck.

Another gunshot echoed elsewhere in the basement. Al-Sistani nodded to one of the bodyguards. "Go make sure the jihadi are ready to sell their lives dearly, then join us in the tunnel."

The Sheik walked up to Suleiman and embraced him. He entered a number code into the timer that would detonate the vest. "There . . . the number to the center of the universe. You will not have to worry about wavering. Twenty minutes will be enough time for the market to tumble; then it will be over a moment after that . . . and you will enter the gates of Paradise."

"I am ready. *Allah-u-Akbar.*"

"Goodbye, Lucy Karp." Al-Sistani walked past her on the way out the door. "Perhaps Suleiman will be kind enough to let you watch the numbers count down on the detonator's readout."

Al-Sistani motioned V. T. to move toward the door. "I'd rather stay and die with Lucy."

"A noble sentiment. But not one I can entertain. Although I believe it is impossible to stop the bomb without the pass code number, I wouldn't want to take a chance on you overpowering my jihadi."

"I'm not going!"

"I'm afraid you are," Al-Sistani said, nodding to a guard who stabbed V. T. with a hypodermic needle.

"What?"

"Just a mild sedative to make you more compliant," Al-Sistani explained as his man tied a rope around V. T.'s neck. "I'll need to talk to your uncle on the way to my jet to see what he wants done with you, and as I said, cell phones don't work here."

They walked out into the hallway, which was filling with a black smoke that made them cough.

"A new sort of tear gas?" asked one of the bodyguards.

"More like a kitchen fire," replied Mousawi. "You better get going. I can handle it from here."

Al-Sistani embraced Mousawi, who took a submachine gun from the bodyguard. "From the first day we met in Iraq and you refused to fight Muslims on behalf of the infidels, I have trusted you best; your place in Paradise is assured," Al-Sistani said quietly, handing him a piece of paper and the vice president's key. "If Suleiman wavers, this is the pass code number and key for the door. Enter and shoot him. It won't matter if he's alive or dead when the bomb goes off. Otherwise, remain here and stop any counterattacks."

"*Inshallah,*" Mousawi promised.

Al-Sistani led the way toward the supply room, pulling V. T. roughly by the rope while the bodyguard followed behind with a gun. Arriving at the room, he pointed to the tunnel entrance. "Hurry. I want to be through the tunnel and out before the bomb goes off."

The guard entered the tunnel first while Al-Sistani kept a gun on V. T. But the man quickly returned. "They're not here."

"What's not here?"

"The flashlights. Suleiman was supposed to leave two flashlights after he cut through the lock."

"Move," Al-Sistani replied impatiently, shoving his way into the tunnel. He peered into the dark. "It goes straight until it reaches the entrance to the church crypts. One of Newbury's men will be waiting for us there. It can't be too far. Let's go."

Al-Sistani went ahead, feeling his way along the wall, with V. T. behind him and the bodyguard following.

Marlene lay prone in the hallway as the smoke filled the space until only the last three feet were somewhat clear. She could hear her would-be ambushers coughing and yelling.

Then one of them emerged, choking violently and shooting wildly down the hall. The smoke cleared for a moment and she got a clear look at his face, his eyes nearly swollen shut from the effects of the burning cayenne.

She shot him just below the navel; the bullet striking the muscle forced him to double over. Her next shot struck him in the top of the head, killing him and knocking him back so that he struck the wall and then sank down into a sitting position.

Marlene was waiting for the second man to emerge when someone else arrived from the other direction, stuck his gun around the corner, and began blindly spraying the hallway with automatic rifle fire. The chance of getting hit was significant, so she snapped off a couple of rounds to cover her retreat behind the filing cabinet.

"Attack," the new arrival yelled to the other man. "Blow yourself up in the hallway and stop the infidels."

With a shout of *"Allah-u-Akbar!"* the second ambusher ran from his hiding place and shoved the burning cart aside while his comrade fired a burst down the hallway. Marlene risked a look around the side of the filing cabinet and saw the suicide bomber grab the detonator cord of his vest. He was fifty feet away and running right at her.

———

Eric Eliaso had been busy back at the stairs. Two shadows appeared on the wall beyond the landing, followed by two men in police uniforms. While one covered the hallway, the other jumped down on the landing, hit the grease, and slid headfirst into the wall where he lay unconscious.

The second *faux* cop, thinking his partner had merely fallen, stepped out onto the landing, his gun at ready. His feet went out from under him, too, and he dropped his gun as he fell to his knees.

"Hold it!" Eric yelled, stepping from his niche with both hands on his gun.

The bad cop hesitated and then grabbed his gun off the ground and shot. The bullet struck the wall next to Eric, who fired twice without looking. When there was no return fire, he saw that he'd wounded the second man, who was attempting to crawl back to the stairs.

Eric left his cover and moved cautiously toward the others. He looked at the first man, who appeared to still be out, and walked over to the fallen man, who lay on his back panting heavily and bleeding from a wound in his side.

A clicking noise behind him caused Eric to turn quickly. Too quickly, as his hard-soled shoes went out from under him. However, the stumble saved him as the bullet intended for his chest caught him in the shoulder and spun him against the wall. He slipped again, sliding down with his back against the wall as a second bullet cracked off the marble just above his head.

Yelling in fear, he pointed his own gun and fired rapidly until it clicked, out of bullets. When he worked up the nerve to open his eyes, he saw that the man who'd been trying to kill him was dead, with two bullet holes in his forehead.

Eric relaxed only to hear the hammer of another gun being pulled back. "Not again," he sighed and turned to point his gun at the wounded man on the stairs, who was shakily pointing his gun at him.

"You out of bullets, muthafucka," the second man pointed out.

"Am I?" said Eric in his best Dirty Harry voice. "Do you feel lucky? Huh? Do ya, punk?"

"What the hell you talkin' about?" The wounded man scowled as he tried to hold his gun steady enough to shoot Eric.

"HOLD IT!" A booming voice froze Eric and the wounded man in place. They looked to the top of the stairs and saw an enormous black man with a handgun pointed. "Drop the guns, or I'll blow your fuckin' brains out."

"So that's how you do it," Eric said, letting his fall.

——————

Clay Fulton stood at the top of the stairs at the head of a team of his men from the District Attorney's Office.

When he had received the call from Jaxon saying that a terrorist plot was going down at the NYSE and the MetroTech in Brooklyn, there wasn't a whole lot more to go on.

"I'm on my way to the Exchange, but you're closer, Clay," Jaxon had said. "I don't know who we can trust there. Apparently, some of the bad guys are wearing NYPD uniforms. But Marlene's over there and involved somehow. . . ."

Fulton rolled his eyes. "Of course."

" . . . Otherwise, Lucy's there, too, and so is V. T. There are also bombs involved . . ."

"Why not . . ."

" . . . and the action is in the basement, that's about all I got."

The next moment, Fulton, who had been standing outside the court-room, burst in to explain what he knew to Karp, and they were both out the door of the Criminal Courts building thirty seconds later, jumping into the office Lincoln Continental with other members of Fulton's DAO team. Minutes later, they were running through the NYSE security gates, badges held high, shouting, "New York PD!" and "New York DAO!"

Once inside, Fulton yelled to the first security officer he saw. "Which way to the basement? We have a possible hostage situation and maybe a bomb. You need to get everybody out of here!"

A second security guard ran up. "Joe, handle the evacuation," he said. "This way to the basement."

As they ran through the trading floors, a few people yelled to ask what was going on, but most were transfixed in front of their monitors. Something was happening in the market. There were a lot of sell-short orders coming in for various equities and Treasury bonds and the Dow Jones was taking a hit. They couldn't be bothered with men running through the Exchange when the market was undergoing some sort of massive downturn.

The DAO team reached the top of the stairs just in time to hear a series of shots. With his big .44 Magnum held out in front, Fulton signaled for the others to stop as he moved cautiously forward to look down the staircase. There he saw a wounded uniformed officer trying to hold his gun steady enough to shoot a wounded white male.

"HOLD IT!" he bellowed. "Drop the guns, or I'll blow your fuckin' brains out."

The white man complied but the uniformed officer refused. "I'm NYPD," he yelled. "This man is a terrorist. He killed my partner."

"Like hell I'm a terrorist," Eric shouted back. "I'm from frickin' Queens, you asshole."

"I recognize that voice," Karp said, pushing to the front and standing next to Fulton. "Eric! What the hell's going on?"

"Hi Butch. Nothing much."

"Watch it!" Fulton shouted and fired twice, blowing the top of the 'police officer's' head off.

"Shit," Eric complained, wiping the other man's blood off his face.

Fulton moved cautiously down the stairs. "Everybody back up a second. Got to make sure this asshole's gone. Dude was going for that little

cord on his belt, which if I'm not mistaken, is probably attached to a suicide vest."

"Fuck me naked," Eric replied. "That would have been a hell of a thing.
But you might not want to have a gabfest here boys, Marlene's back down
that way taking on the rest of them."

As if in answer, there was the sound of a shot. Then many shots.

Fulton ran to the bottom of the stairs with Karp on his heels. "Be careful . . ." Eric started to warn the others, who hit the grease and went down.
"Oh man, that's got to hurt. Forgot to tell you, the floor is slick as snot."

"Thanks," Karp winced. He and Fulton picked themselves up as the rest
of Fulton's team made their way gingerly across the greased marble.

"You going to be okay?" Karp asked Eric.

"Shit yeah, takes more than one bullet to kill a kid from my 'hood. This
baby's gonna leave a nice scar and be worth a few drinks and a whole lot of
sympathy from certain ladies I know."

Karp shook his head as Fulton and his team started moving down the
hallway. *Is everybody in Marlene's family insane?* he wondered.

———

Malovo was starting to get nervous when the call from Al-Hassan finally
arrived. After that, all she had to do was watch the stock-market report on
her Blackberry, and when it fell to the magic number . . .

It was all a matter of timing. If she waited too long to give Azahari Mujahid the signal, the circuit breakers would kick in and the market slide
would stop. However, if she blew it up too soon, trading would have automatically halted while the techies determined what was wrong. Waiting
until the last minute would allow the market to start to crash, then when
the circuit breakers failed to kick in, the techies would be up to their necks
in trying to save what they could. The final blow would be the destruction
of the main computer.

Time for a vacation, Malovo thought. *Maybe Cuba this year. . . .* Her eyes
went to the monitor just as the camera view from the elevator carrying her
men and the janitors should have appeared. It was dark.

A glitch? She flipped the switch to the monitor for the camera outside
the elevator on the nineteenth floor. When the door opened, she gasped. It

wasn't just the lifeless bodies of her men lying on the floor of the elevators, or that three of the "janitors" were obviously well-trained in house-to-house guerrilla warfare. It was the fourth man, a tall man with a black patch over one eye and a scarred face, who sent a chill up her spine.

"Ivgeny!" she hissed in fear and hatred.

Malovo hit the audio switch for the intercom in the investment firm office. "Mujahideen! You are being attacked!" she yelled. "Four men, hold them off! Mujahid, prepare to call the number!"

She glanced at her Blackberry. The market was starting to go down . . . two percentage points already. Just a little longer, and the plan would still work. *In fact, Ivgeny, my love,* she thought, *with you there, this will be like . . . how do the Americans put it? . . . killing two birds with one bomb.*

What in the hell am I doing in this filthy tunnel? William White wondered as he waited for Amir Al-Sistani below Trinity Church.

Like most of the families connected to the Sons of Man, even though his had no seat on the council, the Whites had attended Trinity Church for more than two hundred years. And they were well aware of the coal tunnel located off a little-known passage beyond the old crypts in the basement. In fact, some of the more adventurous boys in those families had played in the tunnels. Legend had it that the old man, Dean Newbury, had once taken his brother, Vincent, into the tunnels and tried to lose him there. It was only after several hours of searching that other family members had located the boy.

White tilted his head and listened, thinking he heard voices coming his way from the dark. He pulled a small gun from his pocket. His orders were to escort Al-Sistani and maybe one or two others out of the church to a waiting limousine, which would take them to a private airfield in New Jersey where a jet waited. Anyone else, he was to shoot on sight. *Who else would be stupid enough to be wandering around in this horrible place?*

He heard the sound of footsteps, and two small figures emerged from the shadows. Not exactly what he was expecting. *Maybe they're hostages.* He'd been told to speak French to The Sheik. *"Qui est là?"*

The answer wasn't what he expected either. "It's the Coal Tunnel Ghost!" one yelled. The other started screaming so loudly that he decided to shoot him just to stop the noise.

He was about to pull the trigger when something struck him hard in the back. So hard that it brought some warm sticky fluid into his mouth. He wiped the moisture with his hand and looked at it. Then he didn't care because he was dead.

"Hello boys," said a tall dark figure.

"Aaah, it's the Coal Tunnel Ghost!" Zak yelled for the second time.

"No it's not, you idiot," Giancarlo said. "It's David Grale."

"In the flesh," Grale said as he stepped on the back of the dead man to pull his knife out. "You want to tell me what's going on up there?"

Marlene stepped out from behind the filing cabinet as the young black man in the NYPD uniform and wearing a vest full of explosives and ball bearings charged toward her. She shot, striking him in the shoulder. Her next shot hit him in the chest and for a moment she cringed, fearing an explosion. Some part of her mind filed away the fact that the explosive was C-4 and hard to set off with a bullet, but not impossible. She aimed low and shot a leg.

It had the desired effect of stopping the charge. The black man fell against a wall, which he used to stay on his feet. Marlene aimed the gun at his head.

"Allah-u-Akbar," he said and yanked the cord to the detonator.

At the same moment, Marlene dropped the gun and pulled the filing cabinet over on its side, falling to the ground behind it. There was a roar and a sound like a sudden violent hailstorm as a thousand hard objects pinged off the walls, floor, and ceiling, with a couple dozen hitting the filing cabinet with a metallic "ponk." The force of the blast knocked the cabinet into Marlene and hurled them both ten yards down the hall.

It was over as suddenly as it had started. Marlene's ears rang and she felt like she'd been in a car crash. She got to her knees and surveyed the scene. Some of the ceiling had caved in, and the walls on both sides of the blast were buckled like someone had taken a giant hammer to them. Bits of ceiling tile, insulation, and, perhaps, clothing burned. But there was little left of the bomber, just a splash of blood, as well as pieces of flesh that she didn't care to look at long enough to recognize.

Smoke hung like a fog six feet down from the ceiling. A large man appeared out of the smoke. He pointed his submachine gun at her.

Behind her a gun roared three, maybe four times . . . it was difficult to tell with her head still ringing . . . and the large man in the suit was driven back into the smoke. Marlene turned to see who her benefactor might be and was surprised to see Fulton crouched with his smoking gun still aimed at the dead man. Behind him was her husband.

"Well, hello Butch," she shouted louder than she meant to. "Wait 'til I tell you what we learned in school today."

Fulton brought them back to reality. "Where are Lucy and the twins?"

Marlene's face looked like somebody had thrown cold water in it. Her eyes hardened. "They've got to be down this way," she said and took off running with Fulton and his team in pursuit.

"Now where's she off to?" a young officer said as he and Karp ran to catch them.

"Mama Bear is off to find her cubs," Karp replied. "I feel sorry for any-body who gets between them."

43

Amir Al-Sistani, The Sheik and future caliph of an Islamic world, felt his way along the coal tunnel like a blind man. He knew it had only been about ten minutes, but the tunnel was oppressive and longer than he had expected. He kept bumping his head and nearly falling, or stumbling into little side openings, but pulling back quickly at the sound of things scurrying there in the dark.

He looked ahead. "There!" he yelled. "I see a light! Allah be praised!" He yanked on the rope to force V. T. to pick up the pace, but all he got was the rope. "Ahmed! Where's the prisoner?"

There was no answer. Al-Sistani turned around but he couldn't see a thing in the dark. "Ahmed? Where are you?"

The only answer was the sound of a struggle and then an odd gurgling sound. "Damn it, Ahmed, answer me!"

"I'm afraid he can't talk right now," said a deep voice. Other voices laughed insanely.

Al-Sistani raised his gun and fired in the direction of the voice. Then someone or something ran past him, clubbing his arm so that the gun fell from it.

Next, someone struck a match. It took Al-Sistani a moment to realize that he was staring into the face of Ahmed, and Ahmed was staring back.

However, the man's head was no longer attached to his body; it was held aloft by a tall, robed man with dark, sunken eyes.

"Allow me to introduce myself," the robed man said. "My name is David Grale, and I will be your host for the rest of your life." He tossed the head of Ahmed to Al-Sistani just as the match went out. The Sheik shrieked and passed out.

"Geez, he screamed just like Giancarlo," Zak scoffed and turned on a flashlight that Grale had given him. "Which is pretty much like a little girl."

"Screw you, Zak. At least I'm not yelling about ghosts every time some-body jumps out of the dark!"

"Oh yeah? Well, at least . . ."

"Boys," Grale interrupted. "I believe your mom and sister may still be in trouble. V. T., are you all right?"

"A little woozy," V. T. said. "I got a nasty bump on the head, and they shot me up with something."

"Do you think you and the boys, can make it to the light up there—that's the entrance to the Trinity Church crypts."

"Sure," V. T. answered. "I won't be much use to you anyway."

"No way," Zak said. "We're going back to help our mom now that we got a posse."

Grale gripped Zak's shoulder. "You're going to do what I say," he growled. "I don't have time to argue. I want you to go sit still in the church until someone comes to find you. If you don't, I will introduce you to the real Coal Tunnel Ghost and you won't like it. Am I clear?"

Both boys nodded.

"What about me?"

The group looked down at Amir Al-Sistani. "I can pay you very well to let me go. I have a jet waiting for me in New Jersey. I'll leave and never come back."

Grale reached down and grabbed the man by the throat to lift him to his feet. "I wouldn't dream of letting you go just yet," he said. "No, 'Sheik,' you and I will be having many long chats this winter. I'm looking forward to learning all about you and some of your friends. Meanwhile, Booger, would you be so kind as to escort Mr. Al-Sistani to our little home beneath the streets?"

"'appy to," Booger snuffled. He grabbed Al-Sistani by the scruff of the neck and shoved him down the tunnel. "'et's go."

Al-Sistani fell to his knees, pleading and begging to be freed. Booger and some of the others laughed, forcing him down the tunnel and into the dark where he continued to scream long after he'd disappeared from sight.

Grale turned to V. T. and the boys. "Off you go. I'll go see if I can find your mother and sister and grandfather."

———

Nadya Malovo watched as Ivgeny and his men fought their way into the nineteenth-floor office. Her men were fighting back from behind desks and posts, but they were up against former Russian commandos with years of experience fighting real mujahideen. It was clear they were outflanking her men.

She looked at her Blackberry. The market was down five percentage points, and she was supposed to wait for four more. She glanced back at the monitor. One of Ivgeny's men was down but so were all but three of hers. Mujahid and Samar were still alive, but they weren't armed and had taken refuge from the flying bullets behind a desk.

Ivgeny could not be allowed to reach the detonator. It was an effective device, but disarming it was as easy as pressing the off button. She was going to have to move the timetable up. She was sure that the market would still slide past the 10 percent mark, and the backup would be destroyed.

"Mujahid!" she yelled. "Make the call now!"

"Screw you!" Mujahid yelled.

"And the horse you rode in on!" added Samar.

"What? Did you hear what I . . ." suddenly she realized that Mujahid had cursed her in English, as had Samar.

Betrayed, she thought. *I knew I didn't like those two.* "Al-Aqsa Brigade! Mujahid and Samar are traitors. Kill them!"

One of her men shot at the traitors while the other two tried to hold off the Russians. Malovo, who knew the number for the pager as well as Mujahid, dialed the number and waited for the detonator phone to ring.

———

Tran peeked out from behind the desk at the detonator, which was twenty feet away. One of the two men who'd been guarding it was dead. The other was ten feet away, shooting at them and the intruders.

The pager rang.

"Maybe you shouldn't have said that," Jojola grinned.

"Yeah, but now I've got to get there before the fourth ring or we won't be saying much of anything anymore." Tran stood and started running for the pager. "Make yourself useful!"

But Jojola was already up and running with him. He flipped his knife around in his hand, gripping firmly on its bone handle.

"Kill them! Don't let them reach the detonator!" Malovo shouted over the intercom as the pager rang again.

The terrorist closest to the detonator stood to get a better shot at Tran. Jojola shouted to draw the man's fire, took two more steps, and hurled the knife with all his strength. The blade caught the man right below his throat, severing his spinal cord so that he collapsed to the ground.

Shit, I've moved faster in dreams, Tran thought. The pager rang a third time. He dove over a desk, his finger extended, knowing that he would be too late. He closed his eyes and prepared to leave the body of an aging Vietnamese gangster. *I wonder what I will come back as?*

Lying on the ground, Tran opened one eye. Only then did he realize that the phone never rang the fourth time.

"You look like you just shit your pants," Jojola said.

"I don't understand. We should all be dead." He looked around. The only men standing were Jojola and the men who'd come to the rescue.

"Sorry," Ivgeny said. "I cut that a little close. The truth is that I forgot to turn it on until I heard the pager ring." He held up a box about the size of a pack of cigarettes with three prongs sticking out at the top.

Ivgeny turned to the video camera. "Hello Nadya," he said. "This is an RX9000, the most powerful handheld jammer you can buy. It has output of 900 megawatts and can jam cellular phone signals up to 30 meters in the right conditions. Your phone service has been cut off. Sorry gentleman. Next time, I remember to turn it on before things get exciting, no? Now, you must excuse me. I have a date with a certain lady."

Ivgeny ran for the stairwell, but Jojola ran too. "Not if I get there first."

Tran sat and looked at one of the Russians. "Next time?" he said. "Next time, somebody else gets to be with the bomb, and I'll show up in the nick of time."

"Justin, please, don't do this," Lucy pleaded. "So many people will suffer."

Suleiman Abdalla looked up, surprised. "How do you know that name?"

"Miriam told me," Lucy replied. "You told her once . . . when you were at her home for *Eid ul-Adha*, the Feast of the Sacrifice . . . in honor of Ibrahim's willingness to sacrifice Ishmael as proof of his loyalty to God."

"She told you that when?"

"Just now. She's here with my . . . I don't know, I guess you'd call her my guardian angel."

Suleiman scowled. "That's crazy! This is a trick. She must have told you at some other time."

"Tell me about it," Lucy acknowledged. "I know it sounds crazy. I used to think I was bonkers—seeing and hearing things. Now, I just accept these spirits, or delusions, or whatever you want to call them, as part of God's plan. And what you're doing is not part of God's plan. . . . It is the work of evil men who lust for power and the death of others."

"You lie," Suleiman said. "Jihad is part of God's plan. If this was evil, it could not happen, because the demons that cause men to do evil are chained in hell during Ramadan."

"Which means that during Ramadan, men cannot claim that Satan or demons made them do something that contradicts the Qur'an. During Ramadan, all evil comes from within. And when you are held accountable for this, there will be nothing to blame it on but yourself. Suicide is a mortal sin in the Qur'an, and no amount of lying or calling it 'martyrdom' can change that. Murder is also a sin. Making war on innocent people, especially women and children, is a sin. No bastardization of the Qur'an by men like Al-Sistani and bin Laden and Rahman can change those truths."

"Shut up! They are great men who understand the Qur'an better than a woman!"

"Better than Miriam? Better than her father, Mahmoud Juma?"

Doubt was written darkly on Suleiman's white face. He looked at the timer. "In five minutes, we will find out who goes to Paradise and who goes to hell. *Inshallah*."

"Do you really believe that?" Lucy glanced out to the hallway. The smoke was getting heavier, but what concerned her more was the big cop scowling at them from out in the hall. "That this is God's will? Was it God's will the way they killed Miriam? She says you were there for that, and you know it was wrong. They cut her throat, Justin. What did she do to deserve that?"

"This is jihad," Suleiman replied. "Innocent people die in war. She will be taken care of by Allah."

"She already has been. But as a martyr, she's allowed to intercede on behalf of others who would otherwise go to hell. She cannot save her husband, your friend Jamal, because his sins were too great. But she can still save you, if you will listen to me."

Suleiman passed a hand over his eyes. He was sweating despite the cool temperature of the computer room. He looked at the bodies of the vice president and the prince, still lying where they had fallen, and at Omar Al-Hassan, sitting in the chair, his eyes open, as if waiting for something to do.

How did this woman know he had spent Eid ul-Adha with Miriam? *Miriam could have told her.* But she also knew about how Miriam died, and only the Al-Aqsa Brigade and Ajmaani had been present then, and they had been together ever since. *No one could have said anything about Miriam's death to an outsider. I don't believe in ghosts. No, but the Qur'an teaches us to believe in angels. Perhaps Miriam is an angel sent to save me.*

"Angel . . . spirit . . . our own subconscious saving us from ourselves, whatever you want to call it," Lucy said, as if she could read his mind.

"I can't stop it anyway. I don't know the pass code number."

"He told you it was the number for the center of the universe," Lucy said. "What would that . . ."

Her question was interrupted by the man outside banging on the door.

"Stop talking in there!"

"Or what?" Lucy shouted back. "You're going to kill me?"

"Be quiet," Mousawi demanded.

"You be quiet. By the way, where's The Sheik? I don't see him here, ready to die with you for Allah. Isn't that always the way with these guys?"

"Suleiman, remember your oath," Mousawi yelled. "Tonight we dine in *bayt al-ridwan!* Do not listen to the infidel witch."

"Tonight the only thing roasting will be you," Lucy shouted back.

Mousawi inserted the key into the lock and punched in the number. The door clicked open.

"Shoot him when he comes in Suleiman," Lucy pleaded. "Miriam says she'll be waiting for you at the gate."

Suleiman looked at Lucy to see if she was lying. But he saw only the truth. As Mousawi began to enter, he shot, but the bullet only ricocheted off the door that the other man was using as a shield. He shot again with the same result.

Mousawi stuck his gun around the edge and fired several times, striking Suleiman and knocking him to the ground. The younger man's gun clattered away as he sank against one of the computer towers.

"I'm going to kill you with my bare hands," Mousawi said to Lucy, but suddenly he stopped as a searing pain shot through the small of his back and his stomach. He looked down; the point of a metal spike protruded from his shirt.

Turning around, Mousawi was struck in the face by a blast of pepper spray. He screamed with rage and shot wildly at an assailant he could hardly see. The shot missed, but an old man fell to the ground as he tried to dodge to the side.

"Grandpa!" the girl in the room cried out.

Mousawi wiped at his burning eyes and gagged as the pepper spray swelled the mucous membranes in his nose and throat. He straddled the old man and pointed the gun down. "*Allah-u-Akbar!*" he croaked.

"Up yours," the old man replied, stabbing upward with his other knitting needle and piercing the big man's groin.

Tossing away the knitting needle, Mariano struggled to his feet with his fists balled. "Come on, you son of a bitch," he yelled. "Put down the gun and let's see what you got."

Mousawi started forward, intending to beat the old man to death with his hands. But there was a roar from down the hall and a blast of air, followed by even more smoke. He slipped in his own blood that covered the

ROBERT K. TANENBAUM

floor. When he opened his swollen eyes again, what he saw was a dark figure emerging from the smoke and the flash of a knife swinging in a wide arc. He grabbed his throat with his hands, but there was nothing he could do about a severed carotid and jugular. He tried to remember the *Shahada* but only got as far as, "There is no God but Allah . . ." before he died.

David Grale knelt beside the old man on the ground. "Are you all right?"

"A little banged up," Mariano admitted. "But I'll be okay if you can give me a hand up. I've got to get to my granddaughter. . . . Who are you, by the way?"

"A friend of the family." Grale offered Mariano his hand. "Ah, and here comes the cavalry. If I'm not mistaken, this would be your daughter and . . . yes, your son-in-law. But as there are police officers with them . . . I must bid you adieu."

Grale melted back into the smoke. Two of the police officers arriving with the others started to go after him, but Fulton called them back.

"We can catch him, Clay," yelled one.

"Yeah, that's what I'm afraid of, and right now, we have a bigger problem."

The other officers followed his glance. Marlene was pushing against the glass door of the computer room, but to no avail. When Mariano had stabbed Mousawi, the door of the computer room had clicked shut again. Lucy was trapped inside with a bomb about to go off.

"Lucy! Can you read the time left on the detonator?" Marlene shouted.

"Yes. Less than three minutes!"

Ivgeny and Jojola raced up the stairwell at the MetroTech, intent on catching Nadya Malovo.

Two of Ivgeny's men were already outside the security office door, having set up a small explosive charge on the lock. At a signal from their boss, they blew the door open.

Rushing in with guns drawn, the men were fired upon by Malovo's last two men. But their shots were wild and they were both shot immediately after they fired—one killed and the other wounded.

"Where is she?" Ivgeny asked, pointing his gun at the wounded man. Before he could answer, they heard the sound of a helicopter approaching. "Never mind," he added and shot the man dead.

"Yours?" Jojola asked as he ran for the stairs marked "Heli-Pad. Authorized Personnel Only."

"*Nyet*," Ivgeny answered. "Mine's on the way, but it's not here yet."

They reached the roof but had to duck for cover as bullets from automatic rifle fire clattered around them. Ivgeny shot back, but it was too late. The black helicopter had already lifted off and was pulling away from the building. Malovo shot at them from the side door. Then she was gone.

"Not again," Ivgeny thundered.

"Not again, what?" Tran asked as he and the remaining Russians arrived on the roof.

Jojola shook his head. "Guess we'll be seeing that bitch again someday."

"Count on it," Ivgeny replied. Another helicopter descended to the roof. "May I offer you gentlemen a ride? I don't want to be here when the police arrive."

"Me neither," Tran replied. "I'm still a wanted gangster, in case anybody's forgotten."

———

"Lucy! We're going to get you out of there baby," Marlene cried, banging on the door in frustration.

"Get on the radio and get somebody who can give us the code to the door!" Fulton yelled to one of the uniformed officers.

Inside the room, Suleiman spoke thickly, blood dribbling from the corner of his mouth. "I'm sorry. I just wanted to belong and serve God."

"It's all right," Lucy replied. "In the end, you tried to do the right thing."

"What does that matter if I've destroyed the world?" Suleiman cried. He looked up at the digital market readout board. "I don't understand."

"What?" Lucy replied.

"It says trading has been temporarily suspended."

"The circuit breakers must have worked! The computer at the Metro-Tech wasn't destroyed." Lucy looked at the detonator, and then yelled to those standing outside the door. "Mom . . . Dad . . . you've all got to go, there's only a minute left!"

"The rest of you get out of here," Marlene demanded.

"Not without the two of you," Karp replied. "Fulton, take your guys and go. Right now, and that's an order. We're staying with our kid, but no one else is going to die here."

"Boss, I can't . . ."

"Get the hell out of here, Clay! Take Mariano with you. . . . Sorry, Dad, but you've got to go, too."

"Everybody out! Clear the building!" Fulton yelled. "Mr. Ciampi, come with me, please." The detective put his arm around the old man, and they took off down the hallway.

Marlene turned back to the computer room. "Think!" she shouted at Suleiman. "Didn't you watch him punch in the numbers?"

"No . . . sorry . . . it's the center of the universe."

"What did he say?" asked a voice behind Marlene and Karp.

"Jaxon!" Karp replied. "Get the hell out of here, there's a bomb about to go off."

"Not without Lucy. I'm the reason she's here. Now what did he just say about the center of the universe?"

"That's the code to stop the timer," Marlene explained.

Jaxon yelled to Suleiman. "Try three-nine-four-nine-two-one-two-seven."

Suleiman looked down at the timer. He'd lost a lot of blood, and his finger was unsteady as he punched in the numbers and then pressed the "Enter" button to stop the countdown. "It didn't work. Twenty seconds."

Jaxon thought again. "Try this! Three-nine-four-nine-three-two-one-two-seven-six."

Slowly, pausing to concentrate, Suleiman punched in the number. "Five seconds," he shouted as he pressed the Enter button again.

Lucy looked across at the three other women in the room. St. Teresa, Hazrat Fatemeh Masumeh, and Miriam Juma. All three smiled as if to welcome her. But the bomb didn't explode, and suddenly everyone was cheering. Marlene and Karp hugged and then embraced Jaxon.

"Uncle Espey, I love you!" Lucy shouted. "How did you know?"

"Easy. It's a riddle, but the first time I forgot to give the compass directions."

"What in the hell are you talking about?" Marlene asked, kissing him on the cheek.

"It's longitude 39°49' east and latitude 21°27' north," Jaxon explained. "The coordinates for Mecca, the center of the Muslim universe."

Karp laughed. "God, you've got to love these guys with a flair for the dramatic."

An hour later, a woozy, disheveled V. T. Newbury arrived at the law offices of Newbury, Newbury and White and rushed past the gaping receptionist to his uncle's office. In his mind, he saw himself leveling a gun at the old man's head and pulling the trigger, splattering the bastard's brains all over his million-dollar view of Midtown Manhattan.

Instead, he entered the room and quickly shut the door. "We were betrayed."

"My God, Vinson, what happened?" the old man said. He was nearly frantic for news of what had occurred at the Exchange. It was obvious that something had gone wrong with the plan—the market had not collapsed, and it was going to take some fast talking to mollify the rest of the Sons of Man council when they discovered how much of their money he'd lost selling off the group's stocks. They could recover from that—their assets went far beyond those in the stock market—more important was whether they'd been found out.

"We were betrayed," V. T. repeated. "The Sheik was carrying out our plan—I wish you'd told me about it first; I nearly got myself shot before he explained it to me. One of the bodyguards was actually a CIA mole. They waited for Al-Sistani to make his move."

The old man squinted suspiciously. "So you know what we planned to do?"

"Yes . . . it was a brilliant idea, but someone talked or the CIA was on to it from the beginning. Karp and his wife, and Jaxon, they were involved, too."

"You understand why we created this event?"

"Yes, yes . . . of course, to save the United States from these fucking immigrants and the uneducated, filthy niggers and spics and Jews. But what do we do now?"

Dean Newbury ignored the question. "How did you escape?"

"I pretended I'd been held hostage. Al-Sistani was gone. It was pandemonium."

"What happened to Al-Sistani?"

"I don't know. He left at the beginning of the assault by the police. He might be dead."

Dean Newbury went to the bar and poured a brandy for himself and his nephew. "Don't worry. There's nothing to tie us to this. We're just a law firm and had no idea that this was going to happen."

V. T. accepted the brandy though the alcohol made the fire in his head burn hotter. "I hope I didn't mess up."

His uncle patted him on the shoulder. "Nonsense, my boy. I'm sorry that I didn't warn you about what was going to happen. There was a lot at stake and, well, to be honest, I wasn't sure you could be trusted."

V. T. looked up with a grateful smile. "Thanks, Uncle Dean. I'm completely on board with this. After all, something needs to be done or this country will be overrun."

"Indeed, and don't give it another thought. . . . You passed the test and we'll recover from this setback to try again." He raised his glass. *"Myr shegin dy ve, bee eh."*

V. T. returned the toast. "What must be, will be."

EPILOGUE

Two days after the attack on the New York Stock Exchange, Roger "Butch" Karp stood looking out the window of his eighth-floor office. Below on the sidewalk, the worker bees were heading back to their offices from long lunch hours while the tourists milled about taking photographs, deciphering street maps, and dodging vendors and panhandlers. Life in the Big Apple continued with few knowing that if things had gone differently, those people on the sidewalks below, as well as everyone else across the United States, would be trying to figure out how to survive with their country in the throes of economic collapse.

According to an official joint press release from the New York Stock Exchange and the NYPD, an attack had been carried out by Islamic terrorists, some of whom had been wearing police uniforms. "The tragic event resulted in the deaths of a senior Exchange executive as well as a half-dozen employees of the exchange." Gotham City Bank floor manager Eric Eliaso was being credited, along with unnamed others, with thwarting the terrorists' intentions of crashing the market.

Trading resumed the next day. However, the Securities and Exchange Commission announced that it would issue new rules and regulations governing hedge funds. It would also launch an investigation into the security lapses, "as well as the investment bank and trading-firm misconduct," that had resulted in the near disaster.

The stock-exchange press release noted a simultaneous attack on a backup computer housed on the MetroTech in Brooklyn. There had been a number of deaths in this incident as well. Though no names were being released, since the matter was still under investigation, the dead included both security officers and what appeared to be home-grown terrorists. Federal agencies would neither confirm nor deny that they had played any role in preventing an apparent bombing attempt. No one was admitting they knew anything about either of the two helicopters seen departing from the building.

One fallout from the attack was the Saudi reaction to the death of Prince Esra bin Afraan Al-Saud. The embassy issued a strongly worded denunciation of the failure of U.S. intelligence agencies to stop the assassination. However, the U.S. State Department pointed out that Saudi intelligence agencies had failed to identify plot "mastermind" Amir Al-Sistani as the brother of a known terrorist who'd tried two years earlier to attack Times Square. The statement implied that the Saudis were not as dedicated to the "War on Terrorism" as they liked to claim.

Various news agencies, starting with the *New York Guardian* in an article by Ariadne Stupenagel, connected the Al-Aqsa Mosque in Harlem and Imam Sharif Jabbar to the terrorists, though the mayor of New York City was quick to point out that most of the people in the congregation had been law-abiding citizens and immigrants. "If there was indeed a relationship between the terrorists and the mosque, it was from a small radical contingent," he said. According to unidentified police sources in Stupenagel's story, Jabbar was apprehended at a private airfield in New Jersey carrying two suitcases filled with cash. He was now facing a variety of state and federal charges, including murder and conspiracy to commit terrorist acts.

For the time being, the mosque was closed; the members of the congregation who wanted to continue as a group were meeting in an old storefront where prayer services were led by Mahmoud Juma. Stupenagel's story had quoted an unnamed source as saying that the body of Juma's daughter, Miriam, had been discovered in the basement of the mosque by police investigators.

"She was the real hero in all of this," said the source, who Karp knew was Lucy. "Information she provided enabled authorities to stop the terrorists before they accomplished their missions, and for that she paid the ultimate sacrifice. Before we condemn all Muslims for the actions of a few radicals, people should know that it was two Muslims, Miriam Juma and Suleiman

Abdalla, who chose to do the right thing, for which we all have cause to be thankful."

That morning, Karp was buzzed by Mrs. Milquetost, who cheerily announced, "Ray is here to see you." Karp was delighted by his receptionist's sudden change in attitude toward his colleague, who he noted had not barged past her and instead waited patiently for her to announce his presence.

The day after the attack on the stock exchange, Karp called Mrs. Milquetost into his office and gave her a stern lecture about discussing office business with others. It turned out that her new boyfriend had been William "Bill" White of the law firm of Newbury, Newbury and White. Or should I say "former boyfriend," Karp thought; the attorney had been reported missing by his father, and there had been no word of him.

She felt horrible, of course. Now, not only had her boyfriend disappeared without a trace or a telephone call, but it turned out he'd been using her to spy on her boss. She was so distraught that even Guma had mercy on her. He'd walked into the reception office shortly after her dressing down by Karp and found her in tears. But instead of piling on, he'd pronounced her name correctly and taken her out for a cup of coffee.

As Guma had risen in her estimation, V. T. had fallen, thanks to his continued association with the firm that employed her former boyfriend. She, of course, had no idea that when Karp found his colleague in Trinity Church with the twins, the two men had managed to fit in a quick conversation about how to continue the subterfuge regarding V. T.'s relationship with his uncle. So far the plan seemed to have worked; V. T. had joined Dean Newbury in issuing a press release criticizing the New York District Attorney's Office for "intimating in the press that the firm of Newbury, Newbury and White was involved in recent events at the New York Stock Exchange."

The DAO had not really intimated any such thing, only releasing a statement pointing out that Imam Jabbar was represented by the firm. "That's all we're going to say about the matter," Gilbert Murrow had said when the press called. "I'd refer you to his attorneys for any further comment."

The Newbury, Newbury and White press release had taken more umbrage at the insinuation that the partners had some foreknowledge of the NYSE attack due to its relationship with Jabbar. "This firm represents a great variety of clients and does not discriminate based on race, religion, ethnicity, or country of origin. The Al-Aqsa Mosque and Imam Sharif Jabbar are clients, and introduced the firm to the late Prince Esra bin Afraan Al-Saud, who was unfortunately one of the victims of these terrorists. We, too, are victims of the criminals who attacked the stock exchange, including attempted murder on partner V. T. Newbury."

Shortly after Guma had entered Karp's office that morning, there'd been a knock at the door of his office that led to the private elevator. Espey Jaxon had arrived to brief him on the latest.

The main character in the events at the Exchange, Amir Al-Sistani, had "disappeared." Jaxon had been trying to reach David Grale, so far with no luck, to try to arrange for the prisoner to be turned over for questioning. "We could learn a lot from him regarding terrorist networks," the agent complained. "Although I suppose that Mr. Grale does not feel the need to abide by the Geneva Convention prohibitions against torture, or the U.S. Constitution, for that matter."

"I think you're right there," Guma agreed. "Grale is in tune more with the Spanish Inquisition than with due process."

"Who knows what will come of that?" Karp added. "It could be that you'll eventually get more information than you might otherwise. When that might be, I don't know. Grale seems to go in and out of his fits of madness, and I think he's serving his own master, not us."

"Well, lucky for us, those urges coincided with our own strategy," Jaxon said.

Although the signs had pointed to an attack on Prince Esra at Grand Central Terminal, Jaxon had not been certain that they'd guessed the location of the attack correctly, and that was why he had asked Tran to let his man implant the GPS microchip. Ivgeny had suggested the janitorial services trick when they informed him that Tran was at the MetroTech building. It was a stroke of luck that as one of his varied business interests, Ivgeny had part-ownership in the Little Odessa Janitorial Services Company. The van had gained him and his team easy access to the building.

Since the prince would also be making a public appearance at the stock exchange, Jaxon had asked Grale if he'd mind keeping an eye out for any suspicious activity in that vicinity. Jaxon had realized that despite the supposedly higher security level, the NYSE would make as good a target as Grand Central.

According to Dirty Warren, who'd filled Karp in later, they'd been fortunate that Booger had been watching the backside of the Exchange building for several days from his panhandling position in front of Trinity Church.

That's where he'd been when he saw the black man with the white face—
the one they now assumed to be Suleiman Abdalla, aka Justin Rhodes Jr.—
enter the church.

The young man had wished him *"Salaam,"* but Booger didn't give it much
thought until he saw him again the day of the attack. First he saw him entering
the church early in the morning when the church first opened its doors; he saw
him again an hour or so later, going into the Exchange dressed in a janitor's
uniform. Suspicious, Booger had entered the church and made his way down to
the tunnel, where he discovered evidence that someone had been inside it. He
followed the tunnel down to its terminus at the stock exchange, where he
found flashlights. He then went to find Grale, who was waiting with his men in
a place that would allow him quick access to the Exchange and Grand Central.

Now, frustrated by his inability to reach Grale, Jaxon joked that maybe he
needed to put the Karp-Ciampi clan in danger. "Then he'll show right up,"
he said.

"Well, you better hurry. After this weekend it's only going to be the boys
and me," Karp said. Marlene had talked her father into a road trip to New
Mexico, where they'd drop Lucy off in Taos. "I think he's more inclined to
save the women, especially Lucy, who he'd like, I think, to be his Queen
Persephone to his Lord of the Underworld persona."

If there were any "winners" from the attack, Marlene's dad qualified; he
seemed rejuvenated, especially when asked repeatedly by the twins to re-
count his "battle with the terrorist."

"Geez, Grandpa," Zak said admiringly at dinner the night after the attacks. "You were just like a ninja with those knitting needles."

"Ninja? The heck with that . . . U.S. Army Big Red One all the way!"

"You were pretty wonderful, Grandpa," Lucy added. "That terrorist,
Mousawi, would have killed Suleiman before the bomb was stopped and I'd
be dead . . . and a whole lot worse."

As Mariano basked in the glory of his grandkids' adulation at the dinner
table, Karp spotted Marlene standing off to the side, watching with tears in
her eyes. He walked over and put an arm around her. "You okay?"

"Yeah, I'm great and Pops is even better. Guess I won't be hearing much
about him being worthless and no good to anyone for a while."

After Jaxon and Guma left, Karp's next visitor was a very nervous Kenny Katz. It had been two days since the end of the Jessica Campbell trial and the jury was still out, and his young protégé was convinced that something was wrong.

"Maybe there's a holdout. Maybe it means a hung jury or even acquittal."

Karp urged patience. "The jury had a lot to consider. If they're taking their time to be thoughtful, that's okay. We did everything we could to present the facts; now it's up to them."

Karp went outside to get a hot dog from the vendor across the street in Foley Square park. A group of the usual street people had set up camp and appeared to be helping themselves to a large selection of cold cuts, breads, fruits, and beverages. He spotted Dirty Warren and Booger among them and walked over.

"Hi Warren," he said. "What's going on?"

"Hey Karp . . . oh boy . . . just a picnic with some of our friends," the little news vendor said. "Some guy . . . fuck shit piss . . . gave Booger forty bucks' worth of food stamps in front of Trinity Church the other day. We decided to . . . your mother's a whore crap . . . throw a party. Join us."

"I've already got lunch but I'll stick around for the company."

"Great! Hey, everybody, look what the . . . balls vagina . . . the cat drug in!" Warren looked up at Karp. "I got one for you. In what movie does Val Kilmer . . . oh boy oh boy . . . say, 'I'm your Huckleberry, and that's just my game?' And in what . . . titties boobs thanks for the mammaries . . . role?"

"*Tombstone*," Karp replied, his mouth full of hot dog. "He was Doc Holliday."

"Ah shit . . . that was too easy."

"Well, today it's just as well; otherwise you might have tripped me up. By the way, if you happen to see David Grale, would you let him know that I'd like to talk to him about a certain guest of his?"

"Sure thing . . . son of a bitch oh boy . . . but I can tell you right now, he's in one of his 'moods' and not easy to talk to. But I'll . . . fuck this shit . . . see what I can do."

Karp was looking out of the window, thinking about Warren and Grale and Al-Sistani, when Murrow entered the office a little after three o'clock to say that the verdict was in. "Dermondy's going to give the alternate jurors and the family a chance to get here, so he wants to bring 'em in at about four o'clock."

Ten minutes before the appointed hour, Karp stood up from his desk and glanced one more time out the window. A swarm of television vans had arrived. They had parked on the sidewalks and wherever else they could find space, and a crowd of people, some curious, others with their signs—or milk crates like Edward Treacher—prepared for the big moment.

Mrs. Milquetost announced the arrival of Kenny Katz. He was still obviously nervous and kept tugging at his tie.

"You ready?" Karp asked mildly.

"I guess. What if we lose?"

"Think positive thoughts, kiddo; we did justice in that courtroom."

Jessica Campbell was already sitting next to Linda Lewis when they arrived. The Guppersteins sat in their usual seats, Ben's arm around Liza, but Charlie was nowhere to be seen. The day after summations, he'd announced that he was withdrawing from the congressional race. "We're going to take some time, assess where we're at, and maybe give it another try when this horrible tragedy is well behind us," he'd said at a press conference that almost no one had attended.

The tension in the courtroom was almost visible as a sort of shimmer in the air when Judge Dermondy entered. He sat down and immediately turned to the attorneys. "First of all, let me say that while this has been an emotionally difficult trial, I'd like to commend counsel on both sides for their professionalism." He then, in a slow but determined drawl, addressed the spectator gallery. "I will be bringing the jury out in a moment, but before I do I want to caution you against any sort of outbursts. I understand that this verdict may be cause for tears or cheers. I will tolerate the first, but I will not tolerate the latter. If you cannot control yourselves, I suggest that you leave now." He looked around the courtroom as if to see if anyone would object—or take his suggestion. Satisfied, he nodded to his court clerk. "Very well, please show the jury in."

As the jurors took their seats, Karp saw that several appeared to have been crying recently. However, the tears had since dried and they sat looking at the judge with their faces set and grim. The courtroom was absolutely still except for the quiet weeping of Liza Gupperstein.

"Ladies and gentlemen of the jury, have you reached a verdict?" Dermondy asked.

"We have, your honor," the jury foreman replied, rising from his seat. He
handed the jury forms to the court clerk, who handed them to the judge.

Dermondy studied them for a moment. "Will the defendant and counsel
please rise."

Jessica Campbell stood, swaying slightly as Lewis put an arm around her.

Dermondy handed the verdict sheets back to the court clerk, who in
stentorian tones began to read: "We the jury in the matter of *The People of
the State of New York versus Jessica Campbell* on Count One find the defendant . . . guilty of murder . . ."

The courtroom erupted. Jessica fainted and her mother cried out. Several reporters dashed from the courtroom with the news as the clerk continued to read the verdict: "three counts of murder. Guilty, guilty, guilty."

As Lewis and court security officers revived Jessica, the Guppersteins
tried to leave but were rushed by the media. "Get away from us, you bastards," Ben Gupperstein snarled.

When the Guppersteins were gone, the court clerk polled the jury—
each juror was asked if the verdict was true and correct. Dermondy then addressed the jury, some of whom had started to cry again. "Your duty here is
done," he said with a kind tone. "You have served faithfully and well and
are to be commended. Go home, hug your children, spend time with your
loved ones. You are excused."

"Your honor, we will be appealing the verdict," Lewis said. "I'd like to
ask the court to set bail pending appeal."

Dermondy denied Lewis's application and remanded the defendant
pending sentencing.

Court security took Jessica by the arms, pulling her gently to her feet.
But she suddenly tore out of the grip. "No!" she screamed, her face con-
torted with rage and fear. "It was Charlie's fault! Fornicator! Adulterer!"
The security team quickly got her under control again, but as she was being
dragged from the courtroom, she went limp and cried out, "Oh God, why
have you forsaken me?"

Ten minutes later, the courtroom was empty except for Karp, Kenny Katz, and Gilbert Murrow, who looked at his watch. "I told the press that somebody would be along shortly to give a statement."

"You two go," Karp replied. "This one was Kenny's."

"Nice of you to say so, boss. But you were right, the jury saw right through the smoke and mirrors to the facts. If I'd had my way, we'd still be arguing the *DSM*."

Karp shook his hand. "Let's just say we made a good team. But I still don't want to go to the press conference. I'm sure you're both capable of dealing with those vultures."

"All right," Murrow shrugged. "You're going to miss a great photo-op." He took Kenny by the elbow and led him down the aisle. "We'll keep it short and sweet," he told him. "Express appreciation for the jury. That it was a difficult trial for all concerned. But that the New York District Attorney's Office believes that justice has been served for Hillary, Chelsea, and Benjamin Campbell. . . . Oh, and remember, thank . . ."

The rest of the conversation was cut off by the courtroom doors. Karp sat still a moment longer. There was something about a courtroom after a verdict. It was as if all that energy and pathos had suddenly gone down a drain, and now the very air was resting.

He stood up. He needed to get home. Tonight, the Karps were going to have a real Shabbat dinner and had invited the Sobelmans. After lunch, he'd received a call from Marlene saying he didn't have to stop by Ferraro's to pick up dessert. A delivery boy had just been by to drop off a cherry cheese coffee-cake.

The thought of it made Karp's mouth water. He was looking forward to seeing Moishe, who'd called the day after the attack. The old man told him about a curious incident at his store several nights earlier. "I thought for a moment I had seen a ghost, a ghost of a boy I once knew. But I went outside and he was gone. I hope that wherever he is now, he has found peace."

Thinking about Moishe reminded Karp of the bar mitzvah class and their discussion about Abraham and Isaac.

"Now the question I wanted to ask you is: If you had been the district attorney back then and God had not intervened to save Isaac, would you have charged Abraham with a crime?"

He glanced over at the defense table and noticed a large manila envelope. Lewis had probably forgotten it, which was none of his concern, but curiosity pulled him a little closer and he noticed there was a name on the outside. District Attorney Karp.

"Well, no," Zak had replied. *"God told him to do it. You have to do what God says!"*

Picking up the envelope, Karp weighed it in his hand, then opened it and pulled out the contents—a single sheet from the sketch pad of Jessica Campbell. It was a detailed pencil drawing from the trial, drawn as if from a perspective hovering above and behind the prosecution table.

The detail and darkness reminded him of the de Goya painting that Lewis had used in her closing. On the left, Katz leaned back in his chair, his eyes fixed on the ceiling—whether in supplication or frustration, it was hard to tell—as Lewis, who had risen from her seat, gestured toward Dermondy.

In the upper right hand, as the focus of the drawing, Karp stood next to the exhibit easel, his hand resting lightly on the photograph of the three Campbell children. He wondered if she'd really meant to create the halo around his head and the photograph or if it was just the way she'd used the eraser. Most of the jurors, drawn as they'd actually appeared, were watching him, though several were crying.

No one was sitting in the defendant's seat. Jessica, in fact, was nowhere in the drawing, though she'd included her sketch pad on the defense table. Looking closely, Karp could just make out a single word written on the pad. *Hineini.* Here I am.

Karp thought about it for a moment. Then he speculated that it seemed as if Jessica Campbell, the radical professor, the ambitious political activist, no longer existed, at least in her own mind, except as an incarcerated murderer in the New York State Department of Corrections. He recalled the question he had put to the students in the bar mitzvah class and Zak's answer. *"Really?"* he'd replied, raising an eyebrow. *"Even commit murder?"*

Karp placed the drawing back in the manila folder. "Not in New York City," he whispered and walked out of the courtroom.